THE RANGERS OF PURPLE HEART RANCH

THE COMPLETE SERIES

SHANAE JOHNSON

THOSE JOHNSON GIRLS

THE RANCHER TAKES HIS CONVENIENT BRIDE

THE RANGERS OF PURPLE HEART RANCH
BOOK 1

CHAPTER ONE

Keaton could hear his heart pounding in his ears. Just like every time he was on the battlefield, the beats synced with the ticking of the second hand of a clock. A calm went over him in the face of the danger that awaited him. He inhaled, the oxygen adding fuel to the bravado that came naturally to him. He was a well-trained soldier, a superbly trained warrior. One of the best specimens of the 75th Ranger Regiment.

Stepping out of his hidey-hole where he'd taken cover after the first shots rang out, Keaton looked around. His sightline was clear, which did not bode well. His spidey senses tingled at the calm and quiet. War was a noisy, frenetic affair.

Something was wrong.

Keeping low to the ground, he poked his head out to gather more intel. The camouflage of his clothes made it so that he blended with his environment. Even his gun was painted green and brown to mix in with the elements.

And then he heard it. A cry. A shot.

They sounded one after the other. Keaton's ears perked like a dog coming alert. Before storming into action, he deduced what he'd learned.

The cry had come from the left side. The shot had come from behind him. The blast from the gun had gone over his head. The cry from a human throat had come before the shot. There was no resulting thump of a body.

A tingle went up to his spine. Keaton rolled over onto his back just in time. A grizzly bear of a man was on him, weapon rising.

That's where the bear went wrong. A rising weapon was completely ineffective. Keaton's weapon was at the ready. His finger already on the trigger, which he squeezed.

The grizzly's body jerked from the direct hit. Pink paint-splattered exactly where his heart would lay if the traitor had one. Keaton fired off another and then another round.

"Hey," growled the grizzly man. "I'm down."

"You know you're on my team, right?" said Keaton.

Griffin "Grizz" Hayes grinned. His incisors glinted in the midday sun like a predator who knew he'd cornered his prey. Keaton knew that look. It was the same look Grizz had given him back in Basic Training when he decided to prank their drill sergeant.

Sergeant Cook never saw it coming. The sadistic sergeant never figured out who'd put Gorilla Glue on the inside of his hat. The entire squad had paid for that prank for months in extra drills in the middle of the night. But it had been worth it to stick it to that demon-born drill sergeant. The red marks of the glue had taken just as long to heal, reminding the soldiers of their revenge every day they ate mud and missed sleep.

So, why had Grizz turned on his best friend now? And why was he grinning after he'd been caught? The spidey tingles crawled over Keaton's skin again.

Keaton didn't remain glued to his spot. He hit the ground just as more shots rang out. Grizz let out a roar of laughter. So, it was a mutiny. His entire team was out to get him.

What for?

It couldn't be the late-night planning session Keaton held them in until well after one in the morning last Saturday. It couldn't be the fact that Keaton changed his mind twice, on which supplier to use, causing them to redo the books over again, and then again. It couldn't be the fact that he'd promised General Strauss that his team would have their Ranger Training Camp ready in just ninety days when the team had originally planned to take half a year to get things in gear, which didn't include any downtime after separating from the military.

The shots coming at him from all four directions told Keaton he was wrong. They'd divided into two equal teams, three on each. But the four remaining men all aimed their weapons at him.

Keaton was undaunted. As the leader of his team, he saw how he could use this mutiny as a teachable moment. A plan formed in his mind. He only had time to come up with two variables in case Plan A didn't work instead of his standard three. With the main plan and two backups, he moved into action.

Mac Kenzie's gaze connected with his. The recognition dawned in Mac's eyes. The two had been in many tough situations together. Enough that they could communicate without using words.

So Mac, or Mackenzie as everyone simply pushed his first and last name together, saw Keaton's entire plan in one glance. But again, Keaton was already locked and loaded a second before Mac rose to the occasion.

Keaton grabbed Mac by the shoulders. Rolling him over, Keaton sprang onto his feet, hefting all of Mac's six foot three, two-hundred-fifty-pound bulk of pure muscle.

"You son of a—" But Mac's words died as his body jerked, taking on pink and purple paint from the assault meant for Keaton.

Keaton swung his weapon up and under Mac's armpit. He took aim and fired, towing Jordan Spinelli and David Porco.

With two down, he had two more to go. He ducked around Grizz, plastering his front to the man's paint-smeared back. In a matter of seconds, Grizz's front matched his back. But not a speck got on Keaton.

From the protection of Grizz's massive bulk, Keaton opened fire on his last frenemy. Russell "Rusty" Hook, who was a perfect shot, went down immediately.

Keaton still didn't lower his weapon. "Surrender," he called out.

"Never," the five men said in unison. "Surrender is not a Ranger word." They all chuckled after reciting the end of the Ranger Creed.

Keaton lowered his weapon. He walked to Mac and helped the man up. Another part of the creed was that they never left a fallen comrade under any circumstances.

Keaton clapped Spinelli on his back and came away with pink and purple paint.

"Told you he had eyes in the back of his head," said Porco.

"Don't be ridiculous," said Keaton. "I have 360 vision. Like a hawk."

"You mean an owl," said Grizz. The man was the strong, silent type women always swooned over. He could often be found reading ancient poetry books. But the weird part was that Grizz actually liked the riddle of words.

"Then I'm a super owl," Keaton countered. "Anyway, I think we can all learn something from this."

Five groans joined the chorus of chirping crickets and birdsong in the forest. Keaton thought he heard a paint gun safety click off.

"This was supposed to be a fun excursion in the midst of your insane work plan," said Mac.

"Don't knock the plan," said Keaton. "The plan is our ticket to not go to desk jobs."

After separating from service, many rangers went on to work in the intelligence community or in top-level security. But none of his guys wanted to work inside. They all craved the outdoors and the freedom to set their own schedules. There was still a lot of action in them. They just no longer had the desire to travel and dodge real bullets.

"The unexpected will happen to us as we move forward building the best training camp in these United States," said Keaton. "But, we'll always be ready to maneuver because we have a plan."

"Oh yeah?" said Rusty. "Maneuver this."

Keaton dodged the paint pellet. It caught him in the forearm, but it wasn't a direct hit.

Rusty rolled his eyes.

"Like a hawk," Keaton grinned.

"An owl," corrected Grizz.

Keaton shrugged.

"You sure about this location, though?" said Grizz. "The Purple Heart Ranch in Montana?"

"I've heard some crazy things happening up there," said Spinelli.

Keaton had heard them too. Soldiers going to heal the wounds they'd received in combat. Yet, in less than three months, each man had winded up in holy matrimony and no plans to leave the ranch. It was kind of like a cult. But Keaton knew the man in charge and knew him to be a top-notch soldier and a decent man.

Marriage wasn't a path Keaton planned to go down. He had a five-year plan before he even thought about marriage.

"We're not living on the land, so none of the rules or hoodoo will apply to us," he assured his men. "Our clients will stay six weeks, at the longest, which doesn't meet their three-month rule."

Apparently, the land of the Purple Heart Ranch had a zoning issue where if a soldier wanted to live on it, they had to be married within three months or hightail it out of there. It was backwoods, for sure. But they needed land in the backwoods to create their state-of-the-art course and facility.

"Good," said Grizz. "Cause myth or zoning, I have no plans for a wife."

There was a chorus of agreement. Except for Mac and Rusty. Mac had given a woman a ring, which she'd rejected more than once. Rusty had divorce papers sitting in his duffel bag. There was one signature on the ream of paperwork. It wasn't his signature.

"Let's get changed and head out," said Keaton. "We've got a lot of work to do and little time to do it. Living at the edge of a rehabilitation ranch and preparing for our first clients will keep us all too busy for dating."

"Whoa, whoa," said Porco, holding his hands up in surrender. "Put dating back in the plan. Those farm girls need a load of me in their lives."

Pops rang out as Porco was painted with a shower of bullets for that comment. With their ire turned away from himself, Keaton took a rare moment to relax and laugh at his brothers-in-arms and their antics.

His edict stood. With the amount of work they had to do in the next three months, none of them, himself especially, had time for dating. The training facility would be his sweetheart for the next five years before he even decided to look for a wife. That was the plan.

CHAPTER TWO

The sizzle of charred beef smelled different when said cow was alive and kicking and not quartered into pieces and placed in a pan. Brenda Vance backed up. She avoided the bull's hindquarters, but she wasn't quick enough to avoid the wood. The plank of the fencing splintered, and a shard of wood caught the side of her forehead.

Blood mixed with sweat and caught in her eye. Brenda swore. Her muttered curse made the younger three of her ranch hands wince. They should all wince. It was their fault the cow wasn't properly secure.

"You all right, missy?" came the gravely, tobacco tarnished voice of the fourth and eldest ranch hand. Manuel Bautista had stepped on this ranch around the time when Brenda had taken her first steps before she'd turned a year old. Like her, he knew this place inside and out. Unlike her, he was not the one in charge.

Brenda bit her tongue before she could utter another curse. Her brother might be a pastor, but she'd learned that his role didn't give her any extra free passes for the next life.

"Don't call me missy." She swiped the blood and sweat with her worn flannel shirt, getting a whiff of the hard work she put in this day. Looking up, she saw that two of the ranch hands' hands barely glistened in the hot afternoon sun. Their brand-new cowboy hats were starched perfect. Their shirts had not a single drop of sweat at the pits.

"It's Miss Vance," she said as she stared down at the blood on her shirt. "Or, boss."

As the elder ranch hand turned back to calm the new bull, Brenda caught the sound of a Spanish curse. Two of the other men chuckled. The skinny blond one in tight jeans that most certainly came from either Old Navy or Urban Outfitters was the one Brenda had nick-named Yankee. The second chuckler, the one Brenda called Frat Boy, had a T-shirt with Greek letters stretched over his brown biceps. He'd claimed his great grandfather was one of the famed Buffalo soldiers. Though Brenda doubted that this kid came from that strong stock when he constantly swatted and yelped when any bug came near him, or any mark landed on any piece of his wardrobe.

The other hand didn't laugh. He pretended to look away. Not to be above it all. His attempt to not take a side was clear. His name Brenda knew. He was Angel Bautista, the nephew of her ornery elder ranch hand.

Angel was young, just out of high school. Born in a time where girls were told they could do or be anything, and they had examples and paths to follow. Angel's uncle had been born during a time when women's places were in the kitchen. Or, if she wanted to venture outside, in the garden.

The other two hands were outsiders. This was a semester internship for them. They'd be back to their city colleges in a couple of weeks' time. Whereas Angel lived here and would need to find and keep work on a ranch. He was stuck between two worlds with two elders to mind. Brenda wouldn't wait long to figure out who the kid would follow.

This was her life, her livelihood, and she needed good hands to keep it going. She'd been herding cattle just as long as she been riding horses. She'd been bruised feeding livestock. Broken a toe while changing out a horseshoe. A broken wrist while on a cattle run which she'd led on her own. You name it, she sprained it, strained, and might even have frac-tured it at some point in her line of work as the overseer on this ranch. And through it all, she'd never missed a day of work.

Brenda had done it on her own the last three years after her parents retired. But in those many years, she'd made the ranch so profitable that she'd grown the herd, thereby increasing the workload and the need for hands to help her.

With these sorry excuses for hands, she might as well be doing it on her own. Manuel refused to listen to her way of doing things, relying instead on the old ways. And the other men followed behind him, even though she was the one who signed their paychecks.

"Maybe you should head back inside the house," said Manuel. "To tend to your injury. It's dangerous work out here."

He left off the end of his sentence *for a woman*. At least he learned one lesson today.

This had all stemmed from her suggestion that they use sugar as well as grain to corral the new bull she'd just purchased so that they could brand it. Sugar would've helped calm the animal down. But it was a new way of doing things, and Manuel had balked. Then the bull had kicked out.

Brenda was too tired to fight. The blood still dripping in her eyes was making it hard to oversee what they were doing. She knew they weren't doing it the way she wanted them to do it. But the bull was branded, signifying that she was the owner. That was the major item on her to-do list for the day, so she might as well call it a day.

She banged through the back door of the big house and froze. The back door led directly into the house's kitchen. Dinner was sizzling in a pan. A perfectly cooked steak alongside roasted smashed potatoes just out of the oven and buttered green beans. The fridge was opened and a body hunched down inside. The door closed, and a man in an apron stood.

"You are truly a gift from God," said Brenda.

"And you're bleeding from the crown of your head," said the man. "But I don't see any thorns."

Brenda touched her hand to her forehead. The warm trickle of blood stained her fingertips. Luckily, there was no pain.

"If I go out there, am I going to find one of the ranch hands dead, Bren?"

Brenda sighed, disappointment clear on the gust of breath. "No, Walter. You won't be giving any last rites tonight."

Brenda's brother, Pastor Walter Vance, grabbed paper towels and pressed them to his sister's forehead.

"Ouch," she complained.

Walter ignored her. This wasn't the first time he'd cleaned her up after she'd broken skin. It had been a regular occurrence in the Vance household when they were kids. Might be one of the reasons he'd gone into the church. "Tell me what happened?"

"Incompetence. Chauvinism. Lazy ranch hands. That's what."

"I thought Bautista was one of the best?" said Walter.

"Maybe twenty years ago. The times have changed."

"Good thing that they have," said Walter. "With all the technology you've implemented into the ranch, you need fewer hands than when we were kids."

Their dad had left the ranch to both of them. But Walter gave up his share to Brenda and turned to the church. She was grateful. Especially since because her brother was not a partner, she didn't have to share with him just how much said new technology cost her, not to mention the new bull. She'd financed it, and the first payment was coming due. She didn't have enough cash liquid to keep up with all the bills and overhead.

"Bren, if something is wrong," her brother said, "you'd tell me?"

No, she wouldn't. "Of course, I would."

Brenda learned long ago that lying to a pastor didn't cause an immediate lightning strike. So, she had time. "As long as you keep coming over and cooking for me, all will be right with the world."

"Maybe you should marry," said Walter.

Brenda's utensils clattered down on the plate. This was one topic where her brother was not evolved. Brenda had no desire to get married. Men slowed her down. Case in point, her ranch hands were slowing her operation.

"You got a ranch full of soldiers next door," said Walter. "Some looking to marry in the next ninety days, as goes the regulations on the ranch land."

Which was why Brenda steered clear of her neighbors at the Purple Heart Ranch. And that included their boundary line, which forced individuals to get married just to stay on the healing ranch. She was sure the arrangement was illegal, yet no one had reported it.

"Didn't one of those soldiers run off with your fiancé?" she said.

Beth Cartwright, the pastor's daughter, had been engaged to Walter briefly. But then her childhood crush who had been MIA returned, sweeping her off her feet with a proposal and an engagement ring.

"Reese is a good man," said Walter. There was genuineness in his voice despite the bitterness of the breakup. "All of the soldiers are."

Walter was far too forgiving. But it was part of his job description. Brenda's job description was rancher. She didn't have time to be someone's wife. She was far too busy with cattle, more repair projects than she could fit on an 8 x 10 sheet of paper – single-spaced, and good for nothing ranch hands who she could see were headed to their trucks before sundown without getting their work done.

No. She was best left to her own devices. She doubted she would ever allow a man to take her hand.

CHAPTER THREE

eaton looked at the passing scenery of the American heartland. The brown, majestic mountains with peeks of various colors. The rolling green pastures that seemed to stretch on into eternity. It surprised him how much this beautiful land mirrored the landscapes of Afghanistan, Iraq, and Syria. The only difference between the two landscapes was that hope and opportunity were in this fresh mountain air. War zones were rife with conflict, turmoil, and hopelessness.

During his service in each of those countries, Keaton had seen men die young. He'd witnessed as women and children suffered on a daily basis. He'd watched as the land was ravaged and torn apart by politics and projectiles.

Driving through the Main Street of this small Montana town, the outlook was night and day. Looking out of the window of his rented red Jeep, Keaton saw children skipping down the streets. Moms trailed behind their youth in yoga pants paired with cowboy boots. A group of old men sat on neighboring porches smoking pipes and spitting tobacco. The earthy smell of baked bread permeated the air instead of the metallic aftertaste of explosive powders.

Keaton could see why the soldiers of the Purple Heart Ranch came here and chose to stay after their rehab. The landscape held the familiarity of where they'd been. But the people showcased the future of what they were all fighting for, a community where they belonged.

For the last six years, Keaton had returned to his hometown after each assignment. The hustle and bustle of the crowded city made him anxious. The tall gray buildings and cold concrete unsettled him. The blank stares of the people on the streets, their tight lips, even the eye rolls of strangers avoiding each other on the sidewalks, made Keaton prickle with worry.

Soldiers looked at each other in the eyes. They spoke plainly. They spoke clearly.

So, no, Keaton had not mixed well with civilian life. Neither had the other men when they'd each gone back home to their city lives. None of them wanted to actively engage in combat any longer. But they still wanted a piece of the action. In this place that looked like a war zone engulfed in peace, Keaton knew that each of them might be able to make a life.

Thirty minutes later, he pulled up to the gates of the Bellflower ranch. He knew he was in the right place when he saw the purple flower insignia on the iron bars. That lily-like flower was the symbol for wounded warriors. In patches of grass just off to the side of the paved path, Keaton saw more of the purple bellflowers. They were a native plant to this area. It looked as though they grew wild on this land. No wonder the wounded vets of this ranch felt at home here.

Driving through the gates and up the gravel path, Keaton saw the ranch was filled with soldiers in various states of healing. Men with prosthetic legs rode hard on horses. Weaving farther down the bend in the road, Keaton saw a garden where men with missing fingers and missing arms tilled the soil. Coming out of a barn were men with burns on their faces, arms, and legs. The soldiers tended to a menagerie of farm animals. Sheep and goats rubbed up against their scarred limbs as though unaware of any injury.

Keaton and his crew were fortunate that they'd return with all their limbs and faculties intact. Had any of them sustained any serious injuries, he knew this would be the best place for any soldier to come and heal. Furthermore, he hoped that any new soldiers aiming to improve their skills would come to the far side of the ranch, where he planned to build his elite training camp.

Keaton parked the Jeep at the big house where the road dead-ended. There were no numbers on any of the homes. The directions he'd been given told him to follow the road until it ended. Hopping out of the Jeep, Keaton saw the man he'd come here to meet.

Dylan Banks emerged from the double doors and marched forward. He was dressed in a denim shirt and khakis. One of his legs was tanned. The other was made of steel.

"Keaton, you made it."

"Good to see you again, Banks."

The two men clasped hands. Scarred palm met scarred palm. Rough fingers gripped and tugged inward. The old friends came in for a hug with many claps on the back. Keaton had served with Sgt. Dylan Banks on more than one mission. The man was sharp and could improvise in difficult situations with the best of them.

"Amazing set up you have here," said Keaton. "I've heard nothing but good things about this ranch."

"We take them all," said Banks. "The tired, the poor, the huddled masses."

"Isn't that the saying on the Statue of Liberty?" Keaton chuckled.

"Well, now we're taking in the wretched refuse like Army Rangers."

Banks struck out an arm, aiming a fist at Keaton. Keaton saw the move coming and held still to receive it. It was all in good fun.

"Ah, is Banksy-wanksy still upset that he couldn't pass the Ranger PFT?"

"Shut it," said Banks, but there was no bite to his bark. "I only missed it by a couple of points. It was the water survival section that drowned me."

"You're from an island."

"I'm from New York City."

Keaton shrugged. The qualifications to become one of the elite Army Rangers were not a joke or a drill. Every month over four hundred eager souls arrived at Fort Benning, Georgia with the hopes that they might have the right stuff to accomplish the challenge. Fifty-one percent went home with their hopes dashed in the mud. The only reason Keaton had survived the training was that he'd prepared for the physical tests like a maniac.

That was what he planned to do with the training camp; train others the way he'd trained to pass the test. Boots On the Ground Elite Training was a dream Keaton didn't realize he had until he faced the nightmare that was the United States Army Ranger school. He knew he could never prepare any soldier fully for that experience. But anyone who passed through his training regimen had a better shot to be in the better half of that percentile.

"By next year, you'll be up and running," said Banks.

"Next year?" Keaton scoffed. "The plan is to open the doors in ninety days."

Banks scratched at the stubble of his jaw as he regarded Keaton. The incredulous look in his eyes said it all.

"It's ambitious," said Keaton. "I know. But I have a well thought out plan that will work if executed properly."

"Of course, you do," Banks chuckled, clapping Keaton on the back again. "I believe you can do it. Amazing things can happen in ninety days, especially on this ranch."

Now it was Keaton's turn to scratch at the stubble on his chin. He knew what that reference meant. Many of the men who came here to heal wound up getting married in that time period. Rumor had it, it wasn't just the zoning laws that governed occupancy on the ranch. Many believed it was something about the land itself.

Keaton was not a superstitious man. Even with that, he had no plans to live on the land. He only needed to work on it. So, the rules and the myths would have no bearing on him nor his business.

"Let's go take a look at the parcel your leasing," said Banks.

They hopped into a golf cart and took off. If Keaton thought the land was beautiful from afar, it was breathtaking up close. Colors kept switching from green pastures, to fertile brown dirt, to a rainbow riot of blooms. Interspersed were horses of brown, white, and black. Sheep with fluffy poofs of hair ... and an array of the rangiest mutts he'd ever seen.

Five dogs barked as they drove by. A few of them had a prosthetic attachment. One even had a wheelchair attached to his hind legs.

"Those are mine," said Dylan. "Well, they're my wife's. But they came with her in the marriage, so ..."

Keaton didn't bother to question the strangeness of this place any further. He kept his gaze trained on the land, making mental notes of how his clients would access the training facilities. At the edge of the ranch, Keaton saw his vision come to life. There, in the untouched land, was where he would carve out a dry patch from a mud pit where his students would learn the joy of crab walking, push-ups, and sit-ups.

Instead of buying lumber, they could chop down a couple of those trees to the right and make a climbing wall. The main thing they had to build was the indoor training facility and bunks. That and the specialty training area, which would take advantage of the mix of terrains from dry earth, to green pasture, to rocky hills, and the creek. That's where they'd put in installations to train special forces for covert missions.

"Can you pull up closer to the creek?" asked Keaton.

Instead of pulling closer, Banks slowed the vehicle. "The creek isn't within our boundaries."

It took Keaton a moment before the words made sense. When they did, his heart sank. He needed that creek for the special forces area. Heck, he needed it as part of the Ranger PFT training. Banks surely had to know that.

"It's owned by the neighboring ranch," said Banks.

"Do you think he'd be willing to sell or lease it for our purposes?" Keaton asked.

Dylan pursed his lips. "Not sure if *she* would. But you can go over and ask her. She's reasonable. Most days."

CHAPTER FOUR

Brenda didn't have an alarm clock in her bedroom. It was the smell of the coffee brewing that woke her. She'd brought herself one of those fancy coffee makers with a timer that magically poured her a cup each morning before the sun came up. Best purchase of her life.

She let the aroma lead her down the stairs like they were fingers in her nose, pulling her along. She was surprised her feet didn't come up off the ground as she made her way to the kitchen and the automatic coffee maker. Pulling two mugs from the cabinet, Brenda poured herself two cups. Like every day of her adult life, she would drink the first one down, letting the hot water burn her tongue and wake up all her brain cells. By the time she finished the first, the second one would be room temperature and ready to savor.

She reached in the fridge for the milk. Only to put the pitcher back. She'd grabbed for the milk that had come straight from the cow instead of the skim milk.

Finally, with her double dose of caffeine in her veins, Brenda ran a brush through her hair. She lost the battle with the tangles, so she gathered her tresses into a ponytail. She pulled a clean shirt over her head and jeans up her legs. Stepping into her boots, she was out the door before the first rays of the new day sun poked over the horizon.

She pulled the notepad from the back of her pocket. Flipping open the pad, she surveyed her list. Most of her chores were the same every day. There was always bale to stack, bale to move, feed to grind, manure to haul, bills to pay, and a fence to fix.

The only fence she was worried over today was the fencing that kept her new prize bull in. She knew the beast was raring to get his job done. But that would have to wait. She had to wean the calves from their mothers and set the newly independent beasts out in their own pasture.

The rooster stretched his feathers as Brenda walked past the coop. He was a slacker like the rest of her ranch hands. None of which were there yet.

Instead of growling about it, Brenda got down to work. She had half her chores checked off her list before the sun blinked a ray open at the horizon.

Brenda climbed on the tractor. It was an older model, older than her. But it worked just fine. She jammed in the specialized key, better known as a screwdriver. The actual key had been lost months ago, somewhere out in her vast acreage. The engine turned over immediately, and she got to work.

By the time she'd worked the land and brought the tractor back, her ranch hands had finally shown up. Late. Again.

Just because she was a woman, they thought they could take advantage of her. Also, because it was late in the season, and most ranch hands had already been hired. She'd gotten the scraps of workers. Manuel was a holdover from her grandfather's time. His nephew was a good worker when he was away from his uncle's gnarled guidance. The other two were pretty much useless outside of being able to lift heavy things. She'd done more this morning than all four of them combined had done all week.

Brenda put the tractor in park. She remembered the specialized key and put it to work at its third job of the day. Twisting her ponytail into a bun, she jammed the screwdriver into her tresses. To keep her hair out of her face. And off her shoulders. And, yes, potentially as a weapon for what she had to do.

"You're late," she said. "Again."

Manuel grinned. "Sorry, honey. But the cattle don't know the difference."

Brenda clenched her fists. But she didn't reach for the screwdriver. Yet. Though she was having very happy visions imagining Manuel's head as an ignition that needed help getting started. Actually, that wasn't far from the truth. The man was stuck in the dark ages of ranching. He needed a jumpstart. But Brenda was sure it was too late for him.

"I'm not your honey," she said calmly. "I'm your boss. But it doesn't look like I'll be that much longer."

"Don't tell me." Manuel's bushy brows lifted. His crooked grin rearranged his wrinkled face into something distasteful. "You're finally getting yourself a husband?"

The three younger men winced. No surprise there. All three of them were born into this generation, where they'd seen women wield power and respect. Manuel was about to get a time and culture shock.

"Let me be clear," said Brenda. "Your services are no longer needed here on the ranch."

Manuel's face contorted into something ugly. It reminded Brenda of the bull receiving his brand. The hiss of pain. The shock of betrayal. The shudder of resignation.

Brenda braced for Manuel to lash out. But he held still. It was the three men behind him that fidgeted like nervous newborn foals.

"You firing me, missy?"

"Good." Brenda stretched her lips into a cruel grin to match his. "I don't have to use smaller words."

His shoulders snapped straight. His fists curled. His mustache twitched. Dark shadows moved across his face as he dipped his head low so that his hat shielded his gaze.

Brenda held her ground. This was her ranch. It was her livelihood on the line. They all could go and find other work, with a man whom they might respect.

Or not. She didn't care. All she cared about was the running of and respect for her ranch.

"Now see here, Miss Vance."

Yeah! He had finally used the word *miss* appropriately. If she had a gold star, she still wouldn't give it to him. Too little, too late. He'd failed. And he was getting expelled.

"Without us, you have no hope of keeping this ranch up and running. It's calving season. It's not a one-man job. Definitely not a job for a woman."

The multitude of checkmarks on the list in her back pocket would beg to differ. But he was right. She couldn't do it all on her own. She would need a hand. Just not his.

She might've trained the younger three. But with the gnarled hand of Manuel having brainwashed them, they were as useless to her as a castrated bull.

"It is no longer your concern," she said.

Manuel curled his lip. His mustached twitched, making him look like the villain in some cartoon. Part of Brenda wanted to laugh. Instead, she looked behind him to see if she might salvage anything.

"If any of you lot are interested in staying, I'm willing to consider retraining."

There was a spark in each of their eyes. Well, the two city boys' eyes. Angel looked away, hiding his feelings on the matter from his uncle and Brenda alike. But Brenda took that as answer enough.

"They won't be led by your apron strings," said Manuel. "You won't make it a week without us. Let's go, boys. We get a weeklong break before she comes crawling back."

The two city boys looked at each other. Then they shuffled back to Manuel's truck. From the corner of her eye, Brenda caught Angel's wince. But he fell in line and trudged back to the truck as well.

"There are no hands available at this time in the season," Manuel said to her. "Can't wait to see you on your knees when you come begging for help."

"Why don't you hold your breath waiting for that to happen," she said.

With a youthful grace that belied his wrinkles, Manuel hopped into the driver's seat and took off. Brenda was about to let out a sigh of relief. She also let the floodgates of worry and anxiety about what she would do open. He was right. Help would be hard to find at this point in the season.

And then the truck stopped. Brenda used her hand to shield her eyes as she peered at the back of the truck. It was halfway to the gate to her property.

Had they come to their senses? Did they want to come back and play by her rules? Would she allow it?

Before she could answer any of those internal questions, Manuel hopped out. He lifted his booted foot and kicked at a weak spot in the fencing. It was the bullpen. The pen that housed her new, pricey bull.

Manuel tipped his hat, hopped back in, and peeled out of her ranch.

The bull was at the center of the pen, and his back was turned. Brenda knew that she wasn't going to make it in time before he escaped. But she had to try. Any damage he might cause, she would be liable for, and she couldn't afford it.

She moved quick. Grabbing a sack of grain with one hand and a bag of sugar with the other, she hopped back on the tractor. She pulled the key from her hair and jammed it into the ignition.

The tractor stalled. She tried again. The bull had turned and was walking gingerly toward the broken fence.

Finally, the engine turned over. Brenda took off. But at twenty miles per hour, she was already too late. Her only hope was to corral the bull before he could hurt himself or anyone else.

Off in the distance, she saw a Jeep turn into her gates. A red Jeep. A red Jeep headed straight toward her bull.

Who drove a red Jeep on a cattle ranch? Of course, Brenda knew that bulls were color blind. But it was a superstition nonetheless.

Brenda gunned the tractor, topping twenty-five miles per hour. She was too late. The bull spotted the red Jeep and rammed into it.

CHAPTER FIVE

Keaton had taken many hits in his lifetime. He'd studied Brazilian Jiu Jitsu where he'd been lifted and thrown bodily across a five-point ring. He'd been kicked in the chest during hand to hand combat training. He'd even had a round hit him in his body armor.

Each hit had rattled him. Each impact had made his vision go blurry. Had made his thoughts scatter, but never too far. Each time, he'd quickly regained his equilibrium and was back in fighting form within a few seconds, a moment at the max.

The great beast barreling toward him was bigger than the pro wrestlers and martial artists he'd faced in the ring. Its hooves tore up the ground each time its feet kicked against the earth to push it faster toward Keaton. Both vehicle and bull were going at the same speed, though the bull may have had a couple of miles on Keaton's Jeep.

In any case, Keaton was not going to outrun this fate. He did the only thing he could. He braced for impact.

Which was a mistake. Tense muscles and tense bones were more prone to injury than relaxed ones. But there was no way he was about to relax. There was an eight-hundred-pound bull headed straight for his driver's side door.

The metal door was no comparison to the armor plate inside a bulletproof vest. Car manufacturers had yet to make a bull proof, well, anything. Metal crunched as the door bent to the bull's will.

Keaton felt the impact on his shoulder and right side. But it was the booming crash that rattled him. The sound ripped his sense of equilibrium in half. He felt that the rug that had been pulled out from under him was the rug on the floor of the entire world.

The bull clearly felt the effects, too. It stood outside the door of the Jeep. Stunned. Its eyes were unblinking. Its breathing slow and ragged. For all the damage it caused the jeep, Keaton was sure the bull had to be bleeding internally.

A dust trail in the distance caught his attention. A tractor was coming toward him. Behind the wheel sat what he could only describe as an Amazonian warrior.

Long, brown hair flew behind her. Her toned arms had the type of muscles a woman got from a hard day's work and not in choreographed kicks and twists at the gym. Her lips were pursed with concentration. Her gaze was focused. Keaton felt the urge to know what the color that determined gaze was.

Instinctively, his hand reached for the door to let him out of the Jeep. He pushed, but the door only went a couple of inches. Not enough for him to scoot his body out.

"Stay put," the warrior woman shouted.

There was so much command in her voice that Keaton did as he was told. The avenging angel put the tractor in park. She leaped out the door before the wheels came to a full stop. Her motion slowed, and it was as though he was watching one of those action movies with the sloweddown fast motion.

No. It wasn't her motion that was slow. It had to be his brain.

He knew she moved quickly, efficiently. But his eyes seemed to want to linger on her motions. Each action she took, his brain set up the replay, like in a football game when a play had to be reviewed.

Her hands raised slowly. Her voice was soothing, calming. Her words were pretty but unintelligible. But their meaning was clear.

Relax.

Everything's okay.

Come with me.

I'll make it better.

Keaton's whole being relaxed. All the pain from the impact dissipated. He was absolutely going to come with this woman who promised to make him better. He felt like a better man just being in her presence.

He tried to open the car door again. Again, it barely budged. Time returned to normal speed, and he caught a flash. It was his warrior angel. She'd flashed her eyes up at him.

They were green, by the way. Green like a blade of grass. A sharp blade of grass that just might leave a nasty cut. So, why did he have the urge to roll around in the pastures of her gaze?

"It's okay, big guy," she said.

Her voice had a dulcet quality. But it was soft as if the feathers were made of steel. It made Keaton's spidey senses tingle. Not over his skin like a premonition of danger. This sensation went straight into his bloodstream like it was a shot of adrenaline. Again, he tried to make his way out of the Jeep and to her.

"I've got this, soldier," she said.

"Let me help," he said.

"You're not part of the plan."

Keaton frowned at that. A plan that he was not a part of? It did not compute. He added a new item to his to-do list; get on board with this warrior angel's plan. Whatever it may be.

Her plan looked like she was going to corral the stunned bull back through the gaping hole in the fence. With a bag of grain and white granules that looked like salt, or maybe sugar.

The bull shook its head as though it was waking from a dream. It blinked a couple of times and then focused on her. Its nostrils puffed out gusts of air.

Was it going to ram her? It had already run into Keaton. He knew at that moment that he would die before he let anything hurt this woman. Whatever her original plan, Keaton was instituting Plan B.

He shoved out of the vehicle. Only for his back to hit the Jeep's door at her annoyed demand that he stay put. He ignored that. His boots hit the ground.

Followed by his knees.

And then his shoulders.

And, finally, his head.

The last thing Keaton realized before he passed out was that the white granules she'd tossed at the bull weren't salt. They were sugar. He wondered if he kissed her pouting, disapproving lips if she would taste as sweet?

CHAPTER SIX

"*I* was able to stop the internal bleeding." Maggie Banks gathered her tools and began placing them back in her veterinarian's bag. "He's going to take a while to heal, which means he's definitely going to be out of commission for the breeding season."

Brenda pressed both her thumbs to her temples. The other four fingers she raised to the Heavens as though in prayer. For guidance? For patience? For a miracle? Probably all three.

As if her short handedness wasn't enough. Now, her prized bull, which she'd sunk most of her liquid cash in, was useless. How was she going to make more babies to replace the cows she would have to separate from the herd and sell? And find the help to do it? Manuel was right. With the size of her herd, this was not a one-man job.

Letting out a moan, Brenda dropped her hands. Her voice was rough and deep. It appeared to have gotten deeper with the hole she was now in. No, that sound hadn't come from her. It had come from the soldier whose jeep had been the unlucky matador's cape in this debacle.

Brenda had propped him up in the shade against the fence. She was a strong woman, but he had been far too heavy to lug inside. He was a big guy, but definitely not out of shape. He had thick legs made for horseback riding, though he clearly hadn't been near a horse lately if a Jeep was his mode of transportation in cattle country and farmland. His arms were the type that could wrap around a barrel and lift it. But she bet he'd likely been using those guns to carry, well, guns. His shirt had come untucked when he'd collapsed, and Brenda had been treated to a view of his six-pack.

Suddenly, she was thirsty for a beer to cool down. From all the exertion. Of corralling the bull.

Her cheeks were obviously flushed because of her anger at her former ranch hands. Still, the cold beer sounded good. But that would have to wait until after her bull was tended to.

"Can I check on *him* now?" asked Maggie.

Maggie had tried to tend to the soldier first, him being a human and all. Brenda had waited impatiently, insisting the man was still breathing, and that was the best they could do. Now that her bull was stable, she gave a head nod, acquiescing that Maggie could turn her attention to the man.

"Sergeant Keaton?" said Maggie.

The man blinked, opening groggy eyes. Cloudy like the sky after a storm. That was Brenda's favorite time; after the rain had washed away all the dirt and dust and left behind a fresh slate. After a storm was the time when things could begin anew. A fresh start. Because the worst had been done.

Sergeant Keaton fixed his clear-eyed gaze on Brenda. There wasn't any hint of cloud. In his eyes, Brenda saw the perfect fresh start.

Brenda felt corralled by his look like her entire body would go wherever he directed. Which was nuts. It had to be that weird Purple Heart Ranch hoodoo. He and Maggie must have brought it onto her land. Well, they'd be getting up and getting off her land soon. She had no need of a husband.

"How many fingers am I holding up?" asked Maggie.

Sergeant Keaton blinked, turning his clear eyes away from Brenda. His gaze went hazy as he looked at Maggie's two fingers. He canted his head, leaning away to peer around Maggie's hand at Brenda.

"Are you okay?" he asked.

Was she okay? He was the one that casually bumped into an eight-hundred-pound bull. And he was asking about her.

"It didn't get you, did it?" he asked.

"The bull?" said Brenda. "No. He got you. And your Jeep."

Brenda's thumbs went back to her temples. Her fingers straightened back up to Heaven. But she knew no miracle was forthcoming to take care of the damage her bull had done to that car. Legally, she was responsible. Even though it was Manuel's maliciousness. Unfortunately, that argument wouldn't hold up in court.

Her land. Her bull. Her responsibility.

"Look," she said, dropping her thumbs when the throbbing continued all around the crown of her head. "I'll file an insurance claim for your vehicle and cover your medical bills."

It would set her back even more. But it was the law. It was also the right thing to do. And her parents had raised her to do right.

"I'm fine," said Sergeant Keaton.

He shifted his big body, trying to get his feet under him. As he leaned forward, Brenda got a clear sight of a strong chest with a dusting of fine hair. Even though his pectorals looked like they were solid as a rock, she was willing to bet that they'd be soft as pillows if she were to rest her weary head upon them.

"Brenda," grunted Maggie, "a little help?"

"Hunh?" Brenda blinked. "Oh. Right."

Maggie had grabbed one side of the soldier. Brenda rushed to his other side. Instead of focusing on righting himself, he grinned down at Brenda.

"You're strong," he said.

"You're weak," she said.

"Am not." He frowned. "I can do fifty-eight pushups, sixty-nine sit-ups, and run five miles in a half-hour."

"Those are the requirements to pass the Army Ranger exam," said Maggie.

"It's not an exam," said Sergeant Keaton. "It's a test of physical fitness, which you can't pass if you're weak."

"Well," said Brenda. "I bet those are great in the army. But they mean nothing on a ranch."

"Can you complete a twelve-mile march with a thirty-five-pound pack on your back?"

"No, but I can drive a herd of cattle ten miles with nothing but a length of rope and a sidearm."

They stood toe to toe now. Sergeant Keaton had a head over Brenda. Brenda was tall. She wasn't used to guys being on her level. Definitely not above it. Despite her attempts to knock him down a peg, she had the feeling she'd met her match.

"Sergeant Keaton," said Maggie. "You should take it easy. You were just in an accident."

"I promise I'm fine." He didn't take his eyes off Brenda as he made the assertion. "No need to file any forms. The car is insured. I got the accident plan."

He did? The one that rental car companies tried to scare customers into purchasing before they handed over the keys even though it was unlikely they'd ever need it? Brenda got the feeling a man like Sergeant Keaton wouldn't fall for that. She had the suspicion that he'd bought the accident insurance on purpose.

Who does that?

"I feel fine," he continued. "But, I'll get checked out by the doctors at the Purple Heart Ranch if it'll stop you two from glaring at me."

Well, that was a load off of Brenda's checkbook. She'd take him up on it. Now, she had two fewer bills to pay. But that didn't answer the question that had been nagging her since she'd seen his Jeep in the distance.

"What are you doing here?" she asked. "Did you get lost?"

"No," he said, testing his balance by stretching those bulging arm muscles. "This is where I'm meant to be."

Something about that statement sent a tingle down her spine. It had the ring of truth to it.

"Meant to be what?" she asked.

"I was looking for you."

"Me?"

"I need something from you."

"From me?" Her voice sounded breathy to her own ears. Brenda was never breathy. And definitely not for some guy. But her breathing was shallow as she hung on his every word.

"I need your land," he said.

The air slapped into her lungs from the gasp. The quick inflation made her head light. All the warmth went cold.

"Just the edge of it," he went on. "Where the creek is. I'll pay its value if I can get it by the end of the week."

The creek? At value? That would be enough to secure her debts, buy another bull, and maybe even hire a decent ranch hand or two.

"You got yourself a deal," said Brenda.

She stuck out her hand. Sergeant Keaton took it gingerly. When his fingers closed around hers, she felt a zing. The force was like the kick from a bull. By the look on his face, she knew he felt it too.

But they'd both been taken down by the same bull.

That was all it was.

CHAPTER SEVEN

"The deal is a no go."

Keaton sat in State Senator, Ginger Chase's office. The pretty blonde stared at her computer screen. Her fingers flew on the keyboard as though she were chasing after the insurgent that was standing in their way. But Keaton's attention was on the beautiful brunette next to him.

Brenda Vance had changed out of her jeans and T-shirt and into a nicer pair of jeans and a blouse. The new jeans were a darker blue and played perfectly against her tanned skin. The blouse, which was buttoned all the way up, still showcased the line of her neck, making Keaton's mouth thirst.

She'd driven them into town in her old Ford F150. The AC had worked, so she'd rolled the windows up and put the radio on. It had been for the best. Keaton was at a loss as to what to say to the woman. Brenda seemed perfectly content with the silence between them. So, he'd closed his eyes and let her take the wheel.

Keaton's rental car company had arrived and towed the ruined Jeep back into town. The owner hadn't been happy when he remembered that Keaton had taken out the insurance policy. Of course, he'd taken out the insurance policy. What responsible adult wouldn't?

Since the rental car company was on the same street alongside the city council building, he and Brenda had decided to kill two birds with one stone and stopped in. No appointment was necessary, as Maggie Banks had called ahead. Ginger was family, she'd said. However, Keaton didn't see any physical resemblance.

"I swear with the backward ordinances in this town, it's a wonder anyone stays here." Ginger's husband, Sergeant Colin Chase, leaned over his wife's chair.

Ginger turned her face up to his. "It kept you here."

"You kept me here," Chase countered.

Keaton looked away as the newlyweds made otter eyes at each other. Chase had come with his team to the Purple Heart Ranch nearly a year ago to find healing and rehabilitation after a mission gone wrong. Now, each of the four-man Fire Team was living on or near the ranch in wedded bliss.

The happiness and love between the two were palpable. It was nice; having someone who you could both depend on, and then go on and kiss. A soft place to fall at the end of a hard mission. Keaton wondered if maybe he'd move his five-year plan up a year or two. Maybe he could make time for dating even sooner.

His gaze latched onto Brenda as she leaned forward in the seat beside him. Her lips twisted in impatience as she cleared her throat. It took a second, and a louder throat clearing, for the lip-locked married couple to focus on the matter at hand.

"You're saying I can't sell my land to a willing buyer because of some ordinance?" asked Brenda.

"No, you can," said Ginger. "Just not as quickly as you'd like. The sale will take six months to go through. And in that time, no new construction can take place by anyone but the owner."

That caught Keaton's attention and broke his study of Brenda Vance's lips. "I need to be up and running in ninety days. My guys will be here tomorrow. We need to break ground by the end of the week to stay on schedule."

He'd planned for some setbacks. But not any of this magnitude. Six months? They couldn't afford to wait around for six months. They'd lose all their contracts, the contracts that would set the business into the black. He hadn't gone to the government to gain land for this very reason. The bureaucratic red tape took time to unravel. But here it was rearing its sticky head.

"There has to be a way around this," said Keaton, his brain already going into tactical overdrive, trying to suss out a workaround.

"Well," said Chase. "There is one way that I can think of."

Both Brenda and Keaton leaned forward eagerly. Before Chase responded, he glanced at his wife. The two shared a knowing look. It was the same silent communication Keaton had with Grizz when they were about to slip into some hairy business on the battlefield. Except there was adoration in this couple's look. Not an any-last-words kinda look he'd often exchanged with his best friend.

Keaton had never had a connection like that with a woman. One where words weren't needed. He'd learned communication was key with the fairer sex. But at the same time, women didn't like blunt honesty.

Whatever nonverbal words transpired between Ginger and Chase, they clearly understood each other perfectly and were on the same page.

Another glance at Brenda and Keaton got the impression she'd clued in on this silent exchange. Her expression changed from eager interest to total denial. She was also no longer leaning forward. She had pressed her body back into the chair, as though she was trying to get as far away as possible from the couple and their impending words.

What was going on?

"If you two are thinking what I think you're thinking ..." Brenda waved her finger at them. Then she waved both hands, as though warding them off. Then she huffed and crossed her arms over her chest in the universal language of back off. "Then, don't even."

Ginger and Chase only smiled. From the little he knew of Brenda Vance, Keaton knew she wasn't a woman who rattled easily. She'd faced down a bull with only a bag of grain and sugar. But looking at her in the chair, she looked completely rattled.

"What's going on?" Keaton asked the question to Brenda. He

wondered if he'd get the message looking into her eyes. But she wouldn't meet his gaze.

"There has to be another way," said Brenda.

"We could get the law changed," said Ginger. "But that would take even longer."

"What if I leased the land to him instead of selling it?" asked Brenda.

"That could work, but it would still take time. Less time. Maybe two to three months before any construction could start."

"Neither of those options work for me," said Keaton. "We have a client booked for ninety days from now. They'll put us in the black for the whole year. We have to be ready, or we'll lose the contract."

He looked around the room. Ginger looked sympathetic. Chase looked amused. Brenda looked furious.

"What's this other way you're not telling me about?" Keaton said.

Keaton directed his comment to Chase. Chase looked to his wife. Ginger looked at Brenda. Brenda threw up her hands and faced Keaton.

"They're suggesting we get married," said Brenda.

Indignation rang through her voice. Her fingers flicked at the air like she was brushing the ridiculous notion aside. The corners of her eyes crinkled, and her brow creased as though the idea was insane.

But Keaton's brain was working, adjusting his master plan. Suddenly, the notion of waiting five years to find the perfect woman didn't seem so necessary. It wasn't ridiculous that he could squeeze Brenda into the plan. He could shift some things around.

Which was insane. Right? It had to be the bump on his head from the bull. Right? Even though the idea made his head stop hurting and his heart race.

CHAPTER EIGHT

"*This* town is absolutely insane." Brenda glared at the flashing red Don't Walk light. She tapped her foot impatiently as the light counted down. Counting was not going to calm her down. She needed to find a green light to get this moving.

"Yeah," Keaton sighed.

He stood beside her on the street corner. He'd had nothing but monosyllabic answers since they'd stormed out of Ginger's office. Well, she had stormed. He'd followed her, walking quietly in his combat boots. Too bad. Brenda was sure they'd sound like thunder rolling in if he was stomping mad.

Why wasn't he stomping mad?

His plans were being thwarted by bureaucratic red tape that should not hold up in a court of law. He clearly wasn't from this part of the country. Even though his muscles looked like they were crafted for bull wrangling.

But the way he carried himself, the straightness of his spine told her he spent more time in taxicabs and Ubers than crouched over a fast running horse. The way his grin held just a little back, as though he hadn't known his neighbors all his life, or maybe he hadn't met each of the people that lived around him. That told her that there stood a city boy through and through.

The light changed to green. Before she stepped into the street, Keaton crossed behind her. His fingers ghosted her low back. Not touching. But close enough that she could feel their impression. Once he was on the side of the street closest to the waiting cars, he fell back into step with her.

He had country manners. A man should always place his body between traffic and a woman. It was a ridiculous notion because if a car jumped the curb, it was barreling into both of them. But the thought was nice.

"Sometimes, I hate this town," said Brenda. "At every turn, someone is insisting you get married. Be it in church, on the Purple Heart Ranch, or at the kitchen table."

If it wasn't her former ranch hand, then it was her brother. If it wasn't her brother, then it was the city government.

"I see," said Keaton.

Two words this time. So, progress.

Keaton shoved his hands in his pockets and hunched his shoulders. He hadn't looked at her since leaving Ginger Chase's office. They still didn't have a viable solution to this mess.

Clearly, marriage was out of the question. It wasn't even a question. The people in this town needed to stop trying to solve business issues with matrimony. It wasn't that easy.

"What if it was that easy?" said Keaton, coming to a stop.

"What if what were that easy?" Brenda asked as she turned to face him.

Keaton's gaze was fixed upon the building in front of them. They were standing at the City Hall. The building was a two-story affair. The mayor and his staff occupied the top floor. On the ground floor was where most civic matters were taken care of. Things like filing lawsuits, paying for violations, and getting marriage licenses.

Brenda's gaze jerked from the building and back to the man standing toe to toe with her.

"What if we did it?" he said.

"Did what?" She couldn't voice it. She could barely even think it. But her mind was already getting away from her.

"What if we got married?"

"Maybe we should stop by the ER," said Brenda. "That was a pretty bad hit you took."

Keaton only grinned. It was a full grin, the kind she was sure he'd give to someone he'd known a lifetime. Why was he giving it to her when he hadn't known her for a day?

It was a dangerous grin. A grin she wouldn't mind seeing for a lifetime. Every self-preserving bone in Brenda's body told her to take a step back from him. Brenda held perfectly still under the assault of that heart-stopping grin.

"I'm fine," Keaton said. "I'm thinking clearly. I'm thinking logically."

He ran a hand through his hair. It wasn't exactly a buzz cut. Which meant he'd been out of the service long enough to let it grow. Brenda wondered what his hair would look like if the locks touched his ears. She wondered what it would feel like if her fingertips brushed the wayward strand of hair that fell onto his forehead.

"Is there really much difference between a marriage contract and a leasing agreement?" he asked. "In a sense, it's all about ownership."

"But in marriage, you would own my property and me."

Something flashed in his gaze. Like a predator flashing his pupils in the dark at helpless prey. Brenda wasn't easy prey. She was always armed. Not with a screwdriver at the moment. But she had her wits about her.

"I would never take anything from you," he said. "I want to build something."

That statement nearly disarmed her. He was a wily one. She'd need to keep her eyes on him. Oh, this man was dangerous. Did she need the money enough to get tangled up with the likes of him?

"We're two grown adults," he said. "Both business savvy from what I can see of your ranch. You were methodical in how you dealt with that loose bull. At least, what I remember of the incident."

His grin went cocky this time. His teeth flashed white at her. Her self-preservation instincts were going haywire. Part of her wanted to run. The confusion was in figuring out the direction. Because most of her body was urging her to crash right into that strong chest and test it for pliability.

"I'm a planner, too," he continued. "Maybe we'd work well together."

Had sexier words ever been uttered by any other man in existence? A man with a plan. And he wanted to partner up. She wondered if he used an old fashioned checklist? Or was he not into paper planners and used a digital organizer on his phone?

Brenda gave herself a shake. Was she seriously talking about marriage? With a stranger? This was not a viable path.

"How can you think we work well together?" she said. "The only evidence we have is from when I told you to stay in the Jeep. You bucked my plan and got out anyway."

Keaton winced. "I didn't understand your plan then. I've told you mine. Tell me yours. Why did you agree to the sale so quickly?"

Brenda swallowed, but the words still escaped her throat. "I need help."

That's not what she'd meant to say. But it came out nonetheless

"I mean the money will help," she tried to course correct. "I've mechanized a lot of the ranch operations. But I still need ranch hands to work with the cattle. And now I'm going to need a new bull for breeding."

"I can help with that," he said. "The hands, I mean. There are six of us. Highly trained Army Rangers. We've been put in tough situations before and came out alive."

"Any of those tough situations happen on a ranch?"

"No, but we're adaptable. Think about it. If we get married, all we'd need is a prenup stating you're entitled to the money for the sale of the creek, and I'm entitled to keep the creek. No other paperwork would be necessary. It's a good plan, and we could both put it into action by the end of the week."

He made it all sound so simple. Brenda would get the money she needed immediately. Plus, free labor. Where was the downside?

CHAPTER NINE

"Hey, Siri, Google what should I include in a prenup?"

"Okay," said the robotic female voice. "Here's what I found with the term prenup."

Keaton winced, as a few heads turned in the coffee shop at Brenda's query. Brenda was entirely oblivious. Her green eyes were completely focused on Siri's findings.

For his part, Keaton was mesmerized by the screen's reflection of Brenda's intent gaze. Her lips pursed as she tapped the screen. She was businesslike as she did her due diligence on her iPhone. When she pulled out a worn memo pad and began making a checklist, Keaton's heart beat so hard he was sure it had turned into a bull ramming to break the fence of his chest.

He was going to marry her. Why didn't that freak him out? It was years ahead of his plan. But she was making a list that ended with the goal of their holy matrimony.

Well, maybe not holy. More like convenient. His convenient bride.

"Looks like we should start by each listing the property we own," she said, turning the page in the memo pad and adding a heading to the new list entitled Owned Property. "And who retains what after the marriage is dissolved."

Dissolved? Keaton took a sip of his tea. The beverage had had time to cool as they sat in the quaint mom and pop coffee shop. But he had trouble swallowing.

"Do you have a planner or any paper to write on?" she asked.

A flush crept over Keaton's cheeks as Brenda regarded him. Her pencil was poised halfway down the sheet of paper where she'd begun making her checklist. He wasn't a paper planner as such. Most times out in the field, a plan wasn't committed to paper. It was discussed, committed to memory, and then executed.

"I don't." He swallowed at the raise in her eyebrows. "I didn't bring any paper with me. I just came to talk to you."

She nodded, closing her memo pad. Keaton balled his hands into fists, so he wouldn't reach out to stop her. The close of her organized checklist felt like a huge casualty loss.

"It's fine," she said, flicking her thumb over her phone screen. "I can make a shared Google Doc instead."

"Good plan," he said. Was it creepy that he felt a thrill at sharing a virtual space with this woman? A space where they would organize their near futures together. Each day ticking off an item on the list.

She began tapping away. Keaton wrapped his fingers around his styrofoam cup. The tepid tea inside warmed under his palms as he watched Brenda.

Her fingers were long and slender. The nails were ragged. It was clear she was a hard worker.

She glanced up at him. He winced under her gaze. Those green blades of her irises were sharp. Keaton felt he'd been caught staring. Because he had been staring.

"You should note the ranch has debts." Brenda sat her phone aside and laid her hands flat on the table.

"Debts?"

"I've always paid cash, but I needed to upgrade and modernize. The ranch made a lot last year, and projections are good for this year."

She sounded defensive. That was the last thing he wanted her to feel with him. Couldn't she see that he wanted to protect her? To be her defender. He wanted to pull her behind him and fight her battles for her. But with the stiffness in Brenda's upper lip, he knew it would not be appreciated. So, he softened his features and leaned in to listen.

"I could've paid it off," she said. "But I'm shorthanded because my ranch hands were awful. Now, my bull is out of commission."

Her hands rested on the table. Just an inch from his. All he needed to do was reach out to brush her pinky finger, the smallest one. But she balled her hands into fists.

"With the money from the sale, I'll be set right," she said. "So, you see, I wouldn't be a liability."

"Of course, you're not a liability," he said.

Keaton did reach for her hands then. He placed his palm on top of her balled fists. Brenda tensed, tightening her hands like she was putting up her dukes, mounting a defense.

Keaton squeezed. In an instant, the tension seeped out of her hands and into him. Instead of feeling her anxiety, it passed through him, like he was a siphon pulling out the bad and pumping in the good.

Their gazes connected. Green meeting blue. Between them was a horizon that stretched on into eternity. The ground shook when she blinked and pulled her hand away.

"Do you have any debts I should know about?" Brenda asked, picking her phone up again.

Yes. He did. He had experienced an acute loss. But it wasn't financial. Keaton glanced at his empty hands before answering her.

"No. No personal debts. The Army paid for my college. I've lived on a base or been on assignment most of my adult life. So, no credit debt or personal loans. My five partners and I have pooled our resources to start this business."

"Five partners? How do you get anything done with six heads?"

"We're a unit."

"Who's in charge?"

"No one really. We all have the same rank."

Brenda stared at him. Her brow crinkled in confusion. White teeth chewed at her lower lip as though she was trying to work out what he was saying.

"We all have different strengths," he said. "I'm a planner."

"Ah," she sighed as though seeing the answer. "So, you're the overseer."

"That sounds severe."

"It's what I do at the ranch," she said. "I oversee the entire operation. I lay out the tasks and assign them to ranch hands."

Yes, that was pretty much Keaton's role.

"Good. It sounds like we're of a similar mind," Brenda continued. "We should get along during our marriage."

Our marriage. Keaton liked the sound of that. He liked the idea of partnering with Brenda. Working with her. Making a detailed plan with items, and lists, and tasks that they would oversee together.

"When do you think we should schedule the divorce?" Brenda's thumb made a swiping motion. The checklist disappeared and was replaced by a calendar.

Keaton heard the sound of tires screeching in his head. He was back in the Jeep, and another bull had rammed into him. This one was bigger.

"Divorce?" The word was bitter on his tongue. He felt an ache in his left shoulder. His gut churned.

"An annulment wouldn't work because that would negate all of our arrangements," she said.

"Right. No annulment. It has to appear real."

Real like seeing her dressed in white, walking toward him. He'd veto the veil because he'd want to see her eyes. Real like saying vows and making promises. Real like sharing a kiss after being pronounced man and wife.

"Three months?" Brenda said. "You'll be done with your construction and up and running by then."

"No." His voice was harsh. Harsh enough to make her look up from her phone and regard him.

"Four months?" she said.

"No." His voice was softer this time. There was even a ring of reason to his tone. "I mean, we should probably look into it more. Make sure there are no legal holes that might trip us up."

"Good point." Brenda tapped more on her phone. "I've filled out the online prenup template with the information I have. We just need to print it out and sign it."

Keaton rose from his seat. His feet were eager to set this plan in motion. The sooner the paperwork was out of the way, the sooner he could figure out a plan to keep his bride around for longer than four months.

"Actually, wait," said Brenda, still tapping away at her phone.

Keaton did not want to wait. If he'd thought five years was a long time, five days now seemed like an eternity. But he was sure they'd have to wait at least that long to get everything in order for this marriage of convenience.

"I'm looking at the requirements for marriage," said Brenda. "Looks like there's no waiting period in Montana. We could take care of this today."

CHAPTER TEN

When she woke up this morning, the last thing Brenda had planned to do was get married. It was not on her chore list. But here she was with a printed prenup in one hand and a marriage license application in the other.

And it all felt like the most normal thing in the world.

Telling Keaton about her financial strife, planning the near future with him, making lists, it all felt natural. He would make a great ranch hand. Under different circumstances, they might even probably be friends. Since they would be married soon, she supposed maybe they probably should be friends. But that would have to wait until later.

Right now, they needed to fill out this application and get in line at City Hall. Not that there would be a line in this small town. Weddings were family affairs here. She was certain they would be the only people knocking on Judge Perry's door.

"Bren? Is that you?"

Brenda stopped in her tracks at the sound of that voice. Keaton, who'd been keeping step with her since leaving the coffee shop, running into the post office to print the prenup, and then crossing the street to City Hall, bumped into her back at her abrupt halt. His hands came to rest on her forearms and then slid down to cup her elbows.

A shudder went up Brenda's spine. Not a cold sensation. It was like warm sunshine breaking through her blinds in the afternoon. She felt the urge to snuggle back into Keaton's hold. To let him hold her. To let him take the lead.

"Who's your friend?"

Brenda stepped out of Keaton's loose embrace to face off with her brother. "Did you follow me here?"

"I was already here when you came in," said Walter.

"Hmmm. Well, what are you doing here?"

"I asked you first."

The two siblings squared off, coming toe to toe. Though Walter was a man of the Big Guy, he didn't take any sass from his big sister. She was not going to get around him to Judge Perry's office without Walter getting a whiff of what she was on about.

She hadn't considered involving her family in this little manner of her marrying for business reasons. It wasn't really any of their business. They'd all left to pursue their heart's desire. It was only Brenda on the ranch pouring her heart and soul into the running of it. And if she wanted to sell a parcel of the land by leasing her heart and soul, then they had no say in the matter.

"Is there a problem here, Brenda?"

The breath of Keaton's voice touched the tip of her ear. Her shiver would've been evident this time. That is if he hadn't brought her back into his loose embrace. Cupping her elbows once more, his chest lightly touched her shoulder blades. They were definitely firm. She resisted the urge to press her back into his chest to see if there was any give.

"Keaton, this is my brother, Walter."

Keaton's hold on her didn't relax after the announcement of their relationship. Walter extended his hand to Keaton. Keaton released Brenda's elbow and took the proffered hand.

"Pastor Walter Vance," Walter introduced himself formally.

"Pastor?" Keaton's voice, strong a moment ago, sounded a bit choked now.

"Don't let the honorific fool you," said Brenda. "He has a bit of the devil in him."

"Aren't you going to introduce me to your new friend, Bren?" said her brother with a devilish grin on his face.

"Walter, this is Keaton … Keaton?"

Oh, wow. She was about to marry this man, and she didn't know his last name. Wait, he'd put it on the prenup. But she didn't dare pull out that document in front of her brother.

"It's Anthony Keaton. Sergeant Anthony Keaton. But everyone calls me Keaton."

"Nice to meet you, Keaton," said Walter. "What are you guys doing here?" He addressed that question to Keaton instead of Brenda.

"What are *you* doing here?" said Brenda.

"Judge Perry is out sick. I was officiating marriages today. But as there are no applications, I was going to head out early."

Walter looked down at her hand. Brenda fought the urge to hide the document behind her back. She was the elder sibling, and she was grown. She didn't have to explain herself to him.

Walter turned his gaze from Brenda and onto Keaton. "You said, Sergeant? You're from the Purple Heart Ranch?"

"Yes," said Keaton. "I'm building a training facility at the border between the two ranches."

"And, let me guess," said Walter. "To stay on the ranch, you need to get married?"

"No." Keaton scratched at his chin. "All the programs from the training camp won't be longer than six weeks. Meaning everyone involved will be exempt from the family status zoning rule."

"So, you'll only be here for about six weeks?" Walter hedged, clearly still looking for the angle.

"No," said Keaton. "I'm here to stay."

"And where will you live?"

Keaton hesitated. He looked at Brenda. They hadn't talked about that part of their plan.

"With me," Brenda found herself saying. "Keaton and I have come to a business arrangement."

"Business?" said Walter. "What business matter has you holding a marriage license in your hand?"

Brenda jabbed a finger in her brother's chest. "You signed your rights for the ranch over to me, little brother. It's really none of your business."

"As your brother, you're right. It's none of my business. But as the only one qualified to marry anyone today, it very much is my business."

The siblings stared each other down. Brenda gritting her teeth, calculating if she would be forgiven for pinching a man of the church. Walter grinning, clearly loving having the upper hand on his big sister.

"Excuse me, Pastor Vance," said Keaton. "I think you have the right to know that your sister and I are going to enter into a marriage of convenience. We've talked about the pros and the cons, the what-ifs and nots, and we come to an arrangement that will strengthen us both together more than remaining separate entities would accomplish. You have my word that I have Brenda's best interests at heart. I'll never do anything to hurt her because her distress is now my business, and I take my business seriously."

Brenda had fallen back during that speech. She'd turned her body so that she could see Keaton as he made these promises, these vows. Doing that left her future husband and her brother squared off.

Brenda's peaceful, yet annoying, pastor brother and her strong, capable Army Ranger who'd faced down a raging bull regarded each other. It was a formidable pairing.

Brenda hated it, she didn't like being the rope in this testosterone tug of war.

Walter broke into a grin. Keaton stretched out his hand. They clasped hands. Walter brought Keaton in for a hug with a manly clap on the back.

"My prayers have been answered," said Walter.

"Hey!" said Brenda.

"Army Ranger, you said?" said Walter. "You're going to marry my sister, and you're gonna work the land? Man, does God move in mysterious ways."

"It's not real," said Brenda.

"Right," said Walter, brushing his sister's comment away with a wave of his hand as he continued to speak to Keaton. "You got a ring?"

Keaton patted his pocket. But no ring magically appeared. They'd prepared all of the paperwork, but forgotten that tidbit in their haste to get to City Hall.

"No worries," said Walter. "The judge always has a spare. Follow me."

Keaton put his hand at Brenda's low back as they walked. Brenda meant to step out of his hold. But their steps matched. Since they were keeping the same pace, she let him keep his hand there.

"Uh-huh, found some." Walter produced two plain gold bands from a drawer inside Judge Perry's office. "Ready?"

"Now?" said Brenda and Keaton in unison.

"Would you rather wait until Mom and Dad can fly up here?" said Walter.

"No," said Brenda. "No."

She knew her mother would insist on making a big production of her only daughter's wedding. That planning would take at least three months. They didn't have time for that. Especially when this marriage was barely going to last much longer than that.

"You want the basic package or the deluxe?" said Walter.

"I want whatever would suit Brenda," said Keaton.

Keaton grinned down at her. That wasn't mischief in his gaze. It wasn't him and Walter against her. It was Keaton and her, and there was no foe in front of them. The way was clear.

"Deluxe, it is." Walter cleared his throat. He pursed his lips and took a deep breath into his nose. He looked upward as though seeking inspiration, much like he did before he began one of his sermons. One of his long sermons. "Marriage, what does that word mean. The scriptures tell us—"

"Switch to the basic package, Walter," snapped Brenda.

Her brother glared at her but complied. "Sergeant Keaton repeat after me."

"I, Anthony Keaton, take thee, Brenda Vance, to be my wedded wife."

Brenda sucked in a breath. As the cool air entered her nose, she tried to slow it down so that it, and the words Keaton repeated, didn't go straight to her head.

"To have and to hold from this day forward, for better, for worse, for richer, for poorer ..."

Well, that was the whole point. This marriage was a means to an end. It would put them both in a better place. It would make them richer instead of poorer.

"To love and to cherish till death do us part."

The breath she'd been holding came out in a gush at that last part. She should've gotten her brother to change that bit. She and Keaton weren't in love. Brenda wasn't even sure if she believed in love. At least not for herself. She'd never had a relationship last long enough that she'd felt cherished.

Keaton took her hands in his. His calloused thumb brushed over her rough knuckles, but somehow the touch was tender. He singled out the fourth finger on her left hand and slid the ring on.

Brenda fought the need to curl her hand into a fist to stop the progression. Once the ring rested at the base of her finger, she felt a heavy weight. Not on her hand. Somewhere else. Somewhere deep in her gut. That feeling in her gut warned her that this ring was not likely coming off.

"Bren," said Walter.

"What?" she snapped.

"Now, it's your turn. Repeat after me."

"I, Brenda Vance, take thee, Anthony Keaton, to be my wedded husband ..."

It took Brenda longer to repeat the vows. She needed to keep stopping to take breaths. To swallow. To clear her throat. But finally, she made it to the end.

"To love and to cherish till death do us part." That last part, she got through without incident.

Her fingers shook as she lifted the ring to Keaton's hand. He reached out with his right hand and steadied her grasp. Together, they slid the ring onto the fourth finger of his left hand.

"You may now kiss the bride."

Keaton's gaze dipped to Brenda's lips. Her hand was still in his. He gave her a light tug. Her body came to his without thought. He let one hand go and wrapped his hand on her waist, urging her closer. Again, her body came to him, closing all distance.

With his thumb, he tilted her chin. Her entire face went where he commanded. Lifting to do his bidding.

Since he'd let go of her hands, they were left suspended in the air. She didn't know what to do with them. She rested them on his chest. Well, at least she had confirmation of her suspicions. Behind those strong pecs, were a soft bit of flesh. Like a firm pillow that could offer both comfort and security.

Brenda felt the strength of Keaton's heartbeat. Her own pounding heart slowed, matching his rhythm, falling behind him. His lips were nearly upon hers. She could taste the sugar and lemon from the tea on his breath.

"We don't need to do that part," she said.

"The kiss is a part of the deal," said Walter.

Brenda jerked her head to her nosy brother. "No, it's not."

"Is too," grinned Walter.

Brenda heard a chuckle. Then she felt the warm velvet press on her forehead.

"There," said Keaton as he pulled back from her forehead. "It's sealed."

It was sealed. She was married. She felt like she was the flap of an envelope that had been glued closed. But something got left out. Theoretically, the envelope could be reopened. But part of the flap would be torn and separated. It would never be the same again.

CHAPTER ELEVEN

Keaton pulled out of the rental car company and onto the main street. As he turned the wheel to merge onto the highway, his gaze caught and held on the gold band on his left hand.

What just happened?

He recounted his steps for the day. He'd arrived at the Purple Heart Ranch. He'd met Dylan Banks. The two of them had toured the land. Keaton had driven next door and gotten hit by a bull. And now, he was married.

The honking horn broke his reverie. Keaton slammed his foot on the brake. The action slowed the car, but not his racing pulse. He barely escaped the second collision. This time with an eighteen-wheeler instead of a bull. But catching the side of the truck as it zoomed by, Keaton saw the advertisement for prime beef illustrated in browns, reds, and white.

Haha, fate was funny.

Was this a sign?

He didn't believe in signs. He was the type of man that collected intel, read the data. When all else failed, he trusted his gut.

This marriage was a means to an end. A business arrangement that would benefit them both. It was temporary.

Keaton had left the main street and the town behind and was headed into the countryside, back to the Purple Heart Ranch, where he was meant to stay the night. He looked down the long stretch of road. There was nothing but green pasture for miles, sharp blades of grass. Instead of feeling the razor's edge, his mind kept turning to the smooth, flat part.

Keaton drove on. His foot pressed down on the gas, and he picked up speed. He felt like he'd missed something. Until Vance ranch came into view.

He had missed something, his turn into the Purple Heart Ranch a few miles back. Instead of a U-turn, he made the right turn into the gates. And there she was. His wife.

Brenda rode astride a horse. She was backlit by the setting sun. She looked part warrior, part angel, all his. Even from this distance, Keaton could see the small band on her left hand glinting in the waning sunlight.

From atop her horse, she commanded the cattle, and they obeyed like they were her obedient soldiers. Keaton parked the truck. This time, he'd rented a Ford F150 like hers.

His feet led him to the fencing that separated his wife from him. It was the fencing that the bull had broken through earlier today. It looked like Brenda had put up a temporary barrier. She'd left wood and nails just outside the makeshift railing.

"What are you doing here?"

Keaton looked up. His gaze caught and held on her lips. He'd come so close to kissing those lips just a couple of hours ago. That mission was now moved to the top of his to-do list.

After they'd recited their vows, Keaton's phone had rung. It was the rental car company letting him know there was paperwork for him to sign and a new car to pick out. Brenda had wished him an awkward farewell and took off. Walter, his new brother-in-law, had clapped him on the back and wished him luck, all with that mischievous grin of his. Keaton could only wonder if the man was truly a pastor or an imp in disguise with the way those two bickered.

"Keaton, what are you doing here? I thought you were spending the night at The Purple Heart Ranch."

That's where he'd meant to go. But here he was. The setting sun cast a growing flame around Brenda. Like a moth, he came closer.

"We're married," was all he could think to say.

"Not for real." Brenda swung her leg over the horse to dismount. She held the reins tight in her hand as she settled a hand on the barrier between them.

"I know it's not real." So, why did those words feel like cotton in his mouth? "I just thought we should probably keep up appearances. Not give anyone any reason to question our union."

Their union. Brenda Vance was his wife. No, Brenda Keaton. Mrs. Keaton. She could pretend it wasn't real. But he'd meant every word of the basic vows they'd recited back at City Hall.

Mrs. Keaton frowned with disapproval at her husband. "Exactly what kind of fake marriage do you think this will be?"

Keaton came to her, standing toe to toe. He wanted to scoop her up into his arms. He wanted to press her body against the fence. He wanted to take his first taste of her lips. But there was a rail blocking complete access to her.

"This is the kind of marriage where the husband, that's me, helps out his wife, that's you."

Since he couldn't reach her through the fence, he took the temporary railing down. Then he bent down and picked up the hammer and nails.

"You want to mend fences with me?" she said.

"It was in the vows, for better or worse. The fence needs to be made better."

"There was also that bit about to love and cherish forever," she countered.

Keaton placed a nail. With one strike, the nail made its way through. If only he could get to the heart of his wife as easily. He knew that finding a permanent route into Brenda's heart would take some serious planning with many evasive maneuvers.

"It's just a fence, Bren."

She bristled at the familiar use of her name. She'd have to get used to it. He planned to become very familiar with everything about her in due time. A time frame that would take longer than ninety days. This plan would run for a lifetime.

"You said you needed hands," he said. "I've got two of them that aren't busy right now. Let me help."

Brenda chewed at her lip as he picked up another nail. "Fine. But I'm not going to babysit you. I have too much to do."

"Like I said, it's just the fence. I can handle – ouch!"

The nail slipped. He'd hammered his thumb. Keaton shook out his thumb. But the motion only dispersed the pain.

"Here," Brenda said, dropping the reins of the horse and taking his hand. "Let me see."

Keaton expected her hands to be rough. In some spots, they were. He didn't focus on the rough patches. He honed into where she was tender.

"It's gonna swell," she said. "It'll probably have a shiner. You swung pretty hard."

"Trying to prove to my wife that I'm of use."

Brenda's gaze lifted to his. Something shifted in her green gaze. It was as though a wind blew, and the sharp edge of her eyes turned to the softer, flatter side of the blade. But the wind shifted again, and the look was gone.

"Come on," she sighed. "Help me put the horse away, and then let's ice this up. We need to get the swelling down if I'm going to use those hands."

She turned just as her cheeks reddened. Keaton bit his tongue. Seems they were both of the same mind.

Brenda gave Keaton a tug with one hand. With the other, she grabbed the reins of the horse. Both man and beast moved at her command.

CHAPTER TWELVE

Brenda rolled over, laying her face in her pillow. She hadn't opened her eyes yet. But she knew it was time to get up. She'd never had an alarm clock. Her body just knew.

But this morning she felt languid. She wanted to stay under the covers and snuggle. Gone was the anxious feeling that she had a million things to do. Absent was the disquiet that she had neglected some chore, and the screws were going to fall off her operation. Missing was the panic that she was running late, always running late, before the sun was even up.

The sun wasn't up. But she had to get up. She had a million things to do. She probably had left a chore off her list.

Brenda rolled over onto her back. It was easy to open her eyes to the new day. Only moonlight showed into her window at this time of day.

Days on a ranch were long in the spring. They began before the sun came up. They ended after the sun went down.

She had cattle to feed. Though the majority of her cattle were strictly grass-fed, she was experimenting with supplemental feeding and watching how it bulked up the cows. It was a project that had put off not only her former ranch hands but her father too. The feeding of cows was a heated subject in these parts.

She would also have to start separating the calves from their mothers soon. They were at the age where they would be branded and taken out to a smaller pasture to start life on their own. It was a bar mitzvah or a sweet sixteen of sorts. Although, instead of getting presents or a new car, they'd get a hot poker and kicked out of their mom's house.

Rubbing a hand over her face, a spot of cold metal went over her forehead and down her nose. The sensation made her shiver. But it wasn't a cold kind of shiver. The prickles running over her skin made her feel warm. When the metallic material got to her mouth, she remembered what it was.

A gold band. A gold wedding band. Because she was married.

There was a creak of the floorboard. The snick of a door opening. The click of a door shutting.

Her husband was awake.

She could hear Keaton moving about the house. He was up already? And she was the slacker still under the covers.

Brenda threw off the covers. She wanted to scramble into clothes and out the door. Unfortunately, she was raised right. She made quick work of tugging her bedsheets into order as her mother had taught her.

By the time the four corners of her bed were maid-service presentable, she heard the *pit-pat* of shower water hitting tiles. She stood in the middle of her bedroom, frozen. Keaton was, as she stood there in her pajamas, in her shower. And if he was like a normal person, he probably wasn't wearing a pair of jeans and a T-shirt in there.

There was a naked man in her shower. And she'd married him. How had she gotten here?

She stared down at the band on her finger. She remembered her brother waving the bands in her face. She remembered the vows both she and Keaton had repeated. Then they'd parted ways, and she hadn't expected to see him again. Until he turned up on her ranch. The rest was a blur.

She'd tended to his thumb. Then she'd offered him some of the leftovers in the fridge because again, she was raised right. Keaton had complimented her on the cooking. She'd accepted the praise. Heating things up to the right temperature was an art, after all.

Brenda had eaten quickly and then begged off. But it had been late. She'd pointed out a room down the hall. Then she'd shut herself into her room. And locked the door. Only to unlock it a second later.

Keaton might be a stranger. But he was her husband. She might not know him well, or at all. But she knew he wouldn't hurt her.

The shower had stopped during her trip down memory lane. Good. He was done. She could slip into the bathroom, then out the door, thus avoiding any need to face him.

With that plan formed, Brenda opened the bedroom door to head to the bathroom. But as she stepped out of her bedroom, Keaton stepped out of the bathroom.

His hair was spiked up. His face was scrubbed clean. There was no sleep in his alert gaze. There was also no shirt covering his bare chest.

Tanned skin was stretched over a six-pack of hard, lean muscle. No, scratch that. There was an eight-pack there. Was that a thing? It clearly was since Brenda was looking at it, staring at it.

"Good morning."

"Huh?" said Brenda.

"You might want to give it a second to cool off before you jump in," he said.

"I wasn't going to—" Her gaze shot up and met with sparkling blue mischief. "What?"

"The shower," said Keaton. "I like it hot. So, there's a lot of steam in there."

"Steam?"

His grin was slow, wicked like he knew where her mind had gone. It hadn't gone anywhere. It was stuck on the man in front of her with his steamy eight-pack, the damp towel draped low on his hips, and his bare feet.

Large, bare feet. You know what they say about men with large feet. Big boots.

"Brenda?" Those large, unbooted feet took a step toward her, and then another. A lean finger reached out for her. Keaton tilted her chin up so that she was looking directly in his eyes. "You good?"

"Hmmm?"

Keaton kept his index finger under her chin. With his thumb, he rubbed at the space under her eyes. "You sleep okay?"

"Hmmm?"

From the hall window, the sun stretched its first rays up from the horizon. The tendril of warmth heated Brenda's cheek. But not as much as the heat from the clear blue gaze of the man who was cupping her cheek.

"You have a long chore list today?" he asked.

"Hmmm. I mean, yes. Feed to grind. Manure to shovel. Fences to mend."

"Hmmm."

Keaton's gaze was on her lips. His index finger still held her chin. Which was a good thing. She was certain that single finger was the sole thing holding her up in the world as she could no longer feel her legs. All sensation had gone to her lips.

She felt completely oversensitive. She needed something to soothe the rising ache that zinged from her upper lip to her lower lip. She flicked her tongue out to moisten them.

Big mistake.

The moisture only served to make her lips even more swollen. Like a balloon that had one too many breaths blown into it. Brenda felt like she was going to pop if she didn't get relief soon.

And the only relief she wanted was the pair of lips that were coming closer and closer—

Ding dong.

The ringing of the doorbell broke them apart. They both looked down the stairs at the door to the house.

"You're far more presentable than I am," said Keaton, his hand waving in front of the damp towel that kept him somewhat modest.

Brenda turned and took the stairs on wobbly legs. By the time she reached the last rung, she had her wits about her again.

Keaton was a distraction. This marriage was a means to an end. She had to get his glistening chest out of her mind and off of her ranch. She had far too much work to do.

Opening the door, she was met with two large male bodies. Unlike Keaton, they were fully clothed. But like Keaton, they had that air about them that reeked of soldier. She turned away from the newcomers and back to the stairs.

"Honey, it's for you."

CHAPTER THIRTEEN

"Working the plan, huh?" said Grizz.

"There were some unforeseen complications," said Keaton as he shut the door and ushered his two friends out.

Grizz and Mac had stared up at him in his towel while Brenda stood in her pajamas on the doorstep. Brenda had offered the men coffee while Keaton had thrown on his clothes. In that time, he knew his men had made up their own minds about what they had seen.

"She looks like a very complex set of curves a man could get lost in," said Mac.

"Hey." Keaton shoved the other man. Mac could've easily dodged the jab, but Keaton's next words stopped him cold. "That's my wife you're talking about."

"Your wife?" both Mac and Grizz said in unison.

"Yeah." Keaton scrubbed his hand through his hair. His fingers caught in the strands. He was due for a cut soon.

"As in married?" asked Mac.

"Yeah," said Keaton. He should probably find a barber in town. Or maybe there was someone next door at the Purple Heart Ranch who did buzz cuts. He'd rather have his hair cut by a soldier than someone he didn't know.

"You been here less than forty-eight hours," said Grizz. "Barely twenty-four."

"And you're not on the Purple Heart Ranch land where this kind of thing is expected," said Mac.

"Like I said," shrugged Keaton, "there was a complication."

"That required a wife?" asked Grizz. His voice was more growl than anything.

Keaton would've expected the push back from Mac, who'd been eager to walk down the aisle since before he'd joined the service. Definitely from Rusty, who was separated from his wife, whom Keaton was sure the man was still in love with. He couldn't understand why Grizz was giving him the push back.

"Yeah," said Keaton. "It's the creek; it's not a part of the land deal with Banks. It belongs to Brenda – that's my wife. This is her land. But the only way we could get past all the restrictions to purchase the land and begin construction was if I was an owner. So, we decided the easiest way was to get married."

The two men stared at him. Mac's mouth worked like he was trying to say something. But no actual words escaped his lips. Grizz simply glared, his nose wrinkled like he smelled something foul.

A door opening and slamming turned Keaton's attention from his men. It was the back door to the house. They each turned to see Brenda, clad in form-fitting jeans, a tank top that hugged those curves Mac should not be noticing, and a cowboy hat on her head, jog down the backstairs. She tipped her hat to them all before heading toward the nearest barn.

Keaton forgot what he was saying as he watched her walk. The woman moved like she was a general, and all in her sight were under her command. Before she got too far away, Keaton saw her reach for something in her back pocket. She pulled out the memo pad. Tugging a pencil from the coils at the top of the pad, she began making marks.

"Easiest way, huh?" said Grizz.

Keaton bit at his lower lip. The sun hadn't fully risen in the sky, but he was suddenly parched. He'd kill for a tall, cool glass of green tea.

"You're really married?" Grizz grabbed for Keaton's left hand. He studied the band on his finger, pressing his thumb over it like he was testing it for realness.

The guilt settled in now. All of the men in his unit looked upon each other as though they were brothers. But Keaton was the closest thing to family that Grizz had. They'd grown up together. Grizz had spent many a night at the Keatons' dinner table and sleeping in a pile of covers on Keaton's bedroom floor. Grizz's home life had been less than ideal.

They'd done almost everything together, including joining the military. Keaton had always assumed that Grizz would've been the best man at his wedding. Only his wedding had been yesterday, and his best friend hadn't been at his side. But Grizz didn't seem entirely put out by it if the grin on his face was any proof.

"You tell your mom?" asked Grizz.

Keaton gulped. His gut shriveled in his belly. His shoulders developed an ache like when he was a scrawny kid back in gym class facing the pull-up bar. Suddenly, he felt four feet tall again.

Grizz cupped his ear and leaned into Keaton. "What was that?"

Keaton cleared his throat to try to make the sound louder. "No," he squeaked.

Grizz threw his head back and laughed. The sound was what a grizzly bear would make before it took its prey's head off. "You're a dead man."

"Well," said Mac, "at least you got to experience love before you died."

"Love?" said Keaton. "It's not like that."

"Maybe not for her yet. But for you?" Mac looked Keaton up and down. "Oh, yeah, it's like that."

Mac Kenzie would know. He'd been in love nearly all his life. With the same woman. But it hadn't worked out the first time. Or the second time. Or the dozens of other times he'd professed his undying love to her after that. Mac had always said that, for him, love was instant and then forever.

Was Keaton in love with Brenda? Had it been instant? The first time he'd seen her, he'd felt the earth move. True, a bull had rammed into him.

He'd been attracted to women before. He'd cared about a few. But those caring feelings had been a faucet left trickling a stream of water. With Brenda, Keaton felt he could barely keep his head above the title wave of water that crashed into him whenever he was near her.

"Yeah," Keaton sighed. "It's like that."

"So, the rumors about this place are true." Mac turned from Keaton to Grizz. "You're gonna get hitched, too."

Grizz didn't back up. He held his ground. "I'm not superstitious. And I'm not marriage material."

"Tell that to Patty."

"What does my sister have to do with anything?" said Keaton.

Mac made a scoffing sound. "You do realize she's in love with him."

"It's just a silly crush." Keaton brushed the notion away. It was normal for little sisters to have crushes on their brother's best friends. But that was years ago. His sister was in college, and she had a boyfriend.

"Patty Cakes is not a little girl anymore," said Mac.

"Hey!" Keaton and Grizz both growled at Mac.

Before the two men could advance, Mac held up his hands in surrender. "What? You both realize I'm taken."

"By a woman who keeps running away from you," said Grizz.

"She's not running," said Mac. "She just has cold feet."

"For almost a decade?" said Keaton.

"I'm giving her time to warm up to the idea," said Mac.

"This doesn't change anything," said Keaton. "We still need to get the camp finished in ninety days. And ... I promised we'd help Brenda with a few chores around here."

"What?" said Grizz. "So, we're ranchers now?"

CHAPTER FOURTEEN

She had been infiltrated. The ranch was under attack. The insurgents were everywhere.

After taking a cold shower in the hot bathroom, Brenda still hadn't gotten the feel of Keaton's fingertips on her face out of her mind. Her mind kept insisting that he had kissed her. She couldn't shake the certainty that she knew what his lower lip felt like, what his upper lip tasted of. It was as though his fingers had transferred the memories directly into her head.

Brenda shoveled a load of manure. But even the rank smell didn't clear her head. She was already behind for the day, for the week, because of all she had to deal with for her former ranch hands' incompetency. And now from Keaton's hands, which had wound up on her body.

She had to set boundaries for this marriage. Boundaries that were drawn at arm's length. Problem was, she'd have to actually come face to face with her husband to make those edicts. For now, she was avoiding him.

It was past lunchtime, and she'd seen not hide nor hair of Keaton. But she knew he was near. Her body felt like an antenna that was picking up his frequency. She felt a constant low hum of his energy. She needed more activity to shuck the excess off.

She should get started on separating the calves for branding. But she turned from that pasture and headed for the bull's pen. Luckily, there was always a fence to be mended on a ranch.

When she came to the broken fence that Manuel had kicked down, and Keaton had lost a fight with a hammer, she saw it was repaired. The big soldier, the one that looked like a bear, was putting away the hammer and nails. His large hands looked untouched by the hammer's face.

"What are you doing?" she asked.

The man straightened to his full height. Which rivaled that of a grizzly bear. He was broad as a bear too, blocking out the midday sun.

"Brenda, right?"

His voice sounded like he'd swallowed a bear. It was low and deep. Brenda felt certain that if he ever shouted, the sound would likely shake the ground.

"Name's Griffin. But everyone calls me Grizz."

"I can see why."

He didn't smile. He regarded her with complete suspicion. Well, he needed to learn she'd faced down … well, maybe not larger men. But she needed Grizz to know that she didn't scare easily, no matter how big her opponent.

"What are you doing, Griffin?"

The only indication he gave that he caught her snub of friendship was the slight raise of his left eyebrow. "Keaton said the fence needs mending. So, I took care of it."

"You didn't have to do that," she said.

"You're Keaton's wife. He's my brother."

"Which makes me your sister?"

Now the right brow lifted to meet the left one. But he still didn't break into a smile or break eye contact with her. This was a test of dominance. Well, this big bear was about to find out that Brenda never blinked first.

"It makes you a part of this team," Grizz concluded.

Brenda gasped. Taking a step back, she blinked at those words. "It's … me and Keaton … we're… it's not real. It's just temporary."

Once again, Grizz held her there under his unblinking, unrelenting, unsmiling glare. For the first time in her life, Brenda squirmed. Not in fear of this man. She squirmed at the lie that had just left her lips.

"Once a Ranger, always a Ranger," said Grizz. "That goes for family, too. Wives, especially. Sisters, too."

With that last statement, Grizz finally broke his glare. But not before Brenda caught something flash in his hard gaze. Something that made his hazel eyes go soft. Brenda opened her mouth to argue but felt it would be a waste of breath.

"Grizz?"

He lifted his head to look back at her.

"Wear a hat," she said. "Or the sun will burn you up."

He lifted an eyebrow but nodded his head. His lip curled. It wasn't exactly a smile. But it wasn't exactly a frown either. "Yes, ma'am."

Brenda walked away from the bear of a man. There were still many chores to check off her list and a shortage of hands to get the work done. There was feed to grind for her special herd of cattle. But when she got to the grinder, the other soldier was there.

"Afternoon, Mrs. Keaton."

Like Keaton and Grizz, this guy was also built like a truck. But unlike the grizzly bear, this man wore a friendly, almost infectious grin on his handsome face.

"It's Brenda."

"I'm Mac Kenzie."

"Mackenzie?"

"Close enough." He shrugged. "You can call me Mac."

"Nice to meet you, Mac. What are you doing?"

"Keaton said I needed to grind the feed." He turned to her new machine, technology which her former hands hadn't deigned to touch. "I Googled how to do it."

Mac patted the machine, which was purring like a kitten as it churned out the goods. It was exactly how Brenda wanted it done. She returned Mac's grin. She decided she liked this one.

"Where's Keaton?" she asked.

"Your hubby said he was cleaning corrals. Whatever that means."

Brenda turned to head in that direction. Mac put a hand to her forearm to stop her.

"Hey, Brenda, welcome to the team." With a wink and a nod, Mac turned back to his work.

A few moments later, Brenda found Keaton. He'd taken his shirt off but was in his undershirt. The white shirt had dirt smudges and spots of sweat in some places.

Brenda didn't focus on those. She got a clear view of his biceps as he set about his work. With his back to her, she was mesmerized by the movement of his shoulder blades and back muscles.

As though he sensed her presence, Keaton turned and caught her staring. Brenda had the urge to run and hide. But she held her ground.

This was her ranch. They'd invaded her space. She was in charge here. Even though these three Army Rangers were doing everything she needed done, the way she wanted it done.

"Everything okay?" Keaton asked.

Brenda had to swallow down a huge lump in her throat before she could respond. She wondered if that lump was her pride. "It's perfect."

Keaton's grin spread wider. He took a step toward her. Brenda took a deep breath and forced more hard to say words from her lips.

"Thank you for your help."

Keaton took another step closer to her.

"I really appreciate it." With one more step, they were toe to toe. "But shouldn't you be getting started on your camp?"

"Change of plans," Keaton said. "I told the guys to put your to-do list first."

"Won't that set you back?" If she reached out, her fingers would meet his bicep and come away damp from the sweat of his hard work.

"We'll catch up. I'm working with six pairs of hands and eighty-nine days. You were completely shorthanded."

There was electricity buzzing between them. That hum that she'd been trying to avoid all day was zinging around her head, in the palm of her hand, in the balls of her feet. More and more, she was feeling powerless against it.

"But now I've got you," she said.

Keaton nodded. "You've got me."

"I haven't been part of a team in a while. It's just been me since my family left the ranch."

"We're your family now." Keaton's hand came up to cup her cheek. They were back where they'd left off this morning. "Hey, Brenda?"

"Yeah, Keaton?"

With her head cradled in his palm, he tilted her head back. The brim of her hat could no longer hide her from him. She felt completely exposed.

"I was thinking," he continued, "maybe I could take you out to dinner? To get to know each other better."

"You mean like a date?"

"Yeah," he grinned. "Call me crazy, but I'd like to take my wife on a date. What do you say?"

Brenda knew she should say no. It wasn't that kind of marriage. It was business. And now he wanted to mix pleasure in. And, oh man, did she want to mix things all up.

She wanted to take a leap with a man like Keaton. Because a man like Keaton would be there to catch her. Heck, he'd likely make plans to be certain she would never fall in the first place.

He'd delegate others to watch out for her. He'd stick around until the job was done. He wouldn't leave her behind. Apparently, it was in the creed.

Brenda opened her mouth to accept when his phone buzzed. The buzz wasn't the normal ring of a cellphone. It was a catchy tune, the kind that would be programmed for a specific caller. It took Brenda a second to place it because she wasn't a *Star Wars* fan, but she was almost certain that was the death march song for the villain of the film, Darth Vader.

Keaton cringed as he jerked his hand away from Brenda. He shoved his hand in his pocket, pulling out his cell phone. He looked at the phone and cringed again.

"I have to get this," he said. "But before I do, I just want to say I'm sorry."

Keaton inhaled and let the breath out slowly. He held the phone to his ear. Then seemed to think better of it because he held the device away from his ear before pressing the Talk button.

"You're married!" The shrill voice carried over the receiver to fill the space between them.

"Hey, Mom."

CHAPTER FIFTEEN

eaton's ear was still ringing from his mother's tongue lashing over the phone. He was sure he knew how she'd found out about his impromptu wedding. Grizz had to know to expect a stealth attack coming his way. Keaton had barely been able to get a word into the conversation.

Not that it had been much of a conversation.

With his father sent on deployment after deployment, Keaton's mom had taken on much of the rearing of her two kids. Having to play both roles, the matriarch and the patriarch, the good cop and the bad cop, the one who cooked dinner and also played catch, Holly Keaton had developed some extra special talents. His mom didn't just have eyes in the back of her head like a normal disciplinarian. No, she could sense when her kids were misbehaving a few blocks away. And when she came to find them, Keaton and his sister Patty always swore they heard the trumpets blaring Darth Vader's *Imperial March*.

"Are you grounded?"

The back door hit him in the rear as he stepped over the threshold. Brenda leaned one hip against the counter as she sipped on what had to be her fifth cup of coffee for the day. Keaton had the urge to take the cup from her hands and replace the ceramic lip of the mug with his own.

The day was over. The sun had set. The only work that needed to be done was the work of slipping under his wife's defenses to get to the heart of her.

"Yup, I'm grounded." Keaton took the steps to close the distance between him and Brenda. But he didn't reach for her cup. She was clearly a caffeine addict. The only way to get rid of one addiction was to replace it with another. "I'm afraid I can't take you to the school dance this weekend."

Brenda giggled. The movement had her lower the cup from her lips on her own. "That's a harsh penalty for a grown man who got married without his mommy's permission."

"I'm sure she'll forgive us after the first grandkid."

The cup slipped from her hands. Keaton reached out and caught it before it hit the floor. He looked up to find Brenda's cheeks reddening. Keaton knew his response was to take the comment back. But he couldn't set his mouth to do it.

"Did you tell your parents?" he asked.

"I will."

Keaton set the half-drunk coffee mug into the sink. "I know you plan for this to be temporary—"

"We," Brenda corrected him. "We plan for this to be temporary."

"Right," he said. "But your family should know what we're up to. You don't want to get in trouble like me."

She turned her face away from him, looking out the large kitchen window at the last rays of the setting sun. "My family isn't concerned about what goes on here. They all scattered as soon as they could and left me in charge."

Keaton reached out to her then. He picked up where they'd left off outside. He lifted her cheek with his index finger. Her green gaze met his. The color of her eyes wasn't the sharp blade of grass now. It was the flat side after a lawnmower, or tractor, or booted foot cut it down.

There was pain in the crinkle of her eyes. Keaton felt the sharpness of the hurt, almost as if it had happened to him. He wanted to take it away from her. He wanted to swallow it down. Toss it away. Whatever it would take to keep it away from her. All he could do was rub his thumb tenderly at the corner of her eye. His tenderness broke her silence.

"I love being in charge," she said.

"Yeah, I got that impression."

She smiled, which caused her eyes to crinkle in a different way now. "I was born to run this place, and I've done a very good job of it."

"I can see that. This operation looks well planned out with clear tasks and objectives to reach an achievable goal."

Brenda preened under his compliments. Her cheeks spread even wider as she grinned. Her warm flesh filled the palm of Keaton's hand as he continued to cradle her face.

And then it was gone. The smile and the light in her eyes blinked out. Her head lowered, coming out of Keaton's grasp.

"My dad's heart just wasn't in this place anymore. He never wanted to be a rancher. He did it for his dad, for his family. Grandpa always said family first."

There was more to that statement. But she didn't say it. She didn't need to. Looking around the kitchen table where eight chairs were evenly spaced around the dining table, it was clear to see that her family wasn't here any longer. Neither were the ranch hands she hired. No one was here for her.

Keaton wanted to wrap Brenda up in his arms. He wanted to lift her chin again and let her know she didn't need to hold it high on her own anymore. Because he was there for her. He'd always be there for her. Temporary was not going to do it for him.

He reached for her. Not her chin. He reached for her elbow. With a tug, she came willingly.

She let him wrap an arm around her shoulders. Her shoulders were stiff, but some of the weight dropped as Keaton pressed his palm's into her shoulder blades. He cradled the back of her head, preparing to tuck her under his chin. But she didn't lower her head. She looked up at him.

Keaton's gaze dipped to her lips. They were parted. The tip of her tongue dipped out to moisten her lower lip.

Keaton was excellent at reading signs in a combat zone. He often got his signals crossed when it came to women and the mixed messages that they sent. Not his Brenda. The messages she was sending were clear. He could cross the bridge. He could kiss her.

He would kiss her. Not a temporary peck. He was going to kiss this woman every day. For the rest of their lives. Starting now.

The back door banged open. Grizz and Mac stormed over the threshold like invaders launching an unexpected, unwelcome attack. Brenda ducked out of Keaton's hold, leaving him feeling shell-shocked.

"Are we indentured servants, or are we going to get fed?" asked Mac.

"I'm neither a maid nor a short order cook," said Brenda.

"Lucky for you, I'm a metrosexual," said Mac.

Brenda held up her hands. "Oh, I don't judge."

Grizz broke into a grin. Keaton noted it was the first time his best friend had cracked a smile since arriving on the ranch. He should ask what was up. But only after he got in a shot for coming between him and his wife.

"It means that I'm a heterosexual male who is not afraid to show my feminine side," said Mac.

Brenda still looked confused.

"It means I'll cook."

Mac headed to the fridge to survey the stores. Grizz turned to the cupboards in search of pots.

"We've already washed up," said Mac. "Why don't you two get cleaned up while we prepare a feast."

Keaton followed Brenda up the stairs. Halfway up, he stopped pretending that he wasn't enjoying the view. She was his wife. What was his was hers, and what was hers would soon be his. If he played his cards right. And Keaton was certain he was figuring out the rules of this game.

"What's on the agenda tomorrow?" he asked.

Brenda turned in the hall just outside her door. "Agenda?"

"Your checklist." Keaton canted his head. He couldn't see the imprint of the memo pad that had shaped the back of her jeans. But the impression of it from him staring all the way up the stairs was burned in his mind. "Tell me, what do you need doing tomorrow?"

"Oh, nothing," said Brenda. "You have your hands full—"

"Didn't we just have this conversation outside? My brothers and I are here to help. You're family now. Your list is my list."

She chewed at that lower lip, but it didn't hide the smile that lifted one side of her face. Keaton's stomach grumbled. But he wasn't hungry for whatever Mac was whipping up downstairs. All he wanted to take a bite out of was the woman in front of him. Starting with that plump lip.

"Our agreement made me part owner in this land," he said. "A small part, yes. But I'm here to stay. Whatever happens between us, I'm not leaving."

Again her lips parted, giving him the universal sign to fire at will.

"Do you want something to happen between us, Bren? Because I—"

His last words were cut off as Brenda's lips crashed into his. Her lips were a curious probe. They tread softly, covering the area of his bottom lip.

Keaton launched a full attack. He brought one hand to her low back and pressed her to him. The other hand, he used to cup the back of her head, angling her mouth for maximum devastation.

But the plan backfired. He'd meant to overwhelm her defenses. Quickly, he saw that he was in the danger zone with this woman.

Through all her outward armor, she was soft and pliable in his hold. At his first strike, she yielded. The thing was, Keaton had crossed into this territory with a white flag of surrender. He'd had no intention of putting up a fight.

He opened to her, letting her invade his senses. Letting her invade his mind. Letting her invade his heart.

The organ in his chest changed its tune and fell into step with her. His every sense was tuned to the tenderness of her touch, the sweetness of her scent, the spicy note at the corner of her upper lip. His mind rearranged its masterplan to do her bidding, starting with that memo pad. His fingers grazed as they slipped from her low back to the pocket of her jeans.

Keaton broke the kiss. He was gratified to see that Brenda clung to him as she tried to recover her wits. Keaton already had his wits about him, and he had her list in his hands.

"If you won't tell me what you need, I'll just have to look for myself."

He opened the pad to find organized lists with checkmarks beside each one. There were dates at the top of each page. When he flipped the page, he didn't see a listing for tomorrow's date.

"I told you," said Brenda, her voice still breathy from their kiss. "There's nothing to do tomorrow. Tomorrow is Sunday. Church."

"Well," said Keaton. "I'll be there."

CHAPTER SIXTEEN

There was a boy in her bedroom.

Brenda had moved into her parents' bedroom after they'd retired. But she'd always felt it was too large for her. She'd purchased a new mattress, but often felt swallowed up by the queen-sized bed. She'd moved out most of their old furniture and felt like she was on an island at the center and needed to send out an SOS.

But she'd outgrown her old room. And she was now the sole owner of this big house. So, of course, she'd taken the biggest bedroom.

She'd brought her clothes and her dresser in there. She'd painted the room in a shade of blue that was supposed to be good for sleep. Looking around the room, she realized that that shade of blue was the exact color of Keaton's eyes.

Keaton, her husband. Keaton, the man who had been sleeping in her bedroom for the past two nights. Her childhood bedroom which was just two doors down the hall.

His large body would certainly fall over the frame of her full-size bed. His muscular arms would likely crush the soft pillows at the head of her bed. His bare feet would slip out of her old comforter.

The man was simply too much for her old room. He belonged in a room the size of her parents' old room. She'd bet if he were in there with her, it wouldn't feel so large. She'd bet it'd feel just right.

She heard the familiar creak of the door of her old bedroom. She heard the floorboards take on the weight of a full-grown soldier. Brenda's breath caught and held as Keaton's footsteps made their way down the hall toward her.

Was he coming in here?

Coming back to finish what he'd started last night just outside this room?

Well, technically, she had started it.

She had no idea what had possessed her to reach up and kiss him. She might be bossy on the ranch, but she was not that girl out in the dating field. She really hadn't had that much experience out in the world of dating. She had always been far too busy on the ranch. And most men didn't appreciate a woman in what was traditionally a man's job.

Except Keaton. He didn't have a problem with her being the boss. In fact, she was almost certain his blue eyes sparkled every time she pulled out her checklist. He seemed eager for her to give him a task to complete.

Yet when she'd taken charge of his lips, he'd expertly slipped the reins of control from her and taken charge. Brenda's lips still burned from their kiss last night. Even surrounded by the calming, blue walls, her body had been far too primed for sleep.

When she heard the bathroom door open, her hand touched her lips that were swollen with want. When she heard the shower turn on, her fingers slid down her heated cheeks. Her hand continued down her throat, which was parched even though a full glass of water sat on her bedside table. Her hand ended at her belly, which grumbled even though she wasn't hungry.

Brenda put her feet on the ground. She was not one to get carried away by a man. She was a strong woman. So, why did her knees wobble as she stood?

She padded to the door and eased it open. The *pitter-patter* of water let her know Keaton was still occupied in the shower. On light feet, she made her way down the hall to her old room.

Even though it was her old room, she knew that opening the door would be an invasion into her guest's privacy. Luckily, the door was cracked open.

Brenda peered inside. The walls in there were a shade of green, which was also said to promote sleep. But the green walls had only made Brenda think of the outside and her chores, and what she had to get checked off her list the next day. All of which meant she hadn't slept much in there.

On the wall hung a picture of her family. Her mom and dad stood together, their arms around each other. Her brother's hand rested on the cross at his neck, his gaze tilted upwards. And there she was, looking off to the side at the ranch.

Brenda didn't doubt for a second that her parents loved her. She knew they believed in her too. She knew with certainty from how frequently her brother was in her kitchen, making sure she was fed, that she had Walter's love and support for what she was doing with her life. But none of them wanted a hand in the family business. It was only her two hands.

Brenda looked away from the family portrait. It was the only thing left in this room that was hers. Everything else belonged to Keaton.

She noted that the bed was made. The sheets pulled tight to the corners like a hotel maid had visited. A green and brown military bag sat at the foot of the bed.

Brenda took a step closer. She knew that opening the bag and peering inside would be the height of ill manners. Luckily, the bag was open.

Inside, she saw a stack of folded clothes in one corner. In the other corner of the bag were two photos. One image was of six men. All in fatigues. All grinning at the off-screen photographer. Three of the grinning faces she recognized.

The other photo was of Keaton and a woman. Again, he grinned at the camera with those sparkling blue eyes of his. Looking closer, she saw that there was a hint of exasperation in the up-tilt of his lips. The girl, a redhead, grinned at him. She had her arms around his neck. Her chin tilted up like she expected to be kissed.

Was this an old girlfriend? Maybe it was his current girlfriend. Whatever she was, it was clear that she was important to him. She had a place in his well-organized bag.

"Hey."

Brenda jolted. One hand went over her racing heart. The other covered her mouth to hold in her yelp of surprise. Here she stood in the middle of her old bedroom in a cami and a pair of men's boxer shorts. The boxers were more comfortable than the flannel when it got warm in the big house.

Unlike the previous morning, Keaton, unfortunately, was dressed. His firm cushion of a chest was covered by a pressed white shirt. Those powerful thighs that made a damp towel look like the height of fashion were draped in dark slacks.

"Am I overdressed?" he asked.

"No," she said, taking her hand from her mouth as she stared. "You look great."

"Thanks," he grinned. "You, too. I'm a lucky man if my wife wakes up looking like this."

Brenda was not the type of woman whose tongue got tied. Except with this man. She swallowed down the knot in her stomach and pushed forth what needed to be said.

"Do you have a girlfriend?"

Keaton lifted a brow at her. Then he lifted his hand and placed it on her waist. With the gentlest of tugs, Brenda came to him. Her body went, but her gaze stayed on the picture in the bag. She had to stay focused.

Keaton's gaze followed hers to the bag. He grinned like a man with a secret he was itching to tell. But he held his tongue.

"No," he said. "I don't have a girlfriend. I have a wife."

"Do you have an ex-girlfriend you're not over?" Brenda prodded.

"No," he said. "There's never been anyone I wanted to hold onto."

His grip tightened around Brenda's waist. His thumbs rubbed tight circles in her sides, making her feel dizzy. The motion loosened her tongue.

"What about the picture in your bag?" she said.

"Picture?" For a man that spoke his mind since the moment she'd met him, Keaton's voice was full of fake innocence.

"All right," she said, pounding a hand against his chest. "I was snooping. But it's my house."

"Our house." His hands came to her back, and he pressed her deeper into the comfort of his chest.

But Brenda stiffened her arms, unwilling to cave into the warmth she knew was at the heart of this man. "Is that what this is? You just want my property?"

"That was what it was about. A means to an end. A convenient arrangement. But I told you, I want more."

Without warning, and without any real protest from her, Keaton claimed Brenda's lips. Her stiff arms collapsed. Her fingers curled around his neck. They had to. She needed something to hang onto as he deepened the kiss and wiped all her good sense away.

"She's my sister," he said when he let her up for air.

"Who?" It took Brenda a second to open her eyes. The world was spinning off its axis. Luckily, she had something strong and reliable to hold onto; Keaton.

"The redhead in the photo. In the bag you were snooping in. She's not my girlfriend. She's not my ex. She's my sister. I'm a one-woman kind of man."

Brenda leaned back and looked into those clear blue eyes. She didn't believe in fate. She believed in a good plan. She'd researched that color of blue that was on her walls. The hue had definitely had a good effect on her this past year. She'd never felt more rested than when she closed her eyes after staring at those walls.

"And," Keaton continued, "I'll have you know that I'm happily dating my wife. You'd better get ready for church, Mrs. Keaton."

With another light press to her mouth, he was gone. Brenda stood in her childhood bedroom and felt like a stranger. Keaton had driven into her life and knocked everything off-kilter.

Even though things weren't going according to her original plan, she felt certain she was on the right path. She had a man who didn't challenge her every thought. Instead, he sought out her advice and consulted her on the way forward for both of them.

And it wasn't just him. He had a team that was loyal to him. And now they were loyal to her by extension. They were going to stay and work the land. For the first time in a long time, Brenda had a team she could rely on.

CHAPTER SEVENTEEN

Keaton couldn't stop rubbing at his bottom lip. The taste of Brenda, his wife, still lingered there long moments after he'd released his hold on her. In his mind, he rearranged every plan he had to date. Now, written in black ink at the top of his master plan, was to have more of her as soon as possible, as often as possible, as long as possible.

"We have a problem," said Grizz.

Keaton was used to hearing those four words in his former line of work. Nothing ever went exactly according to plan on a mission. Typically, when someone said that phrase, his ears went alert. His mind would start buzzing as he mentally made alterations to his plans.

His mind buzzed, all right. But it was more like butterflies flitting around in his head. He wondered what his wife would wear today for church. He wondered if he should introduce her with his last name attached. Though she lived in a fairly traditional town, she had all the hallmarks of a modern woman.

Would she want to keep her own last name? Maybe she'd want to hyphenate? But whose name would she want first? Vance-Keaton or Keaton-Vance? And would he follow suit and change his name? He would if that's what their children would be named.

"Rusty got held up," Grizz continued. "All he would say is it was a family matter, and he'd get here as soon as possible."

"Well, he should take care of that," said Keaton. "Family should come first."

Keaton didn't miss Grizz and Mac's shared look. He just wasn't too interested in figuring out what that look meant. His attention was turned to the stairs as he awaited Brenda's appearance.

"That means we're a man down," said Mac. "It means it's going to set us behind."

"Oh, you're right." The mention of the time frame snapped Keaton out of his stupor. "And now, with the ranch chores, it will set us behind even more."

Keaton rubbed at his chin as he tried to rework the two schedules in his head. He assumed Grizz and Mac were pondering the same logistics when they exchanged another narrow-gazed look.

"You do realize we can't do both and make the schedule," said Grizz.

Keaton removed his fingers from his chin and crossed his arms. "We have to. I promised my wife."

"I thought you said this marriage wasn't real," said Grizz. "Something about a means to an end."

"I never said that." Keaton took a step toward his oldest friend.

"What you definitely said was that you would have this camp ready in a crazy quick time period." Grizz took a step toward Keaton. "You gave your word, and by extension, all of our words. A Ranger does not go back on his word."

"Neither does a husband."

"A real one wouldn't." Grizz met that step until they were toe to toe.

"This is real." Keaton leaned forward until they were nose to nose.

A set of hands came between the two men. Mac gave each a push. When that didn't work, he shoved his body between them.

"Is there a problem?" said a female voice.

The three men turned their heads. All tension left the room as they looked up toward the top of the stairs. Keaton forgot about his friend's aggression. He forgot about the need to rearrange his plans. He forgot how to breathe.

Brenda stood at the top of the stairs. He'd only seen her in either jeans and boots, or in boxers and barefoot. Brenda standing in a simple sundress and sandals made Keaton go stupid.

"You look amazing, Brenda," said Mac.

"Yeah, you look really pretty." There was a gruffness to Grizz's voice like he was annoyed that he spoke the truth.

Keaton was annoyed with them both. They'd given her two of the best compliments. What was left for him to say?

"She's mine," Keaton growled.

Brenda had taken her first step down the stairs. But at Keaton's words, she halted. Her shoulders rotated as though she were about to take a step back. Keaton walked to the landing. He extended his hand up to her and waited.

When her fingertips finally touched his palm, he was left feeling lightheaded. Probably because he'd been holding his breath the long seconds it took her to straighten her shoulders and take the necessary step to reach out to him.

Keaton folded his fingers around Brenda's hand, determined never to let her go. Once again, he tugged her to him, and she came. Keaton tucked his wife into his side, where she belonged as they walked out the door and to his rental.

For a strong woman, Brenda was soft. He knew she would never bend easily. That was fine with him. Keaton had no intention of bending this woman to his will. His goal was to make her melt, to thaw the cold structure she'd erected around her heart. By the flush on her cheeks, he knew his plan was working.

The car ride into town flew by as Keaton continued to hold Brenda's hand in the backseat of the rental. Neither of them talked. At least not with their mouths. He rubbed at her palm while listening to Mac tell some story about their time in Syria.

Brenda rubbed at the space between his knuckles as she stared out the backside window and made noncommittal sounds every so often when Mac paused in his story. Grizz, who was in the driver's seat, kept entirely quiet as he maneuvered the vehicle down the open roads.

Keaton's attention was on the smoothness of Brenda's nails in comparison to the jagged edges of her cuticles. Either she'd broken all ten of her fingernails while out working, or she'd been biting at them from worry. Keaton smoothed his thumb over them again and again as though he could wring out the worry.

The sermon washed over him as well. He sat in the pews beside his wife. Each time they had to rise or bow their heads in prayer, he was obliged to release her hand. He liked it best when they held the Bible between them. Keaton had never been a religious man, but singing hymns and following along the passages, he felt something move him.

After the service, there was a whirlwind of introductions. Keaton would never remember everyone's name. He was so focused on being introduced as Brenda's husband.

"I never thought I'd see the day when Brenda Vance settled down," said one woman, the cloud of her white hair around her heart-shaped face made her look like a pleasant angel. "I thought she was a lesbian."

Keaton blinked. Had he heard that right? He looked up at Brenda, but she was on the other side of the room, encircled by a different bunch of women.

"Now, maybe she'll get in the kitchen and let a man take over that ranch." This was said by a woman with both salt and pepper in her hair. But her lips were pinched as though she'd sucked on a lemon. "Though her cooking skills aren't up to snuff. If you need a home-cooked meal, you come right on over anytime."

Keaton looked from woman to woman. Upon closer inspection, neither of their smiles were genuine. There was a dullness in their eyes, which had only sparked when they'd said disparaging comments about Brenda. "Do either of you actually know my wife?"

The two older women looked at each other. Their shared glance was not one of camaraderie like he and his men would share. There were shields up even as they glanced at each other.

"Brenda is innovating on the ranch, and you're concerned about what she can do in the kitchen?" he said. "With the profit she's making as an overseer, she can hire a cook."

"I thought the rumor was that they had a marriage of convenience?" the White Cloud said to Salt and Pepper.

"It was," said Keaton. "Until I realized I'd hit the jackpot. I have no intention of letting go of my winnings."

Keaton turned from the two women who clearly had two different faces, none of which were genuine. But before he could get too far, he was confronted with a wrinkled older man who looked as though he'd lived his life hard. Keaton could tell he'd been handsome in his younger days because beside him stood a younger, fresh-faced version.

"It might look like profit, but it'll be short-term," said the older man. His voice was rough, as though there was tobacco growing out of his throat.

"How would you know?" said Keaton.

"Worked on that ranch since before little missy was born. Name's Manuel Bautista. This here is my nephew, Angel."

Keaton wanted to cringe when he shook the elder Bautista's hand. He felt a zap zing into the center of his palm. Not a zing of energy. More like a shock that would've warned him to keep away from the electrical box.

When he took the younger man's hand, he felt a tempered hum. Keaton got the impression that Angel Bautista was an untapped source looking for a path. He wondered if he got the younger man away from the energy suck that was his uncle if he might become a force of nature.

"Your little missus—"

"Brenda," corrected Keaton. "Or Mrs. Keaton."

"Right. She thinks she can run that place by herself. But she's going to need help. Now that a man is there, hopefully, you'll be able to rein her in."

"I'm a military man. We prefer to have a strong woman on our side. Only a weak man would be stupid enough to try and rein a woman in. He'd likely wind up snipped like a steer."

The younger man, Angel, snickered. But he straightened his face when his uncle glared at him. Manuel Bautista turned that hard look back on Keaton.

"We'll see if you're up for the task with Miss Vance—I mean Mrs. Keaton. Or if you'll find yourself outside a broken fence like a wayward bull."

Broken fence? "How did you know the bull got out of the fence?"

Manuel shrugged. His wizened face contorting into something on the border of sinister. "Small town. News travels fast."

Angel looked away. The young man bit at his lip and wrinkled his nose, as though there was something foul in the air. Keaton thought he smelled it too. His spidey senses were tingling.

"Anyway," said Manuel, "when you're ready to hire an overseer who knows what he's doing, give me a call."

With another grin that made Keaton's gut grumble, Bautista walked off. Angel hesitated. He looked to Keaton. Then he hung his head and followed his uncle.

"We could use the extra hands," said Grizz, coming up behind Keaton.

"Not the old man's," said Keaton.

"Yeah," said Mac coming up to Keaton's other side. "I didn't take to him either. Too bad you didn't get the kid's info. He looked like he'd make a good worker."

CHAPTER EIGHTEEN

For the second time in her life, Brenda slept late. On Monday morning, she rolled over in her bed only a moment before the first rays of the sun stretched up to the horizon. Brenda stretched her arms over her head, letting out a satisfied groan as her muscles and tendons popped.

She should not get used to this. It was completely unprofessional. She'd have to blame it on the previous day's activities. Walking on Keaton's arm. Sitting with her hand in his. Bearing the brunt of the smile and his sparkling gaze and his deep voice filled with compliments for the entire day. The most taxing had been all the concentrating she'd had to do as she shifted into answering to being called Mrs. Keaton.

True, she'd only been called that twice. And both times had been by her brother who was clearly doing it to needle her. It had needled her. Because she'd liked it.

Brenda had always thought that when she got married, she would keep her last name. It was the name of her family ranch. It was a business decision. When anyone said Vance Ranch, she knew they were talking about her. Now, when the name Keaton was uttered, they were, in part, referring to her as well. Was this divided loyalties?

Unlikely. Most of the ranchers and the townsfolk had always eyed her, and her need to modernize, warily. But nearly every person at the church service took an instant liking to Keaton. It had to be the soldier thing. This town was pretty patriotic.

And all the while that Keaton was winning over her lifelong neighbors and friends, he stuck close by her. If he wasn't beside her with his hand at her back, then his gaze was on her. His smile was aimed at her. His attention was somehow focused on her.

So, it was no wonder she'd slept a bit later than usual. It had been a lot to deal with. She was adjusting to a whole new world.

One where she wasn't entirely sure what her place was. She was a touch confused about her role. And she wasn't completely clear about her duties.

For just the briefest of moments, she felt sorry for Manuel Bautista. Was this what he'd felt like when she'd mechanized the things his generation used to do by hand? But no sooner than the first brush of sympathy touched her heart, did Brenda brush it away.

Even if her footing wasn't sure about her new reality, at least she hadn't kicked a gaping hole in the fencing and let out a raging bull. There were boundaries to this marriage. Even though Keaton's hands had been just a bit outside the lines as his fingers had pressed into her back, rubbed warm circles at her palms, brushed a tendril of hair off her forehead and behind her ear.

And don't get her started on his lips. He had only pressed his lips to her temple a few times during the service. When he'd walked her to her room at the end of the night, he'd only kissed her cheek. But by then, Brenda had been wanting to hop a fence.

She settled for hopping out of bed, shoving into her clothes, and headed out in search of the man who was turning her world upside down. When she got to the other side of her door, she knew he was gone.

Her old bedroom door was slightly ajar. In the bathroom, the shower was damp with use. In the kitchen, the coffee mugs were in the sink, and a new pot of coffee was brewing.

She looked out the window, but the soldiers weren't anywhere within view. Her phone buzzed, and she saw a text from Keaton.

Working on the camp. We'll be back in a couple of hours to help with your chores.

Brenda thumbed the message. She decided not to reply. Her hands were needed elsewhere.

The fences on her property were mended. The boundary lines were set. All was in order. But Brenda knew there was always work to be done. She whipped out her to-do list and began checking off morning chores.

By noon, Keaton and the others still weren't back. She could no longer pretend that she wasn't checking for them, that she wasn't waiting for the company. They had their priorities, and she wasn't at the top of their list.

Besides, she didn't need another set of hands to separate the cows from their calves. Climbing atop her horse, she had the mamas and their babies corralled into a paddock behind the barn where she stored the tagging, branding, and castration gear.

Getting the cattle into the entrance was the easy part. Brenda dismounted from her horse, tying the reins to the outside of the fence before closing the gate. Then she moved amongst the cattle.

Cows had a tendency to want to come out the way they went in. That was the plan. Brenda lifted the lower two rungs on the fencing at the entry. Now the entryway had a fork, one leading back out to pasture, the other leading down a small alleyway to a smaller pen. The trick was, only the calves would fit under the rungs of the second entryway.

Brenda stood just off to the side of the entry as the cows began to head out the way they came in. The mama cows kept with the easy and familiar route to Brenda's left. The calves, who were more wary of humans, avoided Brenda and went to the easier route on her right where their bodies neatly fit under the removed rungs of the railing. Proving once more that ranching wasn't about brute force, just a well thought out plan. The whole separation process from getting the cows into the corral to sectioning off calves took less than a half-hour.

"That's a pretty neat trick, boss."

Brenda paused. That wasn't exactly a man's voice. It still held the tenor of youth. Brenda turned to find Angel Bautista. His head was lowered, causing his worn cowboy hat to cast shadows. His lips were pursed as though he tasted contrition.

"What are you doing here, Angel?"

"Your husband sent me to help. He got my number from someone at church and called me this morning." The kid bit at his lip. It took him a long moment before he lifted his head to meet her gaze. "What my uncle did was wrong. And not just the fence. My mama raised me to respect women. She knocked me upside the head when she heard we left you working the ranch on your own."

"Good for her, but I don't want your help."

"I'm sure you don't want it, but I think you need it. And I want to learn. From you."

"You've got your uncle for that."

Angel shook his head. "My uncle is so caught up in a bygone era when it comes to ranches and women. He's on his third wife, you know. The world's changing, that includes how ranches are running. You're one of the few who are trying to adapt. I've only ever wanted to be a rancher."

"What does your uncle think about this?"

"He doesn't know. He's not the boss of me. I'd like that honor to go to you. Even though you're not the easiest person to work for."

"Hey!"

"But I think the best way for me to learn how is here with you. All I need is a chance."

CHAPTER NINETEEN

eaton sank his hands into the warm earth. The soil here was rich. It moved easily through his fingers as he dug in the trenches. The work was back-breaking, but he could see the rewards he was reaping.

The boundaries of the training camp were finally taking shape. It was all coming together. Not just the camp, but the vision he and his men had had. As well as a vision he hadn't planned on; his wife.

Having Brenda there by his side to see the foundation of his plan coming into view was the only thing that was missing. They'd had to employ the tactic of divide and conquer today. The next few weeks would be hard with all the work they had to do to put their respective plans in motion. For a few days, he'd have to give most of his attention to the camp, but he couldn't wait to get back to the chores on the ranch.

Already, he missed working with the animals, with the Vance Ranch operation, with his life partner who made his heart skip a beat every time he saw her riding toward him on top of a horse. He'd hired one ranch hand to help her out, but he realized he would rather trade spots with Angel Bautista right now and work alongside his wife.

But that wasn't the plan. Brenda had already laid a strong foundation for the ranch. He needed to do the same with the camp.

The sun was setting on this long day. All Keaton wanted was a hot shower, a warm meal, and the feel of his wife in his arms.

Driving across the land, he saw the rest of his life stretched out. He and his brothers would build not only their business but their homes here. His children would grow wild and free, ranging like the cattle. And each night, he'd come home to the most capable woman he knew. And they'd compare checklists.

Grizz and Mac headed inside the big house, where they had each claimed one of the spare rooms on the ground floor. Keaton didn't follow. There was an unsettled air on the ranch. Cows mooed, which was a sound he'd grown used to these last couple of days. But there was a pained note to the chorus of moos. They sounded as though they were in agony.

He walked down a path that led to one of the barns. There were a number of cows out in the pasture. In a smaller pen, were calves. The smaller cattle made sounds that reminded Keaton of a child crying in the night. Standing between the two plots of land was his wife.

Brenda's head was bowed. Her shoulders caved in. Gone was the strong woman he'd met the first time he'd stepped on this land. She looked weary and worn out. Her day had to have been harder than his, especially when she'd only had two sets of hands, and he'd had three. Guilt crashed into him. He should've been there for her.

Keaton wrapped his arms around Brenda from behind. She pulled away from him, jerking out of his hold. When she turned, he saw that there was a branding iron in her hand.

Thank goodness it wasn't hot. But it was aimed at his heart.

Keaton didn't jerk back. He wouldn't mind wearing the Vance brand. It was the letter V with a curlicue at the top like the brim of a cowboy hat. He reached up to the button on his shirt and let it loose.

Brenda watched his action. Her gaze fastened on his bare chest. Could she see his heart pounding on the left side as he waited for her claim?

She lowered the prod and turned back to the fencing. "Don't sneak up on a woman with a branding iron."

"Don't think I'd mind having your mark on me."

Brenda made a scoffing sound as she shook her head. She set the iron down and began arranging some other items that Keaton couldn't identify. All the while, she kept her back to him.

"Rough day?" he ventured.

One of the calves whined low and long, its large brown gaze fixed on her. Brenda tensed at the sound. She shut her eyes and grimaced.

"What's going on with them?" Keaton asked.

"Separation anxiety. We separated the calves from their sows earlier. In the morning, the calves get branded. Has to be done. By law and because otherwise, anyone could claim them. But as you can hear, they don't like being apart."

"I understand the feeling," Keaton said. "I was away from you all day, and I groaned about it enough that Grizz threatened to throw me in the creek."

Keaton reached for Brenda again. She dodged his advance. She gave him her back as she fussed with some other equipment.

"Bren?" Keaton came to stand in front of her. She kept her head down, not meeting his gaze. "What's going on?"

"I have a lot of work to do."

"Did that Bautista kid not help?"

She met his gaze then. Green eyes flashing the hottest part of a fire. "About that. You have no right to hire help for me."

"I couldn't be here for you. So, I sent help."

It was so slight, but he noticed it. Brenda's lower lip quivered. If she'd let any sound escape, Keaton was sure she'd sound just like one of the forlorn calves. Was she feeling abandoned just like the cows?

"I'm sorry, Bren. But I couldn't be in two places at one time. I'm here now."

"I get it. The camp is your dream. The ranch is mine. We have different priority lists."

"You are my list."

He did reach for her then. The separation was clearly causing them both too much anxiety. She didn't fight his hold. But neither did she accept his words.

"You just met me," she said, crossing her arms over her chest but remaining within his embrace.

"And now I want all of you," he said. "There's something between us. You feel it, too."

Brenda shut her eyes and shook her head, but it was a feeble attempt at denial. "It's not real."

"Feels pretty real to me." He leaned in. Just close enough to touch her lips, but he didn't. He needed her to come to him.

"I feel …" Her gaze opened. The blazing green had cooled, but there was still something burning bright. "It's inconvenient. It'll pass."

Keaton let out a harsh laugh, but he did not let her go. He was never letting her go. "You're a hard woman to love, you know that?"

Brenda shook her head. The movement was a tight shake, as though her body didn't believe what she was trying to deny. "You don't love me."

"I'm marching toward it, Brenda. I'm very, very close. And I don't think you're far from me."

She let out a shaky breath. Her fingers, which had been balled into fists under her armpits, crept up to her shoulder blades. She rubbed and squeezed at her forearms. The protective gesture transforming into one of self-comfort.

"You have so many fences up," Keaton continued. "As soon as I get through one, you put up another."

"I'm a cattle rancher," she said. "Fences are my business."

Keaton chuckled as he looked at the obstacle course that was his wife. His heart urged him to bring her closer. But he knew that if he did, she'd put up another fence.

He did it anyway. With his palm at her low back, he pressed their bodies together until a single breath couldn't get between them. He tightened his hold so that she couldn't get away.

"You ever been somewhere and know it's exactly where you were meant to be?" he asked. "When I saw you, I knew I was meant to be here with you."

Brenda didn't answer. The cows had settled for a few moments.

Maybe they'd been calmed by the connection happening just outside the pen.

"I rearranged my master plan for you, Brenda. You're a part of my vision now. I'm bull-headed, like you. I will bust down every fence you put in front of me."

She was soft, pliable now. He felt her will bending. Maybe this would be the last barrier he'd ever have to break through with her.

As if on cue, his phone chimed. Luckily, it wasn't the Vader *Imperial March*, so he didn't feel obligated to answer. But he didn't want another interruption, so he reached in his back pocket for the infernal device.

"Just let me turn this—"

Keaton's words died as he recognized the number. He had to get this call. His hold loosened on Brenda. Like a calf who knew what the new day was going to bring, she slipped out of his hold. Keaton hit TALK on the device. He watched as his wife took one, then another step away from him, gutted that he couldn't immediately follow.

"Yes, sir …? Yes, construction is going well. We broke ground today and … You'll be on the ground for a visit tomorrow …? That's great news. I'll be here to show you around … Look forward to it."

As Keaton pocketed his phone, the cows took up their wailing moos. The sound kept on late into the night. Keaton barely slept a wink in his wife's childhood bedroom as he worried over how the next day would go.

CHAPTER TWENTY

he cries of the cows kept Brenda up all night. They didn't understand why they were separated from their loved ones. In the morning, they'd get another shock when they were poked in the hind with a hot iron. But that's how life was on a ranch. You couldn't stick around on the land without someone finding their way under your skin.

Brenda had grabbed cold leftovers from the fridge and hid in her room. She stayed corralled in her quarters for the rest of the evening. She didn't dare leave the boundary of those four walls the next morning until she heard Keaton rise, shower, and leave out the front door. And so for another day, she started her day behind schedule.

How had it come to this? She'd made every provision to protect her assets in that prenup agreement. But, somehow, she'd missed that her heart could get burned in the transaction.

He was close to loving her? That couldn't be possible. He barely knew her.

Except, he did.

He knew the most important thing about her. He knew that she needed help. He knew that more than anything in the world, she craved someone reaching out a hand to her. He'd done that, over and over again. First with his own hand. Then offering the help of his men. And then hiring the help she'd formerly dismissed.

Brenda couldn't deny that Angel had been a great asset to her the other day. And she'd need his help today with the branding and castrating. Those were her two least favorite jobs on this ranch, and it would destroy her to do it on her own today.

But she wouldn't be alone. She saw Angel's truck parked out front. Because her husband had made sure she had the extra hands she needed. Even though the hand Brenda truly wanted was Keaton's.

You ever been somewhere and know it's exactly where you were meant to be?

Brenda had always known she belonged on this ranch. But for the first time since she'd been here on her own, she felt lonely. She was where she was meant to be. But she wasn't with the person she was meant to be with. He'd left the house without even knocking on her door.

And, yes, she'd wanted him to knock on her door. She'd wanted Keaton to remove that large plank of wood that separated the two of them. Because goodness knew that she was incapable of busting out of the tiny pen she'd corralled herself into all on her own. And she was sure that if she kept bucking away from him at every turn, at some point, he would turn to greener pastures.

It was probably already too late. The first rays of sunlight peaked into her window. Down below, the house was quiet. But in the quiet, she smelled strong coffee, buttery eggs, and toasty bread. Just like the animals she tended to, her husband and his friends had left her sustenance to get through her long day in the fields.

With her tail tucked between her legs, Brenda finally dressed and left her bedroom. She paused on the steps when she heard voices in the kitchen. Neither were the honey tons of her husband's voice. Nor were they the deep tones of Grizz. Or the perpetual laughter of Mac. Brenda rounded the corner to find Angel and her brother.

"Walter, what are you doing here?" she asked.

"Your husband said you needed an extra hand today." Walter piled eggs onto a plate alongside toast. "Why didn't you tell me you didn't have help for the branding? You know I would've come."

Brenda took the plate of food from her brother, taking care to avoid his gaze. At the last second, Walter yanked the plate back.

"Wait a minute," he said, his probing gaze roaming her features. "No, you didn't know that. Did you?"

Brenda shrugged, grabbing the food and going to a seat. "You have your own work. You're living your passion."

"True. But you're my family. I will always make time for you. I make sure you're fed. So, of course, I'm going to make sure you have enough hands to get your work done. Plus, I know branding is your least favorite job here."

Her brother was right. For all her exterior tough act, she hated seeing and hearing the cows cry at the shock of the brand. That's why she'd invested in freeze branding, where liquid nitrogen was used instead of a hot iron. It would still hurt, but research said it would hurt less and was more humane. As humane as burning flesh could be. But it was necessary before she let the calves out to pasture. Otherwise, anyone could claim her cattle as their own.

"I think the three of us can manage," she said after a few bites. "I'm glad Keaton called you. I'm glad Keaton called the both of you."

"That husband of yours is the best hand you've hired, you know," said her brother.

"Yeah, he is. He's helped me more than I can say."

Brenda had spent so much time modernizing and mechanizing so that she wouldn't need all the extra hands. But in the last few days, she'd accomplished more with her husband's hand in the mix. And what had she done? She'd slapped his hand away for helping.

"Bren?" said her brother. "What have you done?"

"Oh, not much," she said, pushing her plate aside. "Just been the pain you know and love."

"Well, that's to be expected."

"Yeah, but will my husband keep putting up with it?" Brenda buried her face in her hands. By the time she scrubbed at her eyes and lifted her head, the two men at the table were looking everywhere but at her.

Neither were used to seeing her uncertain. "All right, you two. Enough with the mushy. Let's get to work."

The visible signs of relief were clear on both their faces. Angel was the first to scurry up and toward the back door. Walter fell into step with her and offered her a mug of coffee.

"There's the sister I know."

Stepping out into the cool morning air, Brenda got her wits about her. She and her husband needed to have a long sit-down and discuss the future of their relationship, along with exactly where the boundary lines would be. She was hoping those lines could soon be erased, and they might end up in the same close quarters. But that would have to wait. She had chores to do.

The first thing Brenda became aware of was the quiet near the barns. The mooing had died down, which was unusual. Many ranchers tried to get the separation and branding done within an afternoon. But as she was short-handed, Brenda had opted for an overnight separation.

But coming to the pasture where the mamas were grazing, there was only the normal amount of ruckus. Across the way in the pen was complete silence. The fencing she'd erected was down. The small enclosure was empty.

Last night there had been fifty calves in there. They all were gone. They'd gotten out.

Fifty calves were a year's worth of income. If she didn't recover them, the loss would put her under. But even worse, the calves weren't branded. Meaning anyone could claim that those fifty were their stock.

"This was done by a man," said Angel. "Not an animal."

Angel straightened from the broken fence. Shame colored the young man's cheeks as he looked up at Brenda. They both knew without saying who'd done this.

"We have to stop him," said Brenda. "Where could he have gone?"

"The only way out undetected is the creek."

CHAPTER TWENTY-ONE

"This is a perfect set up for combat training," said the General as they rode up to the training campgrounds.

Keaton looked out at the parcel of land that he was now part-owner of. Grizz and Mac were at his side. Each man standing higher than ten feet tall. The extra height was due to the horses they were each mounted on. General Strauss had suggested they ride out on horseback rather than take a vehicle. As all four of the men knew how to ride, and the horses were available from the Purple Heart Ranch's stables, they all leaped into the saddle at the chance.

With two days of work, Keaton and the guys had sectioned off each of the unique areas for the camp. The materials would be arriving at the end of the week, along with two of the other men. Rusty was still dealing with his family issues.

But, all in all, it was coming together. So, why did Keaton feel like he'd just run the gauntlet, only to look up and see that he wasn't even halfway through? His shoulders ached as though he'd hefted a heavy load across the land. His palms itched with emptiness. His gaze kept tracking back to the creek.

Rivulets of water babbled over rocks. Those paths were already laid before he'd arrived. It took time to make those pathways in the long-standing river. But now the river and the rocks made a harmonious sound as they continued on their way.

Patience and persistence. That's what won any battle. Including, it would appear, a marital relationship.

"So, you'll meet the deadline?"

Keaton blinked, looking up at General Strauss. With just one contract from this man, he and his brothers would be an instant success. But already they had lost three of the ninety days in his plan, and they were about to lose at least three more with the other guys being held up.

He thought of his brothers who'd put their savings into this venture. He recalculated the amount of work that needed to be done. He had planned for hiccups along the way, he always did. It would take twelve-hour days, seven days a week, to make this deadline. That didn't leave any time to give his wife an extra hand on the ranch.

"What am I talking about?" said the General. "Of course, you will. You always bring missions in on time."

"That might not happen this time," said Keaton.

Keaton took a few steps sideways. But with a jerk of the reins, Keaton stopped the behavior. He lifted his head to look back at the three pairs of surprised eyes.

Well, only the General had an arch of surprise in his brows. Grizz closed his eyes, a pained expression creasing his brows. Mac, ever the romantic, did a little fist pump in the air and then pounded his fist once at his heart.

"My wife needs a hand on the ranch," Keaton continued. "She's my family now. And as you know, as Rangers, we never leave anyone behind."

"Didn't realize you'd married," said General Strauss. "So, the rumors about this place are true, then?" He looked around the land, covering the bare fourth finger of his left hand as though a vine from the ground would leap up and trap him.

"Yes," said Keaton and Mac in unison.

"No," said Grizz, but his protest was drowned out by his two friends that believed in the power of love that could set a man on a new and unexpected course.

"Army Rangers turned ranchers? Now I've seen it all." Strauss chuckled as he leaned over his horse, peering off into the distance. "So, there will be cattle runs?"

"Cattle runs?" said Keaton. "No, sir. The ranch and the camp will operate separately. Only my men will work in both places. We wouldn't ask our clients to help on the ranch with our chores."

"Then why are cattle running on your land?" asked the General.

Keaton, Grizz, and Mac had been facing the General in a semi-circle. The three rangers turned their horses around to get a view of what the general was looking at. When he saw the scene, it took Keaton several more seconds to make out what he was seeing.

"Those aren't cattle," said Grizz. "They're calves."

That didn't make any sense. As a rehabilitation facility, the Purple Heart Ranch didn't have many cattle. What cattle they did have were therapeutic, used to help soldiers regain dexterity where appendages were missing by milking cows. And those therapy animals were all in a pasture on the northern side of the ranch. The soldiers here certainly didn't have close to …

Keaton shielded his gaze to get a better view. That had to be about fifty calves running toward them. Toward the creek and away from Vance Ranch. And they weren't alone.

There was a horseman riding behind them. The rider wasn't a she. He was hunched over the horse with what looked like a lasso in his hands. Every other second, he whipped the rope out toward the scurrying calves. The crackle of sound cut the air. It made Keaton's shoulders tense as much as it made the young calves bleed and move their small legs faster.

The sound wasn't what made Keaton's spidey senses tingle. It was the fact that the rider looked familiar to him. The man kept looking over his shoulder like he was running from something.

The man looked back, and his gaze connected with Keaton's. Recognition happened simultaneously in both men's eyes. Keaton felt that hum of dangerous energy, like an electrical box set to explode.

Manuel Bautista rose the whip over his head. He drove his horse, rounding on the cattle, whipping at their feet until they made a turn away from the creek.

"Plans changed," Keaton said as he tightened the reins in his hands. "Looks like we're going on a cattle run, boys."

CHAPTER TWENTY-TWO

renda pushed her horse. They couldn't drive a vehicle over this part of the land with its changing terrain. If Angel hadn't guessed where his uncle was headed, she would've wasted time going in the wrong direction and losing precious hours in getting her property back.

The horses made their way across the terrain. Angel was riding at her side. He hadn't wasted time in trying to convince her that he had nothing to do with his uncle's treachery. The young man simply swung into action. That's what proved his innocence and his intentions to Brenda. He stuck by her as they rode on, which told her everything she needed to know.

The creek spilled into the edge of the Purple Heart Ranch territory. Just beyond the creek to the east, the land was all open range. If Manuel was able to cross the creek and reached that pasture, there wouldn't be anything that she could do. Anyone would have the right to claim her cattle and her profit margin.

The only question now was, had Manuel taken the calves through the higher ground just above the creek where the terrain was less forgiving but a quicker path to the open territory? Or had he stuck to the lower ground, which would take him through the creek on an easier stretch of land, but it would also add more time to his getaway.

"He went low," Angel called out as though he could hear her inner thoughts. "Trust me on this."

The two of them maneuvered their horses to take the low road. Brenda let Angel take the lead since he appeared to be the best at tracking. Angel's horse made to step in front of Brenda's, but Angel pulled the reins. There was surprise on his face.

Brenda wondered if it was because she was giving her trust so easily and completely to him? Or if it was because she was stepping aside to allow someone to lead her?

In the past couple of days, she'd learned it wasn't all bad to fall into step beside a man. It definitely wasn't a chore with her husband who had developed a habit of giving her the tiniest of tugs to get her to bend to his will.

"You know, I didn't have anything to do with this," said Angel.

Brenda eyed the kid. He reminded her so much of herself at that age, which wasn't that long ago. When she'd turned eighteen, she'd wanted to break free of authority and do things a new way. But unlike her, Angel was smart enough to listen to both the old ways and the new.

"Yeah," said Brenda. "I know. But you know that when we catch him, I'm pressing charges."

Angel nodded. "I understand. Blood can only go so far."

He was right about that. Walter had stayed behind to call the authorities and get a police report filed. Brenda had hesitated to call Keaton. She knew he was in the middle of sealing the deal with the General, whose contract would fund his operation.

She'd dialed the number because Keaton had said that she was his list. She believed him. She still chose to believe that that was the truth when he didn't pick up. Just because he wasn't there for her at that moment didn't mean that Brenda didn't let herself take that any way other than he was tending to his business. Because that's the kind of man she married.

She knew that if she had reached him, he would've been there, riding by her side. Belatedly, she wondered if her husband knew how to ride? A second later, she saw the answer for herself.

They were nearing the border into the free-range territory. The sounds of pounding hooves came at them from the west. Toward the east, she could make out the calves moving steadily toward the boundary.

Manuel was in their midst. Although it didn't look like he was herding them. It looked like he was trying to outrun them.

Upon second glance, Brenda realized it wasn't the calves her old hand was outrunning. It was the sound of the hooves. Four horsemen rode upon Manuel like they were the Four Horsemen of the Apocalypse. Keaton was in the lead, riding his horse. He was the warrior who had laid claim to her heart, and he was not giving up.

When she reached him, she would tell him that he was the owner of her heart. She'd tell him that she'd happily follow his lead. Heck, she'd wear his brand, meaning she'd take his last name full on. Before this, she'd been planning to hyphenate.

Only it was too late.

She was ready to let her husband take his claim on her. But it looked like she'd need to give up the claim to her calves. Manuel and the calves had reached the border. They were in the free-range territory.

CHAPTER TWENTY-THREE

Keaton pushed the horse hard. But the animal didn't seem to mind at all. It had spent much of its time barely running while on the Purple Heart Ranch. It was used as a therapy animal to help wounded soldiers and amputees to heal. But now, it had a real mission.

The four soldiers closed in on the disgruntled, former employee. Keaton was close enough to the elder Bautista to see the whites in his eyes. Though there wasn't much white there to see.

Manuel Bautista's eyes were wide with splotches of red in the corners. He looked the definition of someone who was bloodshot. He was lucky Keaton was unarmed. Though he seriously wanted to pummel the older man with his bare hands.

Bautista dismounted, placing his hands up in the air. At least he knew when he was caught. But it wasn't Keaton and his men that Bautista had to worry about. Keaton heard the sound of more hooves coming toward them fast. The calves ran past Bautista but quickly began to slow now that there wasn't a whip at their hides. The young cows began to nibble at the bounty beneath their feet.

"Mr. Bautista, you seemed to have misplaced my cattle," said Keaton.

"This is free-range area," said Bautista. "These animals clearly wandered off. They're untagged, so by law—"

"By law?" Keaton swung his leg over and dismounted in one smooth move. "What law? You said this is free territory."

Grizz dismounted with a thunderous shaking of the earth. Followed by Mac, whose friendly smile would give a serial killer chills. And the General who would make any man take a step back.

Bautista swallowed hard as he eyed the crew that cornered him. Around them, the calves feasted happily on the grass, completely unconcerned with the aggression swirling in the air. The older man's eyes looked around wildly, likely for an escape. Keaton saw when a flicker of hope brightened his gaze.

With a glance over his shoulders, Keaton saw Angel Bautista coming toward them on horseback. The young man tipped his hat to Keaton. He barely spared his uncle a glance.

"Angel," said Bautista, "you're my blood. I taught you everything you know."

"What's running through your veins is toxic," said Angel. "And I'm thankful I wasn't paying attention to all your lessons. Otherwise, I'd be about to have my hands behind my back rather than have a future as a ranch hand."

"Well said, kid," said the General. "You ever considered the Armed Forces?"

Angel frowned at the General. Then he made a clicking sound and went about rounding up the cattle. Keaton turned his attention to the rider approaching them.

His wife didn't resemble the avenging angel today. There was a sadness in her gaze as she looked down at Manuel.

"The authorities will be here soon," she said. "Walter called them before we left the ranch. You're going to be held responsible for this, Manuel. As well as kicking down my fence and letting my bull out."

"So, that was him?" said Keaton.

Some of Keaton's anger receded, knowing that Bautista was behind the event that introduced him to his wife. Had that bull not run into his vehicle, he might not have found himself attached to the most amazing woman he'd ever met.

Brenda looked down at him. Her green gaze softened when she met his blue eyes. She reached both arms out to him. Keaton reached up to his wife. Lifting her from her saddle, he brought her body against his. When her feet touched the ground, and she stood on her own, he still did not relinquish his hold.

"You okay?" he asked.

"I'm good. You?"

"Yeah." Keaton brushed a stray strand of hair from her forehead, smoothing the worry lines there as he did so. "Just glad we saw what was happening and were able to go into action."

"Me too," she said, leaning her cheek into the palm of his hand. "We might not have got to him in time."

"I'm going to be there for you," Keaton said.

"I know." Brenda rubbed her cheek against his palm. "You are there for me."

Keaton took a moment to caress the softness of his wife's cheek before clarifying his statement. "I mean, I'm going to loosen the deadline so that I can give you a hand on the ranch."

Brenda blinked up at him. She cupped her hand over his. "But, won't that lose you the contract?"

"No, it won't," said the General. "I know ranch life and cattle runs aren't planned as part of the training, but if it's possible for that to change, I think we can work something out about the deadline."

"What are you saying?" asked Keaton.

"This is a need that's not being met," said the General. "Most of the time, my men are in places where we have to use pack animals or are working with farmers and herders. I don't know any other training camp that has this feature."

"It's not a feat—" Before Grizz could complete his sentence, Mac jabbed him in the chest.

"We weren't sure if it was a viable addition," said Mac. "But now that we see you're on board, I'm sure we can work something out."

"I love it," said the General. "Army Ranger training on a ranch. It's genius. Plan an actual cattle run, and I'll be back for that myself."

"You know," said Mac, "we were thinking about adding that to the curriculum ..."

The voices of the two men trailed off as they headed back to their mounts. Grizz dismounted and grabbed Manuel Bautista, dragging him bodily after the other two. Angel had most of the calves in hand and was leading them back the way they came.

That just left Brenda and Keaton, still wrapped up in each other's embrace. Keaton splayed his hand over his wife's low back, reveling in the warmth of her. Brenda leaned her forehead against his chest, then rolled her head until her ear rested against his heart.

"So, we're not fighting anymore?" Keaton asked as he tucked his wife's head under his chin.

"No," she sighed. "I'm not fighting it anymore. You're just too bull-headed."

Keaton chuckled. He nudged the top of Brenda's head with his nose until she tilted her head back. Then he stole her lips in a kiss that left no room for arguments.

"Thank you for rearranging your plans for me," Brenda said when Keaton let her up for air. "Now, how about we go home and make some plans together?"

A low rumble sounded at the back of Keaton's throat. "That has to be the sexiest thing anyone has ever said to me."

"Oh, yeah?" she said. "Just wait until you see the spreadsheets I have planned for us."

Keaton held out his hand. Brenda placed her hand in his. Their palms pressed together. Then their fingers entwined. From this day forward, they would plan together, set achievable goals, and check off lists in the masterplan of their lives. Unlike all of the other plans he crafted, for this one, there would be no Plan B.

EPILOGUE

Grizz was glad the day was over. The authorities had come and arrested Manuel Bautista. The General had signed the contract on the dotted line. All was right with the world again.

As he watched Bautista being carted away, he had sympathy for the guy. Grizz knew what it was like to reach higher than his station. To want something he had no right to. But unlike the old man, Grizz would never take what was not his.

The powers that be thought he had. His superiors thought he'd broken rules and overstepped his bounds. He hadn't. But he had stayed silent as something had gone down. So he was tarnished by proximity.

That was pretty much the story of his life. Even joining the elite Army Ranger force had not shaken the stank of his lower class breeding from his back. The stank wasn't the only thing from his past that was clinging to him. The poverty was back.

The monies owed him by the army were being tied up while his case was under review. Grizz hadn't expected it to take so long. The others had all put in their share to fund the camp. Keaton hadn't pressed his oldest friend. But now that they were on the land, bills were coming due.

Grizz knew Keaton would front him the money. His best friend always had since they were kids. But Grizz hated handouts. He always insisted on earning his own way.

Being an equal member and investor in this venture was his dream. But that dream was turning into a nightmare while he waited for his judgement.

The Sheriff's car disappeared down the road. Bautista had made a bad decision late in life. Bad decisions always planted themselves in frizz's way. They were like land mines he could never see until he was right up on it.

"Hey, Grizzly Bear."

The voice came from behind him. He had learned not to have his back to the enemy. She wasn't the enemy. But she was the greatest danger to him.

Grizz turned to find a young woman standing behind him. All five foot four inches and one-hundred-ten pounds of her. Bright blue eyes filled with intelligence and mischief -a lethal combination. Flaming red hair that rivaled a blaze, a warning not to touch. As if he needed a warning to keep his hands off his best friend's sister.

"What are you doing here, Patty Cakes?" he said.

Grizz had known Patricia Keaton since she was a baby. She's been attached to his leg after her first step. He'd thrilled at being her protector. Coming from the home he came from, he loved the idea of being a hero. And Patty hero worshiped him. Until the day she decided she wanted to be his heroine.

"I came to meet my new sister-in-law and see my two favorite guys," she said. "Don't I get a hug?"

A hug was dangerous. A hug meant that she'd be in his arm. She wasn't all gangly limbs anymore. Patty had curves now. Those curves were headed straight for him.

Grizz took a step back, but it was too late. She was on him. She wrapped her arms around his neck like she would put him in a submission hold. Because he could never say no to her. Except the day when she had asked him to give her her first kiss. He'd told her no. But inside Grizz had felt a growl rise from his gut into his throat.

Mine, that primal beast wanted to shout.

Mine, it wanted to howl now that the woman who fit him perfectly was back in his arms where she belonged.

Grizz ducked away from Patty's hold. In the distance, he saw Keaton headed for them. With his background, he knew he wasn't the guy for a girl like Patty. And with the uncertainty of his future, he knew he would never be.

～

Grizz may be thinking it's not meant to happen between him and Patty.
But Patty has a very different plan.
Watch how these two wind up in a marriage of convenience when
"The Rancher takes his Best Friend's Sister."

THE RANCHER TAKES HIS BEST FRIEND'S SISTER

THE RANGERS OF PURPLE HEART RANCH
BOOK 2

CHAPTER ONE

Four years ago...

"I keep telling you guys that girls are nothing but trouble."

Grizz agreed with the words of his best friend. Not because Keaton was his best friend. It was because Grizz knew the girls eyeing him at this party were mostly underage. True, about two-thirds of them were seventeen with just a few days or months until they were of legal age. The truth of the matter was that their minds were still wrapped around high school issues, final exams, who was dating whom, and what they would be doing for the rest of their lives.

But that's what he got for hanging around at a high school graduation party at twenty-one. Grizz had aced all his exams in high school, he'd had to. It was the only way he would have a future. He already knew what he was doing for the rest of his life. Dating was not a part of the plan.

"I don't plan to get married for at least five years after I'm out of the service." Keaton ran his hand over his buzz cut, courtesy of the United States Army.

Grizz scrubbed his fingers through his short-cropped hair and then across his chin. There was already stubble there even though they'd only been on leave for a few days.

Grizz didn't plan on ever getting married. His mother had always said he had too much of his dad in him. Malcolm Hayes had never been able to stay put for more than a couple of weeks, a month if they were lucky.

Amanda Hayes divorced his father and then proceeded to work all hours of the day and night to repay the debt the man had left them in. His mom's workaholic tendencies also left Grizz mostly unsupervised as a kid. Grizz hadn't gone in search of trouble. But as the child of a single mom, he was an easy target for trouble to find.

"But she's the one." That moan came from the third person in their group. Mac Kenzie also scrubbed his hands through his blond spiked hair. The tendrils were curly when they were long, but after they'd been kissed by a razor, they stuck straight up. The man, who had enough muscle to spare for a weight set, crossed his arms over his broad chest and pouted.

Grizz wasn't the only one trouble had found. But unlike him, Mac's trouble didn't follow him around on the streets. Mac followed his own special brand of torture around begging for her to kick him in the heart again and again.

"It was love at first sight with her," Mac continued. "I knew it the moment I saw her that I would spend the rest of my life with her."

"So, where is she tonight?" asked Keaton. Keaton wasn't being mean. At least not on purpose. He had always preferred things to be concrete. He liked to plan.

Mac kicked at a rock. "She had to work late."

"Seems to me she's more into her job than she is into you," said Keaton.

"For now," said Mac. There was a knowing gleam in Mac's eyes that Grizz only ever saw when the big man was planning something crazy in the field, something that usually blew up all over their faces.

"You asked her to marry you again," said Grizz. "Didn't you?"

Mac didn't answer.

"I take it you got the same answer as the first five times?" said Keaton.

"Wrong," said Mac.

Both Keaton and Grizz turned to their friend with interest in this change of events. Mac's glee was short-lived.

"I've only asked her four times," he confessed.

"Well," said Grizz. "I'm sure the fifth time will be the charm then."

Mac brightened. "You think?"

Keaton and Grizz shared another look. Mac was the jokester of their group. Except when it came to this particular topic. He could never see the irony. He couldn't see anything when it came to this girl. But it looked like he was going to catch on this time.

Mac's features morphed from clear rapture to cloudy confusion and then stormy indignation.

"Just wait until it happens to you," said Mac. "With how tightly you're wound, Keaton, love will definitely knock you on that big head of yours. And I'll bet it'll happen within five years."

Keaton scoffed. He wasn't so rigid as to believe his plans would work perfectly. But, he planned for so many contingencies that things rarely strayed far from his expectations. Anthony Keaton was rarely surprised or caught off guard.

"And you, Grizz," Mac continued, "with how thick you two thieves are? You're going down soon after him."

Grizz didn't bother to answer. He may not have a lot of contingencies in his life plan, but this one thing he knew for sure.

Unlike his father, Grizz had no debts. He owed no one. He handled all of his responsibilities.

But where he resembled his old man was in his inability to hold still. Which wreaked havoc on any potential relationship. Which was why he had never been with a girl for longer than a month. They simply couldn't hold his attention.

Grizz could hardly hold still, which was why the army suited him. After the drilling of Basic Training, which kept him on his toes, he was never bored working twelve-hour days and being on call for the other twelve. He would often wake up in a new and exotic locale. But he craved even more, which was why he and his friends would all be taking the Army Ranger Exam soon.

With his restless spirit, Grizz knew he would never make a good family man. Which was fine, because he'd long ago decided he wouldn't become a father or a husband. He'd be free to travel the world with nothing tethering him to a single spot.

His gaze lifted as though tugged by an invisible force. She was a force to be reckoned with, all right. Wherever Patricia Keaton moved in a room, Grizz could always pinpoint her exact location.

She was dressed in a simple sundress and sandals, but she could've been a model walking right out of a fifties family drama, like *Leave it to Beaver* or *The Donna Reid Show*. Those black and white episodes that seemed far more fantasy than the cartoons on the next channel.

Patty's curly hair sat obediently on her shoulders. The dress hugged her hourglass figure, but not too tightly. Just enough to showcase those curves.

What captivated everyone here was her smile. It was brighter than the setting sun. That's probably why the sun was setting. Because it couldn't outshine her.

Whenever she came near, something always ballooned inside Grizz. A feeling he could never name, that he could never quite put his finger on. And always, like a needle seeking true north, he kept coming back around to be in her presence.

She'd blossomed from the girl in cutoffs and pigtails to become the Homecoming Queen and the Prom Queen. She'd even won a beauty competition a year ago. In the high school yearbook, she was voted Most Liked.

Everybody liked Patty Keaton. What was not to like about her? Nothing.

Except that she was Keaton's baby sister, and Grizz had known her since she was in diapers.

True, he'd been in kindergarten at the time. When his new friend, Keaton, had brought Grizz into his quaint little cul-de-sac after school one day, Grizz had peered into the playpen and saw a bundle of red hair and pink cheeks. The little one who had gripped his finger had fascinated him.

Grizz made daily visits to the Keaton household. Each time, he'd peek into the playpen. He liked watching little Patty Keaton in her sleep. He liked talking to the growing toddler as she babbled on and making her smile. While Keaton had wanted to play soldiers, Grizz had preferred to read to the little girl who listened with rapt attention as he told Dr. Seuss's stories. Patty would smile and grin up at him like he was her hero.

Right now, she was smiling and grinning at some other guy as she walked right past Grizz.

"Mac," said Patty. "You made it."

"Hey, Patty Cakes." Mac swooped her up in a bear hug, lifting her off the ground so that her dress twirled about her long, lean legs.

Grizz wanted to growl. Partly because Mac had her in his arms. Mostly because Mac had dared to call her by Grizz's pet name for her. Grizz had known Patty for her whole life. In the past, he'd always been the first one she ran to. He'd always gotten her grins and smiles.

Mac hardly knew her. He didn't know that she didn't have a sweet tooth and put cinnamon in her tea. He didn't know that she still slept with a stuffed giraffe named Jemmy instead of a teddy bear. Or that she had a smile that made Grizz believe he could wrestle down a bear.

"The Army's been good to you." Patty felt at Mac's biceps. "Look how big your muscles have gotten."

Mac preened under her attention and flexed. Patty's grin widened, showing off that brilliant light in her crystal-blue eyes. The light that turned on when she was up to mischief.

Still, knowing she was up to something, didn't temper Grizz's mood.

"He has a girlfriend," Grizz growled from behind them.

Patty turned her head and looked over her shoulder. Her dazzling eyes came to rest upon Grizz's face. Finally. And there was that ballooning feeling inside of him, pulling him toward her like she was the doorway to home after a long day of work.

"Hey, Grizzly Bear."

"Patricia."

Patty frowned. Using her full name was like pulling her pigtails. Which he hadn't done in years because she no longer wore her curls in pigtails. She no longer wore cutoff jeans and scuffed sneakers like the tomboy she'd used to be.

Patricia Keaton was a tomboy no longer. She wasn't a kid any longer. She was eighteen. A woman grown.

A slow smile spread across her face. Gone was the baby fat in her cheeks. Her high cheekbones were sharp angles that young men started doing acrobatics for. Her once gangly limbs now went on for days, ending in strappy shoes that would likely give normal men a foot fetish.

"Well, I knew you'd make it to my party, Grizz. I can always count on you."

Grizz's gaze slid back to that smile. He'd made her giggle as a kid. He'd delighted her when he'd pushed her on a swing set. She'd grinned up at him as he'd read her the silly poems he'd loved so much as a kid. She'd smiled politely, if uncomprehending, as he'd tried to explain the more complicated poems he enjoyed as a young man.

Patty was the only girl he could spend long afternoons with and not feel the need to rush away. He'd never felt the pressure to be anything more than what he was with her. Likely because they'd known each other so long.

"What about your big brother?" said Keaton. "Am I chopped liver over here?"

"I happen to like chopped liver," she said.

"Because you're weird," said Keaton.

Keaton poked her in the shoulder. Patty ducked and smacked at his hand. The two tussled; Keaton in his sturdy army boots, Patty in her delicate sandals.

She'd had to learn to defend herself as the only girl in a house with a military father, a brother who was aimed for the same path, and Grizz, who didn't understand that girls shouldn't learn how to box. Patty, even in a dress and heels, could hold her own.

At that moment, Grizz saw the girl she used to be. The one he could wrestle with out in the backyard. The one he'd spent quiet Friday nights with watching a marathon of the *Andy Griffith Show* or *Happy Days*. The one he didn't have to think twice about when she rested her head against his shoulder.

Keaton feinted right. Patty had the space to sneak in for a strike. Instead, she stepped back and fell into Grizz. He caught her, bringing her lush body into his. All the fight went out of her. The resistance went out of him as well.

It had been a long time since Grizz had touched Patty. Years since they'd sat close together on a couch while she'd rested her head on his shoulder. This was why.

Grizz's gaze dipped to Patty's mouth. Patty parted her lips. Her pink tongue darted out as she wet those lips. Grizz's hold tightened on her. Everything inside him screaming one single word.

Mine.

"Ha!" shouted Keaton. "Gotcha. Hold her Grizz."

Yes. That's exactly what he wanted to do. Hold Patty tight and never let her go. Tuck her head against his chest so that she could feel how his heart pounded for her. Lift her chin to watch her wet her lips again and then claim her mouth.

Grizz let Patty go. His arms straightened as he shoved her away. Patty wobbled on unsteady feet, and Grizz had to stop himself from reaching for her again.

When his gaze met hers, gone was the brightness in her eyes. The glittering azure had faded into smudges of a blue that could've almost been called gray. Patty stepped away, rejection in her gaze. She gave them all a curt nod and then walked away.

"Why'd you let her go?" Keaton gave him a shove.

The blow from his best friend was light. Grizz's whole body canted to the side like he might fall over from the light tap. He'd just released the one and only thing in the world he wanted desperately but couldn't have. He'd just let go of his best friend's little sister.

"I see you understand me about The One." Mac clapped Grizz on the back. "You are so screwed."

Grizz was so screwed. He had the hots for Patricia Keaton. Mac may have figured it out. Grizz just hoped he could hide his feelings well enough so that his best friend never found out.

*P*atty was going to kill her brother. It didn't matter that he was the best big brother a girl could ever ask for. Keaton never tattled on her. Especially when she didn't eat her veggies. Instead, he'd shown her how to sneak them into the trash when they were sitting at the dinner table, and their parents' backs were turned.

Keaton often let Patty tag along with him and his friends. Mainly because no one ever thought his pack of friends could be up to no good if Keaton's little sister was with them. They were often wrong.

Whenever Patty was up to no good with her own pack of friends, Keaton often wanted in on whatever she'd plotted, certain he could make the plan better. He was usually right about making her plans better.

There was just one plan she'd never let Keaton in on. It was the plan that would determine the course of her life. That was Patty's plan to marry her brother's best friend.

Patricia Keaton was used to getting her way. From a very early age, she knew she possessed the main attributes to get what she wanted in life. With her small hands, she'd felt her chubby cheeks after having them pinched and patted so often as a child. She'd looked in a mirror and stretched her lips wide, trying to see what others saw in her gap-toothed grin. She'd stared in her blue eyes and tried to see the sparkle her mother's friends insisted was there. She didn't see any of it, but she understood that others did and that that gave her an advantage.

Except when it came to Grizz.

Grizz wasn't immune to Patty's charms. He spent a lot of time trying to make her smile. She knew that her giggle brought about his chuckles. She knew that she could hold his attention if she stared into his eyes.

Patty knew Grizz liked her. Just not in the way she liked him. Because she didn't like Grizz. She loved him.

She'd known she'd loved him since her mother had taught her the word. As a child, Patty loved her mother. She loved her father. She loved her brother.

Those same warm and fuzzy feelings were there for Grizz. But they were somehow different, more. Since Patty had learned the word love and learned his name, she knew that Grizz and love belonged in the same sentence together.

From that day forward, she'd decided to learn everything about him. She knew his favorite television shows; he loved the black and white classics like *Leave it to Beaver* and *The Andy Griffith Show* that showcased a simpler time. He loved poetry, from the simple stuff like Dr. Seuss to the complex lyrical stylings of Byron, which she could never wrap her head around. She knew he loved his meat with just a touch of fire like her. But unlike her, Grizz liked a side of vegetables. Even with that flaw, she loved him still and knew they could make it work.

Patty had been hoping that tonight, at her graduation party, Grizz would finally see in her everything she wanted him to see. She'd worn the perfect fifties dress. Her hair was coiled in a bun like Donna Reed. She'd even worn pearls. She was the perfect representation of his perfect wife.

And then her brother had gone and ruined everything.

"Patty, don't be like that," Keaton called after her as she stormed away from their group.

Keaton had always treated her as an equal. Which meant that sometimes he forgot she was a girl. She had never been helpless in a conflict or skittish at the sight of bugs like many of her girlfriends who cried if they got a speck of dirt on their clothing. Patty Keaton could hold her own, be it boy, bug, or beast.

But tonight, she didn't want to be seen as her brother's equal. She wanted to be seen as Grizz's. Maybe that was the problem? A proper girl wouldn't have struck back. She would've retreated.

Even though it rankled, Patty knew what she had to do. She slowed her retreat and let Keaton catch up to her. The moment he caught her, Patty twisted the heel of her shoe and yelped.

"Ouch."

She let her body fall to the ground, making sure to arrange her limbs gracefully as she landed. The party came to a screeching halt. All eyes were on her, but she only cared about the dark eyes looming toward her.

"Keaton," growled Grizz. "What did you do?"

"Nothing." Keaton held up his hands, innocent for once in his life. "I didn't touch her."

Grizz shoved Keaton out of the way. "Careful."

"She's faking it," said Keaton.

Patty faked a sniffle at her faux injury. It was a command performance. One that she was rewarded for when Grizz lifted her up into his arms.

Patty wrapped her arms around Grizz's neck as he turned and headed for the house. With Grizz's focus on the backdoor and his back turned to his friends, Patty couldn't resist. She stuck her tongue out at her brother.

Before Keaton could retaliate, the back door slammed closed. The house was empty. Her mother was across the street at a neighbor's house, secure in the knowledge that nothing would go wrong while Keaton and his friends were watching over the new high school graduates.

Holly Keaton wasn't stupid. She knew that if there was any trouble, her two kids would likely be in the lead of the melee. She also knew that as long as Griffin Hayes was silently watching over the Keaton kids that she had a spy in their midst.

Grizz respected their mom more than he did his own mom. Probably because Amanda Hayes was rarely home, hadn't set a warm meal on the table in years, and taught Grizz how to forge her signature for school documents soon after he learned cursive writing so she didn't have to deal with backpack mail. Grizz had been his own parent for years. The only time he got a break was when he came over to their house where he could get a warm meal out of the oven, a scolding to behave, and a hug before he went home to bed.

Grizz sat Patty on the table. She was reluctant to unfold her arms from around his strong torso. But she did so as he bent down on his knee. This was how she imagined him proposing. But instead of taking her left hand, he took her right ankle and examined it.

"It doesn't look like you broke any skin," he said.

"Can you get me an ice pack?"

Grizz went to the fridge. He pulled the door opened and examined the contents like he owned this place. He'd practically lived here since he was eight, and she was five. Her earliest memories were of him.

When Grizz put the ice pack on her ankle, she hissed. His gaze shot to hers, concern rimming his hazel eyes. That hazel gaze dipped to her lips.

And there it was, proof that he wanted her. Guys always looked at her lips when she talked. The older she got, she knew it wasn't her dimpled grin they were interested in. But Patty had never wanted any boy's lips near hers. She was eighteen and had never been kissed. Because she was saving that honor for the man in front of her.

"Just keep this here," said Grizz, preparing to rise. "I should—"

Patty gripped his hand to hold him in place. He was stronger than her, so he could've moved if he wanted to. He held still. But he averted his gaze.

"Thanks for coming to my party, Grizz."

"Of course, I'm here. Why wouldn't I be?"

"Because things have been weird between us."

Before he'd left for the service, things had been normal between them. The last time they'd hung out was a year ago. They'd curled up on the couch to watch a marathon of *The Patty Duke Show*. One of her favorites, and not just because of her namesake. She loved the twin cousins where one was refined and the other more adventurous. They reminded her so much of herself, especially since it was the same actress playing both roles. She'd leaned into Grizz like she'd done many times as a kid, but for some reason, that night, he stiffened and pulled away from her. He made some excuse about being home in time to see his mom and then darted out of the house.

They hadn't been alone again since.

Grizz didn't respond to her for a long moment. "I wouldn't miss your party for the world. You're practically my little sister."

Patty lowered her head. Her finger pads pressed into the wood of the table as she tried to hold herself together and not pout or shout like she would've only a few years ago when she didn't get her way. She might always be Keaton's little sister, but she was grown now and determined to act it.

Starting now. What happened on the other side of the back door to get her in here alone with Grizz didn't count.

"You're off to college soon," Grizz continued.

That was a topic Patty didn't wish to discuss. She had no desire to go to college. The only degree she wanted was an MRS. She'd been studying at the school of Hayes all her life, and she was ready for the final exam, the one that got her the full time, lifelong job as Mrs. Griffin Hayes.

"You're going to have a lot of new experiences," Grizz went on. "New friends. College boys."

"I won't be busy with college boys," Patty said. "There's only ever been one boy that I wanted."

Grizz pulled away from her. Patty hopped to her feet, all pretense of an injured ankle gone. She was not letting him get away again. Especially not when he was leaving again for training. She was perfectly fine with having a long-distance relationship with him. The key was to get that relationship started. She'd waited all her life to be able to tell him how she felt and have him take her seriously. That time was now.

"Grizz, I think you know how I feel about you."

Grizz shook his head. Patty got the sense that he wasn't denying her words. His gaze appeared as though it were turned inward like he was denying a voice inside his own head.

"Patricia, this cannot happen."

"What's wrong with me?" She couldn't help it. Patty's lower lip trembled.

Grizz's haunted gaze lifted to her, followed by hands that cupped her face. "Nothing. You're perfect."

"Then, why not?" Patty stomped her foot, all pretext of being grown gone. She'd smiled and grinned and gotten all dressed up and worn these uncomfortable shoes. What more was she supposed to do?

Grizz raised an eyebrow at her. Then he sighed. "You're my best friend's sister."

"Then dump Keaton. He's been holding you back."

Grizz tried biting his lip, but that didn't work. A chuckle escaped his perfectly formed lips. There was a hint of stubble there despite the shaving regiment he now put himself through as a member of the United States Armed Services. He'd always been hairy, like a life-sized teddy bear.

"You know Keaton wants what's best for me," said Patty. "Seems to me that that would be his best friend."

"That's cute." Grizz gave her cheek a pinch. Before he could let her face go, Patty cupped his hand with hers, keeping him there.

Grizz shook his head at her, resignation darkened his gaze. He could've pulled away from her hold. He was stronger than her. But he didn't. He ran his thumb across the top of her cheek as he said the words that would break her heart.

"This is not going to happen, Patty Cakes. You're going to go to college, get your degree, meet a nice boy."

"A nice boy? You really want me to break some poor little boy in two?"

She got another one of Grizz's grins for that truthful statement.

"You're the only one who's ever been able to handle me. I'm destined to be Mrs. Griffin Hayes. Have your babies. Be in your bed."

Again his gaze dipped to her lips. She could taste his breath. He gulped, as though trying to swallow down his desire, but hunger remained in his darkened gaze.

As if it had a mind of its own, Grizz's thumb brushed at her bottom lip. As though it was testing what his mouth wanted most. The pad of his finger was rough on her untouched flesh.

Patty parted her lips, ready to beg for him to take her. She knew that if he kissed her then, it would seal the deal. She was so close to having it all.

Grizz exhaled. The small release of air appeared to weigh him down, making his face sink closer to hers. He was close enough for his chest to brush against hers. Inside her heart, Patty heard the gears shifting into place, making room to align perfectly with the man she knew she was destined to spend the rest of her life with.

"Patty?"

They both turned at the sound of Keaton's voice coming from the other room. Patty had no idea why her brother had chosen to come through the front door instead of the back one.

"Mom called from Mrs. Jenkins. She saw what happened and says I have to say I'm sorry. Even though you slipped on your own."

Their mother had eyes in the back of her head. Of course, she saw what had happened between her children. The question was, could she also see what was about to happen between Patty and Grizz?

Patty would not find out. When she turned back, Grizz had evaded her. He slipped out the back door. The last thing she heard was the quiet slap of the door. And then he was gone.

CHAPTER THREE

resent Day

"You're just going to stand there and let this happen to your blood?"

Grizz's lips curled in disgust at the words hurled into the late afternoon air. The words weren't aimed at Grizz, but he felt their impact. Grizz's gaze connected with Angel Bautista. The young man was the unfortunate recipient of the accusation.

Angel's lip curled in revulsion as he turned his back on his uncle. His fists tightened, and a crackling sound emitted from his palms. Brown shells fell to the ground as Angel popped a raw peanut into his mouth.

Manuel Bautista struggled against his handcuffs as he shouted at his nephew. "You're a disgrace to your family."

"No, Uncle," Angel called over his shoulder without turning to meet his uncle's gaze, "that was you."

Just before dawn, Manuel, a former hand of the Vance ranch, had decided his severance package would be the new calves that had been separated for branding. Luckily, before Manuel could get the herd of calves into the No Man's Land that lay beyond the borders of The

Purple Heart Ranch and Vance Ranch, Grizz and his Army Ranger brothers had run him down and caught the thief.

Angel, who had remained loyal to the Vances, had helped hunt his wayward uncle down. Now, the young man walked away from his former mentor, severing the last tie.

"Where do you think you're going, Angel?"

The younger Bautista did turn back at the sound of the deputy sheriff's voice. It wasn't that Deputy Newman's voice rang with authority. It rankled with undue self-importance.

"You're still needed for questioning in this here investigation, boy." The deputy slammed the door with his first quarry inside, then rounded the squad car, gaze intent on new prey.

Angel didn't step back as Newman advanced. He held his ground, his dark head high. But behind his back, Grizz saw the young man's fists clench and release as though he were searching for deliverance. Instead of deliverance, he crunched more shells and was rewarded with another handful of peanuts.

It was the deputy who stepped back. Newman's body coiled away from Angel. His features contorted in horror.

"I'm allergic to those." Newman pointed at the shells surrounding Angel's boots.

"Ah, my bad. I didn't know." Angel's voice rang with false apology.

Grizz failed to hide his grin at the young man. Grizz knew what it was to have a family member's shortcomings projected on to himself, even though he'd never put one foot out of place. The same was happening now to Angel.

"We've already told you Angel's part in the matter," Grizz spoke up. "He helped track down Mr. Bautista and recovered the stolen property."

"Yeah, but it's people like him that we have to watch out for." The deputy leaned into Grizz as though the two were in cahoots.

Grizz leaned away from the man in distaste.

"How do I know the two of them weren't in on it to begin with?" sneered Newman.

"Because we all vouched for him." Grizz waved his hand at the other soldiers helping Brenda lead the weary calves into a pasture in the distance.

Newman's lips pinched. He looked from Grizz to Angel, to the shells on the ground, and then back to Angel. "Don't leave town."

With that edict, the deputy turned on his booted heel and rounded the car to the driver's side. Manuel Bautista glared out of the side window until the engine turned over, and the car pulled off. When Grizz turned back, Angel was gone.

As he watched the elder Bautista being carted away, he felt a twinge of sympathy for the old man. Grizz knew what it was like to reach higher than his station. To want something he had no right to. But unlike the old man, Grizz would never take what was not his.

That was pretty much the story of his life. Even joining the elite Army Ranger force had not shaken the stank of his lower-class breeding from his back. The stank wasn't the only thing from his past that was clinging to him. The poverty was back.

Grizz had sent nearly all of his money earned from the army back home to his mother to pay off his father's debts. After twenty years, his mother was finally free and clear of the mess Malcolm Hayes had buried them under. But that had left Grizz without enough to pay his fair share for the new Army Ranger Training Camp he and his friends were building.

Grizz knew Keaton would front him the money. His best friend always had his back since they were kids. But Grizz hated handouts. He always insisted on earning his own way. Being an equal member and investor in this venture was his dream. But like the other things he'd dreamed he could have in his life, this one too might stay out of his reach.

"Hey, Grizzly Bear."

The voice came from behind him. He had learned not to have his back to the enemy. She wasn't the enemy. But she was the greatest danger to him.

Grizz turned to find a young woman standing behind him. All five-foot-four inches and one-hundred-ten pounds of her. Bright blue eyes filled with intelligence and mischief—a lethal combination. Flaming red hair that rivaled a blaze, a warning not to touch. As if he needed a warning to keep his hands off his best friend's sister.

"What are you doing here, Patty Cakes?" he said.

"I came to meet my new sister-in-law and see my two favorite guys," Patty said.

He hadn't seen her in three years. The Keaton household had not been a second home to him, it had been his dream home. But that door closed when he'd nearly kissed Patty on the night of her graduation.

She'd been a vision that night. She'd taunted his desires. Tested his control. He'd nearly broken when he had her in his arms in the kitchen. And then Keaton had walked in.

If his best friend had seen Grizz with his baby sister in his arms, ready to taste the impish grin that had always fascinated him, Keaton would've banished him from not only his home but his life. And Grizz would've deserved it for even thinking the thought of laying a claim on Patty.

"Don't I get a hug?"

A hug was dangerous. A hug meant that she'd be in his arms. She wasn't all gangly limbs anymore. Patty had even more curves now than the last time he'd seen her. Those curves were headed straight for him.

Grizz took a step back, but it was too late. She was on him. She wrapped her arms around his neck like she would put him in a submission hold. Because he could never say no to her.

Except for the night when she had asked him to give her her first kiss. He'd told her no. But inside, Grizz had felt a growl rise from his gut into his throat.

Mine, that primal beast wanted to shout then.

Mine, it wanted to howl now that the woman who fit him perfectly was back in his arms where she belonged.

Grizz ducked away from Patty's hold. In the distance, he saw Keaton headed for them. With his background, Grizz knew he wasn't the guy for a girl like Patty. And with the uncertainty of his financial future, he knew he would never be.

"Patty Cakes? Is that you?"

Patty dragged her gaze from Grizz to her brother. Keaton opened his arms, and she went into them. Introductions were made with Keaton's wife of a few days, Brenda. While that happened, Grizz allowed himself to finally take her in.

He'd made a deal with himself; he could think about her so long as he didn't see her. And oh, man, had he thought about her over the years. Holding her, kissing her, sometimes just looking into her eyes. Patty had always looked at him like he was a hero. But what kind of hero would go after his best friend's little sister? It would be the height of betrayal. It would be something Grizz's father would do.

"Shouldn't you be in school?" said Keaton.

"Spring break," said Patty.

But there was a hitch to her voice. She wasn't telling the whole story.

"That's a week, right?" said Brenda, excitement rising in her voice. "You'll stay the week with us?"

Grizz wanted to protest. A whole week of avoiding Patty? He would not survive.

Patty's gaze found his. Mischief shone through. "If it's not too much trouble."

Oh, it was trouble. It was far too much trouble. A week with Patty Keaton was going to be filled with nothing but trouble.

CHAPTER FOUR

$\mathcal{P}$atty had always wanted a sister. Brenda was a bit unexpected. She drove a tractor, corralled bulls, and rode horses. The tomboy in Patty screamed to slip on a pair of worn jeans, saddle up, and let her hair fly behind her as she rode through the pastures shouting giddy-up.

Taking in a deep breath, Patty exhaled the thought. She was no longer that wild child. She was a grown woman. A sophisticated, refined, grown woman who would make a soldier a perfect wife. If said soldier stayed around to pay her any mind.

It had been three years since she'd seen Grizz. Three. During that time, she'd caught glimpses of him as she video chatted with Keaton. But Grizz never held still for the camera, often giving her a quick wave, and then excusing himself from anymore face time with her.

Grizz didn't come home for holidays either. Instead, he stayed on base while Keaton came home for visits. Grizz made it a point to visit during the offseason, times when she would be knee-deep in exams and finals. It was like he was purposely avoiding her.

"This here was my prize bull," Brenda was saying.

Patty's attention jerked to the present moment. A large animal swaggered over to where they stood at the fence. The bull was an imposing beast. With its thick legs and broad back. Its nostrils flared as it regarded Patty. A proper lady would've run away at the massive animal's approach.

Patty's gaze connected with the bull. There was a softness to its dark eyes. A weariness about its approach that said *I could hurt you if I wanted to*. Patty knew the bull had no intention of hurting her. She reached out her hand to its horns.

"Careful," admonished Brenda.

But her new sister-in-law was too late. The bull had already bowed its head to allow for Patty's touch. Its hairy head was matted with coarse curls. It huffed out a puff of air that sounded much to Patty's ears as a sign of resignation. She'd heard tired puppies make the same noise.

"Great," sighed Brenda. "He might as well be castrated."

"What do you mean?" said Patty as she scratched at the animal's head.

"This bull was meant to party with all the girls if you know what I'm saying," said Brenda. "But he got into a fight with your brother, and now he's completely out of commission."

"He looks fine to me."

"He's supposed to be a raging bull, ready for business. He should not be letting you pet his head."

"Well, I have a way with big beasts."

Patty's gaze tracked across the field where her brother, Mac, and Grizz were lifting bales of hay. Patty's gaze caught and held on the flex of Grizz's muscles under his damp t-shirt.

Brenda followed the trajectory of Patty's gaze and grinned. "I'll bet you do."

Actually, she didn't.

For the rest of the night, Grizz avoided being alone with Patty. He'd sat as far away from her as possible last night at dinner. He turned in to bed early while the rest of them stayed up to play board games. In the morning, he was out of the house before the sun rose.

Grizz spent the morning out in the barns with the animals. Then he disappeared with the guys over to their training camp around lunchtime. By then, Patty had been on the ranch for over twenty-four hours, and she hadn't spoken any more words to Grizz than that first meeting. Things were not going according to her plan.

It was an old plan, a simple plan. Altered only slightly because she knew that Grizz felt something for her. Confirmed by the way he avoided her at every turn.

Patty's plan was to get Grizz to acknowledge his feelings for her. To do that, she needed to corner him and finish the business they'd started three years ago at her graduation party. She knew that if she got Grizz to give her her first kiss, it would seal the deal on their future happiness.

Turning on her cellphone, Patty checked her email and saw a number of missives from teachers at her school. There were emails about missing assignments. Other notes asked where she was during this exam period. Three emails were from the dean about her failing grades.

Patty deleted them all. They were no longer relevant. Just like school wasn't relevant. Patty had gotten her priorities straight. That's why she was here. She'd wasted three years on a degree she had no use for. Now she was back on track for the only certificate she ever wanted, the one that gave her her MRS.

And now those three letters were again within her reach. The moment she'd known that her brother and his friends were retiring, Patty had started hatching her plan. When she'd learned their location, she got in her car and started driving across the country.

And now she was here. On a ranch. In a kitchen. Unsure of what to do next.

"You must be Patricia."

Patty turned to see a tall man standing in the doorway. The man had what her mother would call a trusting face. His features were relaxed, his smile certain of his place in the world. But there was something mischievous in the lift of his green eyes.

"And you are?" asked Patty.

That grin widened, and he winked one green eye. "I'm your new brother. I'm Brenda's brother. Pastor Vance. But you can call me Walter."

Patty's own grin faltered at the title he put before his name. "Wait? You're a real live priest?"

"I hope so." Walter tugged at his collar, his grin still in place. "Otherwise, your brother and my sister's marriage is a fake."

"You married them?"

"Sure did. They came into the courthouse, marriage license in one hand, prenup in the other."

"Surprisingly, that does sound like my brother."

A prenup might not sound very romantic. But Patty knew that Keaton would've wanted to have a plan and contingencies for his future life in place. She was also willing to bet that the agreement left Brenda with everything if the marriage were to dissolve.

"The two got married to save this ranch and further your brother's grand camp idea," Walter continued.

He'd made his way to the refrigerator and was pulling out vegetables. Carrots, broccoli, and a bushel of leafy greens that made Patty's stomach turn a paler shade of green.

"Though I don't think they appreciate that story any longer. They've basically rewritten their love story as it was love at first sight and not because a bull ran into Keaton's car."

Walter chuckled as he began chopping the rabbit food. Unfortunately, he hadn't pulled out any rabbit meat.

"Too bad for them, I know the real deal. Otherwise, it'd be their word against mine, and they could try and claim spousal privilege."

"Spousal privilege?" asked Patty.

"You know, that law where you can't make a husband and wife testify against each other."

Walter tossed the minced garden scraps into a pan and sprinkled spices. But even the warm herbal scent couldn't entice Patty to consider eating the colorful food. When Walter next emerged from the fridge, he had a steak redder than her lipstick. Now, they were talking.

"Happens more often than you'd think out here," said Walter.

"What?" asked Patty, her eyes on the meat cooking a tad too long in the hot pan for her tastes. "Spousal privilege?"

"Marriage of conveniences. Couples turn up here, and before you know it, they're saying their I do's. The ranch next door is filled with soldiers who've gotten married within months, some within days of arriving here."

"Really?" Patty said as she glanced out the window at one soldier riding atop a horse. Grizz's bearded face was hairier than the animal upon whose back he rode.

"But no need to worry," said Walter. "Your brother tells me your just here for the week before you head back to school."

"Right."

Patty couldn't help but glance back out the window. But this time she looked up in the sky, searching for any sign of lightning. Wasn't lightning supposed to strike if you lied to a priest?

CHAPTER FIVE

Grizz hadn't slept a wink for the last two nights. He'd spent only a week here in one of Brenda's spare bedrooms, but in that time, he'd learned every creak, every groan, every sigh of the old homestead.

There was only silence in the house at three in the morning. But Grizz swore he heard her every shift beneath the covers, her every exhale as she dreamed. What was his Patty Cakes dreaming of? Did his face appear in her head as he tried in vain to rest as hers did in his?

Every night for the past three years, he'd dreamed of Patricia Keaton. Smiling at him. Laughing with him. Sitting beside him and resting her head against his shoulder, something she'd done countless times before. But on that fateful night at her graduation party, Grizz had come to the startling realization that his Patty Cakes was no longer the child he adored, but the woman he desired.

Now, she lay in the room across the hall from him, unguarded, unprotected against those same desires that were still inside of him. Two flimsy pieces of wood and less than twenty steps were all that separated them. This had been much easier when he could keep an ocean between them.

Grizz scrubbed his hands over his face. He pulled at the thick hair on his chin, trying to get his mind right. Barely two days had passed.

How was he going to get to the end of her spring break week without accidentally brushing his fingers against hers and then pulling her to him? Or focusing on her lips as she spoke only to unwittingly find his own mouth pressed against hers? And there was always the threat that she would stand before him and repeat the words she'd said when she first got here; *Don't I get a hug?*

Grizz knew that if she came back into his arms again, he would not let her go.

She'd had three years to get over her little crush on him. Three years to date other boys her own age. Surely, she'd forgotten her feelings for him. But he couldn't take the chance in case she still harbored any thought of the two of them together.

After years of fighting to protect his country, Grizz was weary of combat. He'd grown tired of traveling and tossing and turning on a different mattress each night. He craved any semblance of normalcy. But, he knew that normal could not include an intimate relationship with his best friend's sister.

Grizz dragged his weary, unrested body out of bed while the moon was high, and the sun was still nestled under the cover of the dark sky. He slipped on a fresh shirt and jeans and stepped into his boots.

He knew Patty never rose early. When he'd slept over as a child, Mrs. Keaton would send him into her room to wake her. Patty was prone to kick and punch if roused before she was ready.

He'd never minded her kicks and punches. They didn't hurt. He caught them easily, then tickled her awake. She always woke with a smile for him, eyes shining bright.

Grizz had loved her giggles. He'd loved her smiles. He loved it when she opened those big blue eyes. He never felt more at peace than when she was looking up at him.

Those blue eyes met him as he opened his door.

Her hair was tousled from the pillows. She wore a long nightgown that did nothing to hide the fact that she was now a woman and no longer a child. But what Grizz couldn't take his eyes off of were her pink toes peeking out from beneath her cotton gown.

"Morning," she said.

Grizz's eyes snapped back up to her face. "You should be in bed."

"But I'm wide awake."

"It's three in the morning, Patty. Go back to bed."

Her right brow lifted as the left side of her mouth curled into an amused grin. Grizz was fascinated by the asymmetry of it.

"I'm not a child, Griffin. You can't tell me when to go to bed. Unless you want to come and tuck me in."

Patty took a few steps toward him. Her bare feet padded silently on the floorboards. Grizz felt he was under attack, but something in him would not let him retreat. It took all his willpower to keep his hands at his sides and not reach for her.

She stopped when she was a foot away from him. Her head cocked to the side, like an inquisitive, little bird. If he bent his head down, he could nuzzle against her neck like he'd seen actual love birds do.

"Are you mad at me?"

Grizz's head jerked back, as though she'd slapped him. "No, of course not."

"Then why won't you talk to me?"

"I'm talking to you now."

"We used to be so close, and now you run anytime I come near you."

Grizz opened his mouth, but none of the false, placating words would pass his lips.

Patty's hands rose. His gaze followed them like they were heat-seeking missiles that had locked on their targets. There was no escape. When her soft, warm palms landed on his chest Grizz felt his heart explode inside his chest. He was left in tattered pieces at the slightest touch of her.

"I missed you," she whispered. Her face tilted up. Her blue eyes shone so big, so bright in her perfectly round face.

Just like when they were kids, Grizz felt himself wrapped around her baby finger. He was prepared to indulge her in any whim. To give her

her heart's desire. The problem was, he knew what she wanted, and it was the one thing he had to deny her.

Grizz covered his hands with hers. His rough skin burned as it enveloped her soft flesh. "This cannot happen between us, Patty."

"But you want it to, don't you?"

How had their fingers become entwined? It was not what he intended. He had to break away from her. But he couldn't unravel his digits from the sturdy lacing. Her pinky finger rested heavy against one of his knuckles like it was the key turned into an unyielding lock.

"No," Grizz tried, but his voice was choked.

Patty's smile was slow, even a little wicked as she continued to gaze up at him with guileless eyes. "You've never lied to me before."

Grizz exhaled through his nose. But he needed air to fill his lungs so he could think, so he could speak. The problem was, when he inhaled, all he smelled was the sweet scent of Patricia Keaton. A scent that had haunted and taunted him for three years.

"You know I've loved you my whole life," Patty continued.

"Patty Cakes," he sighed, pulling forth the last ounce of his willpower to get the words out. "It's just a crush."

"It is not."

Patty stomped her foot. Her beautiful face contorted in a fury he hadn't seen since she was an adolescent told by her mother that it was bedtime.

Footsteps sounded at the end of the hall. The knob of a door rattled. It was the door of the master bedroom where Brenda and Keaton slept.

Grizz yanked his hands from Patty's and stepped back just as the door opened.

"What's going on out here?" asked Keaton. His gaze was unfocused from sleep.

"Just a little fight over the bathroom," Grizz called over his shoulder as he made his way down the stairs. "I'll use the downstairs one."

Grizz raced down the stairs, uncaring of his booming footfalls. It would be better to wake the whole house than to be alone one more second with Patty confessing the words he didn't allow himself to dream of.

Her feelings hadn't changed. She still wanted him. He wanted her.

He hadn't said it out loud, couldn't. But he had missed her these last few years. There had been a Patty-sized hole in his life.

Grizz ran his hands over his face. He came away with dirt from the mud at the campgrounds. Fitting because that's who he was, a dirty old man at twenty-five lusting after the little girl he'd once known.

But she's not a little girl anymore, insisted the voice in his head. *She's a full-grown woman who wants you.*

Oh, yeah, thought Grizz. Who's going to tell that to her big brother?

"You're up early," said Keaton.

Grizz dropped the tools in his hands and spun around. He hadn't even heard Keaton drive up to the training campground. Grizz had been so consumed with trying not to think about Patty that he clearly wasn't thinking about anything else either.

"Hey," said Keaton, "what's going on with you and my sister?"

"What? Nothing. Why would you say that?"

Keaton paused, a chainsaw in his hand as he turned to face his best friend. "I don't know? The two of you seem different when you're together?"

Keaton checked the blades of the tool. He hit the ON switch, and the spinning blades roared to life. He shut off the device and looked expectantly at Grizz.

"Come to think of it," said Keaton as he sat the chainsaw down, "I haven't seen you two together in the last two days at all. Are you fighting?"

"What would we have to fight about? We haven't seen each other in years."

"Yeah," Keaton frowned. "It has seemed like the two of you have grown apart. That's too bad."

"It is?" Maybe Keaton wasn't as averse to his best friend and his sister having a relationship after all?

"Something's definitely going on with her." Keaton picked up a shovel and came alongside Grizz. "Why would she choose to spend her spring break on a ranch and not on some beach with her friends? I think some jerk broke her heart, and she's running away. We'll get it out of her and then go wring the jerk's neck. Yeah?"

Keaton clapped Grizz on the back. The force of the impact wasn't hard, but it made Grizz's teeth rattle inside his head.

"Yeah," said Grizz. "Sounds good."

CHAPTER SIX

"That's a nice shirt you're wearing."

"Thanks." Patty gave a wane smile to the guy who'd sidled up to the bar next to her. Her mother had raised her to have manners, even when she didn't feel like using them. Like now.

After their encounter in the hall early in the morning, Grizz had avoided her for the rest of the day. To pass the time, Patty had helped Brenda with tagging the new calves while she and her ranch hand, Angel, had branded and castrated them. Both Brenda and Angel had worried over Patty after the first sizzle of burned flesh. Patty hadn't flinched.

She'd never been a squeamish kinda girl. In fact, she'd enjoyed getting her hands dirty and feeling useful. Something she hadn't felt in the last three years that she'd sat on hard chairs while a professor droned on, and Patty daydreamed about the life she truly wanted. A life beside Griffin Hayes.

"Can I check your tag?"

Patty's head whipped back to the guy leaning casually against the bar. She'd forgotten he was there. "I'm sorry, what?"

"Can I see your tag?" he repeated. "I want to check to see if it was made in heaven? Because someone as fine as you needs a parking ticket."

Patty tried and failed to hide her cringe. She'd heard some bad pickup lines during her time at frat parties. But at least those guys could stick with just one metaphor. She wondered if this guy knew what a metaphor was?

She was a little surprised that she remembered what the word meant since she hadn't paid much attention in English class in high school or her short-lived college career. Grizz had taught her about metaphors when he read her poetry. Most of Dr. Seuss's poetry involved metaphors. The Lorax was a metaphor of anger, and later in the story, hope. So was the Grinch. Patty had often wondered if Dr. Seuss was a depressed soul?

Those metaphorical references she got. Mainly because Grizz was the one explaining them to her, and she always hung on his every word. When her teachers in high school or college tried to cram other dead poets' words into her head, she lost the meaning, and her brain cells collided in an explosion.

Hmm? Was that a metaphor? Patty cocked her head to the side and met with dark eyes.

"I see you get me," said the guy—what was his name?

She hadn't gotten what he'd said or his name? But he thought she had. He apparently thought she was here for his pleasure.

She wasn't.

Patty was tracking another quarry. If she couldn't corral Grizz back at the ranch, then she'd catch him out of that habitat. The guys were due here any moment. Tonight Patty had every plan to tag Grizz as her own.

He couldn't refuse to dance with her if she asked him in front of the others. She knew that if she could just reclaim her old spot inside his arms, he would have no choice but to see her as the woman she was. Then there would be only one more step to her ultimate goal; for Grizz to brand her as his with a kiss.

Her first kiss. The kiss she should have had three years ago at her graduation party. She'd saved herself all these years, knowing that her heart would only ever belong to one person. And it wasn't the sleaze in front of her at the bar.

"Newman," he said as if she'd asked the question. "Deputy Sheriff Nick Newman."

"Patricia Keaton." Patty took his bony hand and shook. A shudder of displeasure went up her arm, and she quickly snatched her hand back.

She couldn't really blame the guy for approaching her. There weren't a lot of single people in the bar. There weren't really a lot of single people in the town.

Tonight the bar was filled with the residents of The Purple Heart Ranch. Patty had met the other men from the neighboring ranch. Each and every one of them here tonight had a ring on his finger. Pastor Vance hadn't been joking when he'd said that the soldiers at the Purple Heart Ranch came looking for healing and wound up married. Each one was more than happy to show pictures of his wife or kid or horse.

Patty liked each and every man and woman she met from there. She wanted to be a part of the group and saw that they would welcome her. She was an army brat who had been blessed to live in the same place her whole life, but she could always easily fit in with anyone in the service. The people at the Purple Heart Ranch were her kinds of people. And she wanted to belong to their club in more ways than one.

The one and only path she planned to take to achieve that goal walked into the bar. Grizz didn't so much as walk as he swaggered. Every female gaze in the bar turned to check him out. Even a few of the wives. Patty knew they couldn't help it even though they were completely devoted to their husbands. Grizz just attracted the female gaze with his pure animal magnetism.

Patty leaned forward to get a better view of the man of her dreams. But she had to quickly jerk back as her nostrils filled with something distasteful. Deputy Sheriff Nick Newman's cologne cloyed her nose.

Didn't he know that a dab went a long way? Apparently not, since it appeared he'd doused himself with the whole bottle. Did he think the scent would attract women? It was having the opposite effect. It was more like woman-repellant.

Grizz's gaze swept the room. Patty knew when he saw her. She could feel the heat of his gaze fall on her cheeks. She didn't expect an encouraging smile from him. She wouldn't have been surprised at a small frown. But the hard glint of anger from his hazel eyes was a surprise.

"Tell me, Patricia Keaton, are you a religious woman? Because you've answered all my prayers."

Patty's stomach grumbled as the cop leaned in. From the corner of her eye, she saw Grizz angle his body toward them. The low hanging fruit would be to let this guy hit on her and make Grizz jealous. But she could never pull that off. Neither did she want to.

The only guy she wanted to flirt with was Grizz. The only guy she wanted to notice her was Grizz. He was noticing her now.

She was looking her best tonight. Since she'd turned eighteen and started on this quest to become Mrs. Griffin Hayes, Patty always made it a point to look her best. All her skirts were tailored. Each dress was only chosen if it flattered her curves, which she never tried to hide. She no longer owned a pair of sweats, not even the cute ones with fancy lettering on the backside. Her tomboy days were long over. If Donna Reed or June Cleaver hadn't worn it, then neither did she.

Except jeans. She couldn't get by without a few pairs of jeans. Which is what she wore tonight. A fitted pair of jeans along with brand new cowboy boots.

Her makeup was done to accentuate her long lashes and eyes. Her lipstick was chosen to make men look at her lips. Which the guy in front of her was doing. But her lips were only for Grizz.

Countless men had looked at her lips, longingly. Not one had ever touched their lips to hers. She only wanted one man to do that, and he was stalking toward her now.

"Come on, angel, let's you and me get out of here." Deputy Newman's palm was hot, but his fingers were cold as they clamped around her forearm. It felt all wrong. But when she went to pull away, his fingers closed like a vise around her.

"You need to let the girl go." Grizz's voice was low. But even with the chatter of the bar, his growl was easily heard.

"What business is it of yours, Hayes?"

Grizz opened his mouth. Then he closed and pursed his lips.

"You got a claim on her or something?"

Grizz's throat worked another moment before he spoke. "She's my best friend's little sister. I helped raise her."

Fury clouded Patty's gaze. Would he never see her for the grown woman she was now? Would he never admit that he had feelings for her?

"Oh, your sister," said the cop. "Hope you don't mind me chatting with your little sister then. She's a nice piece."

Grizz's hazel gaze went as sharp as a shard of wood. But Newman didn't appear to notice. He was far too busy ogling Patty's chest.

"I'm sure you're fending guys off her all the time," Newman continued, still oblivious to the two-hundred-pound soldier who was very near a rage. "But I'm one of the good guys. I'm an officer of the law. She couldn't be in better hands."

"You hear that, Grizz?" Patty said through gritted teeth. "I couldn't be in better hands than his. Unless there was something you wanted to say to me? Maybe you wanted to say it somewhere private?"

"No," said Grizz, letting out a slow breath. "I just came over to check on you."

"Oh. How *brotherly* of you."

"That's what I'm here for."

"Well, you can run along now then."

Grizz held Patty's glare. In it, she knew he was telling her to be careful. She was done being careful. She was done being careless.

She was just done.

She watched Grizz walk off. She turned back to the bar and downed her drink. The virgin peanut butter cocktail gave her a sugar rush that went straight to her head. She wished she could be served something stronger, but she was only twenty. An adult, but without all the privileges of adulthood.

Patty decided she'd done enough adulting for the day. She was calling it a night. She grabbed her purse and headed for the door. Before she could cross the threshold, a hand grabbed her.

Once again, a shiver ran down her spine at the hot and cold of Deputy Sheriff Newman's fingers.

"Where do you think you're going?" he said.

"I'm going home."

"Sounds like a plan. I'll come, too."

"No, you're not invited." Patty stepped out of the bar and into the cool night air. The parking lot was filled with cars but empty of bodies.

"Do you think you can just walk away?"

"No," she said. "I brought my car."

Newman rounded her, planting himself between her and her car. "You led me on back there."

"No, I didn't. I was polite while you entertained yourself with cheesy come-ons."

"Girls like you make me sick." His lip curled, stripping away any hint of handsomeness.

"Girls like me? Seriously, has any woman ever fallen for any of that stuff you were saying? I'm doubting it. Listen, I wasn't being my authentic self back there with you, I admit it. But I also wasn't being an inappropriate jerk. Eyes up here, buddy."

His gaze snapped to hers. For a second. And then they were back on her chest. The guy was clearly a lost cause. It was not her responsibility to try and teach him manners, especially this late in life.

Patty turned to go. Once again, a cold-warm shock held her back.

"You're not going anywhere until I get what I want from you."

Patty turned slowly. More than a couple of times, she'd had to defend herself against a randy man who didn't know how to read the clear signals of a brush-off. Before she used her fists as her brother and Grizz taught her, she decided to give this jerk one last try and use her words.

"I gave you no signals. I'm now clearly stating that I have no interest in you. And here again, I'm going to use my manners and say no and thank you. Now, please let me go."

"Or what?"

Patty clenched her fist. She cocked it back. Before she could raise it, she felt another cold-warm shock. But this time, it wasn't on her arm. It was on her mouth as Deputy Sheriff Nick Newman planted his unwanted lips on hers.

CHAPTER SEVEN

"Are you even listening to me?"

Grizz was not listening to Mac, not even a bit. His gaze was across the room on the television screen over the bar, but his focus was decidedly fixed on Patty. Long before he'd gone into basic training, he'd mastered the art of watching out for Patricia Keaton without letting her know that he was watching her.

Back then, it had been watching her climb the monkey bars when she'd been a head smaller than the other kids. But Grizz never wanted to stunt her independence by stepping in as her safety net. So, he looked the other way.

But he always made sure there was something reflective in his eyesight so that he could see what she was up to. When they were out at the mall when she was a bit older, he'd always scan the food court and know her exact location and those surrounding her. So, watching her in the bar with that jerk of a cop while appearing to not watch her was an old hat to Grizz.

He knew she could handle herself with that buffoon of a deputy. The problem was, Grizz didn't want Newman putting his hands on her. Grizz had no idea how far Patty was willing to push him to admit his feelings for her. He was already at the end of his rope.

"Why don't you just go over there and ask her to dance," said Mac. "You're clearly not trying to get on my dance card."

"Who?" said Maggie Banks, she was the wife of Dylan Banks from the Purple Heart Ranch.

Maggie was swiping through pictures of her son to show Mac and Grizz. Grizz had smiled and nodded obediently when the mother showed him her kid. He liked kids. He often wondered what his kid would look like, especially if they had red hair, blue eyes, and an infectious giggle that made his entire body relax.

He quickly shook himself of that fantasy. He and Patty wouldn't be together like that, much less have kids.

Would that honor go to Deputy Sheriff Newman?

Grizz watched as Patty downed her drink. The frothy concoction made him wonder if it was a virgin peanut butter cocktail, her favorite since she didn't like the sweetness of sodas. He wouldn't get an answer because she slammed the empty glass down on the table and started for the door.

"Oh, I see the boundaries of the Purple Heart Ranch are extending over to Vance Ranch again," said Maggie.

Grizz whipped his gaze back to Maggie. She and Dylan Banks had been the first couple to marry for convenience over at the rehabilitation ranch. Something or other to do with an ordinance that required only families could live full time on the land. There was no red tape on Vance Ranch.

"It's not like that," said Grizz. His fingers balled into fists as he watched Newman follow Patty out the door.

"Looks like it," said Maggie. "What's holding you up?"

"She's Keaton's baby sister," said Mac. "The whole best friend's sister thing. I hear it's a popular story conflict in romance novels."

"It sure is." Maggie's eyes lit up. "We've had that happen at the ranch. But it was two girls who were best friends, and it was the brother that married the best friend. It's one of my favorite of our love stories. But this will be new; a boy's best friend's sister. You should definitely go for it."

"I'm not going for it," said Grizz.

"Why not?" said Maggie. "You clearly have feelings for her."

"I've known her since she was a child."

"She doesn't look like a child anymore. And she also didn't look interested in Deputy Newman. She ... wait, where did she go?"

"She left," Grizz growled.

"With Newman?"

Grizz didn't answer. He rose from his seat without another word. He was out the door in under a second.

The parking lot was dim. There weren't many people on the street at this time of night in the small town. They were either at home or in the bar unwinding. Grizz turned when he heard Patty's voice, followed by the deputy's.

Grizz walked towards the voices and then stopped in his tracks.

"You're not going anywhere until I get what I want from you."

"I gave you no signals. I'm now clearly stating that I have no interest in you. And here I'm going to use my manners and say no and thank you. Now, please let me go."

"Or what?"

Grizz got to them in time to see exactly what Deputy Newman had in mind. Patty's fist was cocked back just like he'd taught her. But Newman's hands were already on her, his lips capturing her mouth.

Patty froze.

Grizz saw red.

Patty's body stiffened. Her eyes went wide with utter shock. Her shock and dismay stunted Grizz into inaction. When Newman pulled away, there were tears in her eyes. It was Patty's tears that yanked Grizz from his stupor.

Grizz stepped to the guy. He grabbed the back of Newman's collar. Before Grizz could punch the man in his face, Newman made a choked sound like he was being strangled. Like Patty's, Grizz's cocked fist remained suspended in the air. But he knew his shock was for an entirely different reason.

Deputy Newman's lips, the lips that had stolen a kiss from Grizz's Patty, were swelling before his eyes. Newman's lips moved, but his words were gurgled, like a fish out of water. Grizz stared in fascination as Newman's lips continued to get bigger and bigger.

"A jerk," the deputy was saying. "A jerk."

"You are a jerk," said Patty, finding her voice again. She whirled the cop around, her fist still cocked. It halted when she saw his increasing lips.

"A jerk," Newman tried again, waving his hands to ward her off. He was patting his pockets, but his fingers didn't seem to be working properly. "A lure jerk."

"Yeah," said Patty. "We get it. But you're not a little jerk. You're a big jerk. That was my first kiss. It was supposed to be with Grizz. Not you. You stole it from me."

Grizz looked back at her. "Your first?"

"Yeah," she sniffed. "It was always going to be you."

"All or jerk," interrupted Newman. "Ebb E Ben."

Grizz wanted to shove the man aside. He wanted to take Patty into his arms and wipe away that tear in her eye. He wanted to hold her to him and erase the memory of anything but his own lips on hers.

Unfortunately, before that plan could be enacted, realization began to dawn.

Angel Bautista tossing peanuts on the ground at Newman's feet.

Patty's frothy drink that she'd downed before coming out here.

The continued swelling of Newman's kiss-stealing lips.

Newman was allergic to peanuts. He was having an allergic reaction. Grizz turned from Patty and began patting the deputy's pockets.

"Uh, Grizz? Why are you feeling him up when I've been coming on to you for years?"

"He's having an allergic reaction. He's allergic to peanuts."

"Serves him right for putting his mouth where it doesn't belong."

"We gotta find his EpiPen, or he could die."

Patty twisted her lips as though in thought.

"Patty."

"Fine." She sighed and went into action. "If it's not on him, maybe it's in his car. I assume that one is his."

A squad car was parked in a No Parking Zone. Grizz helped the swollen deputy to his vehicle. Once there, he let go of Newman.

The man wobbled without Grizz's shoulder to lean on. "Patty, could you?"

Patty looked at him, blue eyes aflame with irritation. She wobbled at the transfer of weight. Grizz turned quickly to get the car unlocked.

"I think he's going to pass out," said Patty.

Grizz slid the key into the lock and turned. He pulled the door open just as he heard a thud. Newman had keeled over. He'd gone down to a knee. Unfortunately, he was now in the direct line of the car door. Which Grizz had yanked open. And smacked Newman upside the head with the metal door.

Grizz and Patty looked to one another. Then down at the fallen man. Then back to each other.

"That was not on purpose," the two said in unison.

The deputy was out like a light. Unfortunately, his lips were still swelling. But he was still breathing.

"Quick, grab the EpiPen," said Grizz as he dropped to his knees to see to Newman.

Patty dashed, emerging a second later with the device. "It was in the dashboard."

Patty held the device up to the street light.

"What are you doing?" demanded Grizz.

"Trying to read the instructions," she said.

"Give it here." Grizz uncapped it and jabbed it in the man's flesh.

Newman's eyes shot open. He gasped in a deep lungful of air, glared at the two of them, and then promptly blacked out again.

This was just great. Newman would have both their hides when he came to. Grizz believed the man vindictive enough to press charges, assault with a door, or some nonsense. Worse, Patty was involved. How was he going to protect her from this?

CHAPTER EIGHT

"Newman, wake up," Grizz shouted at the prone man, still laying on the cold concrete ground.

Patty stood over the two of them, not willing to stoop down to Newman's level. None of this was her fault. He was the thief. He'd stolen her first kiss. If her mother hadn't raised her right, she'd have left him there in his own drivel.

No. She wouldn't have. She'd have punched him first and then called an ambulance. She wasn't sure if they should call one now?

The swelling on his lips had gone down. He was breathing normally instead of wheezing for breath. But his eyes remained closed.

Patty tried to muster concern for his well-being. But she was having a difficult time at it. He still had his life, he was lucky for that. He'd stolen something precious from her.

She'd been saving herself for Grizz all her life, and Newman had come in and taken that from her. He'd put his hot-cold lips on hers. He was lucky all he got was the taste of peanuts. She'd nearly thrown up in his mouth.

"We have to call for an ambulance," said Grizz.

"Isn't the hospital just across the street?"

Grizz looked up. The lights of the emergency room flashed red in the late night. "Help me carry him."

"Me?"

"Who else? I don't want to get anyone else involved."

"Involved in what?"

"Assaulting a police officer."

"He kissed me. That wasn't my fault."

Grizz looked up at her, softening his gaze. "I know, sweetheart. I know. But, guys like him … he could turn this around on the both of us."

"But you saw it. You saw him come on to me."

"Yes, I did."

"I didn't give him any signals other than no." Patty took a deep breath before she started crying.

Grizz straightened, leaving Newman out cold on the ground. He wrapped his arms around Patty, enfolding her in his warmth. Patty clung to him. Inside of Grizz's embrace, her tears felt no need to fall.

"I know, Patty Cakes," Grizz sighed. "And for that, I was ready to knock him out. I'm not entirely sure I didn't purposely hit him with the car door."

"You didn't," she said into his chest, enjoying the feel of the muscles beneath his shirt.

"No, I didn't," he agreed.

Grizz was a big man, with so many muscles that he looked like his body would be hard to the touch. But inside his arms, it had always been soft as a pillow. Patty could've fallen asleep right there. Except …

"We gotta get him some help."

Grizz pulled away from her. Patty bit her lip but didn't offer up another complaint. For now.

Between the two of them, they hefted the deputy up. Grizz did most of the heavy lifting. Patty was no shrimp. She shouldered Newman's weight on her right side. She hadn't been all too keen to help earlier. She'd had enough of Newman's hands on her before he'd fallen to the ground. But she'd keep that to herself.

"Do you really think he'll cause trouble when he wakes up?" she asked as they crossed the empty street.

"If he does, you blame the assault all on me."

"No," she said. "He'll need to take responsibility for his actions against me."

"Fine," said Grizz. "But any damage to him, we'll say that was all me."

"It was an accident."

"They might turn it into a he-said-she-said fiasco," said Grizz. "I won't let anyone put you through that."

Patty ground her molars. She wanted to drop the dead weight she was carrying right in the middle of the street. "Isn't it a he-said-she-said-he-said thing?"

Grizz scrunched up his features as he turned to her. "What?"

"It's both of our words against his."

"Him coming onto you is one thing," said Grizz as they approached the doors to the emergency room. "But the bruises on his head, the fact that he's out cold, and the delay in getting him his meds, that's where it gets hairy. He could see I approached him, ready to knock his lights out. And here he is, lights out."

"I'm not letting you take the blame for me."

Grizz ignored her as they walked into the sliding doors of the hospital. Before they could shout for help in the empty emergency room, a nurse rushed up to them.

"What happened?" asked the nurse.

"He had an allergic reaction," Grizz spoke before Patty could open her mouth. "Peanuts. We found his EpiPen and administered the dose. But he's been out for almost five minutes now."

"We'll take it from here," said the nurse, sliding Newman into a wheelchair

Patty slumped into a chair against the wall. Her shoulder ached from hefting that brute's weight. She sniffed at her shirt and cringed. His cologne was all over her. She wanted nothing more than a hot shower and to forget this night ever happened.

Grizz knelt in front of her. His gaze was soft and filled with concern as he peered into her eyes. With his thumb, he tilted up her chin.

"It's going to be okay," he said.

And just like that, everything was right once again in her world. The smell of Grizz's spicy, earthy scent filled her nostrils. That disgusting kiss had never happened. How could it when the man of her dreams brushed at her lower lip with the pad of his thumb and wiped all trace of it away.

Patty ran her fingers down his strong chin, and he let her. Grizz closed his eyes and leaned into her touch. This was what she wanted. This was what she'd always wanted. To be free to touch him, to hold him, to kiss him.

"I'll protect you," he said into her palm. "I'll always protect you."

Patty knew his words to be true. Grizz had always been her hero. She knew he would lay down his life to protect her. But she didn't want him dead or in jail. She wanted him alive, holding her hand, just like he was now.

The only thing that could make this moment more perfect would be a proposal.

"Excuse me?"

Both Patty and Grizz looked up to find the nurse who'd taken Newman back standing over them with a clipboard in hand.

"Would you and your wife mind giving us your contact information in case the doctor has some questions for you?"

"Oh," said Grizz, "We're not—"

"Of course, we don't mind." Patty took the clipboard and scribbled her phone number on the sheet. Above it, she wrote the words that had peppered so many of her high school notebooks: Mr. and Mrs. Hayes.

Patty had waited forever to have the privilege of writing that phrase. And maybe now, there was a way to make it happen.

Grizz straightened as the nurse walked back to her station. He looked from the clipboard swinging in the nurse's hand and back down to Patty.

"Did you just lie on a hospital form?" Grizz asked.

"Not necessarily," Patty said as she came to standing.

"We're not husband and wife."

"No, not right this minute. But if we were, it would solve our little problem."

"What are you talking about?

"Spousal privilege." Patty tugged him out of the sliding door. Grizz seemed so bewildered that he followed her. "There's a law where a husband and wife can't testify against each other."

"What?" Grizz pulled back from her.

"I was talking to Walter. You know, Pastor Vance. He was joking, but it's a real law. I saw it on television."

"Patty—"

"No, listen. If we get married, they can't make us testify against each other."

"I don't think that's how it works."

"You got another idea? You want to protect me? We should get married. As I hear it, people in this town get married for less."

CHAPTER NINE

Grizz used to hold Patty's hand all the time when she was still in pigtails. Back then, her small, chubby hand wouldn't span his large palm. He'd engulfed her, holding her delicately but securely. The security was more for him than her.

She'd gotten lost once at a county fair. Because she'd gone off and looked at the array of stuffed animals instead of following behind him. When he'd found her ten minutes later, his heart never regained its slow rhythmic beating. From that day forward, it had always sped up a bit whenever her hand wasn't in his.

Grizz's entire world slowed now that Patty's hand was back in his grasp. She still didn't span his entire palm. But he felt her touch span his entire being.

Her palm pressed into his, and he felt swallowed. Her fingers laced with his, and he felt hooked. She gave a tug, and he went where she bade him to go. When he looked up, it was to see a large church bell.

The bell hung silently on its perch. The hour still had another quarter before the alarm needed to be sounded. Relief settled over Grizz's shoulders. There was time.

There were sins he needed to confess. The least of all were the actions back in the parking lot of the bar. The state of the deputy had been the man's own making and not a direct result of anything Grizz had done to him—not that that would be easily believed by the powers that be. But those of that particular power were men.

Grizz needed to confess his real sins to God. He needed to confess the desires he'd harbored for years for the woman whose hand he clung to. He needed to confess the actions he was seriously contemplating right now, taking her as his wife to protect her from what harm may come from earlier.

Grizz hadn't been to church in years. His temple was the cross at his neck. His congregation wherever he dropped to his knees.

When they came inside the building, it was mostly empty. He didn't see a confessional box, likely because this wasn't a Catholic church. The doors to the chapel were open. Grizz decided that would do, and headed toward the pews. But something tugged him in the other direction.

Patty.

Her blue eyes narrowed at him across their extended hands. He could've easily pulled her to him and compelled her to go where he wanted. But it was never that easy with Patty Keaton.

Patty frowned. Her bow-snapped lips pinched in a question. Grizz's answer was to come to her. Fingers still entwined, he fell in step behind her small form. A good little soldier following behind his one true cause; her protection.

There were voices down the hall, and that's the direction they walked. Patty poked her head into a room. Inside, sat a small circle of townsfolk. At the center of the circle was Walter Vance, Brenda's brother.

"When God asks Cain where his brother Abel is, we all know the response," said Pastor Vance.

"'Am I my brother's keeper,'" replied a red-headed young man.

Grizz knew the man to be Reece Cartwright. Beside him sat a lovely woman who smiled adoringly up at him. It was Reece's wife Beth, the daughter of the town's elder pastor.

"That's exactly right, Reece," said Walter, a grin on his face.

Grizz shifted uncomfortably inside the door frame. He'd heard the story of Reece and Beth, and Walter and Beth. Beth and Walter had been engaged. But Beth had always been in love with Reece Cartwright, the soldier who'd gone missing in action a year ago and had been presumed dead. When Reece was found, they learned that his memory was lost, though not all of it. Reece had returned to his hometown, thinking that he was engaged to Beth. Beth had broken off the engagement with Walter to marry the soldier, and when Reece's memory came back, it had worked out.

There was no animosity on Walter's face as he regarded the two. Grizz didn't think he could ever handle Patty gazing adoringly at another guy.

"That answer implies that God does indeed think that Cain is responsible for his brother," Walter preached. "Now, I know this story ends in tragedy, but there's a valuable lesson hidden in here. It's not every man for himself in our society. We are tasked with the care of one another; our mothers, our fathers, our sons, our daughters, our sisters, and our brothers. We were created as a community, and we should care for all."

Around the room, the students at the nighttime Bible study nodded. Walter closed his great book with a decided thunk. "That's enough for tonight, everyone. Thank you for coming."

Reece shook Grizz's free hand as he and Beth made their way out of the door. Beth glanced back at the two of them, a knowing glint in her bright eyes. She whispered something to her husband. Reece turned to look back. The same glint lit his eyes as he chuckled and wrapped his wife in his arms.

As the others filed out of the small room, Walter made his way to Grizz and Patty. "You two missed class."

"We're not here for class," said Patty.

The young pastor looked between Patty and Grizz. Walter's gaze fastened on their joined hands. That same glint caught in the Pastor's gaze. A slow, knowing smile spread across his handsome face.

And then he groaned.

"Does it have to be today?" Walter looked down at his watch. "I had this weekend in the pool."

"What are you talking about?" asked Grizz. "What pool?"

"You know there's a pool about you two? About when you would get married."

Grizz hadn't yet allowed the thought to fully form in his own mind. But he'd allowed himself to be led here. Here, standing before a pastor to bind the one woman he shouldn't have to himself. All under the guise that it was for her protection.

"After we talked earlier," Walter was saying to Patty, "I moved my bet up to this weekend."

Grizz turned to Patty. "What did you two talk about?"

Patty didn't answer. Instead, she gripped his hand more tightly to hers.

Grizz could've easily broken free of her hold. Instead, he rubbed his thumb over her knuckles, locking her grip tighter.

"You've been here for over a week, Sergeant Hayes," said Walter. "You know how this place works with soldiers."

Grizz had heard the tales before they bought the land. But his unit didn't live on the Purple Heart Ranch, so it should not extend to him. Except here he was.

"Can't you two wait until the weekend?" asked Walter. "We could put together something special with all your family. And I could also win the bet. It's just a few days."

"I'm sorry, you're going to lose your bet," said Patty. "But do you think you can marry us tonight? Right now?"

"Why the rush?" asked the pastor. "Oh, I get it. It's your brother, isn't it? Keaton isn't on board with his best friend and his baby sister?"

Grizz gulped. He opened his mouth again. He should be the one doing the speaking. But Patty beat him to the punch again.

"That's it exactly," said Patty. "But we're in love. Have been for years."

She gazed up at Grizz. Those blue eyes that had always felt like home to him, pierced into his heart. Her words were a sieve Something punctured his chest, and all the words he never thought he could say came out of her mouth.

"I love this man with all my heart. I've always known I would spend the rest of my life with him. I've only ever wanted to be married to

Grizz. To be his wife, keep his house, have his children, to be his partner."

Grizz let out a shaky breath as his heart opened wide. There was nothing left inside of him. There was nowhere left to hide his true desires.

His head felt light. Something fluttered in his belly. He was certain that the racing of his pulse would put him flat on his back.

"I love him, and I want to belong to him."

With that last proclamation, Grizz found his voice. It was the one word he tried to keep a leash on. It was the only word that was able to escape his lips now.

"Mine."

CHAPTER TEN

It was happening. It was really happening. Patty was marrying the man of her dreams.

She'd felt Grizz's hands go clammy as they left the hospital. Then dry as they entered the church. They'd become warm as she professed her true, undying love for him. When she'd finally spoken her truth aloud, she'd thought he might shy away from her.

But he hadn't. He hadn't let go of her hand. He'd said that she was his.

They followed Walter down the hall to his office. The small room was more of a closet than anything else. Books wallpapered the walls. Old titles with Hebraic and Latin words on the browning spines.

It wasn't the altar she'd expected to be saying her vows at. She wasn't wearing the wedding dress of her dreams. Instead of the empire waist gown she had envisioned wearing, she was in jeans and cowboy boots. Instead of her hair being in an intricate bun woven with flowers, her tresses were in a high ponytail. Her makeup was done in dark shades designed to be seen in the low light of the bar, not the muted tones for a daytime wedding with flowers all around them.

But when it came down to it, none of that mattered. Patty was standing with Grizz about to say the words that would transform her into Mrs. Griffin Hayes. Her dream might not be in the technicolor wonder of her imagination, but it was becoming a reality. She would grab hold of it with both hands.

"Do you have the rings?" asked Pastor Vance.

Grizz and Patty looked at one another. Grizz's gaze fell to Patty's left hand and the bare fingers there. His forehead wrinkled like a problem was brewing there.

"We don't," said Grizz. "Maybe we should wait until—"

"No." Patty lifted her left hand like a five-fingered stop sign. "Remember, we already talked about how *privileged* we are to be able to do this tonight."

Patty gave Grizz a meaningful glance, a glance that she hoped would remind him of why they were rushing to get this done. She hated that her wedding dreams were finally coming true on the back of a heinous individual like Deputy Doodie Head.

She knew Grizz got her meaning when he scratched at the hairs on his chin with his right hand. Patty grabbed for his hand with her left one, entwining their fingers so that she had him on lockdown from both sides.

"Well, the ring isn't a requirement," said the pastor. "Neither is the marriage license, here in Montana. You just need to be of age, which you both are. And show that you have the mental capacity to wed."

Grizz took in another deep breath. He hadn't taken his eyes off of Patty while Pastor Vance spoke. He seemed to be searching for something. An answer? Permission?

"Patty Cakes, if we do this, it's forever. I won't ever get a divorce."

Patty's heart had been beating wildly since the moment they'd entered the church. It stopped while Grizz was talking. With her heart in arrest, it was difficult to get her lungs to work.

"Patty?"

Tears stung her eyes. Her fingers went lax, allowing Grizz to slip from her hold. But she was too weak to reclaim him.

"Sweetheart, what is it?"

Grizz's arms came around her. Patty went to him. She rested her head on his chest. The sound of his heart beating kicked hers back into gear. Her entire world homed in on the rhythm of Grizz. Her nails dug into his shirt. Her face turned into the center of his chest, and she inhaled, filling her entire being with the spicy, warm scent of him.

"You promise you won't ever leave again?" she said.

"Patty ..." Grizz sighed.

But it wasn't a sigh of exasperation. It was filled with many emotions. Some Patty didn't recognize.

Grizz brushed his fingers across her temple and then gently cupped her cheek. Patty's breath caught as he gazed down at her. There had been a time when he'd hid nothing from her. But when she'd developed boobs, he'd stopped looking at her. She'd started wearing a sports bra for a while, hoping that a uniboob would bring them back together.

It hadn't. It had taken a handful of peanuts and a stolen kiss from the wrong man to get them here. But she'd take it. When Deputy Newman woke up, Patty would be there to thank him. That is if he wasn't trying to press charges against her.

But she didn't want to think of that jerk right now. She put her focus back on Grizz. He still held her in his arms, but she felt tension in those strong muscles of his. Instead of pulling away from her, he pulled her more tightly to his chest.

"I promise," he said.

Grizz's voice was a deep rumble. She felt the truth of his words from the crown of her head to the tips of her toes. The moment was ripe for a kiss, her true first kiss.

"So ..." Walter interrupted the tender moment. "Are we going for the standard vows?"

"No," said Patty. "I've prepared my own."

"You have?" asked Grizz.

"Of course, I have. I've been dreaming about this for years." Patty cleared her throat. She lifted her gaze and looked directly into his eyes. "Griffin Clarence Hayes."

Grizz winced. The only other person who could get away with using his middle name was Patty's mother. If Holly Keaton used a middle name when she called a kid, it could only mean one thing; run because they were in trouble.

Grizz was in trouble. He'd been caught red-handed. One of his hands was still cupping the side of Patty's face. A few strands of her red hair flowed over his fingertips.

"I've loved you since I could say your name. The first time you held my hand, I knew it was where I was supposed to spend my life. I promise to never let go of your hand. I'll be there as your strength since you've been mine. I vow to be your loving and devoted friend, partner, and wife. I look upon you without judgment, without scorn, and always with an open heart and mind."

Patty watched as Grizz's throat worked. His Adam's apple bobbed as he squinted at her. She saw his gaze glisten. Yes, this was it. Just as she'd dreamed.

"Patty, I ..." Grizz cleared his throat and tried again. "Patty, I …" Grizz shook his head and blinked a few times. "I don't know what to say."

"I can help with that," said Pastor Vance, opening his book to the standard set of wedding vows.

"No," said Grizz. "I've got this. Patricia Anne Keaton, I knew you were special the first moment I saw you. I made it my mission to protect you. I haven't been there in a while. You've always looked at me like I was your hero, and I wasn't there for you. I'm sorry."

Patty placed her hand over the hand Grizz still had on her cheek. Then she placed her hand on his cheek. With a push of her thumb, she tilted Grizz's head back, until his gaze lifted to her again.

"If we do this," he continued, "I swear I'll be there for you every day of your life. I won't leave again. I'll protect you with my last breath."

"Those sound like perfect vows to me," said Pastor Vance. "I now pronounce you husband and wife. You may kiss your bride."

Grizz swallowed. Patty watched as his Adam's apple bobbed again and again. There was tension in his jaw, and she knew he was clenching his teeth.

Was he not going to kiss her?

She thought she'd gotten her answer when his forehead came to rest against hers. He let out a long, tortured sigh. The taste of his breath on her tongue was a cruel tease of what he would not share with her.

She'd been patient for what seemed her whole life for this man. And now he was going to hold the one last thing she wanted. He was going to make her wait and—

Grizz's lips were soft as they brushed against hers. So soft that she thought she'd imagined it. But the second touch of his lips was more than a brush, it was a press.

Slipping the hand that held her cheek down to her neck, Grizz tilted Patty's head up. He slanted his mouth over hers and deepened the kiss. It was a good thing he had a hold of her because Patty's knees went weak.

Yes, this was the kiss she'd been waiting for. Being in Grizz's arms, being claimed by his lips, was worth everything. And still, she sensed he was holding back.

She felt it in the careful way he held her. In how he broke the first and then the second touch of their lips before it could go too deep. In the way his fingers fisted at the back of her neck with a need he wasn't satiated himself with. All of that let her know there was more he had to give. He'd given her a lot with this small taste. But when she saw that there was more, she was determined to have all of that, too.

"Congratulations, Mr. and Mrs. Hayes," said Walter. "Now, good luck with telling your brother."

CHAPTER ELEVEN

The ranch was quiet when they returned. The animals had settled in for the night. There were no trucks in the drive, so Grizz had to assume that the others were still out enjoying themselves at the bar.

Good. That meant he didn't have to explain where he and Patty had been. Or what they'd been up to.

Congratulations, Mr. and Mrs. Hayes.

Grizz had never thought he'd hear that title paired with his last name. His mother had gone back to her maiden name a few years after the divorce. Now, the one and only Mrs. Griffin Clarence Hayes unbuckled her seatbelt as he put the truck in park.

Patty had remained uncharacteristically quiet on the car ride from town. She'd sat with her hands folded primly in her lap while he'd driven. She'd rested her cheek against her shoulder as she gazed out the window.

Grizz was unnerved by her calm and quiet. Patty had always been a ball of energy. Her serenity was not natural.

She waited while he came around and handed her out the car, just like he'd taught her to do. A man should always open a door for a lady.

He opened the door to the house. Patty paused before stepping into the open doorway. Her gaze was trained on the ground.

Grizz looked down at the threshold of the doorway. It was a raised hump that divided the inside from the outside. When the meaning of that hump hit him, it became akin to a speed bump for his legs.

Was he supposed to carry her over the threshold? It's what a true married couple would do when entering their home for the first time as man and wife.

But this wasn't their home.

And they were man and wife only on paper. This ruse was all for her protection against that jerk of a lawman. Though ruse wasn't the right word.

Grizz had pledged to protect Patricia Keaton before she could walk. His marriage vows were simply an extension of that original oath. He would keep Patty out of harm's way, and that included if the harm came from being in his arms.

Turning his body perpendicular to the doorway, Grizz crossed his arms over his shoulders and waited for Patty to precede him into the house.

Her gaze narrowed at him in the dim light of the moon. Her lips quirked up, as though she was accepting a challenge. Angling her body towards him, she stepped across the threshold unassisted. But not before making sure to brush her body against his.

Grizz couldn't hide his sharp intake of breath. His nostrils flared as they caught the sweet scent that rested on her skin and rolled off her hair. And now Grizz knew that that same confectionary scent was what she was made of.

The honeyed taste of her from their kiss was still on his tongue. He'd been trying to forget that small sample of her. That was easily done.

It was the second helping of her that he'd stolen that knocked around in his head.

For as long as he lived, he would never forget the soft sigh that breezed over his lips. He would never forget the rightness of pulling her against him. He would never forget the peace he felt pressed against her.

He wanted to wrap himself up in her arms. He wanted to burrow his nose into her neck. He wanted another taste of her. But what shook him to his core was that, by law, he could have more. Because now, he had that privilege.

His stomach grumbled with want. He slammed the door shut to cover up the sound and headed for the kitchen.

"You hungry?" he asked.

Patty shook her head, stopping at the bottom of the staircase. "I'm ready to turn in."

It had been a long day. She was likely still reeling from her encounter with the deputy. Grizz still wished he'd had the opportunity to deck the lawless man before he'd succumbed to his allergies.

He should probably call the hospital to check in on Newman. Grizz wasn't sure how bad allergic reactions went. He was sure the man would be up soon, and then he'd likely go after Patty for revenge.

Grizz wasn't sure if this spousal privilege plan of theirs would work? But it was all they had. Now that they were married, they couldn't testify against each other. This was the only way to protect her. This was his sole job in the world, and he would not fail her.

"I'll walk you up," he said.

They barely fit together side by side as they climbed the stairs. Patty leaned into him. Then she rested her head against his shoulder, just like she'd done when she was a girl.

Her gaze was cast down. The quiet serenity remained on her face. Grizz wondered what she was thinking. He wanted a bit of that peace and quiet for himself. Instead, his mind raced.

Once they reached the second story, he stopped at her door, which was nearest to the stairs. However, Patty let go of his arm and continued on down the hall. She stopped at his bedroom door. Grizz remained at hers.

"Aren't you coming to bed?" she asked.

Grizz opened his mouth. No words would come out. His mind was a hazmat area. Yellow tape, flashing red lights, smoke clouding his vision.

He forced air into his lungs. But his words were choked when they came out. His good sense and his secret desires were locked in combat. "Patricia, that's not happening."

"Griffin, I'm your wife now." She turned the knob on his bedroom door and stood at the edge of the threshold. "This is where I belong."

"This is not that kind of marriage. It's for your protection."

"So what? Are you planning to have it annulled after Deputy Donkey Brains wakes up, and then leave me?"

"No." Grizz was standing before her in just two long strides. "I would never leave you."

"Well, if you really want to protect me, we should make this marriage legal. The way to do that is with consummation."

Grizz shook his head. He reached for her, preparing to march her back to her room. Before he could get a hold of her, she ducked inside his room. She took a seat on his bed, toeing off her cowboy boots.

Grizz stormed into the room. He scooped her boots into his hands. Using one of her shoes, he pointed at her. "That's enough, Patty. Get off the bed. It's time for you to go to sleep."

"I'm fine sleeping right here, thank you very much."

"I'm not playing with you, Patty Cakes," Grizz growled. "I'm going to give you until the count of three and—"

"And then what?" She grinned. "You'll put me over your knee? I've read about things like that in a romance novel. Let's try it."

The boot dropped from Grizz's hand. He was sure his eyes were bugging out of his head. Exactly what had his sweet Patty Cakes been up to since he'd been away? And what had she been reading?

"What's going on here?"

Grizz cursed under his breath at the sound of his best friend's voice. If this night wasn't already trying enough. He was already at the end of his rope. And now here came a huge knot.

Grizz turned to find Keaton standing in the hall. Grizz's best friend looked between his baby sister perched, barefoot, on Grizz's bed. And then back to Grizz.

"We were wondering where you two disappeared to," said Brenda, who stood behind her husband.

"We went to church," said Patty.

"Patty, get off the man's bed," said Keaton. "You're a little too old for sleepovers."

"It's not a sleepover," said Patty scooting back on the bed. "Grizz and I are sleeping together."

Pinching the bridge of his nose, Grizz closed his eyes and let out a long, tired exhale. He hadn't figured out yet what he'd tell Keaton about all of this. He was sure once he explained the situation with Deputy Newman that there might be some understanding. With Patty's narration of the story, Grizz wasn't sure he wouldn't end up in the hospital beside the other man.

Grizz opened his eyes just in time to feel the impact of Keaton thrusting him against the wall. Keaton's calculating blue eyes were a raging storm as they bore down on Grizz.

"Keaton," shouted Patty, "let go of my husband."

"Husband?" choked Keaton.

"It's not what you think," Grizz started. And then stopped.

What was he going to tell his best friend? That he'd married his baby sister as a ruse? That it wasn't real? When Keaton had said those words to Patty, the lie had nearly burned his tongue.

Because the vows he said were real. It was his mission to protect Patty. More than anything in the world, he wanted to be her hero. And he would not leave her. Not even if she had planted herself in the middle of his bed.

"Somebody had better explain," Keaton demanded, his hold still firm on Grizz.

"You know I care about your sister," Grizz began.

"Yeah," said Keaton, tightening his hold. "Like she was your sister."

"No." Grizz shook his head. "I've had feelings for her for a while. I've been trying to keep them from you."

Grizz placed his hands over his best friends and slowly peeled them away. He met with resistance for a moment before Keaton let him go. Grizz took a deep breath and stepped a bit further on the high wire between his best friend and his wife. His feet carried him to the bed where Patty had once again taken her seat. He addressed the next bit to his wife.

"That's why I haven't dated in years. I couldn't stop thinking about Patty."

There. It was out. The words leaving his mouth were like a weight lifting off his soul.

He hadn't dated anyone since he'd almost kissed Patty three years ago. It wasn't for lack of opportunity. His mind had been so occupied with trying not to think of Patricia Keaton that he could never fit anyone else in there. Now, he wouldn't have to fight so hard anymore.

Patty's blue eyes were huge on her heart-shaped face as she regarded him. Her lips were set in a perfectly round O of wonder. She stood and took a step to him.

Grizz's heart thudded hard against his chest with each and every one of her steps. They were only about five or so steps apart. He felt light-headed as he waited for her to get to him. Only three more steps and—

Keaton stepped between them. He turned his back on his sister and faced Grizz. "You two really got married tonight?"

"Yes." Grizz nodded.

"Legally?"

"Walter performed the ceremony at church."

Keaton took a deep breath and whistled low.

"I'm sorry we did it this way. And I'm sorry I didn't tell you what I was feeling for her. But it didn't seem appropriate because—you know —she's your sister. And I've known her all her life. And she was young. But now she's a grown woman."

Keaton balled his hand in front of Grizz's nose. It was the army signal for all motion, including talking, to halt. Ever the dutiful soldier, Grizz did as he was told.

"Wait?" said Keaton. "So, what you're telling me … is we're really brothers now?"

Grizz blinked in surprise.

Keaton clapped him on the back. Then he burst out into laughter. "I can't believe she finally sunk her claws into you."

"Wait?" said Grizz, a bit dazed now. "You knew how I felt about her?"

"Of course, I did," said Keaton. "What? Did you think I'm clueless? I thought it would take until the summer for her to finally break you."

"I had until the end of the week," said Brenda from her post in the doorway.

CHAPTER TWELVE

renda shot Patty a wink as Keaton ushered his wife out the door. The door snicked closed behind the other newlywed couple. Patty and her husband were alone again.

Grizz rubbed at his neck. The poor guy looked dazed. And bruised. The skin there was red from where Keaton had grabbed him.

Patty reached out to Grizz. He let her fingers glide over the sore spot on his neck. She felt his deep inhale. His skin was warm under her fingers. Grizz bowed his head, giving his weight over to Patty's massage.

"So, you haven't kissed another woman in three years, huh?"

Grizz's head lifted. His hazel eyes latched onto her blue ones. His lips, which had been in a hard, pinched line, softened.

"No."

His voice was a soft growl. It made Patty's stomach rumble. She'd said she wasn't hungry before. Now her belly ached for him.

Patty ran her fingers across his shoulders. Up to his neck. Through his hair. "I can help you with that."

Patty smiled her best and brightest smile, her dimples on full display. She knew her eyes were sparkling because she felt an inner light being under Grizz's gaze.

Grizz reached up. But instead of taking her into his arms, he wove his fingers around hers and peeled them from the back of his head. "No, Patty."

Patty's stomach stopped its rumbling. Now it grumbled a hollow protest. Above her belly, her chest tightened as her heart rate slowed.

"That's not how this is going to go," he said.

"But why?" She wanted to stomp her foot. In fact, she thought she did. But her foot was bare and barely made an impact on the soft carpet. "You got Keaton's blessing. You have my permission and consent. What more do you need?"

Grizz cupped her face with his hands. Patty held still for the embrace. How could she not? Being close to this man had been her goal for so long. The chaste kiss he pressed to her forehead, silenced her. But only for a moment.

He released her face and walked to the bed. Patty's heart kicked back into high gear. Was this it? Was it going to happen?

Grizz tore the comforter off the bed. He also snagged one of the pillows. Bending down to the floor, he began making a pallet next to the bed.

"So, we're sleeping on the floor our first night as a married couple?" asked Patty.

"I'm sleeping on the floor. You're sleeping in the bed." Grizz pulled his shirt over his head.

Patty was momentarily distracted by the revelation of his hard, corded abs and the broadness of his chest. She hadn't seen him shirtless since he'd become an Army Ranger. Whatever he'd done in his training had honed his already perfect muscles into weapons.

Grizz was still talking as he balled his shirt up and threw it into an open duffle bag on the floor. It took a second before Patty comprehended his words.

"… and you have to go back to school."

School? Was that his objection? Now would be the perfect time to tell him that she'd dropped out of school. Problem solved.

"Yeah, Grizz, about school—"

"This marriage is not going to interfere with your education."

"Trust me," Patty slumped down on the bed, "that's not what I'm concerned about."

Patty nearly told him that she wasn't going back to school, that she hadn't been back to school in months. But she decided to focus on one argument at a time.

"Well, I am." Grizz came to the edge of the bed and knelt before her. "We were forced into this situation."

"I wasn't forced. I've wanted this my whole life."

Patty looked away from him and out the window. The moon sparkled into the dim room. She'd been told all her life not to look into the sun. She'd never understood how something so beautiful could cause so much pain. But it was fine to look into the moon because it was just a reflection of the sun. No matter how brightly the pale orb shone, it could never hurt her.

Grizz's fingers were soft as they captured her chin. Patty allowed him to turn her face to him. His dark gaze bore into hers, and she shivered.

"You know I care about you, Patty Cakes."

"You know I'm in love with you, Grizzly Bear." She shrugged. "Your move."

Grizz sighed. But the sound wasn't one of defeat. It was one of puzzlement.

"Are you trying to tell me that you don't feel anything for me?" she said.

"I do." He shut his eyes as though it was hard to look at her. "I've been telling myself for years that my feelings for you are wrong."

"They're not. They're—"

Grizz pressed a finger to her lips. It wasn't the gesture that made her hush. It was that she realized he was staring at her mouth like he might kiss her.

And then, somehow, miraculously, her prayers were answered. Grizz brushed his thumb down on the right half of her lip. With the finger gone, he made way for his lips to touch hers. It was just a light touch, the barest of caresses, but the feather-light impact was enough to knock her over. Luckily, Grizz had his arms around her.

He pulled her to him. Her head rested on his bare chest. He buried his nose into her neck and held her tight.

It was heaven. But they were still standing outside the pearly gates. Patty wanted an all-access pass. She reached between them, trying to tug at the top of her shirt.

"Hey, hey," said Grizz. "None of that."

Patty's mind raced and halted at the same moment. It was like a brain freeze, except the temperature went wonky all over her body. Unlike her horrid encounter earlier in the evening with Deputy Dunce, she was sure Grizz was giving off all the signals for Go.

So, why was he shaking his head and stilling her fumbling hands?

"I told you, we're not sleeping together," he said.

"Do you need to have a talk about what's supposed to happen between a husband and wife? I'm sure we can get Keaton back in here."

Grizz tossed his head back and laughed. When he sobered, his face was still soft with mirth. He ran his hands across her temple, pushing a lock of her hair behind her ear.

"This marriage is forever," he said. "But this relationship is new. I want to go slow."

"Slow?"

He nodded. "Maybe take you out on a date."

"You want to date?"

"Is that so strange? A husband wanting to date his wife?"

Now it was Patty's turn to pinch the bridge between her nose. Grizz took her hand in his. He turned her palm over so that her knuckles were facing him. Like a gentleman of old, he brushed a kiss across the back of her hand.

"You've been thinking about this for a long time," he said. "I haven't let myself even imagine it. Let me do it right."

In another life, this would've been cute. For someone who hadn't been waiting three years for this very moment, it might've even been romantic. For someone with patience, she might have been swept off her feet.

He wanted time? Fine, she'd give him time. But the smallest amount that she could manage it. Because Patricia Keaton—no, strike that—

Because Patricia Hayes was determined to get her man, now that she had him. She had every intention of speeding up this little courtship. But she'd play nice. For now.

"Fine," she smiled sweetly.

Grizz gave her a heart-stopping grin of his own, and Patty nearly tossed her resolve. But when he pulled away from her and slipped under the comforter on the floor, her determination shifted into high gear.

Patty slipped one of the straps of her shirt off her shoulders. Grizz's smile slipped as he watched her. His eyes went wider than saucers. He sat bolt up, giving Patty another delicious view of his strong chest and defined six-pack.

"What are you doing?" he demanded.

"Getting ready for bed like you said."

"You can't take off your clothes." He held up his hands, as though they were a stop sign.

Patty ignored his directions. "You did."

Grizz pursed his lips again. She'd missed this, the teasing between them. Even though it had never been on this level with articles of clothing coming off. Now, she'd get to tease him and see his bare chest for the rest of her life. It was a win-win any way she looked at it.

Patty slid the other strap down her shoulder. Grizz followed the fall of the fabric. He shut his eyes tight. Then he turned his back for good measure.

Patty stood and shimmied out of her jeans and shirt. She walked across the room, skirting the pallet he'd made on the floor.

"Patricia," he growled as she came near him.

"Relax," she said. "I'm just getting something to sleep in."

She picked up his discarded shirt from his duffle bag and slipped it over her head. Grizz's scent surrounded her. The shirt was still warm from his body heat. It was the next best thing to being in his arms, which clearly wasn't happening tonight.

Which was fine. There was tomorrow. Then the night after that until forever.

"Okay," she said, once she was under the covers in his bed. "I'm decent."

Grizz opened first one and then the other eye. His throat worked as he took in what he saw.

"Is this going to be our life together?" she mused. "Separate bedrooms like in those old shows you used to watch?"

"Those were the good old times," he said. "Wanna watch one?"

"Sure," she sighed. "Since I doubt there's anything higher than PG-rated that you want to do."

CHAPTER THIRTEEN

Grizz's dreams were fevered that night. The taste of Patty lingered on his tongue. His palms itched to be full of her. Her sweet scent filled his head every time he inhaled. Her soft sighs of rest crashed into his ears all his waking hours.

She was so close, yet so far.

He spent most of the night gazing up at her from his place on the floor. Her arm lay curled on the pillow. Her cheek rested heavily in the crook of her elbow. The cloud of red hair rested on her shoulders. Her beautiful features were soft under cover of night.

Grizz wanted to run his fingers over the fine hairs at her temple. He wanted to brush his lips across her closed eyelids. He wanted ... her.

The scary thing was that he could have her.

She was his wife. His partner. His responsibility. From now until forever.

For years, he'd fought against this particular desire in his heart. Now, it was served up to him on a firm mattress. He need only rise and take what had been freely offered up to him.

Grizz rolled over and came to his haunches. He paused in a low crouch as Patty shifted in bed. Holding his breath and keeping perfectly still during surveillance as his army training had taught him, Grizz waited for Patty to settle. When she did, he rose to his full height, towering over her.

The war was over. The tugging at his heart had been decided. This slip of a woman had unmanned him, and he was admittedly, daresay happily, at her mercy. He just wasn't ready for the victory celebration, as it were.

If he was going to do this, he was going to do it right. Patty deserved a courtship, complete with roses and flowers and romantic poems. She also deserved a man who could take care of her financially. So, with that final thought in mind, Grizz grabbed a clean set of clothes and slipped out of their bedroom.

The cold shower did nothing for him. Not even when he opened his eyes to let the water in. The deluge did not wipe away the vision of Patty, the taste of her, the feel of her.

Grizz wanted his wife.

Instead, he went out to the field and threw his body into manual labor. He'd never fancied himself a rancher, but he liked the physicality of the daily chores. Like Keaton, Brenda had a running list of chores, but only one ranch hand; Angel. Grizz, Keaton, and Mac tried to fill in whenever possible, but with the training camp opening date looming, they couldn't help out as much as they'd like. And with the theft the other day, things had been in an uproar.

Grizz grabbed a box of tools and headed to one of the pastures. Manuel Bautista had managed to free Brenda's young calves from this enclosure and steal them off the ranch while they'd all slept. The enclosure had been a fence Grizz had fixed on his second day here.

Brenda had insisted that none of this was Grizz's fault. Conceptually, Grizz understood that. It hadn't been his shoddy mending work. It had been all Bautista.

Still, in his heart, Grizz felt responsible for nearly losing Brenda her livelihood. Taking out his tools, Grizz worked the hammer and nails to ensure that the young calves would not be separated from them again.

He hadn't learned any of his mending and repair skills from his father. What Grizz knew of construction, he'd learn by watching other men, paying attention to lessons in school, or his training in the army.

What he knew of maintaining a healthy relationship and making a marriage work, he solely knew from the old black and white television shows he'd watched growing up. No, Mr. Cleaver hadn't mended fences or baled hay. But the man had held down a steady job and taken care of his family.

How was Grizz going to do that when he was broke? Sure, his mother was out from under the debt his father had saddled her with after the divorce. That effort had taken Grizz's last cent. Grizz had no problem living hand to mouth. But he couldn't expect his wife and family to do so.

Grizz cursed as the nail slipped, and he hit his thumb. His wife and family. He hadn't even thought about having children. How was he going to take care of his wife and kids?

"What are you doing up so early?"

Grizz turned to see Keaton headed his way. Instead of his normal cargo pants and combat boots, the soldier was decked out in worn jeans and cowboy boots. His typically close-cropped hair was curling around his ears. The man was glowing with the aftermath that could only come from being a newlywed.

"I figured you'd still be in bed with …" Keaton stopped there. His throat worked like a cat with a hairball about to come stateside. The skin at Keaton's neck turned green.

Here was the awkwardness Grizz had been expecting would spring up between himself and his best friend ever since Grizz had noticed that Patty Cakes wasn't a little girl anymore.

"We didn't—" Grizz started.

"Stop." Keaton waved his hands like a frantic red pentagon sign.

"But me and Patty-"

"No, no means no."

Keaton boxed his ears with his hands. He closed his eyes and shook his head like he did when they were boys, and Ron and Hermione shared their first kiss. Keaton didn't want to play wizards and quidditch after that literary moment. He'd also begun to get suspicious of books after slogging through that deathly hollow. Young Grizz had been secretly rooting for the two friends to finally admit to their feelings, and he'd silently cheered when it was displayed between the book's covers.

Right now, Grizz could do nothing but stand and wait for his friend to grow up. Besides, Keaton was right. He didn't need to know the ins and outs of Grizz and Patty's marriage, nor where in the bedroom Grizz had slept last night. His and Patty's was a real marriage, and it would be consummated in due time. After Grizz got his proverbial house in order.

Keaton peeled open one eye. Whatever he saw in Grizz's annoyed countenance must have made him believe all was clear because Keaton opened the other eye and removed his hands from his ears.

"You done?" asked Grizz.

Keaton gave himself one final shake. "Even though I knew this day would come, I don't want to hear any of the details."

"Deal," said Grizz. "You headed over to the camp?"

"Not yet. Maggie's coming by to check on the bull."

"The prize bull who ran into your Jeep?"

"That would be the one."

When Keaton had first visited the ranch, Brenda's brand new breeding bull had gotten out of his pen—courtesy of one Manuel Bautista—and rammed right into Keaton's rental car. Both man and bull had gone down. Keaton was back on his feet, but the bull was laid down in one of the pastures. Its ears were lowered, and its tail was tucked between its legs. Even Grizz, who had no degree in animal husbandry, knew those weren't good signs.

"Brenda doesn't think he'll be able to do his job," Keaton continued.

Keaton grimaced at the assignment. So did Grizz. A bull's job was to breed every female put in its pasture. Both Grizz and Keaton had always been one-woman kind of men. All of the men in their unit were. They were each loyal to a fault.

Grizz turned in the direction of another field where cows and calves were rising in search of the day's sustenance. The females ushered their calves to the choicest spots in the pasture, but it wouldn't be enough. The land was already patchy and barren in spots.

Angel Bautista made his way over to the pasture. On his back, he'd hefted a bag of feed. The feed was to supplement the livestock's diet. The color of the bag reminded Grizz of the sacks of food his mother would get from the neighborhood donation's food pantry when times had gotten rough, and his father was nowhere to be found.

"I've been meaning to ask you," said Keaton, "how's it going recouping that last payment from the defense contract work?"

All of the men in their unit had been severed from the Army at the same time. Each had taken a bit of a break before coming and starting work on the camp. But Grizz had decided to spend a couple of weeks on a contract assignment to make a few extra bucks to pay his share of the investment into the camp. He was still waiting for those funds to come in.

He'd used his last penny to pay off the final debts that his father had left on his mother. Writing that check had made his chest puff up. Now, his chest deflated as his hands patted his empty pockets.

"Still hasn't come through yet?" Keaton clapped him on the back. "I know how these things work. Don't worry. We can just take it out of the profits from the first clients."

It was a kind gesture. The kind of gesture made between brothers. Grizz had no doubt that any of the others in their unit would've made the same offer. Heck, he would've extended the same hand had one of his fellow soldiers been dealt a similar blow.

But it wasn't just about Grizz anymore. Now he had a wife. And he had to care for her. He would not be going to any donations pantry or handout cupboard to take care of Patty. Before Grizz could refuse, Mac popped his curly head from behind the barn.

"I figured you'd still be in bed with your new wife," said Mac.

"Aww, man." Keaton grabbed his stomach and headed away from the two men.

Mac laughed as he watched Patty's brother run off. "Thanks for that, I'm a few bucks richer. I won the bet. I knew the moment little old Patty Cakes turned up here, you were a goner."

Grizz opened his mouth to tell Mac it was none of his business when his cellphone went off. He walked a few paces and answered it. In just an instant, Grizz's ire at his friend was gone. His chagrin over the charity Keaton had offered was put on the back burner.

"Sergeant Hayes? This is Sheriff Declan. We need you to come down and answer some questions about Deputy Newman."

CHAPTER FOURTEEN

Smoke wafted up to the ceiling in the kitchen. The white walls turned a light shade of gray that darkened as the contents in the pan continued to burn. Patty went to the window. Finding the latch, she shoved it open.

The dark curls of smoke made a mad dash to escape. But the late afternoon breeze pushed them back into the kitchen. The acrid smell pushed inside Patty's nose, and she let out a string of coughs. She pressed a dish towel to her face. Then waved it about in an effort to urge the smoke to clear. Eventually, it did dissipate, but the smell lingered.

The veggies in the pan were no longer green. They were black. The long strips she'd cut were all stiff at the edges but soggy in the middle. They were limp with rigor mortis as she moved the pan from the stove to the sink and turned on the tap.

"Darn, you too?"

Patty looked up. Her new sister-in-law stood in the back door, holding it open to usher out more of the singed stench. Brenda was dressed in a pair of jeans that molded to her form. Also molded on her form was mud at her ankles and grass stains on her knees. But Brenda still looked beautiful with her windswept hair and sun-kissed skin.

Brenda was a pretty tomboy, the kind of girl Patty had loved playing with on the playground when she was younger. But Patty had traded her sneakers for kitten heels and her cut-off jeans for sundresses. All in an effort to be Grizz's perfect sitcom wife.

Here she was, Mrs. Griffin Hayes. She was dressed in a sundress that flared from her hips but also had butter stains on the bodice. Her demure bun was unraveling on her shoulders. She'd kicked off her heels just before her failed rescue attempt of the vegetables.

"I'm sorry about this," said Patty. "I'll get it cleaned up.

"I was hoping you'd be the wife who could cook," Brenda said as she came into the kitchen. "I can slaughter the beef. I just can't cook it."

"Oh, no." Patty gave a shake of her head, her curls bouncing happily around her shoulders as though thrilled to be set free. She bent over to the oven where a timer was set to go off in another ten seconds. Patty opened the door and pulled out a perfectly cooked roast. "Meat I can handle. It's just the veggies that always bite the dust under my spatula."

Brenda's nostrils flared in what looked like delight. "I'm a meat and potatoes girl, too. Green is for the cows."

"My thoughts exactly." Patty put the perfectly cooked roast on the stove. The herbs and spices of the meat quickly overpowered the burned veggie stench. "The cows eat the grass, so aren't we getting the benefit of that."

"No," grinned Brenda. "But I love the way you think."

Brenda's eyes lit up like she was looking at her own reflection in a mirror that flattered her appearance. Patty saw her old self when she looked at Brenda. She missed the girl who ran and laughed for days without a care for what boys thought.

"So," said Brenda, reaching for the coffee maker. "You got hitched last night."

Patty pulled the apron over her head. After she balled the buttered up garment into a ball, she nodded in response to Brenda's rhetorical statement. Instead of words, Patty waited to see where her new sister would take this.

"Why?" said Brenda. "I mean, I know you're in love with Grizz."

"You do?"

"It's clear as day. It's clear he has feelings for you, too."

"It is?"

Brenda pulled out a coffee mug and filled it to the brim with steaming dark roast. "What I don't understand is why now?"

Patty tugged at her lower lip. She wanted someone to talk with this about. All her girlfriends from high school had gone off to different places, and they hadn't kept in touch. She didn't have any girlfriends at college since she hadn't been there for months, and hadn't been invested in it since she'd stepped foot on campus. She looked up to her new sister-in-law, wondering if she could trust Brenda with her many secrets.

"I know this place gets to you," said Brenda after a long sip. She turned to the open window and looked out at the lush scenery. "People always said there's something in the land. I never believed it until I met your brother and married him all in the same day."

"Yeah." Patty turned her gaze out to the greenery of the ranch. "Keaton always said he had a five-year plan. And then he got hitched in a day."

"So, what's your and Grizz's story? What happened to get you two down the aisle so fast and with no family present?"

Brenda turned her gaze back to Patty. Her green eyes were friendly. But then they dipped to Patty's flat belly.

"No." Patty covered her stomach. "Nothing like that."

Patty chewed at her lip another second before spilling the beans. The beans of that night of her high school graduation where Grizz had almost kissed her. The beans of last night with Deputy Dog Food. The beans where she and Grizz wound up at the church standing before Brenda's brother. But not the beans about college and her lack of attendance there.

"So, let me get this straight," said Brenda. "You two got married because you assaulted a police officer?"

"We didn't assault him. Newman assaulted me. But it would be his word against mine. Grizz wanted to make sure they couldn't make us testify against each other, and a husband and wife can't testify against one another, so ..."

"Yeah," said Brenda after another healthy sip of her coffee, "I don't think it works like that."

"Too late. We're married. But now I need him to act like we're married. He won't come near me."

"Keaton and I—"

"Ew." Patty threw her hands over her ears. "I do not want to hear about you and my brother. Ew ew ew."

"I was only going to say that Keaton and I had planned a platonic relationship. But after a few days, that went out the window."

"Nope. Still not hearing you."

"All I'm saying is that, like our marriage, your marriage to Grizz happened quick. You gotta give it time. You two also haven't seen each other for years. You need to spend some time getting to know who you are now. I'm sure you both have changed in the time you've been apart."

They had. There were things Patty didn't know about Grizz. And there were definitely things Grizz didn't know about her.

Patty wished they still had the ease with which they'd had when they were younger.

"This roast is going to make a great dinner," said Brenda. "But the guys won't be back for another hour or so. Wanna help me with the calves?"

"Sure."

"You'll need to change out of that homemaker getup." Brenda frowned at the sundress Patty wore. "You got a pair of jeans you don't mind ruining?"

CHAPTER FIFTEEN

Grizz parked the truck. Despite living on the poor side of town and growing up without his own father, Grizz had never been on the wrong side of the law. He'd never seen the inside of a jail cell, nor a police precinct.

Taking a deep breath, Grizz hefted himself out of the truck. He hadn't given Mac or Keaton any of the details of why the sheriff was calling, nor of what had happened before his impromptu wedding last night. He figured he'd handle one thing at a time. Grizz was just thankful that the sheriff had only called him down and not Patty. If there was going to be any trouble, he wanted to be in front of it and have her far out of harm's way.

That was why he'd married her, after all. To keep her out of trouble.

Honestly, that line wasn't flying anymore. Grizz had married Patty because he'd wanted her. He'd wanted her the second she'd become a legal adult. And now that he had her, he wasn't going to give her up easily.

Newman had assaulted his wife. The handsy jerk had kissed Patty without her permission or her invitation. What had happened after that —the delay in delivering the EpiPen dose, the knock on the head with the car door—had been a series of unfortunate events. But events preempted by Newman.

That's what he'd tell the sheriff today. It was Newman's actions. Not Grizz's wife's.

"Excuse me, sir?"

Grizz looked down, and then down some more. Standing before him was an older woman. A cloud of gray hair surrounded her round face. Her eyes were dim, with dark circles under them. It looked as though she'd been crying. Grizz's instincts to protect any woman who looked as though she'd worked her fingers to the bone kicked in.

"Yes, ma'am? What do you need? What can I do for you?"

She offered him a wane smile. "You're the soldier from Bellflower Ranch?"

The Bellflower Ranch was the original name of The Purple Heart Ranch, so called because a bellflower resembled the teardrop emblem of the decorative military award.

"I'm one of the soldiers that work there, yes, ma'am."

"Are you the one who helped my boy the other night?"

"Your boy?"

The older woman nodded. "My poor Nick."

Nick? Nick Newman? As in Deputy Nick Newman, who stole Patty's first kiss away from Grizz.

"I just want to thank you so much for looking after my son the other night."

Mrs. Newman patted Grizz on the back of his hand. Grizz fought the urge to pull away from her. She held firm. Her gaze filled with gratitude and appreciation. And now, Grizz fought the grimace that wanted to crawl over his features.

"Ever since his father left, little Nicky's had a hard time," Mrs. Newman continued. "Especially in the social arena."

Somehow, that fact did not surprise Grizz. Grizz had seen up close that the guy didn't get along with people he perceived were different from him, like Angel Bautista. Grizz also remembered the cop's tacky pickup lines that he'd aimed at Patty. Newman hadn't even been able to read the fact that Patty wasn't interested in him.

"I'm so glad he's found a friend like you."

Grizz gave an internal shake. Then his hands shook, finally wrenching himself free of Mrs. Newman's grasp. When his head began to shake, he stopped. There was a tear in Mrs. Newman's eye.

She dabbed at it with an index finger. Her gaze downcast as she spoke. "Now, we just have to pray that he wakes up."

Pray that he wakes up?

"He's still unconscious?" asked Grizz.

Mrs. Newman nodded. "I do hope you'll stop by the hospital later. I'm sure it'll help to hear a friendly voice to coax him out of the coma."

Coma?

Mrs. Newman patted Grizz's hand. Then she cupped his face and smiled. "I'll bet your mama's proud of you."

Grizz stood in the hall for long minutes after she'd left. He was stunned at the turn of events. Newman was still out cold. And somehow, Grizz had been cast not as a villain but as the hero and protector of the real bad guy.

He wanted to rail against this role. But he couldn't open his mouth. Something held him back.

Grizz watched as Mrs. Newman climbed into a beat-up Honda Civic. She slid the key into the ignition, took a deep breath, and let it out. As she let out the breath, she also allowed her features to crumble.

There had only been a few times when Grizz had caught his mother crying. Each time had broken something inside him and reinforced his determination to pick up the slack that had been dropped by his father. His mother's tears were also the reason why Grizz had never found himself in any trouble with authorities.

"Sergeant Hayes?"

Grizz turned to see Sheriff Declan making his way to him. The sheriff didn't smile. But neither did he look over Grizz with suspicion. The dark-skinned man offered Grizz his hand, and Grizz shook it.

"I'm sorry to bring you out here," Declan began. "We just had a few gaps we wanted to fill in. Since you and Ms. Keaton were the only ones—"

"Mrs. Hayes," Grizz corrected. "Patricia Keaton is my wife."

"Oh." Declan's brows rose. "I didn't know the two of you were married."

"We were married the other night. We were on our way to Pastor Vance when we came across Deputy Newman having some trouble in the parking lot."

"I had heard from the bartender that the three of you left together," said Declan.

"Patty and I left together." It wasn't exactly a lie. Grizz had followed Patty out when he'd seen Newman trailing her. "Deputy Newman was in the parking lot at the same time as we were."

"The bartender also said that Ms. Keaton—forgive me, Mrs. Hayes spent a lot of time talking with Deputy Newman."

Declan's un-accusing, unsmiling features remained placid. Grizz made sure his face gave off the same message.

"Patty's a friendly girl," said Grizz. "She's always made friends wherever she goes."

"So, there was no … tension between you and Deputy Newman?"

"Absolutely not," said Grizz. "I know how my wife feels about me. And she knows how I feel about her. There is no tension in our marriage. If there may have been unrequited feelings on the part of Deputy Newman, you'll have to ask him when he wakes up. But, when we saw the man in need, my wife and I did everything in our power to help him."

Grizz nearly bit his tongue on that last stretch. Both he and Patty had hesitated to offer their immediate assistance. But only for a moment. And then they'd launched into action.

True, their actions had led to the bump on the man's head, but it was the best they could do under the circumstances.

"Do you have any other details you care to give, Sergeant Hayes?"

Grizz shook his head at the sheriff. "That's all I saw. Deputy Newman was having an allergic reaction. I found his EpiPen and administered the dose."

"I was going to call Mrs. Hayes down for questioning." The sheriff scribbled on the pad, but it didn't look as though the letters made any sense. "But as you're her husband, I assume you'll have the same story."

It was a rhetorical question, and so Grizz didn't answer it. He would do anything to ensure that Patty was safe and out of harm's way. If that meant that he would get in trouble for her with the law, then so be it. That's what a husband should do for his wife. That's what any man should do for a woman he cared about.

It grated that with the details Grizz had left out, it would mean that Newman would get away unscathed for what he'd done to Patty. But Grizz was taking no chances.

Newman may have stolen a kiss from her untouched lips, but he'd nearly paid with his life. As far as Grizz was concerned, Newman had gotten off easy with the allergic reaction, the bump, and the day, or more, in bed. When the deputy woke up, if he wanted to make trouble, Grizz would be there to shield Patty.

"If that's all," said Grizz, "I'd like to get back to my wife. We're still newlyweds."

The sheriff looked up with a genuine smile this time. "Congratulations. I'll be in touch when Deputy Newman wakes up. In case there's anything else we need from you or Mrs. Hayes."

Grizz nodded and made his way out of the doors. He knew he hadn't heard the end of this. But he had a brief reprieve from the intrusion of Nick Newman in his life. And he knew exactly what he was going to do with his time.

The drive back to the ranch seemed longer. Grizz knew why. He was eager to get back to his wife. There was nothing standing in his way from dating Patty. So, that was his plan. He'd go in and ask his wife on a date.

His palms sweat as he came up the steps to the back door of the big house. Patty had grown into such a polished young woman. She was always entirely put together from what she wore, to how she spoke, to her hair. She truly resembled the women in the sitcoms he'd loved as a child. They'd always seemed unattainable to Grizz, like a fantasy.

Coming up to the door, Grizz smelled the makings of a delicious feast. Pastor Vance must have come over again to cook. Grizz knew that Brenda had no cooking skills. And if he remembered correctly, Patty wasn't a whizz in the kitchen either. Unless it was to cook hamburgers or steak.

Through the screen of the door, Grizz saw a woman bent over the oven. She wore a pair of cutoff jeans. Her feet were bare. Her hair was down around her shoulders.

She looked nothing like the unattainable fantasy of June Cleaver. She looked like the girl next door. The girl a guy could pal around with one minute, and tell his deepest secrets to the next minute.

The woman straightened, and Grizz saw Patty. But she wasn't the Patty he'd married. She was the Patty he'd known as a girl.

Patty startled when she saw him, nearly dropping the pan in her hands.

Grizz rushed into action, taking the dish from her and setting it on the stovetop.

"Hey," she said.

"Hey," he mimed.

"I didn't expect you back so early."

Grizz could only stare. This wasn't his fantasy. This was the real Patty. The girl he'd sat and watched those black and white shows with. The girl he could talk to about anything.

Most importantly, this was the woman he dared not dream of. And here she was, standing within his reach.

"I look a mess," she said. "I've been out with Brenda all afternoon on the ranch. And now, I've just finished with dinner. Let me go change into something presentable."

"No." Grizz put his hand out, catching her at her midriff. "You look beautiful."

"I look a mess."

"You look like you."

Patty's lips parted. For the first time, Grizz didn't feel the need to run from what he was feeling, to run from her. So, he pulled her to him.

She inhaled sharply as she came to his chest, her heart pressing into his. Her eyes widened, taking all of him in. Her head tilted back, offering herself to him.

Grizz brushed his lips against Patty's. He urged himself to be patient. To take his time with her. To take his time with himself.

But he didn't.

He'd waited so long for this. Denied himself for too much time. Now, he would take what had always been his.

Patty didn't resist. She wrapped her arms around his neck and pulled him down to her. Grizz went willingly. He'd always been wrapped around her finger. Now, he was wrapped around her entire being.

"Patricia?" he said when he finally broke away from her.

"Yes, Griffin?"

"Would you like to go on a date with me?"

She grinned, her eyes shining bright in the setting sunlight. "Sure. I'm available for the rest of my life."

CHAPTER SIXTEEN

atty's heart raced. Her palms were hot. Her breath came fast. She was on a date with Grizz. Sure, they were just sitting on the back porch of the Vance ranch house. But she'd take what she could get.

Much like her wedding, the date wasn't what she had envisioned. First, because he wouldn't let her change her outfit. Grizz insisted that he liked the way she looked. There was grease splattered on her shirt, and her hair was in a messy ponytail. Still, he looked at her as though she were the most beautiful thing in the world. Patty decided to wash and wear the same thing again tomorrow, and then again the next day. Anything to keep him looking at her like that.

She wasn't in one of the flaring sundresses she'd seen Mrs. Cleaver wear. Nor kitten heels that she'd seen Donna Reed putter around the kitchen in. Patty was dressed in a T-shirt and cutoff jeans from helping Brenda earlier in the day with the calves.

Patty had been a natural at herding the small beasts into a new pasture. The separation from their mothers signaled that the calves were grown and had to now make it on their own. Patty, sure enough, understood that. She'd been on her own for the last few months, having unenrolled herself from college and taken the odd job here and there.

The monies from the last year of her college tuition sat in a bank untouched until she could gather up the courage to tell her mother what she'd done.

Not that she needed to tell her mother anything. Her father had left Patty that money. True, it had been earmarked for her education. But it hadn't mattered to anyone that going to college wasn't high on Patty's list. It wasn't even on her list.

Patty had only ever had one thing on her future to-do list. And she was doing exactly that. She was finally doing what she knew she was born to do, serving her husband a well-cooked meal after a hard day of work.

"You never did meet a vegetable you liked," said Grizz.

He grinned as he watched her push around the salad on her plate. The only reason the leaves were granted an appearance on the porcelain was because that's what the sitcom housewives would've done. Patty had dumped a cup of dressing over the greens. However, she still pushed the limp leaves around her plate.

Grizz reached over and speared her vegetables with his fork. He lifted the dripping bit of salad into his mouth, plopped it on his tongue, and chewed.

Patty watched the action, reaffirming her dislike of veggies. How had those green devils of the earth managed to slip into the spot she coveted most?

"Where is everyone?" he asked.

"Brenda and Keaton went for a ride. Mac is over at the Purple Heart Ranch hanging with the guys there."

"So, it's just you and me?"

Patty nodded, liking the sound of that. Then she bit at the bottom of her lip. "Is that okay?"

"Of course, it's okay," Grizz said, cocking his head to the side to look at her.

"It's just …" Patty tugged at the top of her lip. "I wasn't sure you wanted to hang out with me. You keep leaving."

Grizz let out a long sigh. He set his utensils down and reached for her hands. Patty, who'd already eaten all of the meat from her plate, happily put aside the remaining vegetables to take Grizz's hands.

"I'm sorry, Patty Cakes. I know we haven't started this marriage off on the right foot. But all that's going to change now."

"It is?"

Grizz nodded. His hazel eyes bored into hers. Patty had to hold herself still.

It had been so long since he'd let her see past his walls. But now he sat before her, his walls were down. His arms open. He still held her away, but maybe he'd finally bring her inside his embrace.

Grizz opened his mouth to speak. But then he closed it. His gaze narrowed as he focused on something just to the right of her left eye. "You have a mole there."

Patty touched the corner of her left eye, feeling the raised skin there. "Yeah."

"That hasn't always been there."

"No," she said. "It showed up when I was around seventeen or so."

"Figures." Grizz's gaze flicked back to her. "That was around the time I stopped looking directly at you."

He was right. They'd been so close all through her childhood. He'd been her hero, her protector, her friend. And then it all stopped, and he left.

Softness touched the side of her face. Grizz's thumb rubbed at the mole. His large hand cupped her cheek.

"I'm sorry I did that," he said. "That I tried to stay away from you."

"It hurt," she admitted.

"It hurt me, too. Especially when you were always the one person I wanted to spend my days with. It was always going to be you for me."

"I told you so." Her eyes flashed up at him.

The golden flecks in his gaze twinkled with delight. "Sure, when you were seven, and I was ten."

"I was very wise for my age."

Patty rubbed her cheek in Grizz's palm. The span of his hand was so big that she had more than enough space to do it. She could've made a pillow of his hand if he let her, and he was letting her.

Grizz's fingers curled around the back of her head. With a gentle yet insistent tug, he pulled her to him. The twinkle in his eyes caught fire.

"I'm never going to leave you again," he said. "I love you, Patricia Anne Keaton Hayes."

Patty closed her eyes. She wanted to—no, needed to look away from him. The intensity of the emotions on her face was going to knock her down.

Was this why he'd looked away from her as she'd gotten older? Was this why he'd stayed away? She understood the depth of what he was feeling at this moment because she'd been rolling around in it for years. Having it aimed at her now was too much.

"Will you marry me?"

Patty's eyes slammed open. "I already married you."

Grizz shook his head slowly. His eyes were fastened to her lips. Patty knew she was going to be kissed by her husband, kissed very soon and very well.

"No," he said. "I mean a proper wedding. Outside with the sun shining. You in a white gown that's high-waisted and flowing. Your hair all done up with flowers woven in. And family and friends all around us."

He'd just described the wedding of her dreams. A tear trickled down Patty's cheek. Grizz caught the droplet with his thumb and wiped it away.

"Yes," she breathed. "Yes," she said louder. "Ye—"

She was about to shout it so that everyone in the next twenty miles heard her, but Grizz captured her lips. Her shout was pressed between them. She gave him her answer for the third time as he tilted her head back and claimed her mouth. She accepted his proposal again and again as he deepened the kiss. Her arms wrapped around him in a vow of forever. She would have and hold this man from this day forward, and she dared sickness, poverty, or even death to try and come between them.

Grizz was all smiles when he finally broke the kiss after long moments. Patty had not gotten her fill. The sun was still setting, and she wanted to explore more of her wifely duties upstairs. But Grizz seemed in no rush to claim her in all the ways that he could.

"We'll plan for a May wedding," he was saying.

"Why so far away?"

"I don't want it to interrupt your studies," he said. "Your graduation is on the seventeenth of May, right?"

The school's graduation day was set for that particular day. However, Patty would not be walking across that stage.

"Yeah," Patty cringed. "About that ..."

"About what?" Grizz rubbed his thumb back and forth across her chin, his smile was indulgent as he focused more on her lips than the words.

"School," said Patty.

"What about school?"

"Well, there's good news and bad news."

Grizz's thumb stopped its motion, and his gaze rose to meet hers. "Give me the bad news first."

"The good news," she said, ignoring him, "is that we don't have to waste money on weekend conjugal visits."

Grizz narrowed his gaze. "Why not?"

"Well, that's the bad news."

"Patricia ..."

"I dropped out of college."

Grizz sighed, shaking his head. "You are not dropping out of college. We can make this marriage work. We probably need the distance to get to know each other as we are now and—"

"You're not hearing me," Patty interrupted. "I spoke in the past tense."

Grizz cocked his head. He turned his body so that he was facing her head-on. "You dropped out?"

Patty nodded.

"Right before you came here?"

"Well ..."

"When, Patty?"

"The end of last term."

"December?" Grizz sprung to his feet, his boots making a thudding sound as he marched the length of the porch and back to her. "Your mother is going to kill you. You know that, right? And then she's going to kill me."

"On the bright side, we'll die together."

Grizz scowled at her.

"You said 'til death do us part," Patty chided.

"With your mother, it'll definitely be death."

"So what?" Patty shrugged. "You won't be her favorite anymore. Maybe she can dote on her blood-born children for a while."

Grizz scrubbed a hand over his beard, clearly not listening to her. He paced the porch length a second time. He stopped in front of Patty with his index finger raised as though he had an idea.

"We need to call her," he said.

"Oh, no." Now it was Patty's turn to rise and begin her own march. "I'm not dying a virgin."

She made a dash for the stairs that led to the pastures. Grizz caught her around the waist before she could get far. His hold was like iron. In any other instance, Patty would've loved being in his embrace. This was the only time where she fought it.

"Okay, fine," she said. "But, you're telling her."

"Why me?"

"You're my husband. You need to protect me."

CHAPTER SEVENTEEN

Grizz's ear still rang from the tongue-lashing Mrs. Keaton had given them. Patty had gotten the worst of it. Grizz suspected the only reason he got off a smidge easy was that he truly was Mrs. Keaton's favorite amongst the three of them. And now, he truly was her child.

He could hear the happiness in Holly Keaton's voice beneath the scolding. She appeared more upset that she hadn't been a part of either of her children's weddings. But Grizz promised to make up for it by letting her, Patty, and Brenda plan a double wedding this summer, as big and as grand as she pleased. Grizz couldn't say no to the woman who had helped raise him and showed him what real family looked like.

What he did worry about was how to pay for the wedding, plus pay his fair share for the camp, and now taking care of a wife.

He rose the next morning, back stiff from his place on the floor. Despite much coaxing and pouting from his wife, Grizz had insisted on keeping their wedding night sleeping arrangements. He had thought of putting Patty back in her old room, but they'd both vetoed the idea, needing to be close to one another. In the same room if not in the same bed.

Before she'd climbed onto the bed, Grizz had brushed a stray strand of hair out of Patty's face. His face had dipped low to hers. He'd brushed his lips over hers.

Grizz didn't press the kiss. No, that was her. She pressed her lips into him, desperate to take in more of him. Grizz had growled against his wife's lips and pulled back.

"Slow down," he'd said. "We're taking this step by step."

"What if I want to leap?"

"You should know, Mrs. Hayes, that I'm not that kind of man."

Patty had pouted. Once upon a time, Grizz had bowed to her plump lips. Now, he stole a kiss from them.

"This is important to me," he said. "You're important to me. I want to get this right."

"We're right together. I don't think we can go wrong."

He'd twined their fingers together. "Here's my plan. We take it slow over the next week. We go on a few dates. Ending with nothing more than a few kisses."

Patty rolled her eyes, ready to protest. "I'm sure I'm the only wife in the world who has to seduce her husband."

"Not seduce," said Grizz, rolling his body out on the nest on the floor. "I want to be wooed. Flowers, candy, the works. Are you hearing me, Mrs. Hayes?"

He'd gotten a pillow thrown to the chest for that. He'd laughed and caught it. They had gazed at each other, talking quietly until Patty had fallen asleep. It had been just like old times.

The sun peeked above the horizon when he sat up. It had been a restful night of sleep. Likely because he felt at home for the first time in a long time. He had his best friend's blessing, his maternal figure's enthusiasm, and there was his wife lying comfortably in the bed beside him.

Grizz took a moment to simply gaze at his wife. He'd watched Patty sleep many times before. Whether it was waking her up from a deep slumber when they were young or having her fall asleep beside him when they watched a movie in the family room. Patty wasn't a night person as much as she wasn't an early riser. She liked her sleep and would keep her eyes closed for as long as she possibly could.

Grizz took advantage of that fact now as he gazed at her. Her features were soft in her repose. Her hands were wrapped around her pillow as though it was a lover she refused to let go of. She had kicked off the sheets in the night, and her long legs were on display for him. Her lashes kissed the tops of her cheeks, and Grizz became jealous.

He leaned over and brushed a soft kiss to her cheek. She smelled of sweetness with a hint of spice. Her eyes fluttered open, and Grizz felt caught in their depths.

A slow smile spread across her face. She tilted her head up. She didn't crash her lips into his like she had the other day. She waited, as though seeing if he'd meet her halfway.

Like a moth to a flame, he came to her. He brushed his lips lightly over hers. Warmth spread through him. All the stiffness from lying on the floor left him on an exhale. He leaned into her, pressing his chest against hers.

Deepening the kiss, he took his first real taste of her on this, the first day of the rest of their wedded bliss. Joy spread through him as he realized he could do this every day, at any moment, for as long as he liked. He'd lived in a black and white world for so long, but Patty brought color to his life.

She wrapped her arms around him. She tugged him to her, on top of her. Grizz wanted to go. He wanted to devour her. But he pulled himself away. He needed to remember the plan.

What was the plan?

Right. Go slow. Court her. Earn her love.

"I love you, Grizz."

Well, didn't that seal the deal? He had her love.

"This is my dream come true," she said against his lips.

Grizz realized it was his dream too. He'd never dared to see her face in his mind. Still, he'd known that for the last few years, it had always been her. It may have always been her.

Grizz bent his head and tasted her again. She was his dream. His reality. His wife. With that knowledge, the plan went out the window.

With the plan interrupted a knock came at the door. Grizz cursed under his breath as he pulled away from the small piece of heaven that was his Patricia Hayes.

"Go away," she called, bringing a grin to Grizz's lips.

"Whatever you're doing, I don't want to know," said Keaton. "But someone's here at the door for you."

"Then tell them to go away," said Patty as she reached for Grizz.

"It's the sheriff."

Both Patty and Grizz pulled away then. Grizz watched Patty's throat work as the same gulp went down his throat.

CHAPTER EIGHTEEN

Grizz held her hand as they walked down the stairs. His fingers were crushing hers, but Patty didn't complain. Whatever was about to happen, they would face this together as husband and wife, a united front that the law couldn't pull apart.

Grizz let go of her hand and offered his to the sheriff standing in the large living room.

"Good to see you again, Sergeant Hayes," said the sheriff.

"You too, Sheriff Declan."

Again? When had Grizz seen him the first time? Keaton and Brenda sat side by side on a small couch. Mac leaned against the fireplace.

"Any change in Deputy Newman?" asked Grizz. "Has he come out of the coma?"

Coma? When had Newman slipped into a coma? And how come Grizz knew and didn't tell her?

"He's awake, but still a bit out of it." The sheriff's eyes came to settle on Patty. "Your name came up, Mrs. Hayes."

"Me?" asked Patty.

The sheriff's gaze went back to Grizz. "I just have a few questions to ask your wife if she wouldn't mind coming down to the precinct."

Grizz took a step back and put his hand at Patty's low back. Keaton stood at Grizz's right shoulder. Brenda's hand was in Keaton's. Mac pushed off the fireplace, taking lazy steps toward them.

"Can't you question her here, Sheriff Declan?" asked Brenda.

"I want to make it plain," said the sheriff, holding up his hands. "Mrs. Hayes isn't under arrest. There are just a few discrepancies in the story your husband told and what Deputy Newman is saying. We want to get them straight."

"I'm not testifying against my husband," said Patty. "We have spousal privilege."

The sheriff quirked an eyebrow. As did Keaton. But unlike the sheriff, Keaton had more practice in schooling his features when he thought his little sister was up to something, and he wanted in on the plan.

"As I said," said the sheriff, "no one is under arrest. And I don't believe spousal privilege works that way."

"It doesn't matter if privilege applies or not," said Grizz, squeezing Patty's hand. "If you want to talk to my wife, it'll be with me present."

The sheriff looked Grizz up and down. Patty knew that if this became a physical thing that the two men were equally matched. The sheriff had the same big barrel chest as Grizz. The two men shared the same determined grimace. But the sheriff would best Grizz was with the gun at his hip and the badge at his chest.

"Grizz, it's fine," said Patty. "I'll go. Neither of us did anything wrong. We tried to help despite … everything."

Patty saw the flicker of interest in the sheriff's eyes at her words. Oh, man. She was not going to do well in this little chat.

"You want to tell me what really happened that night?" said the sheriff.

Patty inhaled. "I didn't do anything wrong. Neither did my husband."

"But your husband left something out of the story, didn't he? There was a bump on Deputy Newman's head. Know anything about that?"

"That was my fault," said Patty and Grizz at the same time.

The sheriff looked between the two.

"We tried to help him to his car," said Grizz. "To get the EpiPen."

"He was on me," said Patty. "But he's a big guy, and I couldn't hold his weight."

"On you?" asked the sheriff.

"Leaning on her," said Grizz. "I went to search for the EpiPen in the dashboard. Patty couldn't carry his weight, and he fell. That's when I pulled the door open, and it smacked him in the head."

"It was not on purpose," said Patty. "It's not like my husband assaulted *him*."

Again, the sheriff's gaze flickered with interest at her words. Well, the single word at the end of her statement and the inflection she'd put on it.

"And that's it?" asked the sheriff. "That's all you have to add, Mrs. Hayes?"

Patty felt like Sheriff Declan was her history professor trying to coax more about the Battle of 1812 out of her. She didn't care about long ago fights. She could never remember the details.

Except she could remember the feel of Newman's cold hands on her. The smell of his beer-laced breath. The unwanted touch of his lips as they crashed against her mouth.

Patty was sorry that Newman had suffered a medical consequence because of it. She'd much preferred to knock his lights out with her fists instead of her lips. But here they were.

Her gaze caught Grizz's. Patty knew that he could tell what she was thinking. His jaw clenched. She knew that if she didn't keep her mouth shut, he would tell all. And then try and take any of the blame that came.

"No," said Patty. "That's all that happened."

"Deputy Newman is saying that you assaulted him," said the sheriff.

"Grizz didn't do anything," Patty insisted. "He's the one that got the EpiPen and dragged Newman to the emergency room."

"No," said the sheriff. "Not your husband. You, Mrs. Hayes. Deputy Newman said that you assaulted him."

CHAPTER NINETEEN

Grizz's truck came to a screeching halt. If he'd thought he'd gotten an earful from Mrs. Keaton, he was getting a heaping second helping from her daughter. Patty could hardly contain herself on the drive over to the hospital.

"*I* assaulted *him?*"

Patty stomped her foot against the floorboards of the truck. Hard enough that for a moment, Grizz thought the vehicle might break. He sped up after the light went green and took a left turn.

"He kissed *me*." Patty jabbed a thumb at her chest.

"I know, sweetheart." Grizz slowed even more as he took a right turn into town. He liked the feel of that pet name in his mouth.

Patty turned to him as he paused at a stoplight. "You saw us in the bar, right? I was not giving off any signals."

"I know, beautiful."

Grizz let that word roll around his tongue as he turned into the hospital parking lot. He decided he liked sweetheart more. It wasn't Patty's looks that had won him over. It was her spirit, her wit, her strength, and tenacity.

"I'm going to kill him," she growled.

Before Grizz could put the vehicle in park, Patty was already tugging at the door handle. She marched toward the sliding glass doors like a soldier stomping into battle. Grizz hopped out of the driver's side and dashed to her side.

"Honeybun," he tried.

But she eluded his grasp, likely because the pet name wasn't familiar to her yet. Grizz got his arms around her waist just as she reached the reception area. That didn't slow her down.

"Deputy Newman's room?" Patty demanded of the haggard nurse at the desk.

Was it Grizz's imagination? Or did the nurse shudder before she told them a number and pointed to a door at the end of the hall? With even more determination, Patty marched to the room. And paused.

"Slide it on in there, honeybuns."

Inside the room, Nick Newman sat propped up on pillows. A tray of nondescript hospital food was over his lap. Another nurse was spoon-feeding him jiggly, red Jell-O. The look on the nurse's face told Grizz that she was nearing ready to write herself a pink slip. Grizz determined never to call Patty honeybun again.

Newman, whose mouth had been opened wide to receive the congealed square, shut when he spied his visitors. A predatory smile spread over his face when he saw Patty. But when Newman glanced over his shoulders, his gaze narrowed.

"What's he doing here?" asked Nick.

"He's my husband."

"Your husband." Newman sat up higher in the bed, nearly spilling the blobs of Jell-O on the sheets.

The nurse took the opportunity to slip out of the room. Grizz moved aside, giving the nurse a sympathetic grimace. He'd only encountered Newman twice. That first time when he'd tried to lump Angel Bautista in the same category as his villainous uncle, which Grizz was certain was due to racial prejudice. And then again, when the deputy had tried to put the moves on Patty. Each time, the man had tried Grizz's patience.

"You never said you were married," said Newman.

"I also never said I was interested in you."

Newman's gaze slid to Grizz. "Looks like your wife was trying to make an adulterer out of me along with her assault?"

"Assault?" Now it was Grizz who stepped into the room, shielding Patty from any more of this nonsense. He'd been prepared to be the voice of reason, but he was fast losing his patience with this man for the third time. "You put your unwanted lips on my wife's mouth."

"And you knew I had an allergy," said Newman. "Looks premeditated to me."

"You just don't know when to stop," said Grizz. "Do you?"

"I wasn't the married woman flirting with another guy," said Newman. "Hey wait, you said she was your sister."

"I said she was my best friend's sister," said Grizz.

"And I wasn't flirting with you," said Patty. She tried to shove around Grizz's shoulders to get at Newman, but having his wife actually assault this dirtbag was the last thing either of them needed.

"All you women are the same," Newman sneered. "You'll lead a man on and then jerk away when we reach out."

Grizz was nearly across the threshold, ready to throttle the man in his sickbed. A quavering voice behind him stopped him in his tracks.

"Nicky, how dare you say such things."

"Mama?" All the color drained from Newman's face, and he looked truly ill.

Grizz turned to see the gray bun of Mrs. Newman behind Patty. Beside Mrs. Newman stood Sheriff Declan.

Mrs. Newman stepped forward, her small stature loomed large the room. "These people helped you. I thought they were your friends."

"She's the reason I'm here." Newman pointed at Patty. "She at peanuts before I kissed her."

"You kissed her?" Sheriff Declan stood just beyond the door. But his booming voice resonated over all of their heads.

"She led me on," Newman insisted.

"I did no such thing," said Patty.

Grizz looked at the sheriff's calculating eyes. Grizz noted that there wasn't much surprise there. Had the sheriff known that this was his deputy's behavior? Had this been the something more he'd been trying to prod out of Grizz and Patty during his questioning?

Inside Grizz's embrace, Patty was stewing. Her bright blue eyes the hottest part of a deadly fire. It was clear the person she wanted to burn with the flame was lying in the hospital bed. Grizz had half a mind to let her go and claw Newman's eyes out.

Then Grizz's gaze landed on Mrs. Newman. The lines around her eyes looked tired, weary. Her fingers trembled as she clutched at her worn purse. Her back was straight, but her shoulders hunched. In that pose, she reminded Grizz very much of his mother.

Grizz hadn't given his mother much trouble after his father left. He'd watched her work her fingers to the bones going from one back-breaking job in the morning to another at night. When she did pause a moment to look at her son, Grizz saw the worry in her gaze that she wasn't enough to bring the boy into manhood.

"I did not raise you like this," Mrs. Newman said. "You apologize immediately."

"But—"

Newman's protest was cut off with one sharp glance from his mother. Her shoulders snapped back. Her hands balled into fists. Grizz knew this look, too. He'd seen it most often on the face of Mrs. Keaton. It meant *I brought you into this world, and I can take you out.*

Newman's gaze swung to Patty and Grizz. "It's come to my attention that I may have offended you."

"You think," said Patty.

"Patricia," Grizz chastised his wife.

"Thank you, Deputy Newman," Patty said through gritted teeth.

Sheriff Declan stepped past the two of them and entered the room. "Newman, you'll be taking a leave of absence from the force."

"What?" said Newman. "Why?"

"This isn't the first time there's been a complaint," said Declan. "And not just by a woman. By citizens of different racial and religious back-grounds than you as well. You're going to undergo sensitivity training with HR."

"So, I take it, there will be no more questions for me or my wife?" said Grizz.

"No," said Declan. "You and Mrs. Hayes are free to go."

Back in the truck, Grizz pulled Patty's seatbelt tight across her torso. The sound of the metal clicking into place and locking her in was very satisfying. With her strapped to the seat, he pressed a kiss to her lips.

Patty tried to lean toward him, but the belt wouldn't let her get any closer. She let out a frustrated groan, which made him chuckle.

She was well and truly his. There was nothing standing in their way. No threats looming over them. Well, besides the one where he wasn't sure how he would provide for her.

Grizz had no plans to live off her brother's charity. He'd take a job in town to pay his fair share and to take care of her. He would figure something out. In the meantime, he reveled in the sweet taste of her lips.

"Could this count as a date?" she asked.

"Coming to the hospital?"

"We drove from home. There was some discussion. And now we're kissing. All we need is some food and flowers, and I think it qualifies."

"No, this is not how I plan to wine and dine my wife."

"Your wife does not need to be wined and dined. You're the one that wants to be wooed."

Grizz chuckled at that. He leaned in for another kiss. As his lips touched hers, he had serious thoughts of revising his plan to do this all properly. Nothing had been traditional about this marriage so far. Why start now?

CHAPTER TWENTY

$\mathcal{P}$atty was delighted as Grizz kissed her for long moments in the parking lot of the hospital. He kissed her even longer when they'd parked on the ranch. He was still kissing her when there was a knock at the truck's window.

Mac grinned into the driver's side window. Grizz growled, murderously low. The low and beastly rumble didn't wipe the cheek from Mac's grin.

"I know the honeymoon isn't over yet," said Mac. "But your presence is needed at the camp. We're already behind Keaton's crazy schedule, and we need to go over an order for new supplies that weren't in the original budget."

"How much?" Grizzled growled even lower.

Mac shrugged. "Shouldn't be more than a grand after we split it six ways."

"I'll be over in a bit." Grizz sighed as if the weight of the world just came down on his shoulders. After Mac left, Grizz leaned his head back against the headrest in what looked like defeat.

Patty ran her fingers through his hair. It was getting longer now that he wasn't regularly cutting it for the army.

"What's wrong?" she asked.

"Nothing for you to worry about," he said, taking her hand and kissing it.

"Is it the setback at the camp?"

"No, we'll get through that."

"Then what? The money?"

He didn't answer.

"If you need money, you can just use mine."

He lowered his head and looked at her as though she'd just eaten a frog right in front of him. Patty couldn't fathom why? They were married now. What was hers was his.

"I haven't touched most of the money set aside for my senior year of college," she went on. "There's more than enough. You can use it to buy what you need."

"I'm not taking your money."

"It's not my money, it's our money."

"That's the money your parents set aside for your college education."

"Which I never wanted. It was wasted." And then she laughed. "Even without the degree, I still got my dream job. Hey, I am going to want a ring, you know."

"Patricia, no. That is not happening."

"You're not getting me a ring?"

"No." He pulled all the way back from her, slumping in the driver's seat. "Not the ring. I'm not taking your money."

"Why not? Think of it like a dowry of old times. Didn't men marry women based on the size of the money that came with her?"

Grizz's expression soured as though that idea were the foulest lemon he'd ever come in contact with. "I'll take on more defense contract work before I let you lift a finger to support this family."

Now it was Patty's turn to lean back against the passenger side window. "While I appreciate the offer of being a pampered wife, I have no intention of having my husband leave me again for who knows how long and go into some danger zone when I have the money we need sitting untouched in a bank account."

"It would be short term," he said. "Nothing more than a couple of months at most."

"You already promised you'd stay." Patty's bottom lip was already trembling. She'd just gotten him, and now she was going to lose him again. Over something preventable. He was making this choice to leave.

Grizz reached for her hands, but she pulled them away from him. Instead, she reached for the car door handle. As she opened the door, she wondered, was this another metaphor? They said as one door opens, another closes.

She heard the car door slam from the other side of the vehicle. But she was already racing for yet another door. Patty reached the front door of the ranch house and wrenched it open.

She didn't look back to see if Grizz was following her or not. She was truly unsure if he would follow. She raced up the stairs and into their shared bedroom, slamming the door behind her, but leaving it unlocked.

Sometime later, there was a quiet knock at the closed bedroom door. She knew it wasn't Grizz. He might knock, but his large hands didn't know how to be that quiet. Patty had expected Brenda to come to her. She went to the door and found that she was wrong.

Keaton stood on the other side of the door. His hand was raised, fist balled, preparing to knock again. "Can I come in?"

Patty looked past her brother. She didn't see his wife. Nor did Patty see her husband. Leaving the door wide open, Patty went back inside and slumped down on the bed.

She wasn't in the mood for one of her brother's chastising talks. She was in the mood to yell at someone. She'd give Keaton a minute to tell her she was wrong for running away from yet another problem, and then she'd lay in on him.

Keaton sat beside her. His arm lifted and went around her. At first, Patty stiffened. Where was the chastisement? Where were his words about her being irresponsible and not thinking? Instead, he brushed a quick kiss to the side of her forehead.

"Not as easy as you thought it would be, huh?" he said. "He's not an easy man to live with. I should know. I camped out in the desert with him."

Tears threatened Patty's eyes. Keaton's features changed, darkening from jovial to murder.

"Wait." Keaton pulled away from her. "What did he do? Did he hurt you? Did he do ... something you didn't like?"

"What? No. We haven't even slept in the same bed yet. He's been sleeping on the floor."

Keaton turned to look at the floor as though he didn't understand her meaning.

"I know what you're going to say." Patty buried her head in her brother's chest. "That I'm running away from my problems."

"I wasn't going to say that."

"That I shouldn't have dropped out of school."

"You dropped out of school? Does Mom know?"

"That I shouldn't have run from what happened with Deputy Newman and tricked Grizz into marrying me."

"You what? Why am I just hearing this?"

"And that I shouldn't have run from him now. That I should've stayed and talked it out. But he's going to leave me."

"Trust me, if I know anything, it's that Grizz is not going to leave you. He's crazy about you. Has been since we were all kids."

"But he's going to leave to do another contract job because he has no money, and he won't take mine."

"Well, that's just stupid."

"Wait?" Patty looked up at her brother. "You're agreeing with me?"

"Your plan is more sound than his. So, yeah, I'm agreeing with you."

"But he's going to leave me again."

"Again? When did he leave you the first time? Do you mean when we joined the Army Rangers?"

"He didn't come back when you did for breaks."

"Patty, that was because he had feelings for you, and he didn't think he should. He was right. He shouldn't have. He's never looked at a woman the way he looks at you. He never dated in school or when we were in the armed forces. I think it was always you for him."

"He never dated anyone?"

Keaton shook his head. "He always said it was because he had no interest in marrying. And, honestly, I believed that about him. That's really why I thought he stayed away from you because he thought he'd fail like his father did. That's his biggest fear, becoming his father and leaving a woman to shoulder the financial burden of a family. So, yeah, it makes sense that he won't let you pay his way."

"But that's not how family works."

"I know. You know." Keaton left the third sentence, the one that would invoke Grizz knowing, unsaid. Because he didn't know.

"How do I fix this?" Patty asked her big brother.

"I don't think you can. It's a guy thing. Let me talk to him."

CHAPTER TWENTY-ONE

rizz didn't follow Patty into the house. What more could he say? He'd spent so much of his life protecting her, making sure she had everything she needed. But she was right. He had kept his distance. It was the way he knew to care for her.

It was just that he no longer wanted to keep his distance from her. Being apart from his wife, the woman he loved—had loved all his life—made him physically ill. But what could be done? He needed to provide for her, and this was the only way he knew how.

As a kid, Grizz had watched his mother work her fingers to the bone. She had taken to ignoring him. He'd received the love and attention he needed from the Keaton family. Mr. Keaton had shown him what it looked like to take care of a family by going away and deploying to dangerous places. Mrs. Keaton had shown him what it was like to have a mother fuss over him. A young Keaton had shown him what it was like to have a brother who would die for him. And Patty?

Patty had shown him the purest form of love. Patricia Keaton had shown Grizz what it was like to be loved unconditionally, just for who he was. For that, he wanted to give her the world, even if it meant that his life might be forfeited because of it.

Why couldn't she see that that was how he loved her? That was how he'd always loved her. How he always would love her.

"You're breaking her heart, you know."

Grizz couldn't raise his head to meet his best friend's gaze. This was what he'd tried to avoid all these years. This particular confrontation.

"You're breaking mine, too," Keaton continued.

That brought Grizz's head up. "What did I do to you?"

"We said we were out. And now I see you're going back in. Why?"

"Because I'm broke," Grizz finally admitted. "I can't pay my share for the camp. I can't take care of my wife. I have to go back in. It's what a man would do."

"You're an idiot, you know that?"

Grizz wanted to growl. He wanted to punch Keaton in the nose. His best friend had always had things easy; a mother at home, a father who was there, and enough food in the pantry to never worry about going hungry. At Grizz's house, they didn't have a pantry. Everything fit in the fridge or the few cupboards beside it.

"You should've come to the rest of us," Keaton continued. "You should've told us. At the very least, you should've told me. You know I would've covered you."

Grizz was already shaking his head before Keaton finished his sentence. But Keaton would have none of it.

"Don't give me this charity thing again," Keaton scoffed. "You're my brother. Legally now. You've always been family, and this is what family does for each other. This is what Rangers do for one another. We never let one of our brothers fall."

"That's life or death in combat zones."

"And marriage is different how?"

Grizz struggled for a response. He and Patty had already navigated so many minefields this past week. Bombs had gone off at every turn in their relationship. At the end of the day, Grizz did not want to lose this war.

"We've had women taking care of us since before we were born," said Keaton. "Besides, isn't that what they did in those old books of yours; families paid to have their daughters taken off their hands. It's a small price to pay for me to have you deal with Patty for the rest of your life."

But it still wasn't sitting well with Grizz.

"Fine." Keaton pulled out his cell phone. "Then you call my mother and tell her that my sister dropped out, was nearly arrested for assaulting an officer, and is about to be abandoned by her husband after a couple days of marriage."

Grizz cringed away from the phone.

"Actually, no, I'll call her." Keaton brought the phone back to himself. "It's about time I get back on the pedestal as her favorite son. This will definitely knock you off."

Grizz smacked the phone from his best friend's hand. Keaton lifted his brow in mockery. Then Keaton reached for Grizz and brought him into an embrace.

"We're in this together, buddy," said Keaton.

When they pulled away, Keaton punched him in the gut. Grizz doubled over.

"That's for making my sister cry."

"Duly noted," Grizz choked.

By the time he climbed the stairs to their room, Grizz had recovered his breath. Grizz reached for the door just as it opened. Patty stood on the other side. Her eyes were red, her cheeks puffy, her upper lip stiff as she regarded him.

"Hey," he said.

"Hey," she said.

They stood gazing at each other from across the barrier of the threshold.

"Griffin, I want to tell you exactly what's on my mind."

"Okay, Patty Cakes."

"I don't need your protection. I'm a capable woman."

"I know you're more than capable."

"If you don't want to take my money, fine. But you're not in this alone. I'm going to work alongside you."

"No." Grizz gave a determined shake of his head.

Patty sighed.

"I have a better idea," he continued. "We're going to use your money and buy our own house."

Patty blinked. Then she gave a shake of her head as though to make sure she'd heard him correctly. "We are?"

"We can buy something in town, or build it here on the ranch together."

His wife's eyes lit up like the sky after a storm. Glimmers of sunlight sparkled through like rays of hope. Grizz's heart burst open at the sight of it.

"So, you're not going away?" she said.

"No," he said. "I promised. I'm never leaving you again. I love you too much for that."

Patty closed her eyes as though saying a prayer. "I love you too, Grizz."

"I'm sorry," he said. "I'm just so used to taking care of you, that I didn't take a moment to ask if this is what you wanted. But it's going to mean a lot of late nights working on the camp, and maybe even an odd job or two in town. But it will be temporary. Meanwhile, you'll get to live out your dream as a housewife."

"My dream was always to marry you. I achieved that."

She was his dream, one he hadn't dared to think would ever come true. But there she stood. All he needed do was cross the threshold and take what was his.

Patty beat him to it. She leaped over the threshold of the door and right into his arms. Grizz caught her, as he always would. He didn't take a step back. He absorbed her weight. And then he took a definitive step across the bedroom's barrier.

Their lips came together in a heated, possessive kiss. Grizz took possession of what was his, while his wife took possession of what had always been hers. They wrapped themselves around one another, any plans of a long courtship now going out the window.

With a kick of his boot, Grizz pressed the door closed. With the bedroom door closed, all the possibilities for their future lay open before them. Another quiet snick of the lock, and he and his wife made their way into the bedroom. Both eager to make this marriage permanent in every way that mattered.

EPILOGUE

A soft series of dings preceded Mac Kenzie as he shouldered into the door of the establishment. He looked up to find two small white bells tied together with a white ribbon hanging over the entryway. Wedding bells. Fitting as he'd entered a wedding dress shop.

Mac walked into the storeroom as though walking through a cloudy sky of satin, tulle, and a polyester blend of white. Most men would've shrunk back in fear at the sight. Most men would've never crossed the threshold, to begin with. Mac wasn't most men.

It wasn't like he frequented wedding shops. Though when he was in a grocery or convenience store, he might've lingered looking at *Today's Bride* and *Destination Wedding* magazines. It was a habit. His mother was a wedding planner, so he'd been around it his whole life.

He loved watching two people design the start of their lives together. The colors they chose to represent their love. Where they planned to put themselves on display. The menu and cakes they choose to feed their loved ones. You could tell so much about a couple in whether chose a live band or a DJ to host their reception.

The shop proprietress looked up from her phone call and gave him a cheery smile. Mac sat a smoothie container on the counter. She smiled at him gratefully and waved him towards the back.

Mac clutched the other three drinks close to his chest, careful not to spill a drop on any of the gowns on the rack, as he made his way to the backroom; the inner sanctum where brides made the most important choice of their married lives.

Most men did not tread here. Most fiancés didn't anyway. This was a place for sisters, girlfriends, and mothers.

The two women in wedding gowns were both already married. Brenda Keaton and Patty Hayes twirled around in white gowns. Both of their mothers were on their way. Mac, carrying the knowledge of his mother, was a stand-in.

That, and he was their ride. Both of their husbands had foisted the chore on Mac in exchange for doing all of Mac's chores on the army training camp they were building together. Mac was certain he got the better end of the deal.

Brenda and Patty beamed at their reflections in the mirror. Mac winked at Patty in her empire waist gown. It was perfect for her curvy body. But the cut-out patterned dress that Brenda wore didn't sit well on her tall, athletic frame.

"What?" asked Brenda. "You don't like it?"

"No, I do," said Mac. "It's just with your figure and your height, you should go for a princess cut dress."

Mac turned to the stash of dresses he'd laid out before going and grabbing the girls' drinks. He pulled aside the last dress he'd picked out. His fingers had lingered over the dress because it was so familiar to him. Another tall, athletic girl had chosen a similar dress to wear years ago. The fact that Mac had seen it was likely the reason she'd run before their wedding day.

Mac shook off the memory. Not enough to put Lana out of his mind. She was a permanent fixture there. And he had every hope that one day soon, she'd come out of his mind and be with him in reality.

She'd run from him then, and he'd let her. His father had taught him that a caged bird might accept its captor, but what it would always want was flight. Best to open the door and hope that it would return home each day.

And so Mac had opened the door and allowed the love of his life her freedom. He was still waiting for her to return home to him. Truth be told, he was close to hunting her down and dragging her back to him.

But not today. Today, he would help his friends' wives plan the wedding of their dreams. Then maybe, someday soon, he'd have the wedding of his dreams.

Mac turned to Brenda, dress in hand.

Brenda's eyes lit up. "Our new friend just tried on that same dress."

"Your new friend?" asked Mac.

"Yes, I think she said she was a reporter," said Brenda. "Oh, there she is now."

The dressing room door off to the far right opened and a woman stepped out. She had light, bird-like steps that indicated that she might fly away at any moment. Her body was tall and lean. The princess cut dress highlighted the length of her long limbs, making her look both regal and again.

Mac's heart fluttered in his chest as recognition dawned. He was yanked back in time, two years ago. The night he'd seen the woman he loved in her wedding gown. The worst night of his life. The night she chose her career over him. The night she flew out of his life.

"Lana?" he said.

Lana's head jerked up. Her gaze connected with Mac as recognition began to dawn. She gave herself a shake, like a bird whose feathers were ruffled. Her head made tiny, incremental movements as though she couldn't believe what she was seeing.

She inhaled deeply, holding her limbs taut as though readying herself to take flight. And then she bolted out the back door.

Make no mistake that this will be the last time that Lana runs from Mac.
Wanna see how this Army Ranger catches the woman he loves?
Turn the page for
The Rancher takes his Runaway Bride.

THE RANCHER TAKES HIS RUNAWAY BRIDE

THE RANGERS OF PURPLE HEART RANCH
BOOK 3

CHAPTER ONE

"But how can you be sure the beans came from Caldas, Columbia?" Lana Hunt leaned over the counter, pinning the man with what she called her penetrative gaze.

That stern gaze that told the other person that she saw more than they wanted her to was one of the skills needed to be an investigative journalist. There was a fine art to questioning a source, getting them to divulge information without them realizing they were—well—spilling the beans. When it came to information exchange, it was all about asking the right question.

For example, a reporter never asked a closed-ended question like Are these Arabica beans? The interviewee could simply answer Yes or No, and the communication channels would close.

It was best to use an open form of questioning that began with something like *Tell me about these beans.* Or, *Can you relay how you came into possession of these particular beans?* That way, the responder would feel obliged to divulge not only their knowledge but their opinion and feelings, too.

"Another question," Lana said before the bewildered barista could answer the first question.

Lana leaned over the counter, twisting the ring on her finger. The pad of her thumb pushed the small diamond around until it was at the back. Mac said she always did that when she was thinking things over. Lana doubted her fiancé's observation. She hadn't worn the ring long enough to form any habits. It had only been three months since Mac had slid it on her left hand, his brown eyes shining in triumph.

The young man standing behind the counter did not look triumphant as he gaped at Lana. Sweat trickled down his splotchy, side-burned face, and his man bun drooped. Clearly, he was feeling the pressure because he wouldn't quite meet her gaze. He stared, instead, over her shoulder.

Great. She was close to cracking him. Lana placed both her hands on the counter and cocked her head as she went in for the kill. Dogged determination was yet another hallmark of the investigative journalist.

"I happen to know that true Arabica beans are a deep reddish-purple and smell sweet like jasmine flowers."

Research skills were another hallmark of investigative reporting. Lana had studied her material. She inhaled, ready to fire her next missive when she smelled a delicate, flowery smell. Like jasmine. She glanced down at the dark, nearly purple beans.

"All's I know is what it says on the packaging," said the side-burned barista.

Lana looked behind the counter to see an industrial-sized brown container with the words *Arabica Beans* printed on the side. As far as facts went, that one was hard to argue with.

"Come on, lady," called a disgruntled voice behind her. "Take your order and go. Some of us have to get to work."

Lana tapped her credit card on the coffee shop's machine. She declined when it asked if she wanted to leave a tip. Since the barista hadn't given her a tip she might've used to create a news story for her job, she wouldn't return the favor of tipping him for his. Grabbing hold of the tray of coffees, Lana made her way out of the mom and pop coffee shop and into the warm air.

She noticed the world all around her. She might not have gotten what she needed for an exposé on coffee shops passing off inferior beans. But there were still potential stories all around her, all just waiting to be told.

A man walked out of a bank with a locked briefcase clutched in his hand. He looked left, right, and then clutched the satchel tighter. What, Lana wondered, could he be hiding in the bowels of that case?

A young mother pushed a stroller toward the park. She paused to allow a fit jogger to pass her. But when the young, athletic man did, she craned her neck over her shoulder to get a view of him passing. Could there be trouble at home, Lana wondered?

Unfortunately, those potential stories would have to wait a little longer because Lana was late for work.

She dashed into her car, settling the coffee into the passenger seat. Ten minutes later, with one minute to spare, she was riding the elevator up to the third floor of *ChatterZine*. People bustled about inside of the online magazine. The red ink flowed down white sheets of paper as copy was edited. The slicing sound of scissors cut through the air as images were pasted and rearranged for the layout. Interns scuttled and scurried about checking facts, running copies, and getting coffee for their assigned reporters.

With aromatic coffee in hand, Lana made her way to *ChatterZine's* Editor in Chief's office. Reyanna Murphy didn't raise her head when Lana opened the door. Not until the swirling tendrils of warm coffee rose in the air and tickled her nose.

"Arabica beans?"

Lana nodded. "I checked the sources myself."

Reyanna took a healthy gulp. The brown skin of her throat that matched the beans she loved worked as she took in the warm nectar that she worshipped. "Thanks, kid."

Lana wasn't a kid. She was twenty-two. But she didn't check her boss's facts. Initiative was another highly prized skill for an investigative reporter. She just needed Reyanna to take a glance away from the energizing morning brew and see the same fire in her intern.

"Did you finish fact-checking Nichols's story?" asked Reyanna after another sip.

"I finished last night."

It had taken Lana into the evening, well after she should've left the office and gone home. There had been a lot of errors in Nichols's story; factual and grammatical. Lana had practically rewritten the story before she turned it in. She wanted to tell Reyanna that, but Lana suspected the woman knew.

So, why hadn't Reyanna given Lana her own story to write instead of another's to rewrite?

"Andrew Rucker is out again." Reyanna sighed as she gripped her coffee to her chest.

"I hope it's nothing serious." Lana knew full well that the man was likely sleeping off yet another night of illicit delights.

"I'm trying to find something to fill his section."

Another part of investigative journalism was being cutthroat. This was it. This was her chance. "I have an idea for a story."

Reyanna studied her over the rim of her coffee cup. "Your fact-checking has been stellar. I've noticed both Nichols's and Rucker's stories have been… tighter."

Lana smiled demurely, admitting nothing.

"Yes." Reyanna gave a decisive nod. "I think you can handle this story."

Inwardly, Lana jumped up and down. Outwardly, she took a seat across from her boss. She set her mind to determine which story to pitch. An exposé on coffee shops might pique Reyanna's interest, but Lana had no angle. Maybe an investigation into the security of brief-cases. Or an exploration of the satisfaction of today's young mothers in the roles as homemaker and wife.

"There's this woman in the next town over," Reyanna started. "She has twenty cats and—"

"Don't tell me," Lana said, taking out the pen she always tucked into her hair and the notepad that was always in her back pocket. "Animal control is on her?"

"No," said Reyanna. "She makes the cats costumes."

"Oh, I see. So, it's an animal cruelty angle."

"No, Lana. It's a fluff piece about a woman with cats who puts them in funny costumes."

Lana's pen lowered. She sat the blank notepad down on her lap as she struggled to understand the straight lines of the story.

"I want you to go and ask some basic questions, take pictures—lots of pictures. Everyone loves a cat photo."

A fluff piece about cats in costumes? Not an exposé on code violations or a treatise on the plight of today's aging, single woman. Or even a statement piece on how modern feminism is owning a cat.

"Can you handle that?" asked Reyanna.

"Yes." Lana cleared her throat. "Yes, I can."

"Excellent. You can go and interview her on Friday."

"This Friday?" Lana shifted the pen in her hand and twisted the ring on her finger. The diamond met with the ink of the pen.

"Yes, we need the story for the weekend edition."

"This weekend?" Lana twisted the ring the other way, this time meeting the edge of the notepad in her lap.

Reyanna lifted her gaze. "Is there a problem?"

Lana moved the ring up and down, toward her knuckle and then back all the way down. Yes, there was a problem. She had a bit of a family obligation this Saturday.

"No." With one final press of her thumb, Lana shoved the ring firmly back in place. "There's no problem. I just have this family thing. But I can probably wiggle out of it. Or get them to push it back."

"Good. I'm counting on you."

Mac was not going to be happy. But he loved her. Enough to marry her. They were going to spend the rest of their lives together. He couldn't get mad if she wanted to push the start of that forever back by one weekend. Not when it meant she would get a step closer to her dream job.

CHAPTER TWO

Mac Kenzie looked himself over in the full-length mirror. He looked mighty fine if he did say so himself. If ever he was going to do so, he was going to look good enough to break all the girls' hearts, he'd do it in this suit. His wedding tuxedo.

Not that he had any intentions of breaking any girls' hearts. Mac had fallen head over heels in love with Lana Hunt the first time he'd seen her. The first time he'd seen her had been just over there.

Mac turned to look out the window of his childhood bedroom. Well, his summertime childhood bedroom. As a kid, Mac had rarely lived in the same place for more than a few months at a time. With two parents in different branches of the Armed Forces, Mac had been shuttled from base to base and had even spent a couple of years in boarding school while his parents fulfilled their duty to the country.

The only thing that had a semblance of normalcy was his summers, which he spent there, at his grandparent's house. He'd spent every summer there since he was six. His fiancée, Lana, had done the same. She came every summer to stay with her grandparents, who lived next door. Lana's bedroom was directly across from his.

The sun had set. The neighborhood was quiet. The lights of her bedroom were out this evening. She was probably staying late at work. Again.

Mac heaved a sigh as he straightened his tie. He knew he was marrying an ambitious woman. He loved that about his Lana; that she had a single-minded focus. It had taken him years to break through that focus to get her to look up from her newspaper articles and magazine columns. It had taken him even more years to get her to see him as more than a friend.

After much prodding, poking, cajoling, and convincing, she had. The proof was in the ring she'd finally accepted from him. It had only taken him a mere five times in asking. In just a couple of days, she would finally be his forever. Not just for the summers they spent together. They'd be together every day for the rest of their lives.

Without warning, a hand shot over the barrier of the open window sill. Mac jolted. Not from seeing the hand there. He was used to that. Ever since they'd been children, Lana had often climbed into his bedroom window for a late-night chat. It was such an old habit that even now, they both neglected to use the front door of the houses.

But Lana climbing into his window on this night, at this particular time, was his worst nightmare about to come true.

"Lana, no."

Mac grabbed the patchwork quilt his grandfather had knitted him from the bottom of the bed. To work his arthritic fingers, his retired Air Force pilot grandad had taken up the hobby and was quite proud of his work. Mac threw the intricate artwork over his covered body.

"You can't see me like this."

Lana easily stepped over the window sill and into the room. She was dressed in dark pants and a bright blouse. Pants that were now scuffed from her climb and a shirt that held a hint of dampness at the armpits for her efforts. Lana wasn't one of those women that cared for messing up clothes. Clothing was just armor to her, a tool to help her get the job done.

Dark blue eyes narrowed at Mac as she came to standing. She shoved the black tresses out of her angular face to peer up at him. "I can't see you like what?"

"I'm in my wedding tux." Mac tugged the edges of the quilt tighter around himself. "It's bad luck for you to see me like this."

Lana quirked one of her dark brows. "Isn't that myth about the bride in her wedding gown?"

Mac pursed his lips, still not letting go of the quilt. "I'm sure it goes both ways."

"I don't care about that." Lana took a step toward him.

Mac stepped back. Which was entirely counterintuitive. For more than half his life, Mac had been chasing after this girl, trying to capture her into his arms.

"I need to talk to you. Mac, if you're so bothered, just take it off."

Mac lifted a brow at that. He might've spent the last three months wrapped up in planning their wedding, but he'd spent more than enough hours making an agenda for their wedding night. He only had a few more days before he'd see Lana in her wedding dress, and then help her out of it.

As if she saw the trajectory of his thoughts, Lana huffed at him. More than once, she'd accused him of not taking things seriously. She was wrong. He took his vows to her very seriously.

At age six, Mac had vowed they'd be best friends forever.

At twelve, he vowed that he would have his first kiss with Lana.

At age seventeen, Mac had sworn he would marry Lana.

It had taken time, but he'd kept each and every one of those vows. All that was left was the vows he'd prepared as they officially began their lives together. Starting this weekend.

But first, he had to make sure nothing got in the way of the perfect wedding he'd planned for them. And that started with the bride not seeing the groom in his wedding clothes.

Mac made a twirling motion with his index finger, indicating that Lana should turn around. With a huff, she did as he asked. That was the first thing that alerted Mac that whatever she came to tell him might be serious. Lana had always done as she pleased. She was a woman that knew her own mind.

Mac grinned and shed the tuxedo jacket and shirt. At the last minute, he shoved a fatigue shirt from his days in basic training over his head.

Now that the woman of his dreams had finally said yes, he would be separating from the military. He hated to leave behind his Army Ranger friends, but Lana had always been his first priority.

Mac came up behind his fiancée. She settled back into his arms as he slid his hands around her. A sense of rightness lightened his heart as he buried his nose in her hair.

"How was your day at the office, honey?" he said.

"It was good." Lana rested her hands over his. With her left thumb, she twisted her engagement ring around. "I got a story assignment."

Mac whirled her around. "That is amazing. I knew you could do it."

Lana let him pull her into his chest, she snuggled in under his chin at the spot he'd told her was meant only for her. "It's a fluff piece. But it's my chance."

"You're going to nail it."

Mac pulled away. Peering down at her, he saw a light in her blue eyes. He brushed his lips over hers, reveling in the bittersweet taste of her. Coffee and cream, that was his reporter girl.

"I suppose you'll want to work on the story on our honeymoon." Mac sighed, pulling her more snuggly into him. "Fine, but only a few hours. I want most of your time and attention."

"About that..."

Lana squirmed away and out of his hold. She flicked at the ring when she was away from him. Mac felt a prickle of foreboding slither down his spine. She only flicked at her ring when she was unsure of something, which had been every time she'd been asked her opinion on anything to do with their wedding planning.

Lana's indecision and disinterest in the planning hadn't bothered Mac. He'd happily, daresay eagerly, picked up all the slack that was traditionally set for the bride. After all, he was the one who'd been dreaming about this day since they were kids.

"About what?" Mac prodded her.

"About the wedding..."

The shiver that had gone down his spine transformed into a tingle of awareness. Mac didn't think Lana was backing out of the wedding. Though he was the only one who believed they'd ever get close to this day. His friends hadn't even bought plane tickets until just a couple of weeks ago. His parents had scheduled a vacation around the date, just in case.

In truth, Lana had taken a long time to say yes to the engagement. He'd asked her five times over the last two years. But it had taken her three years before she'd agreed to date him. So, there was a marked improvement.

"The interview for my story is scheduled for Friday." Lana shoved the ring up to her knuckle.

"This Friday? Our wedding day?"

She nodded, rubbing at the band around her finger. "I was thinking we could just push the ceremony back a couple of hours."

"Push our wedding ceremony back?"

Lana shoved the ring back down. "Yeah, it could be in the evening instead of the morning. I'll just head out, do the interview, and be back in plenty of time to say *I do*."

Mac's head was spinning as he looked at her. She hadn't taken the ring off. That should soothe him. But it didn't. What had his blood boiling was the change request.

It wasn't the first time she'd asked to push the date back. And each date shift had been due to her work. She'd missed most of the planning appointments because she'd chosen to stay late or follow a lead for her work. Mac hadn't begrudged her until now.

"An evening wedding?" Mac tried not to spit out the words, but they were so distasteful on his tongue. "I planned for an afternoon wedding. The hall is booked. The band, the caterers. Do you know how many people have been invited?"

Just a few dozen of their closest family and friends. Mac had addressed each invitation himself. Lana had been working late that night, fact-checking some story about the dangers lurking in nail salon foot baths.

"I told you not to go through all that trouble," she said. "You're the one that wanted the big wedding. We could've gone to Vegas months ago and got this over with."

"Over with?" Mac nearly choked. "I planned all of this for you."

"No. You did this for you," she said. "What difference does it make when and where we get married?"

"Every difference. We planned this."

"No, actually, you planned this. You want the purple and pink colors—"

"Plum and blush."

"And the roses—"

"Lilacs, not roses."

"And the hundreds of guests."

"It's only going to be seventy-eight. And that's only because your grandmother insisted on inviting the Wallaces from down the street."

Lana huffed. Her hands were balled into fists as she glared at him. She wasn't turning the engagement ring, but he didn't need that to interpret her feelings.

"Mac, this story is important to me."

"Lana, our wedding, which is the starting point for the rest of our lives, is important to me."

"Our life together began years ago. What difference does one day make?"

What difference?

The room was spinning. Mac took a step back, needing to find something to hold him up. Did she really just say those words?

He'd always known that Lana wasn't like the typical girl. She was laser-focused on her career goals. But she'd always made time for him. Yet, now, when he needed her most, she wanted a rain check on their wedding day?

"Look," Lana sighed, "why don't we just elope after I finish the story?"

"E—" Mac choked. He couldn't even finish the word.

"Isn't the important thing that we'll be married?" she said. "I'm just asking for another day."

Mac shook his head. "If we push this back now, next week it'll be something else. Another story. Another excuse. Either you want to spend your life with me. Or you don't."

"I do. I don't see why I can't have a career as well as a husband."

"I don't see why I can't have a wife who puts me ahead of her career."

The moment the words were out of his mouth, he knew he should regret them. Except he didn't. He'd put her happiness ahead of his career. He'd bent over backward to accommodate her choices. He'd made all the choices for this wedding. It wasn't unreasonable for him to want to keep the date.

Lana twisted the ring on her finger. It spiraled up, like a topper being uncorked. The band reached as high as her knuckle. Even in their worst arguments, she'd never lifted it over her knuckle.

Mac held his breath as the band sat at the crease of her knuckle.

Lana balled her hand into a fist. The band slipped just below her bent knuckle. But before Mac could exhale, Lana turned and walked over to the open window.

"I love you," he said before she got a leg over.

Lana turned back to him. "I love you."

This was where he would always bend to her will, agreeing to do whatever she wanted. But on this point, he was not going to budge. Either their lives started on Friday, or they'd part.

They stared at each other for long moments. Neither budging. Finally, Lana lifted her leg over the window sill.

Mac felt himself giving, but at the last second, his back remained straight. "I'll be at the church on Friday afternoon waiting for you."

Lana twisted the ring until the diamond was lost inside her fist. Then she climbed out of the window and was gone.

CHAPTER THREE

*N*ine months later

Lana rode up the elevator to the offices of *ChatterZine*. Like she did every morning, including most weekends, she gripped a cup of coffee in one hand. Though now it was only one cup as Reyanna had gone through a series of bright-eyed interns, whose eagerness dulled within weeks of working for the demanding boss.

Coffee in hand. Pen in bun. Notepad in pocket. Lana took sure steps to her desk. Along the way, she dodged bodies as writers and photographers hurried about inside the office.

As always, the red ink flowed as black copy was stricken across white sheets of paper. Scissors made quick work of photographs and illustrations as the day's layout came together like pieces of a puzzle. Unlike her first year here, this batch of interns stood on the periphery, eyeing the madness with a bit of fear in their eyes. Maybe two of them would make it in this fast-paced, unrelenting, cutthroat world of online reporting. The others would need to take a step back into the world of print.

Lana breathed it all in. This was her world. She was in her element.

So why, with the deep breath, didn't her lungs fully inflate?

Likely because everyone was always out of breath in the world of reporting. Life moved fast in the world of news. To succeed, she had to be nimble enough to catch it. Which meant holding still was for the birds. And so Lana hurried into her seat.

All around her keyboards clacked. It was Lana's favorite sound. The sound of notes being turned into stories.

Though Joe Grist, the political reporter, did jam his fingers into the keys as though his fingertips were jackhammers, and the keyboard was concrete. And Mary James, the fashion reporter, had a habit of uncrumpling the recycled paper in the bin and peering at what others threw away as she waited by the copy machine.

Then there was the new batch of interns, still hovering at the edge of the room. They reminded Lana of old Three Stooges movies when they braved a step forward. They'd bump and bumble into one another while they got facts of the stories wrong.

Lana pulled her keyboard to herself. She hadn't assigned a single one of them one of her stories. Because she didn't have time to do double the work.

"You coming out to happy hour with us?" Warren Blake leaned over the wall of her cubicle. The sportswriter was handsome. Most of the girls in the office were fawning over him.

He kept singling Lana out. Not that she'd once given him an ounce of encouragement. He seemed to view her as though she were a ball that was up in the air waiting for him to catch.

"I can't. I've gotta finish this story." Lana pointed to the screen that held her completed piece for the week.

"I'm surprised that fiancé of yours never comes into this office and drags you away."

Lana twisted the engagement ring on her left ring finger with her thumb. "He's busy."

"Too busy to check in on his girl?"

"He can't. He's overseas. He's an Army Ranger."

"An American hero?" Warren raised a brow as though he was impressed. "Nice one."

Lana nodded in agreement. Mac was a hero and a nice one. Unlike Warren, who constantly hit on a woman who was clearly unavailable.

Well, she was technically unavailable. She hadn't shown up for her wedding. But she hadn't broken the engagement. She hadn't given the ring back. She hadn't even considered it. She fully intended to marry Mac Kenzie.

Some day.

Though she'd probably have to talk to him to determine when that day might be. Or if that day could ever be.

Mac had redeployed last fall, just a few weeks after their summer wedding had been canceled. Lana hadn't heard from him all year. Not since the night she climbed out of his bedroom window for the last time.

"I hope he knows what a lucky man he is," Warren was saying. "If you were mine, I'd sneak away to see you for lunch and happy hour."

Lana didn't answer Warren. She twisted the band on her finger. It was a comfort sitting on her hand all the nights when she wasn't in Mac's arms. When she wasn't seeing his bright smile. Or feeling his warmth as he held her close. Or listening to that deep rumble of laughter that made his whole body shake and then seeped into her and made her laugh.

She'd done what she'd done. And she had no regrets. At least that's what she told herself every night she went home alone.

This career was what she'd always dreamed of. Chasing down a story. Getting the facts out of subjects. Turning that evidence into beautifully crafted prose.

Okay, so the current story she was working on wasn't exactly Pulitzer worthy. But she was still rising to the top. She'd gone from cat stories to dog stories, and now she was actually doing human stories.

Her latest story had been on the man who held the record for the longest toenails. Along with his nightly cleaning regimen. Lana had prided herself for holding the contents of her stomach down as she interviewed the man. She'd aced that story, and she was sure more hard-hitting assignments were on the way.

"Hunt. In here."

Lana's right eye twitched at the sound of her boss's voice. She took another healthy gulp of coffee. The robust brew warmed her belly and gave her the kick of energy she needed for the day ahead. She rose and made her way to her editor's door, passing an intern who looked slightly green around the ears on the way out.

"Nichols is out sick," Reyanna started without preamble.

Too bad for poor old Nichols. Brilliant for Lana. Taking over his stories was how she was moving up in the ranks. Though Lana often wondered why her boss bothered to keep the man on the payroll if he rarely did his job.

"You finished the toenail story?"

"Of course," Lana said, tugging her pen from her bun and pulling her notebook from her back pocket. "It's in your inbox now."

Reyanna offered Lana a rare grin. "I can always count on you."

"What's the story?"

"There's a ranch in Montana where men are marrying women off left and right." Reyanna sat back, crossing her hands over her flat stomach. She'd cringed when she'd said the word *marriage*. "It's being hailed as the modern-day Gold Rush Brides." Another cringe when she said the word *bride*.

Reyanna was unmarried and unattached. She was always in this office when Lana arrived in the morning. The editor-in-chief was still in the chair when Lana went home last each evening. The many times Lana had come in over the weekend this past year, she'd seen Reyanna behind this desk, clacking away at her computer. No wonder the idea of a relationship was foreign to the woman.

"You think it's some kind of cult?" asked Lana.

"Cult or a scam?" Reyanna shrugged. "I hear it has something to do with land ownership. Maybe government tape? The interesting angle is that all the men are soldiers."

Lana's pen scratched across the paper and drew a jagged line on the knee of her pants. She gulped a couple of times before she could speak. "What branch?"

"All of them, I think. It's a rehabilitation ranch for wounded veterans."

Lana let out the breath she held. Mac wouldn't be there. He was neither wounded nor a veteran. He wouldn't be released from the army until the summer.

For the past ten years, they'd met at their grandparents' houses each summer. Either she would climb into his bedroom if he arrived first. Or he would climb into hers.

Lana had planned to take some time off to visit her grands in a few months when the temperature rose and the beaches opened. And if it so happened on a cool summer night that she let her window unlocked and a strapping soldier wanted to climb in, she wouldn't stop him.

Unless he didn't come back. Unless it was truly over between the two of them. Which was possible.

Mac had chased her for years. He might take a step back, but he never backed down. He never gave up each time she rebuked him or tried to slow his roll. He'd always flash that impish grin and come back at her from a different angle.

Which had been exhausting.

Which had been why Lana had backed out of the wedding.

She'd loved Mac—she loved Mac. Not past tense. He was just so determined to have his way and tug her along with him as he did so.

But what if there were no more angles? What if he'd turned and walked in a different direction? He might've even found someone else by now. A girl who wanted to have a huge wedding, and stay home, and be a happy housewife.

Lana hated that girl.

"Hunt? Do you want the marry a soldier story? Or not?"

"Yeah," Lana sighed. "Yeah, I want it."

CHAPTER FOUR

*L*ater that morning, Mac Kenzie lifted his head up and looked out at the wide Montana skyline. Blue sky blended into green pastures. Spotted along the pastures were blotches of brown blobs that were the herd of Vance Ranch, where he currently made his home.

His home was in the sweltering third-floor attic of the ranch's big house, but he'd lived in worse. He'd happily trade the deserts of Afghanistan or the mountains in Syria for the cramped, humid attic any day.

Mac took a deep inhale of the fresh, open-air, and promptly coughed as a dust cloud swirled into his nostrils. The new bull for the Vance Ranch was kicking up a storm in the pen.

It was no wonder why. The animal had gotten a glimpse of the heifers he was about to be locked into a pen with. The new bull was raring to go on his speed dating adventures.

The old bull sat with his bulk on the ground, his large head hanging low. The old bull was bigger than the new bull. But the old bull had taken a mighty blow that left him laid out on his belly. The injured creature lifted his head to glance at his replacement, then slumped back down in defeat.

Mac could relate. In the relationship department, Mac had been replaced by something he didn't view was better than himself. Mac had been replaced by something that wasn't just smaller, it wasn't even his same species.

The love of Mac's life had walked away from him in pursuit of a career.

The injured bull let out a low whine, as though to commiserate with Mac. Mac leaned against the fence in solidarity. Nearly a year later, and he could hardly still believe it himself. But here he was on a cattle ranch while Lana was likely chasing around stories to put in print. Or digital ink, or whatever.

What Mac did know was that he'd chased the love of his life relentlessly for years, and once again, she'd slipped away.

Mac stepped back into the corner as Brenda opened the latch to release the new bull into the females' pen. The females moved quickly, darting out of the way of the randy bull. They might be interested, but none were eager to get caught too soon.

The injured bull sighed again. The veterinarian had told them that cattle have a high tolerance for pain. Much higher than a human.

Mac understood that too. He wore a grin most days, while inside, he felt like his heart was in a perpetual fire that breathing only stoked.

The old bull would heal. He just needed time. Then he could get back to the work of wooing the female cattle next year.

That was Mac's plan. It was an old plan. Most of his life, he'd only get to spend summers with Lana. On the last day, they parted ways, and he had to begin his pursuit again next June.

It had been nine months since Mac's wedding day. It was the middle of spring now. In just a few more months, he'd go in search of her and win her back.

It didn't matter how long it took. Lana was the only woman for him. He'd given her time to work on her career. She had to be missing him now. If she ran again, he would bide his time a bit more. But he'd never give up on her.

A truck pulled up, snapping Mac out of his reverie. When Mac saw who was inside the vehicle, he pushed off the fence and hurried over. Three men filed out of the vehicle.

"Finally," Mac whooped.

David Porco was the first out of the vehicle. He bounded to Mac like a puppy who had been cooped up inside for too long. Which was an apt description of the man with shaggy hair and large, dark eyes.

"Mackenzie," Porco howled as he bowled into Mac.

Mac happily accepted the man's enthusiastic greeting. He was just glad it didn't come with a lolling lick of his chin.

Next was Jordan Spinelli. Spinelli reached his hand out to Mac with a smart smile and a nod. Spinelli was the scholar of the bunch who always had his head buried in tactical books.

Russell Hook came round from the driver's side. Rusty was the eldest of the bunch. But only by a few years. The gray hairs the man sported were from stress rather than time.

"We stopped off at the Purple Heart Ranch," Rusty said after giving Mac a clap on the back. "They told us to come over here. Have we changed properties?"

"It's a long story," said Mac.

"You three have only been here for two weeks," said Porco. "And we hear congratulations are in order? You got hitched?"

"Not me." Mac held up his hands. "Keaton and Grizz."

"So, what they say about the Purple Heart Ranch is true?" said Spinelli. "Soldiers come out here and get married."

The man looked around the rolling pastures as though single women dressed in wedding gowns were preparing to jump out at him. Crazier things had happened. Like their leader, Anthony Keaton getting hitched the same day he'd arrived here.

Mac related the story of how the old bull had rammed into Keaton's truck on his arrival. Though the bull was still laid up and suffering, the animal had knocked good sense into Keaton. He'd looked up to see Brenda Vance riding to save him on a horse, and that had been the end of it. The two married so that she could give him the land the six of them needed to complete their training camp. But Keaton had wound up giving the female rancher his heart.

A few days later, Keaton's baby sister showed up. Grizz had been trying to deny his feelings for Patricia Keaton since the young woman had come of age. But after just a couple of days, Patty had finally sunk her claws into Grizz, and the two turned up married.

If only Lana would turn up here. That would solve all of Mac's problems.

"There's no way I'm staying here," said Spinelli. "I'm too young for a ball and chain."

"You are a ball and a chain," said Porco throwing the man a punch.

"At least you don't have to worry, Rusty. You're already married."

Spinelli had a knack for saying the wrong things at the wrong times. It wasn't that he was insensitive. His brain was often too busy working out big, complex problems that he didn't pay attention to people's feelings.

Rusty let out a low sigh. "Not for long."

No one spoke. They all knew divorce papers were in the works for Rusty and his estranged wife. The papers were signed. But the ink hadn't come from Rusty's pen.

"Come meet the new family," said Mac to break up the tense silence.

The four men went to the other side of the pen, where Keaton and Brenda were keeping an eye on the new bull. Keaton had his arm looped around his wife's shoulder. Beside them stood Patty and Grizz in a tight embrace.

When the two men looked up to see their army brothers, they each tore themselves away from their wives and came forward with open arms. Greetings were exchanged. Backs were clapped. Jabs were thrown, ducked, and counterpunched.

"We need to get you all over to the training camp and show you guys what we've done." Keaton's typically regimented tone was full of eagerness.

"I hear you've relaxed that crazy schedule," said Porco. "Thank you, Brenda."

"We're also helping Bren out here on the ranch," said Keaton. "And now, my mother is demanding a wedding for both her children."

"No worries," said Mac. "I can help with the wedding stuff."

The men all turned and looked at him. The ladies did, too. Brenda with relief in her green gaze. Patty, with doubt in her blue eyes.

"What? My grandmother was a wedding planner. Plus, I'm an evolved man. Come on, ladies."

Planning a double wedding was just what Mac needed to get his mind off his own failed wedding, as well as divert his attention from planning and hoping for what the summer might bring.

CHAPTER FIVE

*L*ana took her last sip of tepid coffee as she pulled up to the gate of the sprawling ranch. For a moment, she doubted she was in the right place. The sign on the wrought iron at the front of the establishment said Bellflower Ranch. It was an impressive piece of ironwork. At its center, was a flower with drooping petals, painted a faded shade of purple.

Lana hadn't needed her investigative journalist skills to tell her that the bellflower and the Purple Heart insignia were one and the same. Her mother had been in the Air Force. It's why, for most of her life, Lana had spent summers at her grandparents' home. Her mother was often deployed, and Lana had been enrolled in a girls' boarding school for the rest of the months.

Ethan Hunt had also been in the Air Force, but he'd died in combat when Lana was quite young. It was how Lana knew that insignia. It hung on the portrait of her father in her grandparents' den.

Veronica Hunt had thrown herself into her work after her husband's death. Lana's mother had become one of the first female fighter pilots and still continued to fly to this day. The last Lana had heard from Lt. Col. Hunt, she was boarding a Thunderbolt in a location that she was unable to disclose. But at least she'd taken a moment to call her daughter.

Driving through the open gates of the Purple Heart Ranch, Lana saw men atop horses, men bent over tending to livestock, men walking about talking with one another. None of them wore fatigues. But she knew that each of them had served.

It was in the way they walked upright, heads high. It was in the way their shoulders were set. It was in the alertness of their gazes. Soldiers at ease but ever vigilant.

That was how Mac had always seemed to her. Alert and ready, even with his easy smile and relaxed posture. Lana had never felt a moment of fear or uncertainty when she had been with Mac. She'd always felt certain that whatever might come their way, Mac would handle it and make certain she was safe.

Lana brushed the warm rush of feelings aside. She had a job to do. Thoughts of Mac were reserved for the moments before she fell asleep at night. That's when she let all thoughts of him run free in her dreams.

Thoughts of what her life might be like if she'd shown up on her wedding day. Thoughts of lazy Sunday afternoons laying in his arms as she rested her head against his chest as he chuckled and made her laugh. Thoughts of what their children might look like if they'd had their wedding night.

Again, she shook herself. Lana reminded herself that she was awake. In her waking hours, she had work to do. A story to write. Not a fairy-tale to weave.

Parking her rental car in front of the biggest house on the ranch, Lana climbed out. She ran her hand over her dark slacks and navy blue blouse. The attire was meant to blend in. Letting those around her think she was just a standard-issue military wife and not a reporter hot on a story.

Yup, Lana was going in undercover.

To complete the look, she pulled the pen from her hair and left her notepad in the car. She hated to leave her armory behind, but her mind was sharp enough to record the details of the conversation she intended to have. Though she'd be loathed to use direct quotes without her pen and paper.

Lying wasn't her favorite aspect of her job, but every once in a while, it had to be done. She had tried to come into the situation clean. Lana had called ahead to try and set up an interview. But the person on the other end of the line had declined. The ranch wasn't looking for any publicity, he'd said.

That had set Lana's investigative radar buzzing. Most cults preferred to work in secret. They also isolated their members. A ranch in the middle of nowhere, Montana was pretty isolating.

Though this place was beautiful enough to steal some of her breath. There was actual space enough to stretch out. The greens of the fields were vibrant. The red brick and brown wood of the quaint cabins were inviting. Nothing like the concrete jungle she barely glanced at every day for the last year back in the city.

As she took it all in, Lana felt her shoulders lighten, her chest lift, and her fingers relax. The swinging seat up on the porch looked incredibly inviting. She wondered if she could take a moment to sit there before—

The door of the big house opened, and two men walked out of the house. One was tall and lean. The countenance of a soldier was in his walk. Even though he walked with a metal leg, he moved forward with purpose.

At the soldier's side was an elderly man. The man was smaller in height, but not in the way he carried himself. The older man's honey golden skin spoke of an ancestry of warmer climes. His smile was gentle, welcoming as he regarded Lana. Something in his gaze told her that he could see right into the heart of her.

"Ms. Smith?" asked the soldier.

Lana nodded, absently twisting the band on her left hand. Smith was her cover name. Lame, but also easy to remember. Lana needed to conserve the space in her head for the details she would have to recall and write down later.

"My name's Dylan Banks, and this is Dr. Patel. We're sorry your fiancé couldn't make it on this visit."

Lana flicked the engagement ring up towards her knuckle. "He was recently wounded. He'll be home soon, and I want to have everything ready for him."

Dylan Banks nodded. Though, his shrewd gaze didn't soften as he regarded her.

"I can see the two of you have been separated for a long time?" asked the doctor. The older man's gaze was soft as he regarded Lana.

"I haven't seen him in almost a year." It was the truth. She hadn't spoken to or seen Mac since that last day that she'd climbed out of his bedroom window. She had expected him to come after her, to plead with her to show up to their wedding.

He hadn't. Which hadn't surprised her at the time. He always took a step back when he was trying to win her to his way of thinking. But he'd always step forward again. In the past, he'd never waited more than a day.

"That's hard on a relationship."

Lana could only nod at the older man's words. She tugged the ring down, twisting the diamond until she could feel its point on the fleshy part inside her balled fist.

"You miss him terribly," said Dr. Patel.

It wasn't a question. Because it was the truth. More and more, Lana wasn't able to keep thoughts of Mac confined to just the nights. He had been seeping into her waking thoughts every morning, often at lunch, and a few timed during the workday.

"You should reach out to him soon," said Patel. With another of his gentle smiles, he turned and walked back into the big house, leaving Lana alone with Dylan Banks.

"What branch is your fiancé in?" asked Dylan once they were alone.

"He's an Army Ranger."

Dylan's brows raised. "We have rangers here."

Prickles started over Lana's skin. Not because she thought Mac would be here. The last she'd checked in on his grandparents, they'd said he was still overseas. They couldn't give more details than that, because Mac could never divulge his exact locations. But what if someone from his unit was here on this ranch? She hadn't thought of that.

"What's your fiancé's name?" asked Dylan.

"Mac—elmore. Macklemore. John Macklemore."

"We don't have any soldiers here with that surname," said Dylan. "The unit of Rangers who are here are all in town right now. Planning for a wedding."

Ah! Now they were getting somewhere. "Because in order to stay here, you have to be married?"

"It's a county ordinance. We could fight it and get the rule changed." The soldier before her relaxed his hands, his own gold band gleaming in the afternoon sun. He smiled at something or someone off in the distance. "But the rule has worked out for all of us who've come to live here."

Lana turned to see a group of women and children walking into a field. The women all looked young, close to Lana's age. A group of men approached from the other side of the field. Two of the women went to the men, walking directly into their embraces.

"All of those couples were married here on the ranch?" Lana asked.

A pleased smile spread over Dylan's handsome face. "Each one of them came here to heal from the war and wound up shackled for their troubles."

"How does that work? Do you bring them all together at a dance or something and see who picks whom?"

Dylan's grin flattened. He turned to face her. "No, we're not a dating service or a matchmaking service, Ms. Hunt."

Hunt? Had he just called her Ms. Hunt?

"Or any other salacious thing your magazine might have dreamed up happens on this ranch."

Oh, no. She'd been found out. She'd pushed too hard with that line of questioning.

"This is a place where people come to heal, and they just happen to fall in love. Since it seems you don't believe that, you won't find a story here. I think it best you be on your way."

So much for undercover.

Lana had bitten the dust. But she couldn't go back empty-handed. This was the first real story she'd been given. She just had to find another way in.

CHAPTER SIX

Mac pulled up in front of the bridal store in town. He parked the truck in front of the red brick building with white trim. The pink sign on the awning read Nancy's Nuptials.

It was mid-day, and many of the townsfolk were about. A few of the faces Mac knew. He waved to Lieutenant Luke Jackson and his fiancée, Elaine, the town's librarian. Luke was the author of epic military science fiction novels. The retired pilot was working on the next book in the series. The last installment of Luke's books finally had the two main characters coming together for some light romance.

Mac wasn't surprised at the twist in the plot. Not when he watched Luke lean down and kiss the lovely librarian before the two entered their favorite Mexican restaurant, likely to take advantage of the tacos that were being served up on this sunny Tuesday afternoon.

Mac tugged at his lower lip. He hadn't kissed a woman in almost a year. Not that there hadn't been plenty of chances. There just hadn't been any desire. There was only one woman he wanted to kiss. She was the only woman he'd ever kissed.

When Lana had climbed down from his bedroom window that last night, Mac had been calm. They'd been down this road many times before. Mac would tug Lana in one direction. She would resist and either pull him in a different direction or simply stand still. But eventually, she would give in and go his way.

After waiting until the morning, Mac had gotten a tingling in his chest when she didn't return to his window. The tingling had turned to clenching when he hadn't seen her the next day. The night before the wedding, something inside him had hardened.

For the first time in their relationship, he'd been too tired to chase after her. He'd been too agitated to hold still. He'd been behind all of the progress in their relationship. If she wanted to move forward, she would have to make the move.

She never came.

Instead of going after her with his tail between his legs, Mac had turned his attention to another mission and went back with his Ranger unit. The job had finished a month ago, but Mac still hadn't returned to find the woman he loved.

Yet.

As angry as he'd been at her abandonment, as heartbroken as he'd been at her broken promise to him, it didn't change what was in his heart. If Mac had doubted it then, he knew it now, Lana was it for him. He'd been a goner that first time he'd seen her standing in the bedroom window that first summer.

He'd seen her standing there each summer after for the next ten years. He couldn't help the hope that she would be back there this summer, and they could rekindle what they had.

His friends thought him a fool to go back for yet more punishment. But as the old cliché went, if loving Lana Hunt was wrong, Mac would simply be a fool. Or something like that.

Summer was just a few months away. But now he had another wedding to plan to take his mind off what may or may not be in his future.

Mac opened the doors for Patty and Brenda to climb out of the truck. Brenda wore a grimace as she looked up at the bridal shop like the whole outing was a chore she wanted to pass off to her ranch hand. Mac knew the born rancher would much rather be riding in the midst of her cattle.

Patty, on the other hand, bounced on her toes as though she were a kid standing before the gates of Disney Land. She let go of Mac's hand as soon as her feet hit the ground and made her way to the shop's door.

A wedding bell over the door jingled as they came inside. That was a nice touch, thought Mac. Inside, the shop was a cloud of fluffy white satin, gossamer, and tulle. Mac breathed in the earthy smell of lavender and the spicy scent of orange blossoms and let out a contented sigh. He felt like he was back home at his grandmother's.

Being near Lana wasn't the only reason Mac loved his summers. Spending his days in his grandmother's bridal boutique also held some of his most precious memories. He loved hearing the delighted giggles of the women who came out of the dressing rooms to show off potential gowns. He looked on eagerly as brides' brows drew together in concentration as they poured over pattern books trying to determine the shade that best represented them and their grooms for their wedding colors. His teeth ached as he'd back away from the sweet treats the brides sampled to determine the best recipe for their wedding cakes.

Mac's father had been a bit worried about the boy who loved running in between the gowns and matching colors and patterns. But Sgt. Kenzie had relaxed each afternoon as he watched Mac line up plastic soldiers and gun down the enemies. The sergeant had thrilled as he watched his son chase in vain after that Hunt girl from next door.

"Welcome, welcome."

The proprietress came out from behind the counter, interrupting Mac's reverie.

"My name is Nancy." Nancy reached for Mac's hand and gave a firm shake. "Which one of these is your lucky lady?"

Mac had a flashback to when he'd been planning his wedding. Lana had never wanted to come on these outings, begging off with the excuse that she had to get work done. She'd also used the fact that Mac was much better at "the wedding stuff" than she was. She had a case because whenever she did come along kicking and screaming, she simply deferred to whatever Mac thought was best. With the way clear and no obstructions, Mac had planned an elaborate do... that had never gotten done.

"I'm not getting married," Mac said. "I'm just here for moral support."

"Oh." Nancy turned to Brenda and Patty. "Well, that's just wonderful. Are you both thinking of gowns? Or would one of you prefer a tux?"

Brenda and Patty looked at each other in confusion. Understanding came first to Brenda's green gaze.

"Oh no," said Brenda, holding up her hands. "We're not marrying each other. Not that there's anything wrong with that."

"She's marrying my brother," said Patty. "I'm marrying the love of my life. We're having a dual wedding since we all eloped, and my mother is demanding it."

"How exciting," said Nancy regaining her composure. "Let's get started. Have you chosen your colors?"

"Colors?" asked Brenda.

"I do love pink," said Patty.

"Pink," Brenda cringed. "Aren't we supposed to wear white?"

"How about periwinkle? It's a pastel and could go with pink, for Patty, and green, which is Brenda's best color."

Three pairs of eyes swung around to gape at Mac.

"Then Patty's bouquet could be filled with pink roses. While Brenda could have a more rustic bouquet with green hydrangeas. What do you think?"

The three women gaped silently for a full two minutes.

"I get the feeling you've done this before," said Nancy. She cocked her head and peered down at his hands. "But I don't see a ring?"

Mac thumbed the bare ring finger of his left hand. He offered Nancy a wane smile in response to her flirtation.

"Have you determined your wedding party size?" Nancy was asking.

"No," said Brenda. "I figured it would just be the four of us who are getting married."

"Oh no," Mac piped in. "I'm going to be someone's best man. And then you also need to plan for three more groomsmen since Rusty, Porco, and Spinelli turned up. It looks like you girls will have to come up with four bridesmaids."

Brenda sighed, reminding him so much of Lana. Mac never thought he would meet another girl that didn't gush and obsess over her wedding day. Even now, Brenda was more eager to return to her cattle operation than to spend her afternoon amongst all this frill.

"And now for the reception," said Nancy.

"Oh, that's easy," said Patty.

"Barbecue," both Patty and Brenda said at the same time.

Though Patricia Keaton Hayes loved her sundresses and strappy sandals, the girl could throw down when it came to putting meat on a grill. Mac felt no need to assist with this part of the conversation.

"All right," said Nancy. "I've got most of the details. Let's start picking out dresses."

Watching the women selecting gowns began bringing up too many memories for Mac. What was he thinking volunteering to help with this? One dress, in particular, caught his eye.

It was a simple sheath dress. Most of the decoration was on the lace and beading of the V neck. The thin fabric of the skirt would skim a tall woman's form. The split on the right side would show a trim leg.

It was similar to the one Lana had picked out, though the straps of this dress hung off the shoulders. Mac didn't approve of that design for Lana. It would take away from the perfection of her collarbone.

He cursed under his breath as his heart skipped a beat at the sudden pang of loss. Mac should've known then that their wedding was doomed. But Lana had insisted on his help, or she would've worn a simple sundress to their wedding.

Mac laid the dress down on the heap Brenda and Patty had collected and turned for the door. He needed some air. "I'll go grab us some grub while you ladies are trying those on."

CHAPTER SEVEN

The green pastures and log-style cabins of the ranches gave way to concrete and brick and mortar buildings as Lana drove her rental into town. The small town reminded her of the one where her grandparents lived and she'd spent her summers. There hadn't been ranches lining the neighborhood streets. But there had been that homey feeling where everyone knew everyone. That feeling where the people walking by looked up and smiled, rather than hung their heads low staring at their phones. That feeling where people crossed the street to say hello instead of going out of their way to avoid any contact.

Lana hadn't been back to her grands' neighborhood since last summer. They talked every Sunday. But one subject was off-limits. That was the subject of her stymied attempt at marriage. Disappointment always buzzed over the connection.

The buzz was now following her as she walked down the street on a Tuesday afternoon. Lana reached into her pocket and pulled out her cellphone. Looking down at the caller ID, she let out a groan. It wasn't her grandparents calling ahead of their regular time.

"Where are we on the story?"

Reyanna never bothered with greetings. Just as she was ruthless on word count, she was economical with all spoken words.

"I didn't get much from the owner," Lana admitted. "But I have a new angle."

"Good. I need you to move up your timetable. Rucker dropped the ball on another story."

Lana bit her tongue from saying *again*. She had no idea how Nichols and Rucker were still employed at *ChatterZine* if they couldn't keep up with the pace. Their lack of professionalism had steadily provided her footholds up the ladder of success. So, she kept her lips zipped.

"I'm giving you the feature."

Lana unzipped her lips and made a choking sound. She did a little tap dance in the middle of the walkway, unable to contain her delight. Around her, the townsfolk smiled indulgently. One man tipped his cowboy hat. A middle-aged woman gave Lana the thumbs-up sign. They had no idea why she was so delighted, but they seemed happy to take part in her celebration.

This was it.

This was her big break.

"I need the story by Friday night to go in Monday's publication. Can you handle that, Hunt?"

"Yes." Lana found her voice. "Yes, absolutely. I'm on it."

"Don't let me down."

"I won't. I'm on it."

But Lana was talking to a dial tone. Reyanna, having got what she came for, was already off the line. Just as she didn't bother with greetings, the Editor-in-Chief had no use for goodbyes.

A few steps down the street, Lana spotted her destination. Nancy's Nuptials. Dylan had said two brides were in town planning their weddings. When Lana had looked it up, she'd seen that this was the only bridal shop in town.

Wedding bells chimed over her head as Lana entered the small shop. She paused just inside the door. A sea of white lay before her. But not just white. There were linens of cream, ivory, and vanilla. On a table with a milk-white cloth lay an assortment of invitations on stock of polar white, pearl white, and snow white. And then there were the dresses on the racks. Fabrics of porcelain, baby powder, and bone hung just above the floor.

Lana was surprised she remembered so many of the shades of white. She hadn't been paying that much attention when Mac had dragged her into a dress shop a year ago. He'd had to drag her in because she'd been more focused on her deadline than their wedding. She hadn't cared to go dress shopping when she had perfectly good sundresses in her closet. But Mac had insisted.

She'd trailed behind him down the racks of dresses, sneaking notes on her notepad for the story she'd been researching. It wasn't until he'd pulled a dress from a hanger that she'd looked up, and then he'd had her full attention.

If Lana had been the type of girl to dream of her wedding dress, that would have been the dress. She hadn't protested when he turned her toward the dressing room to try it on. He had protested when she'd wanted to step out and show him how perfectly the dress had suited her.

"I'll wait," he'd said.

It was one of her biggest regrets that Mac had never seen how pretty she looked in that dress. It was just a simple sheath dress, but it showed off each of her best assets, making her long limbs appear sexy rather than gangly. Her less than generous breasts got a boost from the intricate beading and lacework.

Lana found a dress that was so similar to the one she'd been meant to wear on her wedding day sitting atop a pile of dresses in the shop.

"That would look lovely on you."

Lana dropped the dress as though it had bitten her. She looked over her shoulder to find a petite woman smiling at her. It was clear that this was the shop's proprietress by the subtle calculation in her gaze.

"When's your big day?"

"Oh," said Lana. "It's… we haven't set a date. It's been a bit of a long engagement. He's deployed."

"Another soldier?" The saleswoman's gaze lost a bit of the shrewdness and added a pinch of amity. "Are you another Purple Heart bride?"

The saleswoman didn't give Lana a chance to answer. She scooped up the dress and took Lana by the arm.

"I've done most of the brides' dresses," the woman continued as she steered Lana to the back. "Mostly, with only a couple of days' notice. I'm delighted to get a few weeks with Patty and Brenda."

"The Dumasse girls both had a lot of lead time," said a lean brunette, stepping out of the dressing room in a dress that swallowed her whole.

"Ginger Dumasse is that state senator that suggested you and Keaton marry to get around the land regulations?" That came from a curvy redhead who stepped out in a mermaid style dress that made her look like a modern-day Marilyn Monroe.

Lana ignored the dresses and focused on the details she could use for her story. Land regulations? And a politician was in on this?

"The Dumasse girls married soldiers?" Lana asked after the saleswoman left her with the dress and these two sources of information. "From the Purple Heart Ranch?"

"The town's heiress, Honey Dumasse got caught in a compromising position with Private Mark Ortega," chuckled the brunette as she unzipped the gaudy dress.

"Do you mean she got pregnant and had to marry?" asked Lana.

"Nothing like that at all," frowned the brunette.

"The way I heard it," said the redhead, "she lost her shoe, and Mark found it. Much like Cinderella. Except the ball was a stuffy brunch."

Well, that didn't jive with the story of shotgun weddings and cult-like behavior that Lana was going for. It was far too fairytale-ish. And fairy stories didn't sell magazines.

"I'm Brenda," said the brunette. "And this is Patty."

"Lana."

"Did Nancy say you were marrying a soldier?" asked Patty.

"Yes." Lana held up her left hand. "I'm engaged."

"Congratulations." Both of the women beamed at her.

"Same to you," said Lana, eying their rings. Each woman had two bands on her left ring finger; an engagement ring and a wedding band. So they were already married. "Are you ladies from the Purple Heart Ranch?"

"I own the ranch next door to it," said Brenda, stepping back into the dressing room with a new gown.

"But the magic from there hit both of us," said Patty. Her blue eyes shone with what couldn't be mistaken for love.

Lana needed facts, not feelings. "How so?"

"I was supposed to have a business arrangement with one of the soldiers," said Brenda from inside the changing stall. "I needed money. My soldier needed my land. We even drew up a contract. But then I went and did the girly thing."

"The girly thing?" asked Lana.

Brenda leaned over the top of the stall so that her head was visible. "I looked into his eyes and fell in love. Don't look into their eyes."

Too late, Lana thought, looking down at her own ring. That was what she missed most about Mac. Sitting with him with those clear brown eyes on her as he listened to her with his full attention.

Lana gave herself a shake. It was the middle of the day. Not time to think of Mac. It was time to get the facts for her story. She might be able to do something with the land and regulations angle. But she needed something not so legalese to keep the readers' attention.

Lana turned to Patty, but the redhead was eyeing her in the way of someone trying to remember a dream just as they woke up.

"You look familiar," said Patty. "Have we met?"

Lana was sure she would've remembered the pretty redhead. "I never forget a face. Work habit."

"What do you do?"

Lana decided to keep as close to the truth as possible. "I'm a reporter. I write human interest stories."

Lana thought the woman would push, but Patty's gaze slipped to the dress still in Lana's arms.

"I bet this will look amazing on you," Patty said. "Try it on."

Lana hesitated. The dress was so like the one still hanging in her closet back home. She had no idea why she'd never gotten rid of the dress. Possibly because she still hoped to wear it someday?

She stepped into the changing room and slipped out of her clothes. When she stepped into the dress, it fit like a glove. But she didn't get that tingly all over her skin feeling that she'd gotten with her dress. Still, it was pretty.

"Your new friend?"

Lana tuned into the conversation just beyond the changing room. It sounded like a man had joined Patty and Brenda. The man's voice sounded very familiar.

"Yes, I think she said she was a reporter," said Brenda. "Oh, there she is now."

Lana stepped out of the dressing room. And nearly fell over. There he was.

Well, there his back was. She didn't see his face. She didn't need to. She'd know those broad shoulders anywhere.

When Mac turned, his brown gaze settled on her. Lana made the mistake of looking directly into his eyes. She felt like she was falling. And then she nearly did fall over as the facts paraded through her mind in quick succession.

Mac was standing there.

In a wedding dress shop.

With two women in wedding dresses beaming up at him.

The girls were both already married.

To a soldier.

There stood one such soldier.

Her soldier.

No, not her soldier anymore. Mac was married to one of those women, and now he was planning his wedding.

At the conclusion of the indisputable facts, Lana lifted the wedding gown, turned, and bolted out of the shop.

CHAPTER EIGHT

Mac was having the dream again. He'd been having this dream since he was a teen, and he'd come to truly understand what marriage meant. In the recurring dream, it was his wedding day. Lana was a vision as she came to him. Dressed in a vibrant vanilla white gown. The design was simple, understated, like the woman who didn't like to draw much attention to herself. Lana had always preferred to sit quietly in the background, observing while she recorded the details.

However, an important detail of this vision was wrong. There was no slit in this dress to show off her slender calves. The straps slid off her shoulders, detracting from the heart shape of her collarbone. It was a feature Mac knew all too well as he'd spent countless afternoons kissing the skin there.

Even with those imperfections, Mac couldn't help himself. He reached for the vision, knowing that the moment her fingers met his palm, it would start the first moment of their forever.

She was so close. He could smell the earthy scent of her morning coffee. He could feel the warmth of her startled breath. He could see the navy flecks in her blue eyes.

But the vision didn't reach for him. Mac's dream woman balled her hand in the fabric of her gown. She lifted the hem of the dress. Then she turned and ran.

That's how he knew he was awake.

Lana had slipped out the window when she'd run from their wedding. At least this time, she dashed away from him in a wedding dress. As things went, he could at least call this run through an improvement.

"What just happened?" said Brenda.

"OMG, she said her name was Lana," said Patty. "That was your fiancée's name, wasn't it?"

"Whoever she is, she needs to pay for that dress," said Nancy.

Mac didn't answer any of them. He truly wasn't dreaming. It really was Lana. And she was getting away.

Not this time. Mac set off after her.

Lana had always been a fast runner. Mac knew that as he'd chased her more times than he could remember when they were kids. He'd aimed to best her in races when they were adolescents. He could just barely outpace her as a teen. By the time they were adults, he'd kept up a daily running habit to make sure he could always stay one step ahead of her.

She'd had a head start after he'd been struck dumb at seeing her in the bridal shop. She was dashing through lunchtime traffic in the stolen gown. Cars stopped as drivers watched stunned as a bride ran through Main Street.

Lana looked over her shoulder once to see Mac gaining. He would overtake her in a matter of strides, and she had to know it. She feinted right and took a left. Mac wasn't fooled. He kept his eyes on the prize.

She made a mad dash up steps and darted into the first building on her right. Mac followed, certain she had to have missed the steeple at the top of the building she was now taking refuge inside. By the time Mac entered the church, he saw Lana come to a screeching halt in front of Pastor Vance. The young Pastor looked from the out of breath bride to Mac, who wasn't breathing hard at all.

"Do you two need anything from me?" asked the pastor.

"No," panted Lana, taking a step back.

"Not yet," said Mac, taking a step forward.

Lana whirled on Mac. Her face went through three emotions in the span of one second. Anger. Sorrow. Hurt.

Were those tears in her eyes? That brought Mac up short. It was rare for Lana to cry.

Without a second's hesitation, Mac reached for her. He enfolded her into his arms. She came without protest, but not without a sound.

Lana sniffled as her head came to rest on his chest. She took in a shaky breath and let out a sob. Mac felt his heart breaking and racing at the same time.

He pulled her closer. Held her tighter. Tucked the top of her head under his chin and rested his lips against the top of her head. It had been nearly a year, but she still fit into him.

She always had. Since they were kids and they'd sat next to each other, she'd always fit. Whether they were sitting side by side and their shoulders leaned into one another. Or when they'd gotten older, and she'd sat on his lap as he'd kissed her.

Their limbs had always snapped into place. Their breaths had matched. Their heartbeats had synched.

Mac felt Lana's heart racing against his chest. All too soon, it slowed, coming to beat in time with his.

All was right with the world. This was exactly how things should be. Lana in his arms, her heart in time with his.

He had no idea what had brought her here. No idea what had made her cry. He needed to find out and put a stop to whatever or whoever it was.

Mac pulled her away. Slightly. Whatever her answer to his next question, he had no intention of letting her go.

"What are you doing here?" he asked.

Lana glared up at him. Her eyes flashed. As though in an accusation.

That couldn't be right. He'd never wronged this woman. He'd done everything in his power to please and acquiesce her since the first day he'd seen her.

"Let me go," Lana said.

Nope. Not happening. Not ever again.

"I'm sure you have to get back to your fiancée," she said.

His fiancée? Mac's fiancée was in his arms. In a wedding dress.

Why was she in a wedding dress?

Just as soon as he thought of the question, he realized the answer didn't matter. It didn't matter if she was seeing someone else. It didn't matter if she had said yes to another man.

Lana was his. Always had been. Always would be.

Mac took her hands in his. That's when he felt it. He needed to be sure, so he looked down. And there it was.

"You're still wearing my ring," he said.

With her right hand, Lana tugged at the ring on her fourth finger. With effort, she got the band off. They both stared at her bare finger for a moment, both of their chests heaving as though the act of taking off the ring had knocked the wind out of the two of them.

Lana looked up at him. The same anger, sorrow, and hurt still there in her gaze. She lifted her hand and threw the engagement ring at his chest.

Mac caught the band before it could clatter to the floor. His eyes remained glued to the pale flesh on Lana's finger that the band had revealed.

He knew Lana tanned easily. For years, they would end the summers with her bikini line still visible. Now, it was her ring line that was visible.

Which meant that all through the last fall and winter months that they'd been apart, Lana had not taken his band off her hand.

CHAPTER NINE

*L*ana felt as though she was standing naked in the halls of the church without the ring. Fitting as she was standing near an altar, in a stolen wedding dress, with the man she'd jilted nearly a year ago. Not only had he taken her ring, but he'd also held her —something Lana hadn't realized she'd needed so desperately. And now he'd let her go.

No ring. No hug. No Mac.

Mac had given her his word that he'd love no one but her for the rest of his life. Yet now he had a new fiancée. No—a bride.

Both Brenda and Patty had said that they were already married, and they were only now planning their wedding. Which one belonged to Mac? Lana had no idea which one. She didn't know Mac's type. Was it the lean, brunette-haired Brenda? Or the curvy, redheaded Patty?

For as long as Lana had known him, Mac had only had eyes for her. But neither woman was anything like her. Patty looked as though she'd stepped out of a fifty's pinup poster. Where Brenda looked as though she could hogtie a bull.

Either pairing would make for a good angle to her story. Only Lana didn't care about the story any longer. She just needed to get out of here. But she didn't want to leave without that ring.

Setting her chin, she lifted her gaze and made a miscalculation. Lana looked up and gazed directly into Mac's eyes. She wanted to fold herself back into him. She wanted to listen to his heartbeat. She wanted to hear his words, his laugh. She wanted to look into those laughing eyes that always urged her not to take herself so seriously.

She'd been so serious for more than half a year. She couldn't remember the last time she'd laughed. Either she was hunched over a desk writing. Or she was crying.

"You have a fiancée?" she said.

Mac sighed. A deep, heavy sigh that seemed to arise from somewhere deep inside him. The sigh sounded part relief, part resignation.

"Yeah," Mac said. "I have a fiancée."

She'd known it to be true. Hearing the words come from his lips, she felt her heart splintering into a thousand tiny shards. The pieces pricked at her eyelids, and tears sprung anew. "You should get back to her."

"You're right," Mac agreed.

He reached for her again. Lana's brain didn't even contemplate resisting. She came to him, resting her head on his shoulder and nuzzling into his neck.

Mac's lips trailed down the side of her face. It had been so long since she'd been held. So long since she'd been touched.

Lana tilted her head up and met Mac's lips. It was like they'd never parted. Mac's mouth claimed hers.

When they were together, Mac happily let Lana dictate where they would eat, what movie they would see, how they would plan the weekend. But in two things, he tugged the reins away from her and did not give her leave.

The first was their wedding planning.

The second was in kissing.

Mac was a master at kissing. Which had always puzzled Lana as he swore he'd never kissed anyone but her. She hadn't given in to his kisses until they were eighteen. But even that first kiss had been one for the memory books.

Every kiss after that had been just as perfect. And now, as he kissed her after long months apart, it was the best one yet.

Their kiss wasn't hesitant. It wasn't tentative. It was exacting. Certain. Sure.

It was a meeting of two like minds picking up on an idea that they'd left the night before. His hands splayed across her bareback like he owned her. He slanted his mouth over hers, fitting them together like he was still a part of her.

But he wasn't.

He had turned to someone else.

The thought was a gong in her mind. The ringing of that truth made Lana pull away from him.

Mac let her mouth go, but he didn't let her out of his embrace. That was fine. Lana still needed to be close to him for what she had to do.

She took a deep, heaving breath. Then she slapped Mac across the cheek. Mac's face turned. Though Lana suspected it was more from surprise than the force of impact.

"How dare you kiss me when your fiancée is just a block away."

Mac rubbed at his chin. He opened his mouth wide, rotating his jaw left and right.

"I thought you were a better man than this, Mac Kenzie."

Mac shut his mouth, letting his hand fall to his side. With his hand gone, Lana saw that she'd left a mark. His skin was red from where her palm had met his face.

He peered down at her, as though trying to see her clearly. As the red began to recede from his face, his smile spread. "You think I'm marrying Brenda or Patty?"

Lana flicked her thumb at her fourth finger, only to remember that the engagement ring was gone.

Mac didn't miss the movement. He pulled the ring from his pocket, turning it over in the sunlight from the window. Lana looked away so that he wouldn't see the yearning in her eyes for the band.

"Brenda and Patty are already married," he said. "I was helping with their wedding planning since I've already done it before."

Lana knew that last statement was a dig on her. She ignored it and focused on his earlier statement. "Which one of them is your wife?"

"Neither," said Mac. "Bigamy isn't legal in Montana. Even if it were,

I'm sure Grizz and Keaton would object to me nosing my way into their marriages."

"Grizz and Keaton got married?"

Mac nodded, twirling the engagement ring between his knuckles.

"Before you?"

Mac chuckled at that before nodding. "After all their poking at me, and they go and get hitched before I do."

Lana chewed at the inside of her mouth. She remembered his friends. Griffin Hayes and Anthony Keaton. Then there was the whole leaving Mac at the altar bit. She knew she wasn't their favorite person.

But that wasn't important right now.

"You're not married?" Lana asked.

"I never stopped being engaged," he said. "But I plan on getting married. Very soon."

His words sounded like a threat. A threat aimed at her.

"First," he said, taking her hand and tugging her to the door, "Let's get you out of that dress before the sheriff comes after you."

CHAPTER TEN

"There's only this exit, right?" Mac asked Nancy as he stood at the entryway into the changing rooms. The bridal shop didn't have any men's clothes, so there was no reason for him to be back there while Lana changed out of the wedding dress and back into her regular clothes.

"No," said Nancy as she leaned forward against the counter with interest. "This is a one-lane store."

"Good."

Mac crossed his arms and watched the swing door. He could hear muffled shuffles as Lana went about the change. He couldn't help but note that she herself had changed.

It had been nearly a year since he'd last seen her. Now there were bags under her eyes. The bags had been there before when they were together. Lana had never been the best sleeper. She was a night owl and frequently stayed up late reading, researching, outlining the path she wanted her career to take.

She'd often climbed into Mac's bedroom window in the summers and sat at his desk to do so. Mac would lie on the bed, flipping through wedding catalogs, trying to determine which flowers would best compliment the color of Lana's eyes and would show her off best during their wedding.

"So, that's your fiancée?" said Patty.

Patty and Brenda had each selected a gown while Mac had chased after Lana. The two women had catalogs in their hands, but neither pretended to look down at them. Their gazes were fixed on Mac standing guard at the doorway.

"Yeah, that's her," he said.

"I thought I recognized her," said Patty. "But I'd only seen pictures since she didn't show at the..."

Patty let the sentence trail off. As her voice trailed, Mac's mind wandered back in the past. Memories of his life with Lana swirled around his vision. Arriving at his grandparent's house after a long school year and waiting for Lana's mom's car to pull up a few days later. Walking down to the creek behind their grands' houses, as he and Lana caught up with what had happened during the school year. They were both only children who'd moved around a lot because of their parents' work in the armed forces. Summer was the thing that always remained the same for them.

Even when Mac had gone into the service, he'd finagled his leave to be sometime in the summer months, just so that he could keep their tradition and see her. Even when she'd gotten her first reporting job, she still came back to visit her grandparents and climbed into his bedroom window each summer.

The one and only time she hadn't shown was the day of their wedding.

That hurt had been gut deep. But it hadn't lasted long. By winter, Mac had brushed his shoulders off, knowing that summer was coming. After spring passed, he knew that Lana would come back to him. They always came back to one another.

A hand came down on his shoulder. Mac looked over to find Brenda's serious face. "You okay, Mac?"

Mac nodded, turning his gaze back to the dressing room entrance. "Yeah, I'm good."

He took out the ring that was in his pocket. He still remembered the day when he'd purchased it. Lana was not really one for jewelry. She knew where all of her favorite pens were. But if he looked in her jewelry box, he'd find mismatched earrings, bracelets with broken clasps, and hair barrettes that were still in their wrapper.

But she hadn't lost the engagement ring. She had never taken it off.

"She told you she was a reporter?" Mac asked.

"Yeah," said Patty. "She was asking questions about the ranch."

Mac knew exactly what Lana was doing here. Dylan had mentioned that a magazine wanted to do a story on the ranch, and he'd refused. Apparently, the magazine was prone to sensationalizing the facts for dramatic effect. No one that lived on the Purple Heart Ranch wanted that kind of attention for their families or the soldiers they served.

And then Lana turned up.

Mac was sure she had a notepad in her back pocket and a pen somewhere in her hair. She was here for the story. It always came back to the story and her career.

The door to the changing rooms opened, and Lana stepped out.

"Why don't you two go talk," said Brenda. "We'll grab a bite and have Keaton come pick us up."

Mac barely registered the girls leaving. Nancy disappeared in the back. Mac and Lana were left on the showroom of a bridal shop surrounded by all things matrimonial.

Mac took a step toward her.

Lana took a deep breath but didn't move beyond his reach.

Mac lifted a hand to her hair. The locks curled around his fingers as though they remembered him.

"What are you doing?" Lana asked.

"Looking for a pen?"

She frowned up at him. Her lips parting as though she were going to ask a question. But her lids hooded as his fingers ran all the way down her scalp to end at her neck.

He had her in his hold. He could do with her whatever he wanted. More importantly, he knew that, at this moment, she would let him.

With his left hand, Mac reached farther down. His hand ran along her spine. Over the belt of her jeans and just a little further. There he found it.

"You didn't come here for me," he asked. "Did you?"

He tugged the notepad from her jean pocket and held it up. On the pad, he saw her neat print organized in sections.

"You think this is a cult?"

"Give me that." Lana reached for the pad.

Mac held it out of her way. "You're contorting what's really going on there."

"They're marrying for convenience. For a house or land or money. Which is what marriage is truly about. It's an exchange. It proves that marriage is antiquated and unnecessary in a day where a woman can make her own way in the world."

Mac studied the woman he'd been in love with for nearly his entire life. Her features were slightly contorted, as though she wore a mask. But he saw deeper. "You no longer believe that people marry each other because they're in love?"

"I believe in love."

They stared at one another. The mask she was wearing was slipping. With an inhale, she fixed her features and stiffened her upper lip.

"Anyway," she went on, "it doesn't matter. None of them will talk to me now that they know I've lied to them. I needed this story. It was going to get me a promotion."

Lana rubbed at her left ring finger. Then she balled her hand into a fist when she found the space empty. They both looked down at her bare finger.

Lana frowned as though something was wrong.

Mac couldn't help but feel the same way. Whenever he imagined her over the past year, it had always been with his ring still on her finger. The reality of this situation needed to be fixed.

Mac took another step to her, closing the distance between them. Then he went down on his knee, holding up the ring between them.

Lana tried to straighten her fingers, but they shook as they hung at her sides. She watched Mac, her brown gaze unblinking. Her chest still as if she were holding her breath. Was that hope or fear in her eyes? Probably a bit of both.

"What are you doing?" she finally managed.

"I have a proposal."

Lana's nostrils flared as though she smelled something delicious in the air that she desperately wanted. Her fingers flexed at her sides, balling and unballing as though she wanted to grab for the ring pinched between his thumb and index finger.

"You're going to help me plan Patty and Brenda's wedding," he said.

"Me?"

"You want an in, and there it is."

Still, on his knee, Mac balled Lana's engagement ring in his fist and waited for her answer. He was quite comfortable in this position, having been down on his knees before this woman five other times before. Maybe the sixth time would be a charm. Especially since the promotion at the magazine was something she desperately wanted more than she wanted him.

CHAPTER ELEVEN

*L*ana sank into the cushions of the plush couch. The frills along the sides where she rested her right arm were giving her a headache. It was because of the zigzag pattern of the lace. Her eyes grew weary, tracing the design left, then diagonal, then left again. She much preferred straight lines and fabric made of much sturdier stuff.

"What do you think for the base color?" asked Nancy, the bridal shop owner.

Lana jerked back as another set of patterns was placed in front of her face. The polka dots of pink, checkered squares of cream, and brocades of blues made her temple pulse with agitation. Lana dug her nails into the couch cushions, only to have her fingers tangle in the delicate lace.

Nancy smiled serenely as she turned the pages of the pattern book, as though each slightly different hue deserved its own in-depth discussion. In reality, each page and pattern had had its own discussion. Not that Lana had said a peep for the last five hours.

"We've been looking at these for fifteen minutes, Nancy," said Mac as he flipped through a second pattern book.

Lana looked at the clock. She was startled to see that it had not been five hours. Not even half an hour. They'd been sitting here for only fifteen minutes, and she wanted to tug her eyeballs out.

"That's all?" Nancy smiled over at Mac, batting her false eyelashes.

Strike that. She wanted to tug Nancy's eyeballs out. Instead, Lana contented herself with pulling at the threads of the dainty lace covering the couch.

"It's tough because Patty and Brenda are such different women," Mac said as he flipped yet another page.

Lana flicked her thumb at the underbelly of her ring finger. The movement which usually calmed her nerves did nothing. Her ring finger was still bare.

Mac had her engagement ring in his pocket. She couldn't ask for it back. What would that look like if she did? Asking the man she jilted for the ring back.

She knew she should've given it back to him. That bit of wedding etiquette she knew. But each time she made to take it off, she never made it past her knuckle. The ring had become a part of her. It had made it seem like it wasn't over between the two of them.

But it was. Wasn't it? That's why Mac had taken the ring back and placed it beyond her reach.

"I'm thinking green," he was saying. "A deep, pastoral green. It would represent the ranch for Brenda. But it would go well with Patty's red hair. Don't you think?"

Mac turned to Lana. Lana wasn't exactly sure what they were talking about? What was a base color?

"I think that is a perfect idea," said Nancy, as she beamed at Mac.

Lana scowled at the woman who leaned a little too close to Mac. Mac hadn't asked for Nancy's opinion. He'd asked for Lana's.

Not that Lana had a single opinion of what to do for Brenda and Patty's wedding. She'd had little to do with her own. Mac knew that. This was all for revenge.

"And for the accents?" asked Nancy.

Accents? Were they speaking in foreign tongues now?

"I'm thinking spring tones," said Mac, "since that is the season."

"You really have a knack for this, Mac." Nancy sighed as she rested her chin in her palm and gazed at Mac.

She'd called him Mac. Wasn't it unprofessional to call a client by his first name? No wonder Lana and Mac were the only customers in the store. What bride would bring her groom inside these doors if the help was going to flirt with them?

But Lana supposed Nancy could flirt with Mac. He wasn't engaged. In fact, he was single and had an engagement ring in his pocket. He was fair game.

"It's not a God-given talent," Lana grumbled. "He learned it from his grandmother, who was a wedding planner."

The two looked over at her. Lana may have said the words with a bit too much vehemence. But they were still true.

Mac only smiled. "See that color on her cheeks?" Mac lifted Lana's chin with his index finger. "She turns that color when she gets passionate about something. That's the exact color of blush I had planned for our wedding colors."

Lana turned away from their gazes. Mac let go of her chin, but she still felt his heated gaze on her face.

"Our colors were blush and plum," he continued. "Plum because there's a hint of that color in her eyes. Can you see it?"

Nancy leaned forward, eyes narrowed as she stared at Lana. "Yes," smiled Nancy. "I think I do."

"It was a beautiful setup," said Mac, closing the pattern book. "Too bad you missed it, Lana."

Mac rose from the couch. Lana was surprised that the delicate piece of furniture didn't groan from his misplaced weight. Lana certainly felt unmoored, as though she were a ship at sea who just realized she'd lost her anchor.

Nancy eyed Lana. The woman's raised eyebrow said it all; *you were stupid to let this one go.*

"Are we done here?" asked Lana.

"For now," said Mac. "We'll let you know about the fonts for the invitations tomorrow, Nancy."

A grumble sounded in the quiet shop. It wasn't Lana's stomach. No, the groan had come straight from Lana's lips. She did not want to come back and discuss fonts.

Mac held the door for her as she walked out. The bells above the shop rang, bidding them a good day.

They walked in silence for a stretch. When they were younger, they would often spend the day in virtual silence. Mac would thumb through either a bridal magazine or a military one. Lana would read the day's news stories and do her research. They'd been content with one another's presence.

Now, Lana was a ball of agitation. Mac took the engagement ring out of his pocket. He tossed it up, catching it one-handed. The grass beside him was tall. If he missed, it would be lost forever.

"Would you be careful?" she hissed after another throw.

Mac shrugged. "Why do you care?"

She wanted to say that the ring was hers. She wanted to tell him how it had been her only comfort this past year. She wanted to tell him it made her feel safe when she couldn't hear his voice or feel his arms around her.

In the end, all she said was. "Will you be careful, *please?*"

Mac looked down at her. Everywhere his brown eyes touched her face, she warmed. At last, he slipped the ring on his pinky finger. The anxiety inside Lana settled.

They walked on in silence. His shoulders were less than an inch from hers. Lana held her breath with each of their steps, waiting to see if his forearm would brush hers. It never did.

"We got some good work done today," he said once they were at her car. "But I'm going to need you to pull your weight tomorrow. We've got to determine place settings and finalize the invitations."

Lana didn't hide her groan. "I don't see why you need me. You and Nancy were doing just fine on your own."

"Yeah." Mac nodded, looking back down the street where the bridal shop was. "I suppose me and Nancy could handle this on our own."

Lana grit her teeth. She'd known that there was a possibility that Mac had moved on. But in her heart of hearts, she had never truly believed it.

"But, I want you." His voice was soft, but his words were firm. "And we made a deal."

"You trust me to keep my word?" Lana couldn't hold his gaze. Instead, she looked down at his pocket, where he held her ring captive.

Mac's hand came out of his pocket. But the ring remained. Lana watched his fingers as he reached his index finger towards her. It came to rest at the crown of her head. The pad of his finger traced a tender line down her temple. When he came near to her lips, Mac pulled his hand away.

"See you tomorrow?" he said.

Lana had to swallow a couple of times before answering. "I'll be there."

His brows drew together as he studied her. A white tooth flashed as he tugged his lower lip into his mouth. Finally, as though his decision was made, he gave her a curt nod. With a quirk of his brow, he shoved his hand back in his pocket, and turned and walked away.

CHAPTER TWELVE

Mac stared out at the stars and watched them twinkle. His mind raced in time to the flashing of the starlight as it glinted off the engagement ring he held up to the moonlight.

The sun would rise in less than an hour. Sleep had eluded him. He'd been the same on the night before his wedding. Mac had spent the entire day assuring their families and friends that Lana would show the next day. Then he'd spent the night convincing himself that Lana would show in the morning.

She loved him. He loved her. That was all they needed.

Except it wasn't.

Mac had woken the morning of his wedding with a sense of foreboding. It was the same sense he got the last night of every summer since he'd been six and had spent his first summer with Lana. Even at that tender age, Mac had known that when the summer was over, that a good thing was about to come to an end.

The morning of his wedding, he'd awakened with an empty feeling in his stomach. His heart pounded as he rose from the bed. He felt tingles from his fingertips down to his toes as he'd dressed. Lana had had her own apartment near her job at the magazine, but she'd planned to stay at her grandparents' the night before the wedding. The light across the way had not once turned on that night.

In the morning, Mac had gone to the church and made the announcement before all of his family and friends that Lana wasn't coming.

He'd known where she was. He hadn't gone to her office to talk to her. Because he'd known that if he'd seen her smiling while bent over her laptop typing away at a story, it would've truly crushed him.

Mac had spent hours of his life watching Lana writing her stories, smiling to herself as she came up with a clever turn of phrase. He'd always felt a part of her world. But at that moment, as both their families and friends tried to console him, Mac had felt entirely and utterly alone.

His stomach was empty this morning. Mac bypassed the full fridge in the Vance kitchen. He took deep breaths to calm his racing heart, to no avail. He rubbed his fingers against his pants, but the vigorous movements did nothing to stop the tingles at his fingertips.

The first ray of sunlight had yet to touch the ranch. Still, the day's work had already begun. Mac heard Brenda giving orders to Angel, her ranch hand. Keaton was already up and cleaning corals alongside Rusty and Porco. Which left Grizz and Spinelli headed off to prepare the feed. Even though it was spring, the pasture's grass wasn't green enough for grazing.

Mac decided to join Grizz and Spinelli but pulled up short as he walked past the wounded bull's pen. The animal still lay with his belly on the ground, his tail low. A look of defeat in his gaze as he eyed the rising bull who had replaced him.

The once-proud creature looked miserable as he lay in his weakened state. Just a few weeks ago, he'd been the king of the ranch, raring to do what he was bred to do and make nice with the lady cows. The bull had been blindsided, and now he was passed over and all but forgotten. The path before him, so clear a short while ago, was now uncertain.

"So, she's back," came a disapproving growl.

Mac had been expecting this ever since Patty and Brenda had

learned Lana's true identity. He'd managed to elude his friends the previous night, which wasn't that difficult as they were both newlyweds and preferred to get wrapped up in their wives at the end of each day.

Mac took a deep breath and turned to face Keaton and Grizz. He knew the looks on their faces. It was the same looks they'd worn as they walked with him out of the church on his wedding day. It was the same looks they'd worn after the third time Lana had turned his proposal of marriage down.

"But you're not with her," said Keaton. "So, I assume you told her exactly where she could go?"

"I'm meeting her later today." Mac leaned onto the railing of the bullpen, looking into the glassy gaze of the bull rather than the glares of his friends.

Keaton cursed under his breath. Grizz only stared.

"Don't put yourself through this again, Mackenzie," said Keaton. "You know exactly how it'll end up."

No, he didn't. This time was different. This time she had come to him.

Accidentally.

But she was still here.

"You said the last time was the last time," Keaton pointed out.

"I never said that," said Mac. "You said that."

"Yeah," Keaton agreed. "After she left you at the altar, proving that she didn't want to be married."

Mac held up a finger in protest. "She didn't technically leave me at the altar. She left me at my bedroom window."

Keaton shook his head. He threw up his hands, indicating that he was done. But not before turning to Grizz and jerking his head at Mac. It was the lifelong best friends' version of tapping the other into the fight.

"Mackenzie," said Grizz. "I gotta agree here. This girl has brought you nothing but pain."

"That's not true," said Mac.

It wasn't. Lana was the bright spot of his life. Keaton and Grizz had never understood that. They'd never given her a chance. All they focused on were the times she'd turned his dates down, or his wedding proposals, or their actual wedding.

"She's never going to commit," said Keaton.

"Says the man who had a five-year plan for a marriage," Mac pointed at Keaton. "And the man who never planned to marry at all." Mac pointed at Grizz.

"Yeah," said Keaton. "But Brenda said yes the first time. Then it only took a couple of days for us to fall in love."

That was the difference. Lana had loved Mac. She still loved him. Of that, he was sure. And if he hadn't been, the proof was still in his pocket.

"Lana keeps telling you no or walking away," said Keaton.

"She kept the ring on all this time," said Mac holding up the evidence. Not only had she kept his engagement ring, she'd kept it on her finger, where every man could see.

"You mean that ring that's in your hand?" said Keaton.

"I took it back," said Mac. "I'm not giving it to her until she asks for it."

Grizz crossed his thick biceps over his chest, but the bulges appeared to soften a bit as he relaxed. Some of the tension went out of Keaton's stiff posture. Could it be? Were they coming around?

"Guys," said Mac, "I know you're trying to protect me. But you gotta understand, it's always going to be her for me."

After another long moment of glaring, Keaton threw up his hands in surrender. Grizz shrugged his shoulders, letting his arms fall away from his chest. It was all the permission Mac was going to get.

"I'm meeting her in an hour," said Mac. "She's agreed to help me plan your wedding."

"Our wedding?" asked Keaton. "Is that the best idea?"

Mac ignored the question. It was the best idea unless Keaton and Grizz wanted to plan their own wedding, Mac and Lana were the planners that they'd get. "Mind if I take off a little early?"

Mac didn't wait for a response. He walked to the barn where Brenda kept the horses. As he prepared one of the mare's saddle, he couldn't help but notice that his fingers began to tingle once more. As he mounted the horse, his heart began to race before the creature even began to trot. He took off toward the Purple Heart Ranch, and his stomach began to grumble.

What if she didn't show?

CHAPTER THIRTEEN

*L*ana tucked the ballpoint pen into her loose bun. Her notepad was stiff in her back pocket. She walked the grounds of the Purple Heart Ranch under the bright rays of the new day, not bothering to step into the shaded areas. She had nothing to hide today.

In the front yard of the big house that she'd been summarily dismissed from the other day was Dylan Banks. The young soldier ran after a group of small children. His prosthetic leg didn't hamper him as the young ones raced around him. A pack of dogs wove between the man and children. The dogs were a ragtag bunch of patchy fur, missing limbs, and prosthetics of their own. All of the fur creatures looked as though they'd known their own war zone. But every one of them grinned wide, tongues lolling as though they each had tasted love.

Dylan caught one kid up in his arms. The child was a young boy with cafe au lait skin and a riot of dark curls. Dylan tossed the giggling child up and caught him in sure hands. The child looked nothing like the man, but Dylan's face shown with abject adoration as the child scampered away from him to rejoin the melee.

The clouds shifted, casting Lana in the shadows. That's when Dylan's gaze lifted. His grin tugged downward as his gaze landed on Lana.

"Ms. Hunt?"

Lana winced at the use of her real name. "Hello again, Sergeant Banks."

"Sergeant Kenzie said to expect you. I suppose he was the Macklemore you were referring to."

The cloud hovered over Lana's head, but she could feel the sweat trickling down her back. "I'm sorry I lied."

Dylan's brows furloughed and then released. "Why did you lie?"

Lana tugged the pen from her hair, flicked the cap off, then put it back on. "When I called and told the truth, you weren't interested in having your story told. And…" She placed the pen back in her bun. "I needed the story."

"We're private people here," said Dylan. "Families. We don't care to have our business splayed on the covers of a glossy magazine."

"We're a digital magazine, so no gloss."

Dylan did not return her cheeky grin.

"These men and women have suffered enough," he continued. "We've all found peace here, community. I guess you could say it is a bit cult-like."

He lifted that brow that had been furrowed. But now, a deep frown marred Lana's brow. Was he insulted or joking? For all of her skills at reading people and determining their stories, she couldn't get a bead on this man.

"Anyway, Mackenzie vouched for you," said Dylan.

A small smile played at Lana's lips. She hadn't heard anyone call Mac that in a long time. Most of his friends pushed his first and last name together, making him seem like he was some highland conqueror. Lana had to give herself, and the mental image of Mac in a kilt, a shake.

"He said you were the type of reporter who would get to the heart of the story."

"Mac said that?" Warmth flooded from her heart. It reached around to touch her spine, drying up the sweat that had continued trickling down her back. "About me?"

"Why are you surprised?"

Why was she surprised at anything Mac did? No matter how many times she pushed that man away, he always returned to where she'd left him. Whenever she looked up, he was always there waiting for her. Lana thumbed the bare spot on her left hand, feeling a pang.

"I assume he was the fiancée you were referring to?"

Lana nodded.

"Hmmm." Dylan's mouth went slack as he let the sound tumble from his lips.

"Hmmm?" Lana parroted.

"Just, we've heard a lot about you." Dylan scratched at his jaw as he regarded her.

"Mac told you about me?"

"Since he got here, he's never shut up about the girl he was going to marry. He said the ranch would have no effect on him because he'd already found the love of his life."

Yeah, that sounded like Mac. He'd always been so sure of them. Never a doubt in his mind that they would be together for the rest of their lives. The warmth that had been making a journey all throughout Lana came to a halt. The heat still surrounded her heart, but the beads of sweat returned to her back. There were also some droplets forming on her forehead.

Dylan's gaze stayed on her. His brown eyes pinned her to the spot, asking questions Lana wasn't sure of the answers. She was spared from forming a coherent sentence at the sound of horse hooves.

Looking over, she saw Mac riding atop a beautiful horse. Lana saw his wide grin shining from beneath his cowboy hat. She'd seen Mac in full uniform. She'd seen Mac bare-chested in a swimsuit. But Mac Kenzie, on a horse, with a few buttons of his shirt open, sporting a cowboy hat, made her heart skip a beat, and the sweat gather at the center of her palms.

"Hmmm," murmured Dylan once more.

When Lana looked over at Sgt. Banks, he was no longer frowning at her in disapproval. There was a slight smile on his handsome face.

"Anyway," said Dylan. "I envisioned this place as a haven for the wounded. When men and women come back from combat zones, they, unfortunately, leave a piece of themselves behind in those zones. Aren't you going to write any of this interview down?"

Lana had been too busy watching Mac dismount and tether the horse. It took her another moment to remember that she had a job to do. She snatched the pen from her hair and whipped out the notepad.

"The Purple Heart Ranch is where many soldiers find that healing both in body as well as in their souls."

"But only if they get married?" Lana asked.

"Marriage is not a requirement to come here to heal. It is a requirement if they want to stay. It's a zoning issue, Ms. Hunt. Not a cult ritual."

"If it's a city or state regulation, you could get it changed."

Dylan's grin widened at that. It was a full-on grin. So bright and full of happiness that Lana thought she understood completely why his wife agreed to their arranged marriage.

"We could get it changed," he agreed. "But it has served us well."

It was a beautiful sentiment, it really was. And if she had been a romantic, or was employed by a romance magazine, it would've been the perfect story. Instead, Lana saw the story she had planned unraveling before her eyes. This place was resembling a cult less and less. It was looking more like a community. Much like the one she'd spent her summers in with her grandparents. Much like the one where she'd fallen in love with the boy next door.

Lana watched as Mac walked toward her. Swaggered was more like it. She had always loved watching him move. Especially when his movements brought him closer to her. Truth be told, she didn't mind watching him walk away either. Because she he'd proven that he'd always return to her.

CHAPTER FOURTEEN

Mac took his time getting to Lana. The sun was behind her, enfolding her in its warmth like a lover's caress. He wasn't jealous of the rays. He couldn't be. The way the light danced over her took his breath away.

Lana watched him too. Her lips parted. Her gaze widened slightly. Her nostrils flared. He'd seen that look in her eyes. It had been there the first time she'd noticed that he was more man than boy.

For much of their time together before that instance, Lana's gaze had always been down, eyes darting over words on paper or pictures on a screen. But that summer day, she'd glanced up at seventeen-year-old Mac. Her pen had stopped moving over the pad. He'd seen that flicker of interest in her eyes, the one where a detail or fact had enthralled her.

"You got enough for your story?" Mac asked her.

Lana tilted her head up to meet his gaze. The move allowed the sun's rays to dance along her neck. Her ballpoint pen was held limp in her hand. She bit at her bottom lip. The pen slipped out of her hand, and Mac barely stopped himself for jumping with joy. That flicker of interest had been for him and not whatever angle she was chasing for this story.

"I'll just leave you two," said Dylan. With a knowing grin, the man turned and hurried after a group moving down the lane.

Mac turned his attention back to Lana. She'd picked up her pen and was looking down at her pad now. The flush slowly fading from her cheeks.

"You don't find it strange?" she said.

"What?" Mac asked, coming closer to her. She smelled the same; coffee beans and cream.

"This place." She pointed the point of her pen. "It's just a little too good to be true."

Lana waved the pad and pen around as though to encompass the whole ranch. Mac ignored her reporter's tools and focused on her hair. The midnight tresses caught the sun's rays as her head turned. Mac bit his lip as the darkness lulled him forward, closer to her.

"Maybe the truth is simply a good thing," he said, stealing a step closer to her.

Lana shook her head at him, blue eyes bright against the creamy skin of her cheeks and the dark roast of her hair. Mac was suddenly dying for a strong cup of coffee.

"You always looked at the world with rose-colored glasses," she said.

"I like roses," he said. "It's good to stop and smell them after the ugliness of combat."

He pursed his lips the second after those last few words left his lips. But it was too late. She'd caught his drift.

After Lana had jilted him, Mac had taken on one more mission with the Army Rangers. It had been a difficult one. But he'd needed to have orders, something to follow. Otherwise, he'd have trailed after her.

Mac had never kept many secrets from Lana. However, he always glossed over the particular details of his time in the service. Telling her instead of the scenery of the places he was stationed and the culture of the people he was sent to help. None of the ugliness.

Not because he didn't think she could handle it. He knew she could. Lana was an army brat, like him. Mac just preferred any moment he spent with her to be one of peace or passion.

Lana's gaze lifted to his. She closed the distance between them. She didn't have far to go because, as always, Mac had already closed much of the ground between them. Her hand rested on his cheek. Her warmth transferred to him, flooding his body with memories of holding her, of burying his nose in her hair, of claiming her lips with his own. The wanting of her nearly knocked Mac to his knees.

How had he spent these many months without her? How had he not run after her that day last summer? Why wasn't he kissing her right now?

"Did you get hurt?" Lana asked.

Mac's grin wavered. He took her hand from his cheek, enfolding her fingers with his. "I went in hurt."

Lana's eyelids shuttered. She pressed her lips together and swallowed.

Mac wanted to curse. It had been too long since he'd looked into her eyes. But he couldn't take the words back. They were the truth.

"I didn't want to hurt you, Mac." She shook her head softly but didn't open her eyes. "I just wasn't ready."

Mac stared down at Lana. As he did so, he felt his heart skipping beats at just the sight of her. He felt his chest fill with air, waiting to sigh a longing exhale as he took her in. At her cheek, his fingers started to curl with want.

Mac snatched his hand away from her face and took a step back.

"We'd been dating for years," he said. "Marriage was the logical next step."

Lana's eyes slammed open and then narrowed on him. "We hadn't been dating for years. You had chased after me for years. We'd only officially started dating two years ago. You asked me to marry you on our second date."

"You knew I'd been in love with you for years," he said.

"*You* fancied yourself in love. *I* was still trying to figure out who I was."

"Fancied? Since when do you say words like fancied?"

"It just happened so fast." Lana shoved the pen behind her ear, but the pad she kept in her hand and waved it at him as though it contained evidence to support her angle. "I said yes to a date. You declared that we were boyfriend and girlfriend by the weekend. Then you were down on your knee proposing the next week. I didn't have time to catch my breath."

"Why would you need to catch your breath?"

"Because I wasn't sure." The pages of her notebook fluttered irritably as she threw up her hands. "You had our story all written out. You barely allowed me to add any details. It was all according to your outline."

Mac rocked back on his heels. "Are you telling me you didn't feel the same way that I did?"

"Yes, I did. Of course, I did." Lana shoved the notepad into her back pocket. "Eventually."

Mac's heart stopped skipping beats. Instead, it raced to keep up with the pacing of this revelation. Lana had always been a cautious girl, wanting to know all the details before committing to anything. That's why he'd planned everything; their courtship, their dates, their wedding.

"You said you knew you loved me from that first day when you were six." When she said it, she sounded exhausted, not delighted.

"No, I said I knew I was going to marry you when I was six."

"I didn't know where I was going to be from one month to the next, and you were trying to plan my future."

"I was planning *our* future."

"Sure." She crossed her arms over her chest, her fingers squeezing at her forearms. "With peach base colors and plum accents."

"Blush," he corrected. "It complemented your skin tone." Oh, she had gone too far if she was disparaging his wedding planning skills. "You said you didn't care what I chose. You said that you only wanted to have to show up. And you couldn't handle that."

Lana reared back at those words. Her hands dropped to her sides, and her fists balled.

"I'm sorry," he said.

And he was. For more than half his life, Mac had lived to make this girl smile. He'd hung on her every laugh. He'd cherished every touch. Even now, his heart raced, and his chest begged for air, and his hands itched to be filled with her.

"No," she said through gritted teeth. "I'm sorry. I'm sorry that I hurt you. But even more, I'm sorry that my plan for my life interfered with the plan you had for my life."

She turned on her heel so quickly that her pen lost its hold in her hair. It fell to the ground with a silent thunk. She didn't turn to pick it up. Mac doubted if she even noticed it was missing.

He should let her go. He should at least give her a moment to cool off.

Mac bent down to pick up the pen. He rolled the tool in his hands. Then, he couldn't help himself. He ran off after her.

CHAPTER FIFTEEN

ana stormed away from Mac, needing to put distance between herself and him.

Mac had been relentless in their childhood. Knocking on the door to ask her to come out and play. Even if she said she was engrossed in a book, he'd simply lay on the floor until she gave in and came outside.

When they were teens, he asked her to go on a date with him every Friday afternoon. Even when she said she just wanted to be friends.

Once they'd started dating, he waited only a few days before the first marriage proposal. Even though she was still acclimating to the feeling of her first kiss.

The entire time she'd known Mac Kenzie, he'd pushed and prodded and cajoled until she gave in and did what he wanted. But the problem was that Lana always loved going out and playing with him as a kid. She had the most fun on their dates as a teen. When he'd asked her to spend the rest of her life with him, her heart hadn't skipped a beat. It had settled like it found the perfect spot to set down roots.

However, it was all still a whirlwind. She hadn't been able to catch her breath since she was six years old. Even now, she could hear him behind her as she stormed into the nearest building she came across.

"Mac, stop." Lana whirled around. "Please."

Of course, he kept coming. As though something like her outstretched hand, or the crinkle in her eyes, or her very words would deter him.

"Please."

Wonder of wonders, his steps slowed. He left a foot of space between them. And then, instead of haranguing her, he asked, "Do you want me to leave?"

Just looking at him made Lana's heart rate slow. Her breathing came easier. How was it that he could make her heart race and settle at the same time? How was it that he could leave her breathless and calm her breathing at the same moment? Why was it that she needed both distance and nearness from this man all in the same space?

When she didn't immediately answer him, he took another step toward her.

"Mac," Lana warned, bringing her hands back up. If she stretched her fingers, she'd brush his chest.

"You're upset," he said.

"Because you're making me upset."

"That's not what I want." Mac reached his hand out. Instead of touching her or bringing her close to him, he opened his palm. In his hand was her pen. "Tell me what you want me to do?"

Lana stared at the proffered pen. Her chest rose and sank with short breaths. She took a deep inhale, preparing to tell him. To tell him what? That she wanted him to go away, but kiss her at the same time. That she wanted him to hold her, at the same time that she wanted to punch him in the nose.

She took the pen and shoved it back behind her ear. When she looked up, it was already too late. Mac had closed the distance. His arms were already around her. But he didn't bring her into a tight hold. His hands simply rested on her shoulders.

"Mac," Lana sighed.

"Yes?" His hand cupped her cheek.

Lana felt the cool metal of her engagement ring on the side of her face. She placed her hand over his, rubbing the ring that was on his pinky. It instantly brought her comfort. She knew what she wanted. She wanted it back.

The ring. She wanted the ring back. But did she want what came attached to the ring?

As though he could read her mind, Mac brought his face closer. Too tired to fight, she waited for the inevitable.

He always did this; he wore her down until she gave in to his demands. When the kiss she knew was coming didn't, she frowned up at him.

"I want to kiss you," Mac said. "Is that something you want?"

Lana bit her lip. She knew that if she gave him an inch, he would take more than a mile. He would take her mouth and all of her reasoning.

"Tell me what you want, Lana, and I will give it to you."

Lana closed her eyes and rubbed her cheek against the ring, searching for the peace it had brought her over the year that she and Mac had been apart. That ring had been her security blanket in the storm her life had become without him there to anchor her. It had been the promise that she'd held on tight to.

She wanted the ring back. Would it hurt to have just a small taste of him too?

Lana lifted her gaze. Her blue eyes cleared when they met the twinkle at the center of his brown gaze. Whatever Mac saw in her gaze gave him the answer to the question he'd posed a second ago. His mouth crashed into hers.

Mac Kenzie did nothing by halves. He went all out. He claimed what he knew had always been his as he deepened the kiss.

Lana could deny it all she wanted, but her heart had always belonged to this man. It always would. No distance. No space. No breath would ever change that.

No matter who had outlined their story. No matter when the details got filled in. This was always how the story of Lana Hunt and Mac Kenzie was meant to go.

Mac pulled her into his embrace. His hand slipped from her cheek and came to her low back, pressing her into him. Lana mourned the loss of the ring's cool touch for only a moment. The fire burning between them was too bright for her to care.

The sound of the ringing didn't immediately pull her attention from Mac's kiss. It was Mac's hand moving into her pocket to grab the phone that did it. Before he could pull the device out, Lana had come back to her senses.

She frowned at his actions. Mac only shrugged, not an ounce of guilt in his grin. One arm still fit tightly around her.

"It's my editor," Lana said, snatching the phone from him.

"Send it to voice mail," Mac growled.

"No. I need to take this," she insisted, pushing against this chest. "I want you to please give me some space."

Mac gritted his teeth as the ringing continued. Finally, he relented and let her go. However, he didn't go. He simply leaned against the wall and peered down at her. Lana rolled her eyes and stepped out of the building.

As per usual, Reyanna didn't bother with a greeting. "Lana, what's the update?"

"I got access to the ranch. I'm conducting interviews now."

If the Chief saw just how Lana was conducting her research, she might raise an eyebrow.

"But the story is taking a different direction," Lana continued. "These people living on the ranch, they're families. I'm thinking of spinning it as a feel-good story about healing the heart as well as the body."

Dylan Banks' words had sounded corny to her the other day. The words rang different to her ears now. Perhaps because her heart still pounded from a long-overdue kiss.

"Hmmm, no," said Reyanna. "Healing doesn't sell copies. Scandal does. Let's stick with the cult angle."

Lana glanced out in the field at the families picnicking. She spied Dylan Banks bury his nose in a pretty brunette's hair. Two dogs ran around their feet, and a toddler waddled up to them.

"This story is going to get a feature," the Editor in Chief was saying. "That will solidify your career here at *ChatterZine*."

Behind Lana, Mac came back to the entryway. She felt his presence before she turned to him. The corner of his mouth lifted in that knowing gaze, the one that said, You know you want to, and I'll wait patiently until you change your mind. Lana tried to turn away, but she couldn't escape the heat that still burned in his eyes.

"Will that be a problem for you, Hunt?"

"No. No, it won't."

CHAPTER SIXTEEN

The sun slowly sank down below the horizon. The last ray warmed the sweat at the center of Mac's shoulder blades. He put away the last of the tools. But he kept the screwdriver, tucking it into his shirt pocket. As the other guys piled in Keaton's truck to head into town for a cold drink, Mac jumped into the driver's seat of his own car.

Grizz and Keaton avoided his gaze as they had been doing all day. The two men didn't need to voice their disapproval of where Mac was headed. Rusty and Porco, the two men who believed in love, gave him an encouraging nod. While Spinelli, the brains of the bunch, frowned at Mac as though he had no clue what was going on.

When Mac arrived twenty minutes later, he parked in the lot of the town's only motel. The establishment was a quaint one-story, ranch-style layout. It wasn't a chain, but owned and operated by a family. Hopping out of his car, Mac slung a cloth bag over his shoulder. The heavy square contents slapped at the right side of his shoulder blades.

Mac bypassed the front door. He made his way around the back of the establishment. The small Montana town wasn't exactly a tourist destination. There weren't many people staying. So it was easy to spot the window he wanted.

The curtain was parted, and he saw a figure hunched over a laptop inside. Mac pulled out the screwdriver from his shirt pocket and got to work. It took just a few flicks of his wrist to wrest the window open. He heard a slight gasp as the screen gave way. The window's sill was low enough for him to simply raise his leg and step inside.

Mac took a moment to replace the screen and glass, making sure to tighten the screws securely. He didn't want some crazy stranger trying to make their way in here later tonight. Then he strode into the room like he belonged there.

Because he did. Wherever she was, was where he was meant to be.

Lana only stared. Her beautiful eyes wide, but not exactly surprised. Her cheeks were flushed. Her lips parted. Her slender fingers hovered over the middle keys of the keyboard.

When he was close enough, Mac bent down and brushed his lips lightly over Lana's. Just a taste. He didn't press his suit. He knew she was working. He had work of his own to do.

With a smile and a rub of his nose against hers, he took the two strides over to the made bed. Kicking off his boots, he sat himself down, crossed his legs, and took out the sample book from his satchel. He had to nail the fonts for Brenda and Patty's wedding tonight to get the information back to Nancy, so she could start on the invitations.

The massive book opened with a crack and crinkle of paper. After he'd turned a couple of pages, Mac heard the scoot of the desk chair and the clacking of keys resume. He settled back into the pillows of the bed. The puff of air that escaped the soft pillow carried a whiff of Lana's bright scent. Mac made himself even more comfortable, preparing to stay for a long while.

The scratching of pen on pad, the clicking of nails against keyboard, the soft sighs of concentration that escaped her lips were all welcome sounds to his ears. Pretty soon, Mac was lost looking at fonts of serifs and sans serifs, trying to find a happy medium between the block lettering and curly type to fit the two brides. He was so engrossed in looking at fonts that he didn't notice when the tapping of keys stopped.

The mattress dipped. The earthy scent of tart beans with the sweet hint of rich cream filled his nostrils. Warmth invaded his right side. Mac looked over to see that Lana had joined him on the bed.

"Hey," he said.

"Hey," she said.

They simply gazed at each other for a moment. It was as if the last year had melted away, and they were just the two of them sitting in one of their summer bedrooms again. A rightness settled over Mac, a feeling he knew he was going to fight to maintain.

She'd said she needed space. Being in the same room with her, but sitting a few feet apart was the best he could do. It was Lana who had closed the distance this time.

She tugged at her bottom lip with her teeth. Her throat worked as she swallowed down whatever she'd been about to say. Her gaze dipped, but not to his lips. Her eyes rested on his left hand, more specifically on the pinky finger of his left hand.

Mac saw her rubbing the bare fourth finger of her left hand. Her nostrils flared as she continued to eye the engagement ring. She licked at her lips, as though she were thirsty. Her mouth was right there for the taking. She was ripe for the claiming.

"What are you looking at?" Lana asked.

Mac almost told her exactly what he was looking at and exactly what he wanted to do with what he was looking at. But she wasn't looking at his face. Her focus was on the book in his lap.

"I'm trying to choose the perfect font for the wedding invitations."

"Need some help?" Lana scooted back into the headboard of the bed.

Mac's mouth fell open. "Really?"

"It was part of our deal, right? You help me get access to the ranch, and I help you plan the wedding."

That had been the deal, but Mac hadn't expected her to keep her end of the bargain. He was happy that she hadn't left town now that she'd gotten the interview. Happier still that she hadn't kicked him out of the motel room. Hearing that she was willing to help him with this plan, he… Well, he didn't quite know what to think?

"I don't know how much help I'll be," Lana said. "You know I don't have a knack for any of this."

"Well," Mac leaned forward, pushing the sample book cover over until one side of it lay in her lap. "You could approach it like you would a news story."

Lana's brow lifted, the way it did when she was curious about some detail. "I only just met Brenda and Patty. They're very different women. Keaton and Grizz…" Lana grimaced, tucking her legs under herself, which pushed the sample book off her lap. "I never really got close enough to them. I know they don't like me."

"That's not true," said Mac. The sample book fell to the other side of his lap, forgotten. "They just don't know you."

"All they know is that I keep hurting their friend." Lana tugged the pen from her hair and set it on the side table.

"I was your friend first." He brought his finger to her temple and traced the line of small hairs he found there. "You know me better than them. You know me better than anyone."

"You know me better than anyone, too." She moved closer until their knees bumped. "Are we gonna talk about… it."

"It?" Mac raised a dubious eyebrow at her.

"You know what I mean." Lana dropped her gaze. "Our wedding."

"We didn't have a wedding."

As the sigh escaped her lips, her shoulders deflated. Instead of sinking into herself, she sank into him. Mac had made the first move at every stage of their relationship. But this time, it was Lana who leaned in and brushed his lips.

"I missed you," she said, her voice so soft the only way he knew she'd said anything was the movement of her lips against his and the brush of her breath on his tongue.

"I know," he said.

Lana pulled back, indignation evident on her beautiful face. She punched his shoulder, but she grinned as she did it.

Mac caught her hand in his. Absentmindedly, he rubbed his thumb over her knuckles. He watched as her throat worked when his thumb came to her left ring finger and rubbed the bare skin there. The moment was ripe to offer her the ring again.

Instead of pulling her into his arms and claiming what he knew in his heart was his, Mac let go of Lana's hand. He pulled the sample book back between them. Lana scooted closer, snuggling into his shoulder as they looked at the fonts.

CHAPTER SEVENTEEN

Warmth spread across Lana's shoulder blades. She turned with a smile on her face, preparing to greet the source. Instead of warm, virile man, she met with the rays of the morning's sunlight.

Mac was gone. He'd stayed until late in the night. They'd chosen a font for the upcoming double wedding. Then moved onto writing the words for the invitations that would be printed in the chosen font. From what Lana knew of Keaton, who liked to plan, and Grizz, who liked to brood, Lana thought she'd helped make a good decision with the word choice. There were the details—date, time, place—written in bold. The dress code stated come-as-you-are, as though urging guests to think deeply about their attire.

After the invitations, Lana had assumed the rest of the night would be devoted to catch-up-kisses. But Mac had pulled a long list of things to do for the upcoming nuptials. Lana hadn't known that so much had gone into planning a wedding, being as Mac had taken care of every detail of theirs. They'd gotten another five items crossed off the list.

And then came the kisses. Though the make-out session hadn't been initiated by Mac. He'd stood, as though preparing to leave, and that's when she'd reached up and brought his head down to hers.

Mac had always been the initiator in their relationship. Not this night. He hadn't made any moves on her since he'd cornered her in the barn and asked her what she wanted. Had it been a year ago, he would've already made the plans and kept at her until she'd agreed.

Last night, he'd let Lana control the kisses. He'd let Lana determine how tightly she'd wanted to be embraced. He'd let Lana determine when it was time to stop. Although she couldn't remember why she had. She had no idea how she had survived the last two hundred eighty-five days without beginning and ending every day with her lips pressed against Mac's.

He'd left shortly before midnight. Unlike his grand entrance, he'd used the door upon his exit, wanting to make sure the window was secure as she slept. Lana had hated watching him go. But he'd promised to pick her up tomorrow to have dinner at the ranch.

The clock on the bedside table told her she still had half the day before he arrived. Should she call him…?

No. He said he'd be working on the base training camp he and his friends were building. Maybe she could stop by and…?

No. If there was one thing about Mac, he'd never interfered with her career. He'd never stopped by the office unannounced. Nor had he put up much of a fuss when she'd stayed late. The only time he'd put his foot down was for their wedding weekend when Lana had chosen to chase a cat story over him.

Lana stared at the computer screen. She'd finished the first draft of the ranch exposé. From her research on cults, Lana had gathered that many leaders had a number of personality characteristics in common. Cult leaders were often charismatic narcissists who were hierarchal, unpredictable, and engaged in devious carnal activities with their members.

Not a single one of those characteristics described the Purple Heart Ranch's leader, Dylan Banks. The man, who Lana had learned came from great wealth, was incredibly down to earth, personable, kind to animals, and completely head-over-heels for his wife. The only thing he had remotely in common with the Charles Mansons and Jim Joneses of the world was his desire to be separate from the outside world. And, so, the article focused on the exclusivity of the rehabilitation ranch. It high-lighted the speed at which the residents got married. It pointed to the ranch's psychologist, who also was the church pastor that had married every single man and woman in residence.

In short, it was sparse on facts, loose with substance, and the worst thing Lana had ever written.

She opened a new document on *ChatterZine*'s shared cloud drive and began again. The cursor blinked at the word *cult,* and Lana couldn't figure out what to put after it.

After four taps of the delete button, Lana began again. She started with the women she'd met on the ranch. The veterinarian who was the first bride, Maggie Banks, and her animal rescue efforts. Then there was Eva Demonti, who was finishing up a social worker degree that she planned to put to use with the migrant and immigrant workers in the state. Sarai Cannon was a beauty blogger who's work, which focused on inner beauty and self-love at all shapes, sizes, and colors had really impressed Lana. Those three were just the beginning.

While the men were having their bodies healed, it was the women of this ranch that were changing the world around them. Lana's fingers flew across the keyboard. Once she reached the end, she scrolled back to the top having determined the perfect title; *The Purple Rush Brides.*

She knew in her heart that once Reyanna read the new story, the editor-in-chief would change her mind. It was going to make readers feel good at a time when there was so much strife in the world. Lana was still editing and playing with word choice when there was a knock on her door. She glanced at the time and couldn't believe how much had passed.

"Just a minute," she called as she flipped open her suitcase.

"That means you're not dressed because you were still working," came the deep voice on the other side of the door.

Lana sniffed under her armpits. Coming away with a wrinkled nose, she dashed into the bathroom. "What? I can't hear you."

"That means that not only am I right, but you haven't showered either."

Oh, that man.

"Which is why I told you to be ready an hour before you needed to be."

Lana made a face, even though he couldn't see her. She was not normally late. Except when it came to their dates.

"You're making a face at me, aren't you?" Mac laughed. "I'll be outside waiting for you."

Lana hopped into the shower, throwing water and soap all over herself. She did her makeup as she toweled off. Then slipped into a sundress. She was ready in twenty minutes.

When she stepped out, Mac grinned at her. He stood in a fresh pair of jeans and a crisp collared shirt. The man was truly beautiful. He leaned patiently against the truck like he would've waited forever.

He held his hand out to her. There was not a flicker of concern on his face like he didn't doubt she would come to him. It reminded her of the first time he'd proposed. She'd said no. He'd frowned, but a second later, it was as though she hadn't turned him down, and they continued on with their date.

Mac never doubted that she would be his friend, his girlfriend, his wife. Anytime she'd said no or turned him down, he'd bounced back a second later. Not exactly more determined. He always had the same amount of determination. It was as though he'd always known she would say yes.

Eventually.

Because she always did say yes to him. He'd never really poked or prodded her. He'd take her rejection as his due, and then later try again.

Lana took his hand now. He brought her fingers to his mouth and kissed her knuckles. Then he leaned in and kissed her lips. Just a light brush of skin to skin. He didn't press his claim. He didn't need to. Like always, the eventual moment had come.

She was his. She had always been his. She would always be his.

They drove across the town, as Mac told her about his day. Each time he tried to turn the conversation to her, she turned it back on him. She loved his enthusiasm for the camp they were building and wanted to know all about it. She wondered if she could pitch an angle for the story for *ChatterZine*?

All too quickly, they pulled into Vance Ranch, where Mac was staying. Unlike the Purple Heart Ranch, there were cattle dotting the skyline and hardly any people mulling about. She did see a few familiar faces coming down from the porch of the big house.

With her red hair flying behind her, Patty rushed to Lana and swallowed her up in a hug. "It's so good to see you again, Lana."

Behind Patty, Brenda tipped her cowboy hat. "Welcome to Vance Ranch."

"Thank you for having me," said Lana.

"No, thank you for helping Mac out with the wedding plans," said Patty. "He said you helped word the invitations. It's so good to have a writer in the family."

A deep male voice cleared his throat. Keaton offered Lana a tight grin that did not meet his eyes. "So, when are you leaving, Lana?"

Brenda punched her husband in the shoulder. Patty shot her brother a murderous gaze. Mac rested his hand at Lana's lower back. Lana sank into the warmth he provided her.

In truth, it was a fair question. The story she'd been sent to write was pretty much done. She'd have to get back to work. But the thought of leaving Mac did not sit with her.

"I'm not sure," she said finally. "My work here is done, but I don't have a new assignment yet, so…"

Lana let the sentence trail as she chanced a glance at Mac. He didn't meet her gaze. His eyes were instead focused down on her hand. Belatedly, Lana noted she was rubbing the bare flesh of her left ring finger.

"Mac said you were writing a piece about a cult?" said Grizz.

"That's the angle the magazine wanted," Lana admitted. "I found a different angle."

"What angle is that?" asked Patty.

"Instead of focusing on the men, I decided to focus on the women and how they are changing this community. It's a piece about how marriage isn't about convenience, it's about coming together to make you and the world around you stronger."

"That sounds amazing," said Patty. "I can't wait to read it."

The two pairs turned and started up the steps that would lead into the big house. But Lana held back. Mac turned to look at her.

"Hey, Mac?"

"Yeah, Lana."

Lana scratched at the agitated skin on her ring finger. "Can I ask you something?"

"What?"

"Can I have my ring back?"

Mac cocked his head as he regarded her. He reached down into his pocket without looking. "This ring?"

A sense of relief washed over Lana as she saw the gold band. The diamond caught the setting sun and twinkled as if giving her a warm welcome after being apart for long.

"What do you want it for?" Mac asked.

"It's just…" Lana took a deep breath and let it out slowly. "I've been feeling kinda lost without it. And I want it back with me for the rest of my life. Because I never actually took it off. I never intended to. These last couple of days, I realize just how much I need the comfort it brings me. I love that ring. So, can I have it back? Please?"

Mac's face was impassive as he regarded her. Lana was an ace reporter. She knew how to ask open-ended questions to get her subjects to divulge their knowledge. But in this case, Lana only wanted one answer. And she wasn't sure how or if she'd get the answer she craved.

Before Lana could craft a new set of interrogative questions, Mac slipped the ring off his finger and held it out to her.

Lana lifted her left hand, palm out, waiting for him to drop it into her waiting palm. Mac held up the ring, the band hovering just over her fourth finger. Mac aimed the ring, but before it slid over her nail, Lana stopped him.

"Hey, Mac?"

He lifted his gaze. "Yeah, Lana?"

"Do you think... I mean, would you mind..."

"Yeah?"

"Can I still marry you?"

Mac grinned, slipping the ring on her finger. Lana felt that sense of grounding again. She felt like part of her had been missing, not just for a couple of days, for nearly a year.

"Yes, Lana. Yes, you can marry me."

CHAPTER EIGHTEEN

"Don't you think you should give this some thought?"

Mac didn't need to ask Keaton what he was referring to. The man had never liked Lana. Neither him nor Grizz. Probably had to do with the many times Mac had come to his friends moaning about her latest rejection.

"What thought?" said Mac. "This was always the plan."

Truthfully, there had been some thought. Mac had taken a different tactic this time in his pursuit of Lana. He'd waited and let her come to him. Instead of years, instead of months, it had taken only days to get her back. And this time, she'd proposed to him.

He'd barely eaten last night at dinner because his grin had been so huge. His hands had also been more interested in twining with Lana's than handling his fork. His nose had preferred her robust coffee and cream scent, and his eyes could care less for the perfectly seasoned steak and wilting veggies that had also been burned at the edges. Instead of partaking in the meal, he'd been consumed with Lana, his woman, and once again, his fiancée. Soon, she'd be his wife.

"Gotta agree with Keaton," said Grizz. "You're rushing into this."

Mac kicked a foot up against the railing as he looked on at his two friends in utter disbelief. "Says the two men who married their wives within a week. How am I doing anything different from what you two did?"

"You two just have a history," said Keaton, giving his cowboy hat a flick up and off his forehead.

"It's different this time," said Mac. "You have to see that. She came to me. She proposed to me."

Keaton and Grizz shared a look. Mac was getting tired of those shared looks. The two were best friends and had years of history behind them before they'd met Mac. Mac had never begrudged them their friendship and their silently loud looks. He and Lana had their own inside jokes and telling gazes.

"What about the details?" said Keaton. "Have you talked about where you'll live?"

No, they hadn't. But Mac knew better than to ask Lana to give up that job. It was his only competition for her attention. It had come between them the first time. Now she was likely getting a promotion. Would she leave it? Or would she expect him to go back with her?

Mac looked around at the camp. They had sectioned off the training area. Now that the others had arrived, they were making real progress, and the physical fitness obstacles were nearly all erected. They were going to deliver some serious pain to their first set of recruits, and Mac couldn't wait.

Where would Lana fit into this? A life with Lana had been his dream since he was six. This camp had been his dream since Basic Training. Could he give up one dream for another?

"We haven't talked about that," Mac admitted to his friends. "But, we will."

"You think maybe you should have that chat before walking down the aisle this weekend?" said Grizz.

After the congratulations at dinner last night, Mac and Lana had settled on a weekend wedding. The women had cheered. Keaton and Grizz had shared another one of their deafening glances. Rusty, who had unsigned divorce papers in his bag, looked out the window. Spinelli, a confirmed bachelor who planned to never marry, frowned in incomprehension. Only Porco, who was an admitted ladies' man offered up congratulations.

The back door to the big house had opened, and Brenda's brother had come in with two foil-covered dishes, saving the group's arteries from a steak only dinner. No sooner than he put down the buttery veggies did he learn about the good news. Pastor Vance had joked that he could marry them that night.

Mac wouldn't hear of it. He had to have at least a few items in place for his wedding day. He'd dreamed about this moment all his life. And so they'd settled on the weekend.

There was a gazebo on the Purple Heart Ranch. He could have that place decorated in their wedding colors in a few hours. He knew the flower shop needed a few days to order matching flowers. He'd already put in a call with the bridal shop about place settings that were available within that time period.

And then what?

Don't you think you should give this some thought?

Mac had thought about the wedding day. Had he really thought past that? Had he thought about the future that came after the marriage? The fact of the matter was that he didn't see a future without Lana in it. What exactly did that future with Lana look like?

"I'll catch you guys later," Mac said as he climbed into his truck.

His day at the camp wasn't done, but after the hours he'd put in before Rusty, Spinelli, and Porco finally made it, Mac knew he was due a little slack. Especially if he was getting married this weekend.

After driving across town, Mac parked in front of Lana's motel. He started for the front door, but his path took him to Lana's window. When he came to it, he saw that she had left it open for him to climb through.

Peering inside, he saw her sitting at the small desk, her laptop open. Her left hand was raised. Her thumb ran back and forth over the band on her ring finger. She rolled her neck, letting out a sigh that resonated with deep contentment. As her head moved to the side, Mac caught a glimpse of her computer screen. Instead of a page of words, she was looking at a wedding site.

Mac tripped as he stepped over the window, but caught himself before he hit the ground.

"Hey." She grinned up at him.

"Hey," he said straightening.

"Come see." She waved him toward her screen. "I know you've got the decorations for the gazebo covered, but I was thinking about our reception and—"

"You were thinking about our reception?" he parroted.

"Yeah, and I came across this site as I was looking at centerpieces and—"

"You were looking at centerpieces?"

"Why are you repeating everything I say?"

"Who are you, and what have you done with the woman I love?"

Lana rose with a laugh. She threw her arms around him and kissed him. At the press of her lips against his, Mac forgot any other reason he'd come besides embracing this woman and kissing her senseless.

Mac ran his fingers through her hair. He was surprised when all his digits made it through without obstruction. He pulled away and looked at the crown of her head and then at both ears. There was no pen tucked anywhere.

"Do you want to see the centerpieces?" she asked. "If we order them today, we can get the rush shipping. It'll cost a pretty penny, but I think it fits with the base colors you chose."

Lana gave him another tug toward the desk, but Mac pulled her back into his embrace. "We don't have to do this."

"We don't have to do what?" she asked, tilting her head back to gaze at him.

For the first time in years, he had her full attention. This wasn't a break between research projects. Or a stolen moment between fact-checking. Or a quick kiss goodnight before she reopened her laptop and went back to work. She wasn't even working at the moment. She was planning their future together.

"Our wedding doesn't have to be anything fancy," he said.

Now it was Lana who frowned at him. "Who are you, and what have you done with the man I love?"

The laugh escaped his lips before he knew it was there. Mac inhaled a breath of fresh air and got a lungful of coffee and cream.

"You've been dreaming about this day all your life," Lana said. "I want you to have what you want."

"You're what I want," he said. "You're all I've ever wanted. You know that, right? We could elope, and I'd be happy."

Mac pulled away from her. He peered into the mirror over the desk, eyes wide. Putting his hands to his face, he pushed his cheeks around as though he could rearrange his features.

"What are you doing?" she asked.

"Looking to see what I've done with the man you love. He would never say these words."

Lana giggled at his reflection. He grinned back at her. At that moment, his heart filled with so much love for this woman. His friends had been wrong. There was nothing to worry about. Everything was turning out as it should.

"I wanted to talk to you about something," he said.

"What's that?" she asked as she sat down at her computer.

"Where do you want to live after we're married?"

"With you, of course." Lana's grin was cheeky as she clicked a few keys on the keyboard.

Mac came over and rested his hip at the side of the desk. It was a move he'd done many times in their past, but now he didn't feel that he was in competition with the device. "But where would that be?"

Lana looked up at the ceiling as though she were considering the question for the first time. Her hand went to the top of the laptop as though she were going to close it. Then her gaze narrowed on the screen.

"Oh no," she said.

"What?"

"It's the magazine."

Mac's heart skipped a beat. He blinked rapidly, trying to stave off any flashbacks from their last night together before their wedding. "Is it the new job? Did you get it?"

"It's not about the promotion. It's the story."

So, it would be a repeat of the last time. A new story would take her away from him. But why was she looking at her screen with a mix of horror and anger?

"They printed the wrong story," she said.

"What do you mean, the wrong story?"

Mac came to look over her shoulder. He saw the glossy mast of the magazine who had uprooted his life a year ago. The story Lana had accepted at that time had been about cat costumes. The headline on the screen with her byline now read *The Cult of the Purple Rush Brides.*

CHAPTER NINETEEN

"This is not the story that I wrote," Lana said as she looked around the room.

She expected to see eyes narrowed, lips curled, and fingers pointing at her to get out. Most of the residents of the Purple Heart Ranch looked at her with compassion and concern. Many of the women stood, forming a semi-circle around her. But what comforted Lana most, was the man standing at her back.

Mac hadn't said much after reading the story and then driving her here to the ranch. He hadn't left her side for a moment as Dylan Banks gathered the soldiers and their families to hear about the scathing article that defamed their homestead and way of life.

"Well, it is the story that I wrote," Lana said. "My editor sent me here to tell a story of this place being a cult."

Dylan, whose features had been impassive, tightened as he regarded her. His thumb absentmindedly rubbed at the skin of his wife's neck.

"You gotta admit," Lana said, holding up her hands in her own defense, "on paper, this place is unreal. You each came here and found your perfect match in days. I mean, where else does that happen?"

Lana felt Mac's body warm her back. He'd always said that he'd known she was the one from the first moment he'd laid eyes on her.

Lana hadn't felt that way at that moment. But she'd never felt even an ounce of feeling for another living soul that she did for the man who had always been by her side.

Looking out at the crowd of couples, she saw that each man had that same twinkle in his eye when he looked at his wife. Each wife had the calm, confident demeanor of someone who knew they were cared for and would never have a serious worry for the rest of their life.

No, the whole idea of finding that one person in life who you were meant to be with was not so far-fetched.

"That happens here," Lana admitted. "This place is a miracle. You all are so lucky to have found each other. This ranch, and what it is capable of… well, no one would believe the truth of it."

"Yes, they would," said Maggie Banks, holding up a printed sheet of paper. "They would if they read the article you meant to publish."

Lana had printed a number of copies at the motel before rushing over to the ranch. She needed to show them proof of her deeds. But most of the couples hadn't even read it. They appeared to simply take her word for it. Only Maggie and Sarai Cannon had taken one of the copies.

"This is really well written," said Sarai.

Lana took that as a compliment as the woman was a successful blogger. Lana wondered at the freedom to write what she wanted, without waiting for an editor to assign her a story. Or change the story after it was written.

"I'm going to get the magazine to retract it," said Lana.

"There's no need," said Dylan. "If your readers believe what's printed here, then they won't want to visit. That keeps this place clear for those who really need the healing."

"But…they're lies."

Dylan shrugged. The movement was repeated by nearly every person in the room. Lana felt a shudder cross over her own shoulders.

In her short career, Lana hadn't written the most compelling or hard-hitting stories. But they'd always been filled to the brim with facts. It felt wrong to let this story stand as it was.

She turned to look over her shoulder, seeking Mac's support. He still had his hand at her low back. His shoulder bumped hers. But his gaze was out the window. Far off in the distance, she spied the gazebo where they'd be married in just a few days.

"Mac?"

"You're going back, aren't you?" he asked, his gaze still out the window.

"Just for a day. You know I can't let this stand. I'll be back for our wedding. I won't miss that again."

"Are you going to take the promotion?" asked Mac, finally turning his gaze on her.

"What?"

"You got the story. This will be an advancement in your career at the magazine."

Lana set her mouth to say no, but nothing came out. She took a breath and tried again. "After what they did…" She tried to sound indignant. But it came out husky. "I don't know?"

Mac enfolded her into his arms. She collapsed into him, seeking his calm, confident care. All her life, Lana had been fascinated at digging for the truth, uncovering the facts. All which had impacted her ability to take her own real-life story at face value.

She loved this man. She was going to marry him and spend the rest of her life with him. Of that, she was certain. It was a fact.

What she had no idea of was where that left her career?

CHAPTER TWENTY

The bells tinkled as Mac walked into the wedding shop the next morning. Nancy gave him a wave as she tied up another customer's package with a pastel pink bow. Mac liked the woman's company, but he didn't need her help today.

The bell tinkled again as Grizz's large body filled the doorway. His normally stern face looked uncertain as he gazed around at the frills. He wore a cotton camouflage shirt tucked into khakis. His boots pounded the dainty floor, making Mac think the large man would leave cracks behind.

"You really didn't have to come, Grizz," came the trilling voice of his wife.

Grizz held the door open as Patty flitted into the shop. The petite woman dressed in a light blue sundress looked as though she absolutely belonged in the bridal shop. Just not with her husband.

"This is important to you," Grizz growled. "So, I'm here."

"Well, it is *our* wedding," said Patty.

Grizz shrugged his massive shoulders and then hunched when he saw he was standing near china. "A wedding is just a party."

Both Patty and Mac frowned at that cool assessment. Grizz didn't appear to notice as he sidestepped an arrangement of cake toppers.

"It's a ceremony where the bride and groom make a promise to each other," said Grizz. "I've already made my promise. My focus is on building you a house where we'll raise our family and spend the rest of our lives."

Patty grinned up at him like he hung the moon. Grizz just might be tall enough to reach the rock. He enfolded Patty in his large arms and bent down to meet her kiss.

Behind them, Keaton and Brenda walked in arm in arm. When Keaton saw his sister wrapped up in his best friend's embrace, he groaned.

"You need to get started on that house soon," Keaton moaned. "My delicate constitution can't handle you defiling my sister on a daily basis."

Patty broke the kiss and gave her brother a wicked smile. "Sometimes, twice a day."

Keaton made a choked sound and turned for the door. Brenda snaked her hand around his arm and steered him back into the shop.

"Let's get this over with," huffed Keaton. "I've compiled a wedding checklist from two of the most reputable wedding planning sites. This shouldn't take us long."

Brenda pinched the bridge between her nose. Her husband was a planner. Keaton might not like the idea of picking colors and patterns, but now that Mac had helped with that part, it was simply logistics left, which Keaton excelled at.

Brenda shot Mac an imploring glare. Mac chuckled and shook his head. No way was Mac getting anywhere near Keaton when he had his pen and notepad out. Mac had spent enough time with the man in the Army. Mac had gotten out for a reason. At the top of the list was Keaton's notepad.

Mac kept to the sidelines as he watched the two couples consider, bicker, and compromise over wedding plans. This was how it should be; bride and groom working together to plan the day that would start the rest of their lives together.

Mac looked down at his phone. Lana hadn't called. He knew she was likely still on the plane. He still had no idea what she planned to do once she got to her office. He had no idea if she would take the job or tell them to shove it.

Would she even come back to him?

Would she run again?

A text alert beeped on his phone. Mac looked down to see Lana's name.

Just landed.

That was it. No, *I love yous.* No hint of what she was planning to do. No assurance that she would come back to him.

"Mac, you good?" said Keaton.

Mac looked up to see his friends close around him. Keaton and Grizz had closed around him the last time he'd been left at the altar. They'd closed around him each time Lana had turned down his proposal of marriage. They had the look in their eyes that it was happening again.

"Everything all right with Lana?" asked Grizz.

"Yeah," Mac held up his phone as though it were proof. "She just landed."

"When will she be back?" asked Keaton.

Mac had to focus on releasing the tension in his clenched jaw. "This weekend, obviously."

Keaton and Grizz looked at one another, sharing another of their silent, speaking glances.

"She'll be back," Mac insisted.

His friends said nothing.

Mac felt the tension in his chest tighten. His fingers clenched into fists. The walls of the tiny shop began to close in on him.

"Everything good for this weekend?" said Patty, looking up from one of Nancy's pattern books. "You and Lana need a hand with any of your plans?"

"No," said Mac, backing toward the door. "Everything is good. I'm going to go for a walk."

CHAPTER TWENTY-ONE

The clacking on keyboards made Lana wince as she walked into the building. She only just stopped herself from waving her hands in front of her face as though she were warding off a swarm of bees. The red ink on white sheets of paper made her eyes hurt, and she had to squint. The slicing sound of scissors snipping away at images made her hackles rise. And the pace of the people rushing about made her want to keep still.

Back on the ranch, the people and even the animals had all moved slower. No one rushed. No one shouted. Lana rubbed her thumb down her ring finger and was instantly calmed.

"Hunt, you're back," shouted Reyanna from across the room. "Good. Get in here. I have another story for you."

"Actually…" but Reyanna had already ducked inside her office. Lana ducked and twisted around her colleagues until she was standing before the editor's desk. "I want to talk with you about the last story."

"Great work, Hunt." Reyanna's eyes lit up as she took a swig of her coffee. After she swallowed a grin lit her face. "Our readers are eating it up."

Lana knew the readers would eat up the sensationalized drivel that she'd penned about the Purple Heart Ranch. She'd been hoping to stretch them to eat something more hearty, like the story of healing and strength and love that she'd crafted.

"That wasn't the story I'd hoped to publish," Lana said.

"Oh, I saw the other one," Reyanna frowned into her coffee. "I figured that was the first draft, or you'd gotten stuck watching the Hallmark Channel out in cow country. I didn't even read all the way through it."

"That was the story."

"Cow country?"

"No, the Hallmark Channel. I mean, the touchy-feely story. The article about the strong women and the power of community."

Reyanna studied Lana as though she had grown horns on her head and spots on her chest. "I think there may have been something in that sweet tea you were drinking."

"Sweet tea is a southern drink."

Reyanna's lips paused in a small O with the coffee cup hovering just at her lower lip. "And?"

"Montana is in the Midwest."

"Whatever." Reyanna sat the mug down and ruffled through some papers. Once she found what she wanted, she handed the documents to Lana.

"What's this?" asked Lana.

"The promotion. It's yours."

Lana looked down at the paperwork. It was a contract. At the top of the legalese, in bold, was her new title, Features Writer. There was also a five-digit salary that was closer to six figures than Lana had dared hope. It was everything she'd been working for.

"I need you on this new story," said Reyanna, reclaiming her mug and taking a sip. "There's that reality star, Betsey Blade, who's coming out of rehab."

Lana knew of the star. The woman had been on television since she was a child on the talent circuit. The public had followed her dating life, her breakups, and now her break down. From all reports, it looked like Betsey was on the up and up.

"You want an exclusive on how she's changing her life around for the better?" asked Lana.

"No." Reyanna downed her last drop of coffee and tossed the container in the trash. "I want you there for when she falls off the wagon again. Our readers will love it."

Lana set the papers down on the edge of the desk. With a light gust of wind, they'd easily fall into the bin atop the empty coffee mug.

"You'll have to be there this weekend," said Reyanna. "I'm sure that won't be a problem."

"I can't this weekend."

"What do you mean you can't?"

"I'm getting married."

Reyanna's brows drew together. "I thought you already were married."

Lana should've already been married. She should've shown up that weekend a year ago. She shouldn't have left Mac this morning.

"I'm getting married on Saturday," said Lana, standing. "And I'm not signing the contract. I'll hand in my resignation before the end of the day."

Lana didn't bother offering Reyanna an explanation. She didn't think the editor would understand the angle of her love story with Mac. Neither did Lana bother clearing her desk. There was nothing there she needed. She had no idea where she'd find another job as a reporter. But she knew for certain that sensationalism wasn't the kind of stories she wanted to tell. She'd figure this out. She and Mac would figure this out together.

She did make a quick run to her home. But she packed light. She could send for this stuff later after she'd settled into life on the ranch. There was just one item that she needed to pack. Then she booked the next flight out.

She couldn't wait to tell Mac. She couldn't wait to see him. She couldn't wait to kiss him. She couldn't wait to spend the rest of her life with him.

CHAPTER TWENTY-TWO

The sun shone done on the gazebo that overlooked the small lake that bordered the Purple Heart Ranch and Vance Ranch. Woven around the structure were flowers of blushing pink and ripe plum. The flowers had come in last night, and Mac finished arranging them early this morning. The chairs were set. The altar in place. All that was missing was the bride.

It was nearing forty-eight hours since she'd left, and Lana hadn't called. She hadn't texted since she'd told him that she'd landed. That was two days ago. Mac's phone sat restless and silent in his back pocket.

He stood before the gazebo, where they were to be married later this afternoon. He tilted his face up to the sun, trying to blind the flashbacks from the last time he found himself in this predicament.

Perhaps it was the sun that did the trick. The bright lights washed out the memories of that day. The shinning rays slid down his throat, leaving a hollowness in his chest. Mac was numb in the warmth.

For his first wedding day, Mac had had time to let everyone know that Lana wasn't coming. This time, he only had hours. He didn't move. He took a few minutes to let that sink in.

She wasn't coming.

The sun was higher in the sky now. There was a light breeze picking up. The day was a bit overcast. It looked like rain would threaten.

And still, his cellphone was silent. Not a word. Again.

She wasn't coming.

There was a part of Mac that worried that something had gone wrong. Could she be somewhere hurt? But he knew in his heart that Lana was fine. He could sense in his heart that, once again, she'd made her decision.

She wasn't coming.

Mac would not wait for her. He could no longer hope that this next time when he chased after her, things would be different. Because everything was the same. He was standing at the altar, and she was not coming.

"Here early, I see?" said Pastor Vance.

Mac had never been much of a religious guy. Sure, he went to church on the requisite holidays when he was with his family. He was always in the pews on Sundays during his summers with his grandparents. But other than that, he had little to no interaction with pastors.

Pastor Vance was different. For one, the man was the same age as Mac. He still had all his hair and teeth and didn't spend any time shouting down at Mac with a disapproving glare in his narrowed gaze. Every other word out of Walter's mouth wasn't a prayer or biblical verse, even though he carried a black Bible in his hand. The man was the most down to earth, practical, and patient man Mac had ever met. It was a shame he wouldn't be delivering Mac's vows.

"I don't think there's going to be a wedding today," Mac admitted. "I seem to have misplaced my bride."

Vance pursed his lips. He took a deep inhale through his flaring nostrils as he regarded the purple and pink decorations.

"I don't think Lana wants to get married."

"No?" said Vance. "It sure looked to me that she did that night she proposed to you."

It had looked to Mac that she did as well. He thought he'd done everything right this time. He hadn't pushed or prodded. He'd let her take the lead. So, how had he ended up back alone before an altar?

"Is this about the article that she wrote?" asked Pastor Vance.

Mac didn't answer. He'd read the original article, the scathing exposé full of misdirections and half-truths. When he'd seen those words, Mac had feared Lana had grown into a stranger who he wouldn't be able to respect.

Then he read the second draft. There, in the metaphors and prose she'd penned about strength and courage, was the woman he loved, the writer who should be winning awards. The writer he thought she wanted to be. But if that revision wasn't going to get her promoted, would she revert to the original draft?

"I have a feeling the story is not over for you two," said Pastor Vance. "Plus, I placed a bet that this wedding would be happening today."

Mac wanted to laugh, but his chest felt too constricted. The betting pool about who would get wed and when in this town was a true racket. Mac wondered what the odds on him and Lana had been? Whatever the odds, it looked like neither he nor Pastor Vance would win today.

He looked around at all his decorations, all his plans. He had wanted the wedding of his dreams. But at the end of the day, all that had truly mattered to him was that he had his dream girl at his side. His heart ached because he knew that he would go through this all again if Lana hinted at even a glimmer of hope that they could be together.

Lana Hunt was a part of him, his heart, his soul. There would never be another woman for him.

The sun had reached higher in the sky. Guests would be arriving soon. And she still hadn't called.

Because she wasn't coming.

CHAPTER TWENTY-THREE

The moment the Unfasten Your Seatbelt light went off, Lana shot out of her chair. She didn't have time to count to ten and wait for the kid beside her to wiggle his way out of his seat. She didn't have the patience to take deep breaths when the pregnant woman across the aisle waddled to standing.

From her economy seat in the middle of the plane, Lana wanted to shout that it was her wedding day, and she was going to be late. Though it was clear to everyone there that that might be the case. Lana had stopped home to grab one item; her wedding dress from a year ago. It was now rumpled from sitting in the middle seat for eight hours.

When she'd boarded the plane last night, they'd had to be diverted after a passenger had a heart attack thirty minutes after takeoff. They sat on the tarmac for another few hours before being cleared for take-off again. Only to have a mechanical issue while they were taxiing.

Back to the terminal they went to deplane. By then, Lana's cell phone was dead. She'd rooted in her bag for her charger, but it wasn't there. Had she even packed it when she left the motel? She knew she had an extra back at her desk at *ChatterZine*, but that wasn't her desk anymore.

While sitting in the stalled plane earlier, Lana had decided she was going to go freelance. Either she was going to write the stories that meant something, or she wasn't going to write at all. Right now, she was pretty sure her first report would be a scathing piece on the perils of domestic air travel.

By the time she got booked on a new flight, it was the next day. The shops with cell phone charges were opening their doors just as the voice over the intercom called to announce that her flight was boarding. Weighing her odds, Lana decided to grab her seat rather than grabbing a charger.

Mac would wait for her. He always waited for her. And she was coming for him. Though she was cutting it close.

Halfway through the flight, Lana rose from her middle seat, stepped over the wiggling kid, grabbed her carry on from the overhead compartment, and headed to the bathroom. Once she hit the ground, she would have no time to spare, so she dressed for the part she wanted most in life.

The entire plane stopped and stared when she emerged in her wedding gown.

As a reporter, Lana had always tried to blend into the background of her writing. She wanted the facts to shine. But today, the fact was that she was getting married to the man she'd loved for more than half her life. Today, she was finally writing the story she was meant to tell.

If she could just get off this blasted plane!

Racing through arrivals in pumps, her suitcase rolling in pace behind her, Lana finally reached the parking terminal where she'd left her rental car. Her phone was still dead. Time was ticking away.

She knew Mac would be beside himself. She just had to hope he believed in their love enough, believed in her enough, to wait just one more hour.

Lana tore out of the parking lot and onto the highway. It was a short drive to the ranch. Soon, the long stretch of highway narrowed into a two-lane road with pastures as far as the eye could see. The sight was a far cry from the concrete city she'd been in just two days ago. Something in Lana settled as the green and brown zoomed past her. There was still a sense of urgency to get to Mac, but the heaviness that hung over her shoulders sank down into the seat.

Just a few more miles, and she saw the sign for The Purple Heart Ranch. She made her way into the welcoming gate, passing the pastel flowers that were in full bloom. She drove the car down the dirt path that led right to the gazebo, where she would say her vows to the man she could no longer spend a single day without. She had expected a small crowd gathered. Instead, she saw Keaton and Grizz dismantling the decorations.

"Stop that," Lana said, hopping out of the car.

The two men looked at her agape, their mouths hung open, their gazes going wide. Then they looked at each other. First Keaton's brows raised, arching high as though forming a question. In answer, Grizz lowered one brow in a grimace. Around them, the purple and pink streamers that they had been pulling down hung limp in the silence.

"Why do you look so surprised?" Lana demanded. She didn't wait for their answer. "Where is everyone? Where is Mac?"

"Mac is back at the ranch packing," said Keaton.

"Packing?" said Lana. "To go where?"

Neither man answered. They just exchanged another of those speaking glances between themselves.

"We're supposed to be getting married," said Lana.

"You're running a little late," said Keaton, coming down the gazebo stairs. "We thought you weren't coming. Can you blame us?"

"Am I never going to live that down with you two?" Lana looked between Mac's two best friends. They'd never had this out. Now was as good a time as ever. "You two know how he is. His parents named him Mac for a reason. He can be just like a Mack truck when there's something he wants."

"No one forced you, Lana," said Grizz.

"No," Lana agreed. "That's the point. I had to fight to have a say in my own relationship. Mac decided we were gonna be friends, and then date, and then get married. He just sped along, and I was expected to— what? Sit quietly, and enjoy the ride?"

The two men shared another of those glances. But there were no eyebrow questions raised this time. Both Keaton and Grizz pursed their lips as they regarded one another, as though they were actually hearing what Lana had to say.

"I told Mac no so many times because I wasn't ready when he was."

"But you are today?" asked Grizz.

Now it was Lana who raised her brow in answer to his question. To make sure they understood her point, she pursed her lips and gave a decisive nod of her head.

Grizz relaxed his shoulders. But Keaton was still tense.

"What about the job?" asked Keaton.

"They offered me the promotion," Lana said. "But, they've driven me toward places I didn't want to go in my writing. So, I quit."

When Lana looked up, she saw something she never thought she'd see. Grizz's mouth was stretched wide in a rare smile. Keaton rubbed at his chin with a thoughtful look on his face. It wasn't exactly a smile, but it was close enough.

"Come on," said Keaton. "We'll give you a ride."

CHAPTER TWENTY-FOUR

ac looked at his reflection in the mirror. The man staring back at him looked tired but determined. Behind him, he spied the tux jacket he'd picked out for his wedding today. Instead of tossing it into the suitcase that was open on the bed, Mac reached over and shoved the jacket in a bag for donations along with the collared shirt, tie, and pants he'd planned to wear today. It wasn't likely he'd ever wear the things.

He sat the bag of donations down on the floor next to the trash bin. On the bedside table, he saw the wedding planner book he'd had for years. The binder page opened to patterns featuring the colors he'd chose so long ago. The blush and plum really were the best colors for him and Lana. Two things that you wouldn't think go together, but complemented each other when side by side.

Mac closed the book. It was used so it wouldn't go in with the donations. Instead, he dropped the now useless book into the trash bin.

What was between those pages no longer mattered. Not when the woman who had stolen his heart wasn't invested in the story there. Mac was finally facing facts. Pressuring Lana Hunt to do something when she wasn't ready was a recipe for disaster. The only thing that had ever worked was waiting until she was ready.

Mac heaved a heavy sigh as he closed his suitcase. He'd waited more than half of his life for this woman. He had no doubt he would continue waiting for the rest of it. It was his only choice because he knew that he would love her every day that he drew breath on this earth.

The sound of something tapping on glass brought his attention around. Mac glanced up first into the mirror before him. He had to blink a few times to be certain he was seeing what he thought he was seeing. Still not trusting his eyes, he whirled around to look directly at the window.

And there she was.

Lana was outside his window. Her hair was a bird's nest of a mess. Her makeup was smudged at every corner of her eyes. There were bags above her cheeks as though she hadn't slept all night. But all of those details paled in comparison to the most glaring detail.

When she stepped over the windowsill, Lana stood in a wedding dress. But not just any wedding dress. It was the wedding dress they'd picked out last year. And, despite the mess of her hair and makeup, she looked breathtakingly beautiful.

"Hi," she said, out of breath.

"Hey," he said. Mac had trouble forcing the word out. His eyes were so wide on his face, they made it tough for his mouth to open and form words.

"Can I come in?" she asked.

The question was a moot point as she was already inside. Mac was able to nod his head. Any further words eluded him.

He'd thought she wasn't coming. He'd thought the wedding was off. But there she stood, on the day of their second wedding, looking stunningly disheveled in the dress meant for their first time.

"I'm late," she said.

Again, Mac could only nod.

"I would've called, but there was a heart attack, and no charger, and then the plane broke."

The words coming from her mouth made no sense. It didn't matter much to Mac. He couldn't move his gaze from her lips. He wondered if, when they stopped, if he could kiss her. Signs pointed to probably since she had climbed into his window in a wedding dress on their wedding day.

Lana wrung her hands as she worried her lips. Her thumb rubbed back and forth over the engagement ring on her finger. She looked worried and unsure of herself. Two things that Mac didn't identify with this strong woman.

"You're leaving?" she asked.

Mac blinked, taking his gaze from her mouth and lifting it to her eyes. Lana wasn't looking at him. She was looking behind him at the suitcase on his bed.

"Yeah," he said.

"Mac, please don't." Her face crumpled and tears glistened at the corners of her eyes.

Mac had her in his arms in an instant. The sob that escaped her lips pierced his heart. He tucked Lana under his chin so that her cheek rested right against his chest. That feeling of clicking sounded all throughout his body. Mac recognized the sound as gears fitting together and not a clock that he needed to rush. He would give Lana all the time she needed until she was ready to be with him.

"Please, don't give up on me, Mac."

Give up on her? Where did that come from?

"I quit. I quit *ChatterZine*."

"Why would you do that?" he asked. "You loved that job."

"No, I love you," she said. "I may have figured this out late, but I figured it out. I've been chasing other peoples' stories for so long that I didn't stop to look at my own. It's you. You're my story. My beginning, my middle, my end. The facts of my life don't make sense without you in it."

Mac's lids lowered as he listened to Lana's heartfelt truth. His mouth had gone slack from her confession. So, he still had trouble making any coherent words.

Lana pulled away from him, looking up at him with tear-filled eyes. "Please, don't leave. Stay and give me another chance."

Mac lifted his hand to wipe at the tear trailing down her face. His fingers shook as he did so. "I was leaving the ranch to come to you."

Lana blinked. And then blinked a few times again as though the words weren't coming into focus. "You were coming for me?"

"Of course, I was coming for you. I always come for you."

She blinked a few more times. Slowly now, as though everything was coming clear. Then, without warning, she reached up to him and pulled him down to her lips.

Lana's kiss was bruising, claiming. Mac had no trouble following her lead. He would follow this woman to the ends of the earth.

"You still want to marry me?" she asked when they came up for air, her voice breathless.

"I told you when we were six; you're the only girl for me, Lana Hunt."

Her smile was so bright it dried the tears in her eyes. Then she nodded, her features going business-like. Stepping away from him, she reached up to her hair, where she usually kept a pen. Finding none there, she looked around his room.

"We can start planning for our third and final wedding." She grabbed a stub of a pencil and an old receipt from his bedside table. "We can make it as big and grand as you want. We can invite as many people. No expense will be spared. And I will be there by your side, planning every color, every place setting, everything."

Mac took the pencil and scrap of paper from her hand. "We don't need a new date. We can do it now."

"Keaton and Grizz pulled all the decorations down and—"

"None of that matters," he said. "All that matters is the promise we make to each other to always come for each other for the rest of our lives."

Lana leaned her forehead against Mac. She sighed a deep, contented sigh as she said, "I promise you that."

"I promise you, too." Mac bent his head and sealed that solemn vow with a gentle kiss. "But, I do want this made legal, so…"

Mac pulled away from Lana. He took the few steps to his bedroom door. Turning the knob, he prepared to shout downstairs. But when he opened the door, he saw that there was no need.

Brenda and Keaton, Patty and Grizz, Porco, Rusty, and Spinelli all stood in the upstairs hall. Mac looked beyond them to see Pastor Vance leaning against the railing, Bible in hand.

"Pastor Vance, you said if we needed you?"

The pastor made his way forward, an expectant smile on his face. "It sounded to me like the two of you got through the important parts. I couldn't have written any better vows myself. All that's left for me to do is pronounce you man and wife."

Mac turned back to Lana in her crumpled wedding dress. He was barefoot and in jeans and a t-shirt. It might not be the wedding he'd planned, but it fulfilled his every dream.

EPILOGUE

"Hot, hot, hot!"

David Porco tossed the sizzling piece of bacon from one hand to another. The grease singed the fingers of first his right and then left hand, and so he popped the strip of sweet meat into his mouth.

"Ow -hot." Chew. "Hiss -hot." Chew.

"What do you expect, Porco?" said Mac. "You pulled it straight out of the frying pan."

"Worth it," said Porco. Bacon was his first love. It had narrowly won that position after a long hard-fought battle with honeyed ham. Though Porco often cheated on bacon and ham with pork chops. A little bit of fire was nothing to keep the man from his calling.

Mac shook his head as he regarded his friend, but he smiled as he sipped at his steaming cup of coffee. His gaze didn't linger for long on Porco. It slid to his wife.

Lana Kenzie's head was down, her gaze focused on her notepad. The cup of coffee at her side had long gone tepid. The two were preparing to leave for their honeymoon in just a few hours. Which was why Lana's attention was on her pad.

"You need to hurry and finish that story," said Mac, toying with the pen tucked behind her ear. "We agreed you would not be working on our honeymoon."

Lana tore her gaze away from her words and gazed adoringly at her husband. "Don't worry, I won't. I just need to fix the ending before I submit it. Then I'm all yours."

"You've always been all mine." Mac went in and nipped her lower lip for a kiss.

Porco grabbed another strip of bacon from the pan. He had to repeat the tossing of the sizzling meat from hand to hand again. He allowed this strip to cool as he walked out the back door of the house.

The big house was filled with newlyweds kissing and canoodling in every corner. Porco was thankful he lived across the field in one of the bungalows typically inhabited by the ranch hands. He, Spinelli, and Rusty took up the rooms in the three-bedroom domicile. But Porco had to keep coming back to the big house; it's where all the food was.

He didn't mind maneuvering around embracing couples to get to the fridge. He had every hope that he would be an obnoxious, embracing newlywed someday soon. He just had to find her first.

Since he'd come to this town, he'd begun looking in earnest since he planned to stay here for many years. He was ready to settle down. He just needed to find the right girl, the one who had that certain spark.

"This is absolute manure!"

Porco turned to see Brenda storming his way. Her husband and brother in tow.

Keaton looked down at a stack of papers with concern on his brow. Pastor Vance looked as though he was praying for patience.

"Just who does he think he is to tell me what I can and can't put on my lands," said Brenda.

"Well, Bren," said Vance, "it could just be a huge missed steak."

Brenda's green eyes flared. Keaton winced and gave his brother in a law a subtle shake of the head.

"You know," said the pastor. "Because they're vegans and you're a cattle rancher. I'm just trying to lighten the mood."

"What's going on?" Porco sidled up beside Keaton, giving the siblings a wide berth.

"It's the neighbors again," said Keaton.

As far as Porco knew, the neighbors to the Vance Ranch were the Purple Heart Ranch next door. The two ranches got along fine, often hosting barbecues on each other's land.

"The commune vegan commune next door," Keaton clarified. "They've filed an injunction to try and stop Bren from spraying fertilizer on the pasture that borders their land. Apparently, they're trying to get an organic certification for their vegetables."

Porco turned his nose up at the mention of the word vegetables. He didn't see the need for the food group. Cows and pigs ate grass. He ate their meat. Therefore, he got a daily dose of vegetables.

Too bad his parents had never bought into that argument and kept putting broccoli and carrots on his plate.

"I'm going to fight this, Walter," Brenda was saying. "I've been playing nice for too long. If it's a feud those overgrown flower children want, it's a feud they'll get."

Brenda stormed off. Heaving deep sighs, Walter and Keaton trudged after her. Porco held back. He pitied anyone who stood in that woman's way. He'd seen Brenda square off against a bull. It was the bull who took a step back. Whoever these vegetable farmers were, he did not envy them. Especially, if they grew the hated foodstuffs.

Porco popped the last piece of bacon in his mouth. He headed in the opposite direction. He had a date to get ready for. Maybe tonight he'd finally feel that spark that told him that the woman across from him was the one.

Porco had felt plenty of tingles with the women he'd dated over the past few weeks. The girl he'd be seeing tonight had a fire inside her, and she'd left him feeling warm after their last date. Who knew? Maybe Rosalind would turn out to be the one for him.

Rosalind is not the one for this Romeo.
Porco is about to get his first sight of the girl next door.
Her name is Jules.

She's one of those overgrown flower children who live on the organic, vegan farm next door.
She grows soybeans, loves vegetable dishes, ...and has a pet pig.
Turnt he page for
The Rancher takes his Star Crossed Love!

THE RANCHER TAKES HIS STAR CROSSED LOVE

THE RANGERS OF PURPLE HEART RANCH
BOOK 4

CHAPTER ONE

"Rosalind just broke up with me."

David Porco flicked at the propeller of the drone at his feet. The rotor gave a buzzing whirl of sympathy at his pain. The whir was short-lived as the drone wasn't powered on. Without the engines in gear, the blades barely made a full rotation. Had the device been ignited, Porco was certain he'd get a more resounding response from the drone. He was barely getting a hum out of his friend.

"Didn't you tell me you were going to break up with her two days ago?" Jordan Spinelli's fingers picked over the fuses in the exposed belly of the drone's controller box. "Because you no longer felt *the spark.*"

Spinelli's last two words were said with a sneer of his lips and roll of his eyes. The man's mind was far too scientific to believe in the power of true love, or what Porco's mom called the spark. The flare of feeling across the spine and down to the fingertips. The rise in temperature that wasn't hotter than a fever, and at the same time cooled the entire body. That spark was what let her know that Porco's father had been the man of her dreams. His father had admitted to the feeling too.

Nelson Porco had told his son that the spark had been a racing of his heart. He'd heard his pulse pounding in his ears. His mouth had gone dry, but he'd drooled all the same when he'd caught sight of Hailey Baker, the woman who would just a few days later become his wife.

Porco had been chasing that feeling since he learned that thumping in his chest was called his heart. Anytime it raced or skipped a beat, he investigated the cause to determine if it was the spark. When he'd sat next to Willow Conway in his parents' basement, his heart had raced, but they had been watching a horror movie at the time. He hadn't been scared of the monster rushing at the victims with his bloody blade. No, Porco had caught sight of Annalee Walton sitting - on the floor, and his pulse had quickened to her.

In the skate park, he'd caught Shawna Welsh watching him do a kickflip, and his heart had raced. When he landed, Terri Clarke had winked at him, and he'd drooled after her for a couple of days.

He'd chased that spark of feeling from girl to girl. Sometimes it was strong, and he'd feel heat down in the base of his spine. Other times it was a weak tingling in his fingertip. It was never all-consuming, and the feeling never lasted like it had with his parents.

With Rosalind, his mouth had gone dry, and he'd drooled over the woman at the same time. She was a looker, easily the prettiest girl in the whole town. Although Paige Wiley, who had just moved to town, was giving Rosalind a run for the money in the looks department. Porco had chatted Paige up the other day while he was in town. He'd gotten her number and had asked her out for the weekend. He'd planned to break up with Rosalind before the date, of course. But then Rosalind had gone and dumped him first.

"Why are we even having this conversation?" asked Spinelli. "Just move onto the next one like you always do."

"Like I always do?"

"You've dated three different women since we've been here."

Here was the Vance Ranch in a small town in Montana. Though Porco wasn't sure how the town could be called small when a small ranch spanned farther than the eye could see. Porco and five of his Army Ranger buddies had opened a bootcamp training facility that bordered the Vance Ranch and the Purple Heart Ranch, a rehabilitation ranch for wounded veterans and their families.

The original plan had been to set up living quarters on the Purple Heart Ranch. That was, until the soldiers had learned of a little loophole that bade any man or woman who wanted to live on the Purple Heart Ranch for more than three months be bound in holy matrimony.

The regulation hadn't scared Porco. He wanted to get married. But only to the right girl. Whom he'd only find once he waded through all the firecracker dates and found his final, life-starting Big Bang.

"Your problem is you're always looking at the grass on the other side," Spinelli was saying. "You need to tend your own yard first."

"Well, that's what we're out here doing, isn't it."

Spinelli closed the drone's controller box and handed the device to Porco. There were two drones on the ground, each housed a canister at its underbelly. The canisters were filled with chemical fertilizer for the barren pasture before them.

The two Army Rangers were helping out the owners of Vance Ranch. One of those owners being their former unit commander. Though they weren't on the lands of the Purple Heart Ranch, Sergeant Anthony Keaton had married Brenda Vance the same day he'd met the female rancher. It had been a marriage of convenience at first, one that allowed practical-minded Brenda to cut through the red tape of transferring land ownership of a parcel of Vance Ranch to tactical minded Keaton. Those two individuals had burned through their practical-tactical motivations a few moments after they said *I do* and were fast-tracked on the path to love.

Porco had asked Keaton what it felt like the moment he saw Brenda. Keaton had said he'd seen stars. Spinelli had pointed out the fact that Keaton had just been in a car accident with a ramming bull when he'd looked up to see Brenda racing towards him on a horse. As far as Porco was concerned, that still proved that there was a spark when The One stepped onto life's stage.

"Why'd she do it?" asked Spinelli. "Why'd she break up with you?"

Porco just stopped himself from asking Who? Had he forgotten about Rosalind so quickly? "She said I have a short attention span. She said she wanted to get out before I dropped her."

Spinelli pushed his lower lip up to meet his upper lip as though he could fathom that reason. "She has a point."

Spinelli had a scientific mind. He'd likely think a woman's spine was a looker or her brain had the tempting curves of a backroad. It wasn't that smarts weren't Porco's speed. Nothing made his heart skip like the sparkle of a woman's eyes. Nothing made his hand's itch more than running his fingers through lush curls. Nothing made his mouth water more than the tug of a plump, heart-shaped lip just begging to be kissed.

He'd felt all those things with Rosalind. If given time, could those flares feed into a bigger fire? "There was something there. We did have a spark of... something."

"You and that spark. You do realize that if you light a match, eventually it burns out."

That was Spinelli. The man always had to get scientific and ruin the emotions of the situation.

"Forget about Rosalind," Spinelli called as he mounted his horse, the controller to his drone in one hand, the reins in the other. "We have work to do. Remember, don't get too close to the border. That's the Verona Commune. We don't want any issues with them. Their crops are organic vegetables and..."

Spinelli droned on with his scientific talk as Porco mounted his own horse. They'd promised Brenda that they'd get the west pasture fertilized. The cattle ranch operation was growing, and this field had been running fallow too long. If the expansion was going to continue, they needed this field to produce so the cows could graze.

With a flick of his thumb, the drone lifted up into the sky. Porco kept himself and his mare a good distance behind the craft. The fertilizer wasn't toxic to humans, but he wasn't interested in having the chemicals for breakfast. He'd already had two plates of bacon. If he was lucky, there'd still be some on the stove when he got back.

It might have been a coincidence that he'd been born with that last name. Or it may have been a divine plan. Whatever it was, it was a happy accident that David Porco had grown to love all things pork.

Thinking of the greasy, crispy, sweet delightfulness that was bacon, Porco noticed too late that the drone had veered slightly off course. The craft hovered just over the border, where a wooden fence divided the two ranches. But the fence wasn't necessary to identify the boundary. The grass on the other side was definitely lusher, greener.

The drone flew for another few yards over the lush pasture, raining down the chemical compound. Porco gave the controller a couple of whacks until finally, the drone obeyed his commands and flew straight.

From his vantage point atop the horse, Porco couldn't see any damage that the drone had left on the fields. Just a small spray of fertilizer. With the overgrown weeds in the field, he doubted any of the hippies on the commune would even notice.

No harm, no foul.

He turned his horse away from the green pastures of the neighbors and continued on his journey. His mind was set on how to win back the woman who just might, maybe, possibly be the one. But first, he'd have to call and cancel his date with Paige.

CHAPTER TWO

"Ay, me." Jules Capulano sighed as she looked down at the thriving plants in her garden.

Her woeful sigh wasn't over the abundance of green life surrounding her. Her beloved soybeans had grown nearly tall enough to reach her knees. The leaves stretched out as though to wave at her. The bulbous pods hung heavy as though the beans inside were ready to drop and harvest themselves.

Life was good for the crops on the Verona Commune. Her belly was full every meal from the fresh fruits and vegetables her fellow vegans harvested each day. Her ears were filled with the laughter of the third generation of children running wild and barefoot across acres and acres of land. It was only her heart that was empty.

"Ay, me." She sighed again.

"Oh, no," came a withering sigh that mirrored the tone and tenor of Jules's own voice. "Are you about to enter into a longwinded monologue filled with Elizabethan slang?"

Jules pushed her long, interwoven locks back off her forehead to look up at Romey. Unlike Jules's coiled twists that reached down her back toward the earth, her sister's hair was short and springy, her curls reaching for the sunlight. Romey's butterscotch skin had tanned to caramel under the sun's constant attention.

Since their shared birthday, the Capulano twins woke up with the sun and spent all day in its rays, coming in only once the moon rained its dark light on their parade. While out in the fields, Jules would sprinkle flower seeds as she danced barefoot in the dirt. Where Romey would trough equidistant lines and space out her seedlings in neat little rows.

Their planting methods weren't the only thing different about the twins. Although born identical, it had always been easy to tell the two apart. Jules dressed in colorful sundresses every day of her life, where Romey tugged on funny t-shirts and shorts.

Today's graphic tee displayed two atoms. The bubble over the first element said *I lost an electron*. The second element asked, *Are you positive?*

"If you're going to recite Shakespeare, at least cite *Cymbeline*," said Romey. "There's science in that play."

Jules had heard enough of that little-known Shakespearian play recited by Romey and their historian father, who specialized in the Elizabethan era, when she was younger. The play mentioned a few references to cosmology, which the two would debate endlessly on whether the playwright had read Galileo. Jules retreated to the corner of their cottage home, preferring to read the bard's sonnets instead.

"There's romance, too," Jules insisted. Though she quickly regretted taking the bait.

"Sure there is; adultery, incest, attempted rape, attempted murder, more lies, and deception. I keep telling you, romance belongs on the page and not in real life. That stuff could get you killed. You should be practical about these things."

Practical? Nothing in their lives was practical. Everything had been to the extremes.

Take their parents, for example. In what world would an African American man from the south who was obsessed with all things from Queen Elizabeth's reign fall in love with a radical, white feminist, from a small town in Maine, who'd tried—in vain—to join the Black Panther

Party. If their parents had been practical and hadn't believed in the power of true love, neither Jules nor Romey would be here today.

"Paris said he'd give us a ride to the county fair," said Romey.

"Ay, me," Jules groaned. She should've known this was where the conversation would head.

Paris Montgomery wasn't a bad guy. Far from it. He was kind and jovial. Any girl would love to have his attention. Jules was one of them.

She'd loved playing with Paris when they were kids. The three of them, Paris, Romey, and Jules had grown up close; practically brother and sisters since their parents had founded this commune over twenty years ago. From a young age, Jules remembered the adults joking about one of the twins and Paris falling in love and marrying.

Early on, they'd ruled out Romey. Jules's twin was far more interested in books than boys. And not the romantic books. Romey preferred the nonfiction section of the commune's library. That left Jules. But Jules had only ever seen Paris as a brother. Not a lover.

Love was fireworks in the heart. Love was the eyes shining bright when looking upon the one meant for you. Love was an itch in the palm of the hands to reach out and hold on forever.

Jules's hands met with a hairy back and wrinkled flesh. When she turned to face the newcomer, she had to immediately turn away and wrinkle her nose at the smell.

"Hamlet, how did you get out?"

In response to her question, Jules got an enthusiastic *oink*, along with a wiggle of his fat rump. Hamlet, their pet pig, thought he was a dog. His three-hundred-pound weight slowed him down as he tried to race after them all over the commune, but it never lessened his enthusiasm to catch up to them. What surprised Jules the most was that the pig never seemed to lose an ounce of weight despite how much he trailed after humans and the fact that he was on the same vegan diet as the rest of the families who lived on the lands.

Jules gave the pig a scratch behind the ears and was rewarded with hearty squeals of delight. The pig's murmuring of appreciation was accompanied by a buzzing sound. Bees weren't too common in this part of the commune as soybeans were self-pollinating plants. Listening harder, Jules noted that the sound was coming from above.

Looking up, she quickly found the source of the buzzing. Off in the distance, beyond their property line, a small aircraft flew.

"Is that a toy airplane?" said Jules.

Romey used her hand to shield her gaze before announcing, "Looks like a drone. I guess the soldiers are out playing at war this morning."

There were three ranches in this part of the valley beyond the town. The Purple Heart Ranch was filled to the brim with soldiers, most of them wounded veterans who'd come to the ranch to heal from their time in combat. Jerome Capulano had been a pacifist, but his wife Mariam had been a full-on antiwar advocate. Even though Mariam, along with most of the commune, had waged a decade's long war with the ranch that sat between the Verona Commune and the Purple Heart Ranch.

The Vance Ranch.

The Vances were cattle farmers. The fact that their trade was in meat was bad enough. What was worse was that for years the Vances had been using fertilizer to grow their pastures for their cows to feed on. They had no care for their neighbors who abhorred the use of unnatural chemicals in their foods or near their homes.

Words had been exchanged. There was a rumor that a couple of blows had been thrown between Paris's dad and old Mr. Vance. Jules could easily imagine it. Heathcliff Montgomery had a fiery temper, a booming voice, and meaty fists. Eventually, lawsuits had been filed. Now existed a fragile peace between the current Vance head rancher, who was a woman, and Paris, who'd taken over the leadership position of the commune.

Paris was nothing like his father. The young man had a quiet voice that people hushed to listen to, a ready encouragement for any child he came near, and a thumb greener than the plants that he tended.

He really was a catch. Jules only hoped that someday the right woman would snatch him up. She was not the one to cast that net.

The drone continued zigging off course, heading back deeper into Vance Ranch territory and out of Jules's sight.

"You're trying to change the subject," Romey was saying. "Papa and Paris's dad thought you two would marry. You two have gotten closer these past few months working on the organic certification."

Romey was right about that. Jules and Paris had gotten closer as they'd begun preparations to have the commune's lands certified as organic by the USDA. But working that closely with him day in and out made things crystal clear to Jules.

"I don't love him, Romey. I mean, I love him, like a brother. But I've never gotten goosebumps when I see him. He's never made my heart speed up. Or put butterflies in my stomach."

"All of that is scientific nonsense."

"You have no sense of imagination."

"That's not imagination you're describing. It's a medical condition."

Jules stood, aiming to get away from her sister and her logic. But she knew better. Once Romey did the math and came to a solution, she dug her heels in until everyone became convinced that hers was the right answer. Luckily, Hamlet was a hefty buffer between the sisters.

"Marrying Paris is a good business decision," said Romey. "It was our parents that founded this commune."

"Marriage shouldn't be a business transaction."

"That's exactly what it is. That's exactly how it developed. Disney movies changed all that with its princesses. That's why I prefer Pixar."

Jules didn't bother responding. Just because they were twins and shared the same looks that didn't mean they shared the same brain. Jules was determined to find true love, just like in the storybooks. Just like her namesake. Only without the poison and suicide bit.

CHAPTER THREE

The smells of the county fair were all around him. Growing up in the city, Porco had been to carnivals and amusement parks. He'd been jostled about through the frenzy of busy people rushing their children through the long waiting lines of rides. Or paying fees near the cost of entry to skip to the front of the lines. Only to come off the ride and hurry to make it to the next appointment of hectic diversion.

A small town fair was a unique experience. There was rushing about. But only by the young who were hopped up on sugared candies and fizzy drinks. The adults strolled leisurely, conversing with one another, waving to friends, literally stopping to smell the roses as they checked out a florist's booth.

"There really is no such thing as love."

Porco pressed his lips together rather than to address Spinelli's comment. Spinelli was the smartest guy he knew. The man could compute large equations in seconds without the use of a calculator, or even pen or paper. He could remember minute details and call them forth in the heat of a battle. He was handy with tools and anything mechanical bowed to his whim.

But the man was hopeless when it came to anything to do with the fairer sex. In fact, Porco couldn't remember a single time Spinelli had been out on a date.

"What you're feeling is simply a cocktail of adrenaline, dopamine, and serotonin increasing in levels," Spinelli went on. "It's the same chemicals released on the battlefield."

"So, what you're saying is love is a battlefield?"

"No," Spinelli answered, not even acknowledging the righteous use of the lyrics from Pat Benatar's girl-power anthem. "I'm saying your fight or flight reaction is triggered. There are two choices in that scenario. Ever think you keep making the wrong one?"

Yeah, that had to be why the guy hadn't had a single date the whole time Porco had known him. When he'd met Spinelli, the guy was barely a hundred pounds wet. The heaviest thing on him had been his brain. All these years later, and the Rangers had added what Spinelli had in his IQ to his muscle mass.

Stepping up to a booth that sold battered and fried bacon on a stick, Porco bought two. Spinelli waved the heaven-sent concoction off, as Porco knew the health-conscious man would. Which meant more for him.

His waistline would not appreciate him even if his belly did. Now that he was out of the service, he didn't have to worry about things like weight. Though he doubted it would matter now that the camp was open and they were running drills every weekday and Saturday.

"So, what?" Porco said, picking up the thread of their conversation. "You'll never want to settle down with a woman, buy a house, have a family of your own?"

"I do. But I'd go about both processes in the same way," said Spinelli. "When you look for a home, it has to meet certain specifications; a certain square footage, the right amenities, cost."

"You'd pick the woman you'll marry based on a property report and home inspection?"

Spinelli shrugged. "Isn't that essentially what online dating is? Far more logical than relying on a spike in blood flow."

"I can't wait until love smacks you dead in the face."

"You'll be waiting forever since the concept doesn't have hands. And you're missing the point; you don't love Rosalind."

Didn't he? Porco was no longer sure. He knew he'd felt something with her. Otherwise, he'd be able to get her out of his mind easily. Since he couldn't, he owed it to himself to be sure. He just needed to find her first.

Porco finished off the second skewer of bacon, licking his chops. All along the main street of the fair were more booths touting deep-fried concoctions. Maple bacon donuts. Waffle fried bacon. Bacon stuffed burgers. He'd definitely have to come back and try the chocolate-covered bacon.

But first, he had important business to attend to. He set his feet toward the other end of the park, where he knew Rosalind would be.

He didn't miss the giggles and stares of some women. He sidestepped a few who frowned. Those frowners were girls he'd danced with for a night or dated for a weekend when he first got here. He hadn't felt a spark with Bonnie Jones or Crystal Bates. He didn't believe in keeping a woman hanging when there was no fire between them. He was decent like that.

Up ahead, Porco caught sight of the woman whom he still held a torch for. At least he thought it was a torch. He definitely felt something warm lick up his spine. But he couldn't gauge the temperature from this distance. He needed to get closer.

From this distance, he could see that Rosalind was dressed in her customary plaid shirt with a bit of lace on the collar. Cowgirl chic. She wore a Stetson as usual, so Porco could see her shining blue eyes. Or wait? Were they gray? He couldn't remember.

He could see her long blonde hair. Though the strands hung a bit limp in the midday sun. She was smiling, but the expression didn't quite reach her eyes. Come to think of it, he couldn't remember her smile ever being wider than what he saw now.

"David."

Uh oh. Things weren't good when any of his fellow soldiers called him by his first name. It was much like when his mother said his first and middle name through gritted teeth.

Porco turned to glare at Spinelli. The man looked as though he'd been talking for a while. But Porco's attention had been otherwise occupied.

"I'm just trying to help," said Spinelli.

"By keeping me from the woman who might be The One."

Spinelli let his head roll around his neck, the tendons popping along the journey. "You realize the two of you have nothing in common."

"You realize opposites attract. Isn't that a scientific fact?"

"For magnets. But if one flips around, they repel one another."

"I don't see your point?"

"Yeah, I know." Spinelli rolled his neck the other way. Fewer tendons popped this time. At the end of the journey, his head hung low. He raised his hand in a magnanimous gesture and flicked his fingers. "Go on. You'll lose interest by the weekend. There's a bet on it. I have my money on tomorrow morning."

"Some friend you are." Porco turned on his heel and stormed away.

"That would be your best one you've got," Spinelli called after him.

Porco made up the ground between him and his target quickly. Spinelli was wrong. He and Rosalind were like magnets. He could feel a gravitational pull towards this woman.

Though he was drawn to her, the object of his desire wasn't looking at him. Rosalind was smiling still. Her smile stretched a bit higher this time. Porco wanted to know why? Who had made her smile this big? His glance slid over to Rosalind's companion, and his heart stopped.

It had been a sunny day, but the star shifted. The rays moved across the sky to shine down on the single bright spot before him. Everyone around *her* was cast in shadows in Porco's eyes.

The noisy fairgrounds quieted to a hum in his ears. Overhead, he heard birds chirping the sweetest melody as though they were playing a chorus to make way for *her* appearance on life's stage.

Standing across from the woman Porco thought he'd fallen for was the woman he knew had captured his heart.

She wore a sundress in a riot of rainbow colors. Her skin was a light golden brown, like the battered fried bacon skewers he'd just wolfed down. He'd bet she'd taste as sweet as the honeyed ham. He was determined to find out because one word kept playing in his head over and over again.

Mine.

CHAPTER FOUR

"That natural pomade has done wonders for my hair." Rosalind Carr ran her polished nails through her long, silky hair.

Jules smiled and nodded at Rosalind's words. Her blonde tresses did look much healthier than the first time Jules had met her a few months back at the weekly farmer's market. Back then, the rodeo queen's ends had been split and ragged from all the time spent under hairdryers and the exposure to harsh chemicals and dyes to keep her looking like a natural blonde.

"It's never been this healthy and fine," Rosalind beamed down at her hair, as though she were talking to the strands. "I swear it's grown at least three inches in the last two months."

"That would be the aloe vera plant giving you the moisture," said Jules. "The nettles and rosemary promote growth."

They grew each of the herbs in the southern part of the commune. The soil there was more gritty, which suited the Mediterranean plants best. Harmony Sunshine, Verona's resident herbalist, took pride in getting the most exotic specimens to thrive in the midwest.

"That River Sunshine is a genius," said Rosalind. "Is he here today? I'd love to get my hands on some more."

"River is no longer a he, remember? She transitioned earlier this year and changed her name to Harmony."

It had been a beautiful rebirthing ceremony out at the stream that ran through the northern part of their property. Harmony's mother, a poet laureate, performed a heartfelt spoken-word piece about letting the waters in her son's heart reverse course, and now her daughter lived in harmony. Jules choked up just thinking about it.

"Oh, I don't care if he's gay," Rosalind insisted. She pressed her hand to her heart and spread her fingers wide over her chest as though she was showing that the organ was open. "It's very progressive of him. I mean her? Of them?"

Jules knew that the way she'd grown up was a strong pill for many in this community to follow. In a land of cattle and hog ranches, those who lived on Verona abhorred the thought of slaughter for food or clothes. In a town where the churches were packed every Sunday, the open fields on the commune held shrines to every god, goddess, and pagan saint known to mankind -because they didn't want to leave any deity out.

Many of the townsfolk frowned at their ways. No one had ever raised a fist or a foul word. Well, except the Vances and the Montgomerys. Outside of that ongoing feud, the people of the town had tried often to welcome the residents of the commune, albeit in their awkward, see-look-I'm-openminded-just-don't-go-too-far, kinda way.

"Harmony isn't here today, but we do have some of her products out at our booth."

Rosalind's eyes lit up. She looked up, turning her head in the direction of the Verona booth where they'd laid out a store of fresh produce. If she walked over there, Rosalind would find the homemade hair products she coveted, along with hand-fashioned jewelry, scarves, hats, and other articles of clothing crocheted or knitted from natural fibers, and organic fruits and vegetables.

Jules just hoped Rosalind didn't ask her to accompany her back there. She'd driven with Paris to the fair. For the first time in their lives, there had been an awkward silence between the two of them. They'd both tried to fill that silence with familiar topics like the progress of her soybeans, the upcoming commune community meeting which was always lively with debate, the impending visit from the USDA inspector over the organic seal of approval for their produce.

They'd exchanged only a few sentences. The weight of the words unsaid was heavy in the cab of his fuel-efficient hybrid truck. The tension prickled across her skin, causing her to shiver in discomfort. The tense silence had given Jules a moment to study her longtime friend, who wanted to be her lifelong mate.

Paris Montgomery was handsome. He had a strong chin and high cheekbones that could belong to a model. Though he was never one to go in front of a camera. His body was lean from his plant-based diet, and muscular from his work in the fields each day.

He was a quiet man, had been so ever since they were children. A gentler soul than his fiery father who had been a professional protestor in his youth, Paris preferred plants to people. Jules was much the same. It wouldn't be all bad if she chose to marry him.

Something squeezed in her heart, like the valves of the organ were wringing its hands with worry and anxiety. Perhaps that was why she'd shot out of the passenger seat as soon as he'd parked. Maybe that was why she'd walked away from the booth and made herself scarce for the last hour.

"Oh, no. Not him."

The words hadn't come from Jules's distressed heart. They'd come from Rosalind. The light of excitement over hair care had faded from Rosalind's gaze. Her perfectly plucked brow was now pinched in annoyance.

Had Paris come up to them? Had he come in search of Jules, ready to break his silence? Was he now standing behind Jules? What if he was down on one knee?

There were prickles all over her skin. But these weren't the prickles from before. They weren't uncomfortable pinches. They felt like sparklers dancing up her forearms, sliding across her shoulder blades, and racing down her back.

Jules's heart gave a mighty kick to the front of her chest, as though calling all her organs to attention. Every part of her was on high alert.

Her ears rang clear. Her ten fingers felt a tingle. The soles of her feet were grounded where she stood.

Another mighty kick of her heart. This time she knew that something urged her to turn around. It wasn't a fight or flight sense of urgency. Jules couldn't quite put her finger on what the sensation was. She just knew that she had to turn if she wanted to live.

And so, she did.

First, her head. Her gaze pushed her peripheral vision to its max, trying to get a closer look at what was to come. It was only a glimpse, but she saw the next chapter of her life unfolding as her head, then her shoulders, then her entire body came around.

The man standing over her blocked out the sun, but Jules had never felt so hot in her life. His gaze bored into her, as though it saw directly into her soul. She felt bare and confused at the same time as she felt completely cloaked and understood.

There were no sparks when the man smiled. No, there was an explosion in that devilish grin. A raging fire ignited as everything in Jules shouted two words; *this one*.

CHAPTER FIVE

The first thing Porco had learned to do in Basic Training was to march. Forward March was the command given when standing at a halt. They had been taught to pick up their left foot, taking one step measuring from the heel to the toe. The right arm should coordinate in a swing. Arms straight but not stiff. Hands cupped, thumbs pointing down. A coordinated effort with each soldier moving in unison.

Porco lifted his right foot. His right arm swung at the same time, making his body appear as though it lurched forward, casting him off balance. Each of his fingers stretched out, wanting, needing to grab hold of *her*.

With a few more strides forward, his limbs fell into synchronized motion. Left, right, then left. Porco marched towards his glory.

He was drawn by her hazel eyes. Even from this distance, he saw that there were gold flecks at the edges of her pupils. Their sparkle rivaled that of the sun. Her lips were the perfect shape of a heart, lush and round. He doubted that there was any gloss from a tube coating the flesh there. It had to be her natural coloring. Between her lips and her eyes, her cheeks were flecked with freckles. Not the pale pink he'd seen on other women's skin. The collection of dots was mocha swirls on her caramel skin. Porco had the urge to lean down and sip at the sprinkles.

To get to her cheeks, he'd have to brush away the thick strands of her hair that partially hid her face from view. Much of her hair was coiled up atop her head, but in the back, the dark ropes rioted and fell down her back, reaching the base of her spine. The locks of hair were threaded through like the crochet work he'd seen his grandma make.

Dreadlocks, the style was called. There was nothing dreadful about the way they looked. Porco ached to reach his hand out and test their texture. He wanted to know if they were as silky as they appeared to be.

"Yes, David? Is there something I can help you with?"

Porco's mouth had been agape as he'd taken in the sight of this angel on earth. His lips flattened at the wince at the sound of that voice. He'd expected his angel's voice to shimmer like stardust. Not grind like the gears of a vehicle when downshifted.

Aside from the tenor of her voice was its tone. There was annoyance there, tinged with exasperation.

She was mad at him? But she hadn't even met him yet. And how did she know his name?

Gazing down at her, Porco realized her lips hadn't moved. It was not her voice that had spoken. It was Rosalind. Porco had completely forgotten the other woman was there.

Rosalind shifted, placing her body between Porco's and the woman who had captured his entire attention. With her move, Rosalind also blocked out the sun, casting a shadow on the portion of his dream girl that Porco could still see.

The object of his desire was still gazing back at him beneath hooded lids. Was she shy? Even if she was, Porco saw interest in those sparkling eyes. He opened his mouth to speak to her, but the English language eluded him.

What did one say to an angel?

"I hope you haven't come here to cause a scene," Rosalind was saying.

Porco's angel's brows drew in a frown. Her bright gaze dimmed, and she pulled her lower lip into her mouth. He had to swallow a couple of times, just to reign in some sense. He needed to get rid of

Rosalind. He couldn't even remember why he'd come over to her in the first place.

"I'm surprised you've even come over here to talk to me," said Rosalind. "I figured you'd already be onto the next girl."

His angel's gaze widened at that. Not wanting any more dirt kicked up to mar his character, Porco found his voice. Unfortunately, the first word his angel would hear him utter was a curse. The foul word made her wince, and Porco cursed again, only under his breath this time.

"I'm not here for you, Rosalind," he said, finally turning to address his ex.

One of Rosalind's perfectly plucked brows lifted. Was there disappointment there in her ice-blue eyes? Porco didn't care. He couldn't remember what he'd seen in her in the first place.

On the few dates they'd been on, she'd never missed looking into any window or reflective glass they'd walked by. Whenever he'd reached for her hand, he'd have to first disentangle her fingers from her hair. He couldn't remember a single thing they'd talked about when they were together.

"I'm surprised you even remember my name," Rosalind said. "I heard you'd already moved onto the new girl in town."

Porco glanced at the angel standing behind his ex. Her gaze was averted, as though she were trying not to listen. Of course, she'd heard every word. Not one of them had been flattering towards Porco. He hadn't canceled the date with Paige. And right now, he definitely had different plans.

"That is your reputation after all," Rosalind continued her attack. "Love them and leave them. I just left you first is all."

"I wasn't going to..." Porco didn't finish that sentence. Because that was exactly what he'd already done. But it was only because he'd felt a true spark with...

Wait! Where did she go? Porco turned right and then left and then all the way around. To no avail. His angel was gone.

"You want to date *her*," sniffed Rosalind. "Fat chance. You'll never get anywhere near her."

"Who is she? What's her name?"

"Trust me, I'm doing you a favor." Rosalind chuckled low. She crossed her arms over her chest. Her plucked brows narrowed in triumph. The dark outline of her eye makeup cast her in a sinister light. "That one is completely out of your league."

Out of his league? What did she mean by that? It wasn't like Porco had never struck out before. It just didn't happen often. He had a natural way with women. At the end of the day, he only wanted to have his way with one; the right one.

Could his angel be that girl?

"No, actually, she's not even on the same planet as you."

"Look, Rosalind, I'm sorry things didn't work out between us."

"Save it." Rosalind held up her hand. "I'm going to sit back and enjoy you chase after her and fall flat on your face for once. She'll never date a guy like you."

A guy like him? What did she mean by that? But Rosalind was already walking away, cackling as she went.

Porco didn't bother following after her. He turned and headed left. It had to be the direction his dream girl had gone.

A few moments later he was proven right when he spotted her. Out of his league? To the contrary.

She was standing at the deep-fried pork station looking up at the menu with wide eyes. It was as though the stars were aligning. She was perfect for him.

CHAPTER SIX

Jules grimaced, trying not to inhale too deeply. The smell of meat and sugar frying in day-old oil was doing tricks in her stomach. That, and her head was spinning from the encounter she'd walked away from. For much of the conversation between Rosalind and that man, David was his name.

David.

She liked that name. It was a strong, competent name. To even utter it she had to bite her lip when her mouth formed the V at the center of it.

David.

She didn't say his name out loud now. It whispered in her mind. Still, in reality, she bit her lip. A tingle crept across each of her pinky fingers, moving from her left hand all the way to her right. A shudder skittered down her spine as she stood in the noonday sun.

Her heart thumped. Her mind whirled. It had happened.

She'd always thought that when she felt it -that spark- that it would be like floating on a cloud.

It wasn't.

When she'd come face to face with David, it had been like an explosion. With each step he took nearer to her, smaller bursts of aftershocks had set off all along her body. It was as though her goosebumps had been boobytrapped.

Her breath had left her in a whoosh. Her belly had turned a somersault -not like a child turning a cartwheel. More like a gymnast stomping into the mat after a series of flips where they land with their hands over their heads. Her own knees would not have allowed her to stick such a landing. They'd gone to Jell-O.

He'd looked down upon her with those dark eyes that felt like a flashlight shining directly into her. Jules had wanted to shield her gaze, but she couldn't look away from him.

Once she and David had breathed the same air, everything around her had stopped. She felt weary and energized, and worn and whole, tired and wide awake all at the same time.

So that was him. That was the guy who had made her heart kick into high gear. That was the man her soul recognized as it's missing part. And, to hear Rosalind tell it, it turned out he was some kind of player.

Great. Of all the luck.

Aside from her hair care needs, Jules didn't know Rosalind well. She knew that the woman was strong-minded and independent. As a woman who tussled with raging bulls, wild horses, and randy cowboys for a living, Jules figured Rosalind didn't suffer fools easily. She was the type of woman that men chased after. So if she dismissed David as a lady's man, it was very likely that he was indeed community property.

Jules had lived her life in a community where everything was shared. Her clothes were hand-me-downs. All meals were potluck fare. For once in her life, she'd wanted something of her own.

She'd thought that when she fell in love, it would be once and forever. Not for a moment with a man who had been passed around by the entire town. Her heart had to be wrong about him. Her soul had made a mistake.

Jules let go of her bottom lip. She would not be saying his name again. Not in her mind or in life.

"Hi."

Her two front teeth reached out and snagged the plump flesh at the corner of her mouth. Her heart *tap-tapped* in her chest, ignoring her mind's determination. Heat blasted from her very soul, letting her know that her life would never be the same the moment she turned to that voice.

And she was going to turn around. It was inevitable. Because fate was not going to be ignored.

David towered over her. He was easily six and a half feet tall. She hadn't noticed his height at first. Jules was a tall girl, and most of the boys on the commune barely came up to her chin.

Not David. He had a good foot over her. He made her feel... Well, not small.

Instinctively, she knew that he was the kind of man that would keep her safe and protected. She had the urge to step into his arms and nuzzle her nose right into his chest because that's where her head would fit.

He held out his hand. Had he read her mind? Was he giving her an invitation to do just that?

"I'm David."

Jules gulped once, then twice. Swallowing down her out of control desires. She took the proffered hand. The moment their fingertips touched, she felt another set of explosions go off. This time the blast tripped up her arm and set off fireworks in her heart.

Looking up into his eyes, she could've sworn she saw sparkles reflected back at her. His lips parted as he looked down at her. His hand was warm as it enclosed hers. The aftershocks of the bomb were gone now. All that remained was a warm glow between them.

"My name is Julia."

David smiled like he liked her name. He repeated it quietly, as though testing it out on his tongue. Jules loved the sound of her name coming from his mouth. But something wasn't quite right about the way he said it.

"Everyone calls me Jules."

Yes. That was it. She liked the way he said Jules even better.

"I'm David."

She grinned shyly. "You said."

He nodded, tugging at the corner of his upper lip with his teeth as though searching for something more to say. "Everyone calls me Porco."

Jules wrinkled her nose at that. She knew kids were cruel. Had he been overweight growing up? If the nickname was a taunt, she certainly wasn't going to participate in the teasing.

"I like David."

"Then David, it is."

"David?"

"Yes, Jules?"

"Are you going to give me back my hand?"

They were standing in front of the long lines of the fried food station. People moved around them to get into and out of the line with their crispy, brown foodstuffs. Jules noted that she was no longer having trouble breathing in the oily smells.

"No," David said.

"No, you're not going to give me back my hand?"

He shook his head in the negative, but his lips curled in a smile. A possessive smile. The warmth emanating from that smile made another trek up to her arm and pulsed in her chest. David's nostrils flared as though he'd sensed what he did to her.

"You feel it too, don't you?" he said.

Jules didn't pretend to not know what he was talking about. In answer, she gave a little nod of her head. It was all the movement she could muster being held in his gaze, being held in the palm of his hand.

"I do," she whispered.

David's palm pressed firmly against hers. His thumb rubbed at the skin of her knuckles. Never in her life had Jules felt so cared for with such a simple gesture.

The moment was so big and life-altering. But, also light and natural. It was exactly how she dreamed meeting him would be. Except for the sizzling pig meat surrounding them.

She wanted to get away from here. To be alone with him. To know everything about him. Looking up, she saw an impediment to that desire.

In the distance, she saw her twin. Romey hadn't spotted Jules. Because Romey's face was turned. She was chatting with Paris.

"I have to go," Jules said.

Jules snatched her hand from David. She only got her palm free. But David held onto her fingers.

"You can't go. I just found you."

Her gymnast's heart flipped from one side of her chest to the other, sticking another boisterous landing.

David stepped closer to her. His gaze intent on her face. Then his eyes narrowed on her lips.

The world stopped. Everything centered on him, where his five fingers held onto her, where his dark eyes focused on her. She knew without any shadow of a doubt that her life would be entwined with this man. She just had to take care of one thing first.

"I'll come back," she said. "I just need to handle a family matter first."

"I'll let you go," he said. "But I'm going to wait here for you."

"Right here?" she grinned, looking at their surroundings. The overly sweet scent of deep-fried batter and pork made her senses rear back. David didn't seem to notice.

"Right here." He planted both feet and smiled down at her. "Promise you'll come back?"

"I promise."

That was all it took. David let her go. She could make her escape. Leaving him was the last thing she wanted to do, but she had to go and talk to the two most important people in her life to let them know that her life had irrevocably changed forever.

CHAPTER SEVEN

e was on top of the world. Her last words to him, her promise, felt like a vow. Like a solemn oath that had left him anything but sober. Porco felt drunk as he walked through the fair.

His footfalls were aimless. His only goal, his only care was to will the hands of the clock to move faster. He itched to reach up and push the sundown, tucking it under the cover of darkness so that night might rise, and Jules would return to him.

Jules, his heart sighed.

What an appropriate name for her. She had been a jewel in his eyes. He'd known she was precious after his first glance at her. When he'd come to stand before her, her entire being had twinkled at him, and he'd become lost in her shimmer. Sparking his every nerve ending to life.

Jules, his mind exhaled.

For as long as he'd been dating, he'd never told another girl about the spark he'd felt when he'd met them. Thinking back on it, Porco started to wonder if what he'd felt all those other times had actually been anything other than idle curiosity. Nothing had ignited him before, like what he'd felt standing in her light.

Jules, whispered the hairs along his forearms.

With those eyes flecked with gold at the rim. With that skin of amber and lips of rubies. Her white teeth had flashed pearls as she smiled shyly at him. But he got the sense that she wasn't shy. Only as startled as he was to feel the undeniable pull between them.

He'd seen the moment she'd felt something between them. Her eyes had gone wide with surprise as his had done. She couldn't deny it. Not even after Rosalind's words when she'd turned away from him. That would be the last time his jewel would walk away from him. Porco vowed it.

If she'd doubted him then he would never give her heart another reason to falter, her feet another cause to back away. Porco would show Jules that no other woman would ever touch her shine.

"Hey, Porco. Wanna come on a ride with us?"

Porco looked up to find two women rising up into the sky. A honey blonde girl in a too-tight tank top. And an ebony-skinned brunette with a cowboy hat pulled over her long, wavy tresses. They sat in one booth of the Ferris wheel. The ride lifted them up off the ground, rising toward the sun. Had it been another day, Porco might have leaped onto the ride, causing it to rock. Causing the women to giggle with delight at his daring.

He turned away from them and moved on. That ride, those girls, neither could lift him any higher off the ground than the mere thought of Jules's return. But the sun hadn't given a single inch of its position in the sky.

Jules, his entire being wanted to howl.

"How's Rosalind?"

Porco stumbled to a halt. Rusty leaned against the railing of a petting zoo. The words Vance Ranch were proudly displayed along the fencing. Inside the zoo, young calves roamed the perimeter. Their heads dipped low as their mouths fed at the bales of hay laid next to the wooden posts. Small, eager hands reached between the rails to pet heads and ears.

In the next enclosure were adult cows. Leaning against those rails, watching the cattle eat, were adult humans. Those buyers sized up the beasts, measuring their worth for an upcoming auction.

Rusty cleared his throat. Then snapped his fingers for good measure.

The man looked over at Porco expectantly. Rusty had asked him a question. For the life of him, Porco couldn't remember the place or name Rusty had uttered.

"Who?" said Porco.

Rusty lifted his brows at the single word. He turned his puzzled gaze to Spinelli, who'd stepped up to join them. Spinelli's brows drew together as he regarded Porco, understanding in his intelligent gaze.

"He's already found someone new," Spinelli announced.

Rusty shook his head, pressing his lips together with what Porco knew was disappointment in him. Rusty hadn't dated much. He'd only been with one woman his entire life.

"Not a new girl," Porco corrected. "*The* girl. The last girl. The One."

Spinelli rolled his eyes. Porco was sure it was a perfect three-hundred-and-sixty-degree circle of disbelief. Rusty looked away. The man's belief in The One had been damaged by the divorce papers his estranged wife had sent to him months ago. They sat awaiting his signature, tucked away in his duffel bag.

"I'm serious," insisted Porco. "I've never felt anything like this before. And she felt it too."

"What? The magical spark." Spinelli wiggled his fingers as though at the sky before letting them fall to his sides. "There's no such thing. It's just a heart palpitation. A biological response caused by stress, exertion, caffeine, alcohol, or hormones. The only way that would be magic would be if you're experiencing menstruation, pregnancy, or menopause."

Spinelli had to ruin everything was science and logic. Porco often wondered if the man was nothing more than a robot underneath those clothes. His brawn. as well as his brain too often resembled the cold of metal.

"No," Porco said with certainty. "What's between me and this woman is definitely magic."

"When did you meet her?" asked Rusty.

"Ten minutes ago."

Again, another look between his two friends.

"What do you know about her?" asked Rusty.

"She's beautiful," Porco grinned. But the grin slipped as Spinelli opened his mouth, preparing to rain on Porco's parade. "She's responsible."

The only reason she'd left him was to handle a family matter. So, she held family in high regard. His mother always said to watch how his potential partner treated their parents to see how they would treat him. Although, Porco wasn't sure if Jules had gone off to help her parents or siblings or other relatives.

"Is that it?" asked Spinelli. "Is that all you know about this one."

"The One," Porco corrected. He knew that and that Jules had admitted that she felt it too. That was all he needed to know. "Love isn't science. It's emotion. I felt that spark with her. No, it was an explosion. And she felt it too. She told me so."

The wariness in Spinelli's eyes had Porco clenching his fist. The two of them had never come to blows before, but there was a first time for everything.

"What's her name?" asked Rusty, stepping between the two men.

"Jules."

"Jules?" said Rusty. "Do you mean Jules Capulano?"

Porco frowned. They hadn't exchanged last names. But that didn't matter because one day her last name would be his.

"Jules Capulano?" said Spinelli, his gaze gone from wary to worry. "From the Verona Commune?"

She hadn't told him where she lived. Porco didn't like that his friends knew more about his dream girl than he did.

"Brown skin?" asked Rusty. "Long dreadlocks."

Porco nodded, though he didn't like that Rusty used the word dread to describe her hair. "Yeah, that's her."

Rusty winced and turned away. Spinelli whistled low and wrinkled his nose.

"What?" demanded Porco. What could they possibly have to say against the angel who had set his entire being aflame?

"You know she's vegan?" said Spinelli.

"So, you're racist now?" Porco accused. He wasn't entirely sure what the word meant. He didn't care what race or religion she was.

"Vegan means she doesn't eat meat," said Rusty.

Was that all? Most women were picky when it came to what was on their plates. "So, we'll eat seafood when we go out."

Again, Rusty and Spinelli shared another look that left Porco feeling on the outs about the woman he intended to woo.

"There's no way a relationship between you two would work," said Spinelli. "You're far too different."

So, both of his friends were prejudiced. Great. This was quickly turning into a scene from *Guess Who's Coming to Dinner?* Which made even less sense since both of his friends had mixed heritage in their blood. Spinelli's mother was from South America and his father from Italy. Where Rusty's mother had immigrated from Thailand when she was young.

"Doesn't matter to me what color her skin is or what god she worships or what she eats," said Porco. "She's the one for me, and that's all there is to it."

CHAPTER EIGHT

"Where have you been?" demanded Romey. "Paris has been looking for you."

At present, Paris was chatting with a customer. He held up a crooked looking squash, patiently explaining that even though the vegetable wasn't the prettiest, the taste would be unlike anything the buyer had ever sampled. That was the reason their booth at the weekly farmer's markets had a never-ending line of repeat customers. No grocery store could top the taste of what they pulled from their organic fields.

With the sale made, Paris stuffed the money in the till. He lifted his head and their gazes connected. Jules could see the sharp intake of breath he took when he spotted her. Her breathing remained even. Paris swallowed and then displayed a wide grin as he regarded her. Jules tugged at one corner of her mouth, urging her lips to rise.

Even though Paris stood in the full light of the sun, she felt no heat between them. His attentions left her cool, unaffected. Jules needed to tell him that. She needed to let him know that she had no feelings for him, at least not in that way.

"Are you going to answer my question?" said Romey. "Where have you been?"

"Romey, you'll never guess what's just happened to me."

"What?" Romey scanned her sister's body like a mother would after her child returned after a stint at the playground. "Are you hurt?"

Where the average twins were born moments apart, Romey was the elder twin by an hour. Their mother liked to say that Jules had been a natural homebody and preferred to stay in the familiar fixtures of her mom's belly.

"Romey -no. Stop that." Jules brushed her sister's probing hands away from her body. "I'm fine. In fact, I'm better than fine."

Jules took a deep breath, drawing out the moment. It was a big announcement she was about to make. The biggest admission of her life. It needed the dramatic pause.

"I...am..." Jules took another deep breath, letting go of the last two words with a wondrous sigh. "In love."

Romey's expression didn't change. Her gaze still roamed over her twin as though she were looking for a bruise, a cut, some sort of wound. Finally, she inhaled and then let out a sigh of her own.

"Well, good," Romey said. "I knew that's what you wanted. If you've realized that you can love Paris, all the better."

"No, no, Romey." Jules held up her hands, waving them to ward off such a notion. "I'm not in love with Paris."

"Then I don't understand? I don't see how you're going to marry Paris if you think you're in love with someone else? You haven't shown interest in any other man on the commune."

"He's not from the commune," Jules admitted. "We just met."

"Today?" asked Romey.

Jules nodded.

"Here?" Romey pointed to the patch of dirt beneath their feet.

Jules bit her lip but gave her sister another nod.

Romey regarded her twin for a long moment. Jules could see the wheels turning in her sister's head. While Jules had stayed behind to luxuriate in their mother's belly for that hour, Romey had taken the head start to get the lay of the land. Those additional sixty minutes gave Romey the false sense that she was wiser than her younger sister.

"I think these oils and sugary scents are getting to you," said Romey. "You're not making any sense."

Jules knew better than to try to speak emotions with her science-minded sister. She had to use logic. Although logic didn't actually apply in this matter because Jules had fallen in love, head over heels in love, with a man she'd only just met. A man she didn't know much of anything about.

Except that his name was David. And that his friends were cruel for calling him Porco. Even though pigs were delightful creatures and smart too. as evidenced by her pet pig Hamlet who could always track her down no matter where she was on the commune. Jules bet David was just as smart and loyal as a pig.

But that was all she knew about him. That and that he'd dated Rosalind. And possibly another girl… or two. Or more…

But none of that mattered. What mattered was what she'd felt between them. That had been real.

"Who is this man?" said Romey.

"His name is David."

"David what?"

"I… I um… don't know his last name…yet."

Romey raised a brow. Though they were twins, Jules had never mastered the raise of one eyebrow. Or the lowering of it.

"Okay," Romey said. "What does he do?"

"I, um…" Jules huffed in frustration. Trust her practical sister to ruin it. "Romey, we just met."

"And now what?" her sister asked.

"I don't know? All I know is that he made my heart skip a beat. That's never happened with Paris. That's never happened with any guy I've know."

"But you're in love?" Romey was using her logical voice. The voice that went *if this then that must follow.* "If you're heart skips, then love must follow, right?"

Well, it didn't sound wrong. Before Jules could respond, Romey kept treading down her logic trail.

"What you experienced was likely a heart palpitation, which happens during exercise, heat, or even low blood sugar. It's hot out here, so you're likely overheated. Have you eaten?"

"What? Um… no, not since breakfast."

"And you've been walking, in the heat, with no food in your belly. So, you see, it's not love. It's your body crying for shade, water, and sustenance."

Jules seethed. How had the two of them shared a womb? How, in fact, did they share the same DNA when they saw the world so differently?

"This is why I didn't want to tell you," said Jules.

"Paris is a smart decision," Romey said. "Don't throw your life away on misfiring synapses. All over a man you just met and know nothing about."

Romey reached out to rub Jules's shoulder. The wound wasn't there, her sister had plucked at the center of Jules's heart. Misfired synapses or not, Jules was determined to find David and see what would follow.

She wouldn't get that chance at this moment. Paris was headed toward her. Just as he took his first step in her direction, his gaze shifted. A dark cloud passed over his features as he watched a woman walk down the cleared path of the fair.

Brenda Vance walked past the commune's booth. In both hands, she held leads. Tethered to the ends of each lead was a young calf. Children trailed after the female rancher, unaware that those innocent animals would one day reach their maturity and then be led to slaughter.

Jules wasn't a fool. She knew that was the natural order of things. She simply chose to get her sustenance a different way, the same way the cows did. From the fields.

What upset her was that the Vances tainted those fields with harsh, unnatural chemicals.

As she walked by with her calves and parade of children, Brenda glanced over at the booth finding Paris. Jules held her breath as the generations-old enemies glared at one another. Unlike their fathers who had come to blows, Paris and Brenda only threw daggers with their eyes. That and the legal paperwork each of their lawyers had filed, bound both their hands. The agreement of when, where, and what chemicals could be sprayed had kept the peace so far. But that peace was as tenuous as the thin boundary connecting their lands.

Brenda gave a nod of her head, her eyes ever watchful. Paris deigned to do the same. But it was clear that a line had been drawn in the sand between the two lands. Jules stood firmly behind her family on the commune, the place she'd lived all her life, where she drew her sustenance as well as her livelihood.

There were only two Vances remaining. Brenda's brother was one of the town's pastors. His efforts had lent a huge hand in keeping the peace between the families. Brenda had recently married a soldier, and now she had a small army on her side. A group of tall, well-formed men flanked the cattle rancher. Jules's heart skipped another few beats when she recognized the face of one man in particular.

She'd only seen his shaggy brown hair once, but she'd have easily picked him out of a crowd. She'd been under the direct assault of that grin only moments ago. Seeing it again made her stagger a footstep back now. She took another step back as David's grin slowly fell.

Recognition dawned in his dark eyes as their gazes locked. Happiness, confusion, awe, denial all lit his face at once. Jules had the urge to shield her gaze from the onslaught of his emotions. She didn't get the chance to.

Paris stepped in front of her, blocking her view of David. Jules shifted to catch another glimpse of him. Her heartbeat tripped over itself as she realized they were looking at each other from across an imaginary line in the sand.

CHAPTER NINE

*P*orco stutter-stepped when he saw her, feeling that same draw to run to her and scoop her into his arms. But something had held him back. First, it was Spinelli's grip on his arm. Then the tilt of his head and raise of his eyebrow that told Porco he was missing something.

Yeah, he was missing something. The feel of his woman against him. The touch of her cheek to his. The taste of her lips on his tongue. But there was something he wasn't seeing.

As Porco walked by with his friends, he noted that the people around Jules glared at them. Which was odd. They were all dressed in bright, colorful clothing that harkened back to the sixties and seventies. They looked like they'd stepped out of a history book carrying a banner that said *We are flower children*.

Though that's not what the sign above them said. It read Verona Commune Organic Vegan Produce and Goods. Porco's mind worked hard to comprehend the significance of the sign blaring overhead. It was difficult because his gaze kept returning to Jules. His entire being insisted that he go to her, claim her, make her his in every way. He just needed to figure out what he was missing.

Was it the word organic that should hold his attention? He knew that that was a buzz word touted in the health and fitness industry. All he knew was that when something was labeled organic in the grocery store, it came with a hefty price tag.

There was that word vegan again. It couldn't have anything to do with race. There were people behind those tables of every skin tone. Which meant Porco owed Spinelli and Rusty an apology for calling them racist.

But he had heard that term before? Oh, he remembered. He'd been on the market for a new leather jacket and saw a cheaper model called vegan leather. Was that it?

No. There was something bigger he was missing.

"That's her, isn't it?" said Spinelli.

Porco couldn't speak. He could only gaze at Jules. She was staring back at him. Unlike earlier, her eyes didn't sparkle as she looked at him. Neither was she smiling shyly. Her gaze was clouded and she worried her lip with her teeth.

Something was wrong. So why wasn't he moving towards her? Oh, because Spinelli still held him back.

"Do you see what I mean now?" asked Spinelli.

See what? All Porco saw was the woman, who was very likely to be the mother of his children, standing in a small crowd of colorfully dressed people... who were also frowning and glaring at his group. What was he missing?

A man stepped in front of Jules. He was tall with dark hair. His body was lean, with the type of muscle that Porco had seen on yoga instructors. Porco doubted the man could bench more than fifty pounds if that. Still, the yogi had placed himself between Porco and Porco's woman. That would not do.

"No, no. You can't go there." Spinelli's grip tightened on Porco's arm.

Jordan Spinelli had a big brain and a big body to match. His grip was absolute. But Porco was not above sucker punching his friend if both he and the yogini stood in the way of true love.

"You cannot go over there," Spinelli continued. "Because of the lawsuit."

Lawsuit? What was Spinelli talking about? Porco's brain whirled as realization began to dawn. Hadn't he heard Brenda and her brother going on about a dispute with the neighbors?

"The Verona Commune filed an injunction dictating where and what type of chemicals Brenda could spray on her lands."

Porco did remember that. Vaguely. Something or other about fertilizer and vegetables. He thought maybe the term organic had been used in that conversation.

"That's them," said Spinelli. "That's the Verona Commune."

Here he was, staring down the neighbors from hell. Meanwhile, all Porco could think was that he'd been right next to Jules for months and had been unaware. Oh, fate was a tricky little devil.

"That's why it can't work out between you two. Well, that's one of many reasons."

Spinelli's words made no sense. Porco had no bone in this fight. This was between Brenda, and the leader, who Porco now assumed was the tree standing posed yoga instructor.

This feud had nothing to do with him and Jules. Or what they were feeling towards each other. Right?

Porco looked again to the woman of his dreams. Jules's eyes were squeezed closed, as though she was trying to shut out the same realization he'd just come to. She had to know that he wasn't a part of what was going on between Brenda and Mini Mountain Pose guy.

Jules opened her eyes. Her gaze immediately fell on Porco. What he saw in her brown depths made him believe. There was a spark of hope. It was all he needed to do the impossible.

As part of the Army's premier raid force, Porco had been on numerous missions where he'd infiltrated hostile territory. He'd spent weekends tracking enemy combatants and pulling terrorists out of their beds before their eyes blinked open. He'd run headfirst into dark caves and decrepit cities to rescue prisoners of war and innocent civilians.

Each and every one of those missions had spiked his adrenalin, engaged his flight or fight responses, and made him question his sanity. One thing remained the same every time; he'd never hesitated to take that first step into combat.

But here, in this sedate Montana town, where the biggest threat was the fried oil dough and meats the townsfolk launched at their livers and hearts, Porco faced his toughest battle. He ignored all his training to run headfirst. He turned off his fight response and kept moving forward.

Walking past Jules Capulano had to be the hardest thing Porco had done in his life. But he did it. Because he had the hope that she would meet him tonight as planned. Outside of the scrutiny of their feuding families, away from the lawsuit that tied up their lands, out of the boundaries of who others thought they should date.

With that knowledge, Porco soldiered on. He marched away from the woman who was made for him. With this mission of losing this first battle accomplished, Porco began plotting how to win the war.

CHAPTER TEN

"The nerve of that woman." Paris paced the length of the field. The sun was setting, and the light low. However, his stomping feet never smashed into a single gourd or tomato. The fruits of his labors were always handled with the utmost care and respect. "Did you see her? Parading those poor animals around like that."

"I believe she'd set up a petting zoo for the children at the other end of the fair," Jules said, trying to play peacemaker in a war she'd never wanted in on.

She was surprised the role had landed at her feet. It usually went to Paris, especially while his father had been alive. Now, Jules saw flashes of the fiery Heathcliff in his gentle son.

"That's another thing," Paris went on as though he hadn't heard Jules's tone, which was also unlike him. Paris was one of the most attentive and intuitive people she'd ever met. "Putting those poor babies on display like they were some exhibit."

In addition to being an advocate for clean living and eating, Paris was also an animal rights activist. Though unlike his father, Paris's activism had always tended towards the letter-writing and sign-making campaigns. Whenever anyone had a conflict on the commune, Paris insisted they write out their problems and put them in the Problem Jar. After reading the grievances, disagreeing residents had to come into an Empathy Circle where they would hug it out. That's how problems got solved here. This was the first time Jules had ever seen a hint of violence in his eyes.

"And to put those soldiers on display like that. Did you see them?"

Oh, yes, Jules had seen them. One in particular. It had taken everything in her to not run up to David and wrap her arms around him. The pull towards the man was maddening, unlike anything she'd ever felt.

She'd hated being across a divide from him when she knew in her soul that they should be walking beside each other, hand in hand, fingers twined, hearts matching the same beat. When David had frowned at her across that imaginary line in the sand, Jules had feared it was all over for them before it had even begun.

How could this ever work? He was one of the soldiers staying and working at the Vance Ranch. Her loyalties were to the people of the commune, her family, and friends. The line separating them wasn't imaginary. It was real. That fenced-in border was not to be crossed. There was a legal document that said so.

She'd seen the look of utter dejection on David's face. Jules had felt the same. They'd both touched starlight, only later to feel the burn.

But then, something miraculous happened. The twinkle came back into David's eyes. His chin lifted in defiance, rising higher than that imaginary line in the ground. Higher even than the border that separated them. The look in his eyes told Jules that he still wanted her. The feeling in her heart told her that she wanted the same.

Could this even work? Could she still go to him tonight? Would it mean she was betraying her people if she did? She knew that it would be a betrayal of her heart if she didn't.

"Those soldiers are nothing but mindless, brainwashed automatons," Paris was saying. His pacing doing the work of a trough in the rich soil.

"I heard that the soldiers of the Purple Heart Ranch have been doing a lot of community service work, especially with the youth," said Jules.

"They're convincing children to enlist and become drones like them."

Jules had nothing against the military. Her grandfather had been one of the famed Tuskegee Airmen. Though her father had no designs on service himself, he proudly displayed his father's accomplishments in his home.

"This is so unlike you," she said to Paris. "Why are you so upset?"

Paris took a deep inhale. He let out the air in a long, intoned *Om* as they'd been taught as children. Jules waited patiently until the man got control of himself. She couldn't ever remember seeing him this upset. To say that Paris Montgomery was mild-mannered was an understatement.

"I'm sorry," he said, reaching for her hands. "I'm just stressed. We have a lot riding on this inspection, our entire future."

Jules stared down at their joined hands. When David had held her hands in his, she'd felt a fire ignite inside of her. Paris's hands weren't cold. They were rough, callused from his daily work in the fields. She appreciated everything his hands had done for her over the years. When her parents had passed away, Paris had been there, steady as ever to help them through it. She'd found comfort when he'd held her hands back then. She'd found solace in his arms when he'd offered his shoulder to cry on.

Paris was a good man. A good friend. But he did not light any kind of fire in her.

"Speaking of the future, there's something I've been meaning to talk to you about." Paris chewed at his inner lip. He always did that when he was unsure of himself.

The part of Jules that was this man's friend rose to the fore. She wanted to offer him comfort, even in this. As a reflex, she gave his hands a squeeze. It was the wrong move. She could see the courage gather in his eyes. He opened his mouth to speak and—

"Oink."

Hamlet situated his big body between the two of them, knocking their hands apart. Jules could kiss the pig. In fact, she leaned down and gave his scruffy head a rub of thanks.

"I should probably get him in his pen for the night," she said.

"We'll talk about this later?"

Jules nodded, already leading the pig away. She made quick strides towards the home she shared with her sister. Hamlet kept up on his stubby legs and excess weight.

In the distance, Jules saw the light of the nightly bonfire. Each night her people came together, be it in the communal hall if the weather was poor, or out under the stars. They broke bread, shared anecdotes of their day, told stories of the past, discussed their hopes for the future.

Jules had her own hopes for the future. She just hoped that what she planned to do, and whom she planned to do it with, wouldn't bar her from her seat at the communes table moving forward.

CHAPTER ELEVEN

S he came.

Until he saw her walking through the crowd, Porco had doubted. Not what he felt for her. Not the connection he knew existed between them. But he knew that family was a powerful motivator. If Jules's family was not on board with her seeing him, she might've stayed home.

But she came.

As first dates went, this one wasn't so bad. Porco walked alongside Jules amidst the sounds of the county fair. The wails, screeches, and cries of children who were finally coming down from their afternoon sugar rush. The shouts and giggles of teens testing the boundaries of their independence while inside the cocoon of their tight-knit community were now on the rise. Ever-present was the catcalls of the visiting vendors aiming to pick the last dollar out of eager townies' pockets.

"You hungry?" Porco asked.

Jules tugged at the hem of her sleeve. She'd changed from the brightly colored sundress she'd worn this morning to more muted tones. The dress she now wore was white cloth. There were a few accents of light blue and purple at the sleeve and hem. The softness of the colors cast her in an ethereal glow, making her look like more of the angel in his dreams.

"I ate before I left home," she said. "Most of the foods here don't agree with me."

Right. The vegan thing. No meat.

"We could have a milkshake if you're thirsty."

She tugged again at the blue trim on her sleeve. She'd met his eyes only once, that moment when they'd come face to face for the first time tonight. She'd said hello, gazing into Porco's eyes as if searching for something. Only when she found it, her features had gone pensive, like she was now working out a complex math problem.

"I can't have dairy," she said finally.

"Oh. Well, there's also ice cream."

She found his gaze then. Her eyes sparkled in the moonlight. He felt that he was now the complex math problem she was trying to work out. Porco wanted to tell her that he was a very simple solution.

"We're on a date," he said. "I want to buy you a treat. Is there anything I can get for you?"

Jules pressed her lips together. She glanced up, eyes searching the signs and boards around them. "Well," she said, "Oreos are vegan."

There was that word again. Porco supposed he should ask her exactly what it meant. But he didn't want to offend her or seem stupid. He'd google it later tonight after their date. Though the thought of leaving her at any point didn't sit well with him. This date had only begun, and he wanted it to go on forever.

He watched as she took a tentative bite of the dessert. It wasn't a regular Oreo from a package. It had been covered in batter and deep-fried in oil. Jules's eyes went wide. Her hand went to her head.

"Sugar rush," she said through a wince. "That's more sugar than I'm used to… in a week."

Porco placed his hand over hers, rubbing at her temple. Jules dropped her hands and gave him complete control over her head. Porco had never felt stronger than when he was given charge of this woman.

He massaged the skin at her forehead. His hands cupped her cheek. He gazed down at her, unabashed. He watched the tension slowly seep from her. When she opened her eyes, the golden sparkles there dazzled him.

Porco's heart raced. With his fingers grazing her neck, he felt her pulse pick up. Her breaths came out in quick huffs. He tasted a sweetness that transcended the sugars of the cookie. There was a smear of frosting at the corner of her upper lip. He should bend down to lick that off. Wouldn't want her to experience another rush from the sugar.

Was it too soon? Funny, he'd never asked himself that question before when pursuing a woman. Jules was different. He wanted -no needed to get this one right. She was different. She was special. She was The One.

"You've got something there," he said.

Carefully, he brushed the spot at the corner of her mouth. Grabbing a napkin from a nearby dispenser, he handed the paper cloth to her. As she busied herself wiping at her lips, Porco turned and snuck a lick of his thumb.

Heaven.

"It's funny," he said, as they walked on. "Most first dates take place at a bar after meeting on a dating app."

"Why is that funny?" she asked.

He turned to her, taking a moment when his heart leaped at the sight of her. It hadn't stopped doing that all night. It would probably weaken with all the exertion just being in her presence. It would be worth it.

"We met naturally," he said. "You don't hear a lot of stories of people doing that. Well, except on the Purple Heart Ranch and Vance Ranch. But those are all special cases."

Jules winced at the mention of the ranch. Porco wanted to bite his tongue. They had seemed to mutually agree to keep the subject of their feuding ranches off the table.

"I don't have a cell phone," said Jules. "So, I don't have any apps."

"No cell phone?"

She shrugged. "I live on the commune. Everyone I want to talk to is in shouting distance. Don't look at me like I'm from outer space."

She poked him in the side with her elbow. He had her talking now, relaxed. The more her guard came down, the more he got to know about her. The more he got to know about her, the more he liked her.

"We have a few computers and the internet for work purposes in the community room. But no television."

He blanched at the thought. No phones or television? He wouldn't survive. Except, he had lived like that for stretches of time.

"We didn't always have creature comforts in the army. But if we were at a base, there might be access. Even in the desert or the mountains, many soldiers were able to take college courses or other training between missions."

"All the places you got to see." Jules tilted her head back and sighed. Her gaze was fixed on the stars.

"Do you want to travel?" he asked.

She gave a shake of her head. "I used to think I did. I realized I like the idea of traveling. But everything I need is here. My family, my friends, my work."

"What is your work?"

"I grow soybeans."

Porco wrinkled his nose.

"You don't like beans?"

"Not when I was a kid, no. But I'm willing to give them another try if they're your beans."

Again, her gaze clouded. He'd become a math problem again. More than anything, Porco wanted to add up to her needs.

"Do you know anything about me?" she asked. "About my people and where I come from?"

He didn't know much about the next-door neighbors on the Verona Commune. They were farmers like most who lived in these parts. He'd heard lively music once or twice as he'd driven by; ancient, primal sounds with drums beating and tambourines jingling. It had sounded like a good time. If these were modern-day flower children, he figured he'd have a good time with them. Right now, he was entirely focused on having a good time with the bloom beside him.

"I probably shouldn't be here with you," she said. But her words were whispered, quietly. So softly that they would've easily been lost in the sound of revelry all around them.

"But you are," he said.

Jules worried the hem of her sleeve even more. Porco reached for those slender fingers. Uncoupling them from the fabric, he slid the fingers of his left hand between the fingers of her right one. Not quite down to the knuckle, just to the first line past her fingertips.

"You're here with me."

In her eyes, Porco saw the plusses and minuses of the problem she'd been trying to solve fall away. He slid his fingers down past her knuckles.

"It's what we both want."

With that, Porco let their hands clasp fully. He grasped onto the webbing between her fingers. His palm met hers, giving him another rush of heat that pulsed all through his body. His heart warned him to hold onto this one tight and never let go. Those were instructions Porco intended to follow to the letter.

CHAPTER TWELVE

If she reached up, Jules swore she could touch the stars. She was flying high. Luckily, she was strapped in with a seat belt.

The Ferris wheel rose her and David up higher and higher until the world below appeared small as a puzzle board whose pieces she no longer cared to fit in each space. She was beyond that, above it, making a new picture, playing a new game.

Her heart raced with her feet having left the ground. Her palms were slick with anticipation. Her breaths came in short pants. Beside her, David still held her hand.

Jules had never felt so exhilarated before. She was wide awake but felt like she was moving through a dream. Her thoughts were scattered, but everything made perfect sense. This was exactly where she was meant to be, at this elevation, at this moment, with this man.

Turning to look at her companion, she saw that David wasn't looking at the stars. He was gazing at her. As though she were the brightest thing in the sky. She would never tire of being the focal point of his attention.

"Tell me everything about you," he said.

Jules had never had anyone ask her that. Back home, everyone already knew everything about her. They'd all been there when anything happened. But here was a person who knew nothing about her. She could tell him anything. She could be whoever she wanted to be. All she wanted David to know was the truth of her, who she was down in her core. She wanted him to know and like that person.

"I'm a twin."

The corners of his lips lifted into a delighted grin. "There's two of you."

"No," she chuckled. "Not exactly. Romey and I are very different creatures. She's entirely sensible, where my head is often in the clouds."

David chuckled. "Sounds like my friend Spinelli. He's always telling me to come back down to earth."

"Romey speaks to me in conditional statements." Jules let her voice go more nasally in the know-it-all pitch of her sister, "'Jules, if your head is in the clouds, then you would drown because clouds are made of water.'"

"I've got one for you." David lifted his chin higher as though taking on a superior air. "'Porco, love is nothing more than a spasm of the heart valves, which amounts to nothing more than a medical condition.'"

"Romey's said that!"

David's chuckle mixed with her giggles. Their glee sounded like the perfect harmony. When next she looked over, Jules noted that they sat even closer together than before.

Her soldier's gaze dipped to her lips. Jules's breath caught. Though she didn't watch television or movies, she read her fair share of books. She'd read about what couples got up to on this particular ride. This high up away from prying eyes was the perfect opportunity for kissing.

But he didn't.

"Tell me more," he said.

Jules swallowed, taking a moment to find her voice and hide her disappointment.

"My parents met at the end of the Civil Rights Movement. All of the marches were over. They'd missed a lot of the action. My mother had tried to join the Black Panther Party, but they weren't accepting white women."

Jules grinned, thinking about her fierce, activist mother. Mariam

Capulano always marched at the front of the lines wherever she saw injustice meted out. It didn't matter that she had barely been five feet tall and one hundred pounds only after a Sunday potluck. If she saw an underdog, she was immediately on their side.

"My father was a literary historian. He loved Shakespeare, hence our names; Jules and Romey."

David's grin grew wider. His thumb rubbed lazy circles at the center of her palm. He'd turned his body towards her, giving her his full, undivided, fascinated attention.

"They had us later in life. Instead of raising us in the city, they founded the commune along with the Montgomerys. They wanted to create an idyllic setting where racial and cultural harmony reigned. They both passed away a few years ago."

"I'm sorry."

Her mother had gone first. Her father lost the will to live shortly after burying his wife.

"Anyway, I grew up on the land they bought for us. I have a knack for making things grow. I haven't really done much else. I haven't even dated."

"Really?"

"I grew up with all the boys on the commune. They're like brothers to me. So, I waited."

"Now, I'm here."

David lifted the back of her hand and kissed it. Warmth shot all the way through her. A voice that sang from her blood began chanting, *Yes, this one.*

With the voices in her head and the warmth stretching to every extremity, Jules couldn't think of a thing to say. All she could do was hold onto this man beside her she barely knew but felt like home.

They stayed like that for another cycle of the Ferris wheel. Up and down and around they went. All the while, David held her hand, and her gaze. It didn't feel like staring. It felt like unwrapping the present she'd wanted her entire life.

"It's your turn," she said on the way back up. "Tell me about you."

"I grew up in a big city. Lots of people. I wasn't great at school. Was diagnosed with ADHD. Counselors pointed me to the Army. It was the best thing that ever happened to me. Turned out all I needed was a bit of structure and discipline. Joining the Army Rangers gave me a purpose, something to fight for."

Jules remembered Paris's disdain of the military. He'd been certain that the organization brainwashed individuals. Taking lives to further some hidden agenda.

That hadn't been the case with her grandfather and the mission of the Tuskegee Airmen. Those brave souls had protected people across the globe from a reign of tyranny during the second world war. Now she saw that the army had helped shape the path of the man her heart cried out to. If he hadn't become a soldier, would he have found his way to a ranch in the middle of Montana where soldiers came to heal?

"Now that that life is over, I've opened a training camp with my friends." David grinned, as if at a private joke. "Now I'm the discipliner."

He never seemed to take himself seriously. Jules really liked that about him. She'd grown up around men who debated policy, politics, and philosophy all day, every day. There was nothing heavy about David. He liked to laugh at himself and the world.

"Jules, I need you to know something about me."

"Yes, David?" She leaned in closer. She wanted to know everything about him.

"I've been on a lot of dates. Because I've been looking for The One."

The way he said The One sent shivers along her arms. The hairs at the back of her neck stood at attention, waiting for his command.

"I want you to know that I don't plan to go on any more dates."

Jules had no idea what he meant. She was too busy watching his lips form words. His voice was so silky, like the petals of a new bean sprout.

"This is the last one?" she asked.

"This is my last date. With you."

Her mind raced in the opposite direction of what he meant. The reason she knew it was the opposite direction of where David was trying to go was because as her mind zigged to thinking that he didn't care to pursue anything with her, David was leaning into her.

The first brush of his lips woke something inside of her. She felt like a seedling pushing through the warm earth. Every seed knew it needed to fight hard to get to the top of the soil. Only when it broke free of the earth would it find its true form of sustenance, sunlight.

David's kiss was like the first ray of sunlight. Jules felt herself unfurling for him. She stretched her limbs towards him. She tilted her bulbous head back to drink in more of him. But he pulled away from her, taking his life-giving light with him.

"Tell me you feel it too," he whispered against her lips.

She didn't need to ask him what he meant. It was there burning bright between them. "The spark."

"Tell me I'm the one for you."

Did he really need the words? Couldn't he hear it in her breath, in her blood, in the erratic thumping of her heart?

"Yes, David. I'm yours," she said. "I never want this to end."

CHAPTER THIRTEEN

*P*orco hadn't attended church much while he'd been living here in Montana. His mother had been a social butterfly in her congregation. So much so that Porco knew that the best places for hiding were the vestry and the loft. Only new friends would hide in the sacristy and get found immediately.

While Porco went to church to play, his dad only went to the hallowed halls because a day without his wife was unfathomable. While Jane Porco raised her voiced in the choir, Daniel Porco kept his gaze fastened on her. Their son spent his time between watching the bright light of love that passed between his parents and keeping an eye out for any girl that might look at him in the same way.

Plenty of the girls that came to church smiled Porco's way, and he always smiled back. How could he not? He loved to gaze at the opposite sex, wondering if the next one might be The One. They were all pretty, dressed in their Sunday best. Even today, the sight of shiny Mary Janes set his heart beating.

Jules wasn't wearing Mary Janes as they stepped into the town's church. She had on Birkenstock sandals. Her toenails were painted a deep purple, her heels had a dusting of dirt from the walk through the fairgrounds to the church.

Though her footwear wasn't shiny and new, Porco still felt the thrill from his Sundays prowling the pews. He opened the doors of the church for Jules, knowing he'd never need to search a nave again. He'd found The One.

"Is that you, Porco?" Pastor Walter Vance stood at the pulpit, arranging papers. The tall man looked like he belonged on the back of a horse and not in a sanctuary. He'd been raised on the cattle ranch. Though he'd done his chores every day alongside his sister, Walter had felt pulled for a different calling, as evidenced by the white-collar at his neck.

"You finally hear the voice of God and come to repent all your sins?" Pastor Vance asked with a smile in his voice. The smile dropped when he saw Jules beside Porco. "Ms. Capulano?"

Vance looked between the two of them. His congenial expression moving from friendly, to confused. Then darkening with comprehension and finally crumbling into disdain.

"Oh, no," moaned Vance. "No. No. No." He wagged his finger at them as though they were naughty children. "You cannot ask me to do this."

"We want to get married," Porco proclaimed proudly.

The pastor's shoulders slumped down along with his crumpled features. Porco couldn't understand why? This shouldn't come as a surprise. Everyone in his unit was married. Only he and Spinelli remained. And Porco doubted Spinelli would ever walk down the aisle unless there was the answer to a math problem at the end of it.

Aside from that, Porco had had numerous conversations with the pastor about his desire to find the right woman and settle down. Though he did remember Vance going on about something to do with quality over quantity. Porco couldn't remember the exact details of the conversation because a pretty woman had been walking by. Had he dated her? Or maybe he'd dated the friend she'd been walking with?

None of that mattered. Jules was on his arm. Her warmth danced along his skin until it infused itself in his body. If she wasn't already, she would soon be a part of him. He might've had a lot of dates over his lifetime. All those experiences were what let him know that he'd finally found the right one.

Jules was pure quality. Nothing could be higher. He wanted to spend the rest of his life with her. She'd agreed to do the same with him.

"Do you know who she is?" said Vance, jerking his thumb at Jules. Before Porco could answer, the pastor turned to Jules, his thumb switched direction. "Do you know who he is?"

"He's the man I want to spend the rest of my life with," was her answer.

Porco felt his heart thumping in his chest. It stuttered, making a *ba-bump* sound instead of its normal thump. All too soon he realized, it wasn't just his heart he heard beating. It was her heart too.

He squeezed her hand. He couldn't wait to kiss each digit. Then he would take her lips again.

"How did the two of you even meet?" asked Pastor Vance. Again, before either could answer, he held up his hands like a stop sign. "Don't tell me. You climbed the boundary fence to get to her like something out of *Romeo and Juliet*. Because that's what this is. Your two ranches are feuding."

"But we're not feuding," said Porco. He gazed down at Jules. The same light of adoration shone from her hazel eyes. "I believe everyone will come around when they see how we feel about each other."

That stopped the pastor in his tracks. Though Porco hadn't been paying much attention to the problems between the Vance Ranch and the Verona Commune, he knew that Brenda's brother had acted as the go-between for the two sides. This marriage could be the tie that knotted the two lands together.

"How long has this been going on?" asked Vance.

"We met this morning," said Porco.

Vance sighed, pinching the bridge of his nose. He clutched his Bible to his chest and looked heavenward. His features appeared pensive, as though he was asking the Lord *Why me?*

"Pastor Vance," said Jules, "I know this might seem sudden."

"No, you two aren't the record," he said. "My sister and Keaton only knew each other a few hours before saying their vows. By that math, you two have been dating for a couple of months."

"Then why are you hesitating?" said Porco.

"Because the Keatons and the Vances weren't involved in a generations-old feud," said Vance.

"This feud is between your sister and Paris," said Jules. "The two of them need to work it out. David and I know what we want, and that is each other."

Such elegant words from those perfect lips. If Vance wouldn't marry them, Porco would drive them to Vegas tonight. There would be nothing to keep him from this woman.

"You want to spend the rest of your life with this man," said the pastor, "and all it entails?"

Jules nodded her head. "We'll weather whatever may come."

Pastor Vance turned to Porco. Before he could utter a word, Porco answered him.

"Whatever may come."

"My sister and Keaton with the prenup, I knew what to do there. Patty and Grizz with their unrequited love, easy. Mac and Lana practically married themselves. This one..." Pastor Vance motioned to Jules and Porco's joined hands. "...this one I did not see coming."

The pastor dropped his head. His gaze focused on the Bible in his hands. His thumb pressed on the golden-foiled edges of the pages causing them to flip rapidly under his fingers. As his thumb came to the end of the book, his eyes lit. He looked up at Jules and Porco as though inspiration had struck without reading a single word from the good book.

"I suppose I should offer a bit of premarital counseling," he said, his tone was a mockery of somberness. "You both understand that there are certain expectations in a marriage. There are roles that you must take on."

"Both our parents stayed married until death," said Porco. "We had good role models. Both my mother and father worked and took care of the kids."

"Mine, too," said Jules.

Another thing they had in common. There was so much to learn about this woman. They had a lifetime to tell each other every story and share many more.

Pastor Vance pinched at his lower lip. "What about financial roles?"

"We're both gainfully employed," said Porco. "Jules grows organ beans."

"Organic soybeans," she corrected.

"Right," said Porco. "The bottom line is we both run our own profitable businesses."

Vance pinched at his strong, square jaw. "Okay, how will you resolve conflicts?"

"I feel like I can tell him anything," said Jules. "We already understand each other."

"And if we have a problem we can't solve," said Porco, "we'll just come to you."

The pastor didn't appear to find that funny at all. He cleared his throat, giving his collar a tug. "What about the marital bed?"

Porco felt a rush of heat run through him. His palms warmed where he held her hand in his. Jules was inexperienced. This was her first date. He'd given her her first kiss.

"I'll wait," said Porco. This marriage might be rushed, but he would not rush her into anything.

"Actually," said Jules, tugging shyly at her lower lip, "I'm ready."

"Let's get on with it." Porco had to swallow a few times before he got the words out. He faced the pastor squarely, done with the man's stalling tactics. This marriage was moving forward. Now.

"One more thing," said the pastor. "Where will you live?"

Porco hadn't thought of that. He was staying in one of the ranch hand bunks on Brenda's land. His roommates were Spinelli and Rusty. Not exactly the best situation for newlyweds.

"We'll stay on my farm," said Jules. "My sister and I have our own cabin there."

That worked for Porco. He'd never been a stickler for where he laid his head at night. As long as he'd get to lay it next to Jules, he would not complain.

"You do realize your families will fight this?" Once again, Pastor Vance's shoulders deflated in defeat. But his sigh had a note of hope as it escaped his mouth.

"Or they'll come together when they see that we're in love," said Jules.

CHAPTER FOURTEEN

This was really happening, just like in her dreams. Only this was better.

Jules had never dreamed that her dream man would be so handsome. That his hands would be so soft and firm at the same time. That simply standing next to him would make her feel both powerful and docile at the same time.

She felt a twinge of guilt that her sister wasn't here to witness this. They'd done everything together since they were born. But there had been that hour where Romey had gotten a head start on her. And there was also the possibility that sensible Romey would've tried to talk her sixty-minute-younger-sibling out of this. And there was no way Jules wasn't going forward with this.

"They say that sometimes opposites attract," said Pastor Vance. "I think the reality is that the two forces weren't as opposite as once was initially believed."

He leaned against the pulpit, looking out of the window at the night's sky rather at the two of them. Jules wasn't entirely sure the man was still aware of their presence.

This was Jules's first time in the church. She was far from an atheist. At a young age, her parents had given her and her sister a stack of holy books. Part of their homeschooling was to read them all and make their own decisions. The project included papers, presentations, and a test at the end. Romey's final answer was that God was found in the perfection of nature, while Jules declared that God was love.

"I've found that the happiest couples are rarely the same to outward appearances," Pastor Vance was still philosophizing. Or was he preaching? He might've started the proceedings to marry them. "They are the same on the inside, and that's where you find that you best understand each other's differences."

Outwardly, she and David did appear different. He was a soldier. She was a modern-day flower child. But they'd looked past those differences to the heart of one another and felt an intense attraction.

"Your families are opposites," said Pastor Vance. "Like magnets giving off two negative forces, they repel. But the two of you have turned around and looked at one another to see a different side."

Yes, that was it. They were like magnets. Drawn together, no matter which way you turned them.

David smiled down at her. Like the magnets they were accused of being, he took her hand in his. Jules felt that warmth of electricity zing across her fingertips.

"God is the spark. He's put you two in each other's paths to do His work. I am His servant. Though Lord, I hope you will protect me from my sister."

Once again, Pastor Vance looked up at the ceiling. He let out a long, weary exhale and then made a sign of the cross over his chest. Returning his attention to the couple before him, he gave first Jules and then David a thoughtful gaze. Finally, his face broke into the congenial grin he was known for.

"And now for the vows."

"Wait," said David. "I have something to say first."

Jules's heart skipped a beat. A fluttery feeling crept into her stomach, and she tingled all over. Was he backing out?

"Jules, I know this is crazy; what we're doing. But something in me recognizes you as my home, as my shelter. My mom told me that when I found The One, I'd know it because I'd feel a spark. That's not what I felt with you."

Jules lost her breath. He was breaking up with her. Her first date, her first kiss, her first marriage, and her first break up all on the same day. So why was David clutching her hands tightly, like he planned to never let go?

"It wasn't a spark like my mom said. It was an explosion. It rocked my world. I know I'm not thinking straight, but I don't have a single doubt that this is the right thing to do. I'm not a perfect man, but I know that you are perfect for me."

Jules let out a shaky breath as she regarded this man. Neither had said the word, but she felt it humming between them. That spark, that explosion, that feeling, it could be nothing but love.

True love.

"David, being with you is the most natural thing in the world to me. What's between us, that spark we feel, it's like a seed. I've put it in my heart, and you've put it in yours. We'll grow it with our care and attention. We'll nurture it with time and patience. It will grow strong, and it will feed everyone we love and care about, and then they'll see… they'll see that what we feel is real. It's natural. It's… everything."

David looked down at her with eyes shining so bright that she felt warmed through. She had only kissed him once. Right now, she wanted to do it again. She wanted to do it forever. And very soon, she could.

"Those were perfect vows if ever I heard them," said Pastor Vance. "Julia Starflower Capulano—"

A snort escaped David's mouth, which he promptly covered, only to chuckle again. "Starflower? Your middle name is Starflower?"

"Yes." Jules lifted her chin. "My parents let me pick my own middle name when I was five. What of it?"

David's face sobered. "Nothing. It's beautiful." He winced as though trying to keep an errant chuckle down. Lucky for him, he succeeded.

"Julia, do you take this man to be your lawful wedded husband?"

Jules let go of her annoyance and answered honestly, with all her heart, "I do."

"David Eugene Porco, do you take this woman to be your lawfully wedded wife."

David opened his mouth to agree, but Jules held up her hand to stop him.

"Hold on a moment," she said. "Porco?"

"Yes?" David frowned at her.

"Your last name is Porco? I thought it was a nickname. Like, something cruel that kids called you that stuck."

"No, it's me. David Porco. But I like that you call me David."

Jules nodded her head slowly, as though she was trying to absorb this new detail and let it settle. "So, I'm going to be Julia…Porco?"

"Yes, Starflower. Is that okay with you?"

The grin that she'd found mischievous not too long ago caused Jules's features to pinch in annoyance. What was in a name? Beneath the twinge of indignation at this name-calling interlude, Jules's feelings hadn't changed for this man.

"Yes, it's okay," she croaked.

They both looked at Pastor Vance. The man held his tongue for a long moment. He didn't say the part asking if there was any reason this marriage shouldn't take place to speak now or forever hold their peace. He didn't need to say it. His silence spoke volumes.

When neither Jules nor David voiced any opposition, he continued. " Then by the powers vested in me, I now pronounce you man and wife. You may kiss the bride."

David turned to her. He didn't hesitate. His hands were just as sure as they'd been back up in the Ferris wheel. His lips were just as certain as the first time they'd brushed hers. His sigh of utter contentment when he pulled away from her was just as satisfied as her own.

"Whatever may come," he whispered in her ear. "You're mine now."

"I am," she agreed. "And you're mine."

CHAPTER FIFTEEN

*T*he drive to the commune was quiet. Porco expected to feel differently now that he was married. But he didn't. He felt the same as he had after the first moment he saw Jules.

The same hum of energy skittered across the underside of his forearm, over the pulsing of the veins of his wrist to land in the palm of his hand. The same trickle of warmth pooled in the palm of his hand and radiated out to zing back up his arm and to his chest. The same sense of wholeness settled in his chest, easing the ache that had plagued his heart since he comprehended there was a thing in this world called love.

And now he had it.

While Porco turned the steering wheel with his left hand, Jules's left hand rested in his right one. Her fingertips slid up from his palm and found their way to entwining with his. He folded his thick fingers down over her slender ones, locking the two of them into place.

He'd watched his parents fit together like two pieces of a puzzle for his whole life. His parents never made him feel like an outsider, but even as a kid, Porco was keenly aware that he was one half waiting for a whole. Now with Jules by his side, he felt a connection around the edges of him. The longer he spent with her, the closer he got to her, he felt the two of them snapping into place. He was certain that by morning, he would be made whole.

When he climbed out of the car, the night wind nipped at his back, brushing a cool tendril of air across his shoulders. He brushed it off as he rounded the truck to hand out his wife.

The feel of her hand in his reignited the spark. The cold from the twilight gushed out of him. Porco felt his center of gravity restoring itself.

"This is me," she said, pointing to a small cottage tucked away out in the back of the commune.

The structure was a one-story ranch made with a mix of brick and wood. There was a white bricked turret off to one side with an upside-down ice cream cone painted purple on the top. All it needed was a white flag billowing down and a princess leaning out the window.

"My father built it," Jules said, pride evident in her voice.

Porco wasn't surprised. It definitely looked man-made. It also looked like a strong gust of wind might blow it over. It didn't matter. If that's where Jules lived, then it was now his home too. He'd follow this woman anywhere, even if it was across the threshold of a children's storybook.

"Can you just wait here a second," she said. "I want to warn my sister first. She might've expected me to come home with a stuffed animal, but not a...you." She looked him up and down, eying his chest appreciatively.

Porco preened under her perusal. Under his wife's perusal. In just a matter of moments, he would unveil more of himself for her scrutiny. And he would gently, patiently coax her to do the same for him. For now, he waited on the threshold of her doorstep.

Jules slipped inside the door -the unlocked door. With a shy smile, she shut the flimsy piece of wood in front of his face. Again, he heard no snick of a lock. Looking at the brass handle, he saw no place for a keyhole.

So, not only did no one lock their doors on this land, but they didn't even have locks? That was insanity. It was a change that he would be making in the morning. He had no intention of ever leaving his wife unguarded when he wasn't present. Nor when he let down his guard as he slept with her in his arms.

Another chilling thought took him. If they didn't lock the front doors, then they had no cause to lock bedroom doors. What about bathroom doors? That would need to change. It might be that this would be the first argument they would have as a married couple. Not wanting anything to disrupt his honeymoon night, he would have to let the discussion hold until morning.

A tap at his shoulder brought Porco's attention around. He couldn't make out the figure standing behind him in the dark. He assumed it was a male by the broad shoulders. He became certain the person was male by the meaty fist that struck his eye and snapped his head back.

Porco doubled over, pressing the heel of his hand to his injured eye. Knowing that the threat was still near, he stepped back, putting his body between Jules's door and the assailant. With his instincts kicking in, he straightened, ignoring the throbbing pain of his face. He balled his free hand in a fist and squared off against his opponent.

"Sneaking onto my land?" snarled his foe.

"This is my house." Well, it was his wife's house, and there was that fifty percent marital law. But Porco didn't bother explaining any of that. He had to first contend with neutralizing the menace.

"You must be sniffing those chemicals you poison the land with. If you won't go, I will remove you forcibly."

The man lunged for him. Porco easily outmaneuvered him with only one hand. It wasn't as easy as it looked. The guy was tall, mostly limbs. But there was a cord of power to him. Still, he was no match for a trained Army Ranger.

Porco took him down in two moves. The first move was a swipe with his boots that took out the man's legs. With his second move, Porco was on him. His fist was drawn back, ready to strike. But he stopped when he saw Jules coming towards him, a garden hoe raised for an attack. She wasn't looking at the intruder on the ground. Her gaze was focused on Porco.

"Jules," he said, ducking. "What are you doing?"

"What are you doing trying to break into my house," said Jules.

Though her voice had gone an octave deeper. And when had she cut off her glorious locks? Her hair was short, a puffed-out cloud around her head.

"Romey, stop."

Porco was seeing double. Jules stood in the open doorway of her house. And Jules stood hovering over him with a weaponized gardening tool.

"Romey," said Jules in the doorway. "Put that down."

"He was trying to break into your house," said the man on the ground. Another look let Porco know it was the yogini laying on the ground.

"No, Paris," said Jules coming to stand beside Porco. "I invited him in."

"Why would you invite the enemy in?" asked Paris, now coming to a crouch.

"He's not the enemy," said Jules. "He's my husband."

The other Jules, Romey, let the gardening hoe clatter to the ground. In, Paris, rose to his full height. He took a menacing step towards Porco. Porco's head throbbed from the man's blow, but he was ready to take him on again.

Porco wouldn't have to. Jules stepped in front of him, as though she would protect him. Porco felt another click of their souls fitting into place.

"What's happened?" said Paris. "Has he tricked you? I know this one. Porco, isn't it? They call him that because he's a glutton for female attention."

Jules bristled, but she didn't move away from Porco. "No, that's his last name. Now it's my name, too."

Both Romey and Paris stared, mouths agape as though they were the fish out of water on their own land. Romey was the first to shake off the shock.

"I thought you were just going on a date," said Jules's twin. "How did this happen?"

"It's him," Jules said. "He's The One. There's a spark between us."

Romey's face didn't light up as Jules's was now doing. Romey pinched the bridge of her nose and looked to the stars as if they would provide her any answers.

"You got married?" said Paris.

Jules turned to the man. Was that a touch of guilt on her face? "Yes, I got married."

"But he's a soldier. He's a carnivore. That belt he's wearing is made of leather."

They all looked down at Porco's belt. Paris was right. The belt was leather. So, what of it?

When Paris's gaze lifted from Porco's belt, he looked ready to skin him alive. Not willing to turn the other cheek, Porco took a fighting stance. But Romey stepped between the two men.

"Paris, it looks like you need a visit to the Problem Jar."

Whatever the Problem Jar was, it didn't look as though it sounded inviting to Paris. The man glared at Romey, then Porco, then Jules.

"Paris, I'm sorry," said Jules. "You've been a really good friend to me over the years. But I never felt more for you than deep friendship. I should've told you that sooner."

Under the pale moonlight, Paris's cheeks puffed red in anger. He took a step back from Jules, as though the force of the emotion was unexpected. He turned the full force of that glare on Porco. "You're not welcome here. You will never be welcome here."

Paris turned and walked away. As he made his way up the path, a huge pig made its way down the path. The animal gave the man a wide berth. Its attention caught on Porco, and it trotted over to him.

Porco hadn't seen many live pigs in his life. His father's people were from the country, and when they'd gone to visit, he'd seen hogs roasted over the fire. Which was why he'd learned never to play with his favorite food.

But this pig had decided they would be friends. It nuzzled its snout against Porco's jeans. Insistent until Porco gave his hairy head a pat.

"Well, at least Hamlet likes you," said Romey.

Porco looked up at Jules's sister, her twin. He saw the differences clearly now. Romey had frown lines marring her brow. There wasn't the same light twinkling in her hazel depths. Her arms were crossed over her chest, and her features cast a shade of skepticism in his direction. He'd have to win her over, but he hadn't the first clue how.

"Jules, what is going on?" said her twin. "Tell me you didn't marry a man you just met this morning."

"Okay, I won't tell you that. Even though it's a fact."

Romey sighed.

"Hi, I'm Porco, your new brother." When Romey grimaced at his last name, Porco amended, "You can call me David, like your sister does."

Still no response from his new sister-in-law. She only gaped at him as though she couldn't believe he was real.

"Come on inside," said Jules. "Let's get that eye looked at."

The three of them walked into the house, followed by the pig. Porco was about to voice an objection, his family hadn't even allowed dogs in the house. However, once inside, Porco saw a nest of cushions with the word Hamlet painted over top. Apparently, the pig was not only not food, it was some kind of a pet.

With Jules's hands on his face, he forgot about the pig in the corner of the room. The throb behind his eye eased a bit, but he was sure he'd have a shiner in the morning. He just couldn't believe he'd let that wispy farmer yogini get the drop on him. It had been more than the element of surprise, Porco was off his game because his head was in the clouds because of the woman peering intently into his wounded eye.

"It'll be fine," he assured Jules. "You got any raw meat in the fridge to bring the swelling down?"

Jules's head waggled in that comical way when another person says something utterly ridiculous. But what had he said that was nonsense?

"Paris is right," said Romey. "He won't be accepted here."

CHAPTER SIXTEEN

David was quiet as they drove the short distance from the commune to the ranch next door. Jules had never been on the property. She'd driven past it plenty of times over the years. The main difference was the number of cows that dotted the green pastures where crops and colorful dwellings dotted her homeland.

The light of the moon shone the way as they drove up to the big house. There weren't near as many houses on this ranch as there were on the commune. Far fewer people as well. She felt a stab of disappointment that David hadn't gotten to visit the nightly bonfire on the commune. But Paris's words hung in her mind. Would anyone ever accept him on the land?

She'd always thought of the people of her home as the most open-minded, the most compassionate, the most accepting of differences. And they were. Except when it came to the Vances and how they treated the land.

David wasn't a farmer. He wasn't even a rancher. He was a friend, helping out another friend. He didn't even understand the meaning of the word organic, or vegan for that matter. Was he willing to learn? When he did, would he take her side? Was the thought of making him take aside a problematic way of thinking?

Jules let out a long sigh. Before she'd extinguished all the air in her lungs, she felt warmth kindling in the palm of her hands. David had reached for her hand. He'd engulfed her fingers with his own. At that moment, Jules knew there were no sides. There were only the two of them, standing together, back to back, face to face or side by side to take on whatever may come at them.

Jules looked over at the man who she had changed her entire world for. She wasn't sure what the future held for them, but she knew that being by his side was the right decision. She would give her family and friends time. They would come around. They had to.

At the end of the long drive, David put the car in park. He turned to her with a wary smile. He looked as tired as she felt. The wound beneath his eye was turning a darker shade.

"You alright?" he asked.

"I'm fine," she said, proud her voice held no sign of trembling, unlike her fingers. "We should get that looked at."

She lifted her hand to his face. David caught her fingers before she could touch his eye. He pressed a kiss to each of her five digits.

"Brenda will have some raw meat in the fridge. That and some ice is all it will take."

"I don't understand what you want meat for. Or ice for that matter? You need a warm compress with arnica."

"That sounds like poison," he grinned, brushing her fingertips over his bottom lip.

"Only if you ingest it." Jules watched her fingertips as they glided across his mouth. She wanted to take her hands away and replace them with her mouth.

"Is this our first argument?" David asked, nipping at her index finger. "How to handle the wound your boyfriend just gave me?"

"Paris was never my boyfriend. He wanted more. I didn't. I should've said something a long time ago, but I didn't want to hurt his feelings."

"I'm just messing with you." David pressed her hand to his heart. It leaped the moment her fingers touched his chest. "I don't blame Frenchie."

"His name is Paris." Jules grinned up at David, getting instantly lost in those dark eyes. What were they talking about?

"I'd knock out any guy who tried to come between you and me." David brushed a kiss against her forehead. Then over her eyelid. Then on each cheek. "If he comes at me again, I will knock him across the country."

Jules pulled away from her husband. She set her mouth to tell him that she did not condone violence. But the strength in his tone did something to her belly. It called her a liar.

She was certain she didn't want to see Paris hurting any more than he was. But she liked the idea of David using his strong body to protect her. She was moments away from being fully introduced to her husband's body. They just needed to get out of this truck and to his room. Oh, and there was that matter with his bruise that needed tending to first.

David let go of her hand to climb out of his truck. She watched as he made his way around to her, enjoying the way his long legs ate up the ground to get to her. When he reached her in just a few strides, Jules voiced something that had niggled her on the drive over.

"Paris said you were a glutton for female attention," she said when David had opened the door for her.

David reached into the cab of the truck. He put his hands on her hips and lifted her out as though she weighed nothing. "I told you I'd dated a lot."

"And now you're done with that." Jules wrapped her arms around his neck as he pulled her against him, holding her just off the ground.

"Yes." He held her so that her head was just a hair higher than his. He gazed up at her as though she was the sun and moon and stars combined.

It took Jules a moment to find her voice. "Why me?"

"You know why?" He held her against him with one hand. With the other, he brushed a stray lock back behind her ear. "You feel it too."

She nodded. The spark had grown into a fire between them. With each moment they spent close to one another, it blazed ever brighter. She started to wonder if it would burn them someday.

"Come on," he said, carefully setting her feet on the ground. "Let's get you inside."

They walked hand in hand. They were nearer to the side of the house, so they rounded to the back. As they approached, Jules heard voices. She smelled something sweet in the air. It was an unfamiliar scent mixed with the familiar smell of burning wood and charcoal.

So, the Vance Ranch had bonfires of their own. That settled her anxiety. There would be some familiarity with this bunch.

And then she saw it.

People were gathered around a fire, much like the nightly bonfires on the commune. But unlike the bonfires where people sat with musical instruments on their laps, and others danced around the blaze, there was something in this fire.

Speared on a stake was the carcass of a pig. Its sightless eyes stared at her accusingly. Men poked at it with a stick and sharp knives.

"Hey, Porco, we made your favorite."

Porco raised his free hand and waved. Jules placed her free hand over her mouth to stifle the guttural scream that ached to rise. All laughter around the bonfire faded when they saw her.

"What's she doing here?"

Jules had never met Brenda Vance in person, but she'd seen the woman many times. Brenda rose from her seat and advanced on the two of them. The female rancher looked anything but welcoming.

The fight had gone out of Jules. She was feeling far too queasy watching the animal turning and burning on the fire. "I need to lie down," she said to David.

CHAPTER SEVENTEEN

here was a pain in his neck when he woke the next morning. His eye throbbed a bit as well. But all that pain went away when Porco inhaled.

The flowery scent of lavender tickled the fine hairs of his nose. Followed by the burning bite of peppermint. That overwhelming scent was chased down with a breeze of vanilla, so sweet that he opened his mouth to sample a lick. Instead of an ice cream cone, Porco's lips met with a lush field of silky brown.

Jules lay beside him in his bed, still deep in sleep. They both rested on top of the sheets, covered in their clothing they'd worn on their date. The same clothing they'd worn at their wedding. It wasn't the wedding night he'd always dreamed of, being that he sported a black eye from when he'd tried to carry her over her home's threshold, and she'd thrown up after bearing witness to the reception she'd gotten when they'd arrived at his home.

Porco and Jules's relationship had been rushed, out of order, and out of whack. Gazing down at his wife, he knew that he'd take every step again if it led him to this moment with her in his arms. The disaster of the other day hadn't dampened the spark he felt for this woman. Still, he had no idea what step to take next in their lives.

When they'd come inside the bungalow to his room, she had collapsed on the bed. He'd sat down beside her with a cold compress to his eye since all the meat in the house was cooking in the fire. Besides, she'd had such a bad reaction to the pig roasting that he didn't want to upset her even more.

Before he'd closed his good eye, he'd done a quick google search on the word vegan. His stomach growled even now, remembering its definition. Not only did his wife not eat any meat, she also didn't eat any dairy. He didn't understand how she lived. Certainly not how she had the curves that she did.

Would she expect him to give up meat as well? He was still trying to resign himself to the idea that she wouldn't be making him a plate of bacon and eggs this morning. But one more whiff of her hair and Porco was ready to forgo bacon... for breakfast at least.

He had no idea what to offer her to break her fast? Maybe some home fried potatoes? A salad? If he could find any greens. The only salad he knew how to make was potato salad. And he always put heavy cream in it. So that was a no go.

He knew what vegans didn't eat. But he had no clue as to what they did.

With great reluctance, Porco disentangled himself from his sleeping wife. It was a hardship. Moving away from her felt like tearing himself from a bound book. The pages of their lives may not have started off in the same place. But after being glued together, the story of their lives wouldn't make sense if the pages went missing.

He found the strength to step away from her. He made his way into the bathroom that he shared with Spinelli and Rusty. It looked as though the other two men had already risen and made their way out into the fields. Looking into the bathroom mirror, Porco caught the shiner below his eye. It wasn't as bad as it felt. It was more of his Army Pride that had taken a hit. He'd been cold-cocked by a vegan. How had Paris gotten so big if the male didn't eat meat?

Porco showered and dressed. Keaton had told him to take the day off, but he was used to getting up at the crack of dawn and getting his hands dirty. Outside, the day was overcast. Rain threatened, but he could see the sun peeking out behind the clouds. It could go either way.

"We weren't expecting you," said Rusty. The man wore army fatigues and cowboy boots. It was how most of the soldiers on the two neighboring ranches dressed; a mirroring of their old and new lives. "You and the missus already fighting?"

"No, she's still asleep. We had a long day."

"I'll say," said Rusty. "What with meeting and then getting married right after, it was busy."

"Not you too," Porco sighed.

Rusty had been the only man in their unit that had been married. Though that was soon coming to an end. Not because Rusty wanted his marriage to end. Porco had watched the man fight for his marriage for the last year, offering Veronica anything she wanted. The demand Ronni came back with? She wanted nothing more from him except his signature on the divorce papers. Each morning Rusty struggled, pen in hand, to give her that. Of all of his friends, Porco had thought that Rusty would champion his marriage. Apparently, he was wrong.

"Did you even think it through?" asked Rusty. "Divorces aren't a walk in the park."

"We're not getting a divorce."

Rusty lifted his eyebrows as if to say, *That might be what you think.* His gaze looked up at the clouds. They'd darkened to gray.

Porco's gaze searched the sky too. He knew that behind those clouds the sun would break out at any moment. He just had to wait for it.

"Even if she wanted a divorce," which Porco hoped with everything in him that Jules didn't want, "it wouldn't mean anything. I gave her more than my vow last night, I gave her my heart. It's hers forever. Whether she wants it or not."

"Yeah," said Rusty. "I know exactly what you mean."

CHAPTER EIGHTEEN

ules woke up alone in bed. Which would not be out of the ordinary. Except she had woken a few times in the night and felt the warm, sure heat of David behind her.

Though the previous day had been trying, she'd remembered her reasons for being here with this man in the night. David had held her tightly to him as she'd slept. All through the night, in a strange bed, on land she wasn't sure she was welcome on, she'd felt as though she were fitting into him like a puzzle piece. At the sharp pointed edges of David's body where he ended, she'd begun to curve into him forging a new beginning.

Jules had always felt that something had been missing in her life. Now she knew that something had been a someone. That someone had been him.

So, where was he?

All around the room, she saw evidence of him. A green army-issued duffle bag sat at the floor of the open closet. Inside the closet, jeans and fatigues were organized from the darkest shades to the lightest on hangers. Shirts hung crisp, not only going from light to dark, but also organized by collared shirts, t-shirts, and flannel.

So, her husband was a neat freak. That was good. Though Jules's closet back home was nowhere near this organized and color-coded, everything was at least on hangers and in drawers.

At home. The words echoed into her ears. Was this her new home? Was there space for her here? And what about Hamlet? He was technically her pet. Romey just tolerated his presence. No way was Jules bringing the pig anywhere near this ranch. Her stomach roiled to think back to what she'd seen last night.

Jules rose from the bed. She was still in the clothes she'd worn the other day. In her haste to leave the commune last night, she'd forgotten to pack any of her clothes with her. Her sundress was wrinkled and rumpled. She must look a fright. She was glad at that moment that David wasn't there to see her.

A knock sounded at her door. It seemed entirely wrong that her husband should knock on their bedroom door before entering. If things had gone as planned last night, her wedding night, then David would've probably still been in bed with her. And her clothes wouldn't have been wrinkled from sleep. They'd have been in a heap on the floor.

Jules padded barefoot over to answer the door. On the other side wasn't the man she was expecting. There wasn't a man standing there at all.

"Good morning, I'm Patty." The redhead wore a bright and friendly smile.

"Hi," said Jules. Jules had a vague memory of seeing the woman around the bonfire the other night. When her gaze had slid away from the fire, it had landed on something else red. Yes, she remembered that red hair. "I'm Jules."

"Well, I know that, silly. I'm your official welcome wagon." Patty held a plate in her hands. "Porco said you were vegan. That means no meat, right? Which is a challenge for me because it's all I know how to cook. Luckily, I know how to scramble an egg."

"Well, eggs are meat."

Patty's smile faltered. She looked down at the plate of fluffy, yellow eggs and frowned. Her gaze took in the eggs anew as though she were seeing them for the first time.

"They are?" Patty's voice rang with bewilderment. Then her features crumpled in embarrassment. She slapped a hand at her forehead. "Right, I guess the egg came before the chicken."

She let out a self-deprecating laugh. Jules joined her, not wanting to turn away the first friendly face on this ranch.

"There's also fruit and bagels," said Patty. "Are those okay?"

"Those are fine," Jules lied, taking the plate. Though fruits and bagels were a staple of her diet, the fruit and bagel on the plate were not only touching the eggs, they also sat in a vat of eggy butter.

"Thank you," Jules said. She thought she might content herself with the top of the bagel. But alas, there was cream cheese on the bagel. Still, it was the thought that counted.

"I also brought you some clothes since I didn't see you come in with any bags or anything."

Patty handed over a colorful sundress. Though Patty's offering cost more than Jules's annual clothing budget. Beggars couldn't be choosers. Jules was again grateful.

"The boys are out at the camp this morning," said Patty. "I'm going to get lunch started if you want to come up to the big house. I'm making catfish. You can have fish, right?"

"Nope." Jules gave a shake of her head. "Fish is meat. So..."

"Hmmm." But then Patty brushed it off. "We'll figure something out. Welcome to the family."

CHAPTER NINETEEN

"Yogurt, that's gotta be vegan. Right?" Porco held up the packaged containers. The bright label announced healthy alerts like sugar-free, fat-free, real fruit, and something to do with active cultures.

"No, that has dairy. Dairy is from cows." Spinelli spoke in slow clipped tones as though he were talking to a child.

Porco scowled at his friend. He hadn't asked the man to come along on his grocery store run. Spinelli had hopped into the passenger seat as Porco had started up the truck. At first, Porco hadn't minded the company. Spinelli was a high intellect guy and could help him navigate the labyrinth that was veganism. Porco would've made many more mistakes if his high intellect friend hadn't come along on the errand. Porco just wished Spinelli had a bit more emotional intelligence at the moment.

"If it has a face, it's not a vegetable," Spinelli said for the tenth time.

How was Porco to know what had had a face if it wasn't bleeding in the package? Already he'd had to take out butter from his cart. He'd never realized it came from cows. A packet of tuna had been nixed - because the chicken of the sea was, well, meat. Even a can of brown beans had been blocked because, when they'd turned the can around and read the label, Spinelli pointed out that it was made with bacon seasonings.

Once again, the cruel truth seized him; David Porco had married a woman who'd never tasted and would never want a slice of warm, crispy, salty-sweet bacon. She had a pet pig, for goodness sake. Porco couldn't even think about Hamlet without his stomach grumbling.

"I have no idea what to feed my wife."

It was Porco's job to provide for and protect Jules. Already he was doing a poor job at that. She was even now in his bedroom, which wasn't even his own home, with nothing to wear, which on any other day wouldn't be a problem, and nothing to eat. A fine husband he was turning out to be.

He wanted to give Jules the world. He just didn't know which parts would suit her? A hand came down on his shoulder, giving him an awkward *there-there* pat.

"Just stick to the fruits and vegetables on the outer perimeter, and you'll be fine."

Porco glanced up at his friend. It was a rare show of humanity from the cyborg in the group. Usually, Spinelli was all facts and numbers. Emotions simply didn't compute in his oversized brain.

Just as quickly as Spinelli had offered the fleeting comfort, did he snatch his hand back, clenching and releasing his fists with the same awkwardness. "I mean, even a trained monkey couldn't screw that up."

And the moment was gone.

"She makes my heart speed up, man. She puts butterflies in my stomach."

"That's not love," said Spinelli. "That's a medical condition."

Porco sighed, knowing he'd never get The Cyborg to understand what he was feeling. Spinelli wasn't even listening to Porco any longer. His gaze was fixed on something on the other side of the store.

Still, Porco was thankful for the friend at his side. Thankful that Spinelli was trying to help him care for Jules in the only way his genius friend knew how. Before he'd left the ranch, he'd passed Patty who was at work making Jules breakfast. On his way to his truck, Keaton had insisted that Porco take the next couple of days off. Brenda, who'd stood at her husband's side, had chewed at her lip but remained mute. That was the best Porco could hope from the strong woman; silence instead of a tongue lashing.

He knew his friends would put aside the conflict between the ranches and accept Jules. Especially once they got to know her. Once they looked into her eyes, they'd see she was nothing but kindness. Once they listened to her speak, they'd witness her wit and want to talk with her for hours. Once they heard her laugh, they'd know they'd found a true friend. She would capture their hearts as she had done with his.

"Hey, Porco."

Porco looked up to find a leggy brunette eyeing him like he was on one of the fruit platters he was considering for his wife. He gave the woman a polite nod and turned back to the produce. On a low shelf, he saw a package labeled tofu. The item sounded familiar, though he'd knew he'd never had it before.

"I'm excited about tonight."

Porco glanced up. The brunette was still there. In fact, she was closer to him, all up in his personal space like she had a right to be there. She lifted a hand to him, her finger poised to run over his chest.

There was a sizzle in the air, hovering in the inch between her finger and his exposed skin. It crackled in his ear like electricity. It hummed like the purr of an engine ready to take off.

Porco watched the woman's finger, partly in fascination but mostly in horror. How could there be a spark between them after he'd found Jules? Had he been wrong about her?

Even before the thought fully formed in his head, he'd dismissed it. What was happening between him and this woman was a sizzle, a crackle. Jules had been an explosion.

Jules had made his heart stop.

Jules had invaded his mind.

Jules had felt like she was part of his soul.

When the woman's finger landed on his chest, Porco eyed it curiously. His heart didn't skip a beat. His brain was foggy with thoughts of Jules. His soul was restless, eager to get back to his wife.

His mind wanted her so much that he thought he was seeing things. Standing at the front of the store, Porco saw Spinelli wincing in his direction. Beside his friend, stood his wife.

But it was odd. Every time Porco was in the same space as Jules, his heart sped up. His mouth would water. The palms of his hands would itch. None of that happened now.

Perhaps it was because Jules's hazel eyes sparked in anger. Her pouty lips pinched in disgust. She turned on her heel and marched out the door. Her short, curly hair bouncing in the retreat.

Short curly hair? Not Jules. Uh oh.

"Porco?" said the brunette, leaning into him.

Porco had forgotten she was even there. He tore his gaze from Romey's retreating form. He had no idea what Spinelli had said to Jules's twin to tick her off. Probably something to do with the idiotic feud between the two ranches. Instead of staying, Spinelli hurried out the door after Romey.

"I can't wait to see you tonight," said the brunette.

"Tonight?"

"Yeah, for the concert." Her sultry grin faltered. "Remember?"

"Oh!" Porco's Jules-haze cleared from his brain momentarily. "It's Paige, right?"

"Right," she said, taking a step back from him.

"We had a date tonight. Sorry, I can't."

"Don't tell me you're back with Rosalind."

"Rosalind? No, she dumped me a few days ago. I got married last night."

"Married? You?"

"I actually need to get back to my wife now. She's probably starving. Do you know how to cook tofu?"

CHAPTER TWENTY

hat had she done?

After her full breakfast of air pie and wind pudding, Jules decided she needed a second helping of fresh air. She pulled on clothes that weren't her own and left out of the front door of a house that wreaked of man, to walk across foreign soil that felt so distant from her homeland.

In reality, it was only a thirty-minute walk through the fields of Vance Ranch to reach the boundary line that separated it from the Verona Commune. The green pastures of the cattle ranch turned from green to brown the further she moved from east to west. Only to turn green again, the closer she came to her home.

The small cabin she shared with her sister was settled at the edge of the property. Her mother had chosen that part of the land because the soil was dryer there, not as rich as the land further toward the center of the commune. It was land where beans could thrive.

From this distance, Jules could spy some of her soy beanstalks. She'd taken care not to plant too close to the boundary, not wanting any of her crops to encroach on the Vance Ranch. Still, it looked like the beans had a mind of their own.

On a strip a few yards closest to the border, a patch of seedlings had pushed their way through the dry earth. They shouldn't have been strong enough to have driven through such packed and infertile ground. But push they did through the barren land. Still, it was strange that it was just this small patch of earth that showed life and not further along the boundary.

Jules's mind turned from the tenacious beans to her homeland. She couldn't see the communal fire pit that brought her community together each night, but she thought she could scent the cinders on the wind. She couldn't see the creek she'd swum in naked and unashamed when she was a child but thought she felt its damp waters settle on her brow. She couldn't see the home she'd lived in her entire life, but she felt a connection to it across the short distance.

Did she want to go back home? Did she want to leave this strange land? Did she want to move past these people who were so different than the ones she'd grown up with?

David's grin popped into her mind, clouding her vision. Instead of the light breeze from across the way, she felt the press of his thumb on her cheek. Instead of the dampness of the creek water, she remembered the heat that came when he pressed his lips to hers. Instead of the creaky floorboards of her family's little cabin, she heard the deep rumble of his laughter in her ears.

That's when she knew it. Home was now, and would forever be, wherever he was.

Jules wrapped her arms around herself. Even though she was by herself in a field of barren earth, she knew she wasn't alone. Her husband was out in the world. She sensed that, wherever he was, he was thinking of her at this moment.

The sound of hooves impacting the ground brought her back to the present. Jules's heart sped up, wondering if it was David riding up to swoop her onto a horse and ride off with her. Her heart slowed its beating in disappointment to see that the rider atop the horse sported a ponytail.

Brenda Vance.

Unlike the smile Patty had given her, Brenda Vance scowled when she saw Jules. "I can't figure you out."

Brenda dismounted, still keeping the reins of the horse wound in one hand. Her pretty features were pensive, but her other hand was gentle on the horse's mane. Never one to leave an animal unpetted, Jules stepped closer to the horse and ran her hand over its long nose.

Brenda raised her hand, as though to caution Jules. But the animal dipped its head for Jules's touch.

"He's not the most friendly beast," said Brenda.

Jules shrugged as she ran her hand over the horse's ears. It neighed in delight. "Never met an animal that didn't mind a little affection; be he man or beast."

"Is this where you tell me to spare the lives of my cattle?"

Jules huffed, her laugh humorless. "Even though I was home-schooled, my daddy taught us Darwinism. I know humans are omni-vores; what with the molars and the canines in our mouths. I just choose not to eat meat. I don't judge others who are different than me."

"Well then, you're a rarity in these parts." Brenda turned away from Jules, angling her body so that it was perpendicular to the horse. "I'm judged every day because I'm a cattle rancher with the wrong body parts. Though if I had those other parts, I know mine would be bigger than the male ranchers around here."

Jules giggled at that. Sexism was less of a problem in a community that prized equality, but it still reared its head at times. Like when everyone expected her to marry Paris without a thought of what she wanted to do with her life, her heart.

"What?" said Brenda. "Like you've had to deal with sexism over on your hippie farm of equality?"

"Paris wanted me to marry him. When I married David instead, he kicked me off the land."

"Well, it that isn't the definition of fascism and patriarchy, I don't know what is?"

Jules inhaled deeply and let out a weary sigh. "No. That's not him. Paris is a good man. He's just very focused on securing the future of our land."

Listen to her. Jules was still saying *our land* even though she was standing on the wrong side of the boundary.

"I don't think he ever considered marrying someone that didn't live on the land," Jules continued. "Since we always got along so well, I think he figured I was the best candidate."

"Sounds… sterile."

Jules tilted her head to look up at the tall brunette. "Isn't that the marriage you'd planned for you and your husband."

Brenda opened her mouth to argue. Before any words came out, she winced, as though she thought better of what she planned to say. When she looked at Jules once more, her stern features appeared sheepish.

"You and I," said Jules, "we're probably more alike than you think."

"Maybe," conceded Brenda. Then she wrinkled her nose. "Except for our diet. Where do you get your protein?"

"Same place the cows do; the grass."

Brenda blinked as though she'd never made the connection. Most people forgot that cows were vegans.

"Soybean is high in protein," Jules continued, putting on her farmer's hat. "Studies show it's a great substitute crop for cattle. Especially if you want certified organic beef, which is all the rage these days."

Like the horse, Brenda's ears perked up. But she said nothing. The two women stood there in companionable silence for a moment. In the space between them, it was as though a rift was healing. Fertile ground filling the cracks left by generations before them.

"So, you… and Porco?" Brenda turned her head back to Jules, studying her eyes just like her pastor brother. Though Brenda's eyes had a steeliness to them where Pastor Vance was all softness. "How is that even going to work?"

A grin spread across Jules's face at the thought of her husband. The hunger that was present in her belly had less to do with food and more to do with a desire for him. Jules and David might have a different diet, but one thing she knew for sure was that her appetite would only ever be satisfied by him.

CHAPTER TWENTY-ONE

*P*orco grabbed the brown grocery bags from the passenger seat and kicked the door shut with his booted heel. Spinelli had stayed behind in town, waving Porco off as he trailed after Jules's sister. Had there been interest in the typically discerning man's eyes? Wouldn't that be something if his best friend and his wife's sister ended up together?

The grocery bag wobbled in Porco's arms as he tried to juggle the keys in one hand and his cell phone in the other. He realized belatedly that he didn't have his wife's cell phone number. He didn't remember her bringing one with her as they'd left her house the other day. Then he remembered her telling him that she didn't have one.

It wasn't quite afternoon, just late morning. Porco figured Jules would be up by now. Would she have ventured around the ranch? He tried to imagine the place from her eyes.

Angel, the sole ranch hand that had actually been hired to work the land and animals, was eying one herd of cattle with tags dangling from their ears. The young man's dark eyes were discerning as his pencil scratched on a notepad in hand, writing down the numbers. Porco knew he was determining which cattle were headed for slaughter.

He didn't want Jules to see that. Not after the roasting pig last night.

They couldn't stay here on the ranch. But neither could they live on the commune.

The first order of business today would be to find a place in town where they could live. Or maybe even a starter ranch with land for her to grow her beloved beans. He wasn't a big spender, and he had plenty saved up to make the purchase. Not to mention that the investment in the training camp was already paying off.

Porco would be able to provide for his wife and the family they would have one day. Just the thought of having a family with Jules made his stomach growl with want. Or maybe that was hunger. He needed to get inside and feed them both.

He found her in the small kitchen of the bungalow he shared with Spinelli and Rusty. She was crouched down at the open door of the fridge. Her beautiful features were screwed up in disappointment.

Porco's heart thumped. Not out of desire. The organ gave a sharp kick to his chest. If his heart had a voice, it would be calling him an idiot for failing to provide for his wife.

The inside of the fridge was mostly bare. Aside from a few cases of beer, energy drinks, and packages and packages of bacon.

"Hey," he said.

She glanced over her shoulder, her face lighting when she saw him. "Hey."

Porco's heart stopped its kicking and settled down in a flutter. The blood that had been rushing through his ears sighed now that he had a full view of her face. Julia Porco was the most beautiful sight he'd ever seen in his life. And she was all his.

"You came back," she said.

Every molecule, muscle, and tendon in Porco went slack. The grin that had started to rise went lax. His knees threatened to buckle. His arms went slack, and he nearly lost the contents of the grocery bag.

"You thought I'd left you?" he asked.

They stared at each other for a moment. She sat back on her heels. He stood over her. Finally, Porco sat the groceries on the table and reached for her. Jules came willingly into his arms. She wrapped herself tightly around him, and Porco squeezed her even closer.

He'd been up for hours, but now he felt wide awake. He buried his nose in her thick locks. The scents of vanilla and lavender signaling that no matter where on this earth he stood, he was exactly where he was supposed to be.

"I don't know what I thought?" Jules mumbled into his neck. "David, I don't know how this is going to work?"

Porco pulled back but did not let her go. He cupped her chin in his hand as he gazed into those hypnotic hazel eyes. "Do you want it to work?"

Without a second's hesitation, Jules nodded. The golden flecks in her eyes burned bright. "This all just happened so fast."

He pressed a kiss between her brows. Her eyelids fluttered against his chin. Her soft exhale warmed his neck. He knew then that if her answer had been in the negative, it would not have deterred him. He would've followed this woman to the ends of the earth. Even if that meant a few miles down the road to the lands he was not welcome on.

"David, we are so different. And we don't even know each other, not really."

"What do you want to know? I'll tell you anything. I'll tell you everything."

"Well, you know I don't even have your phone number."

"I'll give it to you now." Still holding her to him with one arm, he pulled out his phone with the other. Then he paused. "I suppose I should get you a cell phone first?"

She grinned down at the device, then bit her lip as she looked back up at him. He was so focused on the place where her tooth had taken her lip. He wanted to do that. Then he realized he could.

Phone forgotten, Porco pressed his lips to hers. Jules gasped at the surprise contact. When her lips parted, Porco took advantage.

He deepened the kiss. He tightened his hold. He pressed his claim.

With his kiss, he wanted to impart his entire being to this woman. He needed her to know that he hid nothing from her. He needed her to know that he would give anything to her, do anything for her. When Porco broke the kiss, finally letting them both up for air, there was one thing he needed to know above all.

"Do you want to go back to the commune?"

Though she was clearly dazed from his kisses, Jules shook her head. "I want to be wherever you are."

Porco rested his cheek atop her head, finding a cushion in the soft coils he found there. "I didn't leave you. I went to get you something to eat."

With great reluctance, he let her go and reached for the grocery bag. Digging into his bounty of produce, he produced one packaged product.

"Tofu?" she said. "You got me tofu?"

"It's soybeans? Right? It's what you grow, so I figured you would eat it."

"Yes," she grinned. "This is what I eat, and I'm starving. Come on, I'll make us lunch."

CHAPTER TWENTY-TWO

"You hate it, don't you?"

Jules watched as David's mouth worked. His right cheek puffed out as he chewed the tofu she'd fried up for him with oil and the available spices. Lips pursing, David's right cheek hollowed as he shifted the bite of food to the left side of his mouth and continued to chew.

"It's not bad," he said, his throat working as he tried to swallow. He tried to lift the corners of his mouth into a grin, but he grimaced instead. He coughed, pounding on his chest. The bite stayed down. David lifted his head, grin firmly in place with his triumph.

"If you liked it," she said, not bothering to hide the suspicion in her tone, "then why not have another bite."

Jules forked a bite of the spongy dish onto her own fork. She raised it to her husband's mouth, airplane style. David's grin of triumph faltered in defeat.

"It's fine," Jules laughed. "It's an acquired taste." She zoomed the fork for a landing in her own mouth.

David's gaze was rapt to her mouth as she chewed. The moment she swallowed, he dipped down to land his lips on hers for a kiss. "I think it's growing on me."

He pressed a kiss to her forehead and then rose from the chair. Tugging open the fridge door, he pulled out a package of bacon. Jules watched in silent dismay as her husband wrapped a strip of breakfast meat around the tofu she'd cooked, and then place it into the frying pan.

"I want you to be comfortable, Jules." Using a spatula, David flipped the sizzling meat wrapped tofu over to the other side.

Jules shifted in the hardback dining room chair. Her nose twitched as the salty-sweet smell of pork permeated the kitchen. "I'm comfortable."

David dished his concoction out of the pan and onto a plate, returning to sit beside her. "I know no one else believes in what we have. But this is real for me."

Jules's gaze was locked on the illogical pairing her husband forked and lifted to his lips. "It's real for me too."

David chewed. His brows knitting together as the food hit his palate. And then, a smile of delight. "It's not bad. I could get used to this."

A drizzle of bacon grease slipped down the corners of his mouth. Jules reached out to him, using her thumb to wipe it away. Repulsion from the pork was the last thing on her mind.

"I love you," she said.

David's grin spread impossibly wider. His eyes lit up. Jules felt the sparks fly from his gaze to hers and settle in her heart. She didn't need him to say the words back. The very look on his face told her his feelings were the same.

She pressed her lips to his. And grimaced. Just as he found tofu to be an acquired taste, she was not jumping on the bacon bandwagon. It didn't matter. She'd trudge through an acre of slop to get closer to this man.

Jules pulled back, gazing into his eyes. She could sit and stare into them forever without an ounce of self-consciousness. Something outside the window tugged at her attention.

"Jules, I love-"

"Is that my sister?"

Jules rose from David's embrace to make her way to the side door of the bungalow. Sure enough, Romey leaned against their truck, speaking to a man. Jules recognized David's friend, Spinelli. The two of them were deep in conversation. Like Jules's gaze had been rapt on David a second ago, Romey appeared unable to take her eyes off the soldier before her.

In fact, her methodical-minded twin was leaning into Spinelli. And—no.

Did Romey just glance down and tuck her hair behind her ear in the universal girl language meaning *I'm interested*? Jules blinked twice, unable to believe her sister was looking up at a man under hooded lashes. Spinelli's full attention was fixed on Romey's face, intent on her every word and motion.

"I tried to tell my sister the same thing," Romey was saying. "This idea of romantic love is nothing but biology."

"Tell me about it." Spinelli tugged at his bottom lip. "Humans were designed to procreate, that's the push we all feel."

"Hmm," Romey agreed, twirling a lock with her index finger. "Though I do think its safest when procreation is done in a committed pair bond. Like wolves, or penguins."

"And owls. Did you know the male courts the female by bringing her dead mice."

"Fascinating," Romey sighed. "So, marriage does make sense in some cases. With the right person."

Spinelli took a step closer. "How would you qualify the right person?"

Now Romey tugged at her lower lip. Her gaze dipped to Spinelli's chest, where his muscles strained under the cotton of his t-shirt. "In most of the world, pairings are still largely transactional. People wed for land, for money, for power."

"I suppose that makes sense," Spinelli agreed. "Though compatibility should probably come into factor at some point. Say, if two people both had the same logical mindset, found interests in the same topics like science… that might make sense."

Romey tilted her head back. "Yes, I suppose it might."

Jules couldn't take the awkward, intellectual flirting any longer. "Hello."

Romey and Spinelli broke apart. Guilt colored each of their cheeks. Behind her, Jules heard David chuckling softly. He might have whispered, "Finally." But she had no idea what he could mean by that.

Romey's guilty gaze shifted from her sister to her husband. Her shoulders straightened, and her finger lifted to point at David. "I just came from the grocery store where I saw him with another woman."

"Well, he wasn't *with* Paige." Spinelli spread his hands in placation. "She came up to him."

Romey turned back to Spinelli. "She was clearly flirting with him."

"You're right. She was." Spinelli turned to David. "But was he flirting with her?"

Romey turned to David. Jules tilted her head, waiting for her husband's answers. He had eyes for no one but her.

"Paige and I had a date for tonight," David said.

Jules heard the sound of ticking. A bomb was set to go off in her chest. David opened his mouth to say more, but she wasn't sure she could handle a second trigger.

"I let her know that I wasn't going to make it on account of I'm married now and entirely off the market."

The bomb went off. But instead of pain, inside, she burst with joy.

"I will never stray," said David. "I'll never need to. You are everything I have ever wanted."

"I believe you," said Jules.

"Jules, you hardly know him," said her sister.

Jules shook her head. She knew this man. She had been waiting for him her whole life. And now, he was here.

"So, that's it?" Romey said. "You're not coming home?"

Jules opened her mouth. And then closed it.

"What about your crops?" asked Romey. "The USDA inspectors are arriving today. They might already be there. This organic certification is what you and Paris have been working so hard for."

It was. And she wanted to see it through. "Paris can handle the inspection. Once we get the certification, he'll calm down. He's never been prone to anger."

As though he'd heard his name called, Paris rounded the corner from the front of the house. Jules didn't see the calm, rational man she'd grown up with. Paris looked red-faced and ready for war.

He was at David's back. David turned, likely from seeing the surprise on Jules's face. Before he could register if the person coming to him was friend or foe, Paris drew his fist and connected it with David's jaw.

CHAPTER TWENTY-THREE

*P*orco's head snapped back from the force of something blunt and angry.

For a moment, he'd thought the earlier kiss from Jules had knocked him back on his rear. He wouldn't have put it past the effect of her. He had no clue how he'd kissed other women and thought he'd found any pleasure in the act. Any and all memories of others were quickly fading from his mind until only Jules remained.

And now there were two of her. Not her sister with the short, springy hair. There were two Jules with caramel skin, flashing hazel eyes, and long spirals snaking over him while he lay on the ground.

Why was he on the ground? Had he skipped some time in this long, endless second day of their marriage, and they were now finally getting to enjoy their wedding night properly? But if so, why were there tears in her eyes? Had he hurt her?

No, that couldn't be it. Because he was the one hurting. His eye was throbbing. Now the right eye along with the left eye.

Jules's fingers over his bruised eye was a balm. Behind her, he heard scuffling. More men charged into the picture. He heard the unmistakable grunt of Grizz and the barking orders of Keaton. But all he could focus on was Jules.

"Wow, Porco. The vegan got a drop on you twice?" That was Keaton. Was that censure in his voice or amusement?

Porco sat up with Jules still draped around him. As his vision came into focus, he saw a tall man with a thin build. The guy looked familiar, but Porco couldn't quite place him. Until he saw the man's balled fist. That he remembered well.

"Paris," Jules hissed. "What is the matter with you!"

Porco had seen Jules smiling. He'd seen her frowning. He'd seen her passionate. He'd seen her confused. He'd seen her disappointed. This was the first time he'd seen her angry.

His produce eating, peace-loving, even-toned wife was a ball of energy. And she was set to launch at the man who'd knocked her husband down. It was taking Grizz and Keaton to hold Paris back from him. Porco got his arms around Jules before she could launch herself at the captive man.

Even with two swollen eyes, this was a battle he had to fight. He'd been prepared to turn the other cheek to Paris after his sucker punch last night. But this was all the zen Porco was going to muster.

"It's all their fault," snarled Paris. "We lost the certification because of them."

Some of the fight to get free went out of Jules at Paris's words. Her hands came to rest on his shoulders. Porco felt his wife's fingers tremble. He turned a murderous glare on Paris. It was one thing to hurt him. He would not stand to have anyone hurt Jules.

But he would have to wait his turn. Brenda stepped between him and Paris.

"You are trespassing on my land," she said. "And you've assaulted one of my residents."

"You assaulted the purity of my lands," said Paris. "The USDA inspector detected pesticides at the boundary between our lands. On our side."

"We stayed away from your land as agreed," said Brenda. "No one sprayed near the border."

A whirring sounded overhead. Up above, soaring through the sky, was a commercial airliner. The timing was uncanny as cold dread washed over Porco. His hands tightened around Jules, certain that if he didn't, she might get away from him.

She tore her gaze from Paris and looked down at him. Concern colored her beautiful face, and she ran a hand over his brow. "David, what's wrong. Are you hurting?"

Porco shook his head, though he felt his insides squeeze. "I did it."

"You couldn't have done anything," she assured him, her heated gaze still on Paris. "None of this is your fault."

Porco swallowed, taking in a deep breath before saying the words that would hurt the woman he loved. Her vanilla scent swirled into his nose. He drunk in her scent, taking in the warm comfort.

"Jules." Her name was a prayer, a balm. He reached for her hands and entwined them with his own.

Jules's concerned melted away. Porco watched as the lines of her forehead creased with something worse than worry. Etched in those lines he saw the markings of dread.

"I was spraying near your lands the other day. I was using a drone. I lost control and it hovered over your land."

Jules blinked, as though she was seeing the scene play out in her mind. "That was you?"

The fear he'd harbored came true a second later. Jules's fingers shook again. This time, anger wasn't the cause. Despair was, and Porco was at its root.

Porco reached for her again, unwilling to let even a breath of space between them. She didn't snatch her hands from him. She gazed down at their entwined fingers as though she was lost.

"It was an accident," said Porco. "I didn't do it on purpose."

"We lost everything," said Paris. "We won't get the certification. Everything we've worked for all these years, gone because of him."

"I'm sorry, Jules," said Porco. "Tell me how to fix it."

"I don't know," she said, defeat in her tone as she rose. "I've gotta go home and figure this out."

"I'll come with you," said Porco.

He took a step towards her. When their gazes connected, he saw that something had dimmed in her eyes. Her focus shifted from him to her sister, and then to Paris.

"I don't think that's the best idea," Jules said. "I need to work this out with my people."

"With your people?"

"I mean, with my family."

"I'm your family."

Jules sighed. His heart broke on her quiet breath.

"I don't want to start another fight," she said. "Just let me go and take care of this. I'll call you later."

Porco watched as his wife walked off with the man who had been his rival just a day ago. He was gratified to see that Jules turned away from Paris when he motioned her towards his truck. Instead, she hopped into the vehicle with her sister. Before they made a U-turn to head off the property, Jules lifted her gaze and connected with Porco one last time before all he saw was the dust kicked up by the tires.

When the truck was no longer visible from the horizon, he remembered. He'd never given her his cell phone number. And she didn't have one of her own.

CHAPTER TWENTY-FOUR

It was just a couple of miles down the road, but Jules felt the separation from David acutely. Every yard was a stab in her chest. Every inch was a slow drip of poison in her veins. Dimly she was reminded that a dagger and a vile of poison were how Romeo and Juliet met their ends in the play.

This would not be how the curtain fell on this particular romance. Jules and David weren't two immature kids who made rash decisions.

Well, their marriage within twenty-four hours had been quick, but Jules didn't doubt for a second that they had the stuff to make it last. There was the spark, that ethereal force that told them both they were meant to be. Jules trusted that force more than anything. It was sent from heaven, so it had to be right.

Besides that divine connection, there was so much to recommend her husband that that boy Romeo didn't possess. David was thoughtful and kind. He was loyal and sincere. He was funny and smart. There wasn't a mean, malicious bone in his body.

Paris had struck the large soldier twice, and David hadn't retaliated. The drone had been an accident. She'd seen the plane correct its trajectory with her own eyes.

But the damage was still done.

Romey drove the truck past their house and down into the fields. The border was still many acres away, they would have to walk the rest of the way. The field of beans looked just as sturdy and bountiful as the day before. To the naked eye, nothing was wrong. Only a test could tell that the roots of her land were now tainted.

"You okay?" asked Romey, coming to stand beside her.

Jules opened her mouth, but nothing came out. Her eyes stayed fixed on the horizon. She couldn't see the boundary that ended the commune and began Vance Ranch, but she swore she could feel the dividing line. David had been here just the other day. His actions had caused an even greater rift between their two families.

"That was a stupid question," said Romey. "Of course, you're not okay."

Romey brought Jules into a hug. At first, Jules was shocked. Though the twins had grown up in a loving family, surrounded by an empathic, huggy community, Romey was not prone to physical forms of affection.

"You really care about him?" said Romey. "Don't you?"

Jules couldn't find the words as she snuggled deeper into her sister's embrace. So, she nodded.

"Then we'll figure out how to fix it. It's just a problem, an equation with variables. We just need to do the calculations to find the solution."

Jules wanted to laugh. There was her pragmatic sister. She half believed that Romey would simply solve for X, and the equation would balance itself out.

"The only solution is to sue, to recoup the profit we've lost now that we don't have the certification."

They hadn't even heard Paris approach. Jules pulled away from Romey to peer at her other lifelong friend. She didn't even recognize the man.

There were lines at the corner of his narrowed eyes where they used to be large and bright. His lips were pinched now. Paris had never been one to grin big and flash his teeth. But he'd always worn a small smile on his face. Dark circles beneath his eyes sat prominently on his high cheeks.

No, he did not look like himself. He looked like his father.

"This is all your husband's fault."

"David said it was a mistake," said Jules. She didn't believe for a second that he would have done this with any malice. For that matter, she didn't think that Brenda would've willfully hurt their prospects.

"It was worse than a mistake," said Paris. "It didn't even occur to him that his actions could be a problem. Those people poisoned our land and our future."

Jules looked around again at her crop. Her beans looked just as healthy as ever. She knew that the chemicals hadn't reached very far, just the small patch at the border. None of the other crops would be affected.

"That's a very dramatic statement," said Romey. "I'm sure we can explain to the inspector about the mistake. If not, we can at least appeal the decision."

Paris shook his head. "Those chemicals will be out of the land in weeks, but it's another three-year wait for us to try for certification again. All because of one careless action, on one patch of land, on the wrong day of the year."

"Ha!"

They both looked over at Romey. Her eyes were lit like when she had solved one of her puzzles in record time.

"That's it," she said. "The variable."

Romey looked at both Paris and Jules expectantly, as if their brains worked on the same level as hers. They didn't.

"Disown our land," Romey said.

Paris' narrowed gaze widened. His mouth slackened. Gone was the ire that had been a constant on his father's features. He looked horrified, like when one of the children on the commune had gotten injured in the field.

"It makes the most sense," Romey continued. "If our patch of land isn't a part of the commune, then the rest of the crops will get the certification."

"I'm not disowning you." Paris's voice was adamant.

"Why not?"

"You're my family," he said as though it was the most natural thing in the world. And it was.

Gone were the lines at his eyes. He still wasn't smiling, but the pinched look had gone from his mouth. The dark circles under his eyes had brightened as his skin had reddened.

Tears struck Jules's eyes. She ran the three steps it took to get to him. And then she was in her friends' arms.

"There you are," she whispered into his chest. "I've missed you so much."

He stood stiff as a board. He tried wriggling out of her hold, but she would not let him go. Jules held on tighter, not willing to let her second-oldest friend go. Soon, his lean body relaxed. His arms came around her and squeezed her back.

"You're our family too, Paris," she said. "David is also my family."

Once again, Paris stiffened in her hold. But Jules refused to let him go.

"That makes him your family," Jules insisted.

"She's right." Romey came up behind Paris and sandwiched the Montgomery inside a Capulano hug. "Their marriage makes him a member of the commune and part of this community."

"And you know what that means," said Jules. "You have two offenses in the Problem Jar. You're going to have to sit with him in an Empathy Circle."

Paris groaned. But he didn't complain. It was a start, and that's all she needed to begin with.

CHAPTER TWENTY-FIVE

It had only been an hour, but it felt like an eternity. Porco stood at the boundary line of the two ranches. Here was the scene of the crime, the mistake that could cost him everything.

The fields he'd treated the other day were already showing signs of life. A few seedlings poked their green heads above the cracked earth. Their leaves unfurled as they reached for the sun's rays.

On the other side of the fence, he saw a few beanstalks that stood a might higher than the others that surrounded it. The growth was slight, but the damage was done. The grass was greener, but it was not better.

"How do I fix this?" Porco asked no one in particular.

He was not alone out in the field. Brenda and Keaton had come to survey the ruins. They were leaning against the rail, heads bent in conversation. It was Spinelli who answered Porco.

"It takes three years for lands to become certified organic," said Spinelli. "It's not a quick fix."

Looking out across the field, Porco could feel Jules's presence. She was so close and yet so far. She'd been there every day tending to her beanstalks, and he hadn't known it. Now he had no idea how he'd live another day without her in his arms.

Spinelli came up to his shoulder, his gaze focused on the beanstalks. "We screwed this one up, didn't we?"

"We?"

"The drone wasn't working properly, that was on me."

"I flew it off course."

"I miscalculated." Spinelli looked across the fields. His gaze was hooded with… was that longing?

A squeal brought both their attention round. Bounding towards them was a fat hog. Porco had no idea how the pig moved so fast on those stubby legs.

"Hamlet?"

As if in answer, the pig squealed. It stuck its snout through the fence. Porco offered the beast his hand, which the pig promptly sniffed and licked.

Wasn't that irony? A pig licking the taste of Porco.

Porco went down to his haunches to scratch the pig's head. Hamlet's snout made it look like it was smiling at him. A soft spot opened in Porco's heart for the pig.

That didn't mean his stomach wouldn't welcome the pig's distant relatives tomorrow morning. Unless it was a requirement for him to bust through this border. Because he knew he would give or give up anything to be with Jules again. Even pork.

In the distance, Porco saw three figures come into view. The first figure he'd recognize anywhere. It was Jules.

The sun took that moment to shine brightly on her face. Time ceased to exist. Distance was no matter. The grass was indeed greener on that side of the fence, and Porco knew that he had to get to the other side.

Shooing the pig aside, he ducked his large body under the fence. Behind him, he heard his friends protest. He paid them no heed. There would be no boundaries in their marriage.

His steps carried him toward Jules. The closer he got, he saw that she was not alone. She was walking with Paris. She was walking arm in arm with Paris. She was smiling up at Paris with those eyes of light.

Porco's steps faltered. Had he lost her? Was it too late?

Paris stiffened. The man must've seen Porco. There would be another fight. Porco had no more cheeks left to turn. He balled his fingers into a fist.

All the fight went out of Porco as Jules turned her gaze onto him. Her smile blinded him. He could feel the love in her heart even from this distance.

She broke the trance, turning back to Paris. She said something to him. Paris sighed, then he kept moving forward. Jules stayed behind, standing shoulder to shoulder with her sister.

Porco ignored Paris, who was striding towards him. He wanted nothing to do with the man, but he would knock Paris down if he dared keep him from his wife. When Paris was just a yard away, the man opened up his arms.

Porco stopped and put his dukes up.

"It's an Empathy Circle," said Paris.

Porco had no idea what fighting stance the man had taken, but he bounced his toes in preparation.

"I'm sorry," said Paris. "I used my fists instead of my words. I've taken a moment to put myself in your shoes, and I see the error of my ways. With empathy instead of anger in my heart, I offer you a hug to mend the hurt I caused."

Porco looked over his shoulder. Spinelli had come through the fence. Brenda and Keaton remained on their side, but their attention was rapt.

Paris was now in front of him. He had his arms opened wide. He was an easy target.

Porco looked past Paris at his wife. Jules was beaming at him encouragingly. Was this what it would take to win her back? He'd rather give up bacon.

Paris waited patiently. Arms still held open. Tentatively, Porco took a step forward. The embrace was stiff, quick. Porco may have given the man a thump on the back that was harder than necessary.

When they broke apart, Porco received the embrace he'd been hungering for. Jules ran into his arms. He caught her up, pressing her to him. They spun in a circle. When the circle completed, he did not put her down. He was never letting this woman go again.

"So, that's it?" Brenda called. "We're good?"

"We're going to have the commune disown our land," said Romey.

"I haven't agreed to that," said Paris. "Our parents left this land in trust to us. It's going to take time and lawyers to work any of that out."

"At least that'll get him off my back," Porco heard Brenda mutter behind him.

"That still leaves you without the organic certification," said Spinelli, his gaze sliding towards Romey.

"I know it's not the most elegant solution," said Romey. "But it should take less than three years, which is how long it will take to get another inspector out here."

"Why not just sell this strip of land to me?" said Brenda. "I don't mind the chemicals. Jules has told me that cows like soybean."

But Paris was shaking his head. "We can't sell it to anyone outside of the families of the charter."

"This place and its land regulations," said Keaton, but he said it with a smile. The regulations on land were what caused his hasty marriage with Brenda that turned into lasting love.

Maybe that was it?

"Sell it to me," said Porco.

"Could work" said Romey. "He is family."

Porco liked the sound of that. Gazing down at Jules, he saw that she liked it too. If they owned this land, it would be out from under the thumb of both the Vance ranch and the Verona commune. They would be the buffer between their two worlds, living in their own cocoon of happiness and peace.

And then the dream sank when Paris told him the value of the land. Porco wasn't hurting for cash. But he didn't have that much in his bank account.

"I can cover the rest."

All eyes went to Spinelli. His gaze kept darting to Romey and then looking away with feigned detachment.

"It's partly my fault."

"We run into the same problem," said Paris. "You're not family."

Spinelli's gaze landed on Romey then. He swallowed, his Adam's apple bobbing before he said, "I could become family."

Romey gasped. Her eyes lit, just like her sister's had the first time Porco had seen Jules. He was standing between the two; his best friend and his new sister in law. The pull between them was unmistakable. There were tiny sparks of energy dancing between the two. Even a blind person could see it.

"It's the best solution," Romey finally said, her voice only slightly breathy. "We can get the certification for the rest of the land. Jules can sell her soybeans to the Vances."

"The Keatons," Keaton pipped in, but no one paid him any mind.

"But you'll have to marry him." Paris stuck his thumb out at Spinelli.

"Jordan is intelligent, gainfully employed, and fit," said Romey, ticking each accomplishment off on her fingers. "What more could a woman ask for?"

"Love?" said Jules from inside the cocoon of Porco's arms.

Romey shrugged.

Spinelli mimicked the movement.

"Love is nothing but a construct," said Romey.

"You can't still believe that," said Jules.

"The marriages on the Vance Ranch and the Purple Heart Ranch all started out as marriages of convenience," said Spinelli. "They've all been successful."

"Excellent point," said Romey, tilting her head like Jules did when she was delighted.

"Thank you." Spinelli gave her a grin.

As if they felt the eyes that were definitely on them, they both wiped the grins off their faces and looked away from each other.

Jules opened her mouth to argue the matter further. Porco turned her, sweeping her back up into his arms so that her feet dangled just below his knees. He pressed his mouth to hers and words failed her.

The spark that had been present between them ignited into a flare. One day the heat they made might dampen into a smolder. Though he doubted it. He was sure it would always be this way between the two of them.

"I missed you," Jules said when he allowed her lips to part from his.

"You never will again," he assured her. "Come on, Hamlet. Let's go home."

The three of them left the others behind to work out the details of the land transfer. He and Jules already done their part. They walked across the acres until they reached the cabin nestled between the two lands who had decided on peace that was now reinforced with love.

Who knew? Maybe someday in the near future, they would even tear the fences down.

EPILOGUE

"She makes my heart speed up, man. She puts butterflies in my stomach."

Jordan Spinelli rubbed his forefinger over his brow. Porco's words made no logical sense. He supposed it was hyperbole, and not meant to be taken literally. But what else were you supposed to do with words if not take them for their definitive meanings?

If Porco meant that Jules made his heart race, then he could mean that she was engaging his fight or flight responses. In which case, his friend's new wife was either a predator who would eat him alive. Or she was prey that he planned to chase after. Neither seemed an ideal situation to Spinelli's mind.

Then there was the bit about butterflies in the stomach; an idiomatic phrase. Spinelli had excelled in school, except when it came to the English language and words that had contrasting meanings when put together in different sequences. He didn't understand how an expression that colloquially meant to make one nervous, could be used to describe love.

"That's not love," said Spinelli. "That's a medical condition."

To be honest, he'd never truly understood the meaning of the word love. The dictionary told it was a deep and intense feeling of affection. A secondary definition was that it was interest and pleasure. Spinelli had always found those denotations lacking. Apparently, he wasn't the only one.

Down at the end of the aisle, he saw a woman's shoulders straighten at his words. Her head gave a nod, as though she were in total agreement with him. Porco was still talking, but Spinelli stepped around him, wanting to get a look at the woman who appeared to share his thoughts.

His feet were moving before he had conscious thought to set them in motion. His ears twitched, like a dog's who heard the high pitch of a whistle from its master calling. His fingers tingled, as though the electricity in the room had increased and become a tangible thing. A chill skittered across the back of his neck, even though he'd stepped away from the refrigerated section of the store.

All the while, he kept moving forward. One step, then another. Closer to her, as if drawn.

What was happening to him? Whatever it was, Spinelli wanted to understand the phenomenon. To study it and pick it apart.

His eyes were glued to the woman, whose back was still turned to him. All he could see of her was her hair. Short spirals of black, bronze, and gold radiated from the crown of her head. As though she was a ball of burning gas and her hair was the radiation it gave off.

As though she sensed him coming near, she turned, and Spinelli stopped in his tracks.

His heart rate sped up. His stomach muscles fluttered. His palms dampened. Was he having a medical condition of his own?

Then her gaze found his. Intelligence shone brightly in her hazel eyes. In the slight smile she offered him, Spinelli felt understood, even though he didn't know this girl. He felt seen, even though this was the first time he'd laid eyes on her. For some reason, she looked familiar to him. But his brain was short-circuiting and he couldn't place her.

They stared at one another. Spinelli spoke six languages. At the moment, he couldn't remember a greeting in any of them.

"Hello," she said.

Spinelli snapped his fingers. That was the word. He repeated it back to her.

And then they stared some more.

She squinted at him as though he was a problem. He could see her mind trying to work him out. Her astute gaze took in his body, taking her time as her eyes roamed over the muscles stretching his shirt. He wanted her eyes back on his face so that she could see that he was smart too.

"You're right," she said finally.

"I am?"

"It is a medical condition."

"What I'm feeling?" The racing pulse. The sweat on his brow. The thrumming in his ears of a single word on repeat. The word sounding like mine.

"Love," she clarified, looking past him. "It's a medical condition. One that my sister's new husband seems to suffer from quite a lot."

Spinelli followed her gaze. Porco was where he'd left him, but his friend was no longer alone. A woman trailed a finger down his chest and Porco looked to be doing nothing to stop it.

"I tried to tell her that there's no such thing as true love."

Spinelli turned back to the woman who he now deduced was Jules' twin sister. How had he not seen that before? Maybe because they looked nothing alike. Romey Capulano didn't have that same starry-eyed look as her sister. There was a sparkle in Romey's gaze that Spinelli could only quantify as brilliant.

"I need to find her and put an end to this marriage." Romey turned on her heel and stormed out.

With a glance at his friend, Spinelli hurried out the door to follow Romey. Like a magnet, he was on her heels, attaching himself to her side. "I'll come with you. I know where she is."

I don't know about you,
but I think what just happened might be love at first sight between Jordan and
Romey.

But these two are going to deny it until there's no other solution before them.
Forget the science and fall in love with
The Rancher takes his Love at First Sight.

RANCHER TAKES HIS LOVE AT FIRST SIGHT

THE RANGERS OF PURPLE HEART RANCH
BOOK 5

CHAPTER ONE

*J*ordan Spinelli gave the tie around his neck a tug. First right, then left. No matter which way he tugged it, it still felt too tight.

"Feeling like a noose around your neck?" laughed his best friend, David Porco.

"No," denied Spinelli, shifting the cloth while looking at his reflection in the mirror. "The knot is just wrong."

With deft fingers, Spinelli unraveled the knot. The color of the tie was a soft shade of brown with touches of orange that pushed it toward gold, but not quite. Hazel, the shade could be called. But the blending of colors didn't come near the brilliance in her eyes.

"Did you know that the necktie actually originated in Croatia?" Spinelli flipped the collar of his dress shirt up and wrapped the cloth around his neck, making a new knot. "It was a handkerchief made of silk worn by the soldiers around the neck. The soldiers were presented to Louis XIV wearing the style, and he adapted it, calling it *à là croàte*, meaning of the Croats."

"Nope, didn't know that," said Porco. "All I know is that I look good in a tux. Wish I'd gotten married in one instead of jeans and a T-shirt. But I was in a bit of a rush at the time."

Porco had married Jules Capulano within a few hours after meeting her. It wasn't an uncommon feat in this particular corner of America. Quickie marriages were all the rage in this small Montana town that boasted a rehabilitation ranch for Wounded Warriors. Most of the residents of The Purple Heart Ranch had married for convenience. But each marriage had turned into something more, a strong partnership filled with love and devotion.

Spinelli pulled the simple ring from his pocket. Devotion, he could promise his soon to be wife. But love? That wasn't on the table. Romey Capulano didn't believe in romantic love. If anyone had asked Spinelli a week ago, he would've said he didn't believe in the notion either.

But then he'd seen her, and his mind had… changed.

He looked at himself in the mirror. The tie was straight, a perfectly balanced Windsor knot where each line hit the right angle. His face was clean-shaven, without a hint of stubble. His dark hair was neatly trimmed, resting just above the collar of his tuxedo jacket. His broad shoulders were back and straight, just as he'd been taught in the Army. So why did his knees feel weak?

"Did you know the tuxedo originated in the Hudson Valley of New York around the year 1888?" Spinelli asked the room of men dressed similarly to himself. They each had a tux handy since weddings were as frequent as cattle runs in these parts. "At the time, it only referred to the white jacket that the elite wore when they went out to dinner. The term later came to include the trousers and other accessories associated with the ensemble, and then it was shortened to tux."

Five pairs of eyes stared at him. Keaton lifted his gaze from a list he was making on a small notepad. Grizz scratched at the stubble on his chin. Mac tore his gaze from the window where his wife stood outside, chatting with another woman. Porco and Rusty sighed in unison as they regarded Spinelli.

Spinelli had never been good at reading facial expressions. He could get by on the basics. A smile meant approval. Though sometimes, it could mean mockery. A frown meant disappointment. A scowl meant anger. Currently, all of his friends' stares were blank. He had no idea what that meant?

"I don't recommend you lead with that explanation on your wedding night," said Rusty.

"Romey is a highly intelligent woman," said Spinelli. "She likely already knows that fact herself."

From the first moment he'd laid eyes on her, standing in the pasta section of the grocery store, Romey Capulano's intelligence had been as clear to see as the perfect diamond he clutched in his palm. He'd been admonishing Porco for his hasty marriage based on the notion that Jules had made his heart speed up and put butterflies in his stomach. Spinelli had aptly diagnosed his friend with, not love, but a medical condition. Across the store, he'd sensed someone agreeing with his words. His gaze had been drawn to Romey. When she'd turned to face him, his entire world had tilted with just that one glance.

"Maybe she knows that fact," said Porco, snapping Spinelli back to the present. "But I bet she'll be interested in other things tonight than a history lesson. By the way, Jules and I are going to clear out and let you two have the cottage to yourself for the night."

"Why would you do that?" asked Spinelli.

The others looked at one another. Mac turned entirely from the window, giving Spinelli his full attention. Grizz's lips twitched as though the big man was trying to hold in a giggle. Keaton held his pencil in mid-air, his checklist forgotten.

"I thought you had *the talk* with him," Porco stage-whispered to Rusty, loud enough so that the people out in the halls of the church could've easily heard.

"I did," said Rusty. "But I didn't pull out any diagrams or equations, so I doubt he was listening."

Spinelli vaguely remembered Rusty bringing up Romey and his upcoming wedding earlier in the week while they were at work. Something or other to do with the mating habits of birds and bees. Though why they were talking about pollination and eggs hatching, Spinelli had no idea. He supposed it was a metaphor. But his mind had never been able to wrap around those. He preferred when people simply said what they meant. That's what dictionaries and encyclopedias were designed for.

"Do you mean sex?" All the tightly held expressions relaxed across the features of his friends' faces. Good, he'd gotten that one right. "Our marriage will be purely platonic."

Five pairs of brows rose towards the ceiling. Five jaws went slack enough to reach the floor. Their looks of surprise surprised Spinelli.

"You all know this is a true marriage of convenience. You were all there when we proposed it."

Just a week ago, the Verona Commune where Romey lived and the Vance Ranch where Spinelli lived had been practically at war. With lawyers and regulations rather than guns and ammo. Porco had made a tactical error when he'd accidentally sprayed chemical fertilizer on the organic farm. That move had lost the commune their certified organic status.

To make amends, Porco offered to buy the strip of land he'd contaminated. That piece of land at the edge of the boundary was where Jules and Romey lived. Unfortunately, Porco didn't have enough to cover it. But Spinelli did. The catch was that in order to buy the land, he had to marry someone from there; Romey.

"This is a purely logical relationship," Spinelli went on. "We're coming together to solve a problem."

"Like me and Brenda did when she wanted to sell me a portion of the ranch," said Keaton.

"Exactly," agreed Spinelli.

Now they were getting it. Brenda Vance and Anthony Keaton had also gotten married on the day they'd met so that she could transfer a portion of her land to the training camp Keaton wanted to establish. It had been a practical, business transaction. Though these days, you couldn't pry the two apart with a shovel.

"Then you're going to need to have *the talk*." Keaton put pencil to pad and began scribbling. "With diagrams and equations this time."

Now it was Spinelli who scowled at his friends. Their grins were all definitely mocking this time. He knew they were trying to imply that he wanted more from Romey than what they had both agreed to. But that wasn't true. He always said what he meant and meant what he said.

He wanted to marry this woman to right a wrong that was partially his fault. It had nothing to do with the golden flecks he'd seen in her almond-shaped eyes. Or the way she bit at her lower lip when she was working out a problem. Or the flare of her nostrils when she came up with an answer.

"This is the best thing to happen," said Porco. "I married the woman who lit a spark in me, and her sister's marrying my best friend."

There Porco went again about that spark. There was no such thing. Spinelli didn't deny that he was attracted to Romey. But it was her mind that he was most interested in. When he'd seen her in the grocery store, he'd been attracted because she had understood what he was saying about love being a medical condition. It was her intelligence, not the fact that her proportions were in the shape of an hourglass.

Thinking about Romey's figure made his heart skip a beat. The knowledge that in just a matter of moments he would take her hand in his and vow to spend the rest of his life with her made his stomach flutter, as though there were butterflies in there. God, he hoped he wasn't coming down with something right before his wedding.

CHAPTER TWO

"I don't see why I need to wear a veil." Romey Capulano used the backs of her hands to fluff the thin scrap of lace up and off her face. "It's not like he hasn't seen me before."

The first time she'd seen Jordan Spinelli was etched in her mind indelibly like the carvings on the Rosetta Stone. Problem was, unlike the translation stone which held the key to deciphering Egyptian hiero- glyphs, Romey was still having trouble puzzling out her initial reaction to the man who'd come to stand before her in the grocery store a week ago.

The first time Jordan had seen her, he'd stared at her as though she had been the key to deciphering an ancient language. With each step he'd taken toward her, comprehension had appeared to dawn in his dark eyes. She'd felt a pull like there was some invisible force between them, intent on entwining their lives like the double helix of DNA. That, she'd wanted to shout to her lovestruck sister, was the true spark. The spark that created life.

And then the two of them had spent the afternoon debunking the idea of love.

Jordan's points about the symptoms of true love being those of a medical condition had been so astute and perceptive that Romey had sighed. When he'd described the notion of passion as a cocktail of adrenaline, dopamine, and serotonin that mirrored reactions on the battlefield, Romey had become heated by his analogy and had needed to fan herself. When he'd determined that the best way to pick a life partner should be in the same manner that someone searches for a home, her knees felt weak.

Jordan Spinelli was the most rational, the most logical, the most calculating man that she'd ever met. She wasn't going to ruin it all by falling in love with him. It was the stupidest thing she could've ever done.

In the mirror, her cheeks heated and turned the blush ruddy. Romey moved her hands and let the veil fall back into place. Only to have her sister pin it back.

"The veil is tradition," said Jules.

"Says the woman who eloped in a sundress and sandals with a stranger she'd only known for a few hours."

"Yes," Jules sighed, her eyes going dreamy. "David is my true love, you know that."

Romey didn't know that. It was impossible for her to know that. Though she and her twin sister Jules might share the same features, they each had two entirely different ways of seeing the world.

All their lives, Jules had had her head stuck in the clouds. She'd always believed in the mythical, intangible idea of true love.

Romey was the more practical-minded twin. Math made her heart flip. Science was her true passion. But now her heart was racing at the thought of a man. It was entirely unacceptable. But she couldn't seem to get it under control.

Every time she thought about Jordan, her mind would fog, her palms would sweat, her lips would tingle. It was embarrassing. Her, Romey Capulano, was suffering the side effects from those silly women who read romance novels about a white knight on a steed come to rescue them. Or a tall, dark, and handsome stranger come to sweep her off her feet.

Romey's feet were planted firmly on the ground. The problem was Jordan had come in to rescue her. Not for love or anything trifle like that. Jordan had fronted the other half of the money to buy her home-stead, the small parcel of land bordering the Vance Ranch and the Verona Commune. The only way the land transfer would work was for Jules and Romey to marry men with money. Their Shakespeare-loving father would've gotten a kick out of that. With the four of them as equal co-owners, they could separate from the commune and it would be granted the organic status it coveted.

It was an elegant solution that she and Jordan had come up with together. Only, now she'd have to see him every day for the rest of her life. Looking in the mirror, Romey saw that her cheeks flushed even redder. But no, that was Patty Hayes brushing blush onto her cheeks.

"Did you know that wearing a veil predates wearing white?" Romey asked. When she got nervous, she always reached for knowledge to shield her. "The ancient Greeks and Romans believed that if a bride wore a veil, it would deter demons from taking over her spirit. They even had bridesmaid's wear veils as well to try and confuse the demons."

"Well, that'll teach bridesmaids or anyone in attendance from trying to upstage the bride," said Patty. She tilted Romey's head to the side and began to work on her other cheek.

"That's the real reason why a father would walk his daughter down the aisle because the veil obstructed her view, and she would bump into things. So, he, or someone, had to walk her down and give her away."

"You don't have to worry about where you're going," said Jules. "I'll be giving you away. And then, tonight after the wedding, David and I are going to make ourselves scarce."

"Why would you do that?" asked Romey.

"So that you and Jordan can... you know... have some time to yourselves."

Time to their selves? They would have a lifetime with each other. Sometimes her sister made no sense.

"Uh oh," said Patty, turning to Jules. "You two have had *the talk*, haven't you?"

The talk? What talk?

"Oh, yes," said Jules. "Laxmi Patel, that's our reproductive health and sexual education teacher on the commune, she was a former tantra instructor. She taught classes on the *Kama Sutra* when we officially entered puberty after our coming of age ceremony."

Oh. *That talk.*

"It's not like that," said Romey. "Remember, this marriage between Jordan and me is practical. We're not in love."

Romey narrowly missed biting her tongue at the statement. She wasn't sure if this was emotional love that she was feeling. It still might be a medical condition. But she was certain it was one-sided. Jordan was far too intellectual to get mixed up in such nonsense.

"Really?" said Patty as she put the final touches on Romey's cheeks. "I've seen the way he looks at you."

"You have?" said Romey. Had her voice gone up an octave with hope?

"That night you invited us over to your land for the communal bonfire, Spinelli couldn't take his eyes off you."

That couldn't be true because whenever she could, Romey had stolen glances at him. He hadn't been looking at her. And when he had looked at her, it was to engage her in conversation about their arrangement. They had spoken practically about their impending nuptials. There hadn't been a single hint of anything more than a business arrangement. Which was what she had always envisioned her marriage to be.

But there had been that moment back at the grocery store. When their gazes had locked for the first time. Had that been a spark in his eyes? Had that been desire curling at his lips? Had his steps brought him to her because he had seen more in her than a like-minded individual? Would he appreciate the fact that they would have the house to themselves tonight, on their wedding night?

Her pulse raced at the thought. Her throat went dry. Her head started to pound erratically until she began to feel faint.

God, she hoped she was coming down with something right before her wedding. A sickness? Maybe madness? Because she wasn't sure she could handle the alternative.

CHAPTER THREE

"Just don't go on about all that science and coding stuff," said Keaton. "Not everyone is as fascinated by numbers as you."

"Brenda loves the algorithm I designed for her to track cattle growth," said Spinelli.

"Yeah," Keaton grinned, getting that far off look that most of Spinelli's married friends were prone to these days. "Well, Brenda's a different kind of woman."

"Whatever you do, just make sure you don't spend all day playing video games anymore," said Grizz.

"Why not? Your wife mopped the floor with my butt in *Call of Duty* last weekend."

A grin tugged at the corner of Grizz's mouth. He got that same faraway look in his eyes as Keaton. "Yeah, but Patty is a different kind of woman."

"Forget these two bozos." Porco took Spinelli by the shoulders and turned him to face him. "If you don't listen to another piece of advice, hear what I'm saying now. Do not ever tell that woman that love isn't real, and all attraction is some chemicals in the brain. No woman wants to hear that."

Around the room, he saw a chorus of bobbing heads nodding in agreement. Spinelli did appreciate the advice his friends were trying to give him about his impending life as a married man. He just deduced that all of them were dead wrong in their guidance.

He and Romey had talked about his work building a virtual reality war game to compliment the training camp's physical fitness courses. He'd gone on and on about coding various aspects of the game, and she'd leaned in, listening with her full attention. She even spoke a few coding languages. True, it was just Python which grade-schoolers could learn. But it went to show that they had yet another thing in common.

When it came to that other thing? Love? Spinelli had never said he didn't believe in love. Just that it was a cocktail of adrenaline, dopamine, and serotonin better suited for the battlefield. That didn't mean it wasn't real. He was certainly feeling a mixture of those charged chemicals coursing through his body as he walked down the aisle of the church.

A rush of adrenaline must've been released because he felt full of energy from his fingertips down to his pinky toes. His heart rate increased, and he felt the blood flowing like a tidal wave through his veins, signaling there was an increase in dopamine in him. Mixed in that cocktail had to be serotonin because his mood was all over the place. He was happy, nervous, anxious all at the same time.

These were the symptoms all of his friends decried was love. If he was experiencing them now, just before his wedding, did that mean that he'd come down with a case of the romance affliction?

He wasn't sure? What he did know was that his soon-to-be wife had spoken aloud her disdain for the notion of love and romance.

There's no such thing as true love.

Those had been Romey's words the first day he'd met her. When he'd been drawn to her. When he hadn't been able to take his eyes off her. When he'd followed her out of the grocery store, unwilling to be parted from her.

He was about to be joined to her in a legal ceremony now. He would have the rest of their lives to figure out what he was feeling. Until then, he'd honor the deal he'd made with her.

"I've got this all under control," Spinelli said. "This will be a practical marriage. You'll see."

None of the men were looking at him any longer. They'd peeled off into the pews to sit with their wives and the families from Romey's commune. The church was decorated with enough flowers to set off the allergies of the whole town. Intermixed with the flowers were gourds, which he'd learned were a symbol of fertility. Streamers mimicking the rainbow hung from the stain glass windows making the religious depictions look as though they were marching in a Pride parade.

All of that escaped Spinelli as the doors at the back of the church opened, and the music began to play.

Spinelli turned, and his heart stopped. That wasn't hyperbole. Or metaphor. Or analogy.

For two full seconds, his heart stopped beating in his chest. His mind blanked. His breath stopped. Was he experiencing an arrhythmia?

He knew he was having a fight or flight response. He wanted to do both. He wanted to fight his way to the woman who'd just entered the doors. He then wanted to fly with her, where no one would question their motives or give advice on how to maneuver the deal they'd struck.

Spinelli had been labeled a genius when he was young. He could do complex math problems in his head. His brain worked in such a way that strings of numbers lined up for him and made sense. With all the codes he cracked, with all the algorithms he'd designed, this was his most brilliant scheme. Getting Romey Capulano to agree to marry him.

"Breathe," Porco whispered in his ear.

Spinelli did. He inhaled as Romey walked slowly toward him. Her veil fluttered around her face. The thin slip of fabric she wore hid nothing. His heart thumped harder, louder, as though it was trying to escape its cage, the closer she got. At least it had started beating again.

It took everything in him to stand still and wait for her. Though he was standing, he felt like his world was upside down. Not head over heels because that was impossible. Just off-center, because his entire axis had shifted and everything was focused on her.

"Who gives away this woman?" asked Pastor Vance.

"I do," said Jules.

Spinelli had hardly spared Jules a glance even though she was the spitting image of Romey. The two didn't compare in his mind. Jules was sunshine on a warm day. Romey was a supernova.

When the veil lifted to reveal her face, Spinelli's breath caught again. His heart threatened to stop and stare. He'd never seen Romey with makeup. He didn't prefer it, but he couldn't deny its appeal.

Her eyes twinkled. Her golden-brown cheeks were warmed. And her lips…

It took everything in him to hold himself back from claiming those lips right now in front of the whole town. Luckily, he knew there was a part in the ceremony that would allow for him to press his mouth to hers. It was the part after the minister declared Romey his before God and all assembled. Spinelli wanted to skip straight to that part.

His gaze caught on something sparkling from her ear. From her ear hung a silver spiral. It was the pattern of a coral shell. But all Spinelli could think was that it looked like a tornado. Possibly because he felt like the delicate spirals hanging from her earlobes could easily knock him over.

"What is it?" Romey asked.

"It just looks like you're wearing the Fibonacci sequence in your ears," he said.

"It is a visual representation of the Fibonacci sequence." She touched a finger to the dangling spirals. "I use it in my work."

"You never told me that." Spinelli stepped closer, wanting to learn more about her work, wanting to learn more about her. "Did you know that Fibonacci's Golden Ratio is used in computer coding and game design?"

A throat cleared behind them. They both swiveled their heads to see Pastor Vance standing between them. The pastor didn't look annoyed as he regarded them, he looked amused.

"Do you mind getting to know each other better later?" asked Pastor Vance. "We have a pressing engagement happening right now."

"Oh, sorry," Romey said, looking out at the crowd of those gathered. Every face in the pews was as amused as the pastor at their little interlude.

Spinelli wasn't sorry. His head was clear. His heartbeat steady. His nerves were calm.

Porco might go on about The One in an ethereal sense. Spinelli knew that Romey was the one for him in every logical sense.

CHAPTER FOUR

ool logic was all Romey needed to get through this. It didn't matter that her makeup was better than she ever could've done herself. It didn't matter that her wild locks were tamed into a sleek bun, sitting obediently at the back of her head. It didn't matter that the white dress fit her like a glove highlighting all of her best assets and making it appear that she had more than she truly did.

This Romey was an optical illusion, a trick of contouring and high-lights. She and Jordan knew the truth. They knew what they were doing here.

So why did her heart skip a beat when the Wedding March started? Why did her fingertips alternate between tingling and numbness as she took her first step down the aisle? Why did she have trouble taking in a full breath when she gazed all the way down toward the end of the aisle and saw him?

Romey's brain scrambled for an explanation. She knew that heart palpations were caused by overheating, or stress, or sugar, or hormones. It had to be one of those factors.

Taking a step down the aisle, she reasoned that she wasn't hot in the dress. The air vents of the church were cool on her back. So, over-heating was crossed out.

Her next step was steady, without a wobble in sight. That was because she knew exactly what she was doing. She and Jordan had made a very thorough plan for this union. There were no unknowns. Which meant she wasn't stressed out.

It wasn't her time of the month. She'd made sure when she'd made the plan for the wedding day. They'd planned for a weekday wedding, on a Tuesday afternoon. Their families and friends had balked at the idea. Weddings should be on the weekends, they'd insisted. But neither Romey nor Jordan saw a reason why? For them, this was business as usual. So why not have it on a business day.

Her sister was still emotional about that decision. Romey had merely shrugged then. She internally shrugged now. Proving that she wasn't having a hormonal episode.

That left sugar. Patty had brought her a glass of sweet tea before she'd begun painting her face. Romey had only taken one sip before getting a head rush at the glass of sugar that was accompanied by a splash of water and a few tea leaves. Growing up on a vegan commune, table sugar wasn't a hot commodity. Those crystals were clearly having a wayward effect on her as she made her way towards her husband to be.

She felt the overwhelming need to fan herself as her soon to be husband came into view. Jordan was dashing in his tux. Romey's mouth went dry, and she wished she could take another sip of that sugary tea.

Her cheeks were heating. She was short of breath. Her makeup was likely melting away from the sweat collecting at her brow. Thank goodness for the veil. She didn't want Jordan to see her like this. But seeing him standing there, waiting for her, did something to her mind. The many brain cells she possessed all scrambled to fall in line with the erratic beating of her heart.

This could not be happening to her. Romey was not falling in love. She was too smart for that. She didn't believe in that.

She needed to get a grip. This wasn't part of the plan. Only... why was Jordan looking at her with his mouth agape? Why was he scratching at his chest? Was he having heart palpitations as well? Maybe they were both sick? Maybe something was going around?

She wished with all her heart that they were coming down with the flu and not… the other thing. A glance to her right and left showed that no other person in the church was experiencing the same symptoms.

As she took her last step, Jordan reached for her. Without hesitation, Romey took his hand. The moment their fingers made contact, something zinged across her fingertips. It bounced off the center of her palm. It zipped up her arms and spread warmth through her chest.

She had to face facts. She wasn't sick. She had simply lost her mind. And she was so screwed.

"Dearly beloved," began Pastor Vance. "We are gathered here today to witness the union of Romey Supernova Capulano and Jordan Jefferson Spinelli."

Jordan raised his brow at the mention of her middle name. Romey waved it away. Her parents had been hippies and allowed her to choose her own middle name. She had been into astronomy at the time.

"We will begin with the vows—"

"Actually, Pastor Vance," Romey interrupted. "Jordan and I have written our own vows."

Pastor Vance chuckled under his breath. He closed his Bible and then made a magnanimous motion with his hand. The bride and groom turned to face their guests.

In the pews was a colorful collective of people. It was very clear to see who belonged to whom. The soldiers and families from the Vance and Purple Heart ranches were all decked out in collared shirts, flannel, and sundresses. Meanwhile, on Romey's side of the aisle, kente cloth mixed with feathered headdresses, and vibrant saris.

The best part was that no one was fighting. Their two worlds were coming together. True, there was still clearly a line of division that was the aisle separating the two sides. But this was a great start.

"As you know," Romey said, "we are both scientists."

"As such, it's research that informs our decisions and our actions," said Jordan.

"So, we decided that there would be no better way to pledge our lives to each other than with scientific research and data."

The crowd of married couples, domestic partners, and friends turned to one another. A few from either side even looked over the dividing line for a clue of what was happening.

"We have crafted our vows as specific objectives based on data." Romey turned to Jordan before continuing. "Jordan, from this moment forth, I vow to respect you for who you are, and show appreciation for who you endeavor to become."

"Thank you, Romey." Jordan nodded to her and then addressed the crowd. "This vow is based on the Theory of Positive Illusions, which shows that it is advantageous to see a life partner in the most positive light instead of highlighting their flaws."

"Exactly," Romey agreed, standing side by side as they addressed their families and friends.

Behind them, Romey thought she heard Pastor Vance utter an *oh, Lord*.

"To further illustrate the efficacy of this vow," Romey continued, "we turn to Michelangelo's Phenomenon, which shows the value in supporting each other's attempts to better ourselves over time as beneficial for the mutual partnership."

"Pretty hard to refute a great such as Michelangelo." Jordan nodded. "Romey, as our lives intertwine, I vow that your choices will always be yours and yours alone. Which means that I will never obstruct your freedom."

There was a snort from the peanut gallery. Romey narrowed her eyes, seeking out the culprit. It looked like a number of individuals on both sides were doing a poor job of keeping a straight face. Well, they could laugh it up. Just give it a couple of years, and they'd see whose marriages were still happy and whole based on a racing heart. Emotions were fleeting. Science was forever.

Whatever was going on with her internally would pass. These vows would ensure they would maintain a mutually beneficial union until their dying days. With that thought, Romey continued.

"Thank you, Jordan. For those of you that don't know that vow of non-obstruction comes from remarkable research based on the Social Construct of Autonomy, which postulates that humans, as social creatures, need and enjoy relationships but also must maintain individuality.

Therefore, there will be no pressuring or guilting or coercing on either of our parts."

Another round of snickers and giggles riffled through the audience. Romey didn't bother to ferret out the guilty parties. She turned from the crowd to face the man that mattered.

Her heart had settled down now. She was breathing normally. Her head was clear. Whatever she'd been feeling earlier had been a passing phase.

"Romey, I vow to treat you with compassion rather than fairness. I vow this because we are a team where one whole and one whole make two and not one."

Just like that, her heart began skipping beats again. Romey had seen these words written down on paper. She'd sat beside Jordan as they'd constructed the pledges. But, for some reason, hearing them spoken out loud, in his deep baritone, changed the meaning of the words.

"This vow is based on Communal Orientation," Jordan continued. "It assures that we won't keep track or tabs. We will both contribute to the relationship based on our strengths and not on a tally system."

Romey expected more heckling laughter. All was silent. Except for her beating heart. The sound of it filled her ears. The only thing holding her up was Jordan's hand, which she belatedly realized, still held hers.

His thumb rubbed lightly across her knuckles. Her fingertips rested in the cradle of his palm. She had the urge to step closer to rest her head on his chest. But that wasn't part of the plan.

"Is that all of the vows?" Pastor Vance stepped forward. "That was very… academic. Do you have the rings?"

Both David and Jules stepped forward with the rings. They both were simple affairs. Just gold bands. Romey had declined the addition of a diamond with all the work she did in the dirt. But something sparkled at her from the band, a tiny, perfectly cut diamond.

"Now, according to God's holy ordinance, I pronounce you man and wife. You may kiss the bride."

Romey and Jordan had discussed each vow. They had footnoted and referenced each theory upon which their lives together would be based. They had not once discussed the kissing aspect of the ceremony.

Jordan still held onto her hand. With his free hand, he lifted his fingers to her chin and tilted her face up. Romey looked up in time to see Jordan's face coming towards her. When his lips met hers, she lost her breath.

He brushed once. Twice. On the third touch, he held, letting his lips linger.

Tiny, illogical sparks of emotion glittered over every part of her skin. Her heart didn't race anymore. It settled down, as though it had found a new home. Despite all evidence to the contrary, it appeared that Romey was wrong. That thing called romantic love might have some validity after all.

CHAPTER FIVE

There was a phenomenon called phantom limb. It was where an amputee felt as though their lost limb was still attached. An itch in a foot that was no longer there. An ache in a wrist where the forearm was gone. Long moments after he'd broken the kiss that pronounced them man and wife, Spinelli could still feel the warm pressure of Romey's mouth upon his lips.

The kiss had been fleeting, but in the all too short space in time that he'd been joined with her at the mouth, he had memorized the curve of her top lip. He knew the precise angle of the divot that marked the right half of her upper lip to the left. He knew the exact internal temperature of her body from the heat given off the slight exhalation when she'd gasped. He knew she'd had strawberries for breakfast.

The kiss had been an hour ago, but Spinelli was still feeling its effects. Still wrapped up in all of the sensory detail. Like it was a phantom limb.

Which was illogical. Romey was not a part of his body.

So why did he feel her absence so acutely even when she sat right next to him at the reception table?

Why, no matter how many times he licked his lips, or pressed them together, could he not shake the ghostly sensation?

"Here's to my best friend, Jordan Spinelli."

Spinelli broke out of his reverie. The sun had set over the Vance Ranch. Picnic tables were arrayed out back of the big house. For the first time ever, the neighbors from the Verona Commune walked freely across the pastures. There hadn't been a single argument between the ranchers and the farmers the entire wedding day.

Porco stood front and center, glass raised to deliver the Best Man speech. The phrase was ironic. In days of old, the Best Man was actually the best swordsman a groom could find. Because a sword might be needed to defend the groom against the bride's family. Bridal kidnapping was a lucrative enterprise throughout history.

In a way, Spinelli had stolen his bride. They could've found loopholes in the commune's charter. With both his and Romey's brain together, no unsolved equation or legalese would've stood in their way.

"Spinelli has always kept us in line with his calculations," said Porco. "His current math has brought him the best problem."

Spinelli hadn't bothered with the math. He hadn't given the charter a single glance. He'd arrived at this solution in the blink of an eye, with flimsy logic, and held to it. He'd stolen his wife, and he had not a single regret.

"His mathematical mind has brought him a woman who will keep him on his toes because her mind matches his own."

Spinelli looked over at his wife. Romey brushed her lip with her fingers, a slight blush touched her caramel-colored cheeks. Spinelli had the insane urge to brush a kiss against those lightly freckled cheeks to determine if they would be sweet and warm like the sugary confection.

"These two think they're solving a problem. But I hope the solution will lead them to see that they are a perfect fit."

Romey turned, as though sensing Spinelli's eyes on her. Her gaze widened when she saw that they were. Her hand jerked away from her mouth and slipped beneath the table.

The strangest thought arose in his mind. He saw himself drawing a sword against anyone who would try to take her from him. Clearly, he'd had too much to drink. Though his wine glass was untouched.

"Jordan, you've tried to talk sense into me more times than I can count," Porco went on. "I rarely listened, but you were always there to pick up the pieces and say I told you so, with a historical or mathematical anecdote that I never understood."

The crowd laughed. Spinelli didn't get the joke. He had done all those things. Porco's statement was factual, not funny.

"You told me Jules and I were incompatible. You were wrong. But you stood by me and tried to help me win her. When you and Romey came up with this idea to marry so that we could all buy the land and save the commune, I thought it was crazy. But then I thought about it and realized you two are perfect for each other."

Beside Spinelli, Romey shifted in her chair. She placed her hands back on the covered table and rubbed at the ring he'd put on her finger. The ring had belonged to his Sicilian grandmother. Sicilians believed diamonds were forged by the fires of love. Egyptians believed the wedding band circle meant that the couple was entering into a never-ending cycle.

Spinelli didn't buy into any of that mythological nonsense. There was reasoning in the ring and its placement. Wedding bands and engagement rings were placed on the left hand's fourth finger because there was a vein leading to the heart, the *vena amoris*. Meaning he'd laid a direct path to Romey's heart. He liked the sound of that science.

"You both are smart, loyal, and no one understands you," Porco was saying. "Except for the two of you. You get each other."

Spinelli knew his friend was going for more laughs at their expense. And Porco was getting them. What his best man didn't realize was that the statement was true.

Over the last week, Spinelli had watched as Romey spoke to others. They often nodded at her with confused expressions. Meanwhile, her every word made complete and total sense to Spinelli.

"Jordan Spinelli, you have been my brother in arms, but now you are my brother-in-law. Romey got a good deal, but I'm the luckiest man in the world."

There were a few jeers from the soldiers in the room. Many cheers from the women. And a cacophony of whoops, jingling bells, stomping, and high pitched yelps from the colorful people of the commune.

Everyone raised their glasses and toasted to Romey and Spinelli's happiness.

Two cakes were brought out after the toast. One was vegan, the other was not. Spinelli brought the vegan cake forward on the table to cut. He had no intention of giving up meat or dairy, but he wanted his wife to be comfortable. It was in their peer-reviewed, fact-checked vows.

"This will be our first joint task in married life," Romey said as she came to stand next to him before the crowd.

Spinelli placed his hand over hers on the knife. A zing went up his palm. He flexed his fingers, pumping them into a fist to shake off the sensation. He needed to get control over himself.

Apparently, Romey was having the same problem with controlling her appendages. Her fingers trembled on the knife's handle. Jordan put his hand back over hers. Her trembling ceased immediately. A calm washed over him at the rightness of her hand in his.

They sliced through the cake, making perfect, evenly spaced triangles. The geometry of it sent his heart racing. They sliced all the way around until they came to the last piece; three hundred and sixty degrees of perfection.

Romey tilted her head back and looked up at him. Her smile was a triumph at their accomplishment. His gaze dipped to her lips. Everything in him told him to lean down and capture her plump top lip. To tease her lower lip. To press her to him until he didn't know where he ended and she began.

Was he truly losing it? Or did the little twinkle in her hazel eyes tell him she wanted the same? Eyes were the window to the soul had always been a metaphor he didn't understand. If one could look into the eyes, they'd see into the brain. Was Romey's brain giving him permission to claim her lips?

It was the catcalls that brought them back to the task at hand. With a heavy heart, Spinelli let go of his wife's hand. With her warmth no longer in the palm of his hands, his fingers shook again. His mouth ached to recapture the pressure from earlier. Because his lips were denied, they tingled even more.

He took a few deep breaths. When that didn't work, he stuffed a slice of the vegan cake in his mouth. Only to come away surprised at the velvety texture of the concoction. He must truly be losing his mind if he found himself enjoying the flour-less, butter-less, dairy-free dessert.

Spinelli had promised Romey a logical marriage. But here he was thinking of ravaging her out under the stars like some love-sick fool. Because, maybe, he was a lovesick fool. Which was the worst thing that could possibly happen to him in this relationship.

He needed to hide his feelings from her. He needed to regain his rational mind. He knew that's what she liked, and Spinelli wanted Romey to like him. He wanted to please her. He wanted to make her heart speed up and her breath catch. He wanted her to want him the way he wanted her. But if he told her that, if he showed that, it would ruin everything.

Spinelli turned away from his wife. His gaze fastened on the top of the cake. There was a decoration there; a tanned groom and a brown-skinned bride topped the cake. Aside from the skin color, there was no likeness to the two of them.

"The top of the cake is traditionally saved to be used at the first child's christening," he said.

"Yes, I know," Romey said. "It's supposed to be good luck if a birth happens in a year."

"Well, we won't need to save ours."

He took the decoration off the top of the cake and placed it in the trash with the other discarded plates. That should let her know he was committed to the logical arrangements within their marriage. Except when he looked at her, she wasn't smiling at him as though they were of two minds. She was staring at the trash can and frowning.

CHAPTER SIX

Romey stared at the plastic couple in the trash heap. They didn't resemble her and Spinelli, not really. The artist hadn't captured Spinelli's strong jaw and massive shoulders that were like a great brown bear's. Neither did the bride figurine look much like Romey. The plastic caricature's hair was smooth, nothing like Romey's springy hair that would never be permanently tamed. And there were no freckles on the molded woman's cheeks.

She couldn't truly blame the artist. Romey's features didn't fit any mold. Most people drew redheads with freckles. Romey's mother had been a redhead. The freckles on Romey's cheeks were brown and not red. Her hair was a mixture of brown and black with touches of gold.

Her father had said his daughters' hair was like flames. Jules had smiled at that, taking the words as a compliment. Romey had frowned at the statement, taking it as fact. Fire didn't have brown in its spectrum.

Romey had had to work all her life to understand when someone was making light and when someone was stating factual information. She wished people only stated facts and conclusions. She had such difficulty with anything else.

Which was why she liked Jordan so much. He only spoke in factual statements. So when he'd tossed the figurine couple into the trash, Romey knew he had no plans to procreate with her.

Had she wanted progeny? She didn't know? She'd never truly thought about it. She'd never truly thought she'd get married. No one had ever shown that kind of interest in her. The few times she thought a boy might have been interested in her looks, he quickly changed his mind after she opened her mouth and gave a glimpse of the contents of her brain.

Romey questioned everything. She thought deeply about everything. She was the girl who, when watching a movie, wanted to talk about and dissect not only the plot but the technical aspects of the films.

For example, whenever the hunky heartthrob was at a school dance, or the action hero stumbled into a night club, it made no sense to Romey that they could have a private conversation with the love interest amid the band or blaring speakers. While the audience was held rapt with attention at the whispered words, Romey's mind couldn't suspend her disbelief. So, of course, she'd gone and researched the technique.

In the film world, the sound technique was known as the phenomenon of Figure Ground. It was a rule in filmmaking that allowed for the singling out of an event that is made to be important and making it the only thing the audience could hear. But just because they made it a rule in celluloid didn't mean it made sense in reality.

The music from two loudspeakers filled the night's air. The tune was an upbeat favorite. The makeshift dance floor filled with cowboys, soldiers, and second-generation flower children.

"Are you all right?"

Jordan's words were spoken quietly beside her ear. Through the cacophony of the music and shouts of the people at the reception, she heard him perfectly. Everything had quieted around her until only his voice, his words were in focus.

He stood as close to her as was possible without touching. But the heat coming off of him made her shiver. Which was entirely nonsensical. How was it that the opposite of normal kept happening when she was with him? For a man that appreciated her intelligence, she found herself tongue-tied at times when speaking to him.

Jordan was so handsome. Smart men shouldn't have that amount of beauty. It was becoming harder and harder for her to concentrate when she looked at him. Her mind kept focusing on the perfect asymmetry of his eyes. The angles of his jaw. The arcs and curves of his lips.

"I'm fine," Romey said.

Jordan opened his mouth. His lips quivered as if he was having the same kind of trouble forming words as she was. Could he be feeling the same effects as her? There was a bit of sweat on his brow. His nostrils were flaring. Did his gaze just dip to her lips?

"Time to toss the bouquet." The shout came from Jules, who was standing just a few feet from them.

Jordan fairly leaped away from Romey. His hand went to his brow. He used the back of his hand to wipe away the sweat. Then he scrubbed his palm over his nose and mouth. When his face emerged, he wore the calm and self-possessed demeanor which had first attracted Romey to him.

She'd been wrong. There was no passion for her there.

Romey allowed herself to be pulled away from her husband. She needed the breathing room from the man. There were times when he made her feel so focused, like when they were researching academic archives for their vows. Then there were times when her mind fogged, like when he flashed her a grin over a discussion of the latest scientific find of an exoplanet that contained water vapor.

Just the thought of him grinning at set Romey's pulse racing, her heart beating, and her mind whirring in a mist of fog.

"Uh oh," said Jules with a grin.

"What?" Romey looked down at her dress, but she hadn't spilled anything on it yet. Which was a miracle. She could never get through a day without dirt finding its way onto her clothing.

"I think you like him." Jules' voice carried over the lyrics easily. Unfortunately.

"Of course I like him," Romey hissed. "I married him."

"No, I think you *like him*, like him."

Romey had always hated those kinds of statements. It was grammatically incorrect to use a verb as its own adverb. And *like* wasn't even a verb.

"I'm not that girl," Romey said. She wasn't now and had never been. Her teenage bedroom had been plastered with the Periodic Table and equations not obnoxious boy band posters.

"No?" asked Jules, sounding genuinely curious. "What if Jordan is that guy?"

But Jordan wasn't that guy. He was a mathematical genius, a brilliant computer coder. Which meant that he was a numbers guy, and not so good with words. Which was what Romey had reasoned that she'd wanted in a life partner. Right?

David came up behind Jules. He slipped his arms around his wife and pressed a kiss to her head. The move was thoughtless but held so much tenderness. Romey had never experienced that kind of care or tenderness from any man except her father. She doubted Jordan would ever make such a move on her. It wasn't outlined in their vows.

Despite herself, Romey had come to like her new brother-in-law. She liked all the men and women on the Vance Ranch. Even Brenda Vance Keaton was growing on her. The female rancher had asked Romey and Jules tons of questions about their soybean crop as she fed it to her cattle, who grazed voraciously on the lands. Brenda was a smart woman, which Romey admired. Not at all cutthroat as those on the Verona Commune had been led to believe.

Romey spied Brenda and her husband Keaton, stealing a kiss as they swayed slowly to the upbeat music. Much of those gathered were couples in loose embraces, or touching, or looking at one another with the same light of tenderness that David looked at Jules. The same love that her father had gazed upon her mother with.

When she found Jordan's gaze, it wasn't trained on her. He was looking off into the distance. His expression was unreadable, as always.

Romey felt another thud in her heart. But this time, it wasn't a pleasurable skipping of a beat. This time it hurt, like tripping over her feet and falling down with a resulting bruise. Had she just made the biggest mistake of her life?

It was too late now. It was done. The music quieted, and all eyes were on her at the center of the dance floor. She was sure whatever woman who would caught the bouquet would find it a blessing. Because that woman would be smarter than Romey. The odds were that that woman would marry a man whom she loved, and who loved her back.

CHAPTER SEVEN

The disease was spreading. Now not only did Spinelli feel a phantom pang on his lips, but it had also moved to his hands. He was repeatedly clenching and unclenching his fists. He rubbed his fingers against his pant legs, seeking the friction there to erase what he'd touched. Nothing helped. No matter what he did, he couldn't get the thought out of his mind that he needed to touch Romey again. To hold her to him. To place his lips upon hers.

He'd almost taken her into his arms before Jules had come up. If Jules hadn't interrupted, what would he have done? He knew exactly what he'd have done. He would've kissed his wife right there, under the stars, in front of everyone they knew, and for no logical reason. Other than he couldn't stop himself.

He had to get himself in order. The two of them had worked so hard on their vows, worked so hard to make this a marriage of mutuality and logic. Now he was going to blow it. All because of that ceremonial kiss.

Spinelli had kissed girls before. Those times had just been the press of skin against skin. All the while, his mind had been elsewhere. Thinking over his latest computer codes and algorithms. Which was probably a factor in the reasoning of why he rarely got a second date with girls.

A wandering mind hadn't been the case when he'd kissed Romey. Spinelli had spent so much time talking to her, getting to know her mind, and her thoughts. So much so that when he kissed her, his mind had been focused solely on her. And now he wanted more. More of her words and definitely more of her kisses.

"It's time for our newlywed's first dance as a married couple."

Across the crowded area, Spinelli's gaze found Romey's. Then they were moving towards each other. He was the moon being pulled into her earthly orbit. There was nothing he could do to resist the gravity of her.

A slow song played over the loudspeakers. The song was sappy and stringy. Spinelli found himself pulling Romey into his arms.

She came to him without protest. Though her brows were knitted in concern. She'd seen through him. She'd seen that the madness of illogic was infecting his entire being. Would she ask for an annulment? Based on reasons of insanity. Because that's what he was experiencing.

She didn't pull away. She pressed her body against his, fitting perfectly into his arms. Just like he'd heard so many romantics say; she fit perfectly.

His large hand spanned the small of her back. She came up to the perfect height if he wanted to lean down and kiss her. Which he wouldn't do. But oh, how he wanted to.

His arms tightened around her. She didn't protest. Her knitted brows relaxed. There was trust in her eyes. More than anything, Spinelli wanted to keep that trust. He wanted Romey to know that she could depend on him. This was just a momentary lapse in his normally clear-minded brain.

Even as he thought it, he heard the lie reverberating in his mind.

"Do you want children?"

At the sound of Romey's words, the hand Spinelli had at her back shook. His fingers curled into the fabric of her dress. It took two deep breaths to get himself under control and release his clenched fingers.

"I'm sorry," she said, shaking her head and looking away. "We didn't discuss that in our negotiations. It was an oversight."

"Do you want children?" He was surprised his voice didn't come across as shaky because inside him, everything was rocking.

Romey bit her lip, lost in thought.

Spinelli held his breath as he watched. He would give anything to be that tooth. The thought of the process of making children with this woman overwhelmed him. At the very least, he'd get to kiss her again. Though the act of kissing wasn't at all necessary to create offspring. Which seemed such a waste.

"I do," she said finally.

"You do?" And then he realized. "Me, too."

Beyond the thought of sharing Romey's kiss and her body, he wanted to see a springy haired kid running around in the fields. He wanted to teach his son or daughter to make planes and build circuits and code games.

"Someday."

Spinelli jerked back to the present. It took him a moment to realize Romey had introduced a qualifier. *Someday.* He needed her to be precise with her language. Exactly how long would he have to wait?

He also wanted to clarify how they would go about it. She could've meant adoption or in vitro fertilization. He did not want a sterile environment when it came to the creation of their children.

"We have our trial period to go through first, of course," she said.

"Trial period?" Again he clutched her closer. Just the thought of this ending was too much for him.

Romey gasped. It was only a slight sound, and she quickly composed herself. But her breath touched his lips, making him hungrier.

"Of course," she said. "This is only the first round of our marriage project. There are bound to be a few kinks along the way that we'll need to work out. Best have that sorted before we add new variables, like children, to the project."

She was right. But he didn't relax his hold on her. She didn't try to pull away.

He couldn't take his eyes off her. There was so much symmetry in her face. The left and right sides of her face weren't complete mirror images of one another, which was impossible in the natural world. But it was darn sure close.

Spinelli had studied the scientific definition of beauty. Romey met all the qualifications. The distance between her eyes was just under half the width of her face. The space between her eyes and mouth was just over one-third the height of her face. She was practically perfect.

That had to be the reason he found himself so attracted to her. She was textbook beautiful.

"You're beautiful."

He hadn't meant to say the words. But they were on his mind. He'd never learned the trick of keeping his thoughts to himself.

"It's the makeup and the gown," she said, still not meeting his gaze. "They highlight my best assets."

Her smile was hesitant. Had he made her uncomfortable? He'd need to keep these overtures to a minimum, preferably none at all. Clearly, Romey wasn't interested in her physical features. Trial project or not, that's not what this marriage would be about.

"Our children will be beautiful with big brains," Spinelli said, trying to cover his attraction and remind her that he was a genius, which was one of the qualities she admired most about him.

"Brains, beauty, and brawn," Romey agreed.

Her hand came to rest on his bicep. He could feel the heat of her palm through two layers of fabric. His muscles flexed under her fingers, eager to show off for her. He wanted Romey to know that he would provide for her, he would protect her, and someday, he would procreate with her.

Her gaze found his then. Spinelli couldn't hide what was in his mind, what was in his heart. He wanted his wife, to kiss her, to hold her, to whisper in her ear.

Whisper what? He wasn't sure. Maybe he could rattle off the golden ratio of the Fibonacci sequence. Surely she would like that since she wore the symbolic spiral of the sequence in her ears.

Before he could open his mouth, whether to rattle off the sequence of numbers or kiss her parted lips, they were pulled apart. The cheering and catcalling turned their attention back to their friends and family.

Every pair of eyes were on them, whooping, whistling, making kissing noises.

"Logical relationship?" shouted Porco. "Yeah, right."

Romey stiffened in Spinelli's arms. She pressed her once parted lips together. Then she turned to him, the cool consideration that had first attracted him firmly in place.

"I think we've provided enough entertainment for them," she said. "You ready to call it a night?"

That was met with more revelry from the group and a few lewd gestures from his friends. Spinelli knew from past experience that trying to explain anything away to this group would amount to nothing. So, he draped an arm over Romey's shoulders and turned them to go.

Rice flew at their backs. Another strange tradition of the wedding ceremony. The throwing of rice was meant to symbolize rain. Which, in turn, symbolized fertility.

There would be no need for fertility tonight. But, Spinelli reminded himself, there might be someday. If he could hold true to the vows he'd made to his wife. Vows that didn't include the thoughtless passion which they were now being heckled about.

It was going to be a hardship, keeping his hands and his feelings from this woman. But he knew that if he wanted to keep her, if he wanted to get to someday, he would have to try harder to master the irrationality that had taken hold of him today. Because Romey was the perfect woman for him -for his mind, his body, and, yes, even his heart. And he would do any and everything to keep her. Even if that meant denying himself the pleasure of her kisses.

CHAPTER EIGHT

$\mathcal{I}$n the early morning light, Romey gathered a handful of her curls. Her fingers tugged at them from the roots, separating her hair into sections. She used a fat-tooth comb and started plucking at the unruly ends, which much preferred to stick together than hang on their own. When she was younger, she'd let her hair lock into permanent plaits, like her sister. But Romey had grown frustrated with the long locks constantly getting in her way as she happily dug in the dirt each day. So she'd shorn them off with gardening shears.

Her father, who placed inner beauty over physical beauty, had shrugged. Her mother, ever non-conforming to the feminine ideal, had beamed at her daughter's uneven and lopsided new do. Jules, who'd at the time liked having a live mirror to gaze into, was distraught, thinking she'd have to do the same. Romey had only cared that her hair was out of her way so that when she leaned over her notebooks to record her data, her hair wasn't getting in the way.

From that day forward, she'd routinely shorn off her locks, ensuring they never grew beyond the nape of her neck. As she combed out the first tuft, she let the lock of hair fall down and saw that it was nearly touching her shoulders. Looking into her vanity, the evidence was clear. It was time for a cut.

So why was she hesitating to reach for the scissors?

On her wedding day, Jordan had said she looked beautiful. Sure, she was wearing a dress that highlighted all that was good on her figure. But it was a dress she never planned to wear again. And her face had been painted to accent certain parts of her features. A long process which she had no time nor inclination to repeat each morning. But she hadn't done much with her hair. Had that beauty he'd noted encompassed her hair?

Romey turned from the scissors, deciding she could go a few more days before a hair cut. Out of the corner of her eye, she spied a makeup kit. She reached for the kit, turning it over in her hands like a penny flipped through the knuckles. It wouldn't hurt to shade the bags under her eyes from her poor sleep last night.

That wasn't vanity. It was practical. She didn't want anyone asking questions or making innuendo about her late-night activities. Because there had been none.

Jordan had retired to her parents' old room, now his room. She had walked into her bedroom. Alone. As was planned.

Jules and David had spent the night out. They hadn't come home last night, and Romey hadn't heard a peep to indicate they'd returned this morning. It was just her and Jordan and the bags under her eyes.

Were the dark circles getting bigger? Would he notice? Would he still think her beautiful this morning in a T-shirt, shorts, and no makeup?

She looked down at the case of eye shadow. Before she could make up her mind whether or not to open it, she spied the expiration date. It was two years expired.

She could go into Jules' room and grab her kit. Whenever they needed to get dressed up, it was always Jules who did Romey's hair and makeup.

Romey tossed the entire kit into the trash. What was she thinking? Primping for her husband? David had agreed to marry her for reasons that had nothing to do with her looks.

The sound of padding footsteps came from the hall. It was followed by a door opening and close. Then the sound of the shower starting.

Romey swallowed. Her husband was in the bathroom, just next door, stepping into a shower without a stitch on. She'd felt Jordan's muscles. What would they look like glistening with soap and suds?

Romey gave herself a shake. She should not be having thoughts like that. She would not. He was her husband, not her lover.

Love and romance were not a part of the equation that they'd calculated together. She had no idea why those variables kept trying to insinuate themselves into this carefully constructed mathematical statement. Because it was null.

Jordan didn't see her that way. He saw her as a smart, competent woman. That's who she was.

Romey scrubbed a hand over her bare face. She shoved a headband over her hair and stood. He said he took her as she was. Well, this was her. Dingy shorts with permanent grass stains. A worn T-shirt of a cat holding a bone with the caption *I found this humerus*. No makeup. No muss. No fuss.

She walked to her bedroom door. When she opened it, she heard the shower stop. She froze, wondering if he'd come out fully dressed. Or if he'd come out in a towel. She was far too chicken to find out.

With quick feet, she hurried to the back door. She wasn't sneaking out. She was late for work. And no, it didn't matter that she was her own boss.

After a few gulps of fresh farm air, Romey began to relax. It was another beautiful day in the paradise that was the Verona Commune. There were all the colors of the rainbow as far as the eye could see. Red and green peppers. A field of purple and blue lavender. Orange and yellow gourds.

Weaving amongst the plants were men, women, and children dressed in blue jeans, Indian saris, African Lapa skirts, and orange Hare Krishna robes. Romey greeted everyone in their preferred salutation. Be it a touch of the palm, a kiss to the forehead, or a bow to the divine within them.

Luckily, there were no remarks on the bags under her eyes. Nor any mentions that she was up early for a newlywed. She was able to make it to her lab with very little conversation.

Before entering the converted barn that was her hydroponic garden,

Romey put booties over her shoes and pulled gloves on her hands, so as not to attract any outside organisms into her workspace. She opened the door and was greeted by a lush garden in the small place.

Unlike outside, there was no soil inside her lab. Her plants instead grew in coconut fibers or Rockwool, which was another mineral fiber. Though there were acres of land outside these walls, Romey could yield just as much and more in the size of this small barn. Another boon was that her plants grew in a fraction of the time it took for the fledging dealing with the elements outside.

Romey controlled everything in this environment from the water distribution to the amount of daylight her plants got to the nutrients absorbed by the roots. She was the mistress of carbon, water, light, glucose, and oxygen in this realm. Everything necessary for a plant to thrive.

There was no factor that she didn't manipulate in here. No string that she didn't pull, or cut loose, to get the results she wanted. Nothing was introduced into this world that she hadn't planned for.

The exterior door opened, allowing real sunlight and a gust of air in.

"Close the door," she shouted at the intruder.

Paris Montgomery's tall form filled the doorway. In the soft light of the morning sun, the bags under his eyes shown darker than Romey's. He came just inside the entryway and shut the door behind him.

"You can come in if you put on the protective gear," Romey said.

"This will only take a second," said Paris leaning against the door frame. "I wasn't expecting you to be at work the morning after your wedding. But then I remembered it's you."

"What's that supposed to mean?"

"You've always put this place first, unlike—"

Romey held up her finger to stop the incoming tirade. Paris had been set to marry Jules. However, that had only been his and Romey's plan. Jules had held out for love. And now she was deliriously happy every second of the day. Romey had found it exhausting to watch this last week. Now she couldn't help thinking about how huge her sister smiled any time she was near, or talked about, or was clearly thinking about the man she'd married.

"Looks like your soldier husband and his friends pulled the right strings," said Paris. "The USDA inspector has rescheduled for early next week."

The commune had failed their organic certification inspection last week when the inspector found pesticides on Romey and Jules' soybean crops. Now that their land was technically no longer apart of the commune, the certification should go through without incident. When it did, that organic stamp of approval would garner the families here a larger profit margin in the markets where they sold their produce.

"That's great," said Romey. "This time, we can get them to swing by here to give a stamp to my hydroponics garden as well."

Paris shuffled his feet on the mat at the door. "Maybe next time. This is all still so new."

"Hydroponics has been around for years, and they're eligible for the organic stamp."

"Romey, let's not make waves. We're on shaky ground as it is. And not everyone is on board with growing food in a lab."

So that's what this was about? Even on her open-minded, everyone is accepted, utopian farmland there were still prejudices. Especially when it came to science.

Well, fine. This was just another problem to solve. If she wasn't going to have the support of her family and friends, then she'd have to substitute another variable to get her hydroponics the approval they deserved.

CHAPTER NINE

The sound of artillery fire filled Spinelli's ears. The grunts and groans of war mixed with gunshots and explosives banged out from the speakers. Flashes and bursts of pixels colored the monitors arrayed on the desks as the heat signatures of soldiers moved around the field of play.

"Rogue Five, can you identify whether the target is hostile?" shouted the unit leader.

"Negative, sir. Identity unclear," was the response.

Spinelli smiled behind his steepled fingers as he watched the game play out on the screens. The first objective of his war game simulation, Tactical Approach, was about identifying the enemy. Players were trapped in darkness, unable to see whether they faced a uniformed soldier, an innocent civilian, or an enemy hiding in plain sight. They would have to rely on logic to smoke out any adversaries by using patterns that would reveal hostility. Because these soldiers were trained mostly with sight, they were losing points.

Another round of fire lit up the speakers in the control room. A high pitched wail signaled friendly fire had taken out yet another team member.

"I'm hit," called the downed man. He'd only lost his life on the game board and not in reality. Still, it was a blow to the team.

Spinelli winced when the remaining soldiers came up against more hostiles dressed in plain clothes. What would they do? They had a myriad of options. Spinelli knew what he would do, but he'd designed the game, so he remained tight-lipped.

"Hold your fire," shouted the team leader.

But the man's voice was drowned out by more sounds of artillery. This time coming from their opponents in the game. The algorithms Spinelli had designed had learned the lessons the soldiers hadn't. The enemy had picked up the patterns of the soldiers' movements, clearly identifying their targets and taking them out one by one.

Spinelli turned to Rusty, who sat to his right. Instead of seeing a grin on his friend's face, Rusty was grimacing and pinching at his brow as he watched the massacre on screen. Spinelli couldn't reason why? The coding he'd programmed had worked brilliantly. The objective had been met, albeit by the enemy and not the self-appointed good guys.

On Spinelli's other side sat Commander Jackson South. Commander South watched his team of elite soldiers on the screen. His brows were drawn as though deep in thought. His mouth was a straight line that left no room for interpretation.

Smiles, Spinelli could identify. Frowns, he understood. Anything in between, Spinelli had trouble with.

He was much better at watching people's actions and predicting future movements. Spinelli's prediction was that the Commander would love his simulation and the challenges it presented his men. He would then sign on for full training, thus bringing in another client for the Boots on the Ground Training camp he and his friends had created.

While the others worked outside on the obstacle courses and drilling, Spinelli had built a state of the art virtual war games arena. He'd been a gamer all his life since his parents had handed him their cell phone as a toddler to keep him quiet. He quickly went through Solitaire and Chess at age two. By age five, he'd mastered every game available on the Gameboy. By his teen years, he'd grown bored with Nintendo and Xbox.

It wasn't until he'd come into contact with a commercial version of a war game known as Full Spectrum Warrior that he'd found a challenge. It took him weeks to beat it. And then he'd hacked the code to play the official, top-secret Army version. Playing that game day and night, Spinelli had come to a life-changing revelation. He'd put down his controller and signed up for JROTC, determined to become a real-life soldier.

Basic training had been a nightmare as his scrawny arm and leg muscles, which had only ever lifted a game controller, strained under the demand. With the hard work and dedication that he'd shown to his gaming and coding escapades, his geeky body had eventually filled out. He'd seen his fair share of combat while enlisted. It was nothing like the games he'd played. That's why he strove to make Tactical Approach fully realistic.

Out in the theater of war, it was difficult to tell the good guys from the bad guys. That and another dozen decisions came at soldiers every single day. Sometimes every hour as they strove to follow orders, complete their mission, and simply survive.

More shouts came from the console, breaking Spinelli's walk down a digital memory lane. The remaining soldiers were backed into a corner and still unable to tell who was friendly and who was the enemy. The unit leader gave the call to surrender. The game was over. For now.

Lights illuminated the game arena, which was nothing more than a large room with pillars for the players to maneuver around or find cover. The men tore off their virtual headgear in frustration. Commander South sat back in his chair with a sigh.

He pursed his lips as he regarded Spinelli. That wasn't a frown. Nor was it a smile. But the man did look pensive. That had to be a good sign. Spinelli decided not to try and interpret. Instead, he began spouting facts, as he wished others would do.

"As you see, the game is realistic," Spinelli began.

"That it is," said the Commander. "The realism is uncanny."

Spinelli let his lips raise in a smile at the compliment. He looked to Rusty to share his good cheer. The man wasn't smiling. He still pinched the skin at his temple, a look Spinelli had seen the hostage negotiator wear when things were not going his way.

"The weapons, the equipment," Commander South continued. "You even put language and cultural nuances into the simulation."

Spinelli had worked hard on all those details. There had been times when making the right gesture while in a hostile zone had saved his life. Any soldier coming into the training facility needed to take all of these things into account for when they went out into the true field of combat.

Commander South slapped his hands down on the console table. "This is not what we're looking for."

Spinelli's head did a comical double-take. Had he heard the Commander right? Had the man said Spinelli's realistic scenarios weren't what he was looking for to prepare his team?

"This is an unwinnable scenario you've crafted here," said Commander South.

"No, it's winnable," said Spinelli. "The men just need to prepare for the eventualities."

"There are tons of eventualities in the real world," said the Commander. "No man could prepare for them all."

Spinelli begged to differ. He could. And when he'd fallen short, he'd added the missed eventuality to his memory bank. All of that knowledge he'd downloaded into this simulation. It was designed to prepare soldiers for every possibility they might be faced with.

"Only a computer could keep all of that intel straight," Commander South was saying.

Spinelli's friends often called him the Cyborg, likening his memory as well as his motions and emotions to that of a computer interface. He knew it was meant to be a joke. But he'd never figured out the funny part.

"They need to be challenged to become better," he said in response to the commander.

"Challenge, yes. Knocked down until they cry uncle, no. I'll tell you what? If there is a different level, one where success is an option, we'll give it another go."

A dumbed-down version? That was a recipe to get people killed. Spinelli wanted to prepare these men and women for whatever may come.

"We'll change out the program and have you and your team visit another day." That came from Rusty. The man was using his reasonable voice, the same voice he used to talk a suicide bomber into taking their thumb off the detonator.

Once again, the voice worked. Commander South gave the two of them a nod. Spinelli managed a nod in return as Rusty walked the man out of the door. Spinelli knew his team needed this contract. But he had no idea how he was going to dumb his game down. He didn't even have the desire to. The only desire he had was to go home and rest his head.

That idea perked him up. If he did go home, his wife would be there. His partner. She'd vowed to listen to him as part of their marriage. Romey was brilliant. Maybe she could help him solve this problem.

CHAPTER TEN

omey inhaled deeply under the late afternoon sun. Clouds moved overhead, casting her in shadow as she looked off in the distance. Twenty feet away stood a colorful target with a green bull's eye. The target was mostly used for archery practice, but Romey had a different use for it today.

She squared her shoulders. With another inhale, she checked the alignment of her spine, visualizing that each disc of her spine was stacked perfectly straight, one on top of the other. It was a trick she'd learned during meditation class as a child.

With another inhale, she raised her right arm. Again, she made sure that her shoulder made a straight line to her index finger, where she held a gun. She took a moment to muse that meditation and guns didn't go hand in hand before she used her thumb to flick off the safety.

Sighting the target in the distance, under a copse of trees, she squeezed the trigger slowly until... BANG.

The feel of the recoil was satisfying. The *thwap* of the bullet hitting its green mark was gratifying. After Paris's easy dismissal of her efforts to get her hydroponic garden certified, she'd felt her anger boiling up until it was ready to explode.

Romey didn't like to feel out of control. She certainly didn't want to hug it out in an Empathy Circle. She wanted to hit something. The target was her best bet.

She decided to make it a little harder and give herself a challenge. Lowering her weapon, she stepped back a few paces. And promptly bumped into a solid mass of muscle.

Romey whirled around. But it was the gun that made it there first. She'd pulled her finger off the trigger, knowing that there would be no foe on her land.

She needn't have worried about the gun going off. The weapon was quickly stripped from her hand. Jordan expertly checked the chamber before flicking the safety back on.

"I didn't know flower children played with guns," he said. "Or with real bullets. I remember seeing a hippie putting a flower in the barrel of a gun."

"We have no issues with the second amendment here."

The clouds chose that moment to part and cast Jordan Spinelli in its full glow. The grin that spread across his face made him look like one of the stars on the posters of the town movie theater. The man was devastatingly attractive.

How had Romey ended up with a man so beautiful? She'd always expected she would end up with a smart guy. A nerdy science teacher. Jordan was smart and handsome, and he liked her for her mind.

Meanwhile, she couldn't stop thinking about what it had been like to kiss him the other day. What would it be like to kiss him today? Out in the field, where no one would see.

There was a sheen of sweat on his cheek. Would the salt of his sweat alter the sweetness of his breath? Or would that little droplet make him all the more savory?

"Romey?"

"Yes?" Oh no, he'd been talking. What had he been saying? He held the disabled gun out to her. "I wasn't going to shoot you."

"I know. I saw that you'd lowered your arm. But old habits die hard."

Spinelli sighed as he looked down at the gun. His head cocked to the side, much like the motion of putting the safety on. But the expression on his face made Romey wonder if he wanted to flick the safety back off.

"Mind if I...?" He made a motion to the gun she cradled in her palm.

"Of course not." Romey handed the gun back to him. "You just have to stay on this track so that the bullets don't get into the field."

Jordan flicked off the safety. He squared his shoulders and eyed the target. Romey didn't hear him taking a breath, but she saw his chest rise before he pulled the trigger. His shoulders bunched at the recoil, causing Romey to let out a small gasp at the play of muscles there.

Again, she gave herself a shake, trying to loose these errant thoughts of objectification about her brilliant husband, who just so happened to have a few attractive qualities. He had a brain. And so did she.

"You know," she said, "I had this idea for environmentally friendly ammunition that biodegrades."

"Really?" Jordan turned back to her. Weapon lowered, target forgotten as she told him more about her idea.

"Yes, well, you know that most bullets are made of lead."

Jordan nodded. "There was a push for more copper-based bullets, which are less toxic to the environment."

"I read that. But what if we made bullets that were not only non-toxic but environmentally friendly. Where the material would turn to seeds and germinate... after... you know."

"After the circle of life, you mean?"

He flashed her another of those grins. Under his perusal, Romey had the oddest inclination. She reached for a lock of her overgrown hair and began twirling it around her finger. Jordan's gaze slid to the movement of her fingers, playing with her hair. After a moment, his eyes slid to her face.

"You're brilliant," he said. Then he cleared his throat. "I mean, the idea is brilliant."

"Thanks."

He swallowed a few times, his throat working as though he was having trouble moving past a lump there. Finally, he turned back to the target, aimed, and fired. His form was magnificent, his aim perfect, but somehow he missed the target. The bullet lodged into one of the surrounding trees.

"I hope that wasn't an ancient, protected tree," he said.

"It's a mistletoe tree. Placing the bullseye here was the parent's way to keep their kids from sneaking off and necking here."

Jordan's brows rose as he looked up at the bloom-less tree. Romey was about to tell him that the tree only bloomed its noteworthy berries during the winter season. But then a branch fell off a nearby tree. A slight wind blew the tumbleweed forward until it rested at their feet.

Romey and Jordan stared down at the berry-less branch. It wasn't as though she believed in superstitions. She was a woman of science. She didn't fret over stepping on a crack, especially not when she had to get to where she was going. It was pretty difficult to not walk under a ladder while repairing a structure. There were tons of affectionate black cats all over this farm who brightened her days.

So, no, she was not at all affected by a branch of mistletoe rolling at her feet. Unless Jordan was?

Romey chanced a glance up at the man. Jordan frowned down at the branch. Then he lifted his gaze.

"I didn't know those trees could grow here," he said.

"Mama Lily can get anything to grow anywhere," Romey said with a touch of pride in her voice. Their resident herb lady had been instrumental in Romey's upbringing in the world of botany.

Jordan nodded, stealing another glance at the wayward branch. Then back at her. "Is your workday over?"

"Yes." Romey nodded, looking away from the branch as it rolled over their feet. "Yours?"

"Thankfully."

"Bad day?"

"Let's just say it didn't go as I planned it."

"Me, too."

"Should we honor our vows and talk about it?"

"I think that would be an acceptable use of our time."

Now back on footing she understood, Romey walked in step with her husband. Things were getting back on track. She glanced over her shoulder and saw that the mistletoe was following their footsteps. The funny thing was, there was no longer a breeze.

CHAPTER ELEVEN

At the end of their wedding yesterday, Spinelli and Romey had crossed the threshold of their home and retreated to their respective rooms. He'd missed her on his way to work this morning. Having her beside him in the kitchen, listening to her relay her day of working in her hydroponic garden left him feeling… full.

He had no other word for the feeling. His mind was engaged in the explanation of her work. His ears were hooked on the sounds of her voice. His eyes were pinned to the movement of her lips.

"Do you see what I'm saying?"

Spinelli swallowed, and then blinked a couple of times. "Yes, yes. Clearly."

"I knew you'd understand," she smiled up at him.

He would understand. If he had heard a single word she'd said, he might have. But he hadn't.

What he did understand was her smile. It clearly said that she was pleased with him. He liked pleasing her. He racked his brain to say something else to please her. But he couldn't think of a single thing. Just the mere sight of the woman and Spinelli slipped into a trance.

"This sauce smells divine," said Romey, bending over the pot of fresh chopped tomatoes simmering in a pan, but not daring to touch it.

They'd picked the tomatoes straight off the vines as they made their way back to their house. Not off any of the vines outside. Romey had taken him into her hydroponic garden. He'd heard her talk about her greenhouse laboratory. This had been the first time she'd let him inside her sanctuary.

Spinelli had been astounded at the sight. Not only was his wife beautiful, and intelligent, she was inventive. Dare he say, magical. He'd never heard of growing plants without soil. But Romey had done it.

They'd only stopped in briefly to gather a few ingredients for their dinner, but he'd wanted to stay longer. He'd have to invite himself back later. Especially if he got to see her eyes light up like they had at his questions over her methods and procedures.

There was so much he didn't know about this woman, his wife. She was a great shot. She could grow anything right out of thin air. And she boiled a mean pot of water. Though if left unattended, she would've likely burned the spaghetti. Fortunately, her one imperfection, being wholly unable to cook, didn't tarnish any of her shine.

"I'm part Italian." Spinelli emptied the noodles he'd rescued into a strainer in the sink. "Can't grow up without knowing how to make sauce from scratch."

"My father's family was from the south, they cooked everything in some kind of pig fat or with a pig's appendage."

From outside the door, Hamlet, their pet pig, squealed. Spinelli didn't think the pig was indignant at his extended family's dietary habits. Hamlet knew he was safe on this commune of vegans. No, the pig was irate about not being let inside.

When Porco and Spinelli had moved in earlier this week, they had both scoffed at the pig being inside of doors. Jules had put her foot down. With three against one, the pig had been relegated outside where it belonged.

"My mom was raised with maids and cooks," Romey continued, ignoring Hamlet's pleas. "Something she rebelled against in her youth, though I wouldn't have minded much. Either way, I got no training in the kitchen other than to pick what I wanted to eat from the ground, rub off the dirt, and pop it into my mouth."

That said, she rubbed a ripe tomato on her shirt and took a bite. Spinelli was far more interested in her shirt. It featured a cat carrying a large bone. *I found this humerus*, said the caption bubble over the cat. Spinelli chuckled. Finally, a joke he understood.

"Hey," Spinelli admonished, as Romey took another bite of the tomato. "You'll spoil your dinner."

She giggled at him but set the tomato down. Spinelli was left to ponder why that trickle of laughter left him feeling warmth across his shoulders. Sound shouldn't have that power. But already, he'd gotten lost at the sound of her voice. He'd become entranced by her words. So it would stand to reason that her laugh would warm him.

Earlier when the mistletoe had landed between them, Spinelli had frowned down at it, wishing it had somehow hung over their heads. He knew the social obligations that standing under a mistletoe imbued. He would've been bound to kiss her. But it lay on the ground and then rolled away.

Romey turned from him. She sliced off the piece of tomato she'd bitten and begun chopping the rest. With that done, she tossed the juicy bits of tomato into a salad. The leafy greens were also from her hydroponic garden. The only thing she hadn't grown was the pasta.

"I actually didn't like spaghetti until I saw the movie *The Lady and the Tramp*," said Romey.

"I know that movie," said Spinelli. "I saw it when I was a kid. Though it took me a couple of views to accept that cartoon animals could talk."

Romey giggled again.

Spinelli wasn't sure what the joke was. If he could figure it out, he'd say it again. "I take it you're referring to the spaghetti scene? The part where they share the same noodle?"

"Yes, that part."

"It's highly unlikely for a strand to be that long."

"Yes, I know. It was all nonsensical. But it was cute."

Spinelli agreed. He dumped the cooked pasta out of the strainer and into a serving dish. With a ladle, he spooned the sauce over the noodles.

"You listened as I shared the woes of my day," said Romey, taking her seat. "By our vow of the Michelangelo Phenomenon, I'm bound to listen to yours."

Spinelli chewed at the inside of his lip as he twirled pasta onto his fork.

"Vows aside, I want you to tell me," Romey said. "Maybe I can help you think it through and come to a solution."

Spinelli smiled at that. There were no ambiguities with this woman. She said what she meant and meant what she said. He reaffirmed that he would tamp down these irrational feelings of wanting to kiss her and give her what she'd asked for; a rational man who was her intellectual equal.

"I built a simulation; a war game. The client said it was too difficult for his team, that they couldn't possibly prepare for the challenges I created. But I believe soldiers need to prepare for every eventuality."

Romey nodded, eyes intent on him as she chewed her noodles. There was a dollop of sauce lingering at the corner of her mouth. Spinelli averted his gaze from the temptation to wipe, or daresay lick, it off.

"War doesn't happen in a controlled environment," he went on. "I don't want to dumb it down in my simulations."

"Is the scenario winnable?" Romey asked.

"Yes, if you prepare."

"So, it's not a Kobayashi Maru?"

"No." Spinelli grinned at the *Star Trek* reference to the unwinnable training exercise that every Starfleet Academy cadet was put through. "It's not a no-win scenario."

"But it would take a Spock to figure it out?" She waved her fork at him as though he'd been naughty. "Not everyone is as smart as you, Jordan. You know that, right?"

He liked that she called him Jordan. Having been in the military for the last five years, he rarely heard his first name. It made him feel human. Especially with a group of friends that casually and jokingly referred to him as a cyborg.

He also liked that she thought he was smart. Even more, he liked showing this woman that he was smart. He'd show her that he was smart enough to figure out how to make Tactical Approach less high-level Spock and more winnable Kirk.

"This sauce is delicious," she said as she reached for another helping of the pasta dish.

Spinelli looked down to see that his fork was in the dish as well. He pulled his fork back. There was already a strand of spaghetti wrapped around his tines. It was a long strand that stretched from his fork all the way to hers.

Spinelli grinned at the thought of the Lady and her Tramp of a dinner partner. When he looked up, he saw that Romey grinned as though she were thinking the same thing.

Then her gaze dipped to his lips. His lips parted, no longer interested in a second helping of pasta. He wanted a huge helping of Romey. But she was pushing back from the table.

"You know what?" She stood up, her chair legs scraping on the hardwood floors. "I'm full."

Without another word, she dashed from the kitchen. Moments later, Spinelli heard the shower going.

Great. He'd gone and bungled it. She had to have guessed that his mind wasn't on their discussion of his work. She had to have seen that all he was thinking about was his carnal desires, and he had no way of hiding that fact from her. Suddenly this felt like the ultimate Kobayashi Maru scenario. He had no idea how he would win in this marriage.

CHAPTER TWELVE

$\mathcal{W}$aking was a struggle the next morning. Romey's dreams kept pulling her back under their warm covers. Part of her knew she was dreaming, but the lines kept getting fuzzier and fuzzier until they became furry.

She was panting in the dream. Her tongue lolled out of her mouth. She was down on all fours, trotting about a back alley. Distressed that she'd get her beautiful brown coat of fur messy. Why did she have paws in her dreams? Why was she sniffing after a scruffy looking gray and white dog with a lopsided grin? Why was she hankering for a meatball?

Romey woke with a start. Her heart was racing. There was drool on her lips. Thankfully her tongue was snug inside her mouth. Her skin was clean, with no hint of fur.

Sigmund Freud had a theory of dreams. The psychologist had postulated that dreams represented an individual's unconscious dreams and desires. They were wish fulfillments behind closed lids. Motivations acted upon in the dark recesses of the mind.

So, did that mean Romey wanted to be a dog? Ridiculous as it sounded, it was better than admitting to the other thing. That she desperately wanted to kiss her husband.

There was another theory of dreams. One where it was postulated that the neuropathways of our brains used the downtime to sort through problems and events of the day that still required our attention. But how did her dream of being Lady make any sense? Jordan was definitely the beautiful coated dog in real life, and she was the tramp who played in the mud all day.

Throwing off the covers, Romey stood. She shook her limbs, trying to shake out the last vestiges of the dream. None of it mattered. It was a new day, and she was going to spend it living up to the vows she'd made with and to her husband.

She dressed quickly, pulling on a black T-shirt that best reflected her mood. On the shirt was a rat outlined in white. Above him, the thought bubble red *Science experiments are fun*. Whenever her family and friends on the commune saw the shirt, they pursed their lips and shook their heads. Everyone was far too emotional to get the joke.

Before leaving her room, Romey pressed her ear to the door. The house was quiet. Jules and David still hadn't returned from their impromptu honeymoon. Romey was sad about it. She needed a glance at her head-in-the-clouds sister to remind herself why she kept her feet firmly on the ground.

Twice yesterday, she and Jordan had been put in situations as though the universe was trying to get them to kiss. Which was ridiculous. Romey believed in God, but she doubted that the entity had any time to design her love life. That was simply preposterous, with the wars, and famine, and strife in the world. God wouldn't be paying attention to her happiness. The entity was far too busy.

If her sister were to tell it, Jules would say that God was love, and that was the deity's primary task. Romey simply couldn't get behind the idea that the creator of all the complex, numerical, symmetry of the world would give a single care over whether or not she and her husband touched lips.

But she couldn't deny the coincidences. As a scientist, she didn't believe in random acts. Everything was served a purpose.

With her ear pressed to the door, Romey heard the patter of size twelve footfalls in the hall. Jordan was up. Sure enough, the patter of water falling in the shower sounded next.

Romey closed her eyes, trying to shut out any imaginings of the man under the spout. Behind her eyes, her imagination, which usually lent itself to growth patterns in nature, went wild.

She imagined the droplets running off his chest. She imagined the suds gathering on his strong biceps. She imagined Jordan lifting his face to the spray and the water raining down on those beautiful lips of his and-

Romey shook herself. She had to get control over herself. This wasn't the type of marriage either of them had signed up for. She was not the kind of woman who men went romantic over. There would be no sweeping of any feet.

Her feet were on the ground, where they belonged. She stood on steady legs. She had work to do. With her resolve in place, she slipped out of her bedroom door -quickly. She didn't want to run into her husband after he got out of the shower.

She left the house so fast, she didn't bother with breakfast or the lunch of leftover spaghetti she'd packed last night. She'd grab something from a vine or tree on her way. She did just that, grabbing a tomato from a vine, she took a bite. But the fresh fruit paled in comparison to the sauce Jordan had made last night.

Still, she needed sustenance for her long day. Her morning would be spent helping the commune kids with their science projects for the town science fair. She'd have to be on her toes with this bunch. They'd been allowed the freedom to run wild and think radically. She wouldn't be surprised if Cinnamon Fairchild was trying to make a time machine to stop all the world's dictators from being born. Nor would Romey be surprised if the device actually worked given the IQ of the girl.

When Romey walked into the schoolroom, she didn't find the kids working on their world-changing science projects. No, she found them behaving like normal, hormone riddled teenagers.

A group of girls and boys stood gathered around a table. The magnifying glasses were moved to the side. There was a bottle at the center of the table. It was spinning.

"Cinnamon, Zion, Winter, Falcon, and Archer, what are you all up to?"

But Romey could guess. They were preteens. They were curious. And the resident midwife had given them all the facts about their reproductive health and how things worked.

Though these kids were allowed to run wild and think freely, they each had a healthy respect for authority and consequences. They all jumped back from the spinning bottle and looked away from Romey's glare. Before Romey could launch in on them about the commune's rule of having anyone under the age of eighteen have a sit-down dinner with both the families before engaging in any type of sexual exploration, the door to the school opened behind her.

Great. Now she would be dragged into the family conversations since the non-sanctioned kissing game was being played on her watch. Romey had no desire to have another talk about birds and bees and the *Kama Sutra*. Her first talk at twelve had left her scared and scarred.

But it was too late. The door opened behind them. Romey looked up to see Jordan in the entryway. He was freshly showered and shaved. He was decked out in a plain, green T-shirt, fatigue pants, and heavy boots. The man was simply stunning. So stunning that Romey's breath caught in her throat.

"Hey," he said.

"Hey," she managed.

"They said I'd find you in here. You forgot your lunch."

Jordan strode toward her. Romey felt her knees weaken as she watched him move. Her own hormones were going haywire inside her blood. As he stretched his hand toward her to hand her her lunch, Romey nicked the neck bottle at the center of the table and set it spinning again.

Round and round the glass went. The children stepped back up to the table to watch. Everyone held their breath as its spinning began to slow. When the bottle stopped, the top landed facing her. The bottom faced Jordan.

Jordan's lips parted. He spoke a soundless word that Romey couldn't make out. Then his gaze rose to hers. He closed his mouth and swallowed hard.

Did he notice? Was he keeping track? This was the third time they had been put in a situation where convention would lead them to kiss. This was no coincidence. God, the universe, some mathematical force wanted her and her husband to lock lips.

Maybe they should? All in the name of science, of course. It could be an experiment. To try to determine what was going on.

Jordan cleared his throat. This time his words were spoken loud and clear. "Enjoy your lesson, kids. I'll see you later at home, Romey."

He sat the bag down next to the bottle. He turned on his heel, and like the soldier he was, he marched out the door.

Romey swallowed her disappointment. She picked up the bottle and tossed it into the recycling bin. Then she directed each kid to their own table and set them to work on their projects. With that done, Romey stepped out for some much needed fresh air.

When next she saw her husband, Romey was determined to have a logical, rational talk with him about these coincidences that kept occurring, and what they were going to do about it. Because she was certain it would happen again, and she was tired of fighting the inevitability.

CHAPTER THIRTEEN

The cold water from the tap rained down on Spinelli's body. He turned the shower dial towards the blue letter C. The ice that came from the shower head wasn't enough to cool him down.

He'd taken a cold shower before he'd fallen into a restless night of sleep after the meatball fiasco. Even when he'd closed his eyes, thoughts of Romey with red tomato sauce coating her mouth, assaulted him. He could not get the thought of kissing his wife out of his mind.

Why had he told her about *The Lady and the Tramp*? He hadn't thought of that movie in years. And what were the odds that after telling her about the spaghetti scene that he'd unravel the world's longest strand of spaghetti, which if they'd been slurping up with their mouths instead of forks, would've led them to kiss just like the cartoon canines in the film.

There was the spaghetti. Then there had been the mistletoe that had fallen between them. And now the pubescent game of spin the bottle. If Spinelli weren't a logical man, he'd swear that everything in the natural and animated world was pushing him towards kissing his wife.

So why was he resisting?

He'd wanted to pull Romey close since the first moment he'd laid eyes on her and seen that intelligent gaze. Eyes that showed they clearly understood him without the need of any dumbing down of his words. Spinelli could be himself with her. No hiding. No changing. Romey got him. And he got her.

Except for this one aspect of their lives together.

He'd been drawn to her that first day in the grocery store. He'd known he'd wanted to get closer to her the more she spoke. That night, he'd hated being parted from her. She was the first thing he'd thought about the next day when he'd woken up. And every day after.

The facts were all there as clear as the pattern of a Fibonacci sequence. The sequence of events showed a clear pattern. The math unraveled to show a simple equation.

Jordan had fallen in love with his wife the first time he'd laid eyes on her. The answer was there in that first meeting. But because he hadn't given voice two the elegant solution, it kept repeating itself. Each interaction after the first was the sum of the previous two interactions, increasing the answer and shining a golden light on the outcome.

It was all so simple. It was love. He let out a laugh at the thought. Water droplets filled his mouth. He didn't spit out the liquid, he swallowed it down like the truth.

So, what did this mean for their marriage and the vows they'd made to each other?

He and Romey had experienced a meeting of the minds in the short time that they'd known each other. But he wanted more. He wanted a meeting in the physical realm. But did she?

He wasn't sure. He'd never been good at reading the emotions of other people. Let alone, the emotions of the opposite sex.

What if she didn't want anything more with him other than what was in their vows? At the end of the day, was a physical relationship required if one found the person who was their match in every other way? He wanted to kiss Romey, and more. But he simply wanted to be in her presence more than anything.

He knew he needed to manage this. This was not the marriage either of them had designed. He couldn't go to her and change the terms so soon. Maybe in a couple of years, he could ask for a reevaluation of their terms.

Spinelli toweled off for the second time this morning. He'd left his clothes back in his bedroom. Since the house was empty, he wrapped the towel at his hips and pulled open the bathroom door. He stepped out of the bathroom and walked directly into Romey.

Her gaze was fastened on the droplets, still streaming off his chest. Was it his imagination, or did her nostrils flare? Was he dreaming, or did she just bite at her bottom lip? Those were signs of arousal, weren't they?

"Hello," she said.

"Hi."

They stared. The sounds of their shallow breathing filled his ears. Spinelli swore he felt an electric spark in the air between them. He was long past denying that the rules of science no longer applied when it came to this woman. From the first moment he'd seen her, he'd felt charged just by being in her presence.

"I'm sorry," he said. "I'll just get dressed."

"Don't."

Romey put up a hand to stop him. Her hand was between them, her palm just a breath from his beating heart. Her fingers curled in and lightly brushed his chest. Spinelli inhaled as though her five fingertips were matches, and she'd struck his skin. He had to look down to be sure she didn't leave a heat trail.

"You are so symmetrical," she said, her fingers tracing over his pecks.

Spinelli held himself entirely still. He was certain now that she was leaving a trail. His skin burned with her light touch. The burning sensation was good. He wanted more.

"It's like you were sculpted from clay," she breathed.

"I work out," he said by way of explanation because Romey liked it when he explained his process. "I used to be scrawny because I only played video games. When I got into the army, I worked hard for this physique."

"It shows." She took a deep breath and blew it out.

The heat of her breath made his insides warm. Spinelli couldn't take it any longer. He captured her hand in his.

That was a mistake. It brought them closer together. All he needed to do was dip his head down and capture her lips. Not in the few years he'd planned, but in the next few seconds.

"Listen," she said, linking her fingers with his, "you need to know that I find you very attractive. It's a simple biological reaction as you are perfectly proportioned to showcase to a female that you can provide for her, protect her, and... procreate."

Now it was Spinelli who let out a low breath. He urged himself to focus on her words. He wasn't one given to much imagination. But the words coming from her lips were giving him ideas of showing Romey what he could do with his perfectly proportioned body.

"I find you perfectly symmetrical as well," he said. "The way your eyes lift at the corners makes me want to measure the angle. I'd bet the distance between your limbs is perfectly ratioed as well. You're like a walking Golden Ratio."

The eyes he admired so much lifted higher at the corners. As did her lips. Romey grinned up at him as though she were delighted.

"Did you just compare me to a Fibonacci sequence?" she said.

"I did."

"That's the nicest compliment anyone has ever given to me."

"You're mathematically perfect," he said.

Her smile dimmed. "Mathematically?"

Spinelli got the sense that something wasn't adding up. She'd said his words were a compliment. So why was she frowning now?

"Mathematically. Of course." Romey tugged at her hand until Spinelli freed her fingers. She pulled away from him, no longer meeting his gaze.

Spinelli wanted to reach out and tilt her head up so that he could see directly into her eyes. Hers was the only gaze that he could get any read on. For the past week, she'd been telling him exactly what was on her mind. She was silent now.

"Did I say something wrong?" he asked.

"No." She shook her head. "No, you made things between us perfectly clear."

Romey gave Spinelli a tight smile, and then she turned on her heel and left. Spinelli stared after her for a long moment. He had no idea what had just happened, but it hadn't ended the way he wanted. He ripped off the towel, shoved into his clothes, and raced after her. He was no longer the master of his mind. His feelings had taken over, and he was glad of it.

CHAPTER FOURTEEN

*R*omey's cheeks were heated as she stepped into the cool enclosure of her hydroponic garden. She put her hands to her cheeks. She couldn't see the redness on her face, but her skin certainly was warm enough to indicate that she was blushing. Despite being a darker tone of skin, her flesh was just creamy enough to redden.

Romey couldn't exactly blame it on her mother. Despite her fair skin, Mariam Capulano never blushed. The woman was fearless. Mariam had tried to join the Black Panther Party...as a white woman. It was her mother that had taught Romey to shoot, that had taught her to never back down to injustice, and to believe in her principles.

It was Romey's father who had taught her that she did have a romantic side. Jerome Capulano had loved the Victorian classics. Despite Romey's best efforts, some of those romantic notions had penetrated her consciousness.

She remembered reading many books where pale-skinned damsels blushed over their knights in armor as they spouted bad poetry up to a balcony window. Romey hadn't blushed when she'd stood toe to toe with her knight, who hadn't been wearing a stitch of armor. She hadn't blushed when she'd made her play for Jordan by telling him how attractive she'd found him. She'd had her wits about her then, but somehow it had all gone wrong when he'd gone and called her mathematically perfect.

In all the Shakespearean plays and sonnets, Romey didn't remember any hero comparing their true love to a math problem. No, those girls got compared to summer days, the winds, and buds in May. With such compliments, it was no wonder that the blood raced to their cheeks to show their affections.

Romey's cheeks flushed now in the privacy of her inner sanctum. Just thinking back over her actions with her husband made her cringe.

Had she really run her hands over Jordan's chest? Had she really told him that he was symmetrical and perfectly proportioned? When she thought about it, her compliments were just as bad as his.

But what had she expected? Romance from two people who had professed to be too logical to believe in such flowery nonsense?

It was just that Romey wasn't so sure it was nonsense anymore.

She had to admit to herself that she did harbor a fantasy of a man falling for her. She did harbor a fantasy of a man sweeping her off her feet. She did harbor hope that she might experience that indefinable notion of true love.

Well, she was experiencing it. There was no other conclusion to draw from the way her heart skipped a beat when she was near Jordan. It wasn't a medical condition. It was attraction. It was desire. And she had no idea how to deal with it. Not within herself. Not to determine if the feeling was there in her husband.

If she confronted him again about her feelings, it would likely dissolve into another think tank on the inner workings of the ventricular system or the rate that the synapses in the brain fired. She didn't know how to talk of love. Which was a hoot, because she could talk about any subject matter. But this—this elusive idea of love—she hadn't the first clue on where to set foot.

The door of the barn opened. In the doorway stood Jordan. His perfectly proportioned figure filled the entire frame. He glanced at her, a fierce determination in his gaze. He took a stride toward her, his heavy boots thudding as they impacted the ground.

"Wait!" Romey held up her hands. "You'll contaminate the plants."

Her brain might be scrambled. But not enough to forsake safety measures for her garden. She might be letting errant thoughts run amok in her mind, but no contaminations would get inside this carefully regulated environment.

Jordan stopped in his tracks. He turned to the sanitation station just inside the door. He bent his large form down to put booties on his boots and gloves on his hands. Once sterile, he resumed his mission toward her.

"I need you to explain it to me," he said.

"Explain what?"

"I called you beautiful, and you ran away from me."

Romey's mouth worked, but no sound came out on the first try. She had the same result with the second try. Finally, she cleared her throat and tried again.

"You didn't call me beautiful. You said I was mathematically perfect."

"That's my idea of beauty. An equation that is both complex and simple. Elegant in the way it balances variables. Challenging yet clear in its expression."

Oh. Well. When he put it like that—take that you summer day girls. She was a complex, elegant, expressive variable.

"That's my idea of beauty." Jordan stepped closer to her.

The distance between them was so slight that she'd need the millimeter side of a ruler to calculate it. Not inches. "It appears that we both find each other physically pleasing, based on our biological responses. Which is completely natural in the animal kingdom."

"Completely natural," Jordan agreed.

"There's also the legal pull as we're married," Romey went on.

"That we are."

They were also now in centimeter territory in the closeness category. Though, in truth, Romey had lost the train of the conversation. All she could see were the lines of Jordan's lower lip. She wanted to trace them to see if there was any pattern to the design.

"When we agreed to get married, we outlined a well-informed, heavily referenced, fact-checked agreement," Jordan said. "I want to toss our marital agreement aside."

Romey's heart sank. Did he want a divorce? Or, more likely, an annulment. He could have that as they'd never consummated the marriage. It would be the cleanest way to get it done.

"I need more," he said. "We're going to have to renegotiate."

"Renegotiate?"

"Yes. There are additional items I'd like to add to this marriage project."

Romey's head was spinning. Was he asking to terminate their marriage or…?

"The first item is kissing."

"Kissing?" She realized she was parroting the man, but her brain was malfunctioning. She was scrambling for any scrap of understanding.

"I want to kiss you," said Jordan.

Well, that was clear. "You do? Now?"

"Yes," he said.

They were still standing within a breath's distance of one another, but they weren't touching.

"Yes, now," Jordan continued. "Then later. I'd like to kiss you a lot."

That was exactly what Romey wanted. She wanted to reach out to him right now and get started. But she was feeling dizzy, lightheaded. For the life of her, her brain couldn't remember how to move a limb. It was too focused on breathing in and out and not taking her eyes off the beautiful man standing before her.

"I'm open to negotiating the amount," Jordan was saying. "If that would make you comfortable."

"A lot is a good amount. I would agree to that term."

"A lot is not a very specific number," he said. "We should probably quantify it, for clarity."

"Or, we could just leave it open to interpretation."

Jordan frowned, as though he didn't comprehend the notion. Before Romey could take it back, the corner of his mouth lifted. The grin that spread across his lips told Romey that, not only did he get it, he wanted the stipulation.

"So," Jordan said, "we're going to do this? We're going to kiss?"

Romey tugged her upper lip into her mouth. She quickly moistened it before doing the same with her lower lip. She desperately wanted to breathe into the cup of her palm and do a smell test, but there was no time. The centimeter of space between them was reduced to the nanoscale.

And then… impact.

CHAPTER FIFTEEN

Spinelli placed his index finger under Romey's chin. Tilting her face up toward him, he took a moment to appreciate the slant of the obtuse angle from her jawline to her chin. He wanted to tell her about the geometry he was seeing in her. But he decided against it.

His first overture with the mathematical perfection of his wife hadn't gone so well. He needed this moment to be perfect, not just for her, but for him as well. Because he'd meant what he'd said.

He planned to kiss his wife a lot. Though they hadn't determined an exact quantity, he had an amount in mind. The number was far too large to encapsulate on a sheet of graph paper.

Looking down at the woman in his care, Spinelli felt a sense of possessiveness come over him. All logic and reason left his mind. He'd vowed to Romey that they were two individuals who would respect one another's autonomy. He realized at this moment that that had been a lie.

There was only one word recognizable in his foggy brain. That word was *mine*.

Without any preamble, Spinelli crashed his lips into hers. The kiss was not quaint, it was awkward and all-consuming. It was exactly what he was, what he felt, and what he needed. His mouth moved over

Romey's hungrily. For her part, Romey met each movement of his lips stroke for stroke.

When Spinelli gave her a fraction of an inch to catch her breath, she was breathless. She looked dazed. He knew that he was both of those things. He was out of his mind. Completely irrational and mindless.

And he loved it. He craved more of it. He wanted a lot of it. No amount of Romey would ever be enough for him.

They had carefully constructed how their lives were going to fit together. And in this one act, they ripped all their carefully laid plans to shreds. There was no going back to the sterile vows they'd made. Things were getting messy, and he was reveling in it.

Spinelli had no idea how long their kiss had lasted. He felt the sun shift over him. But he paid it little mind.

He drank and drank from Romey's mouth, knowing he would never get enough of this woman. Which was entirely illogical. But logic could show itself out the door.

He wanted to rip off the plastic gloves on his hands and hers so that he could feel the softness of her skin. He wanted her fingertips directly on his skin without the sterile layer. But it might be too much. So he contented himself with their kiss.

Spinelli pressed his lips against hers, simply to feel the soft flesh that was his. *Mine*, the word sounded in his head again, like a chant. He knew that one person could not own another. But he needed to possess this woman's body, mind, and soul. Just the legal papers weren't enough. He needed to imprint himself over her very being so that every man, woman, and child would know to whom she belonged.

What had he been thinking? That he could spend his life in a platonic relationship with the most desirable woman he'd ever met? He was an idiot.

"Romey?"

"Hmmm?"

"I have a confession to make."

"Hmmm."

The confession was that he'd fallen in love with her. More importantly, he'd known it for some time. He'd known it since the first time he'd seen her. He needed to confess that he'd fallen in love with Romey at first sight.

Her eyes were closed. Her chin tilted up towards him, still in that perfect obtuse angle. Spinelli couldn't resist. He ducked his head and stole a kiss at the slope of her neck. Romey sighed against him, curling her hands behind his head and pulling him closer.

Spinelli lost himself at the edge of the polygon that was his wife's long, elegant neck. He kissed up her jawline. Slowly, enjoying the precipice of her chin. When he returned to her lips, he remembered he'd been about to tell her something very important.

"Romey?"

"Hmmm?" she hummed, pressing her lips against his.

Once again, Spinelli forgot his train of thought as he looked down at the perfect creature in his arms. Romey blinked up at him. Her brows furrowed, making perfect arcs over her widening eyes. Her hold around his neck loosened as she stared at him. The golden flecks at the edges of her eyes sparkled at him. Spinelli felt like he was looking into the heart of a supernova, and the star was bursting from within. It should've alarmed him. But it didn't. Because when he looked into Romey's eyes, he felt he was seeing into her soul.

But just like facial expressions, the light from a soul was still confusing for him to read. Was that love reflected back at him? Or simply desire? He wasn't sure? He had no barometer to test it.

What he did understand was the grin that spread across her face. It meant she was happy with him. His head dipped to Romey's and stole another kiss—for data purposes, of course. He planned to collect a host of samples from this woman over a very long trial period that was likely to last a lifetime.

So engrossed in the kiss were they that they didn't hear the door opening until the sharp intake of air split them apart. Standing in the entryway to the enclosed garden were Jules and Porco. Spinelli's friend winked at him, while his sister-in-law pointed an accusatory finger at Spinelli and Romey.

"I told you so!" Jules beamed as she waggled her finger at the couple.

Spinelli was busted. He had fallen in love, and he didn't care who knew about it. Unfortunately, he'd have to wait to tell his wife. He didn't want to make more of a spectacle with Jules and Porco present.

CHAPTER SIXTEEN

"*R*omey and Jordan sitting in a tree."

Romey ignored the singsong voice trailing behind her. Unlike other eldest siblings, she hadn't had a year or more to herself before Jules had intruded on her only child status. Her twin had been born the same day and had begun annoying her only moments after her appearance.

"K I S S I N G."

"Really, Jules? Are we twelve?"

Romey had more important matters to tend to. Thinking about the kiss she'd just shared with her husband had to wait a few minutes. Even though she was having trouble pushing the memory down. She could still feel the press of his lips against hers. The rough texture of his thumb on her cheek. The buttery taste of him lingered on her tongue.

Had he had toast for breakfast?

The moisture in the air was not helping her think straight. Neither was the rising temperature inside the garden enclosure. Moisture plus heat equaled humidity. There was far too much of it in the space.

At the temperature panel, Romey adjusted the controls for the heat. When she looked at the temperature, she saw it was at normal levels.

Odd. It was nowhere near as hot as she felt. But still, she wanted to peel out of her T-shirt. She needed a towel to sponge herself off. Perhaps it wasn't the atmosphere in the room. Perhaps it was the residual effects of that K I S S I N Ging with her husband.

Her lips still tingled at the thought. Not just the thought, the memory. Romey had had her first kiss just a few minutes ago.

Well, technically, it wasn't her first kiss. But that fumbling, wet slobber she'd let Sundance Lightfoot plant on her by the creek when they were sixteen no longer counted.

Jordan had been masterful with his mouth. And that thing he'd done with his tongue. Oh yes, she wanted to study that some more. For research purposes, of course.

Who was she kidding? She wanted to experience it again just for the pleasure of it.

"First came marriage, then came love. Next comes the baby in the baby carriage."

Romey stiffened at that. She and Jordan had started a conversation about progeny. Now that they were moving closer to activities that involved creating children, they should probably talk about it later tonight.

Later? The thought of nightfall sent her mind to more carnal thoughts. Would their sleeping arrangements change now that they were kissing? Did she want them too?

She felt like her mind was leaking all rational thought. *Drip* there went an IQ point as she wondered if she could replace the expired makeup kit so that she could make herself pretty for dinner. *Drip,* there went a couple hundred SAT points as she racked her brain over what outfit she should wear when Jordan came home tonight.

Looking down, Romey saw that her hand was wet. Was her brain actually leaking out of her head? Or was there an actual leak in her garden's plumbing system? Romey dropped to her knees to investigate. A single leak in the structure could stymie the entire process.

"For a woman that was getting thoroughly snogged a moment ago, you don't look too happy about it."

From her place on the floor underneath the plant's containers,

Romey let out an exasperated sigh. Not at her sister's poking and prodding. She was used to that.

"Snog? Really, Jules? Are you twelfth century now?" Their father was overly fond of Elizabethan terminology. "I'm very happy about the progression of my relationship with the man I've chosen to be my partner for life. But I'm not going to lose my mind over it."

Of course, just then a drop of water landed splat on Romey's forehead

"Yeah, right," Jules smirked, looking down on her twin.

"Our vows are still intact. We are just adding to them."

"Conjugal visits, you mean."

"Jules, don't be crass."

"Romey, don't be a stick in the mud. Admit it, you have feelings for Jordan. Just say it. It'll make you sound normal."

"It's perfectly natural for one to desire one's husband." Jules traced the lining of the pipe until she found the source of the moisture. There was a clog there.

"Hmm, and love him."

Romey opened her mouth to argue, but another drop of water fell right into her mouth. She coughed and spluttered. The mixture that she used to nurture her plants wasn't toxic, but that didn't mean it tasted yummy.

"There was a bet going, you know," said Jules. "To see how long before passion took over and the two of you jumped each other."

Romey focused on the drip. There might be a loose valve or connection. Or there might be a root mass clogging the reservoir.

"I gave it a week. I can't believe I was so far off. Porco won. He gave it a day."

Finally, Romey found the source of the problem. One plant had doubled up and grown beyond the capacity of its container. Its roots had punctured the container. She'd have to rehouse the big guy. But for now, some duck tape would suffice.

"I'm happy you two realized you're in love."

Romey sat up. She didn't meet her sister's gaze. Instead, she reached for a towel to wipe the residual water from her hands. The dripping had stopped, but there was a puddle of water on the floor. Romey had stopped the symptom, but she doubted that she'd found the source. She'd have to search deeper. The system she'd designed was so interconnected that one wrong move could spell disaster.

"Rome, admit it."

"I won't admit that. It makes me feel out of control."

Jules joined her sister on the floor. "You don't have to control it, Rome. Just let it be."

Romey reached over with the towel and wiped up the puddle on the floor. The stone of the ground stayed moist after the water was gone. Only a bit of heat would lift the rest of the moisture from the surface. Romey decided to let the spot remain. It would evaporate soon enough.

CHAPTER SEVENTEEN

"Assault team, move."

"Roger, that."

Spinelli watched on the big screens as the men moved along the corridor. Weapons were raised. Expressions were pensive, watchful as the men were on high alert.

Beside him, Commander South watched the monitors. His steely expression gave away nothing of what he was thinking of the changes Spinelli had instituted. Spinelli wished the man would wince or frown. But his lips stayed in a straight line as did his eyebrows. He could not get a read on the man.

"West, Nile, cover Jasper. Rice and I will flank."

"Copy that, Red Leader."

Gunshots rang out, sounding like the real thing across the speakers because it was the real thing. Spinelli had recorded the sound and written code to ensure that the sound played with each press one of the players made on the trigger. He'd recorded the sound of a body being impacted as well. Not a real body, but he'd taken pains to ensure the mass he'd used had the same density so that the sound would be realistic. Once a soldier in combat heard that sound, they would never forget it. The game needed to remind them, needed to reinforce to each man and woman the realness of war.

As the team advanced, more problems came there way. But not a multitude of them. Instead of infinite possibilities, Spinelli had used the Golden Ratio of the Fibonacci sequence. The variables increased by the sum of the previous two numbers. So the pressure never let up, but it consistently challenged the player in levels of difficulty.

It didn't look like it was working. On the monitors, the team's heart-beats were up. Their adrenalin was spiked high. They'd conquered the first set of obstacles in their way. But as the hurdles multiplied, the group became taxed. They weren't going to reach their target. Already they were falling back.

The speakers reverberated with the clanging bang of an explosion. Commander South did wince then. His facial features contorted as though he remembered the pain that being anywhere near a bomb renders to the ears and nose as well as the body. Spinelli had gotten the authentic sound of that, too.

The men were blown back. In the real world, they would not have survived the explosion, so the game caused their life forces to deplete. It was over. The men had lost, and it looked like Spinelli had lost the contract.

He glanced behind him at Rusty, who leaned against the wall. Rusty wore the same pensive expression as the Commander. But Spinelli saw defeat in his friend's gaze. Only because Spinelli knew what that particular expression looked like on Rusty's face. Rusty now wore the same expression he'd had as when he'd gotten his divorce papers.

"Good work."

Spinelli blinked. He looked down at the control panel. He didn't remember recording that voice command. Definitely not in Commander South's deep baritone.

"I'm sorry?" said Spinelli. "Come again, sir?"

"I said, good work, soldier. You listened to my instructions, and you incorporated the changes."

Spinelli could only stare at the commander. When he still couldn't comprehend, he turned to Rusty. But Rusty wore the same confused expression as Spinelli.

"There were only able to make it to the next level of play," said Spinelli. "They didn't win the game, sir."

"Exactly," said Commander South. "They were able to advance with the new changes, but they weren't defeated. Now they have something new to work on."

Spinelli still wasn't getting it. When he played a game, he played it to win.

"You know there are battles won and lost in a war. If we succeeded against every obstacle put in our way, we would never learn from our mistakes. This version of the game pushed them. It challenged them to go to the extremes without defeating them. Excellent work."

Commander South held out his hand. Spinelli eyed the outstretched hand with wonder. He'd done it. He'd won the contract. This would be a boon to the camp. Now they could boast a state of the art physical course as well as virtual war games.

"I'm glad you liked the changes," said Spinelli, clasping the commander's hand. "They were inspired by my wife, actually."

"You're married?"

"Yes," said Spinelli. "Only a few days now."

They had been the best days of his life. Today being ranked number one after that kiss he'd shared with Romey. If Jules and Porco hadn't barged in on them, and if he didn't have this appointment to make, he'd still have his wife in his arms. In fact, he had nothing left to do here today, and he wanted to celebrate this victory. There was only one person who he wanted to share his accomplishment with.

"This team got here a few months ago," said the Commander. "And now you're all married?

That was true. The six of them had come to the ranch as single men. Before setting foot on the Purple Heart Ranch's soil, they'd all scoffed at the idea of marriage. Yet here they all were, happily hitched.

All but Rusty. His marriage was over. Despite the lore surrounding this ranch, Spinelli doubted the man would ever marry again.

"I want to show Tactical Approach to the FSW group."

Spinelli opened his mouth, but no words came out. The FSW group? That was the makers of Full Spectrum War, the game that had inspired Spinelli to join the Army.

"I think those fellas would have a lot of use for a mind like yours."

Again, Spinelli opened his mouth, but words escaped him. That had been a dream of his, to work with FSW. The offers hadn't been forthcoming after he was discharged from the Army Rangers. So, he'd gone into business with his friends. But now?

"Walk with me," said the Commander. "I see great things in your future."

Spinelli followed after the commander on wobbly legs. Every dream he ever had and dared not to have was coming true all in the space of one day. It was as though the Golden Ratio had come to life in his world.

CHAPTER EIGHTEEN

"Ouch!"

Romey dropped the knife and brought her thumb to her mouth. The small nick of blood tasted metallic on her tongue mixed with the savory hint of spring onion. Together, the open wound and the ripe onion stung, and she yanked her finger from her mouth.

By the time she pulled her injured finger from her mouth, the blood had dried up. No need for a bandage. She moved to the kitchen sink to shove her finger under a cool spray of faucet water instead.

The first droplet hit her flesh, soothing the wound. From the corner of her eye, she saw red. The flames on the stove rose high. The water from the pot boiled over on the stove.

Leaving the faucet running, Romey dashed into action to save the noodles inside the pot. But it was too late. The contents of the pot spilled over, dousing the fire and spilling all over the stovetop.

"Don't forget the pan of beans," Jules said around a mouthful of popcorn.

On a back burner, the pan of beans was having the opposite problem. All of its water had evaporated. The small green pods were now brown and black as they clung to the bottom of the pan.

"They never stood a chance." Jules adjusted the bowl in her lap. Her feet were propped on another chair as she leaned back, watching her sister's every failing move.

"You could help, you know," growled Romey as she turned all the burners on the stove off.

"And miss the evening's entertainment? Heck, no." Her sister chomped on more popcorn from the bowl in her lap. The grin on her face and sparkle in her eyes told Romey that Jules was, in fact, enjoying the sideshow of this foodie fiasco. "I never thought I'd see the day when you were domesticated."

Romey ignored the words she knew her sister meant as a jab. Looking down at the mess she'd made, Romey huffed as she realized not a single dish was edible. Cooking was not her strong suit.

When she got hungry, she'd simply tug something out of the ground, or out of one of her hydroponic containers, and pop it into her mouth. Raw eating was not just a way of life for her, it was pretty much all she knew how to do. Introducing heat to food was unnecessary. Except now that she had a husband whose lovely muscles could not subsist on raw plants alone.

Of course, Romey knew that a plant-based diet could sustain a man of Jordan's bulk. There had been plenty of studies of vegan athletes. But all of those men and women had lean muscle. Romey liked Jordan's size and shape just the way he was.

To keep him just the way he was, she'd have to learn to take care of him. More than one study showed that a way to a man's heart was through his stomach. So, here she was. Trying to learn how to cook starchy proteins. She wasn't ready to tackle meat.

Romey wasn't an animal activist. She was a complete Darwinist and believed it was a survival of the fittest, dog-eat-dog, kinda world. But if she couldn't cook a bean or a grain yet, to put a piece of red meat in her hands would definitely be animal cruelty.

"Honey, we're home." David's loud voice boomed from the front door, carrying it easily to the kitchen at the back of the house.

"In here," Jules mumble-shouted through another handful of popcorn.

David came in and scooped his wife up out of the chair and into his arms. He planted a long kiss on her lips. "Mmm. Buttery."

Romey wasn't one for butter or oils. There was no need when most of her diet consisted of raw foods. But if fire and condiments are what it took to get her husband to sweep her off her feet like that, Romey was ready to go find a cow.

She heard movement in the other room. The sound of a bag being dropped in the doorway. The *thunk* of thick-soled boots sounded on the hardwoods; Jordan.

He appeared in the entryway of the kitchen. His eyes glanced at Jules and David, still wrapped up in their embrace. He frowned at the two lovebirds.

Was that a look of disapproval? Did Jordan not believe in public displays of affection? Did she? Perhaps if she could get him alone, he might show her the affection he did earlier today in her garden.

Or perhaps that had been a one-time event? They'd agreed to introduce a physical aspect to their marriage. But they hadn't discussed the particulars.

Finally, Jordan's gaze lifted to find her. The frown on his face eased. His brows lowered as he took her in.

Romey stayed rooted while Jordan made his way around the entwined couple to stand before her. He offered her a bright smile. Then he bent down and kissed her cheek.

It was just a simple brush of his lips on her flesh. The contact made her entire face heat. She felt a *thud* as her heart skipped a beat, and then raced to catch up. The muscles in her belly twisted in hunger.

"Hi," he said.

"Hi," she mimicked.

"You're cooking?" Jordan's brows raised, no doubt taking in the catastrophe of her efforts. "I thought you said you weren't good at that."

"I'm not. I'm trying to learn, to improve myself."

His smile went brighter, so bright that Romey felt the urge to shield her eyes from the brilliance of it. She didn't dare. She didn't want to miss a single ray of her husband's shine.

"You're practicing the Michelangelo Phenomenon?"

Romey nodded. Though it wasn't following the letter of the

phenomenon. She wanted to better herself, but not necessarily for their mutual partnership. Romey was making these changes because she wanted Jordan to value her more. She wanted him to see her as more than a partner. She wanted him to see her as a lover.

Though by the burned beans and overcooked noodles, she didn't see her chances looking good.

"It's a trial and error thing," she said. "The first iteration didn't go as planned. But I've analyzed what went wrong. I believe in the second trial, I can improve on my mistakes and have a fairly successful outcome."

Jordan looked past her at the disaster on the stove. Jules and David had unlocked their lips and were doing the same. From the screen door, Hamlet looked inside, took a whiff, and promptly turned tail and trotted away.

Great. She'd completely failed. She was not going to win her husband's heart through his stomach.

"It's fine, Rome," Jordan grinned. "We brought dinner from Patel's. All vegan."

Pastor Patel's family restaurant was one of the few the folks from the commune ate at in the town. Many of the Indian dishes were vegetable dishes. Those that had milk or cream could easily be made without and still tasted delectable.

"Have a seat, ladies," said David, pulling out a chair for his wife. "We're celebrating."

"We are?" asked Jules. "What amazing thing did you accomplish today, my darling husband?"

"Not me. Spinelli."

Romey sat down in the chair offered to her by her husband. He scooted her into the table and then took a moment to unbag the take out they'd brought home. Once the women were served, he took his seat. But no one picked up a fork to dig in.

"Aren't you going to tell her your good news, Spinelli?" said David.

Jordan took in a deep breath. His massive shoulders rising and falling with the movement. "The war game module I've been working on had its final review today…"

"And?" Romey prompted after Jordan took one too many seconds to continue.

He glanced over at her and grinned. The sheer joy and childlike amusement in the expression made her shiver with pleasure. The grin was only for her. She realized he wanted her to be proud of whatever he'd accomplished today. At this moment, she understood why it was called the Michelangelo Phenomenon because her husband looked like a masterpiece as he shared his proud moment with her.

"And they loved it," he said.

"Of course they loved it," said Romey. "You're brilliant."

"No, I screwed up on the first try. But I was able to win them over. That was all because of you."

"Me?"

"I reprogrammed the game with the Golden Ratio from the Fibonacci Sequence." His gaze slipped to the spirals dangling from her ears. "You inspired me."

"That's amazing." Romey found herself rising and flinging herself into Jordan's arms. He caught her and squeezed her. It was too late to feel embarrassed, and she didn't. All she felt was her husband's warmth surrounding her.

"Hey, Jules," said David. "How about a picnic dinner down by the creek?"

"But—"

David grabbed his wife's hand and a couple of containers. He ushered them to the door. Jules, annoying little sister that she was, made kissing noises as they went out the door. A hopeful Hamlet was hot on their trail.

"I am so proud of you," Romey said. She was sitting on Jordan's lap. He hadn't asked her to move. Instead, his arms wrapped tighter around her middle.

"I didn't tell you the best part yet. The Commander was so impressed by Tactical Approach that he wants me to consult with FSW."

Romey had a vague idea of who FSW was. Jordan had talked about his admiration for the group. She supposed she should've been paying closer attention when he spoke about his career and the players. But she had all the time in the world to ask him more about it another time. Right now, Romey was angling how to show her husband just how much she appreciated him with a kiss. But she had never initiated a kiss before.

"It would be a six-month consulting job," Jordan was saying. "They're headquartered in DC"

Romey had been glancing at her husband's mouth, trying to decide how to make her approach. But those two letters threw cold water on her face.

"DC?"

Jordan's gaze had fallen to her mouth. He moved closer, preparing to make an approach of his own. But Romey jerked away.

"You're moving to DC?"

CHAPTER NINETEEN

How had he gotten so lucky? The woman on his lap was the smartest woman he'd ever met. Most men were dazzled by makeup or revealing clothing. His Romey had inspired him with the earrings dangling from her perfectly plump earlobes.

Romey was the most beautiful woman Spinelli had ever seen. There was a light that shone from her eyes that always made it easier to tell what she was thinking. Her heart-shaped mouth would stretch up in a smile when she was pleased. Or it would tug down into a frown when she was thinking. Making it so easy for him to comprehend.

Spinelli loved those expressions the best because he'd wait in anticipation of what she would say. Right now, her gaze was narrowed on him. So much so that a pinprick of light couldn't escape the squint of her eyes.

What could that mean? She had a new idea but was thinking something over?

He thought a new problem was unlikely. Her mouth was drawn in a thin line, neither pleased nor considering. Spinelli wasn't sure what she was thinking, but he got the sense that it wasn't good.

His wife shouldn't be thinking at all in his arms, that's not how seduction went. He might not have a lot of experience with women, but desire he knew. Mainly because he felt it like he had for no other with this woman in his arms. So why was she pushing him away?

"You're moving to Washington, DC?"

Romey climbed off his lap. She didn't retake the seat beside him. She paced a small line in front of him, back and forth with her arms crossed over her chest.

Spinelli might not be good at expressions, but actions he was much better at reading. That pacing and the arms closing her off to him in a protective gesture all read agitation. But what could she be upset about? Maybe he hadn't made things clear, and she needed more details.

"Yes," he confirmed. "For six months. If I get the contract. But it's as good as done. The Commander has many friends high up. I've always hated that aspect of business dealings. Promotion should rely on what you know, not who you know. Would you agree?"

The pacing came to a halt. Romey's head snapped around. She glared down at him. That expressive light he loved so much in her eyes looked like hot, red flames. That was definitely anger in her eyes. But why?

"I'm gathering that you're not happy about this?" Spinelli hedged.

"You think?"

That was the definition of a rhetorical question. She'd asked the question but definitely didn't expect an answer. So, he asked a question of his own. "What have I done to deserve your ire?"

"You're taking a job all the way across the country for six months. You didn't consult me. And you think I'm supposed to be happy about all of this."

Those were all valid points. Points he probably should've considered in hindsight. "I can see where I might've made a misstep in this process."

"Might've?"

"I assumed you'd be pleased as this opportunity would elevate my status in my career, thus elevating our partnership."

"Our partnership?" Her voice had gone up a few octaves. "We're married."

"I know we're married. I was there when we wrote our vows."

"Oh, now you're throwing that vow of autonomy in my face?"

"No, I'm not. That would be keeping score."

Romey's eyes blazed even brighter. She uncrossed her arms from her chest. Her fists balled at her sides. Another motion that Spinelli knew was one of aggression.

He held up his hands. "Not that I'm accusing you of keeping score."

"Well, I am. I'm breaking the Communal Orientation vow right here, right now. You made a unilateral decision that affects our union without consulting me. I am having an emotional response to it."

"That's two. So? We're even?"

If it was possible, Romey's gaze widened further. Her mouth gaped open. Once more, Spinelli had said the wrong thing. He was entirely out of his depths here. He didn't dare bring up another of their vows. He had the suspicion that a logical argument would not work in his favor with his wife so emotional at the moment.

All he wanted to do was share his joy with this woman. Take her into his arms. Tell her he was in love with her. Then kiss her senseless for the rest of the night. It was irrational, but he couldn't think of another thing to do.

He reached for her. She turned her head away from him, but she didn't fight his hold.

"This was supposed to be the happiest day of my life," Spinelli began. "I have the woman of my dreams, and I was offered my dream job."

Romey inhaled. A shudder went through her shoulders as she did so. When she turned to him, there were tears in her eyes.

Spinelli was horrified to see the tears there. Finally, he was reading someone's expressions perfectly clearly. Yet even though he could read her expression, he had no idea what to do about it.

He wouldn't have the opportunity to do anything about it. Romey stormed past him and into her bedroom, slamming the door shut behind her.

<h1 style="text-align:center">CHAPTER TWENTY</h1>

Romey couldn't remember the last time she was this angry. Perhaps when the NASA Terrestrial Planet Finder space missions had been canceled. Or Pluto had been demoted from planet status. Or Douglas Prasher had been denied the Nobel Peace Prize in chemistry for his work on the green fluorescent protein. Oh, that had boiled Romey's onions something good.

But none of those moments could top the feeling of her husband choosing a job over her.

Romey had gone to bed angry, slamming her bedroom door in Jordan's face for effect. The idiot hadn't tried knocking on her door or calling out to her. She'd heard him sigh, and then the thunking tread of his boots on the hardwood floor as he retreated to his own room.

He'd gone back to his own room when she'd planned for them to stay in the same room from this night forward. But no, he was going to have a room in Washington, DC. All to play video games for six months.

Jordan's logical argument played over and over in Romey's mind. He's said it was his dream job. She didn't doubt that it would raise his profile in the virtual war games industry, thus being a boon for their future. She had heard him when he'd said it was temporary.

It was a smart decision. If he'd made it before yesterday when they had taken their relationship to a new level, back then, she might be willing to accept it. But not today.

Today she was an emotional mess.

Jordan hadn't broken any promises to her. Everything he'd decided on was entirely within the bounds of the vows they'd made to one another. Romey wanted to rip up those rational rites.

She didn't want her husband to see her as a positive illusion. She wanted her husband to be delusional in his love for her. She wanted to call Michelangelo and his drivel of supporting a partner's growth a farce. She didn't want her own autonomy. She wanted her life inextricably intertwined with her husband's so that he wouldn't go away, and he would stay with her.

When Romey woke in the morning, heart in hand, prepared to renegotiate her vows with Jordan, she found his room empty.

Her back sagged against the doorframe. Her heart didn't skip a beat at his absence. It slowed as though trying to comprehend the emptiness spreading throughout its chambers.

Romey knew her heart wasn't empty. There was oxygen-rich blood pumping into and out of her valves and headed to her lungs. So why was she having trouble breathing?

It made no logical sense, except that it was nonsense. Because she was in love. She might as well admit to all the foolishness of it. She had nothing left to lose. But she wasn't going to be one of those women that chased after the man. No, if Jordan wanted to talk, he'd have to come and find her.

She supposed he didn't want to talk. Being that he hadn't come after her last night. And he'd gotten up before the crack of dawn this morning to avoid her.

Romey shut her husband's bedroom door and made her way out of the house. The sun was peaking over the horizon as she made her way to her greenhouse. Plenty of the commune's residents were already up, hard at work on the crops that were their livelihood.

In a few hours, Romey would be escorting her science class to the county science fair. But first, she had to tend to her garden. If she could focus, she might determine what the problem was in her hydroponic garden before the whole system broke down.

Opening the door to the greenhouse, Romey heard the sounds of movement. Laying on the floor beneath her containers were a pair of jean-clad legs. Her heartbeat roared back to life, playing a fast rhythm. Whose song died a second later.

The jean-clad legs ended in a pair of Birkenstocks. Her sensible Jordan wouldn't be caught dead in the footwear. Paris slid out from under the containers with a grin on his face.

"Hey," he said. "I came in to find you and saw that your pump was malfunctioning."

Romey looked down at the water pump. Its function was to push the nutrient solution to all of the plants in the system. How had she not considered that it might be the problem from yesterday?

Whatever had happened, it wasn't a problem any longer. The nutrients flowed freely. The plants were already lifting their heads. The system was back online.

"Thank you, Paris. You didn't have to do this."

"What? You think I'd just turn my back and walk away if I saw you were in a bind?" He scoffed, wiping his hands on his pants. "What kind of man would that make me?"

What kind of man, indeed.

Romey looked Paris over. His leaned build was courtesy of all the hours he spent tending to plants in the fields, not hefting guns or taking down bad guys. He had a gentle spirit. He also had a number of academic degrees to match her own.

"Look, Rome, I'm sorry about the other day; what I said about not getting the inspectors in here to certify your hydroponics. This place is as much part of the farm as anything. When they arrive next week, we'll bring them in here."

Tears stung her eyes. Romey wasn't prone to emotional outbursts, but everything inside her was in chaos today. Was his outpouring evidence that she had feelings for Paris?

Maybe she should've married him instead? She and Paris had similar interests. They were both tied to this land and wouldn't leave to spend six months in the nation's capital playing video games. And she was sure that she wouldn't be prone to nonsensical emotions with Paris.

Paris Montgomery was a gentle, passive soul. Except for that time when he'd punched David in the eye over Jules. Twice.

No man had ever punched anyone for Romey. Not that she wanted that. What she wanted was for someone to be passionate enough about her to do it.

"Romey? What is it? What's wrong?"

She blinked her eyelids rapidly. But just like windshield wipers fighting a downpour, she was still having trouble bringing Paris into focus under the deluge of tears.

"Is it your husband? Am I going to have to have words with him? Or maybe use my fists instead of my words?"

"You'd do that for me?" Romey hiccupped. "You'd punch a man for me?"

"Of course, I would if you needed defending."

What a beautiful, passionate statement. So, why didn't that get her heart racing? Paris hugged her tightly in his arms. She didn't feel engulfed as she had when Jordan held her. She didn't have the sense of falling while at the same time knowing she was secure.

"I don't want you to punch Jordan in the nose. I want to kick him in the shins."

Paris pulled back and looked down at her. "Sounds like you're in love with him."

"I am," she sighed.

"You don't sound happy about it."

"Love is awful. It's entirely illogical and unpredictable. It's messy, and sometimes it hurts. The worst part is that I don't think he feels the same way."

"Why would you think that?"

"He's planning to leave me. Well, not leave me—leave me." Wow, she'd just used a phrase to describe itself. "He's going on a long trip without me. I don't want to be apart from him for that long. Just the thought of it makes my heart feel like it's breaking. If he doesn't feel the same way…"

Romey put her hands over her eyes. She tried to wipe away the tears there, but more fell to take their place.

"I've seen the way he looks at you," said Paris. "It's the same way that Porco looks at Jules, like she's the reason he breathes. I've never looked at anyone that way… unless it was a plant."

But Romey knew that Jordan was out in the world, breathing just fine while she was out of his sight. She wanted to believe he loved her, but she wasn't so sure. What she did know is that she would have trouble breathing without him in her life.

Already her heart was throbbing, her lungs felt constricted, her head was a mess. She felt out of control, like an unbalanced equation with too many variables. She had no idea how to solve this problem.

CHAPTER TWENTY-ONE

*S*pinelli pounded at his chest, but it still ached from the inside out. All night and into the day, he couldn't shake the sensation that his lungs weren't inflated properly. Despite taking deep breaths, he felt like he couldn't breathe.

After Romey had slammed her bedroom door in his face, Spinelli had stared at the door frame in shock, uncertain what to do. He'd wanted to knock the door down, burst inside… and say what?

He hadn't a clue what to say to her? He'd offered up a reasoned argument and was met with an irrational, emotional female. Completely unlike the levelheaded, even-tempered, thoughtful woman he'd married.

"You look awful," Rusty said as he came into the control room.

The space was empty this early in the morning. They weren't due to have another training session until later in the day. Spinelli had already uploaded the program and reorganized the arena. Now he sat slumped in his chair.

"I feel awful," he said.

His eyes felt as though there was sand in the corners. Every beat of his heart irritated his chest. His fingers alternated from numb to achy every other minute. His neck muscles ached from trying to hold his head up when all he wanted to do was lie down. Instead, Spinelli let his head loll back against the chair's headrest. That's when he got a look at his friend.

There were dark bags under Rusty's eyes. The man's skin was so pale, it looked like he hadn't seen the sun in days. There was a sickly look around his mouth, as though he could puke at any moment.

"Speaking of awful," said Spinelli, "have you looked in the mirror yourself today?"

Rusty grabbed the seat beside Spinelli. Instead of holding his head high, he let his forehead fall into his palm. A long, weary sigh escaped his lips. "I signed the papers this morning."

Spinelli didn't need to ask which papers Rusty was referring to. It was no wonder the man looked a wreck. His marriage had officially ended.

"I thought you were going to fight for her?" said Spinelli.

"I did everything I could." Rusty opened both of his palms, but there was nothing in his hands. " I reasoned. I pleaded. I even cried. But when a woman's fed up, there's nothing you can do about it."

"Why was she fed up?"

"She said I was never there for her."

"Because you had to work?"

Rusty pursed his lips, shaking his head sadly. "I don't think she meant physically."

What other ways were there to be present for someone other than physically? Spinelli looked over at the glass window of the arena's enclosure. With the lights off, the glass was reflective. Spinelli saw that he and Rusty looked like twins. Did that mean that his marriage was over? That was the last thing he wanted.

"Romey and I had a fight."

"Whatever you did, you were wrong. Tell her you're sorry."

"I don't know what I did wrong?" Now it was Spinelli that held up empty palms. "I told her we won the virtual war game contract. Then I told her about the offer to work for FSW in DC. I outlined the benefits that taking the job would have to our union, and she blew up at me."

Once again, Spinelli leaned his head back against the chair. The pressure was so heavy on the crown of his head that he allowed his eyes to close. In his mind's eye, all he saw was Romey. His inner world felt full with Romey in it. Now that she was out of his reach, he felt empty.

"Oh, you idiot."

Spinelli blinked his eyes open. His head snapped upright until he was eye level with Rusty. His expression was one that was easy to read; curled lip, wrinkled nose, unblinking gaze. The man wore a disgusted look on his face.

"How am I the idiot in this?" Spinelli spluttered.

"Would you really do it? Would you leave your wife?"

The very thought left Spinelli feeling feverish. The weight increased on his forehead and shoulders by the ton. His hands balled into fists with the need to punch through something.

"Never," he said. "It's just for a few months."

"You could do that? You could be away from her for that long?"

Spinelli opened his mouth, but the words stuck in his throat. He thought he'd thought this through. Truthfully, it hadn't occurred to him that Romey wouldn't be with him as he caught hold of this particular dream. He'd imagined her by his side for every moment of it. Didn't she know that?

What if she didn't know that? What if she wouldn't do that?

"I barely made it a night without her," he said. "I love her so much that everything looks gray when she's not there."

He knew that waxed philosophic, but it was true. The green of the commune hadn't looked at all vibrant this morning when he'd stepped outside. He'd done most of his work today in a dimly lit room while looking at a black and white screen. Even his wardrobe was a gray shirt and drab fatigues.

"Does she know how you feel about her?" asked Rusty. "Have you actually told her that you're in love with her?"

Spinelli shook his head. He'd been about to the other day after that kiss. But then they'd been interrupted. And later that evening, before he could admit to his feelings, she'd slammed a door in his face.

If she thought he'd so callously leave her behind, would she even believe that he had real feelings for her? Would a woman as rational and logical as Romey even accept such a notion as fact?

"I can't just tell her this," said Spinelli. "I need to prove it."

"Prove what?"

"That I love her."

Regardless of what she might think of him, Spinelli needed her to know this one thing. He knew just how to present the findings to her. But first, he had to find her.

CHAPTER TWENTY-TWO

Romey stood from her crouch. The tendons in her knees and spine all crackled with protest as she did so. She'd just helped her last student put up their experiment for the science fair. The actual work of lugging the projects inside the church recreation room hadn't been taxing. Keeping the fake smile plastered on her face while her heart was in agony had been.

She wished she could put the temperamental organ in a jar of vinegar and have it congeal like one of those bouncy eggs. Right now, her heart felt like a volcanic mixture just waiting for a teaspoon of baking soda to make it erupt and spill all over the church's linoleum floors.

Love sucked. But she was in it. And she didn't see an escape.

Jordan had stolen into her mind and lodged himself in both her left and right brain. She was emotionally attached to him. She couldn't reason her way out of it.

"We have a late addition to this year's fair," called Pastor Vance from a podium at the front of the room.

It wasn't lost on Romey that the town's church held the annual event. None of the holy men who'd graced these hallowed halls had ever looked at science as a nefarious practice. They encouraged anything that would open the hearts and expand the minds of their flock, especially the young. Romey might not attend church here every Sunday, but she'd always felt at home within these walls.

"As you know," Pastor Vance continued, "the fair is open to young and old. I believe this may be our oldest participant."

The youth participants all left their table to get a look at the old-timer who was their new competition. Behind the children, parents flocked to see the show. Her curiosity getting the better of her, Romey made her way to the edges of the crowd and then gasped at what she saw.

Jordan stood at the front of the crowd. He was dressed in his usual T-shirt, fatigues, and heavy boots. He was surrounded by posters of data readouts and printed charts of colored graphs. He had a pencil shoved behind his ear as he addressed the crowd. It took Romey a moment to tune into his words. Just the sight of him leading a lecture was the sexiest thing she'd ever seen in her life.

"It has been asked many times if love can be quantified," he began. "It's a difficult question as not many agree on what love actually is. Some say it's a physical force. Then there are those who say it is an ethereal experience of the soul. The only consensus is that it can be felt. Well, feelings are electrical."

Jordan turned his back and walked over to his friend Anthony Keaton. Keaton sat in a chair with LEDs attached to his forehead. A square monitor faced the crowd. On the screen, lines ran at steady crests and valleys.

"I'm measuring the levels of dopamine and serotonin present in his brain." Jordan made a motion to a woman to step forward.

When Brenda Vance stepped in her husband's line of sight, the crests went mountain high, barely coming back down into the valleys.

"Notice how the levels increase when the object of love is presented in front of the subject."

Keaton reached for Brenda's hand. When she gave it to him, the lines jumped to the top of the screen. A murmur rose in the crowd as everyone eyed the spikes on the monitor.

Jordan turned from that love-struck couple to another. Dylan Banks from the Purple Heart Ranch stood nearby. He wore a pair of cargo shorts that put his prosthetic leg on display. No one was looking down. All eyes were focused on the wires running under his shirt.

"I've heard it said that when someone falls in love, they feel butterflies in their stomach," Jordan said.

Both Jules and David had made that absurd statement, which both Romey and Jordan had scoffed at. Then Romey had felt the pleasant buzz of insects overtaking her abdomen and learned the error of her beliefs. Though Romey had experiential proof, she watched her husband with rapt attention, eager to see how he'd use science to prove that her feelings were real.

"No butterfly, nor any other insect, could survive in the hydrochloric acid of the stomach."

Romey's stomach clenched at the dismissal. She wanted to shout at Jordan that he was wrong. That she'd felt it.

"What you're actually experiencing is a function of the nervous system. When you see the object of your desire, your body goes into an alert mode similar to the fight or flight mode. Your nervous system releases adrenaline, which shunts the blood away from the gut, causing the muscles there to slow and relax."

Maggie Banks stepped around a corner. When Dylan spied his wife, his eyes lit up, and a secretive smile spread across his handsome face. On the monitor, the readout lines, which had been on a steady plateau up until this point, slumped downward like a butterfly flapping its wings to land on an open flower petal.

Romey wanted to applaud. She wanted to cheer. She wanted to be a part of this experiment so that she might coauthor an academic paper with Jordan on this subject. She could be another of his test subjects because the chemicals in her brain were going haywire. Her stomach muscles were quivering with need. But Jordan wasn't done. And she noted, all through this process, he hadn't once glanced her way.

"They also say that love affects your actions. This is my friend Porco. He loves bacon. But his wife loves tofu."

David sat at a table. A plate rested before him with a few squares that

Romey knew to be fried tofu. David wrinkled his nose at the plate of curdled beans. Yet, when he saw Jules, he dug into the dish with zeal.

"You'll see that Porco isn't hooked up to any readouts," said Jordan. "He's simply making a choice to do something he's not interested in for the one he loves."

Jules leaned over and pressed a kiss to her husband's lips as he swallowed. David dropped his fork and embraced his wife. Jules giggled as he nibbled at her lip.

"So you see, love is a mathematical, logical, rational, scientific fact. I know it to be true because I have experienced it firsthand."

Romey looked up to see that her husband's gaze had found her in the crowd. As Jordan walked over to her, in his hand, he held out a document between them.

"These are my test results when I think of my wife."

Romey unrolled the papers. She couldn't read the results. Her eyes were too full of tears. But she didn't need to see the spikes and plateaus to indicate what her husband thought of her. She knew it in her heart. She didn't need any facts to know what he was feeling. He only needed to gaze into her eyes, and she saw it clearly. But he was Jordan, and so he laid out his findings.

"Romey, I have a confession to make; I believe in love at first sight," Jordan said. "From that first moment I saw you in the grocery store, I knew you had to be mine. It started with the intelligence I saw in your eyes. I felt like you understood me, and that made me want to know you. The more I knew, the more I wanted you."

Jordan lifted a hand to her face to catch her tears. More fell as he wiped them away. Looking into his eyes would've overwhelmed Romey if she wasn't so starved for his affection.

"If there is such a thing as love at first sight," she said, "then maybe there is such a thing as love at first sound. I heard you and David talking in the store. David said Jules made his heart speed up and put butterflies in his stomach. You said that wasn't love, it was a medical condition. That's when I fell for you."

Jordan lifted her chin until her lips met his. It was a light kiss, but its impact was big enough to calm the raging sea inside of her. All went quiet, like a lake after a storm. The still waters of her soul ran deeply for this man.

His gaze raked over her face, taking in every detail, and then returning to gaze a little longer. His expression turned serious. "I'll give up D.C. for you."

"Jordan, no."

He shrugged. "It's not tofu."

"It's your dream."

He shook his head slowly. "You are my dream."

Tears stung her eyes. Her husband may not have punched another man for her, but he was willing to turn his back on his passion to please her. This subject was not closed. It would be open to negotiations.

Maybe he could work remotely? Maybe they could lessen the time frame? Maybe she could go with him for part of it?

She'd vowed to this man that she would support his goals, and she would. They'd figure it out. They were two of the smartest people she knew.

"So, we're in love with each other?" she asked.

"I think all the facts point that way. But we could do with a bit more experimenting, just to be sure."

"What procedures did you have in mind?"

A mischievous grin slid over her husband's face. "I think the next part of our study should be done in a more private laboratory."

"How about my bedroom?"

"Sounds like the perfect setting for this next phase of our experiment."

EPILOGUE

Rusty watched as Spinelli and Romey escaped out the doorway. Their absence was noted, but no one said anything. Everyone was far more interested in Spinelli's love experiments. Couples hooked each other up to the devices to get actual proof of what they felt for one another.

It had never occurred to Rusty to question his feelings for Ronnie. It simply was. It was something he'd known about himself to be true. Just as he knew he was a soldier. Just as he knew he could disassemble and reassemble any firearm put in front of him. Just as he knew the right words to say to defuse any crisis situation.

Rusty had talked suicide bombers out of their vests. He'd talked guntotting assailants into laying down their arms. He'd talked a few men and women down off ledges. He was very good at getting people to see reason and do what he wanted them to. Except when it came to Ronnie.

The woman had a mind of her own and a will of iron. Two of the things he loved most about her. When she got a notion in her head, it was hard to talk her out of it. Even for the trained crisis negotiator.

For months, Rusty had pleaded with her to reconsider her decision to end their marriage. She hadn't budged. In the end, she'd stopped taking his calls and answering his emails. Rusty hadn't spoken or heard from his wife in weeks.

The strain had taken its toll. It was clear she wasn't going to change her mind. She wasn't going to come back to him. There was nothing left in his bag of tricks. Nothing in his training taught him to talk a woman into staying married when she no longer wanted to be.

So, he'd picked up a pen and finally given her what she wanted. Watching the ink flow from the pen onto the divorce papers had been like signing over his soul. As he watched the ink dry, a cloud had shrouded his shoulders. He felt like he'd just returned from combat, and now he was missing a limb.

No prosthetic could replace what Rusty had lost. He'd spend the rest of his life a widower, knowing that the vibrant woman who was his wife was living a full life without him.

Looking around the room, his eyes were assaulted with the oppressive sights of love. Couples laughing. Couples kissing. Couples play fighting. It was too much for him to bear witness to. So, he slipped out a side door.

The sun was starting to set on this day. Not that it mattered. Day bled into night, which bled into weeks and then months for him. This was how he was going to spend the rest of his life; a shell of his former self.

Suddenly, anger boiled inside of Rusty. He wasn't even thirty years old yet. He still had a full life to live. He owed it to all the people whose lives he'd saved to live it.

His phone buzzed in his pocket. Still holding onto his resolve, Rusty took the device out. At the sight of the name on the caller ID, his heart hammered in his chest, his breath left him, buzzing bees raged in his belly.

"Veronica?"

"Russell? I need you."

~

*Find out if Rusty can win back the only woman for him in
"The Rancher takes his Last Chance at Love!"*

RANCHER TAKES HIS LAST CHANCE AT LOVE

THE RANGERS OF PURPLE HEART RANCH
BOOK 6

CHAPTER ONE

*R*usty Hook turned his cell phone over and over in his palm. His palms were sweaty, and there was a tremor in the ring finger of his left hand as the plastic case of the phone scraped against the gold band on his hand. His wedding band lifted a fraction each time the phone case bumped against it, but the ring kept its spot low on his finger, where it had been for the last five years.

"In a situation like this, we'd follow the first three principles of hostage negotiation."

A woman in fatigues stood at the front of the classroom. Her blunt fingertips pointed at the colorful slides of a Powerpoint presentation as she went through her points. Her gaze flicked over at Rusty as she spoke.

"Those principles are to contain, isolate, and negotiate," the soldier went on. "The method was successfully executed during an operation in Afghanistan where Sergeant Hook negotiated the safe return of four young boys stolen to become child soldiers."

Rusty didn't raise his head to acknowledge his part in the training presentation. Though this was his class on crisis management tactics while in the theater of combat, his eyes were on the wedding band contained on his finger. It sat isolated in that spot. There was no room to negotiate its release from his hand, even if the woman who put it there had asked him to take it off.

"You could argue that Sergeant Hook tacked on the principle of surrender when he demanded the release of the children in his negotiations."

If only that tactic worked with the female species. For months, Rusty had tried every negotiation tactic he'd ever employed to win back one hostage. But he couldn't seem to contain her, as she refused to stay in one place. He had no opportunity to isolate her, as they were always on opposite ends of the country, or sometimes the world. She wouldn't talk to him to negotiate any terms of surrender.

Until a few days ago.

His phone vibrated in his hands. He'd turned the ringer off while he sat in the presentation. He didn't accept the call. One look at the caller ID button told him that that particular call could wait. He had to keep the line open for the call he truly wanted.

"Negotiations account for ninety-seven percent of safe release cases. When those tactics don't work, the escalation tactics of using chemicals to flush out the enemy, or sharpshooters to wound or kill, have a far less success rate."

A few days ago, Rusty had gotten a call. It was an unexpected call as he'd been trying to flush out this particular adversary for months. When he'd seen her name on the caller ID, it had been like a round straight to the heart. He'd answered before the first ring was complete and set to giving her anything she wanted.

"If you can get the combatant to talk, the best place for you to be is not with them, but up high and out of sight."

Rusty scoffed at that. Being apart from his estranged wife was the last thing he wanted. Getting her onto his territory was his number one goal. She was coming here, driving from wherever she had been hiding out from him.

Just the thought of her driving that death trap she refused to give up gave Rusty a case of the jitters. He was sure she hadn't changed the oil since the last time he'd done it for her. She didn't know how to put more air in a tire, much less think about rotating them. What if she broke down on one of these long Montana backroads with no service station for miles?

"And lastly, as Sergeant Hook has taught us time and again, you have to be willing to walk away from any negotiation."

Rusty's head jerked up at that. Had he uttered those words? He had no intention of ever walking away from Ronnie. No matter how far she ran from him. But she wasn't running anymore. She was coming back to him.

Not to get back with him. The divorce papers she'd sent months ago had made her stance on their marriage clear. But she needed him for something. Whatever it was, he was going to give it to her. He wouldn't be able to help himself. Married or separated, his every instinct still was to give her the world.

With the presentation over, Rusty ducked outside before any of the workshop participants could corner him. The sun was reaching its peak on this fall day in Montana. Behind him, he could hear the grunts of men and women as they were put through their paces on the obstacle course of the Boots on the Ground Training Camp that prepared soldiers to undergo the arduous rigors of the Army Ranger School.

For a long time, Rusty had felt that the time he spent in the mud and climbing over barriers had been the hardest thing he'd ever done. Harder even than his many tours and missions in war-ravaged foreign lands. He'd been wrong. The hardest moment of his life was waiting for his phone to ring.

"Why didn't you pick up my call?"

Rusty looked up at the man coming toward him. Anthony Keaton's blue eyes were locked on the phone in Rusty's hands.

"Oh," said Keaton. "I see."

Rusty let out a long sigh as he flipped the phone once more in his palm. He'd turned the ringer back on. But the phone remained silent.

"That's happening today?" asked Keaton.

Rusty gave a nod, not trusting his voice. Which was funny. He was a trained hostage negotiator. More than half of his skills were in talking. This had been one problem he'd never been able to work out. Likely because he was the hostage in this situation.

He felt powerless. The uncertainty of his future plagued him. He'd never been on this side of the table in a crisis situation.

"Why don't you take the day off?" said Keaton. "We've got this."

"No," said Rusty. "I need something to occupy my mind while…"

He held up his phone as though it would finish the sentence for him. It still remained silent, allowing the ellipsis of Rusty's sentence to drag on. Keaton clapped him on the back, three times as though to put an emphasis on that punctuation.

"She didn't say what this was about?" asked Keaton.

Rusty shook his head. He noted that Keaton didn't use his wife's name. There had been a time while they'd served together that every other word out of Rusty's mouth had been about Veronica. As his tours got longer and more frequent, he'd spoken her name aloud less and less. That never changed the fact that she was still in his every waking thought, his sleeping ones as well.

"You don't think she's changed her mind?" Keaton's words were measured and slow. His expression told Rusty that he was trying to sound nonchalant, but Rusty caught the barely masked note of hope in his friend's voice.

Keaton liked Ronnie. All the guys in his unit liked his wife. Everyone who met her liked her. Rusty just wasn't sure why his wife had stopped liking him.

He wished Ronnie had changed her mind. It had taken him months to finally see the writing on the wall. It all became clear to him when he'd received the divorce paperwork with her signature on the line.

It was more than the fact that she'd signed the paperwork. It was how she'd signed it. Where Ronnie had always placed a heart over the I in her name, it was now just a solid, black dot.

"Well, we're all good here at camp," said Keaton. "But Dylan and Dr. Patel had been asking for you to help with a matter up on the Purple Heart Ranch."

That was as good a place to be as any. Rusty remembered his first day here on the Purple Heart Ranch; the rehabilitation ranch for wounded veterans. His team of six had been lucky in that they'd walked onto the ranch without any physical injuries. Though they all had scars. Rusty's injury was internal. He'd come with a broken heart.

The funny thing was that this ranch was renowned for more than only healing injuries of the wounded. The soldiers who stayed often found their true love while rehabilitating their bodies.

Rusty knew the ranch's matchmaking magic would never work on him. He'd found the love of his life years ago. His problem was that he lost her and he didn't know why?

He mounted one of the horses they kept to move from the training camp to the ranch. He tucked his phone in his pocket and gave a tug of the reins to get the animal moving. But as the horse took off, the communication device slipped from Rusty's pocket. The clomping of the horse's hooves as they galloped away muted the ringing of his phone.

CHAPTER TWO

$\mathcal{R}$onnie Hook pursed her lips at the sound of the phone ringing in her ear. By the fourth ring, she was gritting her teeth. When the beep that indicated the answering service had engaged, she blew out a disappointed breath.

There was silence after the beep. Rusty never bothered to record a voice message, not even when they'd dated. He wasn't the share-your-feelings type. He certainly wasn't a leave-a-recording-of-your-thoughts type.

If he needed to leave a message, he'd hold it in his head until he saw her. When they'd married, he'd barely made it through the home phone message she'd insisted on recording. He'd even frowned at the mounted device hanging on the kitchen wall, certain no one of importance would ever call. He'd sounded stilted as they recorded the outgoing message.

Hi, this is Veronica...and Russell.

Sorry, you missed us... but stay on the line.

To cast a message for...the Hooks.

They'd gotten a lot of chuckling compliments for that message. Well, only about five since hardly anyone ever used the landline's number. But that voice message had been the encapsulation of their relationship.

Ronnie was the bubbly romantic, while Rusty was always measured and practical.

It had been that calm, quiet attitude that had drawn her to him when they'd first met. Ronnie's life had always been a deafening hurricane with the large family she'd come from. She'd been born smack dab in the middle of seven siblings. Her oldest sister and youngest brother got all of the attention, while Ronnie was often forgotten. Mainly because she always had her nose in a book, and often chose obscure places to read, like the linen closet, or under the kitchen cabinets, or the crawl-space in the attic. But those places were where she could find quiet and solitude in the madhouse that was her home.

When she'd gone off to live with Rusty, all had been blessedly quiet. There had also been a good deal of solitude. It took years before the lonely silence became a problem—years before she felt his long absences acutely. By then, it was too late.

Ronnie would not be dealing with his silence any longer. She hit redial on her cellphone. The phone intoned the numbers Ronnie knew by heart. Rusty hadn't changed his phone number since they were dating. Even though he preferred text messages, he'd always answered on the first ring.

Once again, the phone rang and rang in Ronnie's ear. Four rings, a beep, and a standard voice message from the female computerized voice telling her to leave a message at the tone. Ronnie pressed End and pushed her phone away from her.

"Can I get you anything else, hon?"

Ronnie looked up at the waitress. She was a middle-aged woman with gray at the roots of her hair. Her smile was matronly, but her figure was anything but. The waitress, Marla as told by her name tag, had the slender form and height that Ronnie had always wished for but never rose to.

Ronnie only barely crested five feet, and a lot of that was achieved by the riot of brown curls atop her head. She had a slim waist, but above her belly was cleavage one cup size away from making her top-heavy. To balance that out, her hips were what was kindly referred to as good for childbearing.

Ronnie was an hourglass where she'd always wanted to be a vase. Vases held roses. All hourglasses ever held was sand.

But Ronnie didn't hold her figure against Marla. The waitress had given Ronnie extra guacamole on her burrito, so Ronnie was leaving her a big tip.

"No, I'm done," Ronnie said. "I'll take the check."

Marla tore a slip and placed it on the table. But when she went to pull away, one of the bangles on her wrist caught Ronnie's satchel. The avocado in Ronnie's stomach turned as she watched her bag fall the short distance to the hard floor.

Marla reached for the bag and caught the straps. Relief flooded the older woman's face. Ronnie's features pulled tighter together in absolute horror.

Though Marla had saved the bag from its date on the pristine floor, the contents of the bag spilled out. There was only one thing inside of Ronnie's bag. Ronnie shuddered when it impacted the unforgiving ground.

There wasn't the shattering crack of glass breaking. Nor was there the metallic clang of precious jewelry hitting the floor. There was simply a thud, the sound of the hard spine of a book fracturing as its pages were ruffled.

As though the book was aware it had been caught naked out in public, the covers squeezed its pages back in. For a second, Ronnie thought the book would stand upright, but it teetered on the edge of its spine. Ronnie held her breath, hoping against hope that it would land on its face, thus hiding the cover.

But no. The book fell on its back. Hiding the blurb of the story inside the pages. Most people judged the book by its cover, anyway.

Marla's perfectly plucked brows rose to her gray hairline as she looked down at the vivid jewel tones of the cover. When Ronnie had printed it at an Office Depot Store, she was surprised at how bright the colors turned out. So bright that the couple depicted in the image looked orange.

"Is that one of those alien romance novels?" asked the man in the booth across from her. "I heard about those." He gave her a wink before dipping his tortilla chip into a bowl of salsa.

Ronnie sat frozen in her seat. She vacillated between the shame at Marla's pinched gaze and outrage at the man's lascivious stare. The dueling emotions didn't allow her to move to pick up the book.

"I'll just cover that up for you." Marla reached for a napkin, then the book.

As the waitress held the book gingerly, the pages fluttered again. Inside, Ronnie saw a copious amount of red markings, notes for mistakes on the manuscript. So much red that the book looked as though it was bleeding. Marla slid the injured tome back into Ronnie's satchel, as though it were a bandage, and placed it on the table.

Ronnie didn't meet the woman's eyes as Marla collected her dirty dishes. Ronnie was used to the judgment over her reading material. As a kid, she had had many a book yanked from her hands by her parents, her siblings, teachers, and librarians.

You're not old enough for that, said her mother.

That's mine, said her older sister.

That's above your reading level, said the librarians.

That's not on the assignment we're working on, said her teachers.

But with the invention of the ebook, no one could see what she was reading. Ronnie had downloaded hundreds of romance books and devoured every single one of them. So much to the point that she thought she could write one herself.

And so she had.

Using a pen name, of course. She might love the romance genre, but she didn't need any more grief from her family and friends about her reading habit, or now her new career. Her book just needed a professional cover, one not created by her in Microsoft Word. It also needed a qualified editor, which would cost money she didn't have...yet.

She looked down at her phone. It wasn't like Rusty to not answer her calls. Definitely not like him to not call her back.

But she had no claim to him any longer. They'd been separated for nearly a year. They were getting a divorce. She'd signed the papers months ago, but Rusty had been dragging his feet.

That had frustrated Ronnie, until now. She needed him to cosign a business loan so that she could get the money to make her dreams come true. After that, he would have to let her get on with her life. And he would get on with his.

Ronnie was here to get two signatures from him. The first on a loan. The second on the divorce papers.

She hadn't wanted to do this face to face. Rusty had a habit of talking her into what he wanted. That was his job as a hostage negotiator. But she'd held still and quiet in this relationship too long waiting for him to come home to her. Meanwhile, he went all around the world solving crisis after crisis, while back at home, she stewed alone in the silence.

Love shouldn't be quiet. Ronnie didn't want to go back to the quiet, and there was nothing Rusty could say to make her turn around. Now, she had something to say, and she'd written it all down in a book. A book with a bright cover and bleeding words that she wanted to share with the world...after muting the color a bit and cleaning up the manuscript.

Ronnie knew where Rusty was staying; a place called the Purple Heart Ranch. It was just a half-hour drive away. She grabbed her purse and her book and headed out to her car.

Climbing inside her old Chevy named Old Bessie, the engine wheezed as Ronnie turned the key. After a few false starts, the engine roared to life. And by roar, it let out a grumble that made a few pedestrians jump back.

The check engine light came on as Ronnie pulled out onto Main Street. But Bessie was reliable. The old girl would get her to her destination. Once Ronnie had her first royalty check from her published book, she'd get her car a complete internal makeover.

CHAPTER THREE

he ride across the green pasture did much to settle Rusty's mind. There was something about being up on a horse that sent power up through the legs. Many of the riders he encountered on the way to the Purple Heart Ranch had lost limbs. But astride the therapy horses, it was clear to see that their wounds hadn't broken their spirits.

It wasn't just the horses that helped these men and women take back the power of their lives. Soldiers and veterans worked in a garden, digging gnarled and mangled fingers into rich soil and pulling up vegetables they produced through hard work. Men and women with scars and burn marks tended to livestock that cared not for their looks but for the care and attention given.

This place was a paradise for service members and their families. It was a place that Ronnie would've loved to live in. Maybe if he brought her here, she might fall in love with the ranch and back in love with him?

Rusty brought the horse down to a slow trot as he approached the stables. Before Rusty could dismount, he got waved down by Dylan Banks and Dr. Patel. Rusty climbed down from the horse and handed him over to one of the ranch hands. Then he approached the two men.

Dylan Banks stood in a pair of cargo shorts. The cool fall breeze wisped through the gears of his prosthetic leg. Dark circles formed a half-moon under his eyes, but the man looked too joyful to be tired. Rusty knew Dylan awaited the birth of his second child. The smile on his face was that of a man who had everything in life he ever wanted. Once upon a time, Rusty had known that smile for himself.

After shaking hands with Dylan, Rusty turned to the smaller man beside him. Dr. Patel wore a serene smile as ever. The man also wore a tweed jacket, making him look more like a college professor than a psychologist. What did look out of place was the hint of concern in his gaze.

"We're glad you're here," said Dylan. "We could use a man with your skills."

"Is there a problem?" Rusty's particular skillset was only ever called upon in times of trouble. It often involved a ransom note, suicide vest, or hostages. None of that was in alignment with this healing ranch.

"We just had a new patient come into the clinic," said Patel. "He's come off a rough mission and has a past documented TBI."

TBIs, or traumatic brain injury, were the bane of a soldier's existence. Just as in sports, there were often collisions of linebackers and forwards, bombs exploding, and hand-to-hand combat were murder on the brain. The problem in the military was that for a long time, these sneaky wounds went undetected and silently degraded the health of many a serviceman.

"He was starting to improve," said Dylan, his expression going grave. "But then he got word that his wife had signed divorce papers."

Rusty remembered that particular gut punch when he'd received those documents in the mail from the woman he'd sworn to love and protect his whole life. He'd never been diagnosed with a TBI, but that moment he'd felt as though the pieces of paper were shrapnel burning his fingers.

"We thought with your area of expertise, along with your recent experience with... you know." Dylan looked away instead of saying the D-word.

"I understand," Rusty chimed in, not meeting either man's eyes. "Just say the word, and I'm happy to have a chat with him."

Rusty tried to inject cheer into his voice. That failed. Because he'd failed. His number one job had been to make his wife happy, and he'd failed.

He caught Dylan's eye then. Dylan had found the love of his life here on this ranch. So had many of the soldiers who lived here. Each marriage was strong and happy. Back at the Vance Ranch, the same thing had happened. Each of his friends had fallen madly, hopelessly in love, and gotten married only days after meeting the woman they hadn't dared to dream of.

Maybe that could happen to Rusty. But he'd have to clear Veronica out of his heart. And there simply wasn't a broom large enough for the task. She was in every nook and cranny of his chest.

Dylan gave Rusty a clap on the back. Then he turned and took off. Likely in search of his wife and child.

Dr. Patel, however, stayed behind and eyed Rusty closely.

Rusty and his team had never been through the Purple Heart Ranch's healing program. They hadn't come here wounded physically. His team had come with the express purpose to train soldiers at their camp. But they'd gotten close to the residents, including the resident psychologist who liked to meddle in not only everyone's mental state but in their affairs of the heart as well.

"How are you doing these days?" said Patel.

Rusty wasn't used to being the one to answer questions. He was the one who did the talking and listening in a hostage negotiation.

"I hear you signed the divorce papers?"

Rusty nodded. "I did. A few days ago."

"I also hear your wife is coming for a visit."

There were no secrets in this place. You told a wall a private matter, it would carry over to the next roof by the end of the day, and every human, child, and animal would know your business.

"She says she needs a favor," said Rusty. "I'll always do anything for her, regardless of whether we're legally married or not."

"Just because you sign a document, that doesn't mean the heart stops wanting what it wants."

Wasn't that the truth? Rusty knew he would never love another woman again in this lifetime. Even though he'd signed the papers, he still considered Veronica his wife.

'Til death, he'd pledged.

'Til death, he meant.

"If you need anything, I'm here for you," said Patel. And with that, the older man turned on his heel and headed toward the ranch's clinic.

Rusty watched him go. He had to admit he was a little surprised. He'd expected more probing and prodding from the psychologist. But that was it.

Maybe there was no hope for Rusty's situation? He patted his pocket for his phone. It had been thirty minutes since he'd last checked for it. His hand ran over the smooth fabric. There was no rectangular indentation in his jeans.

His phone wasn't there. His sole connection to Ronnie was gone. What if she'd called and he'd missed it? Panic set in.

Rusty turned to retrace his steps. He had ridden the horse for a long distance here. It could be anywhere.

He looked up and got distracted by what he saw. A man was on the roof of the barn. The man walked dangerously close to the edge. Rusty didn't think, he acted.

He raced inside the structure, climbing up until he was at the roof. He stepped out onto the roof and called out to the man.

What had Dylan said his name was?

"Randy?" The man didn't answer to that.

"Ray?" Still no response.

"Reggie." That was it. But still, the man didn't answer.

That was a bad sign. When the party didn't speak, it meant they'd already given up hope. Much like how Ronnie had stopped speaking to Rusty. She'd given up hope on their marriage a year ago and simply stopped responding to his pleas for another chance.

Reggie took another step and looked over the side. The roof was high enough that a break of some body part was likely. But he didn't step over. He only peered down. Maybe the man just wanted attention?

Suddenly Reggie turned to look over his shoulder. He peered at Rusty as if he was just noticing him for the first time, even though Rusty had been calling out to him.

"Listen, Reggie, let's talk about this."

Reggie reached up to his ears. He pinched his fingers into first the left and then the right ear, pulling wireless earbuds out. "What are you doing up here?"

"I'm here to help, Reggie," said Rusty.

"My name is Paul. I'm here to fix the roof. Who are you?"

Rusty was just a few feet from the man. He'd had his hands outstretched, trying to portray a non-threatening posture. But he let that go under this revelation.

"You're a roofer?"

Paul nodded.

"Not a soldier?"

Paul shook his head.

Rusty let out a sigh. He felt like a complete idiot. Here he was trying to save someone who was just doing their job. And it appeared they'd obtained an audience. There was a small crowd gathering down below. In the crowd, he saw a familiar head of curly brown hair.

Ronnie?

He didn't think. He took a step toward her. And fell off the roof.

CHAPTER FOUR

When Ronnie pulled up to the Purple Heart ranch, she assumed it would be like any base she'd ever lived on. She'd lived on a lot of bases. Such was the life of a military wife.

But the houses she drove by looked modern and not like something from three decades ago. In a lot of the military housing she'd experienced, the appliances were older than her parents, and the laundry room had to be entered into with a gas mask due to the rank smell of unclean socks and underwear come back from overseas.

Here on this base, that wasn't a base at all but a ranch, couples strolled by, sneaking kisses. Children played ball with a group of dogs running between their legs. A gathering of women sat off to the side, sipping drinks out of decorative mugs. Smiles warmed their faces.

As Ronnie drove by, one of the women looked up and waved. Ronnie ducked her head and focused on fitting her oversized Chevy into the parking space.

Military bases were always a tight-knit community. The wives there were often the stitching holding the fabric together. Ronnie missed having that group of friends most. She was still in touch with the wives she'd befriended over the years. But email and phone calls just didn't do it. And that's why she had no intention of moseying up to those women to collect more people who would eventually be pulled away from her in the line of duty.

"Hi!"

Ronnie looked up to see the woman who'd waved to her, standing at her driver's side window. There was a small bump beneath her shirt that could only be from pregnancy.

"Can I help you find where you're going?"

The woman's voice was pleasant. Not that Ronnie would've expected anything different from a military wife. Even though this wasn't a base, its people still had all the hallmarks.

The women at the table leaned back, eying the two of them. Ronnie didn't second guess their welcoming smiles. She just didn't want to get attached to something temporary. She would only be here for a couple of days at most.

"I'm looking for someone," said Ronnie.

"What's their name?"

"Russell Hook."

The woman's face split into a beatific grin. "Oh, you're Rusty's wife?"

"No. Yes. Not anymore. Can you tell me where he lives?"

Her smile didn't dim at Ronnie's denial. "He doesn't live on this ranch. He lives next door on the Vance Ranch. But he works here. It's just a hike to get to the training camp. Let me find someone to drive you over there."

Ronnie followed the woman, Maggie she learned her name was. She also learned that Maggie had a son and a daughter on the way. She learned that Maggie had lived on the ranch for a couple of years now.

Ronnie let Maggie go on as she tried to keep at least a foot of distance between herself and the friendly woman. The friendship that beckoned between them would not survive after Ronnie completed her business here. And that business would conclude as soon as she got Rusty's signature, once she found him.

And then she saw him.

Rusty stood on top of a roof. He had his hands outstretched. It was a posture she knew well. It was the same posture he'd used when she'd told him she wanted a divorce. He'd tried to talk her down. He'd tried to use his hostage negotiation tactics on her.

He'd used her name over and over again. He'd tried to get her talking, to keep an open line of communication between them. But by then, there had been nothing more to say. She couldn't bear to watch him leave another time. So that time, she'd left.

It didn't look like his tactics were working now. The man near the ledge appeared to be ignoring Rusty's attempts to save his life. The man was standing very close to the edge.

"Should we call someone," said Ronnie.

"That's the roofer," said Maggie. "What's Rusty doing up there?"

The roofer finally turned to acknowledge Rusty. Ronnie couldn't hear what the exchange between the two was. She was far too focused on her soon to be ex-husband.

He'd lost weight. But even with the loss of the pounds, his shoulders were still as broad as a bear's. She knew exactly where the warmest spot in his chest was where she could hibernate all winter.

Except they never got to hibernate all winter. He was always called away. She was always left alone, moving, setting up a new life, new friends where she would wait for him to come back so they could repeat the whole process again.

Not anymore. She'd turned away from that life. No, she wasn't exactly happier. Yet. But she would be. Soon.

Ronnie was about to turn away from Rusty on the roof when their gazes connected. Ronnie's heart did that flip every time she was in his presence. The flip hadn't gone away even when things had gone silent between them. Her mind might be made up, but her heart had never gotten with the program. Even though it broke every time he got spun up and walked away from her to go on a mission.

Her heart flipped again when Rusty took a step toward her. It flipped because Rusty didn't seem to remember that he was on a slanted roof and not solid ground. With a second step toward her, his feet came out from under him, and he fell.

Rusty landed with a sickening thud to the ground. Ronnie ran toward him, her heart in her throat. When she got to him, he lay immobile on the ground.

There was a crowd around him. Mostly other large males. Likely soldiers. With their big bodies, it was hard to break through them to get to Rusty.

"Make space," said an older man. He was thin with brown skin and a slight accent. The men let the man through, and he reached for Rusty's wrist. "He's breathing. Let's get him to the clinic."

Luckily, her position made it easier to get around the crowd and follow them. Ronnie raced behind them. Rusty's hand dangled between the men who carried him. It was his left hand that dangled. On his ring finger sat his wedding ring. There was a speck of dirt that muted its shine. Ronnie itched to reach over and wipe the spot clean.

"I'm sorry, ma'am. You can't come in."

Ronnie looked up at the imposing soldier. He wasn't one from Rusty's unit. She hadn't seen any of those guys here.

"I'm his wife," she said. It wasn't a lie. They were still married. Rusty hadn't signed the papers. She didn't think he ever would. Now, she was glad of it. But how could she prove that she was who she was?

Ronnie lifted her left hand, only to remember that she'd taken her ring off months ago. It was in her suitcase, inside a hidden compartment with other valuable items. Did she have time to run back to her car and grab it?

"Let her through," said the older man.

The brawny soldier stepped aside, allowing Ronnie to pass. She walked into the room where they laid Rusty out on a bed and stopped just inside the doorway. Rusty lay motionless on the bed, and all Ronnie could do was stand there and stare.

For years, she'd craved silence from her large family so she could escape into a world of books. She'd found that silence with Rusty, and then got restless from his absences. Now here he was, a captive audience, and all she wanted him to do was wake up and shout to make a ruckus.

"Mrs. Hook?"

Ronnie blinked at the elderly man with a stethoscope in his hand. "Yes?"

"I'm Dr. Patel. It doesn't look like anything is broken. But it was a nasty fall. We'll need to wait until he wakes up to be sure."

As though Rusty had heard the older man's command, he started doing just that. His eyes blinked open. His gaze focused on her. His lips split in a wide grin.

"Am I dead?" he asked.

"No, you're alive," said Dr. Patel.

Rusty frowned, his gaze still on Ronnie. "You mean, this isn't heaven?"

"No," chuckled Dr. Patel, "you're on the ranch."

"But she's here, my angel."

Rusty reached his hand up and pulled Ronnie to him. Ronnie didn't resist. Later she'd tell herself that it was because it proved his arms weren't broken. She didn't know what excuse she'd give for why she allowed the man she was trying to divorce to press his lips to hers and kiss her soundly.

CHAPTER FIVE

He was having the dream again.

Each night since Rusty had met his wife six years ago, he'd dreamed of pulling her close and kissing her. Sometimes, in the dream, she would laugh as she kissed him back. Sometimes, as he lay there with his eyes closed, she would sigh and rest her head on his chest.

She did that now in the dream; she sighed as he pressed his lips to hers. Her breath was sweeter than sweet tea. With a hint of avocado. It was Rusty's new favorite treat.

In his dream, he pushed her hair out of her face so that he could get better access to her mouth. There was nothing like Ronnie's big buffet of curls. Her hair was a smorgasbord of spirals. No two coils were alike. The top twisted one way while the back of her frizzed in the opposite direction. Rusty would get lost as he brushed the waves out of her face so that he might claim her lips.

His favorite dream was the one where he tugged back her hair with one hand and handed over a present with the other. The present was a key. The key was to their dream home.

It's what he'd worked for their whole lives together. No more renting a small apartment where they could hear the neighbors every conversation. No more base living where everything was temporary, and as soon as they'd get comfortable, they'd be leaving again (with PCS stickers stuck to more and more of their possessions).

In his dream, Rusty had saved up to buy Ronnie the two-story single-family home of her dreams, complete with a room for a library and a reading nook. Ronnie would look at the house and then turn and kiss him. Just like she was doing now.

Though this dream was far more vivid than the others. He could smell the perfume that she always wore. He felt the silk of her skin as he cupped her cheek. The sweet taste of her had morphed into something spicy; salsa and guacamole.

That was an odd detail that had never come up in the dream before. And the fingers he ran his hair through felt straighter than normal. But what he did recognize was Veronica's sigh.

Rusty lived for the sound of that sigh of contentment. He hadn't heard it in years. He'd forgotten what it sounded like. But in this dream it all came back to him; the sound of his wife happy and in his arms where she belonged.

A voice cleared somewhere in the distance. How was that? There had never been another person in these dreams. And definitely not a male.

"I beg your pardon." Dr. Patel's voice came from far away, but way too close for this to be in Rusty's imagination. "But, I have to check our patient and make sure everything is intact."

The kiss broke on a gasp. Rusty opened his eyes. And there she was.

Veronica was only a couple of inches away from him. Her wild hair was tamed back into a ponytail. The tendrils were rioting at the edges. But still, she was here. Live and in the flesh… and pulling away from him.

Her eyes blazed brightly. Her cheeks flushed pink. Her lips pursed together, as though they were being scolded for that kiss.

That kiss.

How had that happened? The last thing he remembered was falling from the roof. No, the last thing he remembered was seeing her face in the crowd. Then there had only been the drive to get to her.

Gravity had put a damper on that. Rusty wasn't sure if he was hallucinating or if this was real life. So he let his training kick in, and he asked.

"Are you real?"

"I…" No other words came from her mouth.

Rusty felt the brush of air from her lips. Real or imagined, he knew he was keeping this version of his wife. He would find a way to contain her, to keep her close to him. That was the first step in any hostage negotiation.

"You had a pretty bad fall there, soldier."

Rusty didn't look up at Dr. Patel. He dared not take his eyes off Ronnie. What if she disappeared again.

He had to find a way to move to the next step of hostage negotiation and isolate her. His gaze never left Ronnie as Dr. Patel checked for breaks and sprains in his bones. And then Rusty got his wish. Once he was all checked out, Dr. Patel left the two of them in the room alone.

"Hey," Rusty said.

"Hey," Ronnie said, avoiding his gaze.

"About that kiss—"

"You were dazed," she said, waving his words away.

He was dazed, dazed by her. Ever since the first time he'd seen this woman and her wild hair and huge grin, he had been taken. So taken that he never wanted to be parted from her.

"You don't have to apologize," she said.

Rusty had no intention of apologizing. He'd meant every nibble, every touch of his lips against hers.

"I'm here to talk business. Not about us."

Us? Just as much as he missed kissing his wife, Rusty missed being an us. They weren't an us any longer. Rusty had held out for as long as he could, but he'd eventually given in and signed those divorce papers that separated that monosyllabic word that had tied them together.

"What I need is for you to sign the divorce papers. Since I know you haven't done that yet, I need a favor."

That pulled him up short. Should he tell her that he had signed the papers like she wanted him to? Show her that he was still capable of giving her what she needed. Or should he hold his tongue and see what this favor was? See if there was any leverage he could gain to show her that he was still what she needed?

"I need money," Ronnie said, still not meeting his gaze.

When Ronnie had first called asking for his help, Rusty had wondered for days what she might ask for. He'd assumed she was coming for the divorce papers. Money was the last thing he'd expected to hear. She still had access to all of their banking accounts. He'd never withheld anything from her.

"I told you, whatever alimony-"

"I don't want alimony." Ronnie held up a hand. "I want to take care of myself."

When they'd been dating, Rusty had loved that independent spirit of hers. Ronnie had always insisted on contributing to the family coffers. The problem was she couldn't hold a job. Mainly on account of there always being a book in her hands.

"I want to get a business loan," she continued. "But I'm having problems getting approval since I haven't had steady employment in the past five years as we moved around a lot."

"I don't understand?" Rusty rubbed his palm against his temples. A headache from the fall was starting to grow there. "Why would you take money from strangers at a bank and not out of our account."

"It's not our account. You earned that money."

"You worked for it as well," Rusty insisted. "The life of a military wife is hard work."

"I don't want to argue." Ronnie held up her hand and closed her eyes.

Rusty waited until the pained expression went away. He knew better than to antagonize the person he was trying to negotiate with. He had to find her pain points and show that he was the man to solve them.

"What do you need, Veronica?"

"I just need you to cosign a loan with me."

Easy enough. And the loan document would present another tie to her. He'd take any rope she'd toss his way.

"I know it's an imposition," she said. "It's the last thing I'll ask of you as your wife."

The last thing as his wife? Because she thought she was still his wife. She thought he hadn't signed the papers. But he had. The truth was they were no longer man and wife. But she didn't have to know that yet.

CHAPTER SIX

onnie watched the expressions on Rusty's face. When she'd told him about her intentions to get a business loan, his gaze had narrowed as he searched for understanding in her words. His eyes widened in surprise when she'd declined to use the joint accounts from their marriage, accounts filled with the money he'd earned by risking his life. Didn't he know she couldn't touch that, not when she'd decided to leave him? She'd felt bad enough that she had told him she wanted a divorce before a deployment.

Ronnie had spent those last months in a constant state of despair, expecting to get a knock on the door at any minute. As a military wife, that fear had always been in the back of her mind. But as she'd done for years, she'd soldiered on, just as her husband did during his service. She'd marched forward until she'd hit a brick wall.

Now she sat within reach of her soon to be ex-husband, and she wanted nothing more than to feel his head for bumps from his fall. But that was no longer her right.

Oh, Ronnie knew Rusty would let her. If she had doubted, that kiss they'd shared made his feelings crystal clear. He still wanted her.

Well, she still wanted him. But wanting each other would not solve their problems. So she sat back in her chair.

What do you need, Veronica?

Rusty had always been a rock. No, not a rock. He'd always been like the tree in her parents' backyard. The tree she'd climb early in the morning and sit nestled in its strong branches while she wiled the day away between the pages of a novel.

That was Russell Hook. He was the strongest, sturdiest man she'd ever known. He just couldn't give her what she needed.

Looking at him now, he looked like that same massive tree with thick roots. No matter where they went, it was always Rusty that felt like home. Being in his arms a moment ago had been the first time Ronnie had felt settled in a year.

Ronnie gave herself a shake. This was why she hadn't wanted to see him in person. Things always got confused when she was in his physical presence. They'd never had trouble with the physical aspects of their marriage. It was the emotional aspect where they lacked.

After their first year of marriage, she and Rusty hadn't connected on an emotional level again. After they'd said *I do*, the romance had stopped. They'd settled into a married life of routine. One where he'd split himself in two.

At home, Rusty would kiss her senseless when he was in her presence. On missions, Rusty kept a wall of duty between them that led to a silence that stretched beyond an ocean.

Ronnie knew there had to be a cone of silence surrounding the details of his missions. But that's not what she wanted to get to the heart of. She wanted to get to her husband's heart. Unfortunately, it was buried beneath the layers of his body armor.

"Business loan?" Rusty asked. "What business?"

"I've written a book."

"You have?" His eyes brightened with awe and pride. "That's amazing? I'm so proud of you."

Ronnie's shoulders went back under his praise. There was a part of her that wanted to whip the book out and show it to Rusty, splotchy cover, red marks, and all. But there was another part of her that hesitated. The part of her that hid her romance novel addiction between the covers of a classic tome. The part of her that fist-pumped the air when the eReader was born, and she didn't have to hide so blatantly anymore.

"About what?" Rusty asked. "Life as an army wife?"

"Sort of," Ronnie hedged. Her romance novel did feature a soldier as the hero. The woman he pursued would become his wife by the end of the novel. Which made her character an army wife.

"Oh, I know. It's about the trials of growing up in a large family."

Ronnie cocked her head to the side as though she could see the pages of her book turning. She had grown up in a large family, and that had informed much of her life.

"That's in there, too," she said.

"Tell me more."

But she was tongue-tied.

"Will you let me read it?"

"No." The word was resounding, like slamming a hardback book closed.

"No?" Rusty said, genuine hurt on his face.

"It's not something you'd enjoy reading," she said.

"If you wrote it, I'd enjoy it."

Ronnie bit her lip. "Well, it's not published yet. That's what I need the money for. There are editing costs. And I need to buy cover art. It's all adding up."

"I'll pay for it, whatever the costs."

"No. I want to do this on my own. I can't keep relying on you."

"I'm your husband. It's in the job description."

"You're not my husband anymore." Ronnie turned away from the pain that furrowed his brow. "You won't be soon enough. I can't rely on you anymore."

"You can always rely on me, Veronica. I will always be here for you."

It was words like that that made her heart flip. But Rusty only said things like that when their relationship was in dire straights. The overtures only came out when times were bad. That wasn't the type of romance Ronnie wanted.

"All I want is your signature." She had to force herself to say the next part and inject steel into it. "Actually, I want your signature twice. First, to cosign the loan. And then, when that's secure, I want you to sign the divorce papers."

Rusty pursed his lips as he regarded her. His gaze was dark. She'd never seen that look on his face.

Ronnie had already used all of the steel in her voice. She didn't have much left for her spine. Rusty was an expert negotiator. He had the skills to talk anyone into or out of anything. He never used those tactics on her. But now he was backed against a wall, being forced to do something he didn't want to. Ronnie was certain he was about to pull out all his hostage negotiating stops.

"All right," he said.

Ronnie blinked. Then cocked her head to peer at him. "All right?"

"It's a deal."

"Deal? Deal as in you mean you'll do it?"

She had expected push back. She had expected him to try to contain her, to isolate her, and then negotiate. She knew the tactics. She knew his tricks. He should've been trying to keep her talking, getting as much information as possible. But he hadn't pried when she'd told him she didn't want him to read the book. He wasn't asking for any details. What was his game?

"We'll go to the bank in the morning," he said. "I'll sign the loan."

"You will?"

"And then in a week, I'll sign the divorce papers."

"A week? Why a week?"

"Because you'll stay here for those seven days and give us a second chance."

There it was. The containment, the isolation, the negotiating leverage he sought. But she knew it was useless.

"It's not going to work, Russ."

Rusty had been the tree that provided her with stability. The roots she knew was her home wherever they were transplanted. The shade that protected her from the elements.

But that was it. Trees weren't inherently romantic. They didn't spout overtures of love. They sprouted leaves. They didn't sweep a girl off their feet. For that, she'd have to climb. And the only place she had to climb was out of this marriage and into a new life of her own.

"Then you have nothing to lose," Rusty said. "You'll have your loan. And in a week, if you haven't changed your mind, we walk away with a clean break and never have to see each other again."

That thought pulled her up short; *never have to see each other again*. Ronnie wanted the divorce. But the thought of never seeing Russell again hadn't occurred to her. But that is what divorce meant.

"Deal?" he said, holding out his hand.

Ronnie stared at his hand. "Fine."

She put her hand in his. He closed his fingers around hers, and she felt engulfed, safe, secure. And then he let her go, and the feelings went with it.

What had she just gotten herself into?

CHAPTER SEVEN

*R*usty shook out his hand. It was no use. Even all these hours later, he still felt the imprint of Ronnie's hand in his. It was no wonder. The woman was apart of him, had been since the first time he'd pulled her to him and kissed her.

When he'd been deployed for months, that sense of attachment to her had gotten him through many scrapes and long nights.This last year, as he'd felt her slipping away more and more each day, he'd felt himself go hollow in the spots she used to fill.

He'd wanted her back with him. Tucked back into his side. Snuggled back into his chest.

She was back. But she wasn't with him.

Rusty pulled the door to the bunkhouse closed, leaving Ronnie inside. A part of him wanted to lock the door so that she wouldn't escape. Unfortunately, the lock only worked to keep people out, not in.

Ronnie could leave at any time. And she would. Just as soon as she learned what he'd done.

It was the worst thing that could have happened. Just as Rusty thought he was getting what he wanted, he'd lost the one thing that could change it all. He couldn't find the signed divorce papers.

After months of lugging the thin stack of papers around in his duffle bag, he'd taken them out a few days ago and signed them. The last thing he remembered is stuffing them in an envelope, but he couldn't bring himself to mail them. He'd thought he'd left them on his dresser. When he went into his room, the package wasn't there.

He'd searched the kitchen while Ronnie got settled in Porco's old room. He'd even gone into Spinelli's old room to search. Both Porco and Spinelli were now living with their wives in the cottage on the Verona Commune. Rusty had been the only one in the house for the last couple of days. With each room, he came up empty-handed.

That day when he'd signed the settlement had been such a blur. He couldn't remember much of it. Maybe someone else had come in? By the time he'd finished his search, it had been late. Everyone up at the ranch house would be asleep. Ronnie hadn't left the room after she'd closed the door, indicating there would be no talking between them.

The silent treatment had been her one and only weapon in their marriage. They both knew that if he could get her talking, she'd cave to his requests. Not that Rusty ever made outlandish requests of his wife. All he ever asked her to do when she was upset, or frustrated, or despondent was to stay with him. To wait it out until things got better. Now was that time.

Rusty knew that if he could just talk to his wife, face to face, he could make this better. Ronnie would have to face him today. They had the meeting at the bank later this afternoon. But before the talking, he had to find those papers.

The sun was rising on Vance Ranch as he walked the path from the bungalow to the main house. Ronnie would still be sleeping. She was a night owl, as that was the best time for reading. She wouldn't be up for a few more hours.

Rusty took his time walking the pastures. This morning he couldn't help but take the ranch in with new eyes. Would Ronnie love living someplace like this? There were tons of places for her to curl up and read her books. He'd always dreamed of building her a homestead that was all hers where they could raise their children; curly-haired kids whose noses were always in a book like their mother.

Now, maybe he'd get the chance to make that dream come true. He had seven days to convince her to stay his wife forever. But first, he had to make sure that the paperwork that would dissolve their union could be found and destroyed.

Mac and Lana sat on the porch eating a breakfast of steak and eggs. Mac chewed his meat while gazing at his wife. In his hand was a wedding catalog. Aside from his work training soldiers at the camp, and his helping out here at Vance Ranch, Mac also was a wedding consultant on the side.

Lana typed on a keyboard with one hand. In the other, she held a steaming mug of coffee. The aroma of the beans tickled Rusty's nose as he approached. She didn't look up from her keyboard. He knew she was working on a story about the troubles veterans were having as they tried to reintegrate into civilian life.

"I hear you had a sleepover last night," said Mac. His brows waggled like a dastardly villain in a cartoon.

"It's Ronnie," said Rusty.

"Oh, good," said Lana looking up from her computer. "So, you guys are back together?"

Lana had met Ronnie a few times. The last time had been when Lana had stood Mac up for the wedding. Ronnie had missed the impromptu ceremony a few months ago that had taken place inside a bedroom after Lana climbed into the window.

"We're giving it another shot," said Rusty. At least that was the plan. This would be the negotiation of his life, and he was prepared to pull out all the stops to win his wife back. Just as soon as he found the one thing that would tear them apart.

"That's great, man." Mac clapped him on the back. "So, why don't you look thrilled? I thought this was what you wanted."

"It is. I am. I just—have you been in the bungalow recently?"

Both Mac and Lana shook their heads.

"I misplaced something important. An envelope. You haven't seen one laying around."

Again they both shook their heads.

"You hungry, Rusty?" Patty poked her head out of the screen door.

Grizz filled the frame behind her. He rested his hand on her belly. When he did that, the small bump there became noticeable.

"No," said Rusty, eyes on the baby bump at Patty's midsection. "I'm just looking for something I lost. Have you seen an envelope laying around?"

The couple looked at each other and shook their heads.

It took Rusty a few minutes more to extricate himself from the two couples and their attempts to ply him with food or get details about Ronnie's return. Once he escaped, he turned and headed out to the pastures.

He found Brenda, Jules, and Romey in one of the fields spreading seed. Rusty knew the women were growing soybean plants on the pasture as a supplement to the cows' diet. What he marveled at was how the three lifelong enemies were getting along.

Brenda's hair was pulled back into a ponytail. Her green eyes sparkled as she laughed at something Jules said. Jules's hair was also pulled into a ponytail, but instead of straight strands, her hair was a collection of silky coils. Romey, whose hair was a riot of curls that stretched to the sun, shook her head at the laughing women.

"I can't believe the cows have taken to eating soy," said Brenda.

"Well, they're not our husbands," said Jules.

"In a way, our husbands are eating soybean," said Romey. "Since these are what the cattle consume."

"Hey, Rusty," said Brenda. "You looking for the guys? They headed over to the camp already."

"Actually, I wanted to talk to you, Bren. I misplaced an envelope sometime over the past few days. Have you seen anything laying around? Or," Rusty gulped, "been to the post office recently?"

"My brother was here the other day, and he took a bunch of mail to the post office."

Brenda's brother was a pastor. How ironic would that be if Pastor Vance was the one to dissolve Rusty's marriage.

CHAPTER EIGHT

*R*onnie stretched her limbs in the comfortable bed. Spread out like a starfish, her toes and fingertips weren't able to reach the four posts. It was luxurious.

She was used to sleeping alone. Rusty had been gone most months out of the year. What she wasn't used to was sleeping in sheets that didn't smell like her husband.

These sheets smelled like another man. They had the sweet tang of bacon on the pillow. She'd bet this had been David Porco's old room.

That was another thing she had missed about the separation from her husband. Military life, even though it came with all its trials and tribulations, came with a built-in tribe. No matter where she went, there was always a military family that would welcome her.

She'd particularly liked all of Rusty's team. From the ultra-organized Keaton to the broody Grizz, who she could talk poetry with. She'd missed the laughter of the prankster Mac. She'd missed explaining social nuances to Spinelli and steering her girlfriends away from Porco.

Ronnie might miss them, but she was surely using them. They were the subject of the next books she was writing. She'd planned a whole series featuring soldiers who would find their soul mates after their last deployment.

Each man would get his own story and a woman to compliment him. Spinelli would get a witty woman who could match his analytical mind. It would be funny if Porco got matched with a woman who was a vegetarian and didn't like bacon. For Mac, Ronnie wanted to write a second chance romance with the fiancée who'd stood him up. Grizz needed the girl next door type. Someone like Keaton's little sister Patty, who clearly was in love with him. Ronnie's biggest challenge was figuring out what kind of woman might ensnare the heart of Anthony Keaton. That woman would have to first snatch the checklists out of his hands and get him to look her in the eye. Ronnie wasn't sure such a strong woman existed.

The thought of giving those men love stories of their own after all they'd done to keep their country safe made Ronnie's heart fill. Unlike in the real world of military life, these books would be filled with long, lovey-dovey conversations where the calls didn't drop. There would be gifts in the mail that were delivered on an important date and not weeks or months later—or worse, not at all. There would be no wounds or injuries when the soldiers came home.

Ronnie knew she was writing a fairytale series. But no reader wanted to read the truth. The anxiety of waiting. The loneliness of long nights. The silence when a scheduled call was missed or didn't go through. The heartbreak when orders came that would separate loved ones and new friends over and over again.

No. None of that was romantic. So that's not what she wrote.

Ronnie pulled her laptop into the bed with her and began typing some more notes for the next story. An hour later, she looked up to see that it was approaching ten in the morning, nearing the time she and Rusty were due at the bank. She pulled on a robe as she padded around the bungalow, noting that Rusty wasn't at home.

He'd likely gone to work. No surprise there. She had no idea how the man planned to woo her back when he fell back into the same routines. At least he wasn't in any danger with his new job on the training camp. But it proved to her that he would never change.

His work had come before her when they were married. She'd signed up for that and knew she'd have to wait her turn. But when he'd taken on another assignment after they agreed he wouldn't reenlist, that had been the final straw.

The doorbell rang, jarring Ronnie out of her reverie. She tightened the robe around herself and went to open it. She expected one of the guys to be on the other side of the screen. Each man had spent time in their home when she and Rusty were married. Greeting them in a robe would be no big deal.

On the stoop stood a handsome man Ronnie had never seen before. When he lifted his head, she saw that there was a collar around his neck.

"Hi, I'm Pastor Vance."

Ronnie pulled the edges of her robe closer together. "I'm Veronica. Rusty's…"

"Wife?"

Standing in front of a pastor, wearing a robe, while in the home of a bachelor, Ronnie thought she should have felt vindicated by being called someone's wife. But instead, she grimaced. "Not for much longer."

The pastor's gaze swept down to her left hand, where she held her robe together. Pastor Vance wasn't leering at her. He was looking at her ring finger. Her left-hand ring finger to be exact. The one where a wedding ring should reside. All that was there was a tan line.

"Is Rusty here?" asked the pastor. "I seem to have collected a piece of mail that belongs to him. I would've mailed it for him, but there's no address."

"I'll take it." Ronnie took the long envelope from the man. She thought that was it, but the pastor lingered in the open door. "Is there something else you needed?"

"I have a habit of putting my nose in where it doesn't belong," he said, more to himself than to her. "I know the two of you are contemplating divorce. That's a big decision."

"I've already decided."

Pastor Vance's gaze was like lasers. His brows dipped, as though they were turning the knobs of his irises to focus. Did he see her lips tremble as she made the proclamation? Did he catch the wince at the edges of her eyes anytime she acknowledged the D-word?

"Rusty has sought counsel with me."

That surprised Ronnie. Rusty had never been a very religious man. She knew he believed in God, but he preferred to keep his own counsel rather than reach out to anyone else.

"I know he loves you very much."

Ronnie huffed. Everyone was constantly saying that. She knew Rusty loved her, intellectually. The problem was she could no longer feel that love.

"You don't believe that?" asked the pastor.

"I know he loves me. I love him, too. It's just not enough."

"What more do you want?"

"Passion. Romance."

"Ah."

"Let me guess." Ronnie let go of the edges of the robe to place her hands on her hips. "You think that's fanciful?"

"To the contrary," the pastor leaned against the door jam. "The Bible is filled with many romances. Adam and Eve, Abraham and Sarai, Isaac and Rebekah. But the story I think is most apt to your situation is Jacob and Rachel."

Despite herself, Ronnie leaned in to listen to Pastor Vance's words. She was a sucker for a good story. And she did remember the story of Jacob and Rachel. It was the first Romeo and Juliet story, but instead of a balcony, Jacob had to toil in the fields for seven years to earn the hand of the woman he fell in love with. When it came time to reap his reward, Rachel's father played a trick on him.

"In the end, Jacob had to work twice as hard to win his lady love," the pastor was saying. "There is something romantic in hard work. To persevere through adversity shows passion. Don't you think?"

Rusty was a worthy man. Ronnie would never deny that. He had worked hard all these years. But he put more care into his career goals, working twice as hard at it than their relationship. At the end of the day, there was no passion left for her, no time for romance. And Ronnie knew that she needed those things to be happy.

"I think, Pastor Vance, that you're leaving out an important detail of that story. The first seven years Jacob worked, didn't he wind up marrying Rachel's older sister first?"

The pastor pursed his lips. "Well, there is that minor detail. But that wasn't the point."

"I think the point is that even if you work hard for something, it doesn't mean you'll get what you want in the end."

CHAPTER NINE

*R*usty looked in his rearview mirror for the twentieth time. Ronnie's car was still behind him. Not that he would miss Old Bessie. There was a cloud of smoke coming from her back end and the muffler that announced itself from a mile away.

Bessie had come with Ronnie into their wedding. Rusty had been trying to get rid of the old girl since right after the I do's. But Ronnie had insisted on keeping the gas-guzzling, Check Engine blinking, unreliable heap parked out front of the door.

At first, Rusty had grinned at her loyalty to the heap of oxidized metal. But after the third break down, one when he was overseas, he'd put his foot down and insisted on replacing the death trap with a newer model. Rusty decided patience would be the avenue to take to get rid of the old jalopy.

The joke was on him. His soon to be ex-wife sat comfortably on the exposed springs in Old Bessie's driver's seat. Meanwhile, Rusty was the one looking at them both in his rearview mirror.

Ronnie had insisted on driving herself to the bank. She'd always been an independent woman. That was something Rusty had loved about her. She'd come from a large family, where he'd been an only child. His independence had come naturally where Ronnie had had to fight for every morsel of solitude and autonomy she could come by.

He'd thought that had been a strength in their union; that she didn't mind being left alone. For five years, he'd given her the peace and quiet she'd craved. He'd bought her an eReader and had never once balked at the monthly credit card bill when there was always an extra digit beside bookstore charges. Those charges were often more than the electric or gas bill. But if it kept his wife happy, he was happy to do it.

Rusty had given her everything she wanted. And he still had no clue why she was walking away from him. Or rather, lagging behind him.

He'd slowed his speed to allow her to catch up with him. Yet, she kept letting others pass between them. Keeping at least a car length or two between them.

Rusty took a left turn into the bank's parking lot. Cutting his engine, he waited for Ronnie to park her car beside his. Old Bessie grumbled and growled as she came into the lot. Ronnie pulled into the farthest spot. Rusty jogged over to the old Chevy in time to be there to open the door for her, but he was too late.

Veronica gave the metal door a shove. It squeaked on its ancient hinges, as though it were loathe to give her up. Rusty couldn't blame the old beast.

Ronnie stepped out in a sundress. The yellow of the garment made her skin shine brighter than the sun. Her normally wild hair was tamed back into a bun atop her head, but a few tendrils rebelled and curled around her neck. Rusty couldn't take his gaze off the hem of the dress, which brushed her knees. His fingers clenched with each swish as she walked toward him.

"You got everything you need?" Ronnie asked.

No, he didn't have everything he needed. He didn't have the one thing he knew he needed in his life. The only thing he needed was her. The woman he loved was standing in front of him, within arms distance, and he couldn't touch her.

He couldn't say that. So, he nodded.

He couldn't touch her either. So, he waved his hand for Ronnie to proceed into the bank.

As Rusty stepped into the establishment, his training kicked in. His eyes scanned for tactical weaknesses and advantages. The glass door closing behind him was the only entrance. Though he assumed there would be another exit behind where the tellers worked. There was only one security camera. But the red light to indicate that the device was on was blank. Meaning it was either out of service or someone had forgotten to turn it on.

This place would be a robber's paradise. But not in this town. Of course, there were a few bad apples in the community. There were in every community. But in a town where everyone knew everyone else, crime wasn't a booming business due to the lack of anonymity.

Still, Rusty was ever vigilant. His most prized treasure was inside these four walls. He shadowed Ronnie as they waited in the reception area for their appointed time.

There was a small line inside the bank for the tellers. There was no glass partition separating tellers from their customers like in most cities. A bowl of lollipops sat in front of both of the two tellers. They smiled when the adults took the candies at the conclusion of their business.

A new adult stepped into the bank. This man didn't look like he had two pennies to rub together. His hair was a bird's nest. His clothes were wrinkled, and his sneakers caked with mud that smelled rancid, as though he'd just walked through a horse stall.

The tension fairly crackled in the air when the tellers became aware of him. Rusty edged his body closer to Ronnie, who appeared oblivious. She was thumbing through the documents in her bag.

The man walked up to the teller and leaned into the counter. "I need my money."

His hands were empty. There was no bulge in his waistband, meaning he likely wasn't armed. Still, Rusty stayed alert.

"Do you have an account with us, sir?"

The man sighed. He pinched the bridge of his nose as though a headache pained him. "My wife takes care of the paperwork. She left me because I couldn't get the money."

"I'm sorry for your financial woes, sir. But I don't think we can do anything about that."

The man released the hold he had on his nose and slammed his hand down on the counter. The teller jumped. Ronnie finally looked up.

"Something's wrong with my head," he said. "They don't believe me, so they won't give me the money."

"I'm sorry—" The teller began but didn't finish.

The man turned on his muddied heel and stormed out of the bank. He flashed Rusty a look as he went out the door. Rusty stared at the closed door for a few moments, making certain the man didn't come back inside. The tellers were in a tizzy during that time but soon settled. That scene might play out more regularly in a big city, but he was certain it was an anomaly in such a small town.

"Mr. and Mrs. Hook?"

Rusty's heart kicked up at those words, the homeless man all but forgotten. This would likely be the last time he'd hear Ronnie called that. A thorough search of the ranch had not produced the missing divorce papers. Pastor Vance hadn't answered the phone when Rusty had called the church earlier.

Beside him, Ronnie bristled at the title, but she gave a curt nod of her head to the short man with spectacles that approached them. He had a few wisps on his balding head. The buttons on his suit strained to keep his belly contained as he reached out his hand to Rusty.

"I'm Mr. Denton, the bank manager." Mr. Denton's handshake was clammy. He winced as Rusty's hands gripped his and squeezed. The man rearranged his features to smile at Ronnie.

Ronnie offered her hand, but Mr. Denton was already turning into his office. He swept his hand in front of his paunch, indicating that Ronnie precede the men. Ronnie's hand dropped to her side, and she stepped in and sat.

"What's this loan for?" Mr. Denton asked, his gaze fixed on Rusty as he spoke. "A new home? Are you expecting a new addition soon?"

Rusty's tongue tied when he tried to speak. He had trouble forming the single syllabic word that would answer that statement. Because more than anything, he wished it could be true.

"No," said Ronnie. The two lettered word settled like a bomb going off. The shrapnel tore at Rusty's insides. "It's for a business loan."

"Oh," Mr. Denton grinned. "What kind of business are you getting into, son?"

Denton pulled out a stack of clipped papers and sat them on the desk before Rusty. Then he grabbed a heavy-looking pen and clicked it open.

Rusty could feel the heat rolling off of Ronnie. During his time overseas, he'd had to hold his tongue as men spoke for women who clearly had other ideas. The tide of cultural change was slowly shifting in the Middle East. It had turned decades ago here on his home turf. Perhaps Mr. Denton hadn't gotten the memo?

"I…" Ronnie said the single word pointedly, letting it draw out until Mr. Denton turned his attention to her. "…am going into publishing."

The banker looked from Ronnie to Rusty. His thick brows pushed together in confusion. After a moment, they separated as though understanding dawned. "Have you written a cookbook, my dear?"

Rusty had neither the time nor luxury for the grimace that threatened. He sat forward, blocking Ronnie from the man who had painted a black and white bull's eye just above the bridge of his nose.

"My wife is a brilliant storyteller," said Rusty.

That was pretty much all he could say. Ronnie always wove the most fantastic of tales when she lay in his arms at night. Or when the phone line between them had a good connection. Listening to her simply tell him about her day drowned out the noise of the combat zone outside.

"Fiction books?" said Mr. Denton, his brows pulling together again to mark the target on his forehead. "Oh, well, I'm sure it's not one of those bare-chested books in the grocery store. Can you believe they have the audacity to sell that smut where kids can see them?"

"Did you know that romance books are a billion-dollar industry?" said Ronnie. "There are women all over this nation making living wages, or more, and supporting their families off of writing those love stories."

"Is that what you've written?" The banker screwed up his nose. "A romance novel?"

Ronnie swallowed and bit her lip.

Mr. Denton put down his pen and began pulling the documents back to himself.

"What I wrote..." Ronnie began, then stopped. She licked her lips as though she were making a decision about something. "It's about life in the military through a wife's perspective."

The banker's gaze brightened. He slid the paperwork back on the desk. "That sounds remarkable. An excellent way to support your husband in his endeavors."

Ronnie pursed her lips together and kept her mouth shut for the rest of the meeting. It wasn't like her, and Rusty wanted to know why. More importantly, he wanted to get his hands on the book she'd written. Maybe it would provide some clues as to what had gone wrong in their marriage and how he could fix it.

CHAPTER TEN

The check in her hand didn't feel as freeing as she'd thought. She slipped it into her canvas bag. Inside that canvas bag, Ronnie had prepared documents and charts. She had research about how the romance industry was indeed a billion dollar a year industry. She had printouts of success stories of women like Norah Roberts, Debbie Macomber, and her favorite, Robyn Carr. All housewives who had made a career of writing those books Mr. Denton had sneered at.

Robyn Carr was Ronnie's idol. Because just like Ronnie, Mrs. Carr had been a military wife. She'd traveled from base to base, never staying anywhere too long, but carrying a romance novel as her best company. When Carr put pen to paper, she created a world that warmed the hearts of millions.

Those success stories were nothing to sniff at. But that's what most men did. Some women, too, as evidenced by Ronnie's waitress the other day.

Romance novels were a viable and respectable industry. So why hadn't she admitted that was the business this check was going to fund? Why hadn't she spoken up when Mr. Denton had put it down?

"You know, I'd love to read your book when it's ready."

Ronnie jerked at the sound of Rusty's voice. He was standing outside her car door, leaning against the hood. They'd arrived back at the ranch. Rusty had trailed behind her as she'd driven Old Bessie. She'd seen him through the puffs of smoke Bessie blew back at him as they cruised down the streets.

"It still needs work." Ronnie fidgeted with the keys. Her gaze darted to the canvas bag, where the mock-up of the first draft of her book sat.

She'd brought the prototype to the loan meeting. But she was glad she hadn't taken it out of the bag. The guy on the cover wasn't exactly bare-chested. He had on a shirt. But it had a few buttons open. She was certain if stuffy old Denton had seen it, he'd shove the loan documents back in his desk and show them the door.

Ronnie cut the ignition. As she yanked the key out, the car let out a huff of air that mirrored her emotions. She gave the steering wheel a pat of commiseration before stepping out of the vehicle.

"When's the last time you took her to a mechanic?" asked Rusty.

"Bessie's fine."

"She's coughing up fumes, which for a human means a symptom of sickness. She needs to see a doctor, which for a car is a mechanic."

"You got me the loan, Rusty," she snapped, rounding on him. "The health of my car is not your concern."

Rusty let out a long, weary sigh through his nose. His features were strained, but Ronnie could tell he was pulling for patience. He never used to do that with her.

When they were first married, there had always been a light in his eyes when he'd looked at her. Like the sun rose and set on her face. For the past year, when they spoke, he'd eyed her warily, as though he were waiting for her to pull down a shade of darkness between them.

"Even though we're not married anymore," he said, "I'm always going to be concerned about you."

Rusty stood directly in front of the sun. She wanted to shade her eyes as she looked up at him. She felt the darkness prickle at the back of her neck.

"We are still married," she said, surprised to hear the tremble of need in her voice. "For now, that is. Until you sign the divorce papers."

A flicker went across his features. Ronnie couldn't tell if it was defiance or defeat? The thought of the first emotion raised her ire. The thought of the latter emotion made her shiver.

"Seven days," he said. "You said you'd stay for a week, and then I'll sign."

Rusty's voice was monotone as he spoke, lifeless. It sounded like a threat when he said it this time. It sounded as though he was leaving her now. The thought settled like acid in the pit of her stomach.

"Seven days," she repeated. "And then you'll sign."

"You have my word."

Ronnie nodded. She turned from him, taking a step toward the bungalow. But Rusty's hand fell to the small of her back. When it did, a weight settled inside of her. Something that had been out of place clicked back into its spot.

"Why don't you come up to the main house," said Rusty. "You didn't get a chance to say hi to the guys. They want to see you. They want you to meet their wives."

Ronnie hesitated. Her life as a military wife had been a revolving door of new people every few months. Finding a friend that she connected within the last couple of weeks of being stationed at a base, only to have them leave or Rusty get new orders and then lose touch. She wanted off that roller coaster. She wanted roots where people stayed put, and no one would leave in the middle of the night.

She stepped away from Rusty's hand. They were only separated by a foot, but she felt like she was free falling. "I'm tired after today. I'm just gonna go and lay down for a bit and then get to work."

"On your romance novel?"

She should've known he'd figure it out. Ronnie had bought her fair share of bare-chested covers during their marriage. She'd never left them out for Rusty to see. Or so she thought. Clearly, she hadn't been as careful with her reading materials as she'd thought.

"Don't start."

Rusty held up his hands. "I wasn't going to. You made some good points back there at the bank. It sounds like you've researched this business."

Had she heard a note of derision in how he said the word business?

Rusty had never commented on her reading material before. He'd never snatched a bodice ripper from her hands like others had.

"But if it's about us, I would like to read it?"

"It's not about us," she insisted.

"Military wife?"

"There are thousands of military wives in the world."

"You were always amazing at weaving stories and tales," he said as though he didn't hear her. "Maybe if I read your book, I can finally figure out what I did wrong."

"You didn't do anything wrong, Russ."

"Then why aren't you in my arms right now?"

Ronnie didn't miss the hint of anger in his voice. She had no words to answer the bewilderment in his eyes.

"Why did we fail, Ronnie?"

She pursed her lips. She'd never been able to vocalize what had gone wrong between them. All she could ever tell him was that something was missing. She'd thought that missing piece had been him. But here he was, standing in front of her. And like he said, she wasn't in his arms.

"I thought we were fine."

"Of course, you thought that. You were never there."

"I was out building a life for us."

"I was at home living a life without you."

"Is there someone else?"

Ronnie's gaze went wide. "Is that what you think of me?"

"I don't know what to think?" Rusty raked his fingers through his hair. It had grown long now that he was out of the military. "One day, things are fine, and the next, you're shoving papers in my face and telling me you don't want me in your life."

"I never said I didn't want you in my life."

"Well, that's what happens when people get divorced. It's a dissolution. A separation of two things that are no longer connected."

That's what she wanted, right? To be separate from him. To be apart from him. To be on her own. That's what she'd felt all these years. But the thought of not seeing him again, ever, terrified her.

Ronnie looked at Rusty's hands. Those strong capable hands that had always grounded her. When he'd touched her, she'd felt rooted again, like the tree she'd always climb and read her books in. He was keeping his distance now. Which was what she wanted, right?

"I've only ever tried to give you what you wanted," Rusty said, exhaustion in his voice. "I just don't know what that is anymore. And I'm not sure you do either."

Ronnie steeled herself for a long argument. One where he kept her talking, using his negotiating tactics to try and determine a way past her defenses. One where he made it seem like he was acquiescing to her every demand, only to see that he'd played her right into his hand.

Rusty clamped his mouth shut. He turned on his heel and walked away from her. Leaving Ronnie alone as the sky above her began to darken.

CHAPTER ELEVEN

*R*usty stomped on the jack. Old Bessie's big, clunky body raised inch by inch as though she were reluctant to expose her underbelly. With the car sufficiently jacked up, Rusty grabbed his tools, slid under the behemoth, and got to work.

He was greeted by the sight of rusty pipes. Lubricants wouldn't work to smooth things over with this muffler. It was welded to the rusted pipes and would need to be hacked off.

Great.

Rusty grabbed for his hacksaw and began cutting into the faulty piece of hardware. The sound of metal banging against metal wore off the last vestiges of his anger. No, anger was the wrong word for what he felt.

Frustration was more like it. And a healthy heaping of confusion.

Rusty wasn't used to facing a problem he couldn't solve. The United States Military had invested too much into his training to ensure that he was well equipped to deal with any negotiation matters that came before him. But in none of his textbooks had he ever come across how to deal with women.

More times than not, men were the hostage-takers in the theater of war. Males were also more likely than women to take their own lives in crisis situations. The most used tactic during these confrontations was to get the hostile to talk. Talking, and airing out their feelings, is not what most men are known for. Still, more often than not, the strategy worked.

Rusty had talked people down from high ledges. He'd talked them out of suicide vests. He'd talked them into releasing hostages. The problem was that he was the hostage in this situation with Ronnie. And he'd developed Stockholm Syndrome.

Ronnie had stolen his heart the first time he'd laid eyes on her wild hair. He hadn't seen her eyes as her head had been buried between the covers of a book. When she'd lowered the book, his world had tilted. She could've hog-tied him and carted him off then and there. She'd captured his attention, and he didn't want to be let go.

The problem was Ronnie was all too ready to let him go. She'd been cutting all ties to him for the past year. Rusty had tried to tighten the knots, but no matter how hard he pulled them, the binds wouldn't hold.

Using the wrench, he tightened the bolts on the new muffler. Its smooth face looked out of place amidst the dirt and grime of Bessie's underbelly. She clearly needed an oil change. And the front tires were low on air.

The car was a death trap waiting for a bump in the road to take it down. Had Ronnie been driving this hunk of metal like this without any maintenance or repair since the last time he'd seen her? She never let mechanics touch it because they'd tell her the truth; that the car should go to the junkyard in the sky.

Rusty had always done the maintenance himself under the cover of night when he was home. When he wasn't home, he'd always made sure a buddy checked on the state of the car for him. He knew Ronnie had been staying with her parents for the last few months, so he'd had no way of checking to see if her Check Engine light was on.

He slid from under the car. After releasing the jack, he pulled open the driver's side door. He still had a spare key. He used it to start the engine up.

Old Bessie purred, like a cat who'd just had a good belly rub. No smoke or grumbles came from the rear of the car. The Check Engine light didn't turn on either.

That was a small blessing. It still left the tires to be replaced, and the oil changed. He wondered if he'd have time to tend to that maintenance before she woke up.

Here he only had a few days left to talk her back into being his wife, and he'd spent all morning fixing her car. But he didn't know what else to do? He didn't know what to say to her? Not a single page from any of his training manuals would help him.

Rusty rubbed a hand across his forehead. The back of his hand slicked quickly across his flesh. He turned his hand over to see that there was grease on his knuckles. There was grime on his shirt.

He yanked the shirt over his head. Turning it inside out, he wiped the grime from his head and headed around the car. He opened the passenger door to set the seats right again when a book fell out.

The paperback landed in the dirt, just shy of an oil spill. Rusty reached out and rescued the book before the cover could be spoiled. Ronnie regarded books as precious items that should be set up high. Using his shirt, he brushed the dirt from the cover. What he found beneath the thin layer of grime perplexed him.

The book featured a nearly bare-chested man clutching a woman on the cover. The pose was on the provocative side. But not much racier than anything he'd seen on the grocery store shelves next to magazines.

Grocery store shelves? Rusty heard the stuffy banker's voice in his head. He remembered Ronnie's shoulders bristle with tension at the man's words. Rusty couldn't understand why? It wasn't like she read any of those bodice ripper books.

In their home, the shelves had been lined with the classics. He'd often catch Ronnie reading two books at a time. One inside the other, in fact.

Rusty's eyes scanned away from the indecent couple and caught the title of the book. *Seduced by the Sergeant* was written in a bright, curly script that hurt his eyes. The title was in stark contrast to the jewel tones surrounding the couple.

His eyes quickly darted away from those words down to the bottom of the book. There he found the author's name; V.E. O'Brian

V? E? It couldn't be. But they were. Those were Ronnie's initials; Veronica Elizabeth. O'Brian was her maiden name.

V.E. O'Brian. That was her. This was Ronnie's book.

Rusty's hands shook as he held the book in his palms. It felt like a bomb. A slight wind blew, rustling the pages. The rustling sounded like a bomb ticking down to an explosion.

He should put the book down. Carefully. He should step away. Slowly.

Rusty opened the covers to a random page and read the first line he saw.

Ryker pulled her close, smashing her tender bosom against his rock hard chest. Vanessa struggled in his hold, but it was no use. She was helpless to escape the sergeant's captivity.

"Let me go," Vanessa pleaded.

"Your pretty mouth says no," Ryker growled. "But your lush body says yes."

His lips crashed down to hers in a brutal claiming. Vanessa felt as though she were being pulled under by his passion. Never had she experienced such a sensation. She wanted more. But she couldn't-

"Rusty?"

Rusty slammed the covers of the book closed and pressed it to his chest. He turned his head to look over his shoulder.

Veronica stood at the door to the house. Her gaze wasn't on him. It was on the back end of her car. With her attention diverted, Rusty took the opportunity to wrap the book in his shirt.

"What are you doing to my car?"

"I fixed the muffler."

Ronnie frowned. Her head snapped to him. Ire was bright in her gaze. But as her eyes dipped to his bare chest, the look in her eyes softened. Rusty saw when she caught herself looking. Her lips pressed together, and her gaze shuttered.

"I didn't ask you to do that," she huffed.

"Just because we're not together anymore doesn't mean I'm not going to concern myself with your safety."

"I can handle my own car maintenance."

"Yeah, your mouth is saying one thing, but your actions say something else entirely."

Her eyes flashed up at him. A tiny breath escaped her mouth. Rusty had seen that expression many times. It typically led to her coming into his embrace for long, luxurious moments of kissing.

Ronnie blinked and gave herself a shake. But even as she walked to the driver's side door, she seemed flustered. "I'm heading into town to run some errands."

"You'll be back for dinner."

Ronnie's hand froze on the driver's side door handle. Her gaze rose to his. There hadn't been a question in his statement. It was more of a command.

Rusty was ready to open his mouth and take it all back when she swallowed. Her lip trembled as she bobbed her head and then disappeared into the interior of the car.

Rusty said nothing as he watched her go. Once Ronnie and the old Chevy were ambling quietly down the drive, he pulled out the book. Unwrapping it from his shirt, he peered down at the garish cover.

She had written those words. He'd just used them against her. Maybe this was the text he'd been looking for; the negotiation tactics he'd need to win back his wife? With the book in hand, Rusty headed round the back of the house and started studying the first page.

CHAPTER TWELVE

onnie took the long road into town in silence. Complete and utter silence. Bessie didn't grunt or grumble once after she pulled away from the ranch. The only sound that rang out in the car was the sound of Rusty's voice in Ronnie's mind.

Yeah, your mouth is saying one thing, but your actions say something else entirely.

He'd never spoken to her like that. Sure, she'd heard him speak like that to others. To men and women who were below him in rank. There had been many phone calls she'd overheard or times on base when she'd happened by her Rusty giving orders.

In fact, the first time they'd met, she'd remembered he'd taken that tone with someone. She'd been reading a book about a pirate and a lady he'd absconded with. Rusty's deep baritone had made her heart kick in her chest and brought her head up from reading her book. It was his friendly smile and his gentlemanly manners that held her attention.

You'll be back for dinner, he'd commanded. Demanded.

Just exactly who did he think he was? He certainly wasn't the boss of her. If Rusty thought he could give her orders, he had another thought coming.

Though there had been something about the timbre in his voice. It sent a shiver over her shoulders just thinking about it.

In fact, it made her think of another man. It made her think of Sergeant Ryker Catch from her novel. That was exactly something he would say to the heroine Vanessa. Right before he swept her off her feet and into a heated kiss.

Rusty wasn't that type of man. He didn't have Ryker's devil-may-care attitude. Rusty would only ever pick a woman up if she was in danger, and after he had her express consent and permission to handle her body in such an intimate fashion.

Chivalry wasn't dead. It was just bogged down and knotted up in a mess of political correctness and changing cultural norms.

Ronnie shook the memory off of Rusty's words and their effects. It was anger she'd heard in his voice. Rusty was still upset that she wanted the divorce. But there was nothing he could do—certainly not in five days—to change her mind.

The car ride into town was smooth. He'd not only fixed the muffler, he'd reset her seat back into its prime position, a feat Ronnie had had trouble with. Now the car cradled her low back. It was the same feeling as when Rusty splayed his hand on her low back, that feeling of being rooted.

That was Rusty. He sprouted roots, where she wanted adventure. He was good for fixing her car, fixing things around the house. Practical things. Not the romantic things she wrote about. There were no candle-light dinners, or long walks, or gazing into each other's eyes.

There were Skype calls in low lighting. There were long stretches of silence when he was on a mission. There were always other people in the background when they did have a strong enough connection to see each other.

Ronnie had thought she had what it took to be a military wife. But she'd been wrong. She knew Rusty was no longer in the service, but she also knew that hadn't been the plan. He'd planned to serve at least another five years. She never would've lasted that long. She was certain as soon as the divorce papers were signed, he'd sign right back up for the service.

Putting the car in park, Ronnie tugged her satchel out of the passenger side of the car. She had a long to-do list today. At the top of the list was to find a photographer and cover model for her book. Now that she had the money, she didn't have to rely on stock photos.

The smells of fried foods and slow-cooking soups greeted her nose as she stepped out of the car. Ronnie's gaze immediately swung back to the Mexican restaurant she'd visited the other day. Though her roots were Irish, her tastebuds thought they were from the south of the U.S. border.

Stepping through the entryway, Ronnie sidled up to a booth inside the taco joint. She made sure to choose an area different from the first one she'd sat in the other day. She hoped she wouldn't see the judgy waitress from her first meal here.

An older couple sat across from her. Their brown skin was wrinkled, but there was a youthful look to the both of them. The woman wore a colorful sari clueing Ronnie in that their ancestry was from India. Looking closely at the man, Ronnie realized she recognized him. He was the doctor who had tended to Russell after his fall.

Dr. Patel held his wife's hands, grinning like a wolf. Mrs. Patel looked down demurely, then up through thick eyelashes. Adoration and love was clear on their faces

Marla, the waitress from the other day, stepped up to the Patels's table. "Here's the check, Pastor Patel."

"Oh, no," said Mrs. Patel as she snatched the slip of paper away from her husband. "I invited this handsome devil on this date, so I'm paying. Unfortunately, for me, he's not a cheap date."

"No," chuckled Dr. Patel, "but I'm worth it, my darling."

"Yes, that you are."

Pastor Patel kissed his wife's knuckles. "You'll forgive me that I don't see you home. I have to get back to work."

"As long as you're home by dinner. No more late nights. You promised."

"I will rush home to be with you before the sun sets." Dr. Patel bent down and kissed his wife's temple. When he straightened, his gaze caught Ronnie's. "Mrs. Hook, how nice to see you again."

Ronnie hadn't been called Mrs. Hook in a long time. It had been a running joke with her and Rusty, where she imagined herself as Wendy married to the pirate.

"Hello, Dr. Patel. Or is it Pastor?"

"I am both," he said. "This is my wife. Deeksha, this is Russell Hook's wife."

"Lovely to meet you, my dear," said Mrs. Patel. "Your husband is such a kind soul."

Ronnie decided not to correct the older couple on her marital status. Besides, she was right. Rusty was a kind soul. His manners weren't why she wanted a divorce. His long absences and shortcomings in the romance department were.

Dr. Patel gave his wife another wave as he walked out of the door. But Mrs. Patel wasn't eyeing her husband. Her gaze was trained on Ronnie's computer screen, where bare-chested men were on display.

Ronnie decided that was the perfect time to come clean about her marital status. "Russell and I are separated."

"Is that a dating site?" asked Mrs. Patel.

"No, I'm not dating." The very idea of dating another man didn't appeal to Ronnie. From now on, she preferred to keep men between the covers of a book rather than step out onto a real-world stage. "I'm looking for a cover model."

"Are you a writer?"

"I am."

"Let me guess; romance novels?"

Ronnie searched the woman's gaze for judgment. When she found none, she answered tentatively, "Yes."

"I love romance novels," sighed Mrs. Patel.

"You're a pastor's wife."

That came from Marla. Ronnie had forgotten the woman was nearby. Marla turned from the table she'd been bussing with raised brows. What Ronnie didn't understand was why Marla's brows were raised at her and not the pastor's wife.

"There are many love stories in the Bible," said Mrs. Patel.

Marla sniffed at that, looking anything but cowed.

Ronnie hoped Mrs. Patel wouldn't pull out any examples. She'd already had this discussion with Pastor Vance, and happily-ever-afters hadn't faired so well with the biblical characters.

"But I prefer the more contemporary tales," Mrs. Patel continued. "I especially love the ones with the males who shift into wolves." She giggled like a schoolgirl. "Do you write those?"

"No," said Ronnie. "I write military romances."

"Fitting, since your husband is in the military."

Ronnie wanted to balk at that. Her books were not based on her life with Rusty. Sure, the hero was a soldier. And sure, a lot of the book had the hero and heroine separated with him off fighting. And maybe her heroine was a writer. But that was where the similarities ended.

"Mrs. Patel," said Marla. "I had no idea you read smut."

"Smut?" said Mrs. Patel. "Romance novels are far from smut. They are about women's empowerment. The modern love story is the one where women are the heroes of their own stories. These tales deal with women's issues, women's goals, their growth, and their pleasure."

"B-but," sputtered the waitress. "But they set unrealistic expectations for young girls."

"Unrealistic, how?" asked Mrs. Patel.

"They're not about real men," said Marla. "No real man in this world knows the first thing about romance. The women who read these will face disappointment all their lives if they believe such nonsense."

Ronnie had been Team Mrs. Patel for the duration of the discussion. Now she was torn. Marla made a good point. The men in romance novels were figments of women's imagination. Even she knew that as she penned her hero. She knew Rusty would never behave the same way that Ryker would.

"If it's romance that you want," said Mrs. Patel, "then you need to tell your partner. You can't expect him to know. You have to show him, which is why sometimes I take my husband out on dates so he can know what I like."

Now it was Ronnie and Marla who shared a disbelieving look. Tell a man what you want? And then expect him to deliver? That was a true fantasy!

CHAPTER THIRTEEN

"*I*s this what women want?" Rusty pointed to the book on the console. The spine of the tome cracked in answer as he pressed the splayed pages open. Though Rusty wasn't sure if the crackling sound was a resounding no or a heartfelt yes?

The men who looked over his shoulder made grunting sounds and coughs. Again, Rusty was unsure if their unintelligible words were in agreement or discord. For his entire career as a hostage negotiator, he had been the talker in the group, the one with the answers. It was the first time he was at a loss for words.

"*'Ryker used his powerful forearm to swipe the romantic dinner off the floor,'*" read Keaton. His no-nonsense tone was at odds with the words from Ronnie's book. "*He scooped Vanessa up to his powerful chest—*"

"You shouldn't use the same word twice in the same paragraph," Spinelli spoke up. "It sounds repetitive and leads to the reader's dissatisfaction."

"*'He scooped Vanessa up to his powerful chest and took her mouth against his. Vanessa struggled against him but soon realized the fight was futile. He was right; she did want this. There was nothing more for her to do. His strength was more powerful than hers.'*"

"That's the third time." Spinelli held up a finger. "What? She used powerful three times. She needs an editor. Or a thesaurus."

"*His strength was more powerful than hers. Ryker was going to take her.*"

That was the end of the chapter. Keaton didn't turn the page. They all knew what would happen next.

"What happens next?" asked Spinelli. "Where is he taking her?"

Keaton and Rusty shared a look.

"He's taking her upstairs," said Keaton.

"For what?" said Spinelli. "Who's going to clean up that mess they just made?"

Rusty didn't bother trying to explain. Spinelli had a habit of taking things very literally, and Rusty didn't want to go any further down that road with the man. Besides, he still hadn't had his first question answered.

"Do women really want that?" he asked. "Do they want a man to, well, manhandle them? Do they want him to take charge and not seek any of her input? Do they want to be dominated like this?"

Rusty would never think of pulling Ronnie to him and kissing her if she'd turned away from him. But the inner monologue of her heroine didn't protest when the hero's powerful lips met hers. In real life, Ryker Catch's actions would be considered sexual harassment, possibly even assault.

Except the Vanessa character was consenting. Consenting in her mind. But how was a man to know that? Why didn't she just come out and say that that's what she wanted?

"It seems like these are the character's inner wishes," said Spinelli.

The man wasn't great at reading emotions. He was far more analytical. But he had a point.

"It gives a checklist of how to woo a woman who wants to be wooed but says she doesn't," said Keaton. "I'm glad Brenda just comes on out and tells me what she wants."

Rusty did envy his friend that. Brenda Vance Keaton was a no-nonsense woman who always said what she meant. She had to be. She bossed a whole ranch of men around.

Spinelli's wife, Romey, was also pretty straightforward when she spoke. Romey was a scientist, used to data and measurements. So she had to be exact when she spoke.

Ronnie had always had her head buried in books. She often had a pile of books around her and would read more than one at a time. Words were like a buffet for her. She wanted to use them all, even if she seemed to get stuck on the word *powerful*.

"Though sometimes it feels as though Brenda wants me to guess," said Keaton, peering closer at the book.

"I wish I knew what Romey was thinking when she gets quiet," said Spinelli, also leaning in to focus on the words on the page.

"Maybe we should keep reading," said Keaton, already making a note on his checklist.

Rusty turned the page to the next chapter, and there was that word again. *Vanessa lay her hand against Ryker's bare chest. His heart beat powerfully.*

Powerful. Should Rusty be more powerful in his relationship with her? He'd tried to be accommodating for the last few months. He'd tried to figure out what it was that she needed so that he could provide that for her.

Ronnie had said she wanted more romance in their life. But was this it? In this book, the heroine was constantly getting put into danger, which the hero would rescue her from. Rusty spent his career trying to ensure the world was a safer place for not only his countrymen but for his wife. He was not about to put Ronnie in harm's way.

"I suppose I could do a candlelight dinner," Rusty said, noting the elements of the scene they'd just read.

"You should do the part where he buys her clothes," said Keaton, bringing up how the previous scene in the novel had started.

The Ryker character had brought Vanessa a designer gown. Though how the man could afford such an expensive piece of clothing on a soldier's salary was beyond Rusty. The man also lived in a mansion and seemed to have a lot of leisure time between his missions, both falsehoods. But this was her fantasy.

This was her fantasy? That a powerful man would make her dinner, and buy her clothes, and spirit her away to his huge house, and spend free time he shouldn't have with her. This was Ronnie's fantasy. This was what she wanted.

"What about the part where she's in danger?" said Keaton.

In the next chapter, where they are upstairs, and Ryker was kissing Vanessa *powerfully*, the bad guys from Ryker's last mission burst into the house and interrupt the amorous activities. Never mind that ten known insurgents would never make it out of the deserts, past Homeland Security, and into a major U.S. city.

"How can you replicate that?" asked Keaton.

"You could stage a home invasion during the romantic dinner," said Spinelli.

It seemed like a lot, but Rusty was willing to try. He was willing to do anything to get his wife back. If dinner and danger were what she wanted, then that's what she was going to get.

"Oh, and wear a suit," said Keaton.

"A suit? I don't have a suit. I only have my military uniform."

"Chicks dig the uniform," said Keaton.

Rusty gave a sigh. A willing sigh. He had a lot of work ahead of him before Ronnie got home tonight. But if all went well, maybe she would realize he could give her exactly what she wanted.

CHAPTER FOURTEEN

Ronnie could hear the laughter from the big house before she turned off the engine to her car. She saw the group roaming around on the big porch. They were all smiles. Most of the faces were familiar.

Grizz was the first familiar form she recognized. It was hard not to. The man was the size of a bear. Resting against his large form was a small woman. The flaming red hair marked the woman as Patricia Keaton.

Ronnie had seen the attraction between the two the times she'd visited the Keatons for holidays. Grizz had tried to keep his distance from his best friend's baby sister, but like a perfectly plotted romance novel, little Patty had gone and bagged herself a bear of a man. Ronnie made a mental note for the next characters in her book to use elements of this love story.

Sneaking an embrace as they came up the steps were Mac and Lana. Ronnie had worried if the two would ever make it down the aisle, but it looked like they had. Not that Ronnie was surprised. The no-nonsense journalist and the romantic wedding planner were exact opposites, making them the perfect foils for each other.

Though they hadn't always been in constant contact, those four had been constants in Ronnie's life when the whole team gathered. But she wasn't part of the team anymore. She was the one who'd left this time.

She'd be leaving again soon. But the next place she settled, Ronnie was determined to grow roots. She would find her forever home and her forever friends that she would keep for the rest of her life.

Turning away from the friends of her past, Ronnie trudged up to the front door of the bungalow. The door was unlocked. Of course, it was. This was a ranch filled with military men who had signed up to give their lives for their country. Of course, they would do tenfold for their loved ones. Only an idiot would dare trespass on this land.

Inside, the house was dark. But a glow from the dining room caught Ronnie's gaze. She headed in that direction, lulled by a peculiar scent.

In the small, candlelit dining room stood Rusty. He was decked out in full military regalia. At first, Ronnie took in the delectable sight of him.

Russell Hook had always filled out that uniform nicely. The gold buttons down his torso highlighted the sparkle in his eyes. The floppy cap on his head took away some of the seriousness of the ensemble

She had always loved seeing him fully decked out like this. But those times were few and far between. Mostly when…

"Oh, no," Ronnie dropped her canvas bag and rushed to him. "Who died?"

"Died?" Rusty had been grinning. But that cocky look dissipated from his features. "No one died."

"But you're in your full uniform. You only wear that when you've lost a soldier."

Rusty let out a weary sigh and looked skyward. "I didn't think of that."

His gaze fell past her and looked off to the side. Ronnie followed his gaze down to the dining room table. An elegant tablecloth was laid on the scratched wood surface. The candlelight that had led her in here cast a glow on the spread of her favorite foods.

"No one died," said Rusty. "I made you a special dinner."

"You made this?"

"I had it delivered."

There was a veritable Mexican buffet on the table. Rice, beans, queso, and guacamole. The spices of peppers and cilantro filled the air.

"Mexican's still your favorite, yeah?"

"Yeah."

Ronnie's stomach grumbled with want. She'd just had a burrito for lunch. Her stomach appeared to have quickly forgotten that meal and was ready for another.

"And I brought you this."

Rusty held up a gown. It was unlike anything Ronnie would've bought for herself. It was a pastel, princess cut affair that wouldn't go with her skin tone and wouldn't flatter her figure.

"Rusty, what's going on?"

"Don't ask any questions. Just put it on."

Ronnie flinched at his tone.

Rusty cursed under his breath, jerking his hand back. But then his resolve seemed to steel, and he held the dress out to her.

"I don't understand what's happening here?" Ronnie said. "Is this because of our argument the other day?"

"You know what," he said, clenching the gown in his fist. "You talk too much."

Rusty dropped the gown to the floor. He turned to the table, pulling his forearm to his torso as though he was about to swipe the food off the table.

"Rusty, no." Ronnie grabbed his forearm before he could take his anger out on the savory-smelling guacamole.

She had no idea what had gotten into him? He rarely displayed any anger. What was going on here?

She didn't have the chance to ask him. Rusty gripped her forearm and swung her into his chest. His powerful chest. It had been a long time since she'd been in this space.

Rusty's hand slipped down to the small of her back. That sense of relief flooded through Ronnie. She felt her soul rooting into the ground.

No. Her soul was rooting into this man.

No. Not rooting. She felt she was reconnecting into the soul where she had once flourished.

Rusty's lips took hers in a claiming kiss. His mouth crashed into hers, brooking no argument. Allowing no room for escape. It was more forceful than any kiss they had ever shared.

At first, Ronnie pressed against his chest. This was so unlike him. He'd always been gentle with her. Passionate, yes. But never unyielding.

Instead of letting her go or loosening his grip, Rusty's hold tightened around her. A low growl escaped his mouth. It sent a shudder of desire through her. Any resistance went out of her.

Ronnie couldn't remember why they hadn't been doing this since the first day she'd gotten here. Oh wait, they had kissed that first day. When he'd fallen at his first sight of her. Then he'd opened his eyes, called her an angel, and took her lips.

Rusty had been back from overseas for months. They'd wasted all that time apart when they could've been together and kissing. Ronnie pulled him to her now, deepening the kiss.

She couldn't remember why she'd insisted on their separation? Something or other to do with romance? Who needed romance when they had this much chemistry between them?

But no. Chemistry wasn't the issue. When the kiss broke, when the day changed to night, the problems would still exist. What problems were those again?

The problem was that he always left. There was always another mission, an upcoming deployment, and he'd leave. He'd come home. It would be like a honeymoon all over again. They'd fall back into the routines, and at some point, he'd leave again. He always left.

"Russ, please," she said against his lips.

Rusty pulled back from her, but he didn't let her go. His gaze searched hers, eyes screwed in confusion. "This isn't what you want?"

Ronnie opened her mouth to say she didn't want this. That she didn't want him. But it was a lie.

She wanted him. She just didn't know how to have him. How to keep him. Because he would leave again.

"I followed everything to a T, Veronica."

"Followed? Followed what?"

Rusty rested his forehead against hers. "Ryker made Vanessa dinner and bought her a dress."

Ryker? Vanessa? Where had Rusty heard those names?

"He kissed her even when she said she didn't want him to. But in her head, she did."

"How would you know that? Have you been reading my book?"

"Yes, I read it." Rusty still hadn't let her go. He was gripping her shoulders now. "It was the only way I could figure out what you wanted."

Ronnie pulled out of his hold and glared at him. "How could you? That was private?"

"Private? You put our lives on the page. You were about to share it with the rest of the world."

"*Seduced by the Sergeant* is not about us."

"Oh, yes, it is. But in the book, you gave me a chance. You won't in real life. Why?"

Ronnie turned away from him. The spices in the salsa hit her nose and caused it to wrinkle. The peppers made her eyes water.

"Why, Ronnie?" Rusty demanded.

"Because you're captive on the page. Because there you won't leave me."

"Leave you? I've never left you."

Ronnie turned away. Those peppers were really hot and doing a number on her eyes. Her stomach was in knots, letting her know that it would not hold down any of this food.

Rusty reached out to her, but this time it was Ronnie who turned to leave. However, as she did, a large figure clad in black burst through the door.

"This is a break-in," he growled in a low voice. A low, familiar voice.

"Grizz?" said Ronnie. "What are you doing?"

Grizz pulled the dark mask from his face. He looked from Ronnie to Rusty. "Sorry, man. I tried."

Ronnie looked between the two men, then at the dinner, and then the dress on the floor. Rusty had just manufactured a romantic evening, complete with a villain breaking in to interrupt an intimate moment.

Had it been on the page, it would've worked. But as this was her real life, the grand gesture fell completely flat.

CHAPTER FIFTEEN

Rusty slept badly after last night's debacle of a romantic date. When the sun's rays touched his cheek, and he could no longer lay in bed, he rose. When he looked out the window, he felt he'd been tricked. Rain fell in heavy drops as the sun shone brightly.

He hated days like this. They were a contradiction. A rainstorm on a cloudless sky. That was much like his life these days. The skies were clear one moment, and then a storm came from out of nowhere in the next.

As he made his way down the hall, he saw that Ronnie's door was closed. There wasn't a single sound of stirring from within. He didn't knock. He wouldn't know what to say.

He'd fought hard for her over the last year during their separation. He'd caved and given her what she'd told him she wanted when he'd signed those missing divorce papers. He'd thrown caution to the wind when he'd acted out what he thought she wanted but left unsaid.

None of it had worked.

Rusty left the copy of her book on the dining room table. The table was cleared of all the dishes he'd had prepared for her. They were covered in foil or enclosed in Tupperware in the fridge.

Ronnie must have done that sometime after he'd stormed off last night. She didn't like to leave a mess. She couldn't sleep if dishes were left in the sink.

In fact, the entire place was orderly. The floors were swept. The appliances shone spotless. There were the pair of running shoes he'd misplaced a week ago lined up next to the door.

Rusty bent down and ran his hands over the lip of the shoes. She'd even tucked the strings inside. He couldn't help but smile.

Despite the fact that the woman drove him mad sometimes, he couldn't imagine his life without her. He knew she wanted to be with him. That had been desire in her gaze when she'd looked up at him. Before the surrender, serenity had settled on her features when she was in his arms. When his lips met hers, he'd felt his entire being latch into place, like a lock that had been missing the catch and finally fell back in place.

But then she'd pulled away.

Ronnie had said he was the one to leave, but she was always with him no matter where he was in this world. His every action was to secure her future. She was the one who'd thrown it all away. And for what?

"Found this," said Keaton when Rusty made his way to the training camp.

Keaton deposited a muddied cell phone in his hand. Rusty hadn't thought about his phone since he'd had Ronnie in the bedroom beside him for the past few days. The phone had been his only connection to her for the last year. It was useless now, having been left to the elements for days.

"So, the romance thing didn't work for you?" said Keaton.

Rusty shook his head. His chin lowered to his chest. He was glad he was looking down. His head was spinning, and there was a dull ache in his heart. He shouldn't have come to work today. He couldn't negotiate his own body into working correctly. He'd be of no use to anyone.

"I'm surprised," said Keaton. "It worked wonders for me and Brenda last night."

If the grin on the man's face wasn't clue enough, the wiggle of his eyebrows told Keaton had had a very enjoyable evening with his wife last night.

"I wore my uniform for Romey," said Spinelli. "She practically ripped it off me. Then later asked me to put it on again."

Rusty wanted to be happy for his friends. Just a year ago, when his marriage was falling apart, both of these men had sworn marriage was the farthest thing from their minds. Now, here they both were, happily married and having romantic evenings with their wives at his expense.

"What's this I'm hearing about romance novels?" said Mac, coming up to join their group. Grizz and Porco were a step behind him.

"Ronnie wrote one," said Grizz, scratching at the dark whiskers on his chin.

"Ronnie writes smut?" said Porco, popping a strip of fried bacon in his mouth.

"It's not smut," said Rusty.

"It's actually not," Grizz agreed. "It's the story of two people who you wouldn't expect to be together. Against all odds, they find each other and work through their problems to be together."

The way Grizz phrased it, the book sounded like a fairytale. Like make-believe.

"And there's bedroom stuff?" said Porco, popping another strip of bacon in his mouth.

"It's not about that," said Keaton. "It's about how they first work against each other and then work together to achieve their happy ending."

"I felt it was more of a woman's journey of self-discovery where she learns to believe in herself first and then open herself to love," said Grizz.

"Really?" said Spinelli. "I felt it was more of a treatise on the human condition."

The final piece of bacon was held before Porco's open mouth. He didn't slide it in his pie hole. Instead, he gaped at each of the men standing around him in utter disbelief and confusion.

"And yeah," said Keaton, "there's bedroom stuff. Man, I learned a few things."

"Hey." Rusty reached over and punched his friend in the chest. "That's my wife you're talking about."

"It's actually your wife's character," said Spinelli. "Which is why I don't understand why that scene last night didn't work. You played on all of her inner desires."

"The problem is, I don't think Ronnie knows what she wants," said Rusty.

"Do you know why you want her?" asked Spinelli.

Rusty frowned at the question. Then he opened his mouth to state the obvious, only to find that it wasn't so obvious. Why was he going through all this trouble to try and keep someone who wanted to run away from him? Why had he caught her in the first place?

He remembered the first time he'd seen her. Her smile had knocked him back. But it wasn't just her looks.

They'd talked for hours that first night. Well, she had done most of the talking. He'd listened. He loved listening to her. But had he fallen in love with her because he wanted a storyteller?

When he was near her, it just felt right. She felt like home to him. She set his world right. Not just with how she ran their household. He happily put his life in her hands and let her arrange it, so long as he got to care for her. He wanted to give her the world, but since that was too big, he'd given her his heart.

And she had handed it back to him.

"You're not going to give up," said Keaton. "Are you?"

The spinning sensation came back to him. So much so that Rusty couldn't even lift his head to look his friends in the eyes. He'd tried everything. He had nothing left to give because there was nothing the love of his life wanted from him.

CHAPTER SIXTEEN

onnie gathered her research notes into one arm. She tucked her laptop in the other and went out onto the deck of the bungalow. The sun had dried the droplets from the freak rainstorm from the morning. She loved it when it rained on a sunny day. The contradiction delighted her.

She'd stayed up late last night to put away the dishes Rusty had laid out on the table. Her stomach had been tied in such tight knots that she couldn't eat a bite. Now she brought the food out onto the deck, but she still couldn't bring herself to eat a single bite.

She couldn't believe the length he'd gone to last night. Flattery and anger were still warring in her head. Rusty had never done anything like that before. Likely because he'd never known that it was her fantasy.

What was it that Mrs. Patel had said? She had to take her husband out on dates to show him what she wanted. But shouldn't he just know?

Ronnie supposed not. Even though Rusty had read the details of her dream date, he'd still gotten it wrong.

She pushed last night out of her mind. She had too much work to do. Work that would ensure her future; a future that didn't include Rusty.

She set her research notebooks, model photographs, and miscellaneous paperwork aside. Tapping the keys to open her Word document, Ronnie read through her manuscript.

The end still wasn't sitting well with her. Ryker and Vanessa had been through every obstacle she as an author had thrown at them. Forces had tried to keep them apart, but they always found their way back to one another time and time again.

She was nearing the end of the story. This was the climax. This was the last challenge they would face. But something was off.

For this final climax, Ronnie couldn't find a way to get her hero and heroine back together. Everything she tried read as forced and unplausible. The ending was playing out more like a tragedy than a romance.

Ronnie closed the Word file and pulled up an Excel spreadsheet. She needed to give the creative side of her brain a rest. So she decided to do some administrative work instead. In the rows and columns of the spreadsheet were names and fees for book editors. The problem was that Ronnie wasn't sure which type of editor to choose.

There was a list of developmental editors who would go over the structure of her book and tell her whether it was good or not. But what if they didn't like her story? What if their suggestions would lead to a rewrite of her work?

Then there were the line editors. Their job was to look closely at her sentence structure. Ronnie hadn't paid the best attention in English class. She'd preferred to read the assigned books rather than fuss over the grammar and repetition of words. What did it matter how many times you used a word if it was the right word for the scene?

It didn't stop after the line editor. There were also copy editors and proofreaders. Then beta readers and ARC readers. It was overwhelming. And would eat into most of her funds. Not to mention that most of the editors she'd contacted were booked up for months in advance. Which meant she wouldn't be turning a profit anytime soon. No profit meant no money for rent and necessities.

She didn't want to go back to her parents. Though all of her siblings had homes of their own, her parents' house was grandparents central. There were always people over. Ronnie would get even less peace there than when she was a child.

All she wanted was a quiet place where she could get her work done. She could stay here with Rusty. Not that he'd want her here any longer after last night's argument.

That had been their worst fight ever. In the past, when they'd disagreed, Rusty would listen quietly, trying to patiently and logically negotiate with her. Last night he'd been emotional. His final words to her had been filled with anger. And all that after he'd tried to give her the romance she said she wanted.

But what he'd done hadn't been real. It had been from the pages of a book. Her book. He'd tried to give her what she wanted only to find out it wasn't what she wanted from him.

She didn't like Rusty manhandling her, where he'd always been gentle but passionate. She didn't like him bossing her around, where he'd always talked things through with her.

So what did she want from him?

Ronnie scratched at the hollow spot at her low back. She remembered when he'd pulled her to him. He'd settled his hand there, and she'd felt that sense of security. He'd pressed his lips to hers, and she'd felt light like nothing could touch her. But now she was left insecure and weighed down with indecision.

"Hi, Ronnie."

Ronnie looked up to see Patty waddling toward her. The woman's belly wasn't protruding, but her pregnancy was getting more and more noticeable. Patty wasn't alone. Lana was with her. Along with Keaton's wife and the two twins who were married to Porco and Spinelli. They had platters in their hands.

"We brought lunch," said one of the twins. She was the one with the longer hair; Jules was her name. Jules put a plate of squishy white blocks before Ronnie. Ronnie leaned back in her chair at the unfamiliar fare.

"And sandwiches," said Brenda, putting down ham and cheese sandwiches in front of the edible sponges.

"To each his own," Jules muttered as she plopped a squishy blob in her mouth.

"We came for gossip," said Lana, taking a seat beside Ronnie. "We heard what happened last night."

Ronnie groaned. Partly because she didn't want to rehash what had happened last night. But also because she didn't want a back porch full of women who she'd have to leave in a few days.

"Did Rusty really get decked out in his uniform?" Lana asked.

Ronnie nodded as she closed her laptop. The smell of ham had her reaching out for a sandwich. She flipped over a slice of bread and smeared guacamole on it.

"I thought it was sweet," said Patty. "They tried to recreate your book for you. Your book was fabulous, by the way."

"You read my book?" said Ronnie around a mouthful of savory ham.

"To help Grizz get into character," said Patty after taking a bite of her own sandwich. "Thank you for not stabbing him, by the way."

"You're welcome," Ronnie mumbled, her mind still on the fact that others had read her book. She wondered if everyone on this ranch had passed around the copy. She wanted to let them know it wasn't the final version.

"I didn't read it," said Romey, the twin with the shorter, springy curls. "But Jordan recounted it for us. He has a photographic memory."

Beside her, her sister Jules looked skyward, fluttering her lashes. "I loved the part where Ryker finally drops to his knees and admits he can't live without Vanessa."

"That's because you're a hopeless romantic," said her twin.

"Guilty," said Jules, plopping another spongey blob into her mouth.

"There were a few grammar errors," said Lana, her tone delicate. "I could help you with those if you like. I worked at a magazine for years."

That's right, Lana was a writer. The two had had a great conversation about Jane Austen's heroes years ago. Captain Wentworth was Ronnie's favorite while Mr. Tilney was Lana's. Mr. Darcy didn't rank in the top five for either woman.

"We could also get Sarai Cannon to take a look, too," Lana went on. "She's another writer. She lives next door on the Purple Heart Ranch."

"What are you going to do about the cover?" said Patty, her voice wasn't as delicate as Lana's. Patty had always been a straight-forward kinda girl. "I think it should be a bare-chested man. You can use my husband if you want."

"I don't know, Patty," said Brenda. "Grizz is putting on pregnancy weight alongside you."

Patty threw a bread crumb at Brenda. The tall ranch woman ducked the missive with ease. They all were laughing at the antics. Like old friends.

Ronnie sat in the circle of laughter. It washed over her like an unstoppable wave. Because Ronnie couldn't stop this from happening. She liked these women.

"Since last night didn't go well, are you and Rusty still getting a divorce?" That came from Romey, Spinelli's wife. It was clear the two were meant to be. She was just as direct as her husband.

"Are you already dating someone else?"

Ronnie was looking down. She didn't know the women well enough by voice to know who'd asked that. The thought of dating anyone else had never occurred to her. The women must have seen the revulsion on her face at the idea.

"Do you still love him?"

Ronnie didn't lift her gaze. Her lips pursed as she fought to keep hold of the answer. But she was sure the women saw her chest beating an answer against her tank top.

"Why not try to make it work? Rusty is such a good guy."

Rusty was the best guy. But when he left, when he turned to his work over her, it hurt more than she could bear. One night of candles and pretty words weren't enough to smooth that over.

And that's when she knew that romance wasn't what she wanted. What she had always wanted—what she had only wanted—was his presence. For him to stay with her and never leave. For him to not put himself in danger to give her the life he thought she wanted.

She knew that was selfish. She could never speak those words aloud on a base. But she wasn't on a base any longer. She was on a ranch.

And so she looked up. She opened her mouth to speak what was truly in her heart. And there he was.

CHAPTER SEVENTEEN

*R*usty had no idea what to expect when he came back home that afternoon. It certainly wasn't the entire community of women gathered in his back yard. He could barely handle the one he wanted to gather into his arms.

Ronnie rose to greet him. "Hey."

"Hey," said Rusty, standing in the back door. He felt as though there was a boundary line between the inside of the house and the outside. The distance was short to Ronnie, but he was certain the ground between them was laid with land mines.

"You're home early," Ronnie said, biting her lower lip.

Rusty's gaze tracked the movement. His hands itched to bring her to him. His mouth watered to taste the spot where she'd bitten. But even more, his heart pounded at the words she'd said to him.

There was something so domestic about the way she'd said that word; *home*.

Rusty had come home. In a place they shared together. He'd come back sooner than he'd planned. He couldn't help himself. Whenever he returned from a mission or a deployment, he spent his every waking hour with her, unsure how long his stay would last.

Sure, he left. It was part of his job. But couldn't she see that his every move was always to get back to her? He wanted nothing more than to hold her in his arms for the rest of his days.

Ronnie's arms were crossed over her chest. She hugged herself, providing the comfort he wanted to give. She didn't want his comfort because she thought it was transitory.

"I didn't mean to interrupt." Rusty motioned to the women seated in chairs.

None of them made to move. The other wives watched him and Ronnie as though they were a live-action soap opera.

"I can leave." The words grated as they passed Rusty's lips.

His heart had taken up permanent residence in Ronnie's soul. Yet she was trying to evict him. It was a doomed mission. Because he wasn't going to leave. It was impossible. She was a part of him, and he was never giving that back.

"No!" Ronnie took a step toward him, her hand stretched out to him.

Rusty's first instinct was to gather his wife up in his arms and pull her to him. But those instincts had failed him last night. So he shut his mouth, and he held his place.

They stood before each other. The silence should have been awkward, but it was familiar. He stared into Ronnie's eyes, searching for something.

And then he found it.

Something had changed there. It wasn't something new. It was something old. There was an openness he hadn't seen in a long time. In that opening was a light. Just a small glimmer. But he recognized it.

It was hope.

Rusty's heart had been beating sluggishly all morning. Now it kicked into gear. His mind raced with negotiation protocol. Contain her. Isolate her. Skip talking negotiations and make her surrender with seduction.

"They brought the welcome wagon," said Ronnie, gesturing behind her to the women around the table.

Rusty lifted his gaze to look over Ronnie's head. The women were all leaning in. Rusty narrowed his eyes to slits as he looked at each woman in turn. His intention was to communicate to them all to get lost.

Not a single one of them moved.

It wasn't that his threatening glare was out of practice. He'd stared down insurgents only months ago. He dealt with the ire of wanna-be Rangers crawling through the mud and obstacle courses of the training camp each week. He managed Keaton on a daily basis.

But so did each of these women. One of his friends' wives on her own, he might be able to scare off with a look. All of them?

"Ladies, our husbands will be arriving home soon," said Brenda. "We should probably get these leftovers to them so they can have an appetizer before dinner."

The other four women didn't move a muscle at Brenda's subtle command.

"Up!" Brenda snapped her fingers, which worked to kick the women in gear. Keaton would be so proud.

Their movements were slow and grudging, especially Patty's. Though Rusty had seen her move quickly the other day when Grizz chased her through one of the fields. Soon, but not soon enough, they all started back up the path to the main house.

"I thought you weren't keen on making new friends," Rusty said once he and Ronnie were alone.

"They didn't give me a choice."

She was contained and isolated. But he had no idea how to get her to surrender. He ached to simply take her in his arms, but he'd learned his lesson.

"Ronnie, I'm sorry about last night."

"I know."

"I thought that was what you wanted; for me to take charge like that and not give you a choice."

"Me, too," she said, shaking her head as though clearing fog. "But it's just a fantasy. It doesn't work in real life."

"What do you want in real life?"

She looked up at him. Her eyes were clear. The spark of hope Rusty had seen a moment ago reached the edges of her pupils.

Was it enough? He wasn't sure. So he held his ground, but he spoke his truth.

"I love you," Rusty said with a shrug.

"Yeah, I know." Ronnie mirrored his shrug. "I love you, too."

"So, why are we…" Rusty motioned at the distance between them. "Why isn't that enough for you?"

"Because you make me feel like a balloon."

"I…what?"

"Every time you come around, I get inflated. You puff a little more into me each time. Then when you leave, I deflate until it feels like there's nothing left of me. Then you come back, and the process begins over again until I'm left sagging and formless."

Her hands motioned up and down her lush curves. A deflated balloon is the last thing Rusty would compare Ronnie to. But he doubted complimenting her body was the right tactic at the moment.

"I forgot who I was." She looked down at her hands as though they didn't belong to her. Then she turned to her open laptop on the table. "I think that's why the book isn't working. I'm confused about what love looks like."

Ronnie turned back to him. The hope in her eyes had dimmed and only despair showed through. Rusty wanted to tell her that love looked like a man willing to do anything to make a woman smile. Love was fighting so hard you couldn't see straight.

"At least I *was* confused about what love is," she said. "Then you fixed my car. And you co-signed my dream. And you made a complete fool of yourself last night."

Yeah, and it looked like that, too.

Ronnie closed the distance between them. Rusty's arms reached out to contain her. He pulled her into his body to isolate them from the rest of the world. His hands negotiated the curve of her spine until they came to rest at her low back. Ronnie's sigh was pure surrender as she closed her eyes and rested her head against his chest.

"This is what love feels like," she said.

Rusty wasn't sure what she meant. He wasn't even kissing her yet. He didn't feel the need. He had her close. That was all he wanted, to keep her close and safe in his arms. And so he did.

Rusty wrapped Ronnie up in his arms, and he held onto her. Tightening his hold with every minute that passed. She didn't offer a single mumble of protest.

"Russell?"

"Yes, Veronica?"

"I want to negotiate terms."

"Terms for what?"

"Reconciliation."

Rusty pulled her even tighter. If she were the sagging balloon she complained of, she would've burst. But he'd put the pieces of her back together.

The sun peeked from behind a cloud. As it did, a light rain started to sprinkle as the rays shone down. For once, Rusty didn't mind the contradiction. All the grit and grime of the past year washed away from his hard exterior to leave behind a bright afterglow of happiness.

Ronnie, however, jumped in his arms. Rusty tightened his grip. He'd let her go once. That was never happening again.

"I have to get my things from the table," she protested

It took Rusty a couple of strides to get to the table and swipe everything up in his arms. Ronnie relieved him of her laptop, tucking it under her shirt for protection, lucky piece of technology. When he got inside, he looked down at the documents in his hands.

Notebooks that looked well worn. Spreadsheets with names and figures. Photographs of shirtless men. Rusty looked past the shirtless men and his gaze rested on a familiar envelope.

"Oh, that's yours. Pastor Vance brought it by a couple of days ago. I'm so sorry. I completely forgot to give it to you."

Rusty's fingers trembled as he held the missive. Unfortunately, he was holding it upside down, and the documents slipped out. Ronnie sat the laptop on the kitchen table and bent to pick up the documents. Her face fell when she realized what she held.

"These are the divorce papers," she said.

Rusty said nothing.

"You signed them?"

CHAPTER EIGHTEEN

The documents trembled in her fingers. The pages fluttering like wings upset by a sudden wind. Ronnie held tight lest they get away from her.

She glanced at her signature on the document. The V in her name looked like a checkmark. A tick in the box in her bid to dissolve the union between her and Rusty.

Although the V had almost become a W. Her hands had shaken as she'd put the pen to paper. She'd nearly asked for a new signature page. She'd been sure Rusty had seen her hesitancy in her scrawl. She'd been sure that that's what had kept him from placing his signature beside hers.

There had always been some part of her that never expected to see this. But there it was, in black and white. There was no wiggle in Rusty's signature. The pen marks were straight and sure.

Their marriage was over. Just after the very second when she thought it was saved.

Ronnie released her hold on the document. The pages fluttered to the floor, landing in a resounding thud. She wrapped her arms around herself. She felt as though she was going to float away. Why hadn't she thought that this was the conclusion of her actions?

She wanted to take the papers and rip them up. She wanted to burn them out of existence. The sound of a tear brought her mind back to the present. Rusty's powerful hands were rending the document into two. Then he took the two halves, and for good measure, he tore those bits to shreds as well.

"It doesn't make a difference," he said. "It never had, not even when I signed it."

Ronnie could only stare at his hands. Those powerful hands that could rip a stack of papers, but could also make her feel grounded and safe. Those hands came up to her face and cupped her chin.

"I gave you my vow," Rusty continued. "No inkblot can ever take that away."

"You signed." Even as she said the words, she recognized they had no weight. The only weight she felt was Rusty's hand slowly moving down to anchor at her back.

"I did," he nodded. "I thought I had no more cards to play, so I gave in to your demands."

"I was wrong."

"Yeah, I know."

A strangled laugh escaped Ronnie's throat. A soft chuckle left Rusty's lips. He rested his forehead against hers.

"Russ?"

"Yeah, Ron?"

"I know what I want now."

"Tell me."

"I want to be with you."

A slow grin spread across Rusty's handsome face. He lifted his head from hers. In doing so, his lips brushed lightly across hers.

"No, not physically." Ronnie shook her head. "I mean, yes, physically. But I want more than that. You stopped talking to me when you came home from overseas."

"I did?" There was confusion in those two words.

"You closed yourself off to me. And I understand some part of why. You saw awful things overseas, and you wanted to protect me from it.

But I lost a part of you when you shut me out. I don't want to be shut out anymore."

Rusty didn't immediately respond. He didn't let her go either. He held her in his arms as he turned her words over in his mind.

"You're right," he said finally. "I didn't want any ugliness to touch you from my work. I did everything in my power to make the world safer for you. If I could, I'd have built a wall around you to make sure the bad guys never got close to you."

"I don't want to be locked away unless you're with me."

"I can arrange that," Rusty grinned. "We could live here."

"In the bungalow?"

"No. Here on the ranch. We each got an acre of land as part of the deal we signed. Mac, Grizz, and I are going to build houses. I'll build your dream house. We can go out later, and you can choose a reading tree."

Ronnie's eyes lit up at that thought. Plus, a home where she got to put down roots. Friends that she never had to say goodbye to. And Rusty working just a few miles down the road and home every night.

"Yes," she said. "Under one condition."

"Name it."

"Little Patty Keaton is pregnant," she said.

"She's Patty Hayes now."

"I want to be pregnant, too."

Rusty swallowed. His gaze did a slow scan of her body. Before his eyes came back to her face, he said, "Let's get started."

Ronnie found herself being swept off her feet then. She grinned into Rusty's lips as he pressed his claim. She gave herself over to his command, ready to yield to his every directive.

The chiming of a cell phone interrupted the mood of the moment. As if to punctuate the intrusion, Ronnie felt a buzzing against her thigh, which was pressed against Rusty's pant leg as he held her up.

"I thought this thing was dead." Rusty shifted his hold of her to one arm and reached in his pocket for his phone with the other. "Let me just..."

He looked at the screen and his features pinched. Ronnie knew that look. It was the look he got whenever he was being called in to be spun up for a mission.

"It's okay," said Ronnie, wiggling to get out of his hold.

Rusty set her down as he thumbed a button on the device, but he didn't let her go. "Dr. Patel? What is it?"

Rusty's voice wasn't curt, even though their amorous activity had just been interrupted. Rusty sounded genuinely concerned. Ronnie couldn't hear the other part of the conversation. But she watched Rusty's expression turn grim.

He winced when he looked back at her, his expression turning pained. Ronnie knew that look too. Their amorous activities were about to be postponed.

"I'll be there as soon as I can." Rusty clicked off and turned to her. "I'm sorry, Ronnie, but one of the vets has gone missing. He's had some psychological problems. They asked if I can help find him."

"I understand." And she did. Her raging hormones could take a back-seat while her husband went to save someone's life. Especially since he'd given her a brief of his mission. And also because it wouldn't take him overseas, just down the road.

"I'll be back soon," he said.

"I'll be here," she said.

"I love you."

For the last year, those words had weighed heavily on Ronnie's heart whenever he said them to her. Today, they made her feel like she could fly. "I love you."

Rusty pressed his lips to hers. A soft gentle kiss that was heavy with promise. He grinned at her as he pulled away. "I have you back."

It was a whisper. She wasn't sure if it was for him or for her, but she held onto those words. He did have her back. And she had him back. She would have him with her for the rest of her days.

CHAPTER NINETEEN

For almost a year, Rusty had wracked his brain for the words that would convince his wife to give their marriage a second chance. He'd scoured old textbooks and documents on negotiation strategies and tactics to use to his advantage. In the end, the thing that had worked had been giving Ronnie what she thought she wanted, only to see that it was the last thing she cared to have.

Which was funny, when he thought of it. Rusty had fought the inevitable for months. And the moment he let go, she came back to him. He'd had Ronnie back in his arms. He'd kissed her senseless, and she'd given in to his desires.

He had no idea how he'd just walked away from that dream come true and out the door. Especially when his being called away at a moment's notice, and his long absences had contributed to the downfall of his marriage. That edict of military life was a difficult one when a man had a family. The balance was near impossible. But this time, when duty called, it wouldn't pull him too far for too long.

The Purple Heart Ranch had a brother missing. The soldier needed his help. The United States Military never left one of their own behind. Not even when they were on home soil.

"Private Reggie Williams was last seen at 0800 this morning," said

Dylan. "We became aware that something was amiss when Private Williams missed his check-in at the clinic."

Rusty looked down at the photograph of the man. In the picture, Private Williams stared straight ahead, no smile on his face as was the way in a military photograph. This was the man Dr. Patel and Dylan had asked him to lend a hand with the day Ronnie got here.

Private Williams looked like every fresh-faced soldier. There was that light in his eye that he was eager to serve his country. Along with the lift to his chin that he wanted to be cast in the role of hero. They all did. They all were. But war clipped many men and women's capes.

"I feel obliged to share with you the Reggie was experiencing post-traumatic episodes over our last few sessions," said Dr. Patel. "He was having trouble keeping his grip on the present moment."

The collective sigh that went through the room of soldiers was silent. It was the heaviness in the air that touched Rusty's ears. Each man had their own demons that they battled with after leaving the service. Some were external scars. But most were hidden deep in their chests.

"So, he thinks he's back on the battlefield?" asked Keaton.

"No," said Dr. Patel. "Private Williams wasn't flashing back to combat. He's been reliving his conflicts with the red tape of the government."

Dr. Patel explained how Reggie Williams had been denied some of his benefits. The type of injury Reggie experienced, a traumatic brain injury or TBI, was still a new diagnosis in the military. TBIs left many a soldier disabled after their time in service. However, because they were rarely diagnosed during combat, because it could put the brakes on their career, many soldiers left the service with the injury in tow and no records of its initial appearance. This made claiming a TBI as a disability after separation a daunting task.

"Private Williams feels that if he had the disability and the added benefits it came with, then he could've afforded to buy his wife a home and she wouldn't have left him."

Rusty scratched at his chest. The man's story was tragic. A few more knocks to the head, and it could've been the unhappy ending for anyone gathered in the room. There was a resolve on each man's face to find their injured brother.

"We've called you all in here to help with the search because…" Dylan took a deep breath before continuing. "It appears someone has broken into the weapons locker."

The stance of each man in the room changed in a split second. The level of danger raised up to the roof. Each man had a family on this land that he was willing to lay down his life for.

"You're saying we have an armed man, who is trained in combat, and experiencing episodes in bureaucratic conflict?" Rusty ticked each issue off with his fingers.

"That's the right of it," said Dylan, his expression grave.

"You think he's gone back to his wife?" asked Keaton.

"She's clear across the country," said Dylan. "And she has a protective order against him. I think he's likely gone to the VA in Fort Harris to confront them over his financial woes."

It was that phrasing that sparked Rusty's memories. His mind flashed back to just a couple of days ago. The man he'd seen inside the bank. That man had not been the clean-shaven soldier in the picture. He'd looked like a homeless man. But it was the eyes that connected the dots.

"I think I know where he is," said Rusty.

CHAPTER TWENTY

onnie pulled up to the bank. Unlike the first day here, her car didn't screech when she pressed the brakes to stop. Bessie was riding like a car ten years younger thanks to Rusty. Ronnie patted the steering wheel before she stepped out of the driver's side door.

Taking the uncashed bank check out of her purse, she headed to the glass doors. She no longer needed the bank's money. Perhaps this was why she hadn't cashed it. Perhaps she'd known there wouldn't be a need for it.

She had two editors lined up to clean up her words in Lana and Sarai. She'd settled on Porco as her male model, much to the ire of the other men. And she'd also learned that another wife on the Purple Heart Ranch was good with marketing. She'd need to spend a fraction of the money to bring her book to the world.

And that fraction would come from the joint bank account she shared with her husband. This book was as much his tale as it was hers. Just as his service had been just as much hers.

To top off finally claiming her authorial dreams, she was also getting her dream home. Ronnie didn't care about the specs of the place. The only requirement she had of her dream home was that her dream man live in it with her.

Rusty would be there for her. Not just physically. He'd pledged to be there for her emotionally as well. And, she hoped, there would be more romance tossed in. She could even do with being swept off her feet and manhandled every now and again. So long as her husband was the man to do it.

The divorce papers were in the trash bin where they belonged. Rusty wasn't gone. He wasn't deployed. He was just a couple miles down the road looking for a missing soldier.

He was coming back. To her. To their home.

This could be their home, a place with roots to plant themselves forever. They could finally start a family together. Oh boy, did she want to get to work on that endeavor. But first thing's first.

Ronnie clutched the check in hand and headed into the bank. She sought out the chauvinist banker, but he wasn't at his desk. Mr. Denton was standing with a customer. But the haughty sneer wasn't on his face today.

His features were a mismatched hodgepodge. His eyes were large, open so wide they nearly touched his hairline. His lips were rounded in a small, pinched O. His cheeks were flushed red. He was sweating from his brow and shaking from his shoulders down. Put all together it looked like fear.

Ronnie knew she'd guessed Mr. Denton's mood right when his gaze darted to her in the doorway. His gaze narrowed, as though imploring her to help him. That was a weird turn of events. What could she possibly do to help him? Other than give him back the check she no longer needed.

Ronnie held up the check as though to indicate to Mr. Denton that that's what she'd come to do. That's when the customer standing in front of Mr. Denton turned around.

Ronnie recognized him instantly. He was the scruffy looking man who had been in the bank the day she'd gotten her loan. That man had walked out of the doors empty-handed. His hands weren't empty any longer.

"Don't scream," the man said, waving the gun at her. "Don't run, and no one will get hurt."

"Okay," Ronnie said soothingly.

Her back was against the closed glass door. She knew she couldn't reach behind her and yank it open faster than a bullet could catch her. She also knew that calm was the best defense in these matters. Rusty had taught her that.

Rusty? She wished he was here with her now. He would know how to handle this situation. He'd talked men out of suicide vests and down from high ledges. What would Rusty do in this situation?

Contain. Isolate. Negotiate.

They were all contained in the four walls of the bank. There were five of them in isolation. Ronnie, the gunman, Mr. Denton, and the two tellers. Luckily, there were no other civilians inside. Now it was time to negotiate.

"Maybe I can help?" said Ronnie, taking a step closer to them. "You need money? That's why you're in the bank. How much do you need?"

The gunman's gaze flicked to the check-in her hand. "I don't want your money. I wouldn't take money from a woman."

That's when she saw it. This man may look disheveled, but his shoulders were erect. His head was high. His posture perfect. Only one type of man had that countenance in him at all times.

"You're a soldier, aren't you?"

The gunman didn't answer. He turned the gun back on the bank manager. "I just want what they owe me."

"We don't owe you anything," said Mr. Denton. "We're not the U.S. government or the VA. You need to take your issue there."

The sound of the safety flicking off brought whimpers around the bank. Mr. Denton shut his eyes. Tears streamed down his cheeks.

"I was right." Ronnie took a step closer, still keeping her hands up. "You are a soldier. You having some trouble with your VA paperwork?"

He didn't look at Ronnie. But his jaw tensed, letting her know she'd struck a nerve.

"I know what it's like to deal with all that red tape and paperwork," she said, trying to keep her tone friendly. "I've got permanent paper cuts to prove it. I'm a military wife. My husband is Sgt. Russell Hook. Do you know him?"

The gunman's jaw relaxed, but he didn't speak.

"What's your name, soldier?"

It took forever, but he answered. "Private Reggie Williams, ma'am."

This was good. If he gave his name he was less likely to hurt them. He'd also called her *ma'am*, which meant his manners were still intact. Polite people didn't usually go about shooting others.

"I can help you with the paperwork. I've gotten pretty good at it. What do you say we get on the phone and talk with someone from the VA?"

Reggie turned to face her. They were only a few footsteps away from each other now. His hand began to lower as his gaze rose to her face. But when the front door of the bank slammed open, Reggie's gaze flicked away from her, and his hand raised.

"Get away from my wife."

Ronnie looked up to see Rusty. His broad shoulders darkened the doorway like an avenging angel. Ronnie's instinct was to go to him and fold herself into his chest. But she couldn't move. There was a hand around her neck and a gun pointed at her temple.

CHAPTER TWENTY-ONE

usty's life had flashed before his eyes many times in the theater of battle. It was the same set of scenes each time an explosive had gone off too near him. Or a bullet whizzed past him. Or a hostile got a caged look in their eyes when the negotiations soured.

Each time the end looked like it was near, Rusty's mind would rewind and do a life review. He never saw a single scene of battle or his time of service in that split second. His family featured prominently, his mom and dad's faces taking a good twenty percent of that single tick of time.

His military brothers' faces flickered for a tenth of that second. The five men were all smiling and laughing. There was not a hint of remorse from a single one of them. They'd each known the cost of their service could add up to the ultimate sacrifice. They'd each gotten up each morning prepared to tender that bill if duty called.

Still, each of those memories, those of his family and his friends, were but a fleeting instant. The remaining balance of that split second accounting of Rusty's life was spent on Ronnie.

Ronnie with her head buried in a book. Ronnie with the light of laughter in her gaze. Ronnie with a flare of desire in her eyes.

Funny that not a single flash he saw of her showed any of the ire that had come between them in the last year. He supposed that time in their lives wasn't worth remembering. She looked at him now with absolute horror in her wide eyes.

Her face was ashen, a sickly white. Those lush curls radiated out from her crown, but a piece of steel held some of the curls back. The steel was a gun.

A man held a gun to Ronnie's temple.

Rusty's training should've kicked in. He should be trying to get the man to talk. He should remember that this was a fellow soldier who was in need of help. But all Rusty saw was red.

He'd been trained in all forms of hostage negotiation, including what to do in terms of a bank robbery. He knew that the last place a negotiator wanted to be was inside the establishment. It would've been best to set up outside and out of sight. To call in and establish communication via phone.

Rusty's feet didn't budge from the doorway. He shut the door behind him so that no one else could come in. He'd contained the threat. They were all isolated together. All that was left to do was negotiate.

"Point it at me," Rusty said calmly.

Reggie Williams flinched. It was as though the man's brain had heard the command of a superior and was warring against disobeying a direct order. "I just want what they owe me."

"We're fine," said Ronnie. "Everything's fine. This is my friend, Reggie."

There was a tremor in Ronnie's voice. She'd gotten the man's name out of him. That was good. She must have remembered what Rusty had told her about hostage negotiations. The old adage for a hostage to make themselves familiar with their captive.

But, like the tremor in Ronnie's voice, as she introduced her new friend, there was also a tremor in Reggie's hand. The hand that held the gun to the head of the person Rusty held most dear in the world. That thrust the potential of Reggie's and Rusty's friendship down the drain.

"He's upset over his disability," Ronnie continued, her voice growing stronger. "I told him I could help him with the paperwork because I'm good at that."

"I just want what I'm owed," said Reggie, the tremor of uncertainty still in his voice.

"Private Williams, I'm going to need you to stop pointing the gun at my wife and train it on me."

"She's your wife?"

Reggie lowered the gun a fraction. Rusty's instinct was to charge the man and grab Ronnie. But there was still a chance the gun would go off in the kerfuffle, and she might be hurt. Too risky.

"My wife left me," said Reggie, lowering the gun another fraction.

"I left him, too," said Ronnie, turning slightly in the gunman's hold. "But I came back. We talked it out. Now we're back together, stronger than before."

Ronnie wasn't looking at him, but Rusty knew the words were meant for his ears. She was using her story time voice. The one Rusty could listen to for hours and be lulled into a peaceful respite. It was working on Reggie.

"I can't talk to my Janie," Reggie said. "She put a restraining order on me."

Rusty felt for the guy. He really did. But the gun was lowered to Reggie's side. Ronnie was out of danger.

Reggie was no longer looking up. He was looking off in the distance, thoughtful. Rusty could've used his words and negotiated a peaceful end to this scene.

Instead, he charged the man.

CHAPTER TWENTY-TWO

When Rusty had rushed past her, Ronnie's life had flashed before her eyes. The reel was all too brief. Images of her family flickered, much like an old cinema reel gaining speed.

Ronnie saw her mother frowning at the jewel-coated romance cover of *The Flame and the Flower* in her twelve-year-old hands. But instead of the scolding Ronnie had insisted she'd gotten, she now remembered that her mother had slipped her a worn copy of Judy Blume's *Forever...* Her mother had insisted that if she was going to read romance, it shouldn't be of men ripping a woman's bodice. It needed to be one that featured smart girls learning there was no shame in their bodies.

There was a flash of Ronnie's sister looking angry after Ronnie had snuck a book from her stash. But the annoyance of her memory died and was replaced with her sister handing her the first book in that series and recouped book four, with a promise to lend Ronnie that work after she'd caught up.

There was a glimmer of her English teacher's disapproving face as she looked over Ronnie's textbook to see a romance novel inside the pages. But instead of the chiding Ronnie recalled, she recollected that the woman had slipped her a copy of *Pride and Prejudice*, insisting that if

Ronnie was going to read romance, then it needed to be quality literature.

After all of those retouched reflections, there was nothing but flashes of Rusty. Rusty's mouth tugging into a grin. Rusty's eyes lighting with desire. Rusty's hands pulling her close.

The sensation of safety, of security, flooded Ronnie as the reel of her life played on. But there was no end to the reel. The last image was not of his face. It was of his chest. Because that's what she saw now.

Ronnie was pressed into Rusty's chest, held close to his beating heart. His hand was at her lower back, giving her that sensation of being rooted. Because he was her home, her present, her future.

The images of him hit her so hard, so fast that Ronnie was breathless when she looked up and was treated to the reality of his handsome face. Her husband was there in the flesh. Whole and unharmed and holding her.

He wasn't grinning down at her. His gaze flared, but with anger. His hold on her was more painful than pleasurable.

"What are you doing here?" he shouted. "You could've..."

He didn't complete the sentence. Instead, he pulled her back to him. His hold was even firmer, a padded lock Ronnie doubted she would ever break. She knew she'd never want to.

"I came to return the check," she said as she rubbed her hands up and down her husband's back, trying to infuse the sense of safety and security she always felt when he did the same to her.

After long moments, Rusty gave. But it was less than an inch. As she had predicted, his hold on her didn't break as she squirmed to get a look at the aftermath.

Mr. Denton was seated in a chair, a handkerchief pressed to his forehead as he dotted away the sweat on his brow. And perhaps a few tears from his cheek. Tossing the check-in his face or ripping it up would be anticlimactic after having saved the man's life.

Reggie Williams was on the ground. He wasn't being held. Keaton and Dylan Banks stood over him. Reggie's head was in his hands, his body rocked with tremors, his face contorted in misery.

There was resignation in his light eyes. He'd given up. Despite what he'd just done, the crime he'd committed, and the danger he'd caused, Ronnie felt sorry for him.

"He needs help," she said.

Rusty sighed. The sound was weary, as though there was some give. But still, his hold on her remained absolute. "He'll get it. He has to face the wrong he's done here today. But then, after, help will be waiting for him at the Purple Heart Ranch. He's a brother. We don't leave our brothers behind. Even if we want to beat the crap out of them."

Rusty pulled her closer. Then Ronnie was airborne. He'd swept her off her feet and was whisking her away from the danger. He didn't set her down until they were outside the building.

The cool breeze of the day lifted the curls of her hair. Her bottom was cold as steel as Rusty sat her on the hood of Old Bessie. Once she was perched onto the car, he finally let her go.

Rusty took a step back from her, and a tremor went through his body. He looked as though he might swoon.

"Russ?"

"My work has never touched you before," he said. "You've never been in danger of being a hostage."

She wanted to tell him that that wasn't true. That she'd been a hostage as long as she'd known him. A willing one that had fallen for the man who'd captured her heart. But she doubted he'd care to hear such romantic overtures at the time.

"You're my world, Veronica."

Or maybe he had some overtures of his own he wanted to dish out. Ronnie was here for that.

"You took my heart hostage from the first moment I saw you. I knew that no matter what happened, I would forever be yours. I became your hostage, body, and soul."

Part of Ronnie wished she had a pen and paper to write this purple prose down. But she knew that each word Rusty uttered was being written on her heart.

"Whatever terms you want in order to stay," he continued, "name them, and they're yours."

Ronnie held her arms open. Rusty came inside them. He wrapped his arms around her, resting his hand in the place it belonged at the small of her back.

"What I want is to live with you happily ever after."

"Ever after, I can promise," he said. "Happily I might fall short of from time to time."

"It's okay. I've learned the value of having a good editor."

Rusty sighed as he pressed his lips to hers. Ronnie had kissed her husband before, thousands of times. But this kiss was different. It was more. It was the first chapter in the sequel to their life's story. And Ronnie knew that his new journey would be a sweeping, epic romance for the ages.

EPILOGUE

Keaton could hear his heart pounding in his ears. Just like every time he was on the battlefield, the beats synced with the ticking of the second hand of a clock. A calm went over him in the face of the danger that awaited him. He inhaled, the oxygen adding fuel to the bravado that came naturally to him. He was a well-trained soldier, a superbly trained warrior. One of the best specimens of the 75th Ranger Regiment.

Stepping out of his hidey-hole where he'd taken cover after the first shots rang out, Keaton looked around. His sightline was clear, which did not bode well. His spidey senses tingled at the calm and quiet. War was a noisy, frenetic affair.

Something was wrong.

Keeping low to the ground, he poked his head out to gather more intel. The camouflage of his clothes made it so that he blended with his environment. Even his gun was painted green and brown to mix in with the elements.

And then he heard it. A cry. A shot.

They sounded one after the other. Keaton's ears perked like a dog coming alert. Before storming into action, he deduced what he'd learned.

The cry had come from the left side. The shot had come from behind him. The blast from the gun had gone over his head. The cry from a human throat had come before the shot. There was no resulting thump of a body.

A tingle went up to his spine. His wife launched herself at him, a paintball gun raised and aiming for his heart. Keaton lowered his weapon and took the missive. The impact made him stagger, but not as much as when Brenda flung herself into his arms.

"Surrender," she said against his lips.

"I never stood a chance," he growled against her mouth.

More shouts rang out behind them, but Keaton ignored the ongoing battle. He'd have waved a white flag of triumph if his hands weren't full of the glory that was his wife.

"Man, you're supposed to have my back," yelled Mac.

Keaton lifted his head to find that Mac was in the same predicament as he was. Lana had fired a number of shots right at his heart as well. Now, her gun was lowered, and she was in his arms. There was a grin on Mac's face as his wife tended to his superficial wounds.

Porco and Spinelli were sitting on the sidelines. The Capulano twins had taken them out in the first few minutes of the paintball game. The two flower child, grown women had sniper sharp aim. Keaton had been ducking them before he'd fallen for his wife.

His little sister sat on the sidelines with Grizz. Well, Patty wasn't so little anymore. Her belly was so big that Keaton worried she might burst at any moment. Beside Patty, Ronnie lounged in the cradle of Rusty's arms. Ronnie's swelling belly was just visible in the outline of her top.

"This was supposed to be a fun excursion in the midst of your insane work plan," said Mac.

"Don't knock the plan," said Keaton.

The plan had been to build the best Ranger training camp in the States. They were well on their way to surpassing that goal. Boots on the Ground was the most sought after school for those wanting to join the 75th Regiment.

But the unexpected had happened. The men had been outmaneuvered. They'd come to this land a tight unit. They'd grown into a strong community and were planting deep roots with the women who'd conquered their hearts. But perhaps, that had been the plan all along.

ALSO BY SHANAE JOHNSON

Shanae Johnson was raised by Saturday Morning cartoons and After School Specials. She still doesn't understand why there isn't a life lesson that ties the issues of the day together just before bedtime. While she's still waiting for the meaning of it all, she writes stories to try and figure it all out. Her books are wholesome and sweet, but her are heroes are hot and heroines are full of sass!

And by the way, the E elongates the A. So it's pronounced Shan-aaaaaaaa. Perfect for a hero to call out across the moors, or up to a balcony, or to blare outside her window on a boombox. If you hear him calling her name, please send him her way!

You can sign up for Shanae's Reader Group and receive a FREE NOVELLA in this world at

https://shanaejohnson.com/ReaderGroup

ALSO BY SHANAE JOHNSON

The Brides of Purple Heart

On His Bended Knee

Hand Over His Heart

Offering His Arm

His Permanent Scar

Having His Back

In Over His Head

Always On His Mind

Every Step He Takes

In His Good Hands

Light Up His Life

Strength to Stand

His Grace Under Pressure

The Silver Star Ranch Romances
His Pledge to Honor

His Pledge to Cherish

His Pledge to Protect

His Pledge to Obey

His Pledge to Have

His Pledge to Hold

The Flying Cross Ranch Romances
His Vow to Love

His Vow to Treasure

His Vow to Adore

His Vow to Trust

His Vow to Respect

His Vow to Defend